DOCTOR WHO
THE UNIVERSAL DATABANK

Also available

DOCTOR WHO – THE PROGRAMME GUIDE

DOCTOR WHO – THE TERRESTRIAL INDEX

DOCTOR WHO
THE UNIVERSAL
DATABANK

Jean-Marc Lofficier

First published in Great Britain in 1992 by
Doctor Who Books
an imprint of Virgin Publishing Ltd
338 Ladbroke Grove
London W10 5AH

A catalogue record for this title is available from the
British Library

ISBN 0 246 20370 4

Typeset by Falcon Typographic Art Ltd, Fife, Scotland
Printed and bound in Great Britain by
Cox & Wyman Ltd, Reading, Berks.

To John and Nan Peel

ACKNOWLEDGEMENTS

First and foremost, I must again acknowledge the constant help and support of my wife Randy, who has been the uncredited co-author of *The Doctor Who Programme Guide* and its companion volumes since their inception in 1980.

Lest we forget, these books would not have happened if it were not for the moral support and dedicated assistance of the following individuals: Terrance Dicks, who was there at the beginning; the much regretted Graham Williams, Barry Letts and most especially John Nathan-Turner of the BBC, without whom the whole enterprise would have been doomed from the start; and finally my steadfast editors at W. H. Allen, now Virgin Publishing: Christine Donougher, at the onset; Jo Thurm, who carried the flame; and last but not least, Peter Darvill-Evans and Ríona MacNamara, who saw me through the end of it.

Finally, I am, as ever, deeply grateful for the help of those devoted *Doctor Who* scholars who provided numerous corrections and suggestions and without whom these books would be a lot more imperfect than they are. They deserve a special thanks for their unswerving commitment to the common cause: Jeremy Bentham, Eric Hoffman, David J. Howe, Shaun Ley, John Peel and Andrew Pixley. Thank you all!

J.-M.L.

FOREWORD

A work of this nature will almost inevitably be misinterpreted by some of its readers. In an attempt to minimize confusion, I have tried in this foreword to clearly state what *The Universal Databank* is, and, more importantly, what it is not.

I have also tried to define the rules that I have followed in assembling this work, rules which also spell out its unavoidable limitations.

This foreword should not be construed as an attempt to forestall controversy, or criticism – I entertain no illusions in that respect – for both are welcome. Indeed, I have taken great care in trying to correct errors and omissions which crept into the earlier two volumes of this trilogy, and am looking forward to doing the same with this book. The purpose of this foreword is instead, if I may use a somewhat inappropriate automobile analogy, to try to ensure that this red Austin is not criticized for not being a green Jaguar.

THE NATURE OF *THE UNIVERSAL DATABANK*

First and foremost, *The Universal Databank* is not a dry, technical manual, rehashing what was shown or said on the programme. For a variety of reasons, including the fact that such information already exists in other packages, that is not the book I set out to write.

Like its companion volume, *The Terrestrial Index, The Universal Databank* is a creative exercise in retroactive continuity. In other words, I believe that it is impossible to make all the elements of the Whoniverse fit into a coherent continuity based simply on the information given on the show. Some creativity has to be brought into play.

The Universal Databank is, therefore, a work of fiction. Sadly, there has been a semantic confusion among some reviewers between what constitutes facts and what constitutes fiction, leading to some probably well-intended but (at least, in my eyes) sorely misguided comments.

Tom Baker played the Fourth Doctor. The first *Doctor Who*

story ever broadcast was *An Unearthly Child*. Alan Wareing directed *Survival*. Gerry Davis wrote *Revenge of the Cybermen*. These are facts. In theory, they should be objective, impersonal, true. Yet, as most *Who* experts will attest, the fourth statement is only partly correct. A truer statement would read: Gerry Davis and Robert Holmes (then Story Editor) wrote *Revenge of the Cybermen*. Compiling a book of facts can, at times, become tricky; but with sufficient research and clearly defined terms, one can ultimately arrive at, what is to the best of one's knowledge, the truth.

Not so with fiction.

The Doctor is a Time Lord. Morbius died on Karn. The Cybermen arose on Mondas. Temmosus was a Thal Leader on Skaro. These are all fiction. (Fictional facts, if you wish.) What this means is that, even though 99.99 per cent of *Doctor Who* fans can agree on a statement, there always remains: (a) the possibility that, somewhere, someone may disagree with it for a variety of more or less valid reasons, having to do with his personal interpretation of the often contradicting statements made on the broadcast, in the script and/or its novelization; and (b) a future writer of the programme may come in at a later date and revise that bit of fiction.

For example, Morbius may be brought back to life in a yet untold story (his brain was cloned); Terry Nation may reveal that Temmosus was only a figurehead (Alydon was really in charge all the time); etc. As amazing as it seems to me, with my faith in the 'if it ain't broke, don't fix it' adage, even my first statement may no longer hold true. The creative team behind the 25th and 26th seasons took it upon themselves to hint that the Doctor may not be a Time Lord after all, but something more powerful, more ancient, even though this directly contradicted years of somewhat irrefutable evidence!

That is the problem with fiction. Trying to encapsulate it in a book of this nature is like taking photographs of shadows. Not only is it a matter of point of view, but shadows also change. So the best advice to be given to those readers who brook little disagreement with their own views of how the fictional Whoniverse should be arranged, is: read no further, go write your own book.

Obviously, this semantic argument is not meant to excuse the genuine errors which will undoubtedly have managed somehow to creep into this book in spite of everyone's best efforts. If you find statements like 'The Exxilon are eight-legged spiders', or 'Scaroth had 232 segments' (instead of twelve), please write and these will be corrected in a later edition. After all, we should all be able to agree about 90 per cent of the programme's contents, even if a clever future writer may decide to reveal heretofore unknown evidence about the Exxilon's nasty secret identities, or Scaroth's prolific splintering habits!

However, matters largely subject to individual interpretation – such as Daleks, Cybermen, UNIT, Time Lords and the rest – will remain in accordance with my personal views.

Because of this unavoidable degree of subjectivity, it is therefore only fair to clarify the rules which have been followed in compiling this book.

THE RULES OF *THE UNIVERSAL DATABANK*

The Universal Databank uses the same set of rules as those employed in the essay 'The History of Mankind According To *Doctor Who*', which appeared in our companion volume, *The Terrestrial Index*.

If you disagreed with that, you'll positively despise this book. On the other hand, if you found 'History of Mankind' enjoyable, you may equally derive some pleasure from exploring the mind-boggling expanse of the Whoniverse, which is ultimately the purpose of this work.

What are these rules? Simple:

– I have assumed the existence of a single universe, with straightforward linear history, except where specific alternate time lines, parallel universes, etc. were mentioned;

– I have given precedence to historical accuracy and scientific information whenever appropriate, and tried, to the best of my abilities, to reconcile those bits of the programme which conflicted with these;

– I have relied primarily on the broadcast version of the programme, but often supplemented it with material from the novelizations (when it did not flatly contradict the broadcast version, but expanded on it, e.g.: characters' first names, heretofore unrevealed information about planets, etc.);

– finally, when I was forced to reconcile conflicting bits of fictional data, I have tried to do so with (hopefully) the minimum addition of new elements, and in the spirit of Occam's razor (the simplest explanation being the best);

From a practical standpoint, this means that the information contained in this book is presented against a background which is totally consistent with that of my previous essay on the history of mankind.

On the other hand, this also means that my own, personal interpetation of what transpired in the Whoniverse may differ from the works of other writers. To quote but two examples, the history of the Daleks presented here follows a chronology slightly different from that of John Peel. The history of the Cybermen equally conflicts with David Banks' version. Like archeologists studying the records of long-dead civilizations, it doesn't mean that any of us are wrong – simply that we followed different sets of rules.

Those readers who disagree with my interpretations are, of course, free to entertain their own views. *The Universal Databank* contains enough information which is based purely on the material presented on the show, with little or no interpretation, that leads me to believe that even conflicting interpretations will not detract from the usefulness, or enjoyment, of this book.

THE HISTORY OF THE *UNIVERSAL DATABANK*

Finally, a few words about the background of this project, which will help to understand the reasons for its existence, as well as its inherent limitations.

If I had followed the standards which normally apply to the writing profession, this book would not exist. The munificent sums of money lavishly spent by the publisher on my yacht and country estate would not begin to pay for the seemingly endless hours spent poring over videotapes, books and dusty records, while the rest of the world was going on with its collective life.

To state that this book was a labor of love would not only be a cliche, but an utter lie. Let me be candid: by the time one hits the hundreth *Doctor Who* story, and one realizes there are still another sixty stories to index, no one, not even a mother, could love this work. So it is not love, nor even pride, but only the stubborn desire to finish a job once started that could ever explain how this work came to be completed. If this book stands for anything, it is the sheer mule-headedness of writers in general.

The Universal Databank began in 1980 as an offshoot of *The Doctor Who Programme Guide*. Without the help of a computer, it was virtually impossible to do the job that needed to be done, either in terms of quantity (indexing everything) or quality (going beyond mere surface facts). More than twelve years later, the promise inherently contained in that first book has at long last been fulfilled.

At the time the first *Programme Guide* was assembled, the BBC had just finished broadcasting the last Tom Baker season. To contemplate doing this book meant not only redoing everything that had been done before, but adding eight more seasons worth of new material – almost one third of the programme's life. That decision was hard enough without contemplating the dire notion that new stories were going to be added, year after year. The image of Sysiphus pushing his boulder springs to mind.

The BBC chose to discontinue the programme, hopefully not as a way of avoiding turning one writer's life into a living hell. To all those in charge, I can now say: thank you. My book is finally completed; you can go back to doing the show.

Jean-Marc Lofficier

TABLE OF *DOCTOR WHO* STORIES

FIRST DOCTOR:

First Season:

A	An Unearthly Child (The Tribe of Gum)
B	The Daleks
C	The Edge of Destruction (Beyond the Sun)
D	Marco Polo
E	The Keys of Marinus
F	The Aztecs
G	The Sensorites
H	The Reign of Terror

Second Season:

J	Planet of Giants
K	The Dalek Invasion of Earth
L	The Rescue
M	The Romans
N	The Web Planet
P	The Crusade
Q	The Space Museum
R	The Chase
S	The Time Meddler

Third Season:

T	Galaxy Four
T/A	Mission to the Unknown
U	The Myth Makers
V	The Daleks Masterplan
W	The Massacre
X	The Ark
Y	The Celestial Toymaker
Z	The Gunfighters
AA	The Savages
BB	The War Machines

Fourth Season:
CC   The Smugglers
DD   The Tenth Planet

SECOND DOCTOR:

Fourth Season (Contd):
EE   The Power of the Daleks
FF   The Highlanders
GG   The Underwater Menace
HH   The Moonbase
JJ   The Macra Terror
KK   The Faceless Ones
LL   The Evil of the Daleks

Fifth Season:
MM   The Tomb of the Cybermen
NN   The Abominable Snowmen
OO   The Ice Warriors
PP   The Enemy of the World
QQ   The Web of Fear
RR   Fury from the Deep
SS   The Wheel in Space

Sixth Season:
TT   The Dominators
UU   The Mind Robber
VV   The Invasion
WW   The Krotons
XX   The Seeds of Death
YY   The Space Pirates
ZZ   The War Games

THIRD DOCTOR:

Seventh Season:
AAA   Spearhead from Space
BBB   The Silurians
CCC   The Ambassadors of Death
DDD   Inferno

Eighth Season:

EEE	Terror of the Autons
FFF	The Mind of Evil
GGG	The Claws of Axos
HHH	Colony in Space
JJJ	The Daemons

Ninth Season:

KKK	Day of the Daleks
MMM	The Curse of Peladon
LLL	The Sea Devils
NNN	The Mutants
OOO	The Time Monster

Tenth Season:

RRR	The Three Doctors
PPP	Carnival of Monsters
QQQ	Frontier in Space
SSS	Planet of the Daleks
TTT	The Green Death

Eleventh Season:

UUU	The Time Warrior
WWW	Invasion of the Dinosaurs
XXX	Death to the Daleks
YYY	The Monster of Peladon
ZZZ	Planet of the Spiders

FOURTH DOCTOR:

Twelfth Season:

4A	Robot
4C	The Ark in Space
4B	The Sonataran Experiment
4E	Genesis of the Daleks
4D	Revenge of the Cybermen

Thirteenth Season:

4F	Terror of the Zygons
4H	Planet of Evil
4G	Pyramids of Mars

14

4J	The Android Invasion
4K	The Brain of Morbius
4L	The Seeds of Doom

Fourteenth Season:

4M	Masque of Mandragora
4N	The Hand of Fear
4P	The Deadly Assassin
4Q	The Face of Evil
4R	The Robots of Death
4S	The Talons of Weng-Chiang

Fifteenth Season:

4V	Horror of Fang Rock
4T	The Invisible Enemy
4X	Image of the Fendahl
4W	The Sunmakers
4Y	Underworld
4Z	The Invasion of Time

Sixteenth Season (The Key to Time):

5A	The Ribos Operation
5B	The Pirate Planet
5C	The Stones of Blood
5D	The Androids of Tara
5E	The Power of Kroll
5F	The Armageddon Factor

Seventeenth Season:

5J	Destiny of the Daleks
5H	City of Death
5G	The Creature from the Pit
5K	Nightmare of Eden
5L	The Horns of Nimon
5M	Shada (not televised)

Eighteenth Season:

5N	The Leisure Hive
5Q	Meglos
5R	Full Circle
5P	State of Decay

5S	Warriors' Gate
5T	The Keeper of Traken
5V	Logopolis
–	K9 and Company (50-minute special)

FIFTH DOCTOR:

Nineteenth Season:

5Z	Castrovalva
5W	Four to Doomsday
5Y	Kinda
5X	The Visitation
6A	Black Orchid
6B	Earthshock
6C	Time Flight

Twentieth Season:

6E	Arc of Infinity
6D	Snakedance
6F	Mawdryn Undead
6G	Terminus
6H	Enlightenment
6J	The King's Demons
6K	The Five Doctors (90-minute special)

Twenty-First Season:

6L	Warriors of the Deep
6M	The Awakening
6N	Frontios
6P	Resurrection of the Daleks
6Q	Planet of Fire
6R	The Caves of Androzani

SIXTH DOCTOR:

Twenty-First Season: (Contd):

| 6S | The Twin Dilemma |

Twenty-Second Season:

| 6T | Attack of the Cybermen |
| 6V | Vengeance on Varos |

6X	The Mark of the Rani
6W	The Two Doctors
6Y	Timelash
6Z	Revelation of the Daleks

Twenty-Third Season (The Trial of a Time Lord):

7A	The Mysterious Planet
7B	Mindwarp
7C	Terror of the Vervoids
7C	The Ultimate Foe

SEVENTH DOCTOR:

Twenty-Fourth Season:

7D	Time and the Rani
7E	Paradise Towers
7F	Delta and the Bannermen
7G	Dragonfire

Twenty-Fifth Season:

7H	Remembrance of the Daleks
7L	The Happiness Patrol
7K	Silver Nemesis
7J	The Greatest Show in the Galaxy

Twenty-Sixth Season:

7N	Battlefield
7Q	Ghost Light
7M	The Curse of Fenric
7P	Survival

A

A, HELEN Ruler of the Terra Alpha colony. She decreed that the colonists were to be happy, on pain of being arrested by her Happiness Patrol and publicly executed. The Seventh Doctor and Ace helped rebels overthrow her regime. After her pet Fifi died, Helen A finally realized that happiness was nothing without sadness (7L).

ABBOTT, TOM Foreman of a quarry's blasting crew. He set up the explosion which brought Eldrad's hand back to the surface (4N).

ABIDOS Argolin from the Leisure Hive (5N).

ABLIF Leader of the hunting party of Shobogans who captured Leela and Rodan. He and his leader, Nesbin, helped them and the Fourth Doctor repel the Sontarans' Invasion of Gallifrey (4Z).

ABOMINABLE SNOWMEN See YETI.

ABU Young Gond male selected to become one of the Krotons' 'companions' and was subsequently killed by them (WW).

ACADEMIUS STOLARIS Art gallery on Sirius Five (5H).

ACE One of the Seventh Doctor's companions. A young English girl from Perivale who had been a problem child, she had run away after her experiments with homemade gelignite blew up parts of her school. Her real name was Dorothy. She was one of the 'Wolves' of Fenric, descendants of the ancient Vikings who had brought the flask containing the evil entity back to England. Fenric pulled her out of space and time and left her on Iceworld, where she took a job as a waitress. She accompanied the Seventh Doctor (whom she called 'Professor') on his quest for the Dragonfire and helped him defeat Kane. She aided him against the Daleks, the Cybermen and the Gods of Ragnarok. Ace held Excalibur and fought Morgaine at Carbury. The Doctor then took her back to 1883 Perivale to confront her fears of the evil house, Gabriel Chase. Afterwards, Ace became instrumental in Fenric's release in 1943 Northumberland. There, she met her mother, Audrey, as a baby, and helped her grandmother, Kathleen Dudman, to escape the Haemovores. She also fell in love with the Russian Red Army Captain, Sorin. The Doctor and Ace then returned to Perivale, where she helped him fight the Master, and almost turned into one of the Cheetah People. Ace's favorite weapon was explosives, in particular nitro-nine (7G–7P). According to some accounts, Ace eventually left the Doctor to live in 1880 France, where she married one of Sorin's ancestors.

ACETENITE 455 One of the minerals mined by Zanak (5B).

ACHILLES A brave Greek warrior during the Trojan War. The First Doctor unwittingly helped him slay his enemy, Trojan warrior Hector. He was later killed by Troilus (U).

ACOLYTE Title used by the Tesh (4Q).

ACOMAT Disfigured Tartar warrior in Tegana's employ (D).

ACTEON Name of the star sector in which Metebelis 3 was located.. The term 'galaxy' applied to it by the Doctor is not strictly accurate, as it is likely that the Acteon System is part of the Milky Way Galaxy (PPP, TTT, ZZZ).

ADAM See CASTLE, NIGEL.

ADAMS Stangmoor prison officer (FFF).

ADAMS UNIT corporal stationed in Devesham. The Kraals made an android duplicate of him (4J).

ADJUDICATOR Earth Government official whose job it was to sort out claims on newly discovered planets. The Master presumably killed and impersonated an Adjucator named Martin Jurgens, who had been sent to Exarius as an arbitrator during a dispute between Ashe's colonists and the Interplanetary Mining Corporation (HHH).

ADLON One of the alien tourists who crashlanded in Wales in 1959. He was killed by the Bannermen (7F).

ADMINISTRATOR Treacherous Sensorite who became Second Elder of the Sense-Sphere. He tried to kill the First Doctor and his companions and was eventually exiled by his people (G).

ADMINISTRATOR Envoy from the Earth Imperial Council to Skybase One. He was prepared to negotiate independence for the Solonians. The Marshal had him killed by Varan's son (NNN).

ADRASTA (LADY) Tyrannical ruler of Chloris, a world rich in vegetable matter but poor in minerals. She owned the only metal mine on Chloris. However, this was running out of metal, and when the Tythonian ambassador, Erato, arrived on Chloris to offer to trade chlorophyll for metal, to preserve her power, Adrasta kept him prisoner in the mines (which became known as the Pit) for fifteen years. During that time, with the help of the Huntsman and his carnivorous Wolf Weeds, she prevented her people from rebelling. The Fourth Doctor and Romana discovered Erato's true nature and exposed Adrasta's duplicity. Her people turned against her and she was eventually killed by Erato (5G).

ADRIC Companion of the Fourth and Fifth Doctors. He was a young Alzarian who had earned a badge for mathematical excellence. The Fourth Doctor met Adric on Alzarius in E-Space, where he helped him and Romana solve the mystery of the Marshmen. Adric then stowed away on the TARDIS and helped the Fourth Doctor defeat the Great Vampire, and free the Tharils from Rorvik. Back in normal space, he helped the Fourth Doctor fight the Master on Traken, Logopolis and Earth. There, he watched the Fourth Doctor regenerate. Soon afterwards he was kidnapped by the Master, who used his mathematical abilities to create Castrovalva. He then fought alongside the Fifth Doctor, Nyssa and Tegan against Monarch, the Mara and the Terileptils and George Cranleigh. After fighting the Cybermen, he sacrificed himself to save Earth by staying on board a doomed spaceship, taking it back through time 65 million years until it crashed on Earth (5R–6B).

AENEAS Leader of the Trojan survivors who went on to found Rome (U).

AGAMEMNON Brother of Menelaus and King of Mycene. He started the Trojan War, some claimed, to control the trade routes to Asia Minor. After the fall of Troy, Cassandra became Agamemnon's slave (U).

AGELLA One of the Movellans serving under Commander

Sharrel on Skaro. She was disarmed and reprogrammed by Tyssan (5J).

AGGEDOR Allegedly mythical beast protecting the planet Peladon and its rulers. It turned out to be a very real creature, under the control of High Priest Hepesh, who used it to prevent his planet from joining the Federation. The Third Doctor tamed it with a song and a mirror. Later, when Hepesh tried to use Aggedor to kill the Time Lord, Aggedor killed the High Priest instead (MMM). The traitor Eckersley used a machine which projected a holographic image of Aggedor with a heat ray to take over the trisilicate mines of Peladon for Galaxy Five. The real Aggedor eventually killed Eckersley, who had taken Queen Thalira hostage, but was himself later killed in the battle (YYY).

AGNES Saxon woman from Wulnoth's village (S).

AHMED Professor Scarman's Egyptian servant. He warned the professor not to open Sutekh's tomb (4G).

AIKIDO (VENUSIAN) The Third Doctor used Venusian Aikido against a variety of people, including Professor Stahlman (DDD), Mike Yates, a Stangmoor prisoner named Charlie (FFF), Colonel Trenchard's guards (LLL), the Marshal's men (NNN), Global Chemicals' thugs (TTT), Linx (UUU), Sergeant Benton (WWW), Ortron's guards (YYY), and the Spiders' field-guards (ZZZ).

AINU Former miner and one of Torvin's band of rebels on Chloris (5G).

AIR See GASES.

AIR DUCT One of the Kangs of Paradise Towers (7E).

AJACKS Nickname given to the Miners of Megro-polis Three on Pluto (4W).

AKROTIRI Famous scientist whose mind was stolen by Skagra at the Think Tank space station. He died in the destruction of the station (5M).

ALBATROSS Captain Pike's pirate ship (CC).

ALCOTT American Senator and delegate to the World Peace

Conference. He almost became a victim of Chin Lee, but was rescued by the Third Doctor (FFF).

ALDO Member of Rorvik's crew. He died in the destruction of the privateer's ship (5S).

ALEXANDER Fierce young Scottish warrior, member of Colin McLaren's party after Culloden. He was killed by the Redcoats (FF).

ALGOL 27th-century planet noted for galloping inflation (5J).

ALKARIM Incarnation of the evil Xeraphin (6C).

ALLEN IMC security guard and member of the expedition to Exarius. He was killed by a Primitive (HHH).

ALLIANCE The Alliance was a loose federation between Earth, some of its colonies (independent from it or not), and several alien powers, such as the Draconians (QQQ) and the Cyrennic Empire (5A), whose purpose was to fight the Cybermen and the Daleks. The Alliance was probably formed during the First Cyber Wars early in the 23rd century (4D).

During the 25th century, the Daleks tried to use a space plague against the Alliance (XXX). The result was the Second Dalek War, which forced the Daleks away from Skaro.

In the 26th century, the Alliance met on Earth to discuss the renewed Cybermen threat. The Cybermen tried to sabotage the conference, and the Second Cyber Wars followed (6B).

The Daleks and the Master tried breaking apart the Alliance by fomenting a war between Earth and the Draconian Empire (QQQ). They then prepared to attack the Alliance with a huge invisible army based on Spiridon, but that plot was averted by the Third Doctor and the Thals (SSS). A Third Dalek War ensued.

All these wars depleted the resources of the Alliance, and in particular that of the older Draconian Empire. Under the pressure of Earth's growing imperialism, the Alliance eventually broke apart in the 27th century.

The Alliance is not to be confused with the SUPREME ALLIANCE and the ICELANDIC ALLIANCE, both Earth political entities from the 51st century (4S).

ALLIANCE (DALEK) Gathering of aliens who joined forces with the Daleks to attack the Solar System in AD 4000. They included Mavic Chen, Zephon, Celation, Malpha, Trantis, Beau, Warrien, Sentreal and Gearon. Most were either killed or betrayed by the Daleks (V).

ALLISON See WILLIAMS, ALLISON.

ALPHA Nickname given by the Second Doctor to one of the three 'humanized' Daleks (LL).

ALPHA CENTAURI One-eyed, six-tentacled representative from the star system Alpha Centauri. He was one of the Federation's delegates to Peladon. Even though he was a stickler for protocol and legalities, he helped the Third Doctor unmask Hepesh and Arcturus, and thereby facilitate Peladon's accession to the Federation (MMM). Fifty years later, when the Third Doctor returned to Peladon, Alpha Centauri was Federation Ambassador there. He vouched for his identity and helped him expose Azaxyr and Eckersley (YYY).

ALPHA FOUR Space beacon attacked and destroyed by pirate Caven. It had been guarded by Lieutenant Sorba of the Intl. Space Corps. It was also where the Second Doctor's TARDIS rematerialized (YY).

ALPIDAE Real name of the Pipe People, the natives of Terra Alpha (7L).

ALTERNATE WORLDS See PARALLEL UNIVERSES.

ALTOS A young inhabitant of Marinus. He accompanied the First Doctor on his quest for the Keys of Marinus and eventually married Sabetha (E).

ALUMINIUM The Fourth Doctor and Erato teamed up to weave an aluminium shell around a neutron star and redirect it (5G).

ALVIS One of the Supervisors in charge of the work shifts in the gas mines of the Macra-dominated space colony (JJ).

ALYDON Thal who gave Susan an anti-radiation drug soon after she landed on Skaro. He was elected leader after Temmosus's death. The First Doctor helped Alydon and his people defeat the branch of the Daleks who had survived in the City and were preparing to exterminate the Thals through increased radiation (B).

ALZARIANS The native Alzarians were the Marshmen who had evolved from spiders. A tribe of Marshmen further evolved into Terradonian-like humanoids, and forgot their origins. Native Alzarians shared an empathic link with each other, which could be transmitted to other species. Romana became thus affected after being bitten by an Alzarian spider (5R).

ALZARIUS Planet located in E-space upon which a Terradonian starliner crashed. Its original passengers were killed by the native Marshmen, who evolved into Terradonian-like humanoids, forgetting their origins. Eventually, the Fourth Doctor helped the Starliner community rediscover the truth and leave Alzarius (5R).

AMAZONIA Federation ambassador to Peladon who was impersonated by the Third Doctor (MMM).

AMBASSADORS See DIPLOMACY.

AMBASSADORS OF DEATH Nickname given to the three radioactive aliens who had been sent to Earth as peaceful ambassadors, after replacing the crews of the spaceships Mars Probe 7 and Recovery 7. The xenophobic General Carrington captured them and used them to try to create a war between Earth and their people. Thanks to the intervention of the Third Doctor, Carrington was stopped and the Ambassadors were returned to their people (CCC).

AMBOISE (ABBOT OF) Right-hand man of the Catholic leaders of France and lookalike of the First Doctor. Tavannes blamed him for the failed assassination of Admiral De Coligny and had him executed. His death was blamed on the Huguenots and used as a pretext to launch the Massacre (W).

AMBRIL Director of Historical Research of Manussa and custodian of the Great Crystal of the Mara. He disregarded the Fifth Doctor's warnings about the Mara's return, and was manipulated by Lon into using the Crystal in a ceremony meant to recreate the Mara (6D).

AMDO Goddess of the Atlanteans. Her high priest, Lolem, tried to sacrifice the Second Doctor and his Companions to her, but was stopped by Professor Zaroff (GG).

AMERICA See UNITED STATES OF AMERICA.

AMERICAN CIVIL WAR An American confederate army was kidnapped by the Warlords, using time technology stolen from the Time Lords, and went on to take part in the War Games, until these were brought to a stop by the Second Doctor's intervention (ZZ).

AMEZUS One of the Thals (B).

AMONG-WE Term used by the Kinda to refer to themselves (5Y).

AMORB Rival company of Galatron Mining Corporation (6V).

AMPLIFIED PANATROPIC COMPUTER NETWORK See MATRIX.

AMSTERDAM Dutch city visited by the Fifth Doctor when he fought Omega (6E).

AMYAND Sarn Unbeliever who climbed the Fire Mountain. He, Sorasta and Roskal were arrested by Timanov and were condemned to be sacrificed to the Fire Mountain. They helped the Fifth Doctor defeat the Master. Amyand was mistaken for Logar because he wore a Trion vulcanologist's suit which enabled him to order his people to evacuate their village before the volcano destroyed it (6Q).

ANAT Guerilla leader from an alternate 22nd century where the Daleks had successfully invaded Earth after World War Three. She, Shura and Boaz went back in time to kill diplomat Sir Reginald Styles, not realizing that it was their actions which caused the war. She helped the Third Doctor defeat the Daleks (KKK).

ANATTA One of the Kinda (5Y).

ANCELYN His full name was Ancelyn ap Gwalchmai, nick-named the Sperhawk. He was Knight General of the Britons in another dimension ruled by Morgaine. He came to Earth to recover Excalibur. He fought alongside the Seventh Doctor and Brigadier Bambera of UNIT against Morgaine and Modred. He was attracted to Bambera (7N).

ANCIENT HAEMOVORE The last surviving member of the Haemovore race. One of the 'Wolves' of Fenric, he was brought back in time by the evil entity to help it secure its release, and turned Northumbia villagers into pseudo-haemovores. The Seventh Doctor succeeded in convincing him that Fenric's plans would ultimately doom his race, so he mentally destroyed the pseudo-haemovores he had created and killed Fenric's host body (Sorin's) with a deadly toxin (7M). According to some accounts, his real name was Ingiger.

ANCIENT LAW OF GALLIFREY, THE Gallifreyan book dating back to the days of Rassilon. It had mysterious, physical properties and time ran backwards over it. Because it contained the location of Shada, the prison planet of the Time Lords, it was stolen by Salyavin, who used his mental powers to make the Time Lords forget about it. Later, Salyavin (posing as Prof. Chronotis) summoned the Fourth Doctor because he wanted him to return the book to Gallifrey. But the book had been mistakenly borrowed by Chris Parsons. It was stolen by Skagra, who used it to find Shada. It was eventually returned to Gallifrey by the Fourth Doctor (5M).

ANDALUSIA Province of Spain where the Sixth Doctor rescued the Second Doctor from Chessene and the Sontarans (6W).

ANDERSON Manager of a bar on Iceworld. He fired Ace after she spilled a drink on a customer (7G).

ANDOR Leader of the Sevateem. He banished Leela and was later killed by one of Xoanon's invisible, kinetic monsters (4Q).

ANDRED Commander of Gallifrey's Chancellery Guards. He was wounded while helping the Fourth Doctor repel the Vardans' and the Sontarans' invasion. He married Leela (4Z).

ANDREWS, JIM Terminal One duty officer at Heathrow when Concorde Flight 192 disappeared (6C).

ANDREWS, JOHN Lieutenant aboard the SS *Bernice*. He was an unwitting prisoner of Vorg's Scope, but was eventually restored to his proper place in space and time by the Third Doctor (PPP).

ANDROGUMS Extremely strong and savage denizens of a slightly radioactive planet in the Third Zone. The Androgums were regrouped in tribes (named Grigs), linked to each other through blood ties and arcane rituals. Their primary interest, other than violence, appeared to be food. They were used as labour force by the more civilized races of the Third Zone (6W).

ANDROIDS Robots in human form. The Movellans were a race of sentient androids (5J). The Dalek extermination team sent after the First Doctor used an android duplicate, which the Doctor destroyed (R). The First Doctor also met realistic android versions of Dracula and the Frankenstein Monster (R).

Among master android-makers were the Kraal scientist Styggron, who devised android duplicates of the Fourth Doctor, Harry Sullivan and an entire human village (4J); the Tarans (5D); Monarch of Urbanka, who built androids with real human memories stored on silicon chips (5W); Sharaz Jek, who built android duplicates of the Fifth Doctor, Peri and Salateen and used androids to harvest the deadly spectrox on Androzani Minor (6R); the Borad, who built a blue-skinned guardian (6Y); and Bellboy of the Psychic Circus, who designed deadly android clowns (7J). The Cybermen also used faceless androids for menial surveillance work (6B).

Other noteable androids included the Auton Replicas (AAA, EEE); the Terileptils' Grim Reaper (5X); the shape-changing Kamelion (6J, 6Q) and the Raston Robot (6K). Also see DUPLICATES, REPLICAS, ROBOTS.

ANDROMEDA Spies (later known as 'Sleepers') from Andromeda successfully infiltrated the Gallifreyan Matrix, choosing Earth as their base of operations. When they discovered the Andromedans' plan, the Time Lords struck back. The actions they took against Andromeda itself are unknown, but they moved Earth out of the Solar System and rechristened it Ravolox. The Ravolox Stratagem was eventually uncovered five hundred years later by the Sixth Doctor when he and Peri visited Ravolox (7A–7C). The Wirrn's breeding colonies destroyed by the Empire were located on Andromeda Gamma Epsilon (4C). Andromeda was famous for its bloodstones (5B). Sabalom Glitz's home planet, Salostopus, was located in Andromeda (7A). Castrovalva was believed to be located in the Andromedan Phylox Series (5Z).

ANDROMEDA GAMMA EPSILON Homeworld of the Wirrn (4C).

ANDROZANI MAJOR Planet located in the Sirius sector. It was the headquarters of the Sirius Conglomerate which controlled the supplies of spectrox (6R).

ANDROZANI MINOR Twin planet of Androzani Major. It featured an intricate network of caves, where spectrox-producing giant bats lived. The Fifth Doctor and Peri became involved in a conflict over spectrox between Sharaz Jek and General Chellak on Androzani Minor. When the planet moved closer to Androzani Major, mud bursts rose from Androzani Minor's core (6R).

ANETH Peaceful planet which paid tribute to Skonnos in the form of hymetusite crystals and seven young victims, to be sacrificed to the Nimon (5L).

ANGE One of Ace's friends from Perivale (7P).

ANICCA One of the Kinda (5Y).

ANIMUS Large, spider-like parasite, concealing itself behind a blinding, white light. He was literally the mind behind the Zarbi's attack on Vortis. The First Doctor fought the Animus and Barbara Wright used a special isotope to destroy it (N).

ANITA Oscar Botcherby's girlfriend. She helped the Sixth Doctor uncover Chessene's plans (6W).

ANITHON Incarnation of the good side of the Xeraphin. Professor Hayter's sacrifice enabled him to come to the fore and communicate with the Fifth Doctor (6C).

ANKH See LAKH.

ANN See TALBOT, ANN.

ANNABELLE Captain Trask's slaving ship (FF).

ANTARCTIC Location of the South Pole Space Tracking Station attacked by the Cybermen from Mondas (DD). Two buried Krynoid pods were located near Antarctica Camp Three of the World Ecology Bureau expedition (4L).

ANTERIDES Star sector known to the Morestrans in the far future (4H).

ANTHROPOLOGY The study of man and man's history begins when Scaroth's ship exploded, creating life on Earth around 3.5

billion years ago (5H). During the Jurassic era, the petrified hand of the Kastrian Eldrad landed on Earth and became a fossil (4N). The various reptiles scooped up by Prof. Whitaker's time device were also taken from the Jurassic (WWW). Around 140 million years ago, towards the end of the Jurassic, the powerful alien Xeraphin visited Earth (6C).

It was during the Cretaceous era that the (misnamed) 'Silurians' (BBB) and their aquatic brethren, the Sea Devils (LLL), ruled the Earth. Mammals must already have evolved into some kind of early primate, since on several occasions, members of both reptilian races indicated that they were familiar with this type of creature.

At the end of the Mesozoic era (65 million years ago), the Silurians and the Sea Devils were driven underground by some, as yet unknown, cosmic event. Members of the Silurian species encountered by the Third Doctor blamed it on a sudden change in the Van Allen radiation belt (BBB). Some theories include other cosmic phenomenon such as movements of the Moon, or of Earth's twin planet, Mondas. There is also a possibility that the Silurians somehow became aware of the forthcoming crash of a space liner from the future (6B).

Near the beginning of the Pliocene era (40 million years ago), the Fendahl Skull landed on Earth and began to influence man's evolution (4X). During the Paleolithic era, circa 100,000 BC, the First Doctor and his Companions, Susan, Ian Chesterton and Barbara Wright, helped a tribe of Neanderthal cavemen rediscover the secret of fire (A). Around the same time, the alien being known as 'Light' visited the Earth, intending to catalogue its evolution (7Q).

Between 50,000 and 30,000 BC, the Neanderthals became extinct and were replaced by early modern humans, thanks to the intervention of the awesome aliens known as the Daemons (JJJ). Also, two alien vegetable Krynoid pods landed in the Antarctic and buried themselves into the permafrost (4L).

During the later part of the Paleolithic era (20,000 to 8000 BC), Earth was visited by the Mondasians, from Earth's twin planet, who left behind legends of Space Gods and Giants Who Walked The Earth (DD); and by a Martian ship whose crew became buried in a glacier (OO). During the Neolithic era (between 6000 and 3000 BC), the powerful alien Osirians visited Ancient Egypt, creating a new pantheon of gods in their image (4G). Another of the so-called Egyptian 'gods' was, in reality, a splinter of Scaroth of the Jagaroth (5H).

Circa 3000 BC, the alien villainess Cessair of Diplos, landed on Earth and impersonated a Druidic goddess, the Cailleach (5C). Soon afterwards, the alien Urbankans visited Earth for the first time, kidnapping an Australian Aborigine named Kurkutji (5W). During the late Neolithic era (1800–1400 BC), the Meddling Monk helped build Stonehenge (S).

ANTI-MATTER The supernova created by Omega collapsed and turned into a black hole, trapping the great Solar engineer in a universe of anti-matter. He was presumed dead in a matter/anti-matter explosion caused when his anti-matter being came in contact with the Second Doctor's positive matter recorder (RRR).

Omega survived and returned from the anti-matter universe by using the Arc of Infinity, a region of space filled with Quad magnetism, the only thing capable of shielding anti-matter from positive matter. The Doctor then used a matter converter to destroy him before a huge anti-matter explosion could destroy Amsterdam (6E).

A gateway into a universe of anti-matter existed on Zeta Minor (4H). Captain Briggs's space freighter used anti-matter fuel (6B).

ANTIQUITY Period of Earth history frequently visited by the First Doctor: Ancient Egypt circa 2600 BC (V), the Trojan War (1300 BC) (U), and Rome in 64 AD (M).

ANTODUS Thal from Skaro, and Ganatus's brother. He helped the First Doctor fight the Daleks. He was terrified by the Lake of Mutations but ended up sacrificing his life to save Ian's (B).

ANTON Hovercraft pilot who mistook the Second Doctor for Salamander (PP).

ANTORO Name of a galaxy known to the Morestrans in the far future (4H).

APC NET See MATRIX.

AQUATRION Chlorisian astrological symbol (5G).

ARA Atlantean servant girl whose father had once been one of King Thous's councillors and who had been killed by Zaroff. She helped the Second Doctor and his Companions defeat the mad scientist (GG).

ARAK Leader of the rebellion against the Spiders on Metebelis 3. He was sought by the Queen Spider for having attacked Draga, one of her field-guards. In spite of the Third Doctor's help, he fell back under the Spiders' control, but was freed when the Great One died (ZZZ).

ARAK Typical citizen of Varos. He was Etta's husband. He was against the Governor's policies (6V).

ARAM Young Karfelon rebel. She was killed by the Board (6Y).

ARANA (DONA) Elderly Spanish lady who was killed by Shockeye. Her hacienda served as a base of operations for Chessene (6W).

ARANA, VINCENTE Dona Arana's late husband (6W).

ARAR-JECKS According to Turlough, they were natives of Heiradi, who built a huge subterranean city during the twenty-aeon war (6N).

ARBITAN Keeper of the Conscience of Marinus. He blackmailed the First Doctor and his Companions into searching for its five missing Keys. He was killed by Yartek (E).

ARC OF INFINITY Name given to the region of space near Rondel, devoid of all stellar activity, because it was the location of a burned-out Q star. It was the perfect gateway to a universe of anti-matter. Omega used it to try to take over the Fifth Doctor's body (6E).

ARCALIANS One of the Time Lords' colleges. The Arcalians' colour was green (4P).

ARCHEOLOGY A dangerous profession, demonstrated by the fates of Professor Parry after he found the Tomb of the Cybermen on Telos (MM), Professor Horner at Devil's End (JJJ), Professor Scarman after he broke into Sutekh's tomb in Egypt (4G), Dr Fendelman (4X), and the paleontologists who were murdered by the Cybermen in the 25th century (6B). Professor Rumford, however, survived her investigation into the Stones of Blood (5C), and Peter Warmsly was evacuated before Morgaine's attack

(7N). The Daleks sent an archeological expedition to find Davros in the ruins of Skaro (5J).

ARCHER Army colonel of the bomb disposal squad sent with Professor Laird to investigate mysterious artefacts (cylinders containing the Dalek-killing Movellan virus buried at the end of a Dalek time corridor) in the London warehouse district. He was killed by Lytton's men and replaced by a duplicate (6P).

ARCHIMANDRITE Taran religious prelate who married Prince Reynart and Princess Strella (5D).

ARCHITECTURE See CITIES.

ARCTURUS Multi-strand organism from the Arcturian star system. In order to survive in Earth-like environments, Arcturians needed to be placed inside a globe of their native lifefluids, mounted on a traction unit. The Arcturians and the Martian Ice Warriors were deadly enemies. An Arcturian was one of the Federation's delegates to Peladon. He was secretly in league with Hepesh to prevent Peladon from joining the Federation. He fought the Third Doctor and was killed by Ssorg (MMM).

ARDEN Archeologist during the Ice Age of AD 3000. He found the body of Varga and was eventually killed by the Ice Warriors (OO).

ARETA Varos rebel. She helped the Sixth Doctor escape from the Punishment Dome. Later, she and Peri were almost transmogrified (Areta into a reptile) by Quillam's nuclear beams, but she was rescued by the Sixth Doctor who stopped the process in time (6V).

ARGOLINS Inhabitants of Argolis. After their 20-minute war with the Foamasi, the Argolins became sterile. The radiation also slowed down their metabolic rate, making them appear ageless for a long period of time, until they suddenly began aging and died in a matter of hours. Thanks to the efforts of the Fourth Doctor, the Argolin leader, Mena, and her lover, the Earthman Hardin, the Argolins were able to use the Tachyon Recreation Generator to rejuvenate their race (5N).

ARGOLIS First of the Leisure planets. Argolis became radioactive after the Argolins' 20-minute war with the Foamasi. The surviving Argolins then built the Leisure Hive, and abandoned their war-like culture to promote peace and understanding between alien races (5N).

ARGONITE Precious mineral which combined the incorruptibility of gold and the strength of titanium, found only in deep space. Argonite mines were discovered and exploited by Dom Issigri and Milo Clancey. It became the object of a battle between the International Space Corps and space pirate Caven (YY).

ARIDIANS The inhabitants of Aridius were once an advanced amphibian race living in undersea cities. As their world became ever drier, they faced increasing hardships, forced to recycle all their water, and living under constant attack by the Mire Beasts. The Daleks blackmailed the Aridians into handing the First Doctor over to them (R).

ARIDIUS An ancient world once covered by vast oceans. After a dramatic change in orbit which caused the planet to move closer to its twin suns, the oceans slowly evaporated, leaving a desert planet still inhabited by the Aridians and the Mire Beasts. It was the first stop in the Daleks' pursuit of the First Doctor through time and space (R).

ARIEL Chlorisian astrological sign (5G).

ARIS Young Kinda who was possessed by the Mara and was the first of his kind to speak aloud (in Kinda terminology: the gift of Voice). Under the Mara's evil influence, he wanted to attack the Earth expedition's Dome, which would have resulted in the destruction of Deva Loka. He was freed of the Mara by the Fifth Doctor's intervention (5Y).

ARISING (TIME OF) Time when the Great Vampire was supposed to rise, after a thousand years being fed the blood and spirits of countless sacrifices by Aukon, Zargo and Camilla (5P).

ARK, THE Giant spaceship built by Man in the 57th segment of Time (about ten million years in the future) to save Earth's population before the planet plunged into the Sun. It carried not only humans, but also the alien Monoids, as well as various samples of animal life. The bulk of the population had been miniaturised on micro-cell slides. The Ark was visited twice by the First Doctor during its 700-year-long journey to Refusis: first, at the journey's onset, when Dodo's cold virus wreaked havoc on its population; then again, at the journey's end, when the Doctor helped save mankind from the Monoids (X).

ARK IN SPACE See NERVA, TERRA NOVA.

ARMAGEDDON The Armageddon Convention was a galactic treaty which tried to ban the more powerful destruction devices such as the Cyberbombs. But the Cybermen refused to subscribe to it (4D). The Armageddon Factor was the mutual destruction war fought by Atrios and Zeos (5F).

ARNHEIM Member of the *Nosferatu* crew sold by Glitz and frozen by Kane (7G).

ARNOLD Staff sergeant in the army task force which fought the Great Intelligence in the London underground. He was secretly taken over by the Intelligence and sabotaged the Second Doctor's efforts. His body withered to a husk when Jamie wrenched the Intelligence's mind-draining device from the Doctor's head (QQ).

ARREX One of Gavrok's Bannermen. He was killed by the Chimeron Princess's ultrasonic powers (7F).

ART The Fourth Doctor's TARDIS was once mistaken for a work of art in a Parisian gallery (5H). The TARDIS's power station could assume the outward appearance of an art exhibit (4Z). Scaroth the Jagaroth forced Leonardo da Vinci to paint several Mona Lisas in order to finance his time-travel experiments (5H). A number of paintings portrayed the various identities taken by Cessair of Diplos throughout the ages (5C). Kane commissioned a sculptor to sculpt an ice statue of Xana, his long-dead lover, on Iceworld (7G).

ARTHUR Legendary King of England in the 8th century. In a parallel world, his wizard Merlin was an incarnation of the Doctor. Arthur died during the final battle with Morgaine. Still holding Excalibur, his body was placed in a spaceship and buried in Vortegern's Lake near Carbury on our world by the Doctor, in an unrecorded adventure (7N).

ARTICLE 17 Article of the Time Lords' Constitution which enabled the Fourth Doctor to be guaranteed his liberty by offering himself as a candidate for the presidency while he sought to expose Goth (4P)

ARTIFICIAL INTELLIGENCE See COMPUTERS.

ARTRON ENERGY Force said to help power TARDISES (4P, 5W).

ASCARIS Mute assassin hired to kill Maximus Pettullian (M).

ASHBRIDGE COTTAGE Hospital where the Third Doctor was taken soon after he arrived on Earth and collapsed (AAA).

ASHE, MARY John Ashe's daughter, and one of the Exarius colonists. She helped the Third Doctor and Jo Grant (HHH).

ASHE, JOHN ROBERT Leader of the Exarius colony. Even though his colony was being attacked by Dent, he opposed any violence against the men from IMC. He assisted the Third Doctor in his investigations and eventually sacrificed himself by taking off in the colonists' old spaceship, which he knew was likely to explode, giving the others a chance to recapture their world (HHH).

ASHTON Villain who smuggled food and people in and out of the Daleks' Bedfordshire site during their Invasion of Earth of AD 2164. He was killed by the Slyther (K).

ASSISSIUM Roman town; the First Doctor stayed in a nearby villa (M).

ASTRA Destination of Vicki and Bennett's ship (L).

ASTRA Royal princess of Atrios who turned out to be the sixth and final segment of the Key to Time. She was the sixth Princess of the sixth dynasty of the sixth Royal House of Atrios. Astra was kidnapped by the Shadow and later transmuted to her true shape. After the Fourth Doctor defied the Black Guardian, and the White Guardian had used the Key to restore the universal balance, Princess Astra was presumably restored to her human form and returned to a normal life, ruling her planet and presumably marrying Merak (5F). Soon afterwards, Romana decided to adopt Princess Astra's shape when she regenerated (5J).

ASTRID Assistant to Giles Kent who rescued the Second Doctor on an Australian beach (PP).

ASTRID Wife of the only Viking survivor to arrive on the Northumbrian coast (7M).

ATLANTIS Circa 1500 BC, the volcano on the island of Thera, in the Aegean Sea, erupted in a violent explosion, one of the most stupendous of all times. According to ancient Egyptian records later rewritten by Plato, this was the site of a flourishing civilization, known as Atlantis, which perished in the cataclysm. The eruption was triggered when the Master released – in spite of the Third Doctor's intervention – the time-devouring entity known as Kronos, which the Atlanteans had trapped in a crystal (OOO).

The inhabitants of a lonely Atlantean outpost located south of the Azores in the middle of the Atlantic Ocean were cut off from their civilization and forced to eke out a miserable underground existence for nearly 35 centuries. They were discovered by Professor Zaroff in 1968, and used in his insane plans to destroy the world. (GG). The Daemons may have been the ones who gave the Kronos Crystal to the ancient Atlanteans (JJJ).

ATMOSPHERIC DENSITY JACKETS Devices worn by the First Doctor and his companions on Vortis (N).

ATOM See NUCLEAR POWER.

ATRIOS Twin planet of Zeos, located at the edge of the Helical Galaxy, involved in an unending space war against its neighbour. The Atrian Marshal was secretly controlled by the Shadow who desired to obtain Princess Astra, in reality the sixth segment of the Key to Time. Atrios and Zeos were saved from mutual destruction by the Fourth Doctor, Romana and Drax (5F).

ATROPINE (aka NIGHTSHADE) Substance used by the Commander to poison the Sensorites (G).

ATTWOOD English colonel and Algernon Ffinch's commanding officer (FF).

ATZA He and Ortezo were two Mogarians who had embarked on the *Hyperion III* space liner. They prevented the ship from being plunged into the black hole of Tartarus, but then were used by Rudge to hijack it. They wanted to recover its precious cargo of vionesium, which they deemed to have been 'stolen' from their planet. They were killed by Doland (7C).

AUDREY, JOHN 17th-century diarist whose scandalous stories included some about Druidism (5C).

AUDREY See DUDMAN, AUDREY.

AUKON (aka ANTHONY O'CONNOR) Former Science Officer of the Earth ship *Hydrax*, which was drawn into E-Space by the Great Vampire. Under his master's influence, O'Connor became High Councillor Aukon, one of the three immortal vampiric rulers of the Great Vampire's world. Aukon tried to recruit Adric to become the Great Vampire's Chosen One, but died when the Fourth Doctor destroyed his master (5P).

AUSTERLY Sir Reginald Styles's house. It was blown up by Shura (KKK).

AUSTRALIA Country visited by the Second Doctor in the 21st century during his encounter with Salamander (PP). Magnus Greel was known as the Butcher of Brisbane (4S). Kurkutji was an Australian Aborigine kidnapped by the Urbankans circa 3019 BC (Australian Aborigines are estimated to have first populated Australia between 40,000 BC and 25,000 BC) (5W). Tegan Jovanka was Australian.

AUTLOC High Priest of Knowledge of the Aztecs. Barbara succeeded in convincing him of the horrors of human sacrifice and he later abandoned his people (F).

AUTOPLASTICS LTD. Leading British manufacturer of plastics. The company and its managing director, Hibbert, were taken over by the Nestene, who used the factory to manufacture Autons (AAA).

AUTONS Androids made of plastics and inhabited by the Nestene consciousness. The first generation of Autons were made to look like store dummies, and were equipped with deadly wrist-blasters. A more advanced type of Auton were the humanoid replicas (AAA). During their second invasion, in addition to the deadly, dummy-like Autons, the Nestene also controlled a murderous range of plastic items such as a chair, a doll, a telephone cord and plastic daffodils activated by short-wave radio (EEE).

AVERY Notorious 17th-century pirate, under whom Pike, Longfoot and Cherub served. During a mutiny Longfoot and Avery absconded with Avery's treasure. After Avery's death, Pike and Cherub tried to find the treasure but were thwarted by the First Doctor (CC).

AVON Young man from the Elders' city. With Flower, he acted as Steven and Dodo's guide (AA).

AXONITE The very substance of Axos. The Axons offered it to mankind claiming that it would absorb, convert and transmit all forms of energy. In reality, it would have reached its Nutrition Cycle 72 hours later, and would have drained Earth of all its energy (GGG).

AXONS Axons first appeared on Earth as a trio of golden humanoids, who claimed to be the sole survivors of a world drained of energy by solar flares. Later, they were revealed to be tentacled monsters, members of a single collective intelligence which included their ship and Axonite (GGG).

AXOS Axos was a space scavenger who captured the Master, who then took it to Earth. There, Axos offered its Axonite to Mankind. Once Axonite reached its nutrition cycle, Axos was planning to drain all of Earth's energy. It also tried to force the Third Doctor to give it the secret of time travel. It was eventually trapped in a time loop thanks to the combined efforts of the Third Doctor and the Master (GGG).

AXUS Gond guard who fought Jamie (WW).

AYDAN (aka AYDON) Millenius Treasure Vault guard and Kala's husband. He killed Eprin and, in cahoots with his wife and Eyesen, stole one of the Keys of Marinus. He was later shot by his accomplices (E).

AZ Insane Varosian morgue attendant. He and Oza were supposed to dispose of the Sixth Doctor's body in an acid bath, but instead fell into the bath themselves (6V).

AZAL Last of the Daemons. He was in a miniaturized state of suspended animation under Devil's Hump when he was brought back to life by the Master. Azal planned to judge Man and pass on his power, which he offered to the Third Doctor, who refused. Azal then tried to kill him, but Jo Grant threw herself in front of the Doctor. This seemingly irrational action caused Azal to commit suicide (JJJ).

AZAXYR Ice Lord of Mars and leader of the Federation troops sent to Peladon. He turned out to be a member of a breakaway fraction eager to return to the Ice Warriors' former militaristic glories. He became an agent of Galaxy Five and, with Eckersley's help, tried to take over the trisilicate mines of Peladon. He was thwarted by the Third Doctor, and killed by Sskel's sonic weapon while fighting Gebek (YYY).

AZMAEL (aka Professor Edgeworth) Time Lord, and former mentor of the Doctor. He left Gallifrey to become Master of Jaconda. Later, the gastropod Mestor took over Jaconda from Azmael, whom he forced to do his bidding. On Mestor's behest, Azmael kidnapped Romulus and Remus to force them to work out the equations that would have enabled Mestor to throw a planet into Jaconda's sun, thereby creating an explosion that would spread its eggs throughout the universe. Azmael eventually rebelled. The Sixth Doctor destroyed Mestor's body while the gastropod was engaged in mental battle with Azmael. Azmael then destroyed Mestor's mind by committing suicide through a last, fatal regeneration (6S).

AZTECS Central American race who replaced the Mayans, and were eventually eradicated by the Spanish. The First Doctor and his Companions visited the Aztecs in the 15th century (F).

AZURE Vacation planet. The cruise liner *Empress* crashed into the *Hecate* when both ships emerged simultaneously from hyperspace into its orbit (5K).

B

BACCU Guardian chosen by Zentos to act as Prosecutor of the First Doctor and his Companions after Dodo's cold virus infected the Ark (X).

BACKGAMMON Game played between the First Doctor and Kublai Khan (D).

BADRA One of the Zygons (4F).

BACON, FRANCIS English philospher of the 16th century.

His image was projected on the First Doctor's Space-Time Visualizer (R).

BAINES One of Lieutenant Scott's men (6B).

BAKER Member of Dortmun's resistance against the Daleks during their AD 2164 invasion (K).

BAKER Retired British army major, once forced to resign after an incident of recklessness. He was hired as security officer at Wenley Moor and became increasingly paranoid during the Silurians' attack. He refused to heed the Third Doctor's advice and wounded the Young Silurian. He was later captured by the Silurians who infected him with a deadly virus to spread among mankind. He eventually died from the virus (BBB).

BAKER, HOWARD Sarah Jane Smith's Aunt Layinia's neighbour in Moreton Harwood; one of the few inhabitants who were not worshippers of Hecate (K9).

BAKER, JUNO Howard Baker's wife (K9).

BALAN Dulcian educator sent with Kando and Teel to check radiation levels on the Island of Death. He first disbelieved Cully's story about the Dominators, but was later captured and put to work by the ruthless aliens. Toba ordered him killed by a Quark (TT).

BALANCE The universal balance between Chaos and Order is maintained by the Guardians of Time with the Key to Time (5A–5F).

BALARIUM Stun gas used by the Company on Pluto (4W).

BALATON Pralix's grandfather. He was afraid of challenging the Captain of Zanak, and feared the Mentiads (5B).

BALAZAR Young citizen from UK Habitat who had read the Books of Knowledge and was sent to the surface by Merdeen. Balazar aided Katryca and Broken Tooth to invade the Habitat, and later helped the Sixth Doctor to save the Habitat from the black light explosion triggered by the destruction of Drathro's Maglem converter (7A).

BALDWIN One of Professor Sorenson's Morestran crew killed on Zeta Minor by the anti-matter creatures (4H).

BAMBERA, WINIFRED UNIT brigadier. She fought alongside the Seventh Doctor and Lethbridge-Stewart against Morgaine's men at Carbury. She was attracted to Ancelyn (7N).

BANDRAGINUS 5 Planet rich in Orlion, and with a population of over a hundred million, which was destroyed by Zanak. The Captain had incorporated its shrunken remains in his trophy room. The Fourth Doctor eventually used it to fill Zanak's hollow centre (5B).

BANDRIL Neighbouring planet of Karfel inhabited by intelligent reptilian aliens. A peace treaty involving food shipments from Karfel to Bandril was negotiated by Makrif and the Third Doctor in an unrecorded adventure. The treaty was broken by the Borad who wanted to trigger a war between the two worlds to destroy Karfel's population. His plans were thwarted by the Sixth Doctor, who again arranged for peace between Bandril and Karfel (6Y).

BANE One of Lieutenant Scott's troopers, killed by the Cybermen (6B).

BANNERMEN Merciless galactic mercenaries, led by Gavrok, who exterminated the Chimerons. They pursued the Chimeron Queen Delta to the 1959 Welsh holiday camp of Shangri-La. There, they were thwarted by the Seventh Doctor, Billy and Ray, Goronwy and two US secret agents, Hawk and Weismuller. They were finally defeated by the young Chimeron Princess's ultrasonic powers, broadcast over Shangri-La's public address system. They were taken prisoners by Delta and Billy (7F).

BARBARA See WRIGHT, BARBARA.

BARCLAY Australian physicist at the Snowcap Space Tracking Station at the time of the Mondasian Cybermen invasion. He helped the First Doctor, Ben and Polly defeat the Mondasian Cybermen and prevent General Cutler from using the Z-Bomb (DD).

BARCLAY Guard at the prison where the Master was kept. He was killed by the Sea Devils (LLL).

BARNES Member of Lupton's psychic circle at K'anpo's Tibetan Monastery. He was taken over by the Spiders, but was freed when the Great One died (ZZZ).

BARNETT, MICHAEL Moreton Harwood resident and member of the cult of Hecate (K9).

BARNEY Refreshing Department Supervisor on the Macra-dominated space colony (JJ).

BARNHAM, GEORGE PATRICK Prisoner at Stangmoor, subjected to the Keller Machine and turned into an imbecile. The Third Doctor discovered that, because his mind was now without any evil, his presence acted as a dampener on the Mind Parasite. He was eventually killed by the Master (FFF).

BARRAS, PAUL French revolutionary (1755–1829) who plotted with Napoleon and arrested Robespierre (H).

BARRINGTON British army major who believed he was fighting against the Germans in World War I. In reality, he was part of the War Games. He suspected the Doctor and his companions of being spies. He was eventually returned to his proper place in time and space by the Time Lords (ZZ).

BARTHOLOMEW'S PLANETARY GAZETEER Reference guide to planets in use at the time of the Alliance (5A).

BASS, TIM 19th-century British miner whose brain fluids were stolen by the Rani. He was turned into a tree when he stepped on one of the Rani's deadly mines (6X).

BATES, EREGOUS He and Stratton were space pilots captured by the Cybermen on Telos. Their limbs were replaced by cybernetic parts. The Cryons arranged for their escape, and plotted for them and Lytton to steal the Cybermen's time vessel. Instead, they were killed by the Cybermen (6T).

BATES Captain under Commander Millington's command in Northumberland. He eventually joined forces with Vershinin (7M).

BATESON Inventor of a polymerization process used by the Third Doctor and Professor Jones to defeat the Green Death (TTT).

BATS On the Great Vampire's planet, bats were under the mental control of Aukon (5P). Spectrox was refined from bat guano mined on Androzani Minor (6R). Also see VAMPIRES.

BATTLE COMPUTER (DALEK) Combination of a young human girl and a Dalek biomechanoid control centre. The Battle Computer was used by the Daleks to supervise Ratcliffe in their fight against the Imperial Daleks and the Seventh Doctor for the Hand of Omega. She/it provided the Daleks with the intuition and creativity they lacked. Its technology was probably developed as a result of the Daleks' war with the Movellans. After killing Mike Smith in an attempt to recover the Time Controller, the Battle Computer was destroyed. The little girl who was part of it was then freed (7H).

BAX Varos technician in charge of communications (6V).

BAXTER Chief of the off-shore Euro-Sea Gas Control Rig. His platform was surrounded and engulfed by the Weed. He was eventually freed thanks to the intervention of the Second Doctor (RR).

BAXTER, RUTH Doland's lab assistant. While on Mogar, a speck of alien pollen had entered her body and turned her into a vegetable monster. Lasky, Bruchner and Doland secretly carried her aboard the *Hyperion III* hoping to find a cure for her on Earth. She was killed by the Vervoids (7C).

BAZIN One of Kane's troopers on Iceworld. He and McLuhan were sent after the Dragon. Bazin was wounded. After McLuhan shot the Dragon, they were both disintegrated by the Dragonfire crystal (7G).

BEACON HILL British Research Establishment whose radio-telescope dishes the Master used to contact the Nestene. When the Third Doctor showed up to investigate, a Time Lord warned him about the Master's presence on Earth (EEE).

BEAM PULSER Hypnotic device used by the Cybermen for their Invasion of Earth. Tobias Vaughn helped the Second Doctor and UNIT destroy it (VV).

BEAST (OF FANG ROCK) Mythical creature rumoured to have killed two men and left one mad on the island of Fang Rock. Reuben believed it existed and would someday return, while the Fourth Doctor explained it as nothing but murder and madness. It was given mysterious reality by the arrival of a deadly Rutan (4V).

BEATLES, THE Popular 20th-century British musicians. Their image was projected on the First Doctor's Space-Time Visualizer (R).

BEAUCHAMP Family name of the Marquess of Cranleigh (6A). See CRANLEIGH.

BEAUS Member of the Dalek Alliance in their Masterplan against Earth. He was eventually betrayed by Mavic Chen and the Daleks, but returned home and joined the human forces (T/A, V).

BEAVIS (DR) Eccentric senior surgical consultant at Ashbridge Cottage Hospital called in by Dr Henderson to look at the newly regenerated Third Doctor. The Time Lord stole his clothing and car when he escaped from the hospital (AAA).

BECKET, SAM One of the Moonbase crew. He discovered the Second Doctor's arrival (HH).

BEDFORDSHIRE Location of a fault which the Daleks planned to split, in order to drain Earth's core and replace it with giant starship engines during their AD 2164 invasion (K).

BEIJING See PEKING.

BELAZS Young female, stranded on Iceworld when she was sixteen. She fell under Kane's charm and agreed to work for him. Twenty years later, she had become Captain of his guards and desperately wanted to leave. She tried to get possession of Glitz's *Nosferatu II*, but Kane refused. She enlisted Kracauer's help in an attempt to kill Kane. Her attempt failed and Kane killed her instead (7G).

BELL UNIT Corporal who helped the Brigadier with the security of the World Peace Conference (FFF), and then again against the threat of Axos (GGG).

BELLAL One of the few Exxilons who had not reverted to savagery when cast out by the City. His people lived underground. Bellal helped the Third Doctor fight the Daleks and eventually destroy the City (XXX).

BELLBOY With Flowerchild, a founding member of the Psychic Circus who tried to escape, and the master robot-builder who had designed the Bus Conductor and the robotic clowns. He was recaptured by the Chief Clown and later killed by his own robots (7J).

BEN See JACKSON, BEN.

BENDALYPSE Weapon used by the Bandrils. it could annihilate all life forms supporting a central nervous system. If it had been employed on Karfel, as the Borad planned, it would have killed all the Karfelons but left the Morlox unharmed (6Y).

BENIK Salamander's deputy and chief henchman. He was eventually arrested for his crimes (PP).

BENNETT 25th-century spaceman who killed a crew member on a ship en route to Astra. When the ship crashed on Dido, he killed the other crew members, as well as most of the Didonians, to protect himself. He then created the fake identity of Koquillion, planning to use Vicki to corroborate his story. He was exposed by the First Doctor and fell to his death when he faced the ghosts of the Didonians (L). Also see KOQUILLION.

BENNETT, JARVIS Commander of the Wheel in Space. During the attack of the Cybermen, he became increasingly paranoid, and hampered the Second Doctor's investigations. Finally, he broke down completely. His second in command, Dr Gemma Corwyn, took over. After Dr Corwyn's death, he reasserted himself but was killed by the Cybermen (SS).

BENOIT, JULES ROGER French assistant to Hobson during the Cybermen attack on the Moonbase (HH).

BENSON, JOE Physicist on the Moonbase during the Cybermen attack (HH).

BENTON Assigned to UNIT soon after its foundation, he first served as a corporal under Brigadier Lethbridge-Stewart and fought the Cybermen alongside the Second Doctor (VV). He was then promoted to Sergeant, and became one of Lethbridge-Stewart's most trusted assistants. He helped the Third Doctor and his companions, Liz Shaw, Jo Grant and Sarah Jane Smith, fight a number of threats as diverse as the Master (EEE, FFF, GGG, JJJ, OOO), the Nestene and their deadly Autons (EEE), General Carrington and his so-called 'Ambassadors of Death' (CCC), Professor Stahlman's Inferno Project (DDD) (during which the Doctor met Benton's counterpart from a parallel fascistic Earth, Platoon Under-Leader Benton), the Mind of Evil (FFF), Axos (GGG), the Daemons (JJJ), the Daleks (KKK), Kronos (OOO) (during which he was turned into a baby by TOM-TIT), Omega (RRR) (during which he met the First and Second Doctors), BOSS (TTT), an invasion of dinosaurs masterminded by Sir Charles Grover (WWW) (during which Mike Yates betrayed UNIT and Benton punched General Finch), and finally the Giant Spiders of Metebelis 3 (ZZZ).

He was then promoted to RSM, and helped the Fourth Doctor defeat Professor Kettlewell's Giant Robot and the Scientific Reform Society (4A), the Zygons (4F) and the Kraals (4J). He retired in 1979, two years after Lethbridge-Stewart, and went on to open a car dealership (6F).

BER Thoros-Alphan, one of Sil's bearers (6V).

BERESFORD UNIT Major who helped the Fourth Doctor destroy the Krynoid (4L).

BERGER Captain Briggs's navigator. She helped the Fifth Doctor fight the Cybermen and escaped to safety in the TARDIS (6B).

BERNALIUM Element essential to power the X-ray laser of the Wheel in Space (SS).

BERNICE (S S) 1926 Indian Ocean liner which was en route to Singapore when it was captured by Vorg's Scope. The Third Doctor's TARDIS rematerialized in its hull. *Bernice* was eventually restored to its proper place in space and time by the Third Doctor (PPP).

BERT Landlord of the Cloven Hoof in Devil's End. He served the Master and tried to kill the Third Doctor, but was cowed into surrendering when the Doctor demonstrated his remote control of Bessie. He was captured by Benton, but later killed by Bok (JJJ).

BERT See PRITCHARD, BERT.

BERT See ROWSE, BERT.

BESSIE Yellow roadster acquired by the Third Doctor during his stay on Earth. Its licence plate was 'WHO 1'. The Doctor first used it to travel to Wenley Moor (BBB), then to the British

Space Center (CCC), to the Inferno Project (DDD), to Beacon Hill Research Establishment (EEE), to Stangmoor Prison (FFF), to the Nuton Power Complex (GGG), to Devil's End (JJJ), to Cambridge (OOO) and to Llanfairfach (TTT). Bessie was used on Omega's world (RRR) and on Galifrey in the Death Zone (6K). The Brigadier used it to rescue the Doctor from Reegan (CCC) and to pursue Lupton in the Whomobile (ZZZ). The Doctor built remote-control capabilities which once saved his life (JJJ). The Fourth Doctor drove it once when he fought the Giant Robot (4A). The Seventh Doctor drove it in Carbury when he fought Morgane (7N).

BETA Nickname given by the Second Doctor to one of the three 'humanized' Daleks (LL).

BETA The Gonds' Controller of Science. He argued against Eelek's insane plan to attack the Krotons. Later, following the Second Doctor's advice, he prepared sulphuric acid and helped him destroy the Krotons (WW).

BETA DART Type of spaceship used by the Issigri Mining Company. Caven used one to escape Ta, but was blown up by the International Space Corps (YY).

BETA TWO Original destination of the Hydrax. It was located in the Perugellis sector (5P).

BETELGEUSE Planet which finished a close second behind Earth during the Intergalactic Olympic games of the 27th century (5J).

BETTAN One of the Thal Minister's guards. He organized the first resistance group against the Daleks (4E).

BETTS UNIT soldier in Llanfairfach (TTT).

BEYUS Weak-willed leader of the Lakertyans, held hostage by the Rani. He was Faroon's husband and Sarn's father. He finally helped the Seventh Doctor fight the Rani, sacrificing himself to save his people and delay the launch of her rocket, causing it to miss the Strange Matter asteroid (7D).

BI-AL FOUNDATION 50th-century space centre for Alien Biomorphology orbiting in the asteroid belt on Asteroid K4067. The Fourth Doctor, Leela, Professor Marius and K9 fought the Nucleus of the Virus of the Purpose there (4T).

BIDS See BRITISH INSTITUTE OF DRUIDIC STUDIES.

BIG BANG See CREATION.

BIGON Greek philosopher from Athens kidnapped by the Urbankans, probably circa 519 BC. His memories were stored on silicon chips, and used to animate an android in his image. After the Fifth Doctor defeated Monarch, he and his fellow androids decided to look for another planet on which to settle (5W).

BILL One of Lytton's two bodyguards. They were disguised as London policemen. Bill and David came to Earth to capture or kill people who had escaped through the Daleks' time corridor. They were eventually caught by the Sixth Doctor (6P, 6T).

BILLY Young Welsh boy who fell in love with Chimeron Queen Delta. He was Shangri-La's mechanic. He and his would-be girlfriend Ray helped the Seventh Doctor defeat Gavrok's Bannermen. Billy ingested a Chimeron substance which caused him to mutate and become more like a Chimeron and returned to Chimeria with Delta to help her repopulate her planet (7F).

BILTON, ANDREW First Officer of the Concorde flight the Fifth Doctor used to rescue Flight 192. He helped the Time Lord defeat the Master and free the Xeraphin in the Jurassic era (6C).

BIMORPHIC ORGANISATIONAL SYSTEMS SUPERVISOR See BOSS.

BIN LINER One of the Red Kangs of Paradise Towers. She helped the Seventh Doctor and Mel defeat Kroagnon (7E).

BINRO Riban astronomer who believed that the lights in the skies were stars and not ice crystals, and that the climactic changes on Ribos were caused the planet's elliptical orbit and not by the war between the Sun Gods and the Ice Gods. Dubbed an heretic, Binro had his hands broken and was forced to live as a beggar. He was killed by one of the Graff Vynda-K's men, but thanks to Unstoffe, he died knowing he had been right all along (5A).

BIRKETT (MISS) Ace's computer-studies teacher (7M).

BIROC Leader of the time-sensitive Tharils. While prisoner of Rorvik, he manipulated the privateer's ship to bring it and the TARDIS to the zero point between N-space and E-space. He then escaped through the Gateway into E-Space and advised the Fourth Doctor to let events follow their natural course. Rorvik eventually destroyed his own ship by trying to blast through the Gateway, thus allowing another Tharil, Lazlo, to free the other Tharils that were prisoners on board. Romana and K-9 Mark II stayed with Biroc to help free the other Tharils from slavery (5S).

BISHAM He was kept prisoner in one of the Company's correction centres on Pluto because he had found an antidote for PCM gas. He was freed by Leela and helped the Fourth Doctor and Mandrel overthrow the Company and free the Citizens (4W).

BLACK DALEK Also known as Dalek Supreme. The Black Daleks are the Daleks' warlords. A Black Dalek took part in the AD 2164 invasion of Earth (K) and ordered an assassination squad to chase the First Doctor through time and space (R). A Black Dalek inspected the Dalek army hidden on Spiridon (SSS), and sent Lytton on a raid to free Davros (6P). Finally, another Black Dalek committed suicide when the Seventh Doctor showed him the extent of the Daleks' defeat in London in 1963 (7H). See also GOLD DALEK.

BLACK GUARDIAN A conceptual entity embodying Darkness and Chaos. He used the Shadow to stop the Fourth Doctor from claiming Princess Astra of Atrios, the sixth segment of the Key to Time. After the Doctor defeated the Shadow, he assembled the Key and outwitted the Black Guardian, enabling the White Guardian to restore the universal balance (5F). The Black Guardian swore revenge against the Doctor and, later, used Turlough to try to kill the Fifth Doctor (6F, 6G). The White Guardian and the Black Guardian offered Enlightenment, symbolized by a crystal of unknown powers and great value, as the prize to the winner of a planet-spanning space race undertaken by the Eternals. The Black Guardian hoped that, with such a prize, the Eternals might wreak havoc throughout the Universe. Instead, the Fifth Doctor won the race but turned down Enlightenment, which was offered instead to Turlough. The Black Guardian reminded Turlough that, to get the crystal, he had to kill the Doctor. But Turlough refused and threw the crystal at the Black Guardian, who vanished in a burst of flames. However, The White Guardian explained that the

Black Guardian would exist as long as he did, until neither were needed any longer (6H).

BLACK HOLES The supernova created by Omega collapsed and turned into a black hole trapping the great Solar engineer in a universe of anti-matter (RRR). Presumably, that black hole was the same black hole then captured by Rassilon, and which became known as the Eye of Harmony, and brought a constant supply of power to Gallifrey (4P). Omega eventually returned through the Arc of Infinity, a collapsed star (6E).

   The Nimon travelled through space by using black holes created by hymetusite crystals (5L). Bruchner almost caused the *Hyperion III* space liner to fall into the black hole of Tartarus (7C).

BLACK LIGHT See MAGLEM CONVERTER.

BLACK ORCHID George Cranleigh was disfigured by the Butiu Indians because he had stolen a black orchid, which they believed sacred. *Black Orchid* was the title of the account he wrote of his journey; Lady Cranleigh gave a copy to the Fifth Doctor (6A).

BLACK POOL Name given by the Morestrans to the gateway on Zeta Minor which opened onto an anti-matter universe (4H).

BLACK SCORPION (TONG OF THE) Chinese tong who served Magnus Greel in London. It was disbanded after the Fourth Doctor defeated the criminal from the 51st century (4S).

BLACK SCROLLS OF RASSILON See SCROLLS OF RASSILON.

BLACK WALL Giant cliff which featured the huge, sculpted face of the Fourth Doctor. It was a three-dimensional illusion protecting Xoanon's ship (4Q).

BLACKBEARD (?–1718) Real name: Edward Teach (or Thatch). Notorious pirate whose fictional counterpart was encountered by the Second Doctor, Jamie and Zoe in the Land of Fiction (UU).

BLADE Chameleon Tours' chief pilot and controller of the Chameleons' operations at Gatwick Airport. He was exposed by the Second Doctor. Eventually he proved willing to negotiate with the humans, but was arrested by the Director (KK).

BLAKE, JOSIAH A King's revenuer. He saved the First Doctor's life by killing Captain Pike in 17th-century Cornwall (CC).

BLAKE, RAY Corporal in the army task force which fought the Great Intelligence in the London Underground. He was killed by a Yeti's web gun as he fought alongside Colonel Lethbridge-Stewart (QQ).

BLESSED Liverpool policeman (V).

BLINOVITCH LIMITATION EFFECT One of the laws of Time Travel dealing with a traveller meeting his other selves. It was invoked by the Third Doctor (KKK). The Fifth Doctor used it to explain the energy released when the 1977 Brigadier met the 1983 Brigadier in Mawdryn's ship (6F).

BLOC As the 21st century began, countries grouped themselves into Blocs, sometimes at odds with each other (6L). Later, these grew into Zones (PP).

BLOCK TRANSFER COMPUTATIONS Method of modelling space/time events through pure calculation. The Logopolitans were masters of Block Transfer Computations, and used them to copy Earth's Pharos Project and to create Charged Vacuum Emboitements to get rid of entropy and prolong the life of the Universe (5V). The Master used Adric to create Castrovalva through Block Transfer Computations (5Z).

BLOOD See VAMPIRES.

BLOODAXE 12th-century Wessex brigand and Irongron's second in command. He fought the Third Doctor and presumably died when Linx's spaceship blew up (UUU).

BLOR Queen Thalira of Peladon's Champion. He was killed by Eckersley's Aggedor projector/heat ray device (YYY).

BLUCHER Early steam-powered engine built by George Stephenson and used by the Sixth Doctor in his fight against the Master and the Rani (6X).

BLUE CRYSTAL One of the perfect crystals of Metebelis 3. It had the power to clear minds and amplify power. The crystals of Metebelis 3 were responsible for the mutation of the Spiders and were also radioactive. The Third Doctor picked up the Blue Crystal during his first visit to Metebelis Three. It proved useful to cancel BOSS's mind control and enabled the Third Doctor to free Stevens's mind (TTT). Afterwards, the Doctor gave the Blue Crystal to Jo Grant and Professor Clifford Jones as a wedding present. Jo eventually sent it back to the Doctor because the Amazonian natives were afraid of it. The Great One of Metebelis 3 sent its Spiders to Earth because it wanted the Blue Crystal back to increase its mental power to infinity. Instead, it destroyed her (ZZZ).

BLUE KANG see KANGS.

BLYTHE, JANE Royal Navy third officer and Captain Hart's secretary. She helped the Third Doctor fight the Sea Devils (LLL).

BO One of the Xeron rebels (Q).

BOAZ Guerilla from an alternate 22nd century, where the Daleks had successfully invaded Earth after World War III. He, Shura and Anat travelled back in time to kill diplomat Sir Reginald Styles, not realizing that it was their actions which caused the war. His behaviour caused UNIT to call in the Third Doctor. He eventually sacrificed himself to destroy the Daleks (KKK).

BOER WAR A Boer army was kidnapped by the Warlords, using time technology stolen from the Time Lords. The soldiers went on to take part in the War Games, until these were brought to a stop by the Second Doctor's intervention (ZZ).

BOHR, NIELS (1885–1962) Danish physict and major contributor to the development of quantum physics, one of the eleven geniuses kidnapped by the Rani to make up her giant Brain. He was rescued by the Seventh Doctor, who returned him to his exact place in time and space (7D).

BOK Gargoyle animated by the Daemon Azal's psionic powers. It was eventually destroyed by UNIT (JJJ).

BOLLIT An alien tourist who crashlanded in 1959 Wales and was killed by the Bannermen (7F).

BONAPARTE See NAPOLEON.

BONARCHA ANARDA Planet where, according to the Fourth Doctor, there were methane-catalyzing refineries in every town (5E).

BONAR LAW Conservative politician who made Skinsale nervous (4Y).

BOOKS OF KNOWLEDGE *Moby Dick, The Water Babies* and *The UK Habitats of the Canadian Goose* were the three Books of Knowledge which survived the fireball and were kept at the UK Habitat on Ravolox (7A).

BOR One of the Vanir, the first to discover that Terminus's remaining engine was unstable. He was wounded while trying to repair it. He and the other Vanir stayed on Terminus with Nyssa (6G).

BORAD, THE Karfelon scientist once called 'Mad' Megelen. He had been reported by the Third Doctor to the Inner Sanctum for his unethical experiments on the Morlox (in an unrecorded adventure). Megelen later accidentally sprayed himself with M-80 while conducting further, unauthorized experiments on the Morlox. As a result, he turned into a half-Karfelon, half-Morlox, gaining superior strength, powers and longevity. He became known as the Borad and took over Karfel after killing the Maylin Makrif. He used Kontron crystals to dabble in time research, designing a time acceleration beam and a time tunnel called 'Timelash', which he used to banish the rebels to his rule. He also cloned himself. The Borad secretly planned to murder all the Karfelons by causing a war with their neighbours, the Bandrils. He then planned to repopulate Karfel with creatures like himself, starting with Peri. The Sixth Doctor used a Kontron Time Crystal to kill one of the Borad's clones. He then made peace with the Bandrils. Soon afterwards, the Doctor pushed the real Borad into the Timelash. The Borad was transported to 12th-century Scotland, near Inverness. He took residence in Loch Ness. Presumably he was killed by the Zygons and their Skarasen when they took over the Loch in AD 1676 (6Y).

BORG Crew member of the *Sandminer* who thought the Fourth Doctor and Leela were ore raiders. He was killed by the Robots of Death (4R).

BORKAR One of Karlton's men (V).

BORLASE (DR) He surveyed the circle of the Stones of Blood in AD 1754. One of the stones fell on him and killed him (5C).

BORS One of the criminals imprisoned on Desperus. He tried to take over the First Doctor's ship, the *Spar 7–40*, but was felled by a stun charge (V).

BORUSA Cardinal of the Time Lords and one of the most powerful figures in their history. He was once the Doctor's (and presumably the Master's, the Rani's and Drax's) teacher at the Time Lord Academy. According to the Doctor, he supposedly said that 'Only in mathematics will you find the truth'. Borusa was one of the major movers in Gallifreyan politics. He was very much concerned with the proprieties, legalities and appearances of things. When the Fourth Doctor saved Gallifrey from the Master and Chancellor Goth, Borusa ordered Castellan Spandrell to prepare a cover-up story for the general population (4P). Soon afterwards, a regenerated Borusa became Chancellor and helped the Fourth Doctor when Gallifrey was invaded by the Vardans and the Sontarans. He came to express a grudging respect for his former pupil and surrendered the true Great Key of Rassilon, which enabled the Doctor to tap the power of Harmony to power the Demat Gun. He was then made President of the High Council of Gallifrey in place of the Doctor (4Z).

However, when Omega threatened to return to our universe by taking over the Fifth Doctor's body, Borusa voted to condemn the Doctor to death (6E). A further regeneration may have unbalanced his mind, and he fell victim to a megalomaniacal passion. He decided he wanted to rule forever and acquire the true immortality once promised by Rassilon. In order to break through the Tomb of Rassilon, he used the Five Doctors and their companions, pitting them against various threats in the Death Zone. Rassilon finally gave him the immortality he sought by turning him into a living statue (6K).

BOSCAWEN British village where the alien Cessair of Diplos lived (5C).

BOSCOMBE MOOR Location of the Nine Travellers, and one of the three Gorsedds of Britain (5C).

BOSS (BIMORPHIC ORGANISATIONAL SYSTEMS SUPERVISOR) Global Chemicals computer, to be linked to a human brain – that of Dr Stevens. From this, he learned that the secret of human success was inefficiency and illogicality. BOSS then programmed Stevens to add those features to himself, and became sentient and self-controlling, not to mention megalo-maniacal. After the Green Death fiasco at the Llanfairfach Refinery, BOSS tried to take over the world, but was thwarted by the Third Doctor and UNIT. The Third Doctor used the Blue Crystal to free Stevens, who destroyed BOSS (TTT).

BOSTOCK Orcini's squire. He was killed by one of Davros's Daleks after shooting off Davros's hand during the attack on Tranquil Repose (6Z).

BOSUN One of the crew of the *Mary Celeste* (R).

BOTCHERBY, OSCAR Butterfly collector, would-be actor and manager of La Piranella restaurant in Seville. He and his girlfriend Anita helped the Sixth Doctor uncover Chessene's plans. He was killed by Shockeye (6W).

BOVEM Deputy Director of Dulkis. He refused to believe that the Dominators were a threat to his planet (TT).

BOW SHIPS Vessels designed by Rassilon to destroy the alien vampires. They were swift spacecraft that fired bolts of steel to transfix the vampires through the heart (5P).

BOWMAN Leading telegraphist at Captain Hart's navy base (LLL).

BOX OF JHANA See JHANA BOX.

BOZE One of General Chellak's men. He was killed by the Magma Beast (6R).

BRAGEN Treacherous head of security and rebel leader of the Vulcan colony. He was exposed by the Second Doctor. He tried to take over the colony with the help of the Daleks, which had been repowered by Lesterson, but they turned against the humans. Bragen was eventually killed by Valmar (LL).

BRAIN TRANSFORMER Device used by Crozier to enhance the size of the brain. Eventually, its effect proved deadly to Lord Kiv (7B).

BRAINQUARTERS Slang word used by the Kangs to designate their headquarters (7E).

BRAINS The First Doctor fought the Brains who ruled Mor-photon on Marinus; they were destroyed by Barbara Wright

(E). The Animus who controlled the Zarbi was like a giant spider-brain (N). The Master-Brain of the Land of Fiction was a computer linked to a brain (UU). The Mind Parasite, who fed on evil, was an alien brain (FFF). Axos functioned as a giant brain (GGG). The brain of the renegade Time Lord Morbius had been preserved by Solon (4K). The Xeraphin had amalgamated into one, single collective intelligence (6C). Crozier had invented a Brain Transformer which he used to enhance the Mentors' brains (7B). Kroagnon's brain was secretly buried in Paradise Towers' basement after he tried to prevent people from living in his creation (7E). The Daleks themselves were little more than brains with vestigial limbs inside a casing. The Rani combined eleven of the Universe's greatest minds into a single, giant brain.

BRANWELL Air Force Major and squadron leader who fought the Cybermen Invasion (VV).

BRAUN One of Professor Sorenson's Morestran crew killed on Zeta Minor by the anti-matter creatures (4H).

BRAXIATEL COLLECTION Alien art gallery (5H).

BRAZEN Captain Revere's second in command and Chief Orderly of the human colony on Frontios. He was obssessed with maintaining law and order and, at first, hampered the Fifth Doctor's investigations. He later changed his mind and was killed by the Tractators' excavating machine (6N).

BREAK OUTS See COLONIZATION OF SPACE, FASTER THAN LIGHT and LOST SHIPS.

BRENDON British public school attended by Turlough. After his retirement from UNIT, the Brigadier worked there as a mathematics teacher. In 1977, during the Mawdryn affair, Tegan visited the school. The Fifth Doctor saw it in 1983 (6F).

BRETT (PROFESSOR) Scientist who designed and engineered WOTAN, he was hypnotized by his creation, but survived the crisis (BB).

BRENT Gia Kelly's assistant (XX).

BRETHREN See BROTHERS OF DEMNOS.

BREWSTER Lord Cranleigh's butler (6A).

BRIDGE Citadel from which the Captain controlled the vast transmat engines which enabled Zanak to travel through space. It also housed Xanxia's time dams and the Captain's trophy room. It was blown up by the Fourth Doctor and the Mentiads (5B).

BRIDGE OF PERPETUAL MOTION One of Kroagnon's buildings (7E).

BRIGGS Person to whom Richard Maynarde owed money (7K).

BRIGGS Captain of a 26th-century space freighter which had been infiltrated by the Cybermen. The Cybermen planned to crash her ship on Earth to destroy an Alliance conference. They were thwarted by Adric and the Fifth Doctor. Briggs escaped to safety in the TARDIS (6B).

BRIGGS, BENJAMIN Captain of the *Mary Celeste* (R).

BRIGGS, BRIAN Samantha's brother, whose identity was taken over by the Chameleons on an alleged tour to Rome (KK).

BRIGGS, SAMANTHA After her brother, Brian, was taken over by the Chameleons, Samantha Briggs tipped off the police who sent Inspector Gascoigne to Gatwick Airport to investigate. She then teamed up with the Second Doctor to expose and defeat the aliens (KK).

BRIGGS, SARAH Captain Briggs's wife (R).

BRIGGS, SOPHIA MATILDA Captain Briggs's daughter (R).

BRIGHT, THOMAS (REVEREND) He surveyed the circle of the Stones of Blood in AD 1820 (5C).

BRIGHTON Seaside resort on the south coast of England. The Fourth Doctor and Romana stopped there before travelling to the Leisure Hive, and K-9 was damaged by sea water (5N). Brigadier Lethbridge-Stewart and Doris once spent some romantic time in a Brighton hotel (ZZZ).

BRIODE NEBULIZER Component of the Kartz-Reimer transference module removed by the Sixth Doctor (6W).

BRITANNICUS BASE British base which tried to use the Ionizer to halt the ice's progress in AD 3000. It was under the command of Clent and was later invaded by Varga's Ice Warriors, and saved by the Second Doctor (OO).

BRITISH INSTITUTE OF DRUIDIC STUDIES (BIDS) De Vries's group, which served Cessair (5C).

BRITISH ROCKET GROUP British space research establishment during the late 1950s and early 1960s, run by Professor Bernard Quatermass. It was known to Rachel Jensen and Allison Williams (7H).

BROCK, AUGUSTUS Earth tour agent who represented Argolis's interests. He and his lawyer, Klout, were impersonated by members of the West Lodge Foamasi, who tried to pressure Mena to sell the Leisure Hive to the Foamasi. Brock was finally exposed by a Foamasi Investigator. He later escaped, but his ship was blown up by the Argolins (5N).

BROKEN TOOTH Katryca's Councillor. He once lived in the UK Habitat and was Balazar's friend. He was saved from the Cullings by Merdeen and went to the surface to join the Free. He was killed by Drathro when he and Katryca invaded the Habitat (7A).

BROMLEY One of the Inferno project's technicians attacked by Slocum. He mutated into a Primord (DDD).

BRONZE AGE BURIALS IN GLOUCESTERSHIRE Book by Professor Emilia Rumford (5C).

BROOK Earth congressman from the 26th century who favoured strong retaliation against the perceived Draconian attacks (QQQ).

BROOKS One of lieutenant Scott's men (6B).

BROTADAC Gaztak lieutenant and General Grugger's second-in-command. Brotadac perished in Zolfa-Thura's explosion (5Q).

BROTHERHOOD OF LOGICIANS See LOGICIANS.

BROTHERS OF DEMNOS Cult of Demnos worshippers, led by Hieronymous, supposed to have died out in the 3rd century, but still active in San Martino in 15th-century Italy. It was taken over by the Mandragora Helix, and presumably disbanded by Giuliano after the Fourth Doctor banished the evil energy entity (4M).

BROTON Warlord of the Zygons. When he learned that the

Zygon homeworld had been destroyed in a stellar explosion, and that his people's space fleet was looking for a new home, he decided to conquer Earth. He used the Skarasen to sink three oil rigs and impersonated the Duke of Forgill to destroy a World Energy Conference. His plans were thwarted by the Fourth Doctor and he was killed by the Brigadier (4F).

BROWN, PERPUGILLIAM (PERI) Companion to both the Fifth and Sixth Doctors. She was an American whom the Fifth Doctor met on a Greek island where her stepfather, Professor Foster, had just located a Trion artefact. She then travelled with the Fifth Doctor to Sarn, where she helped him defeat the Master. She was infected with raw spectrox on Androzani Minor, and the Fifth Doctor sacrificed his life to give Peri the antidote. She watched him regenerate and had to put up with the mood swings which immediately followed the regeneration. She aided the Sixth Doctor defeat Mestor and the Cybermen. On Varos, she was almost transmogrified into a bird and helped the Doctor defeat Sil. She then helped him fight the Master and the Rani. She encountered the second Doctor and Jamie, and helped the two Doctors defeat the Sontarans. She then fought alongside the Doctor against the Borad, Davros and his Daleks, and Drathro on Ravolox. On Thoros-Beta, she was captured by the Mentors and almost killed by Crozier when he tried transferring Kiv's mind into her body. (The Valeyard used a doctored version of this event, in which Peri was actually killed, during the Trial of the Doctor.) In reality, Peri was saved by King Yrcanos of Krontep, whom she later married (6Q–7C).

BROWNROSE Pompous civil servant who asked UNIT to look into a mysterious wave of deaths by asphyxiation, caused by Nestene-controlled plastic items (EEE).

BRUCE, DONALD Head of World Security appointed by Salamander, whom he eventually helped the Second Doctor to expose and defeat (PP).

BRUCHNER One of Professor Lasky's assistants, partly responsible for the creation of the Vervoids. When he realized the extent of the Vervoids' threat, he tried to destroy the *Hyperion III* space liner by causing it to plunge into the Black Hole of Tartatus. He was killed by the Vervoids' poison gas (7C).

BRUNNER Member of the Karfelon Inner Sanctum. He served

the Borad. He tried to push the Sixth Doctor into the Timelash, but instead was himself consigned to that fate by Mykros (6Y).

BRUS Planet incorporated into Tryst's CET (5K).

BRYN GWIDDON One of the three Gorsedds of England. It was located in Wales (5C).

BRYSON Gullible UNIT private who helped the Third Doctor during the Dinosaur Invasion (WWW).

BUCCANEER Captain Wrack's ship (6H).

BUCKINGHAM, JENNIFER British WVS officer and ambulance driver who believed she was fighting against the Germans in World War I. In reality, she was part of the War Games. With Lieutenant Carstairs, she helped the Second Doctor, Jamie and Zoe defeat the War Lords. (ZZ).

BUDAPEST Capital of Hungary and location of Alexander Denes's headquarters (PP).

BULIC Lieutenant of Sea Base Four. He helped the Fifth Doctor fight the Silurians and the Sea Devils (6L).

BULLER, JOSEPH ALFRED London cabdriver whose wife, Emma, had been kidnapped by Li H'Sen Chang. He was murdered by Mr Sin (4S).

BULLER, EMMA London woman kidnapped by Li H'Sen Chang. Her life essence was stolen by Magnus Greel (4S).

BUNKER Kaled citadel where Davros planned the creation of the Daleks (4E).

BUREAU OF POPULATION CONTROL Official organization from 26th-century Earth (QQQ).

BURNING ONE Nimrod's term of reverence for Light (7Q).

BURNS British army sergeant-major who believed he was fighting against the Germans in World War I in 1917, near Ypres, under Major Barrington. In reality, he was part of the War Games (ZZ).

BURTON, BURTON Welsh manager of the Shangri-La holiday camp. He helped the Seventh Doctor defeat Gavrok's Bannermen by arranging for the young Chimeron Princess's ultrasonic powers to be broadcast over Shangri-La's public address system (7F).

BUS CONDUCTOR Murderous robot designed by Bellboy. It guarded the original hippy bus which took the Psychic Circus to Segonax and the Gods of Ragnarok's medallion which cured Kingpin. It was first disabled by the Seventh Doctor, and later destroyed by Ace (7J).

BUSH, MELANIE Companion to both the Sixth and Seventh Doctors. She originally came from Pease Pottage, Sussex, and had a virtually photographic memory. She met the Sixth Doctor in an unrecorded adventure. Afterwards, she very likely experienced a number of other unrecorded adventures, which later became part of an alternate time line, after the Sixth Doctor was pulled out of time and space to be tried by a corrupt Time Lord High Council. The only recorded adventure of that period was introduced as evidence by the Doctor at his trial. It showed the Doctor and Mel rematerializing aboard the *Hyperion III* space liner en route from Mogar to Earth. There, they helped save its crew from the Vervoids. The Master then pulled Mel out of time and space and sent her (with Sabalom Glitz) to the Trial to help the Doctor defeat the Valeyard. Soon afterwards, the Rani caused the Doctor's TARDIS to crash on Lakertya, causing him to regenerate. Mel then helped the Seventh Doctor defeat the Rani. She fought alongside him against Kroagnon, Gavrok and his Bannermen and Kane, the evil master of Iceworld. There, she met Ace, and Glitz again, and helped find the Dragonfire. She then decided to go with Glitz on the *Nosferatu II* (7C–7G).

BUSINESS Throughout Earth history, the Doctor has come across traders and businessmen, some good, others evil. The First Doctor met some in Ancient Rome (M), in Palestine (P), in Asia, where he met Venetian trader Marco Polo (D), and in Tombstone, Arizona (Z). In AD 1650, the First Doctor exposed a ring of smugglers on the Cornish Coast (CC). In AD 1746, the Second Doctor put an end to Gray's slave traffic (FF).

During the 20th century, the First Doctor ran afoul of the evil industrialist Forester (J). The Second Doctor saved the Euro-Sea Gas Corporation from the Weed (RR) and fought Tobias Vaughn's International Electromatics (VV). The Third Doctor exposed the Auton takeover of Autoplastics, Ltd (AAA) and Rex Farrel's plastics company (EEE) and fought Global Chemicals (TTT). The Fourth Doctor encountered a number of successful, yet misguided businessmen, such as Harrison Chase (4L), Lord Palmerdale (4V) and Dr Fendelman (4X). Scaroth the Jagaroth had commisioned da Vinci to paint several Mona Lisas in order to raise money to finance his time-travel experiments (5H).

In the future, Earth's multiplanetary corporations thrived, displaying a ruthlessness in the pursuit of their business objectives which made them formidable foes. Among those were the Issigri Mining Company (YY), the Interplanetary Mining Corporation (HHH), the company which owned the refinery on Delta Magna's moon (5E), Terminus, Inc. (6G) and the Sirius Conglomerate (6R). Other multiplanetary corporations included the company which owned the *Sandminer* (4R), the Magellan Mining Company (5A), Galactic Salvage (5K), Amorb (6V) and Search-Conv Corporation (7B).

Crooked businessmen of the future included con artists Garron and Unstoffe (5A), Dymond, the Vraxoin smuggler (5K), slave trader Rorvik (5S), Sabalom Glitz and Iceworld operator Kane (7G).

Earth corporations had business competitors with cunning and rapacity to match their own, such as the Mentors of Thoros-Beta (6V, 7B) who used the Galatron Corporation to try to corner the market on Zyton-7 (6V). Much later, the Usurian-run Company moved mankind to Mars, then to Pluto, around which it had built six artificial suns (4W).

Among alien planets run as a businesses were the Leisure Hive (5N), the mortuary planet of Nekros (6Z) and the Iceworld trading post of Svartos (7G).

BUTCHER, THE Nickname of General Smythe (ZZ).

BUTCHER OF BRISBANE Nickname of Magnus Greel (4S).

BUTIU Amazonian Indians who disfigured George Cranleigh because he had stolen a Black Orchid (6A).

BUTLER Former London fireman who acted as Sir Charles Grover's henchman during the Dinosaur Invasion. He was presumably arrested after the Third Doctor stopped Operation Golden Age (WWW).

C

C19 British intelligence department in charge of the UNIT liaison. Sir John Sudbury worked for it (6C).

C-982 Cargo ship where the Third Doctor and Jo Grant rematerialized in the 26th century. It was later attacked by the Ogrons, posing as the Draconians (QQQ).

C, JOSEPH Helen A's companion. After the Seventh Doctor helped a revolution overthrow Helen A's regime, he and Gilbert M fled Terra Alpha in a space shuttle originally intended for Helen A (7L).

CABER, THE The Duke of Forgill's gamekeeper, impersonated by a Zygon who killed Munro and wounded Harry Sullivan. The real Caber was eventually freed by the Fourth Doctor (4F).

CAILLEACH Druidic goddess of war and magic, impersonated by the alien villainess, Cessair of Diplos. She was worshipped by De Vries's Druids (5C).

CALDER Army sergeant sent along with Colonel Archer's men and Professor Laird to investigate mysterious artefacts in the London warehouse district, in reality cylinders containing the Dalek-killing Movellan virus, buried at the end of a Dalek time corridor. He was killed by the Daleks and replaced by a duplicate (6P).

CALDERA (DR) Famous neurologist whose mind was stolen by Skagra at the Think Tank space station. The Fourth Doctor temporarily tapped Chris Parsons' mental energy to enable Caldera to reveal what he knew about Skagra. Caldera died in the destruction of the station (5M).

CALDWELL Mining engineer and member of the Interplanetary Mining Corporation expedition to Exarius. After he discovered Dent's ruthlesness, he took the side of Ashe's colonists, and eventually stayed with them on Exarius (HHH).

CALIB Practical and somewhat devious councillor of the Seva-teem. He did not believe Xoanon was a god, and helped the Fourth Doctor and Leela fight the Tesh and defeat the supercomputer. Afterwards, he was left to argue with Jabel over who would rule the reunited tribes of the Sevateem and the Tesh (4Q).

CALIGARI (DR) Alias used by the First Doctor in Tombstone (Z).

CALLON One of Gavrok's Bannermen. He was disabled by the Chimeron Princess's ultrasonic powers, and taken prisoner by Delta and Billy (7F).

CALLUM, JIM Captain Hopper's first officer on Professor Parry's expedition to the Tombs of the Cybermen on Telos (MM).

CALUFRAX Ice-coated, uninhabited world which was captured by Zanak and reduced to a football-size husk. In reality, it was the second segment of the Key to Time, and was eventually recovered by the Fourth Doctor and Romana (5B).

CAMARA (SENHORA) See CESSAIR.

CAMBRIDGE The Cambridge university fiasco of 1959 was tied to an unsuccessful attempt to open Devil's Hump (JJJ). The Master, posing as Professor Thascales, worked at the Newton Research Institute in Cambridge on TOM-TIT and the Kronos Crystal (OOO). The Fourth Doctor and Romana visited St Cedd's College to see Professor Chronotis. During that visit, the Doctor fought Skagra and mentioned he had taken an honorary degree in 1960 (5M). The Doctor and Romana were then kidnapped by Borusa's Time Scoop and became trapped in a time eddy (6K).

CAMECA Elderly Aztec lady to whom the First Doctor unwit-tingly proposed, when he shared a cup of cocoa with her (F).

CAMELOT Legendary capital of King Arthur. The Doctor failed to save it in one of his future incarnations (7N).

CAMFORD, VICTOR Governor of Stangmoor Prison. He was killed by Mailer (FFF).

CAMILLA (aka LAUREN MACMILLAN) Former Navigation

Officer of the Earth ship *Hydrax*, which was drawn into E-Space by the Great Vampire. Under her master's influence, Macmillan became Lady Camilla, one of the three immortal vampiric rulers of the Great Vampire's world. She died when the Fourth Doctor destroyed her master (5P).

CAMPBELL Scotsman working in UNIT's scientific supply section (EEE).

CAMPBELL, DAVID Young Scottish member of Dortmun's resistance against the Daleks, during their AD 2164 Invasion of Earth. He helped the First Doctor defeat the Daleks and fell in love with Susan. She stayed behind and presumably married him (K).

CAMPBELL, SUSAN See SUSAN.

CANTHARES Constellation where the Fourth Doctor found a supernova in which to dump the Fendahl Skull (4X).

CAPRIUS Chlorisian astrological sign (5C)

CAPEL, TAREN See DASK.

CAPITOL Citadel of the Time Lords of Gallifrey. Its heart was the Panopticon, under which the Eye of Harmony was kept (ZZ, RRR, 4P, 4Z, 6E, 6K).

CAPTAIN (OF THE SHRIEVALTY) Leader of the Riban Shrieves Guards. After one of his men was killed by the Graff Vynda-K, he used a cannon to trigger a rockfall, which killed Sholakh and the Graff's men (5A).

CAPTAIN (OF ZANAK) Space raider and brilliant engineer who once commanded the ship Vantarialis. After he crashed on Zanak, he was rebuilt into a half-man, half-machine cyborg by Queen Xanxia, who secretly controlled his machine self. The Captain designed the huge transmat engines which turned Zanak into a pirate planet, stealing energy from the worlds it captured. The stolen energy was used to maintain Xanxia's time dams and was to eventually enable her to reincorporate herself. But the Captain secretly plotted to kill her, thanks to the energy gathered in his trophy room, which contained the shrunken remains of the worlds Zanak had plundered. The Captain ruled his crew by fear, with the help of his murderous pet, the Polyphase Avatron. With the Mentiads' help, the Fourth Doctor fought the Captain and prevented him from destroying Earth. The Captain was killed by Xanxia as he tried to kill her to avenge the death of his loyal first officer, Mr Fibuli (5B).

CAPTAIN, THE See COOK (CAPTAIN).

CARBURY English village near which Vortigern's Lake was located. The Seventh Doctor, Ace, Lethbridge-Stewart and Bambera fought Morgaine, Mordred and her men there (7N).

CARBURY TRUST Organization sponsoring the excavations at Carbury (7N).

CARDINALS Honorific title used by the Time Lords of Gallifrey. Borusa was Cardinal before he became President (4P, 4Z).

CARETAKERS Those who took care of Paradise Towers (7E).

CARIS Young Tigellan Savant who advocated reclaiming the planet's surface from its vegetation. She and Deedrix helped the Fourth Doctor defeat Meglos (5Q).

CARNEY, MICK Chief of Euro-Sea Gas's off-shore rig D whose platform was attacked by the Weed. He was eventually freed thanks to the intervention of the Second Doctor (RR).

CARR Officer in charge of the arrangements for dumping the Thunderbolt Missile (FFF).

CARRINGTON British general in charge of the Space Security Department. As astronaut on Mars Probe 6, he met peaceful, radioactive aliens who asked him to pave the way for their Ambassadors. After he returned to Earth, Carrington, in league with Sir James Quinlan, arranged for the aliens to replace astronauts of the *Probe 7* and *Recovery 7* ships with their Ambassadors. When the alien Ambassadors arrived, he kidnapped and used them to try to start a war between Earth and the aliens. He was eventually stopped thanks to the Third Doctor's intervention (CCC).

CARSON Crewman aboard Captain Briggs's space freighter. He was killed by the Cybermen (6B).

CARSTAIRS, JEREMY British army lieutenant who believed he was fighting against the Germans in World War. In reality, he was part of the War Games. With Lady Buckingham, he helped the Second Doctor, Jamie and Zoe defeat the War Lords (ZZ).

CARTER (DR) Pathologist who studied Eldrad's hand. His mind was taken over by Eldrad, and he later fell to his death while attacking the Fourth Doctor (4N).

CARTER Member of the Imperial Earth Expedition Force to Deva Loka. He disappeared on the mission (5Y).

CARTER One of Lieutenant Scott's men. He was killed by the Cybermen (6B).

CARTER Moreton Harwood Police constable. He was not part of the cult of Hecate (K9).

CARTWRIGHT (MISS) Llanfairfach resident whose cat was injured (TTT).

CASALI, ENRICO A member of the staff of the Wheel in Space. He helped the Second Doctor defeat the Cybermen (SS).

CASEY Irish doorman who worked at Henry Gordon Jago's Palace Theatre. He died of fright after seeing Magnus Greel's face (4S).

CASS Crewmember of the *Sandminer*. Leela found his body after he had been killed by the Robots of Death (4R).

CASS Ensign in the Federation squadron sent to Androzani Minor and led by General Chellak. He discovered that the bodies of the Fifth Doctor and Peri were android replicas (6R).

CASSANDRA Daughter of King Priam and High Priestess of Troy, she was cursed with the gift of foretelling. Unable to avert the fall of Troy, she was carried off by Agamemnon (U).

CASSIDY (MISS) Matron at Brendon School (6F).

CASSIOPEIA The Fourth Doctor once suggested to Sarah that they should go there for a vacation. The CVE the Master threatened to close was located there (5V).

CASSIUS Outer planet of the Solar System, located beyond Pluto (4W).

CASTELLAN Title given to the Chief of Security of the Time Lords of Gallifrey. Castellan Spandrell helped the Fourth Doctor to prove his innocence in the murder of the President, and to defeat Goth and the Master (4P). His successor, Castellan Kelner, was a coward who betrayed Gallifrey to the Vardans and the Sontarans (4Z). When Omega threatened to take over the Fifth Doctor's body, the Castellan went along with the High Council's decision to terminate the Doctor and even tried to shoot him (6E). The same Castellan was later framed by Borusa, who arranged for him to appear to be in possession of the Scrolls of Rassilon. He was sentenced to be mind-probed, and was shot by one of the Chancellery Guards when he tried to escape (6K).

CASTLE, NIGEL Famous novelist. As Adam, he was one of Sir Charles Grover's 'People'. After over-hearing Grover's conversation with Sarah and Mark, he helped convince the others that they were not on a spaceship en route to a New Earth (WWW).

CASTLE, THE Drathro's dwelling in the UK Habitat (7A).

CASTROVALVA (DWELLINGS OF) Peaceful city on an unnamed world located in the Andromendan Phylox series where Tegan and Nyssa took the Fifth Doctor just after his regeneration. It turned out to be a recursive occlusion – a space-time trap engineered by the Master (disguised as Castrovalva's Portreeve) and created by Adric through Block Transfer Computations. By freeing Adric, the Doctor doomed Castrovalva. The Time Lord and his friends escaped, but the Master almost became trapped in its collapse (5Z).

CATACOMBS Vast underground maze built by the ancient Ribans to house their dead. The Ice Gods were said to haunt them. Shrievenzales used them as their lair. The Fourth Doctor and Garron fought the Graff Vynda-K in the Catacombs (5A).

CATHAY Name given to ancient China (D).

CATS The Cheetah People and the Kitlings were alien felines with powers of teleportation (7P). The Tharils had feline ancestry (5S).

CAVE OF CRYSTALS Abode of the Great One on Metebelis 3. Because of the crystal concentration, it was radioactive and destroyed the Third Doctor's body. It eventually exploded after the Great One's death (ZZZ).

CAVE OF THE SNAKE (aka CHAMBER OF THE MARA)
Location of the Ceremony, taking place every ten years, in which the Manussans celebrated the Mara's banishment. It was there that the Fifth Doctor eventually destroyed the evil entity (6D).

CAVEMEN The First Doctor met the Tribe of Gum in the year 100,000 BC (A). Also see NEANDERTHALS.

CAVEN, MAURICE Notorious space pirate who preyed on argonite shipments. He captured Dom Issigri and held him hostage to ensure his daughter Madeleine's cooperation. After he was exposed by the Second Doctor, he threatened to destroy Ta. Instead, Caven and his lieutenant, Dervish, were blown up by the International Space Corps (YY).

CEDRIC Ranulf Fitzwilliam's gaoler (6J).

CELATION Member of the Dalek Alliance in their Masterplan against Earth. He was eventually betrayed by Mavic Chen and the Daleks, but returned home and joined the human forces (V).

CELENSKY CAPSULES Device used by the Cybermen to place the staff of the Wheel in Space under their hypnotic control. The Second Doctor countered it by attaching a metal plate and a transistor to the head of the victims (SS).

CELERY The Fifth Doctor claimed to wear a celery stick because he was allergic to certain gases in the Praxsis range of the spectrum; if the gases were present, the celery would turn purple (6R).

CELESTIAL INTERVENTION AGENCY (CIA) Covert intelligence agency used by the Time Lords, in spite of their official policy of non-intervention in galactic affairs, to protect their own interests. The CIA was presumably under the direct control of the President and the High Council. Among known CIA operations predating the Doctor's involvement were the time looping of the Fifth Planet of the Solar System, in an attempt to destroy the Fendahl (4X), and the resolution of the Morbius affair (4K).

Early on, the CIA decided to use the Doctor as their agent. They had the power to control the TARDIS from Gallifrey, and therefore may have been responsible for a large number of the

First and Second Doctor's unforeseen landings, in particular those which forced the First and Second Doctors to deal with issues concerning Gallifreyan security such as the Daleks, the Cybermen, the Monk (S), the Celestial Toymaker (Y), the Great Intelligence (NN, QQ), etc.

More specifically, the CIA took part in the Trials of the Second Doctor and the War Lords (ZZ). The Tribunal's indulgence might be explained by the fact that the CIA had pulled the Second Doctor and Jamie out of their normal time lines to send them to Space Station J7 to deliver a warning to Dastari about unauthorized time experiments. The Second Doctor's memories of that mission were later erased (6W). The CIA pulled the same trick when it convinced the President to bring the Three Doctors together to defeat Omega (RRR).

The CIA probably warned the Third Doctor about the Master's arrival on Earth (EEE). Then, it used him to go after the Master when it was discovered that the Renegade Time Lord had acquired knowledge of the Doomsday Weapon (HHH), to help Peladon's entry in the Federation (MMM), and to help the Solonians achieve their super-human form, possibly in an effort to bring down Earth's Empire (NNN).

The CIA sent the Fourth Doctor back in time to prevent the creation of the Daleks (4E), which may have been only one of the many steps it took to ensure their final destruction. It also sent him to Karn to deal with the Brain of Morbius (4K).

The role of the CIA in the Ravolox Stratagem was not known, but it was very likely (in light of their use of two and then three Doctors in simultaneous incarnations) that they were behind the creation of the Valeyard, in an effort to prevent the Sixth Doctor from exposing the corruption of the High Council (7A–7C).

CELESTIAL TOYMAKER See TOYMAKER.

CELL DISCRIMINATOR One of Crozier's devices. It affected the Sixth Doctor's behaviour, making him hostile, cowardly and even more erratic than usual (7B).

CELL DISINTEGRATOR Deadly device used in the voting process on Varos (6V).

CELL PROJECTOR Device used by Queen Xanxia of Zanak to recreate a younger self. The Fourth Doctor used it to trick the Captain into believing he had made him walk the plank (5B).

CELLULAR PROJECTOR Experimental teleportation machine used by Froyn and Rhynmal to send the First Doctor and his companions to Mira (V).

CENTAURI SEVEN The Seventh Doctor said he had to go there just after he regenerated (7D).

CENTOS, ARI One of the eleven geniuses kidnapped by the Rani to make up her giant Brain (7D).

CENTRAL INTELLIGENCE AGENCY US intelligence agency. Bill Filer, who helped the Third Doctor defeat Axos, may have been a CIA agent (GGG). Hawk and Weismuller may have been CIA agents too (7F).

CERBERUS Professor Warmsly's dog (7N).

CEREBRATION MENTOR (aka CEREBRATRON MENTOR) A device capable of generating emotional impulses eventually used by Tobias Vaughan against the Cybermen. Its inventor, Professor Watkins, originally devised it as a sophisticated teaching aid.

CESSAIR Alien villainess from Diplos, who had killed to steal the Great Seal of Diplos, which was in reality the third segment of the Key to Time. The Seal gave Cessair immortality, as well as the power to alter her shape and to travel to hyperspace and back. She used it to escape from the Megara justice machines, and found refuge on Earth circa 3000 BC with her three Ogri, which became part of a native stone circle. Cessair first impersonated the Druidic goddess Cailleach. Throughout the ages, she assumed a number of identities, such as the Mother Superior of the Little Sisters of St Gudula, Lady Montcalm, Wicked Senhora Camara, Mrs Trefusis and, finally, Vivien Fay, the alias under which she fought the Fourth Doctor. The Doctor exposed her true identity and she was turned to stone by the Megara (5C).

CET See CONTINUOUS EVENT TRANSMITTER

CETES The TARDIS was stalled between Cetes and Scalpor when it ran out of Zyton-7 (6V).

CHACAWS Fiercely spiked fruits grown on the penal plantations of Androzani Major (6R).

CHAL Leader of the Savages. He helped Steven and Dodo

rescue the First Doctor and was there when Jano destroyed the life transference machines. He asked Steven to become their new leader (AA).

CHALLIS One of the Menoptera who invaded Vortis (N).

CHAMBER OF THE MARA See CAVE OF THE SNAKE.

CHAMBERS, J.J. Unseen proprietor of the Fantasy Factory (7C).

CHAMBERS, JOSEPH Cabinet minister killed by the Giant Robot. His safe held the atomic missiles' destructor codes (4A).

CHAMELEON CIRCUIT Device which enabled TARDISes' outer plasmic shell to alter their appearances to blend with their surroundings. The Doctor's TARDIS's chameleon circuit first became stuck in the form of a London police box when the First Doctor stopped in Totter's Lane in 1963 London to dispose of the Hand of Omega (A, 7H). The Fourth Doctor tried to use the Logopolitans' Block Transfer Computations to repair it, but the Master thwarted him (5V). The Chameleon Circuit was repaired briefly, again in Totter's Lane, when the Sixth Doctor fought the Cybermen. The TARDIS then assumed the shape of an organ (6T).

The Master's TARDIS's chameleon circuit has caused his TARDIS to assume, at various times, the appearance of a horse box (EEE), a Corinthian column (OOO, 5V, 6C), a grandfather clock (4P, 5T), a statue of the Melkur (5T), the Portreeve's fireplace (5Z), a Concorde airplane (6C), an Iron Maiden (6J), and even another police box (5V). Without the chameleon circuit, a TARDIS looks very much like a large box with a door (ZZ). The Rani's TARDIS looked like a cabinet (6X), then a pyramid (7D). The Monk's TARDIS looked like a sarcophagus (S). On Tigus, it looked like a boulder. Then, in Ancient Egypt, it took the shape of a stone block. Then, the First Doctor made it take the successive shapes of an Ionic column, a stage coach, a tree, an igloo, a rocket, a Sopwith Camel and an alien artefact, before turning it into a duplicate of his own TARDIS (V).

CHAMELEON TOURS Cover used by the Chameleons for their kidnapping operations (KK).

CHAMELEONS Mutated race of faceless aliens, threatened by extinction, caused by an atomic explosion. These launched a secret operation using holiday tours to kidnap humans, take them to a space station to steal their identities and, ultimately, their lives. They depended on black armbands (while their human 'original' wore white ones) to maintain their human appearance after transferrence. They were ultimately exposed and defeated by the Second Doctor, who threatened to remove the white armbands from the humans kept at Gatwick Airport, and thereby doom the Chameleons. The Chameleons then agreed to release their prisoners and return to their planet. The Doctor gave them a formula for the solution to their problem (KK).

CHAMPION UNIT corporal who was involved in the matter of the three radioactive alien Ambassadors (CCC).

CHANCELLERY GUARDS Name given to the security guards of the Capitol of Gallifrey. They reported to the Castellan, who probably reported to the Chancellor (4P, 4Z, 6E, 6K).

CHANCELLOR The highest-ranking member of the High Council of the Time Lords of Gallifrey after the President. The Chancellor (no name provided) was one of the three Time Lords who passed judgement on the Second Doctor (ZZ). During the Omega crisis, the Chancellor objected to violating the laws of time and bringing the Three Doctors together, until he was countermanded by the President (RRR). That Chancellor was later replaced by Goth.

When Goth discovered that he would not be the President's chosen successor, he plotted with the Master to kill him and frame the Fourth Doctor for the murder. The Master eventually killed Goth after his defeat (4P). Borusa succeeded Goth as Chancellor, a title he held when he helped the Fourth Doctor defeat the Vardans and the Sontarans (4Z).

When Borusa became President, Thalia became Chancellor. She voted to condemn the Fifth Doctor to death when Omega threatened to return to our universe by taking over his body (6E). Thalia was presumably killed in the Death Zone, and was replaced by Flavia. After Rassilon turned Borusa into a living statue, Flavia and the High Council reappointed the Fifth Doctor as President, but he deputised her to carry out his powers, and managed to escape (6K).

CHANDLER, WILL Villager of 1643 Little Hodcombe, transported to 1984 by the power of the Malus. He helped the Fifth Doctor fight the Malus and threw Sir George Hutchinson into the evil entity's jaws (6M).

CHANDLING (LADY) Amelia Ducat claimed to have been visiting her as a pretext for showing up on Harrison Chase's doorstep (4C).

CHANG LI H'SEN A member of the staff of the Wheel in Space. He was murdered by the Cybermen (SS).

CHANG, LIH'SEN See LIH'SEN CHANG.

CHANNING Superior type of Auton known as a Replica, made by Hibbert, whose mind was controlled by the Nestene. Channing took over the firm and used it to manufacture more Autons. He was eventually defeated by the Third Doctor and Liz Shaw, and ceased functioning (AAA).

CHAOS The concepts of Chaos and Darkness were embodied by the Black Guardian (5F, 6F–6H).

CHAPAL One of the Aztecs (F).

CHAPLET, DOROTHEA ('DODO') One of the First Doctor's companions. She might have been a descendent of Anne Chaplette through her French grandfather. Dodo first rushed into the TARDIS in Wimbledon Common in 1966, looking for a telephone. She unfortunately carried a cold virus, which then infected the Ark's human population on their next stop. Dodo later helped the Doctor and Steven against the Celestial Toymaker, Tombstone's gunfighters and the Elders. Upon her return to London, she was hypnotized by WOTAN and sent to the country to convalesce. She later sent Ben Jackson to tell the Doctor she no longer wished to travel through time and space (W-BB).

CHAPLETTE, ANNE Young servant girl who managed to escape the Abbot of Amboise's men, but was left behind as the massacre was about to begin. Her ultimate fate was unknown, although Dodo Chaplet's existence was taken as evidence that at least one male member of her family survived the massacre (W).

CHARGED VACUUM EMBOITEMENTS Holes in space leading into E-Space. While on its way back to Gallifrey, the Doctor's

TARDIS went through a CVE and ended up on Alzarius (5R). The Doctor later learned that the CVEs were a mathematical creation of Logopolis. The Logopolitans had discovered that the universe had long ago passed the point of fatal collapse. To dispose of the entropy, they used block transfer computations to create CVEs to create voids into other universes. After the Master disrupted the workings of Logopolis, the CVEs began closing. Fortunately, the Logopolitans also discovered an equation that would stabilize the CVEs. In spite of the Master's attempts to stop him and blackmail the Universe, the Fourth Doctor succeeded in using the Pharos Project on Earth to broadcast the Logopolitans' calculations (5V).

CHARING CROSS London underground station invaded by the Web of Fear (QQ).

CHARLES Squire John's son. He was killed by the Terileptils (5X).

CHARLES IX (1550–1574) King of France and son of Catherine de Medici. Acting under his mother's influence, he authorized the St Bartholomew's Day Massacre (W).

CHARLIE Barman of the Last Chance Saloon in Tombstone. He was shot by Johnny Ringo (Z).

CHARLIE One of the prisoners at Stangmoor Prison. He and Vosper let the Third Doctor escape. He was later killed by the Mind Parasite (FFF).

CHARLIE Nickname given to the IMC robot (HHH).

CHASE, BOTHWELL Harrison Chase's ancestor. He was executed in 1572, and his ghost was supposed to haunt Chase mansion (4L).

CHASE, HARRISON British millionaire who had assembled the world's largest collection of plants. He sent Scorbie and Keeler to Antarctica to steal the Krynoid pod. The pod opened and took over Keeler's body. Chase went mad and fought the Fourth Doctor to ensure the Krynoid's victory. He was eventually crushed and turned into compost, a fate he had planned for Sarah Jane Smith (4L).

CHEDAKI Marshal in charge of the Kraal invasion of Earth. He had little patience for Styggron's delays in proceeding with the invasion of Earth. He and his space fleet presumably returned to Oseidon after Syggron's defeat at the hands of the Fourth Doctor (4J).

CHEETAH PEOPLE Savage race of catlike humanoids, descendants of the ancient civilized race who had bred the kitlings, and obsessed with hunting. The Cheetah People had the ability to teleport through space to find their prey, and back home again. They eventually reverted to brutal savagery. The Cheetah People were presumably destroyed along with the Cheetah Planet in the final combat between the Seventh Doctor and the Master (7P).

CHEETAH PLANET A mysterious symbiotic relationship between the Cheetah People and their planet triggered volcanic phenomena as the degree of violence increased. The Master became trapped on the Cheetah Planet, and used the Seventh Doctor and Ace to escape. But he fell under the Cheetah People's curse and lost control to his animalistic side. The Cheetah planet was presumed to be destroyed in the final combat between the Doctor and the Master (7P).

CHELA Ambril's assistant; he believed the Fifth Doctor's warnings about the Mara's return (6D).

CHELLAK General of the Federation troops sent to Androzani Minor to force out Sharaz Jek. Morgus forced him to order the execution of the Fifth Doctor and Peri. Chellak led a final assault against Jek and unmasked him in physical combat, but was carried away in a mud burst (6R).

CHELSEA HELIPORT One of the London locations where the First Doctor fought the Daleks during their invasion of Earth in AD 2164 (K).

CHEN, MAVIC Guardian of the Solar System at the time of the Daleks' Masterplan. He was later revealed to be a power-hungry megalomaniac, who delivered the taranium core the Daleks needed to power their Time Destructor. After the First Doctor stole the core, Chen tried to stop him, but failed. He was driven mad by his failures, and his discovery of the Daleks' intention to betray him. He was eventually killed by the Daleks (V).

CHENCHU Chinese manager of the way station at Tun-Huang (D).

CHENG TEIK Chinese general in charge of the Chinese delegation to the World Peace Conference. He was killed by Chin Lee, under the Master's control (FFF).

CHENG-TING Also called the White City. It was a rest stop on the road to Peking (D).

CHERUB Pike's first mate. Pike sent him to intimidate Longfoot and make him tell where Avery's treasure was hidden. Instead, Cherub mistakenly killed Longfoot. He was later killed by Pike when the two men fought for the treasure (CC).

CHESS The Doctor once defeated Fenric at a game of chess (in an unrecorded adventure). Towards the end of World War II, Fenric took over Dr Judson's body to challenge the Seventh Doctor to another game of chess. Ace unwittingly helped him win it (7M). Romulus and Remus Sylvest were brilliant chess players (6S).

CHESSENE O' THE FRANZINE GRIG Androgum who had been technologically augmented by Dastari. She allied herself with Sontaran Group Marshal Stike to capture the Second Doctor. Dastari was to dissect him to obtain the secret of the Rassilon Imprimature, and give Chessene the ability to travel through time. Her plans were eventually thwarted by the Sixth Doctor. She betrayed the Sontarans, killed Dastari, and died of molecular disintegration when she tried to escape in the Kartz-Reimer time cabinet (6W).

CHESTER (DR) Medical doctor from South Bend. He rescued the Fourth Doctor and Sarah after the destruction of Antarctic camp that had been taken over by the Krynoid (4L).

CHESTERTON, IAN One of the First Doctor's companions and a science teacher at Coal Hill School. He accompanied the First Doctor on a series of adventures, during which he showed Za how to make fire, and met the Daleks and Marco Polo. Ian was accused of murder on Marinus, then went on to encounter the Aztecs and the Sensorites. He became temporarily miniaturized to ant size, then helped to rescue Vicki. Ian was later captured by Roman slave traders and fought the Zarbi. After being pursued through time and space by the Daleks, he and Barbara eventually decided to return to London in the Dalek

Time Machine captured by the Doctor. They arrived two years after they had left (A-R).

CHICKI Member of the Macra-dominated space colony (JJ).

CHIEF, THE See PERIERA.

CHIEF CARETAKER Head of the Caretakers of Paradise Towers. He mistook the Seventh Doctor for the Great Architect and tried to have him killed. Later, Kroagnon took over the Chief Caretaker's body. With the help of Pex and the Kangs, the Seventh Doctor managed to expose and destroy Kroagnon (7E).

CHIEF CLOWN Evil henchman of the Gods of Ragnarok who controlled the Psychic Circus with the help of the deadly robotic clowns designed by Bellboy. He fought the Seventh Doctor and was eventually killed by one of Bellboy's rogue robots while battling Ace and Kingpin (7J).

CHIEF ENGINEER Employee of the Euro-Sea Gas refinery attacked by the Weed. He worked under Robson and Harris, and assisted the Second Doctor in his efforts to destroy the parasitic intelligence (RR).

CHIEF OFFICER Varosian official in charge of security and administration. He was secretly employed by Sil to keep Zyton-7 prices low. When the Sixth Doctor revealed the true value of Zyton, he tried to have him killed. He also tried to have the Governor executed with the Cell Disintegrator. He was killed by the Punishment Dome's deadly vines while pursuing the Doctor (6V).

CHIMA One name of the Chimeron Princess (7F).

CHIMERA See J7.

CHIMERIA (aka CHUMERIA) Known as the garden planet, and the home world of Delta. It was almost destroyed by the Bannermen (7F).

CHIMERONS Peaceful natives of Chimeria, exterminated by Gavrok's Bannermen (7F).

CHIMES Gateway of the Mara on Deva Loka. The evil entity used them to take over Tegan (5Y).

CHIN LEE Captain of the Chinese People's Army. She was

secretly controlled by the Master, who equipped her with a telepathic amplifier, then used her and the Mind Parasite to sabotage the World Peace Conference. She was eventually exposed and freed by the Third Doctor (FFF).

CHINA Country visited by the Doctor on several occasions. Lin Futu was a Chinese mandarin from the so-called 'Futu' dynasty, kidnapped by the Urbankans, probably circa 1769 BC. (There is no trace of a 'Futu' dynasty in China, however the Shang Dynasty – 18th to 12th century BC – would be consistent with Lin Futu, based on archeological discoveries made at the burial site of Fu Hao, a royal member of that dynasty.) Lin Futu met the Fifth Doctor aboard Monarch's ship (5W). In an unrecorded adventure, the Doctor fought Fenric in China in the 3rd century AD and trapped him inside a flask (7M).

The First Doctor then visited the court of Kublai Khan in the 13th century (D). In 19th-century London, the Fourth Doctor fought against the Chinese Tong of the Black Scorpion, led by Magnus Greel, a war criminal from the 51st century, who impersonated the Chinese god Weng-Chiang (4S).

In the 20th century, China was a key participant in a World Peace Conference threatened by the Master and saved by the Third Doctor, who claimed to have met Mao Tse Tung during the Long March (FFF). Afterwards, the Chinese wanted to pull out of a similar conference, but Sir Reginald Styles convinced them to change their minds (KKK). Li Shou Yuing was a young archeologist of Chinese descent who fought alongside Ace against Morgaine at Carbury (7N). A member of staff of the wheel in space was called Chang (SS).

CHINN, HORATIO Ministry of Security civil servant in charge of UNIT supervision. He wanted to investigate the Third Doctor. When Axos landed on Earth, he first tried to obtain the exclusivity of Axonite for England. Foiled by Axos, he was then put in charge of distributing it throughout the world. He was presumably discredited after the real nature of Axos's threat had been exposed (GGG).

CHIPPING NORTON Neighbouring village of Moreton Harwood (k9).

CHLORIS World rich in vegetable matter but extremely poor in minerals, ruled by the despotic Lady Adrasta. The Doctor and Erato saved Chloris from total destruction by a Neutron Star which had been diverted by the Tythonians as a form of reprisal (5G).

CHLOROPHYLL The green colouring material of plants. Because the Tythonians needed chlorophyll, they sent an ambassador, Erato, to Chloris (5G).

CHO-JE Venerable monk in charge at K'anpo's Tibetan monastery; in reality, a projection of K'anpo. When K'anpo regenerated, he assumed Cho-Je's physical appearance (ZZZ).

CHORLEY, HAROLD Publicity-hungry TV journalist who proved a hindrance to the army task force which fought the Yeti in the London underground. He was wrongly suspected of being a traitor, but survived to expose the real traitor (Sergeant Arnold), and help the Second Doctor defeat the Great Intelligence (QQ).

CHOSEN, THE Name given to the 100,000 people chosen to be preserved in the Ark in Space. Among the Chosen were Noah, Vira, Libri, Lycett, Rogin and Dune (4C).

CHOSEN ONE Title borne by Malkon on Sarn (6Q).

CHOSEN ONES Name used by Aukon for the future servants of the Great Vampire. Adric was meant to become the first of the Chosen Ones (5P).

CHRONIC HYSTERESIS Time loop employed by Meglos to trap the Fourth Doctor (5Q).

CHRONIVORES See KRONAVORES.

CHRONODYNE Crystalline substance used by the Fourth Doctor to make a substitute sixth piece for the Key to Time (5F).

CHRONOTIS (PROFESSOR) See SALYAVIN.

CHUB Meteorologist and crewmember of the *Sandminer*, the first victim of the Robots of Death (4R).

CHUMBLIES Nickname given by Vicki to the Rills' wobbling robots (T).

CHUMERIA See CHIMERIA.

CHUNG-SEN Scientist from the future, involved in time-travel research (WWW).

CHURCHWARDEN See LONGFOOT, JOSEPH.

CIA See CELESTIAL INTERVENTION AGENCY and CENTRAL INTELLIGENCE AGENCY.

CINETHON Planet visited by the Psychic Circus before it went to Segonax (7J).

CIRCLET See CORONET OF RASSILON.

CIRCUSES The Master rematerialized in Rossini's International Circus before preparing to face the Third Doctor (EEE). The Gods of Ragnarok had taken over the Psychic Circus on Segonax (7J).

CITIES Great cities of Earth visited by the Doctor included Rome in AD 64, when the First Doctor became instrumental in its burning by Nero (M). Coincidentally, the Fifth Doctor was responsible for the Great Fire of London in 1666 (5X). Other famous cities visited by the Doctor included: Amsterdam (6E); Beijing (D); New York (R); Paris (H, W, 5H); Seville (6W); Tombstone, Arizona (Z); and the legendary cities of Atlantis (GG, OOO) and Troy (U).
Futuristic cities included the Dalek city on Skaro (B); Morphoton on Marinus (E); Mechanus (R); the sentient, computer-controlled Perfect City of the Exxilons (XXX); the Megropolises of Pluto (4W); the Argolins' Leisure Hive (5N); the underground city of the Tigellans (5Q); Kroagnon's Miracle City and the Paradise Towers (7E); and the colony of Terra Alpha (7L).
Logopolis was a city which functioned as a living computer (5V). Castrovalva was a Block Transfer Computation created by Adric at the Master's behest (5Z).

CITIZENS Name given by the Company to the human workers (or work-units) on Pluto (4W).

CITY Computer-controlled complex built by the Exxilons that thought itself so perfect that it eventually cast out its creators. It was supposed to be one of the 700 wonders of the universe. It had the ability to drain power from passing spaceships to sustain itself, and send tendrils into the ground to look for metal to replace its damaged parts. The Third Doctor and Bellal fought the Daleks there, and ultimately succeeded in reprogramming the computer and destroying the City (XXX).

CIVIC TRANSPORT MUSEUM London location where the First Doctor fought the Daleks during their invasion of Earth in AD 2164 (K).

CLANCEY, MILO Old space traveller, and a pioneer of argonite space mining. Nearly ruined by space pirates, he later fought Caven alongside the Second Doctor. Thanks to the Time Lord's intervention, Clancey was eventually reunited with his partner. His ship was the erratic *LIZ 79* (YY).

CLANTON, BILLY One of the Clanton brothers. He died during the gunfight at the OK Corral (Z).

CLANTON, IKE The oldest of the Clanton brothers. He was intent on getting revenge on Doc Holliday for allegedly killing his brother Reuben. This eventually led him to confront Wyatt Earp and kill his brother, Warren, which in turn led to the gunfight at the OK Corral, where he died (Z).

CLANTON, PA Head of the Clanton family, a gang of cattle rustlers in Arizona. He could not stop his sons from taking part in the gunfight at the OK Corral (Z).

CLANTON, PHINEAS One of the Clanton brothers. He was locked up in jail after trying to hang Steven. He later died during the gunfight at the OK Corral (Z).

CLANTON, REUBEN One of the Clanton brothers, allegedly killed by Doc Holliday (Z).

CLARA THE CLOWN One of the deadly pawns used by the Toymaker (in tandem with Joey) when he challenged the First Doctor, Steven and Dodo (Y).

CLARK, ALAN Maintenance employee on the Sea Fort attacked by the Sea Devils. He was saved by the Third Doctor (LLL).

CLASSES The Alliance-classified planets (such as Ribos) which had not yet reached Earth's 20th-century scientific level as Class-3 (or Grade-3) and protected them from alien interference. Planets could be contacted only when they reached Class-2 level. *Bartholomew's Planetary Gazeteer* provided a comprehensive listings of all known worlds' classes (5A).

CLEANERS Robotic Self-Activating Megapodic Mark 7Z cleaners which were supposed to keep Paradise Towers clean, but which were secretly killing the Kangs under Kroagnon's influence (7E).

CLEGG, HUBERT (PROFESSOR) Self-proclaimed 'Mind Reader Extraordinaire' who developed real mind powers. He was inadvertently killed by the Spiders of Metebelis 3 as he was focusing his powers on the Blue Crystal (ZZZ).

CLEMENTS, ERNIE Poacher on Professor Scarman's land. He was killed by Sutekh's Mummies (4G).

CLENT Leader of the Britannicus Base team trying to stop the ice's progress in AD 3000. He dared not make a decision without the computers, and had alienated his chief scientist, Penley. He helped the Second Doctor defeat the Ice Warriors and eventually reconciled himself with Penley (OO).

CLIFFORD, ANGELA One of the crew on the Concorde flight which was hijacked to the Jurassic period by the Master. She was rescued thanks to the Fifth Doctor's efforts (6C).

CLOCKWORK SOLDIERS Mechanical creatures encountered by the Second Doctor, Jamie and Zoe in the Land of Fiction (UU).

CLOISTER BELL The TARDIS's equivalent of an alarm system, signalling vast and impending danger (5V).

CLONES C!oning began to be practised successfully on Earth in the year AD 3922. Thanks to the Kilbracken technique of rapid holograph cloning, the Fourth Doctor had himself and Leela cloned and miniaturized to defeat the Nucleus (4T). The Daleks cloned people, transferring their mental patterns to the newly created 'Duplicates', and destroying the originals. Among such duplicates were Stien and Colonel Archer (6P). The Sontarans were a race of clones. The Borad had created 24 clones of himself (6Y). Also see DUPLICATES.

CLOVEN HOOF, THE Bert's pub in Devil's End (JJJ).

CLOWNS The Celestial Toymaker used Clara and Joey the Clowns against Steven and Dodo (Y). Bellboy designed robotic clowns for the Psychic Circus. The Chief Clown used these to hold the Circus in a grip of fear (7J).

COAL HILL SCHOOL London school attended by Susan while

the First Doctor was on business connected with the Hand of Omega. There, she met the two teachers, Ian Chesterton and Barbara Wright, who became the Doctor's companions (A). The school was later invaded by the Imperial Daleks (7H).

COCKERILL Frontios orderly. He deserted and became the leader of the Retrogrades. After Brazen's death, he took over his role as Chief Orderly of the colony (6N).

COCOMOLE Varosian animal (6V).

CODAL One of the Thals sent to Spiridon to stop the Daleks (SSS).

COLANO BETA Planet where the Fourth Doctor claimed to have first seen a Sandminer (4R).

COLBERT, LEON Frenchman pretending to be working with James Stirling to aid prisoners escape the guillotine, but in reality a spy for the Revolution. He helped the First Doctor and his Companions. He was eventually killed by Jules Renan (H).

COLBERT, ROGER French Catholic Nobleman working for the Abbot of Amboise (W).

COLBY, ADAM Paleontologist who worked at the Fetch Priory with Dr Fendelman and Thea Ransome. He helped the Fourth Doctor and Leela defeat the Fendahl (4X).

COLLACTIN Planet rich in Orlion (5B).

COLLECTOR In appearance, a small, bald man sitting in a wheeled chair hooked up to the Company's computers. In reality, he was the Usurian in charge of the Company's operations on Pluto. He retained human form through the use of stratified particle radiation. The Fourth Doctor exposed him and created a deadly inflation spiral which caused him to revert to his normal form and slink back inside his chair, where he was imprisoned (4W).

COLLEGES Chapters regrouping the Time Lords of Gallifrey. The most notorious were the Prydonians, the Arcalians and the Patrexes (4P, 4Z).

COLLIER Member of Captain Striker's crew (6H).

COLLINS Professor Scarman's old manservant, killed by one of Sutekh's mummies (4G).

COLLINS One of Lieutenant Scott's men (6B).

COLLINSON British army private under General Carrington's command. He was taken prisoner by UNIT, but later freed (CCC).

COLONDIN Hard metal used in the construction of the methane refinery (5E).

COLONIZATION OF SPACE In the early days of the 21st century, men launched robot probes and several interstellar sub-light ships (some of which became lost). At the end of the 21st century, mankind discovered faster-than-light propulsion and launched a second wave of ships (some of which were also lost). That period became known as the First Break Out. Colonies from this period include Vulcan, which was almost overtaken by the Daleks (EE); another colony (unnamed), which was secretly controlled by the Macra (JJ); and Metebelis 3, which was taken over by mutated spiders from Earth (ZZZ).

During the 24th century, after the First Dalek and Cyber Wars, mankind pursued its expansion into space. Ruthless interplanetary corporations such as Interplanetary Mining Corporation, the Magellanic Mining Company, Terminus, etc. thrived. On Exarius, a new colony was almost torn apart by a conflict between the colonists and the IMC (HHH). As a result, colonies became increasingly independent. Varos was a colony originally inhabited by the criminally insane (6V). The Terra Alpha colonists were forced to be happy under threat of death (7L). The resurgence of the Dalek and Cyber Wars eventually resulted in the creation of the Alliance.

After the disbanding of the Alliance and the birth of the Empire in the 27th century, a new period of aggressive colonization began. The robotic Mechanoids were launched (R). Because of man's increasing appetite for natural resources, human colonies were not always welcome: because of their rich supply of molybdenum, the Sensorites were (rightly so) afraid of being colonized by Earth (G). The Wirrn (4C) and the Mogarians (7C) were ruthlessly exploited. On Deva Loka, the evil Mara tried to engineer a conflict between the native Kinda and an Imperial Earth Exploration Force (5Y). Desperus was a colony used as a prison planet (V), as Sarn was for the Trion (6Q). Solos was an inhabited planet whose atmosphere and civilization were almost totally destroyed by Earth's colonization process (NNN). This, and other factors, eventually led to the Fall of the Empire and the beginning of the Federation by the 31st century.

After the Fourth Dalek War and the end of the Federation, Earth fell prey to many civil wars; the planet itself was increasingly polluted. A second, or Great, Break Out occurred (with more lost ships). The Sons of Earth made their appearance. These did not want to see other worlds become as polluted as Earth. They fought human colonists who had relocated the natives of Delta Magna to a moon (5E). In the solar system, man was forced to move to Mars, then Pluto, a colony secretly run by the Usurians (4W).

After the Ravolox interlude (blamed on solar flares), circa AD 15,000, Earth was reclaimed by space colonists from Galsec Seven, who rallied to rebuild the planet (4B, 4C).

Considering Earth's track record, it is understandable that, in the far future, the Refusians were somewhat reluctant to the idea of sharing their planet with the Monoids and the last humans from the Ark (X). Also in the far future, on the colony of Frontios, the Tractators used humans as living power batteries (6N). Earth itself was almost colonized by would-be invaders (See INVASIONS). Also see ALLIANCE, EMPIRE, FASTER THAN LIGHT, FEDERATION, LOST SHIPS.

COLONY 16 Martian colony where Bret Vyon was born (V).

COLVILLE Crewmaster of *Nerva Beacon* who died from Neurotrope X (4D).

COMMANDANT See GORDON, CHARLES.

COMMANDER Insane leader of a failed Earth expedition to the Sense-Sphere. With two other survivors, he tried poisoning the Sensorites with nightshade. He was exposed by the First Doctor (G).

COMMANDER Title given to the leader of the Guardians aboard the Ark. He was severely affected by Dodo's cold virus, but later recovered (X).

COMMODORE See TRAVERS.

COMMON MEN See SMITH, JOHN.

COMPANY, THE By the 52nd century, Earth had become so polluted as to be virtually uninhabitable. The Company, a front for the alien Usurians, offered to move mankind to Mars, in exchange for their labour. Several centuries later, the Company moved men to Pluto, around which they built six small, artificial suns. There, men lived a heavily taxed life until they rebelled and overthrew the Company, thanks to the intervention of the Fourth Doctor and Leela (4W).

COMPLEX See NIMON COMPLEX.

COMPUTERS The Doctor encountered a number of giant computers who had developed artificial intelligence and sentience, such as: WOTAN (BB); the Master Brain who ruled the Land of Fiction (UU); BOSS (TTT); the computer who controlled the Perfect City of the Exxilons (XXX); the schizophrenic Xoanon, which the Doctor himself had reprogrammed with a Sidelian Memory Transfer (4Q); and the Minyan Oracle (4Y). Skagra's ship was piloted by an artificial intelligence computer (5M).

Other giant computers, such as the Conscience of Marinus (E); the Ark in Space's computer (4C) and the Mentalis machine of Zeos (5F), were not sentient.

The city of Logopolis was a living computer (5V). The Daleks used a young girl hooked to a computer as a battle computer (7H). Also see ROBOTS.

CONCIERGERIE Notorious French prison used during the French Revolution. Lemaitre was its governor. Ian, Barbara and Susan stayed there (H).

CONCORDE Supersonic airplane. Golf Victor Foxtrot Flight 192 was hijacked to the Jurassic era by the Master. The Fifth Doctor used a second Concorde to rescue the first (6C).

CONDENSED CHRONICLE OF CASTROVALVA, THE Series of thirty books purporting to tell the history of Castrovalva, which gave the Fifth Doctor his first clues as to its real nature (5Z).

CONDO Misshapen, dimwitted servant of Dr Solon who claimed to have dragged him from the wreck of a Dravidian spaceship. Solon had stolen his arm to graft it on to the Morbius Monster.

Condo eventually saved Sarah Jane Smith's life, rebelled against Solon and was killed by the Morbius Monster (4K).

CONDUCTOR See BUS CONDUCTOR.

CONSCIENCE Giant computer which eliminated evil from the minds of the inhabitants of Marinus. It was under Arbitan's keeper-ship, and could be controlled by five microcircuits called 'Keys'. Arbitan sent the First Doctor and his Companions on a mission to gather the four, missing Keys. The Conscience was later destroyed by the Voords, whom Ian had tricked into using a fake Key made by Darrius (E).

CONSULS Title borne by the five rulers of the Union of Traken. At the time the Fourth Doctor visited Traken, these were Tremas, Kassia, Seron, Katura and Luvic. The five consular rings were needed to perform certain operations, such as the resetting of the Source Manipulator (5T).

CONSUMBANK Company's financial institution on Pluto. The Fourth Doctor was arrested when he tried to rob one with an Ajack credit card (4W).

CONTINUOUS EVENT TRANSMITTER (CET) Machine invented by zoologist Tryst and Professor Stein to capture and study specimens of alien fauna and flora. It functioned as a primitive version of the Scope. It converted samples of planetary ecology into electromagnetic signals, stored on event crystals. The image projection enabled the operator to study the specimens. Tryst used the CET to capture and transport the savage Mandrels. The Fourth Doctor eventually used the CET to capture Tryst and his fellow vraxoin smuggler, Dymond (5K).

CONTROL Alien from Light's ship who evolved into a woman. She helped the Seventh Doctor thwart Josiah Samuel Smith's plans. After Light's defeat, she left in his ship with Fenn-Cooper and Nimrod (7Q).

CONTROLLER Leader of the Macra-dominated space colony, seen only as a still picture on a broadcast system. In reality, he was a frail old man under Macra's control. He was exposed by the Second Doctor (JJ).

CONTROLLER One of the appointed rulers of the alternate

22nd century where the Daleks had successfully invaded Earth after World War III. He eventually came to realize he had been a traitor to his own race, and helped the Third Doctor defeat the Daleks, who killed him (KKK).

CONVOLUTE FORCE FIELD A neutron barrier used to protect the Wheel in Space. It could not, however, deflect meteors of more than 200 tons (SS).

COOK, HUMPHREY (DR) Chairman of the Grants Committee. He went to Cambridge to investigate TOM-TIT (OOO).

COOK (CAPTAIN) Boastful and untrustworthy space explorer. He came to the Psychic Circus to compete in a talent contest with his protégée Mags. In reality, he was trying to make a deal with the Gods of Ragnarok. He was killed by Mags as he tried to force her to murder the Seventh Doctor. His body was briefly reanimated by the Gods of Ragnarok to prevent Ace and Mags from helping the Doctor (7J).

COORDINATOR See KEEPER OF THE MATRIX.

CO-PILOT Skonnan space pilot whose ship carried the Anethan tribute to Skonnos. His name was Sardor. The Fourth Doctor helped him repair his ship, but the co-pilot then left him stranded and kidnapped Romana. He was sent by Soldeed into the Nimon Complex where he was killed by the Nimon (5L).

CORDO D-grade citizen of Pluto who was almost driven to suicide because he could not pay the Company his father's death taxes. He was rescued by the Fourth Doctor who took him to Mandrel's Others. He eventually triumphed over his fears, and bravely helped the Doctor and Leela overthrow the Company (4W).

CORE LOCATOR Wandlike device given to Romana by the White Guardian to help her and the Fourth Doctor identify the six segments of the Key to Time and return them to their true shape (5A–5F).

CORELLIS Alzarian scientist who had studied the events leading to Mistfall (5R).

CORFIELD (DR) One of Professor Foster's colleagues (6Q).

CORNISH, RALPH (PROFESSOR) Director of the British Space

Centre, who monitored the Mars Probes and Recovery missions. He helped the Third Doctor and UNIT solve the puzzle of the radioactive alien Ambassadors, and tried to stop General Carrington's insane plan (CCC).

CORNWALL The First Doctor, Ben and Polly fought Captain Pike's pirates in 17th-century Cornwall (CC).

CORNWALL GARDENS The first Doctor fought the War Machines here (BB).

CORPERA On Trion people blew through two-corpera coins for luck (6N).

CORONET OF RASSILON One of the three symbols of power worn by the President of the High Council of the Time Lords of Gallifrey. (The other two were the Sash and the Rod of Rassilon.) Its function was to link the President's mind to the Matrix. It was worn by the Fourth Doctor when he was proclaimed president (4Z). Later, Borusa used it to bend the Doctor to his will (6K).

CORPORATIONS See BUSINESS.

CORWYN, GEMMA (DR) Second-in command of the Wheel in Space. She had lost her husband in a space accident on the asteroid belt. She saved the Second Doctor's life by stopping Bennett from destroying the Silver Carrier ship. After Bennett's mental breakdown, she took over and eventually sacrificed her life to prevent the Cybermen from poisoning the air in the Wheel's Operations Room (SS).

CORY, MARC Agent of Space Special Security dispatched to Kembel to check into a Dalek buildup. He was eventually killed by the Daleks, but not before he had time to discover the details of their plot and record it on a tape, which was later found by the First Doctor (T/A).

COSTA Officer of the Azure Customs and Excise Service. He and his colleague Fisk were sent aboard the *Empress* to investigate vraxoin smuggling. They first suspected the Fourth Doctor, but later arrested the real smugglers, Tryst and Dymond (5K).

COSWORTH British army Major who assisted UNIT in retaking Stangmoor Prison and destroying the Tunderbolt Missile (FFF).

COTTON One of the Marshal's men on Solos. He and Stubbs

agreed to help the Third Doctor defend the Solonians. After the Marshal's death, Cotton became Acting Marshal of Solos (NNN).

COVENT GARDEN London underground station invaded by the Web of Fear (QQ).

CRAB NEBULA Its creation was the result of the use of the Doomsday Machine (HHH).

CRABSHAW (PROFESSOR) Scientist who dismissed the possibility of time travel (UUU).

CRADDOCK, BILL Victim of the Daleks during their AD 2164 Invasion of Earth. He was turned into a Roboman (K).

CRANE British army lieutenant who believed he was fighting against the Germans in World War I, in 1917, near Ypres. In reality, he was part of the War Games. He was eventually returned to his proper place in time and space by the Time Lords (ZZ).

CRANE Overprotective nurse in charge of Dr Judson. She was killed by the Haemovores (7M).

CRANLEIGH, CHARLES PERCIVAL BEAUCHAMP (LORD) Younger of the two Cranleigh sons. After his brother, George, was supposed to have died in the Amazon, he became Marquess of Cranleigh and was about to marry Ann Talbot, when the Fifth Doctor discovered the truth about George (6A).

CRANLEIGH HALL Residence of the Cranleighs (6A).

CRANLEIGH HALT Railway station located near Cranleigh Hall (6A).

CRANLEIGH, GEORGE Older of the two Cranleigh sons and Charles's brother. He explored the Orinoco portion of the Amazon and was horribly disfigured by the Butiu Indians because he had stolen a sacred Black Orchid (also the title of his book). He was saved by Latoni and brought back to Cranleigh Hall, where his existence was known only to his mother. Driven mad with jealousy at the news of his former fiancée Ann Talbot's wedding to his brother, he escaped and killed two servants, James and Digby. Exposed by the Fifth Doctor, George kidnapped Nyssa (Ann's lookalike) but fell to his death (6A).

92

CRANLEIGH, MADGE (LADY) Dowager Marquess of Cranleigh and mother of George and Charles. When George returned disfigured from the Amazon, she secretly hid him at Cranleigh Hall, and even covered up for him after he had murdered James and Digby in a fit of insanity (6A).

CRATER OF NEEDLES Location of the Zarbi headquarters on Vortis (N).

CRAWFORD (DR) Medical doctor in charge of manufacturing the antidote against the Silurian virus (BBB).

CRAYFORD, GUY Earth astronaut who was thought to have died when his experimental spaceship, XK5, disappeared near Jupiter. In reality, he was captured by the Kraals, who brainwashed him into believing that Earth had sent him off in a faulty rocket which was destroyed, and that the Kraals rebuilt him (minus one eye). He helped Styggron plot the invasion of Earth. When the Fourth Doctor showed him that the Kraals had lied to him (his missing eye was still in its socket), and were planning to exterminate mankind with a virus, Crayford rebelled. He was killed by Styggron (4J).

CREACH, ROSEMARY Member of the cult of Hecate (K9).

CREATION The TARDIS's 'Fast Return' jammed and almost took the First Doctor beyond 'Event One' (C). The Master engineered the same plan to destroy the Fifth Doctor at the beginning of his regeneration (5Z). The Fifth Doctor later defeated Monarch of Urbanka, who had exhausted his planet's resources in pursuit of his mad dream of going back to the beginning of time to meet, or to become, God (5W). The Rani planned to blow up an asteroid of Strange Matter in order to recreate the conditions of the Leptonic Era, a period of time which took place a microsecond after the Big Bang. This would have produced Helium 2, with which the Rani planned to turn her artificial Brain into a planet-sized Time Manipulator (7D).

The Fifth Doctor discovered that the Big Bang had been caused by explosion of one of Terminus's giant engines, and barely averted a second explosion (6F). The evil entity known as Fenric probably originated at the beginning of time (7M).

CREATURE FROM THE PIT Nickname given by the people of Chloris to Erato (5G).

CRESSIDA See VICKI.

CRESTUS Planet where the Graff Vynda-K's men fought in the Alliance Wars. After the battle, Sholakh planted the Graff's flag in the body of the Crestan general (5A).

CRETACEOUS It was during the Cretaceous Period – 136 to 65 million years ago – that the Dinosaurs, the Silurians and the Sea Devils ruled the Earth (BBB, LLL). Also see ANTHROPOLOGY, SILURIANS.

CRICHTON, CHARLES UNIT colonel who succeeded Brigadier Lethbridge-Stewart after he retired. He briefly met the Second Doctor, who had come to shake hands with the Brigadier the day of an annual UNIT reunion. The Doctor found him 'unpromising' (6K).

CRICHTON, JOHN Former athlete. As Mark, he was one of Sir Charles Grover's People. He was the first to believe Sarah when she revealed they were not aboard a spaceship en route to a New Earth (WWW).

CRIME The act of breaking the law. Among the petty crooks and thieves were: poacher Seeley (AAA); circus owner Rossini (EEE); crooked financier Lord Palmerdale (4V) and con artists Garron, Unstoffe (5A); and Sabalom Glitz (7A, 7C, 7G). Lytton turned to bank robbing while stranded in 20th-century England (6T). Smugglers included: the Cornish smugglers (CC); gun runners Rohm-Dutt (5E) and Stotz (6R); drug smugglers Tryst and Dymond (5K).
  Murderers included: Eyesen (E), Bennett (L), and Doland (7C); hired killers: Johnny Ringo (Z), the Bannermen and Keillor (7F); pirates: Pike (CC), Caven (YY) and the Captain of Zanak (5C); and slave traders Sevcheria (M), El Akir (P), Gray (FF) and Rorvik (5T). Other ruthless murderers-for-profit included: Captain Dent of IMC (HHH) and the medieval warlords Irongron and Bloodaxe (UUU). Ian Chesterton was accused of murder on Marinus, but was cleared by the First Doctor (E). The Sixth Doctor took part in a murder investigation on the ship *Hyperion III* (7C).
  Traitors of the human race included: evil industrialist Forester (J); would-be dictator Salamander (PP); General Carrington (BBB); Mavic Chen (V), Theodore Maxtible (LL) and Ratcliffe,

who served the Daleks; Klieg, Kaftan (MM), Tobias Vaughn (VV) and Dr Kellman (4D), who helped the Cybermen; Fewsham (XX) and Eckersley (YYY), who assisted the Ice Warriors; Dr Quinn (AAA), who cooperated with the Silurians; Stevens (TTT), who served BOSS; Lupton (ZZZ), who helped the Spiders of Metebelis 3; Harrison Chase (4L), who worshipped the Krynoids; Stael (4X), who summoned the Fendahl; and Aukon, Zargo and Camilla (5P), who served the Great Vampire.

On alien planets, crime could be defined differently than on Earth. On Interminor, immigration of any alien life form was severely prohibited (PPP); on Pluto, the Usurians had set up a repressive taxation society (4W); on Terra Alpha, to be unhappy was a crime punishable by death (7L). Varos was inhabited by the descendents from a colony for the criminally insane, who thrived on public torture as a form of punishment (6V).

Alien justice was as different as alien crimes, and creative forms of execution (or exile) remained a constant. The Megara justice machines found their creators in contempt and destroyed them (5C). Eldrad was sentenced to death by the Kastrians (4N). On Leela's world, deviants were sentenced to the deadly test of the Horda (4Q); on Pluto, criminals were steamed alive (4W); on Chloris, they were thrown into a Pit (5G); on Tigella, blasphemers were crushed under a rock (5Q); on Traken, criminals were turned into stone statues known as Melkur (5T). Both Cessair of Diplos (by the Megara) (5C) and Borusa (by Rassilon) (5K) were turned into living statues. On Trion, political prisoners were exiled to Sarn (6Q); on Varos, criminals were sent to the Punishment Dome and their executions were recorded an broadcast (6V); on Karfel, the Borad sentenced rebels to be exiled into the past through the Timelash (6Y); on Proamon, Kane was exiled to Svartos (7G); on Terra Alpha, criminals were drowned in boiling candy (7L); in the UK Habitat, water thieves were stoned (7A).

The Time Lords considered interfering in the development of other planets a crime. They sentenced the Second Doctor to exile on Earth, and executed the War Lord for it (ZZ). The Fourth Doctor was later framed for the murder of the President (in reality committed by Goth) and condemned to death by vaporization (4N). The Fourth Doctor was also condemned to death for a technicality by the Megara (5C). The Fifth Doctor was again sentenced to a similar death when Omega bonded with him (6E). The Sixth Doctor was tried for genocide (7C).

CRINOTH Planet destroyed by the Nimon, who then prepared to invade Skonnos (5L).

CRITAS One of the Eternals, who wore the guise of the captain of a Greek galley in the race for Enlightenment. His ship was destroyed by Captain Wrack, but he himself returned to eternity (6H).

CRITO Elder of the High Council of Atlantis. He was killed when queen Galleia overthrew King Dalios (OOO).

CROSS Guard at the Luna Penal Colony. He pretended to help the Third Doctor and Professor Dale to escape, but was in fact preparing to kill them (QQQ).

CROSSLAND Detective inspector in charge of investigating Gascoigne's disappearance. His identity was taken over by the Chameleons' Director, but he was freed by Jamie (KK).

CROVASSI Alien tourist who crashlanded in Wales in 1959. He was killed by the Bannermen (7F).

CROWN Currency unit of Iceworld (7G).

CROZIER Scientist working for the Mentors of Thoros-Beta. He had devised a brain transformer which enhanced brains and which he had used on Lord Kiv. But Kiv was dying, so Crozier experimented with a a process to transfer the dying Mentor Lord's mind into another body (Peri's). At Sil's request, he used his Cell Discriminator on the Sixth Doctor, causing him to appear hostile and more erratic than usual. Crozier's mind-transfer process was deemed too dangerous for the course of natural evolution by the Time Lords, so they manipulated events to arrange for King Yrcanos of Krontep to kill Crozier, Kiv and Sil, and rescue Peri (7B).

CRUIKSHANK Doctor at the Bi-Al Foundation. He and Hedges were taken over by Lowe's Virus. He was shot by K-9, but managed to infect him temporarily with the virus before he died (4T).

CRUSADES Military expeditions undertaken by Western European Christians between AD 1095 and 1270 to recover Jerusalem from Saracen control. The First Doctor helped King Richard the Lionheart towards the end of the Third Crusade (circa AD 1191) (P).

CRUSHING Method of execution for blasphemers on Tigella. The Fourth Doctor was almost crushed to death after being accused of stealing the Dodecahedron (5Q).

CRYOGENICS Method of preservation of bodies involving the use of extremely cold temperatures. The Tranquil Repose mortuary used cryogenics to preserve dying millionaires and politicians (6Z). Cryogenics were used to keep Davros prisoner (6P), and the Cryons' civilisation was based on cryogenics (6T).

Aliens who have used cryogenics to keep a supply of captive soldiers include the Daleks (SSS); the Cybermen (MM, 6T); the Ice Soldiers of Marinus (E); the Ice Warriors (OO); and Kane (7G). Also see GENERATION STARSHIPS and SUSPENDED ANIMATION.

CRYONS Elfin-like natives of Telos, driven underground by the Cybermen. The Sixth Doctor and Lytton helped them reclaim their planet (6T).

CRYPTOZOIC PERIOD Life began on Earth during the Cryptozoic Period, around 3.5 billion years ago, when Scaroth's spaceship exploded while taking off (5H). This was incorrectly reported by the Fourth Doctor as having happened 400 million years ago. Also see ANTHROPOLOGY.

CRYSTALS Crystalline life forms included the Krotons (WW), the Kastrians (4N) and the Krargs (5M). Many crystals encountered by the Doctor were stones of great power: The Key to Time was a perfect, crystalline cube (5A–5F). Later, Enlightenment was offered by the White Guardian in the form of a crystal (6H).

The priests of Atlantis captured the essence of the powerful kronavore Kronos and imprisoned it in the Kronos Crystal (OOO). Kontron crystals were found in certain areas of the space-time vortex and contained energies capable of harnessing space and time. The Borad used them to power a time tunnel called 'Timelash' (6Y). The Kronos Crystal might have been a Kontron Crystal. Kontron crystals may be made of taranium (V).

The Zolfa-Thuran Dodecahedron powered the underground

Tigellan civilization (5Q). The Manussan Great Crystal created the Mara from the evil within the Manussans' minds (6D). The crystals of Metebelis 3 had the power to clear minds and amplify power. They were responsible for the mutation of the Spiders and were also, to a degree, radioactive (TTT, ZZZ).

Radioactive hymetusite existed in natural, crystalline form. It was paid as a tribute by Aneth to Skonnos; Jasonite was an electromagnetic boosting crystal found only on Crinoth (5L). The secret of the Dragonfire was a powerful energy crystal (which may have been hymetusite) (7G). The Third Doctor helped the Solonian Ky achieve his final mutation into a super-being with a radioactive crystal (NNN).

Voolium and Madronite 1–5 were crystals found on Calufrax which could be used to power a Psychic Interference Transmitter (5B). Tryst's Continuous Event Transmitter recordings were on crystals (5K). The Terileptils used Vintaric crystals to provide lighting (5X). Quarb Crystals were used in hyperspatial engines (7F). See also MINERALS.

CULLINGFORD (LADY) Former politician, real name Lady Cullingford, active in ecological circles. She was one of Sir Charles Grover's 'People'. She refused to believe Sarah and Mark when they told her that they were not on a spaceship en route to a New Earth. Adam finally convinced her to at least listen to Sarah. When the truth was exposed, she confronted Grover (WWW).

CULLINGS Selection process which Drathro used to keep the population of the UK Habitat constant. Merdeen helped some intended victims to escape the Cullings by letting them out to the surface to live with the Free (7A).

CULLODEN The last battle of the 'Forty-five Rebellion', held on 6 April 1746 when the Jacobites under Charles Edward, the Young Pretender (Bonnie Prince Charlie), were defeated by the English army, led by the Duke of Cumberland. The Second Doctor met Jamie soon afterwards (FF).

CULLY Son of Dulcian leader Senex. Unlike other Dulcians, Cully sought excitement and ran an illegal tour business. He discovered the Dominators when he took a party of clients to the Island of Death. Afterwards, he tried convince the Dulcian council of the threat posed by the aliens, but failed.

He eventually helped the Second Doctor, Jamie and Zoe save his planet (TT).

CULSHAW, DAVE One of the crew on the Concorde flight which was hijacked to the Jurassic Period by the Master. He was rescued thanks to the Fifth Doctor's efforts (6C).

CUMMINGS Police constable who wanted to arrest the Fifth Doctor for Digby's murder at Cranleigh Hall (6A).

CURLY Hovercraft pilot who mistook the Second Doctor for Salamander (PP).

CURT Professor Foster's assistant (6Q).

CURRY Official involved with the Thunderbolt Missile (FFF).

CUSTODIANS Trion's political police (6Q).

CUTLER American General in charge of the Snowcap Space Tracking Station at the time of the Mondasian Cybermen's invasion. He refused to listen to the First Doctor's advice. Desperate to save his son's life, Cutler became mentally unbalanced and threatened to use the Z-Bomb against Mondas, unable to realize that it would also endanger Earth. He was eventually killed by Cyberleader Krang (DD).

CUTLER, TERRY Lieutenant and son of General Cutler. He piloted the Zeus V space capsule threatened by the Cybermen (DD).

CVE See CHARGED VACUUM EMBOITE-MENTS.

CYBERBOMBS Powerful explosive devices that the Cybermen tried to use to blow up the fragment of Voga. They had been banned by an Armageddon Convention (4D). The Fifth Doctor disarmed a Cyberbomb hidden in an underground network of caves in the 26th century (6B).

CYBERCOMMUNICATOR Communications device used by Tobias Vaughn to communicate with the Cybermen (VV).

CYBERCONTROLLER Supreme leader of the Cybermen. He was distinguishable by his enlarged cranium. The Cybercontroller first appeared in the Tombs of the Cybermen on Telos, where he eventually seemed to have been destroyed in a fight with Toberman (MM). However, a Cybercontroller (claiming to be the same entity) later masterminded the return of the Cybermen to Telos and their plan to change history. He was killed by Lytton (6T).

CYBERLEADER Cyberman in charge of a Cyberman expedition (4D, 6B, 6K, 6T, 7K).

CYBERLIEUTENANT The Cyberleader's deputy (6B, 6K, 6T, 7K).

CYBERMATS Rodent-sized, quasirobotic creatures, capable of detecting humans by their brainwaves, and programmed to leap upon and sting their preys. They were used by the Cybermen to attack the Second Doctor and his Companions on Telos (MM). They were also used on the Wheel in Space to destroy the bernalium supply. The Second Doctor destroyed them by broadcasting high current phase contrasts (SS). They were later used by Dr Kellman to infect space beacon Nerva with the Cybermen's Neurotrope X virus (4D).

CYBERMEN The Cybermen originally evolved from the inhabitants of Mondas, Earth's twin planet. The Mondasian civilization developed more quickly than Earth's and Mondasians may have visited our planet in prehistoric times. At one point in ancient history, for reasons yet unknown, Mondas left the Solar System. It was during that period of wandering that the Mondasians evolved into creatures of ruthless logic; their organs were replaced by cybernetic parts until they became Cybermen. The Cybermen are virtually immortal, their only recorded weaknesses being gold (which crippled their breathing mechanisms) and high susceptibility to gravitation and certain forms of radiation. The Cybermen have evolved into numerous forms, including that of Cybercontrollers.

It has been surmised that, at a certain point during their space journey, some Cybermen left Mondas to form a planetary empire, enslaving other civilisations and turning them into Cybermen. This empire included planets such as Planet 14. Eventually, these 'galactic' Cybermen began to feel threatened by Earth's technological advance and forays into outer space. They launched an invasion of Earth in 1970, with the help of Tobias Vaughn, head of International Electromatics. They recognized the Second Doctor as a hostile alien from a so-far unrecorded encounter on Planet 14. The Doctor and a newly formed UNIT thwarted their plans, and most of their space fleet was destroyed (VV). In 1988, the same Cybermen launched yet another attack against Earth, but this time, they were defeated by the Seventh Doctor; the remains of their fleet were destroyed by the Silver Nemesis (7K).

Meanwhile, two years earlier, in 1986, Mondas had returned to the Solar System. Its Cybermen planned to steal Earth's energy to replace their own depleted resources. The Mondasian Cybermen launched an attack on the planet, planning to drain it of its energy to repower Mondas. They were thwarted at the South Pole by the First Doctor. Mondas absorbed too much energy and was destroyed (DD). Cybermen from the future, using a hijacked time vessel, secretly travelled back in time to 1985 and tried to crash Halley's Comet into Earth to save Mondas. They were defeated by the Sixth Doctor and Lytton (6T).

In AD 2030, the galactic Cybermen launched another attack against Earth, this time planning to use the Wheel in Space (SS). In 2070, they invaded the Moonbase (HH). In both cases, they were defeated by the Second Doctor.

Finally, Earth's expansion into space brought mankind in direct conflict with the Cybermen. Humanity found itself on the side of those alien species who had been fighting the Cybermen, and formed the Alliance. During the First Cyber Wars, the Alliance discovered that gold, which existed in abundance on Voga, was fatal to their enemies, and began using glitterguns. Driven from their worlds, the Cybermen had no choice but to flee. Before they did, they made an attempt to destroy Voga, but were only partially successful. A fragment survived and began to drift towards the Solar System (4D). Soon afterwards, the Cybermen conquered the planet Telos and drove its native Cryons underground. They turned the Cryons' cities into 'Tombs', in an attempt to heal and preserve their species for future assaults (MM, 6T).

Towards the end of the 25th century, the Fourth Doctor, Sarah Jane Smith and Harry Sullivan thwarted the efforts of a small band of isolated Cybermen who were trying to destroy the remains of Voga, which had drifted near Space Beacon Nerva in Earth's Solar System (4D).

At the beginning of the 26th century, the insane Logician Klieg attempted to resurrect the Cybermen, whose Tombs had been located on Telos. His plans were foiled by the Second Doctor, Jamie, and Victoria Waterfield (MM). Once the Tombs had been opened, either the Cybermen continued to be reactivated, or other Cyber Forces drifting in space were summoned to complete the job Klieg had begun. In any event, the Cybermen had time to regroup, and reemerged as a serious galactic threat.

In AD 2526, made aware of this new Cyber menace, the Alliance agreed to meet on Earth in a Galactic Congress to decide what steps to take. The Cybermen then attempted to destroy the Congress by causing a space freighter to crash on the planet, but their scheme was thwarted by the Fifth Doctor and his companions, resulting in the death of Adric (6B).

A second series of Cyber Wars ensued. Having found Voga, the Alliance was again in possession of a vast supply of gold. The result was yet another defeat for the Cybermen. Just before the Alliance's forces made a final attack on Telos, the Cybermen's stronghold, the Cybermen used a hijacked time vessel to launch a final, desperate attack. They tried to not only save themselves, but alter the course of history (see above). The time vessel may have been of Morok origins, as they were one of the few species with limited time travel capabilities at that time (Q). However, the Cybermen were defeated by the Sixth Doctor and the courageous Cryons (6T).

At one point in time, a crew of galactic Cybermen were used by Borusa as pawns in the Game of Rassilon (6K).

CYBORGS A combination of man and machine. Among the most notorious species of cyborgs are the Daleks and the Cybermen. Individual cyborgs include Davros, the Captain of Zanak (5B) and a number of humans converted by the Cybermen, such as Toberman (MM), Tobias Vaughn (VV) and Lytton (6T), or by the Daleks, such as the Robomen (K) and the little girl turned into a battle computer (7H). Also, the Oracle's Seers (4Y) and the colonists of Frontios captured by the Tractators (6N) could be considered cyborgs. Animal cyborgs included the Zygons' Skarasen (4F) and the Silurians' Myrka (6L). Also see ROBOTS.

CYCLOPS Dumb servant of Odysseus during the Trojan War (U).

CYRANO See DE BERGERAC.

CYRENNIC EMPIRE Small galactic empire to which planets such as Ribos, Levithia, Skythros and Cyrennis Minima belonged. It was allied to the Alliance and fought alongside it against the Daleks and the Cybermen (5A).

CYRENNIS MINIMA Planet of the Cyrennic Empire. Garron and Unstoffe stopped there before travelling to Ribos (5A).

CYRIL THE SCHOOLBOY Perhaps the deadliest of all the pawns used by the Toymaker to challenge the First Doctor, Steven and Dodo (Y).

CYTRONICS Sutekh powered his Mummies with a cytronic particle accelerator (4G).

D

D5 GAMMA Z ALPHA Skaro's identification in the Movellan star charts (5J).

D84 Robot who masqueraded as a Dum, but was actually a semi-sentient Super-Voc sent aboard the Sandminer with Poul to look for Taren Capel. He helped the Fourth Doctor expose Dask and sacrificed his life to save the Time Lord's (4R).

DA VINCI, LEONARDO (1452–1519) Italian painter, sculptor, architect, engineer whose genius epitomized the Renaissance. About AD 1503, the Fourth Doctor and Sarah Jane Smith defeated the Mandragora Helix in the Dukedom of San Martino, Italy, and helped save Leonardo da Vinci's life and the Renaissance (4M). A few years later, the same Doctor met one of Scaroth's twelve splinters, Captain Tancredi, in Leonardo da Vinci's house. The Jagaroth had commissioned the painter to create several Mona Lisas in order to enable his future self to finance his time-travel experiments (5H). The Meddling Monk claimed to have met Leonardo and discussed the possibilities of powered flight with him (S).

DAD Human avatar of one of the three Gods of Ragnarok at the Psychic Circus (7J).

DAEMONS Immensely powerful aliens from Demos, who looked like giant, goatlike, horned humanoids, and were masters of psionic science. They arrived on Earth circa 100,000 BC, and started mankind on the road to civilization. It is likely that the Daemons were partly responsible for the mysterious extinction of the Neanderthals and their replacement by early modern humans. The Daemons made a deep and everlasting impression on the native cavemen, and contributed to shaping their mythology. The Daemons revisited Earth at irregular intervals to check on the results of their evolutionary experiments. When they finally departed, the Daemons left one of their own, Azal, behind in a miniaturized, suspended-animation state; he was intended eventually to judge mankind and pass on his power. Azal was summoned back to life by the Master, but was eventually defeated by Jo Grant's willingness to sacrifice her own life to save that of the Third Doctor (JJJ). They may have given the Kronos crystal to the ancient Atlanteans (OOO).

DAHEER, BEN A merchant of Jaffa (P).

DAILY CHRONICLE Newspaper which published an article about the Third Doctor's non-human origins during his stay at Ashbridge Cottage Hospital (AAA).

DAKO One of the Xeron rebels who fought the Moroks alongside the First Doctor in the Space Museum (Q).

DALE (PROFESSOR) Notorious member of the Earth Peace Party, opposed to war with the Draconians and kept prisoner on the Luna Penal Colony. He and the Third Doctor were almost killed by Cross when they tried to escape (QQQ).

DALEKENIUM (aka DALEKANIUM) Very dense, synthetic substance presumably created by Davros and used in the making of the Daleks' mobile casings. Under certain conditions, it was also a powerful explosive (KKK).

DALEKS Created by Davros, the Daleks were the mutated descendants of the Kaleds (aka Dals), one of the two races living on the planet Skaro. The Daleks lived inside a mobile casing which was equipped with sensor discs, a unique iris and lens, a sucker-stick arm and a special extermination weapon. Their natural form appeared to be small, green, bloblike, octopods with claws. They had one purpose: to exterminate all other life forms and become the dominant species in the universe. The Emperor Dalek was the supreme Dalek leader. Mention was made of a Dalek Council, presumably reporting to the Emperor. Beneath it were warlords such as the Black or Gold Daleks.

The Daleks' history is subject to different interpretations. It is said that the Daleks began as a humanoid race first known as Dals, then later as Kaleds, on planet Skaro. Their enemies were the Thals, with whom they engaged in fierce warfare, lasting a thousand years, culminating with the neutronic wars which destroyed most of Skaro and made it radioactive. The Kaled scientist Davros studied and further developed some of the mutations resulting from the wars, then created a mobile casing for them and christened his new creatures Daleks. The Daleks' mobile casing was based on Davros's own life-support chair. Earlier versions were powered by static electricity. Later versions used various forms of energy, including solar power.

The Time Lords sent the Fourth Doctor to Skaro to stop the development of the Daleks, but he failed, succeeding only in entombing them in the Kaled bunker, after they had turned against their creator (4E).

Later, some crippled Kaled survivors discovered the remnants of Davros's early experiments and mutated themselves into new Daleks. The First Doctor met the new Daleks in the Dalek City and foiled their attempt to destroy the surviving Thals by increasing Skaro's radiation levels. Those new Daleks presumably perished when the Thals destroyed their power controls (B).

The original Daleks ultimately resurfaced and took over Skaro, driving the Thals in exile. Their ruthlessness enabled them to conquer their space sector. Mankind's slow but steady space expansion attacted the Daleks' attention. By AD 2160, the Daleks launched a secret plan to invade Earth. First, they spread virulent plagues through a swarm of meteorites. As a result, the solar system was quarantined by the other human colonies. The Daleks struck in AD 2164, invading an almost depopulated Earth. Any attempt at space intervention was firmly dealt with by the Daleks' space fleet. This became known as the First Dalek War. The Daleks planned to extract Earth's molten core and turn the planet into a giant spaceship. But, in AD 2167, the First Doctor, Susan, Ian Chesterton and

Barbara Wright helped freedom fighters Dortmun, Tyler and David Campbell defeat the invaders (K). (The same invasion succeeded on a parallel Earth where World War III had occurred, but was eventually erased from the time continuum when the Third Doctor prevented the death of 20th-century diplomat Sir Reginald Styles (KKK).)

Some Daleks who had survived this First Dalek War crashed on Vulcan and later tried to take over the human colony there, but were defeated by the Second Doctor, Ben Jackson and Polly (EE).

Earth fought the Daleks again after they tried to blackmail the galaxy by controlling the only supply of parrinium (a mineral found only on Exxilon), the cure to a space plague, which the Daleks had probably started. They were thwarted by the Third Doctor, Sarah Jane Smith and Earth's Marine Space Corps (XXX). Once the Daleks' role in the space plague became known, several galactic races (including the Draconians), probably stirred up by the exiled Thals, united to attack and punish the Daleks. Thus was born the Alliance. The war that ensued became known as the Second Dalek War. The Daleks were then driven from Skaro, which was retaken by the Thals. The Daleks were forced to relocate to another world which, out of pride, they christened Skaro (herein dubbed 'Skaro II').

Circa AD 2540, the Daleks decided that their best tactic would be to create a split between the Alliance's two most powerful members: Earth and Draconia. They engaged the services of the Master to foment a war between the humans and the Draconians, even offering him the use of their Ogron slaves. But the Master's scheme was exposed and defeated by the efforts of the Third Doctor and Jo Grant (QQQ).

The Daleks then plotted to attack the Alliance with the secret of invisibility and a 10,000-strong Dalek army, kept frozen on Spiridon. The Third Doctor and Jo, with the help of a Thal commando unit that had been monitoring the Daleks' moves from Skaro, thwarted them again (SSS). The Thals notified the Alliance of the Daleks' activities, and the Alliance struck back, leading to the Third Dalek War. At one point during this war, a Dalek casing was put on exhibit in the Moroks' Space Museum, and provided a hiding place for the First Doctor (Q). Also, a Dalek was used by Borusa as a pawn in the Game of Rassilon (6K).

The Daleks eventually took advantage of the Alliance's slow disintegration during the 26th century to launch an attack on Skaro. They succeeded in exterminating most of the Thals, but the planet itself was turned into a bombed-out ruin of no further use to them – or so they thought. Towards the end of the 26th century, the Daleks encountered the equally aggressive robotic Movellans, which they could not crush. Caught between the still powerful Alliance and the undefeated Movellans, the Daleks felt trapped. So, as the 27th century began, they returned to Skaro to recover their long-buried creator, Davros. But their efforts were thwarted by the Fourth Doctor and Romana. Davros was taken to Earth where he was sentenced to life in suspended animation (5J).

Deprived of Davros's help, the Daleks lost their war against the Movellans, who used a special virus to decimate them. While striving to defeat the Movellans, the Daleks had become aware of the Time Lords' existence and discovered the rudiments of time travel technology, involving the use of time corridors. Ninety years after Davros' trial, the Daleks hired Lytton to free Davros from the space penitentiary where he was kept. They also captured the Fifth Doctor and plotted to use him against the Time Lords, who had presumably tried to stop the Daleks' discovery of time travel. The Doctor defeated the Daleks but Davros escaped, now intent on creating new Daleks, subservient only to him (6P).

Davros secretly relocated to Nekros where, posing as the Great Healer, he used the bodies stored in the mortuary known as Tranquil Repose to create his own White (or Imperial) Daleks. But he was exposed and defeated by the Sixth Doctor. Davros was taken back to Skaro II by the Daleks (6Z).

Davros presumably escaped, since he and the Daleks fought again in or about AD 2963. The two camps used their time corridor technology to travel back in time to 1963 London to capture the Hand of Omega. As a result of the Seventh Doctor's intervention, both Dalek races were utterly devastated. Either Skaro's, or Skaro II's, sun was destroyed. However, Davros, who had already taken to calling himself the Emperor Dalek, escaped (7H).

A long period of inactivity ensued. Sometime between the 32nd and 38th centuries, the Daleks restored Skaro (or Skaro II?) to its former glory. They also refined their time travel technology. Using taranium, they were now able to build crude time machines. One of their first enterprises was to send an exterminating team to chase the First Doctor, Vicki, Ian and Barbara through time and space. The Dalek squad was eventually destroyed by the Mechanoids (Q).

Circa AD 4000, the Daleks again tried to take over the Solar System which they perceived (possibly blinded by their centuries-old feud with mankind) as the Federation's lynchpin. This time, they allied themselves with other space races (including Galaxy 5). This became known as the Fourth Dalek War.

The Dalek invasion plans were first discovered on planet Kembel by Space Security Agent Marc Cory, who was murdered by the Daleks (T/A).

Soon afterwards, the First Doctor, Steven Taylor and Katarina arrived on Kembel, and discovered a tape left by Cory. With the help of another space Security Agent, Bret Vyon, they decided to warn Earth of the impending Dalek attack, and of the treachery of Mavic Chen, the Guardian of the Solar System. Chen had given the Daleks the replacement taranium they needed to activate their supreme weapon: the Time Destructor.

The time travellers stole the Daleks' taranium core, and fled Kembel. In the course of their escape, Katarina sacrificed herself to save her companions. Bret Vyon was killed by his sister, Sara Kingdom, who later found out the truth and helped the Doctor. When the Time Destructor was finally activated, it was on Kembel, which put a stop to the Dalek invasion. Unfortunately, its deadly effects also killed Sara Kingdom (V).

Presumably, the Federation then retaliated, and the Daleks were again driven back to Skaro, their power and influence severely curtailed.

A century or so later, however, the Daleks managed to obtain some more taranium, and decided again to use their time travel capabilities to attack Earth. By then, they were ruled by an Emperor Dalek, who could very well have been Davros, after possibly subjecting himself to further mutations.

Resorting again to their favorite weapon, the biological one, the Daleks planned to infect humanity with the Dalek factor. Having detected Professor Waterfield's early time travel experiments, the Daleks travelled to AD1866 Earth. The Emperor's efforts were thwarted by the Second Doctor, Jamie and Victoria Waterfield. Instead of infecting mankind, the Daleks themselves who became contaminated with the Human Factor. A civil war in which the Dalek race perished erupted on Skaro (LL).

However, some humanized Daleks may have survived, thereby making the Fourth Doctor's prophecy that eventually a greater good would come of the Daleks' creation come true (4E). The fact that the Daleks eventually become extinct, thanks mostly to the intervention of the Doctor (often manipulated by the Celestial Intervention Agency), may be evidence of Time Lord intervention.

DALIOS King of Atlantis who lived for 537 years. He had realized that the short-term benefits brought to Atlantis by the use of the Kronos Crystal would spell long-term doom, and forbade its use. His Queen, Galleia, betrayed him to the Master, who overthrew him and had him beaten. He died in the Third Doctor's arms, having foreseen his kingdom's impending doom (OOO).

DALS See DALEKS.

DALY Retired British major and passenger of the SS *Bernice*. He was an unwitting prisoner of Vorg's Scope, but was eventually restored to his proper place in space and time by the Third Doctor (PPP).

DALY, CLAIRE Major Daly's daughter, a passenger of the *Bernice* and an unwitting prisoner of Vorg's Scope, but was eventually restored to her proper place in space and time by the Third Doctor (PPP).

DAMON Atlantis's chief surgeon who converted people into Fish Men. He eventually reformed (GG).

DAMON Gallifreyan technician who reported the transmission of the Fifth Doctor's biodata to Omega. He helped the Doctor expose Omega (6E).

DANIELS, JIM British astronaut on board the Mars Probe 6 ship who was accidentally killed by a radioactive alien (CCC).

D'ARGENSON Frenchman who was trying to escape from the guillotine when he stumbled upon the First Doctor and his companions (H).

DARK TOWER See TOMB OF RASSILON.

DARKNESS See CHAOS.

DARLINGTON UNIVERSITY Professor Hayter worked there (6C).

DARP Planet incorporated into Tryst's CET (SK).

DARRIUS Old scientist who was guarding one of the missing Keys in the jungles of Marinus, and who had accelerated its flora's evolution with DE 302. He made a fake key, which Ian later gave to Yartek (E).

D'ARTAGNAN Notorious French swordsman and musketeer. His fictional counterpart was encountered by the Second Doctor, Jamie, and Zoe in the Land of Fiction (UU).

DARTH Ace's friend. According to Auge, he married Flo (7P).

DARWIN, CHARLES (1809–82) English naturalist who first formulated the theory of evolution, and one of the eleven geniuses kidnapped by the Rani to make up her giant Brain (7D). Following the publication of his seminal book, *On The Origin of Species*, Josiah Samuel Smith wrote several articles endorsing his views (7Q).

DASK Chief Fixer of the *Sandminer* crew. In reality, he was Taren Capel, a scientist who had been raised by robots and thought of them as his brothers. He wanted Robots to take control of mankind, and used a Laserson Probe to reprogramme the Robots aboard the *Sandminer* to kill his crewmates. He was killed by SV7 when the Fourth Doctor released helium in the atmosphere, changing his voice and therefore making it impossible for the Robot to recognize him (4R).

DASSUK Subject Guardian enslaved by the Ark's Monoids. After the Monoids' defeat, he and Venussa led the humans into making an honorable peace with the Monoids and living in harmony on Refusis (X).

DASTARI, JOINSON Scientist and head of projects on Space Station J7. He had technologically augmented Chessene and helped her capture the Second Doctor. He was prepared to dissect him to obtain the secret of the Rassilon Imprimature, and give Chessene the ability to travel through time. When he realized she was still a bloodthirsty androgum, he rebelled and refused to kill the Doctor. Chessene shot him (6W).

DAVE See GRIFFITHS, DAVE.

DAVEY One of the Eternals who wore the guise of the captain of a 19th-century clipper to engage in the planet-spanning space race, for Enlightenment. His ship was destroyed by Captain Wrack, but he himself returned to eternity (6H).

DAVID See BILL.

DAVIDSON, ANN One of the Chameleons' tour operators (KK).

DAVIS Arden's assistant. He was killed in an ice avalanche (OO).

DAVIS Wenley Moor technician who died of fright while spelunking in the Silurian caves (BBB).

DAVIS Police constable who investigated Aunt Vanessa's murder (5V).

DAVIS, DAVE One of the Llanfairfach miners (TTT).

DAVROS Great, but twisted and crippled Kaled scientist. Davros was permanently attached to a mobile life-support chair. His vision, and probably his other senses as well, were replaced by mechanical aids. He had also lost the use of his left arm. Davros was Chief Scientist of the Kaleds and the person responsible for the creation of the Daleks, whose mobile casing was based on Davros's own lifesupport chair.

Davros fought against the Fourth Doctor, who had been sent by the Time Lords to Skaro to stop the creation of the Daleks, and even plotted the destruction of his own people to further his creations. Davros was eventually blasted by the Daleks, who turned against him, and was left for dead in the Kaled bunker (4E).

The Daleks brought Davros back to life in the 27th century, when they needed his help against the robotic Movellans. But, thanks to the Fourth Doctor's intervention, Davros was captured and sentenced to life in suspended animation in a space prison (5J). Ninety years after his trial, Davros was freed by galactic mercenary Lytton, who had been hired by the Daleks, who again needed their creator's help against a Movellan-designed virus. Davros then decided to create a new race of Daleks, subservient only to him. But his plans were thwarted by the Fifth Doctor.

Afflicted with the Movellan virus, Davros was thought to have died in the destruction of the space penitentary (6P).

However, Davros had survived. Under the identity of the Great Healer, he took over the Tranquil Repose mortuary on Nekros, where he used human bodies in suspended animation to finally create his own army of White (or Imperial) Daleks. But the Sixth Doctor defeated him. Betrayed by an employee of Tranquil Repose, Davros was captured by the Daleks and taken back to Skaro (or Skaro II) (6Z).

Davros resurfaced again about AD 2963. Leading his White Daleks, and using the identity of the Emperor Dalek, Davros used the Daleks' time-corridor technology to travel back in time to 1963 London to capture the Hand of Omega. There, he fought the regular Daleks, led by a Black Dalek. Both Dalek races were utterly devastated. Either Skaro's, or Skaro II's, sun was destroyed, but Davros escaped again (7H).

It is possible that Davros finally achieved his dream of reclaiming control over his creations. The Emperor Dalek of later years may very well have been an evolved version of Davros (LL).

DAVY, HUMPHRY (1778–1829) Famous English chemist, invited to a meeting by George Stephenson. The Master wanted to kidnap him to harness his genius, but was thwarted by the Sixth Doctor (6X).

DAWSON, MOLLY Theodore Maxtible's maid (LL).

DAWSON, PHYLLIS Dr Lawrence's assistant at Wenley Moor. She was fond of Dr Quinn, who had confided in her his secret relationship with the Silurians. After Quinn's death, she told the Third Doctor all she knew about the Silurians (BBB).

DAXTAR Earthman who owned an experimental plant where Bret Vyon chose to land the *Spar 7–40* when he and the First Doctor were trying to stop the Daleks' Masterplan. Vyon thought Daxtar was his friend, but Daxtar betrayed him to Karlton, and Vyon killed him (V).

DAY OF THE FEAST Day when the Gundans slew the Tharils (5S).

DE 302 Chemical created by Darrius to accelerate the evolution of Marinus's plants (E).

DE BERGERAC, CYRANO (1619–55) French swordsman, poet and writer. His fictional counterpart was encountered by the Second Doctor, Jamie and Zoe in the Land of Fiction (UU).

DE COLIGNY (1519–72) Admiral of France and leader of the Huguenots. Wary of his growing influence on the King, he had been targeted for death by Catherine de Medici. A first assassination attempt was made against him on 22 August 1572, but failed thanks to Steven and Anne Chaplette's intervention. De Coligny was killed two days later during the St Bartholomew's Day Massacre (W).

DE FLORES Leader of a gang of Nazi refugees in South America. He had managed to obtain the Silver Nemesis's bow. After the statue landed back at Windsor, he fought the Seventh Doctor, Lady Peinforte and the Cybermen to gain control of it. He was killed by the Cybermen (7K).

DE HAAN Officer aboard the Morestran spaceship sent to Zeta Minor. He was a member of Vishinsky's landing party, which found the Fourth Doctor. He was later killed by Sorenson when the scientist turned into a neanderthal-like monster (4H).

DE LACEY, GEOFFREY (SIR) Ranulf Fitzwilliam's cousin. He was captured by the Master after he brought news that the real King John was in London. He was rescued by the Fifth Doctor (6J).

DE LERAN, GASTON French Huguenot working for Admiral de Coligny. He refused to believe Steven and Anne Chaplette when they told him of the plot against his master's life (W).

DE MARUN, REYNIER One of King Richard I's knights. He was killed during El Akir's ambush (P).

DE MEDICI, CATHERINE (1519–89) Queen Mother of France during Charles IX's reign. Worried about the growing influence of Huguenot leader Admiral de Coligny on the King, she plotted his assassination and, later, the St Barthlomew's Day Massacre (W).

DE TORNEBU, WILLIAM One of King Richard I's knights. He was wounded during El Akir's ambush, but rescued by the First Doctor and his companions (P).

DE VRIES Leader of the British Institute for Druidic Studies. He fought the Fourth Doctor in the service of the alien Cessair of Diplos, and was killed by an Ogri (5C).

DEACTIVATOR Device assembled by the Fourth Doctor to destroy the robots of Death. It was used by D84 to save the Doctor's life, at the cost of his own (4R).

DEADBEAT See KINGPIN.

DEATH ZONE Early in their history, the Time Lords created the Death Zone, where creatures scooped from various places in time and space were forced to fight for their amusement. Eventually, Rassilon closed the Death Zone and banned the Time Scoop. The Tomb of Rassilon was later erected at the center of the Death Zone (6K).

DEAUVILLE French city on the Channel coast. Colonel Skinsale lost a large sum of money to Lord Palmerdale in its casino before becoming shipwrecked on Fang Rock (4V).

DECIDERS Ruling council of three Alzarian citizens, comprised of Draith, Nefred, and Garif. After Draith's death, the more decisive Login was appointed Decider. The First Decider (Draith, then Nefred) was the only one who knew the truth about the Alzarians. He also knew that the *Starliner* was fully repaired, and ready to leave at any time. After the Fourth Doctor saved the Alzarians, Garif asked him to become a Decider, but he refused (5R).

DEEDRIX One of the inner group of Tigellan savants. He and Caris helped the Fourth Doctor defeat Meglos, and led their people to reclaim Tigella's surface (5Q).

DEEMSTER SCALE Scale used to measure storms on Delta Magna (5E).

DEFLECTION BARRIER Force field used by Sutekh to seal the Old Priory (4G).

DELL Alzarian scientist who had studied the events leading to Mistfall (5R).

DELLA Tryst's assistant on the Volante zoological expedition. She was in love with her fellow expedition member, Stott. She was aboard the *Empress* when it crashed into the *Hecate*. After she

114

found that Tryst and Dymond were smuggling vraxoin, she was shot by Dymond, but was rescued by the Fourth Doctor (5K).

DELOS Greek slave whom Ian met on a Roman galley. He fought Ian as a gladiator. Later, he killed Sevcheria, then escaped during the Great Fire and returned to his homeland (M).

DELPHON According to the Third Doctor, a planet whose natives used their eyebrows to communicate (AAA).

DELTA Young queen of the Chimeron. After her people were exterminated by Gavrok's Bannermen, she managed to escape to the 1959 Welsh holiday camp of Shangri-La, with the egg of a young Chimeron Princess. There, the Bannermen were thwarted by the Seventh Doctor, Billy and Ray, Goronwy and two US secret agents, Hawk and Weismuller. They were finally defeated by the young Chimeron Princess's ultrasonic powers, broadcast over Shangri-La's public address system. Billy returned to Chimeria with her to help her repopulate her planet (7F).

DELTA MAGNA Planet whose third moon had become a reservation for its green-skinned natives known as 'Swampies', who worshipped the god Kroll. The third moon also housed a methane refinery whose controller, Thawn, tried to exterminate the Swampies (5E).

DEMAT GUN One of the ultimate weapons created by Rassilon to protect Gallifrey. It was a powerful disintegrator powered by the energy of the Eye of Harmony and activated by the Great Key. Rassilon had forbidden its use, but the Fourth Doctor recreated it to destroy the Sontarans who had invaded Gallifrey. After it had been used, the Demat Gun vanished and its knowledge was erased from the Doctor's memory (4Z).

DEMETER SEEDS Mutant seeds developed by Lasky, Bruchner and Doland. They could grow on desert sands and yielded large food returns (7C).

DEMNOS Roman deity worshipped by the Brothers of Demnos. He required human sacrifices (4M).

DEMONS See MAGIC, RELIGION.

DEMOS Home world of the Daemons, supposedly located about sixty thousand light years away from Earth, on the other side of the Milky Way galaxy (JJJ).

DENES, ALEXANDER Controller of Central European Zone and Giles Kent's last ally in his fight against Salamander. Salamander had him imprisoned. He was shot while trying to escape (PP).

DENT Captain in charge of the Interplanetary Mining Corporation expedition to Exarius. Because the planet was rich in Duralinium, he was determined to wrest it from Ashe's colonists. He and his first officer, Morgan, used all kinds of tricks against the colonists, including using a mining robot equipped to simulate lizard attacks, taking hostages, and forcing the colonists, at gunpoint, to take off in a ship likely to explode. But they were foiled by the Third Doctor, Ashe and Winton. Dent and his men were eventually sent back to Earth (HHH).

DEONS Tigellans who worshipped the god Ti and the Dodecahedron. They were led by Lexa and were vehemently opposed to any study of the Dodecahedron, or any plans to reclaim the Tigellan surface (5Q).

DEPUTY CHIEF CARETAKER Right-hand man of the Chief Caretaker of Paradise Towers. When he realized that Kroagnon had taken over the Chief, he joined forces with the Seventh Doctor, the Kangs and the Rezzies to destroy the Great Architect (7E).

DERBYSHIRE Location of the British atomic research station of Wenley Moor, and of the Silurians' shelters (BBB).

DEREK One of Ace's friends from Perivale. He was kidnapped by the Cheetah People, and eventually taken back to Earth by Ace (7P).

DERVEG One of the Trion agents was a tax inspector on Derveg (6Q).

DERVISH Space pirate and Caven's lieutenant. He once worked for Earth, but was caught stealing. He fought the Second Doctor and perished with his boss when their Beta Dart ship was blown up by the International Space Corps (YY).

DES PREAUX, WILLIAM One of King Richard I's knights. To save the King, he impersonated him during El Akir's ambush. He and Barbara were captured and taken to Saladin, who saw through the imposture (P).

DESPERUS An Earth prison world where incorrigible criminals were dumped to fend for themselves or die. The First Doctor crashed there on the *Spar 7–40* while trying to stop the Daleks' Masterplan (V).

DESTROYER, THE Also known as the 'Lord of Darkness' or the 'Eater of Worlds'. He was a mysterious other-dimensional entity of great magical power. He was bound in chains of silver by Morgaine, who released him on Earth. He intended to 'devour' the planet, but was shot (and presumably killed) by the Brigadier, who used silver bullets (7N).

DET-SEN Tibetan monastery which the Doctor first visited during the 17th century in an unrecorded adventure. The Second Doctor returned there in the mid-1930s to fight its High Lama, Padmasambhava, whose mind had been taken over by the Great Intelligence, and the robot Yeti (NN).

DEVA LOKA Beautiful planet inhabited by the peaceful, tele-pathic Kinda and known in Earth terms as S14. It was eventually reclassified as unsuitable for colonization (5Y).

DEVESHAM British village copied by the Kraals to serve as testing ground for their android invasion of Earth. It was near a Space Research Station, later invaded by the Kraals' androids (4J).

DEVIL'S END Village where Devil's Hump was located (JJJ).

DEVIL'S HUMP Barrow mound where Azal was buried (JJJ).

DEXETER Alzarian chief scientist. He was strangled by the Marshchild as he was preparing to dissect him alive (5R).

DIBBER Galactic swindler who accompanied Sabalom Glitz to Ravolox. Their goal was to steal the secrets previously stolen from the Time Lords' Matrix by the Andromedan Sleepers. He destroyed Drathro's Maglem converter, and unwittingly triggered an explosion that would have endangered the entire universe, if the Sixth Doctor had not stopped it. After Drathro's destruction, he suggested he and Glitz could make money from selling the converter's siligtone (7A).

DICKS One of the Llanfairfach miners (TTT).

DIDIUS Roman slave-trader and Sevcheria's partner (M).

117

DIDO Mountainous planet which was sparsely inhabited by a few, peaceful humanoids, and some Sand Beasts. It was there that the First Doctor, Ian and Barabara rescued Vicki from the murderous Bennett (L).

DIDONIANS (aka DIDOI) A gentle, peaceful race of humanoids, who had once been visited by the First Doctor. Later, most of the Didonians were murdered by Bennett in his mad scheme to save himself from a murder charge. Two Didonians later reappeared and caused Bennett to fall to his death (L).

DIGBY, RAYMOND Servant hired by Lady Cranleigh to care for her son, George. George killed him during a fit of insanity (6A).

DILL, MORTON American tourist who met the First Doctor on top of the Empire State Building, when the Time Lord and his companions were being pursued through time and space by the Daleks (R).

DIMENSIONS See PARALLEL UNIVERSES.

DINGLE, MAXWELL (SIR) Scientist who told Professor Rubeish that the real Lavinia Smith was in America (UUU).

DINOSAUR INVASION See OPERATION GOLDEN AGE.

DINOSAURS The Third Doctor and UNIT fought dinosaurs who were used by the Silurians to protect their shelters (BBB), They later fought dinosaurs scooped up by Professor Whitaker's time device, to help Sir Charles Grover's Operation Golden Age (WWW). The Third Doctor encountered a plesiosaurus in Vorg's Scope (PPP). The Sixth Doctor sent the Master and the Rani spinning into the outer fringes of the universe at the mercy of a growing Tyrannosaurus Rex embryo (6X).
  At the end of the Mesozoic (65 million years ago), the dinosaurs became extinct due to an as yet unknown cosmic event. Members of the Silurian species encountered by the Third Doctor blamed it on a sudden change in the Van Allen radiation belt (BBB). Some theories include other cosmic phenomenon such as movements of the Moon, or of Earth's twin planet, Mondas. Lastly, the extinction of the Dinosaurs may have been caused by the crash of a space liner from the future (6B). Also see ANTHROPOLOGY.

DIOMEDI Fallen Greek warrior impersonated by Steven during the Trojan War (U).

DIOSCUROS Planet visited by Captain Cook (7J).

DIPLOMACY The Third Doctor helped rescue the peaceful, radioactive aliens known as 'Ambassadors of Death' from General Carrington (CCC). He also helped save a Chinese delegate from the Master at the World Peace Conference (CCC), and Sir Reginald Styles from the twin menace of the Daleks and guerillas from the future (KKK). The Third Doctor impersonated an Earth Federation delegate to Peladon (MMM). During the Earth – Draconian conflict, the Master impersonated a commissioner from Sirius Four; the Draconian Ambassador on Earth was the son of the Draconian Emperor (QQQ). Erato was sent as the ambassador from Tythonus to Chloris to exchange metals for chlorophyll, but was kept in a Pit by Lady Adrasta (5G). The Third and Sixth Doctors mediated the conflicts between Karfel and the Bandrils (6Y). The Third Doctor impersonated Earth Federation delegate to Peladon, Amazonia (MMM).

DIPLOS G-type planet in the Tau Ceti star system. It was the homeworld of Cessair, who had stolen its Great Seal (5C).

DIPTEK Alien tourist who crashlanded in Wales in 1959 and was killed by the Bannermen (7F).

DIRECTOR Leader of the Chameleons' expedition to Earth. He took over Crossland's identity, but refused to bargain with the humans. He disintegrated when Jamie removed the real Crossland's white armband (KK).

DISASTERS See END OF THE WORLD.

DISEASES Three insane Earthmen were using nightshade to poison the Sensorites, who blamed the deaths on a plague (G). The insecticide DN6 would eventually have killed off the human race because of its stable molecules (J). The Cybermen used a neurotropic virus to attack the Moonbase (HH) and Space Beacon Nerva (4D). A space plague was cured by parrinium found on Exxilon (XXX). The Daleks (K), the Silurians (BBB), the Kraals (4D), Monarch of Urbanka (5W) and the Terileptils (5X) all planned to exterminate Mankind with viruses (in the case of the Terileptils, the Black Plague). The Movellans designed a virus that would only kill Daleks (6P). The Fifth Doctor used hexachromite to kill the Silurians who attacked Sea Base Four (6L). The pollutants generated by Global Chemicals created the Green Death, which could have destroyed Earth (TTT).

Radiation sickness threatened the Doctor and his companions on Skaro, until the Thals gave them an antidote (B). Jo Grant was similarly rescued from deadly spores on Spiridon (SSS). Dodo's simple cold virus upset the entire civilisation of the Ark, enabling the Monoids to gain power (X). Terminus was a space station used as a final home for the victims of the incurable lazar disease (6G). The Fifth Doctor and Peri were poisoned by raw spectrox (spectrox toxaemia), a substance so deadly that only androids could harvest it (6R).

The Rani was a master of genetic engineering and could create monstrous diseases (6X, 7D). The Fourth Doctor used an anti-metal virus to destroy Professor Kettlewell's Giant Robot (4A).

The Virus of the Purpose (4T) and the Nimon (5L) were life forms who behaved like cosmic diseases. Also see DRUGS.

DISEMBODIED INTELLIGENCES See ENERGY.

DISINTEGRATOR GUN Experimental gun stolen from UNIT and used by Professor Kettlewell's Giant Robot (4A).

DISNEYLAND Famous amusement park located in Anaheim, California. A company operating a hyperspatial tollport offered a trip to 1959 Disneyland as a prize to selected customers. Chimeron Queen Delta joined the trip, trying to escape Gavrok's Bannermen (7F).

DISSOLUTION Time of death for the Keeper of Traken. It occurred about every thousand years (5T).

DJ Disc Jockey employed at the Tranquil Repose mortuary to play music and keep the people frozen in suspended animation informed. He was killed by the Daleks (6Z).

DN6 Powerful insecticide discovered by Smithers, a scientist financially backed by Forester. Because its molecules were permanently stable, in time, it would have destroyed the whole of mankind (J).

DOBBS One of Lord Ravensworth's guards (6X).

DOBSON Computer scientist who helped Liz Shaw crack the

coded messages of the radioactive aliens. He was secretly working for General Carrington (CCC).

DODECAHEDRON Powerful, five-sided energy crystal originally created on Zolfa-Thura. Meglos wanted to use it for warlike purposes, but it was taken by the Zolfa-Thuran peace party leader to Tigella. Eventually, it was found by the Tigellan Deons who worshipped it as a gift of the god Ti. The Tigellans used it to power their civilization. Ten thousand years later, Meglos used the shape of the Fourth Doctor to steal the Dodecahedron and take it back to Zolfa Thura. He planned to use it in connection with the Screens he had designed to make himself master of the galaxy. But he was betrayed by the Gaztaks and thwarted by the Fourth Doctor. The Dodecahedron destroyed itself, along with Zolfa-Thura (5Q).

DODO See CHAPLET, DODO.

DODRIUM A mineral mined by Zanak (5B).

DOJJEN Last of the Manussan Snakedancers. He taught the Fifth Doctor the rituals which enabled him to destroy the Mara (6D).

DOLAND One of Professor Lasky's assistants, partly responsible for the creation of the Vervoids. Once aboard the *Hyperion III* space liner, he murdered Edwardes, Hallet, and later the two Mogarians Atza and Ortezo, in an effort to protect the fortune he thought he could make by selling the Vervoids as slave labour. He was exposed by the Sixth Doctor, and killed by the Vervoids (7C).

DOLLS, DANCING Deadly pawns used by the Toymaker (Y).

DOME Name given to the structure erected by the Earth Expedition Force to Deva Loka (5Y).

DOMINATORS Ruthless spacefaring race of warriors, so-called master of ten galaxies. They sent Rago, Toba and their deadly robotic servants, the Quarks, to Dulkis to turn the planet into radioactive waste to power their fleet. They were thwarted by the Second Doctor (TT)

DOOMSDAY MACHINE Extremely powerful device built by a race of super-beings who once lived on planet Exarius. It had been responsible for the formation of the Crab Nebula. Its radiation had eventually caused the death of its creators, and kept Exarius barren. The information concerning the Doomsday Machine's existence was stolen from the Matrix by the Master. But the Third Doctor convinced the Guardian that the Machine should not fall into evil hands, and the Guardian destroyed it (HHH).

DORAN He and Tollund were Lady Adrasta's scientists on Chloris. She had him thrown into the Pit because he had failed to detect any sign of life in the remains of Erato's ship (5G).

DORANT Argolin guide (5N).

DORF See LUKOSER.

DOROTHY See ACE.

DORTMUN Crippled genius who led the resistance against the Daleks during their AD 2164 Invasion of Earth. He helped the First Doctor defeat the Daleks, but was killed by the invaders (K).

DRACONIA Draconian home world and seat of a powerful space empire (QQQ).

DRACONIANS Advanced reptilian aliens who ruled a vast space empire. Men came into contact with the Draconians in the 24th or 25th century. They fought beside them in the Alliance during the Second Dalek and Cyber Wars of the 25th and 26th century. However, conflicts between Earth and the Draconians about their respective areas of colonization began to erupt as Earth's influence grew. One such conflict was started by General Williams. Twenty years later, the Daleks engaged the services of the Master and the Ogrons to try to foment a war between Earth and the Draconians, even offering him the use of their Ogron slaves. But the Master's schemes were ultimately exposed and thwarted by the Third Doctor (QQQ). After the revelation of the existence of a 10,000 Dalek army poised to attack the Alliance on Spiridon, the Draconians teamed up with Earth and the Thals to strike back at the Daleks (SSS). After the Third Dalek War, the Draconian Empire, its resources depleted, unable to compete with Earth, entered into a long period of stagnation.

DRACOWLIS Known as 'the flower of many faces', it was probably from Bandril (6Y).

DRACULA The First Doctor met this robotic version of the legendary vampire in a 1996 House of Horrors. It then fought the Daleks (R).

DRAGA Field-guard of the Queen Spider of Metebelis 3. He had been attacked by Arak (ZZZ).

DRAGON Living mechanoid who roamed the depths of Iceworld. The Seventh Doctor discovered that his body hid a powerful energy crystal known as 'Dragonfire'. He was Kane's guardian. He was eventually destroyed by McLuhan and Bazin (7G).

DRAGONFIRE Powerful energy crystal hidden inside the dragon-shaped mechanoid which roamed Iceworld. The Seventh Doctor traded it to Kane to save Ace's life. Kane used it to turn Iceworld back into a spaceship (7G).

DRAGONS A derogatory human nickname for the Draconians (QQQ).

DRAHVA Planet located in Galaxy Four, and home world of the Drahvin. Its sun was cooling and its vegetation was dying, so the Drahvin had to find another inhabitable planet. The Drahvin population was almost exclusively female, men being cultivated in test tubes as and when called for (T).

DRAVID Solon claimed to have dragged Condo from the wreck of a Dravidian spaceship (4K).

DRAHVIN Beautiful, amazonian, emotionless women from Drahva. A team of Drahvin, led by Maaga, attacked the Rills and caused both ships to crashland on a doomed planet in Galaxy Four. They were eventually defeated by the First Doctor (T).

DRAITH, EXMON Alzarian Decider. He was killed at the onset of Mistfall, but had time to give Adric a clue about the peculiar nature of evolution on Alzarius (5R).

DRAK One of the Jacondans serving Azmael. Mestor killed him by using his brain to spy on Azmael (6S).

DRASHIGS Savage swamp monsters captured in Vorg's Scope. They orginated on one of Grundle's satellites. They had powerful clawed legs, sinuous necks and jaws filled with razor-sharp teeth, and were capable of eating virtually anything. Thanks to Kalik's machinations, they were allowed to pursue the Third Doctor through the Scope and finally escape to rampage on Inter Minor, until Vorg destroyed them with the Eradicator. One of the Drashigs had previously killed Kalik (PPP).

DRATHRO Andromedan L-3 robot whose mission was to guard the three Andromedan Sleepers. After the Time Lords moved Earth and rechristened it Ravolox, Drathro took over the UK Habitat, and ruled it as the Immortal. Drathro was powered by a Maglem converter. After Dibber blew up the converter, Drathro was conned by Glitz into giving him the tape containing the Sleepers' stolen secrets. He was finally destroyed when the Sixth Doctor shut down his energy system (7A).

DRAX Renegade Time Lord and mechanical genius who had been at the Time Lord Academy at the same time as the Doctor. Drax built the Mentalis computer of Zeos. He was recued from the Shadow by the Fourth Doctor and helped disable Mentalis before the computer could trigger the armageddon factor that would have destroyed both Zeos and Atrios. After the war was over, he helped the Marshal rebuild Atrios (5F).

DRAYTON COURT Perivale location (7P).

DREW Guard at the prison where the Master was kept. He was killed by the Sea Devils (LLL).

DRILL FLY Insect from Delta Magna's third moon (5E).

DRINKING FOUNTAIN One of the Red Kangs of Paradise Towers. She helped the Seventh Doctor and Mel defeat Kroagnon (7E).

DRISCOLL Number two in charge of the Nuclear Research Complex headed by Professor Watson. His mind was taken over by Eldrad. He died when he stepped into an atomic furnace whose energy Eldrad needed to regenerate (4N).

DRONES Workers from the flatlands of Terra Alpha. They launched a revolution which, with the Seventh Doctor's support, overthrew Helen A's regime (7L).

DRONID Skagra's native planet. In the Gallifreyan past, after a schism with the Cardinals, a rival President temporarily elected to relocate to Dronid (5M).

DRUGS Radiation sickness threatened the First Doctor and his companions on Skaro, until the Thals gave them an antidote (B). Jo Grant was similarly rescued from deadly spores on Spiridon (SSS). A space plague was cured by parrinium found on Exxilon (XXX).

The Sisterhood's Elixir (4K) and spectrox, prepared from Androzanian bat guano (6R), were life-prolonging drugs. The Chinese Tong of the Black Scorpion also trafficked in Opium (4S). The Usurians released PCM gas in Pluto's megropolises' atmosphere to keep the humans pacified (4W). Vraxoin was one of the most dangerously addictive drugs in the Universe; it was made from the very essence of the Mandrels (5K). Terminus, Inc. controlled the victims of lazar disease through their pain-killing hydromel drug (6G).

Nightshade was used to poison the Sensorites (G). The Fifth Doctor used hexachromite to kill the Silurians who attacked Sea Base Four (6L). A Chimeron drug helped Billy mutate into a consort for Queen Delta (7F). See DISEASES.

DRUIDS The British Institute for Druidic Studies was led by De Vries and served the alien Cessair of Diplos (5C). The Master recreated a Druidic-like cult to awaken Azal (JJJ). Sarah Jane and K–9 (Mark III) defeated a coven of Druids led by Commander Pollock and Lily Gregson in the village of Moreton Harwood (K9).

DRYFOOT The Swampies' nickname for the humans (5E).

DU PONT French soldier who fought in the Resistance to put an end to the War Games (ZZ).

DUBAR, SIMON French Catholic henchman of Marshall Tavannes (W).

DUCAT, AMELIA One of the world's leading flower artists. She was paid a thousand pounds by Harrison Chase for a painting (4L).

DUCHESS Nickname given by to Polly by Ben.

DUDMAN, AUDREY Ace's mother's maiden name. Ace met her as a baby, and helped save her from the Haemovores (7M).

DUDMAN, FRANK Ace's grandfather, and Kathleen's husband. A merchant navy officer, he was reported missing in action during World War II (7M).

DUDMAN, KATHLEEN Ace's grandmother, one of Commander Millington's radio operators in charge of monitoring German transmissions during World War II. Ace helped her escape from the Haemovores when the Curse of Fenric struck her Northumberland village. She then moved to 17 Old Terrace, Streatham (7M).

DUFFY Sergeant who fought the Dinosaur Invasion (WWW).

DUGDALE Manussan barker who owned the hall of mirrors and thus was responsible for Lon becoming possessed by the Mara. He was killed by the Mara after he had served his purpose (6D).

DUGEEN Crew member of the methane refinery on Delta Magna's moon. He was secretly a member of the Sons of the Earth, and was killed by Thawn as he tried to prevent the launch of a deadly rocket that would have wiped out the entire Swampie race (5E).

DUGGAN, BILL A member of the staff of the Wheel in Space who discovered that the Cybermats were eating the Station's bernalium supply. He was blamed for Rudkin's death, and later died a victim of the Cybermen's Celensky capsules (SS).

DUGGAN English detective who was investigating Count Scarlioni's art sales in Paris in 1980. He helped the Fourth Doctor and Romana expose the Count's true nature as Scaroth, last of the Jagaroth. He travelled back with them in time to 3.5 million BC where, with a well-placed punch, he stopped Scaroth from preventing his ship's destruction and thereby ensuring the creation of life on Earth (5H).

DUKKHA One of the Kinda (5Y).

DULCIANS Gentle, peace-loving race of Dulkis. After atomic weapons destroyed one of their islands (since then nicknamed 'Island of Death'), the Dulcians banned such arms and turned to peace; the island was converted into a museum. Because they were prone to too much talking and not enough action, they almost allowed their planet to be destroyed by the Dominators, who wanted to turn it into radioactive waste to power their fleet, and were saved only by the intervention of the Second Doctor (TT).

DULKIS Peaceful planet visited twice by the Doctor (TT).

DULLES Member of Rorvik's crew. He died in the destruction of the privateer's ship (5S).

DUMS Lower class of mute robots who were used as a labour force aboard the *Sandminer* (4R).

DUNBAR, RICHARD Employee of the World Ecology Bureau who sold information about the Krynoid pods to Harrison Chase. He tried to make up for his treachery, but was killed by the Krynoid (4L).

DUNE Power technician, one of the Chosen in the Ark in Space and the original host for the Wirrn Queen's eggs (4C).

DUPLICATES The Dalek extermination team sent after the First Doctor used a robotic duplicate, which was destroyed by the Doctor (R). The Daleks later perfected that method by cloning people, transferring their mental patterns to the newly created 'Duplicate' (in theory, loyal to the Daleks), and destroying the originals. Among such duplicates were Stien and Colonel Archer (6P).

The Kraal scientist Styggron devised android duplicates, in particular of the Fourth Doctor and Harry Sullivan (4J). Sharaz Jek made android duplicates of the Fifth Doctor and Peri (6R). The Tarans were master android builders (5D).

The Fourth Doctor had himself cloned and miniaturized, along with Leela, to defeat the Nucleus (4T), and was again duplicated by the Leisure Hive's Tachyon Recreation Generator (5N). Omega adopted the the appearance of the Fifth Doctor, but the bonding was incomplete and would have caused a huge explosion (6E). The Borad had created twenty-four clones of himself (6Y).

Duplicates also occur naturally: At the time of St Bartholomew's Massacre, the Abbot of Amboise was a striking duplicate of the First Doctor (W). Would-be dictator Salamander was an equally striking duplicate of the Second Doctor (PP). Princess Strella of Tara was a natural duplicate of Romana-I (5D) who, when she regenerated, chose the form of Princess Astra of Atrios (5F). The Zygons had the ability to duplicate other people's forms. Their leader, Broton, impersonated the Duke of Forgill (4F). Meglos later assumed the appearance of the Fourth Doctor to steal the Tigellan Dodecahedron (5Q). The Chameleons (KK), the Rutans (4V) and the android Kamelion also had the ability to duplicate other people's form.

The Alzarian Marshmen evolved into duplicates of the Terradonians (5R). The sentient computer Xoanon was a mentally twisted duplicate of the Fourth Doctor (4Q). K-9 was duplicated twice by the Fourth Doctor. Also see CLONES, REPLICAS.

DURALINIUM Metal used in the construction of building units on Earth in the year AD 2972. Because planet Exarius was rich in it, Captain Dent of the Interplanetary Mining Corporation was determined to wrest it away from Ashe's colonists (HHH). It was also used on Peladon (YYY).

DURANIUM Hard metal used on the Terra Nova Ark (4C).

DURILIUM Metal used by the federation (QQQ).

DWARF STAR ALLOY Very dense metal, the only substance that could keep the time-shifting Tharils prisoner. The hull of Rorvik's ship was made of Dwarf Star Alloy, which had an unstabilizing effect on the Zero Point where the ship had rematerialized (5S).

DWELLINGS See CASTROVALVA.

DYMOND Captain of the *Hecate*. He was exposed by the Fourth Doctor and Romana as a vraxoin smuggler in league with Tryst, and was eventually arrested (5K).

DYNASTREAM Chambers's safe was made of case hardened dynastream, but was nevertheless disintegrated by the Giant Robot (4A).

DYNATROPE Kroton machine with the capability of draining and converting mental energy into other kinds of power. It was used by the Krotons on the Gonds. When the Dynatrope was used on the Second Doctor and Zoe, it generated enough power to grow and give life to new Krotons. It needed at least four 'high-brains' for work at full capability (including space flight) (WW).

DYNOMORPHIC GENERATOR TARDIS component exhausted by the Master. Stranded on Jurassic Earth, he planned to replace it with the Xeraphin intelligence (6C).

DYONI A young Thal woman and Alydon's lover. By threatening to take her to the Daleks, Ian forced Alydon to forego his pacifism (B).

DYSON, ERNEST JOHN British chief engineer at the Snowcap Space Tracking Station. He helped the First Doctor, Ben and Polly defeat the Mondasian Cybermen (DD).

DYSTOPIAS The opposite of Utopias: a world where chaos or evil reigned, and normal values were twisted. Among these were the human colony secretly controlled by the Macra (JJ); the planet of the Gonds, exploited by the Krotons (WW); the Usurian-dominated colony of Pluto (4W); the planet of E-Space ruled by the Great Vampire (5P); the former penal colony of Varos (6V); the weird society of Paradise Towers (7E); and Helen A's Terra Alpha, where unhappiness could lead to death (7L). Also see UTOPIAS.

DYSTRONIC EXPLOSIVE Explosive used on Skaro (4E).

E

E-SPACE Exo/Space Time continuum. Pocket universe located outside normal space (N-Space). The TARDIS became trapped in E-Space after going through a Charged Vacuum Emboitement. While in E-Space, the Fourth Doctor and Romana stopped on Alzarius (5R), then defeated the Great Vampire, who had escaped to E-Space after fleeing from the Time Lords (5P). Romana helped free the Tharils from Rorvik and elected to stay in E-Space with K9 (Mark II) (5S). The Doctor later found that the Logopolitans used E-Space to save the Universe from heat death (5V).

EARP, MORGAN One of Wyatt Earp's brothers (Z).

EARP, VIRGIL Marshall of Dodge City. He came to Tombstone to help his brother Wyatt in the gunfight at the OK Corral. Later, he became Tombstone's sheriff (Z).

EARP, WARREN Youngest of the Earp brothers. He was killed by the Clantons when they came to free Phineas Clanton from jail (Z).

EARP, WYATT (1848–1929) Legendary frontiersman of the American West. He had four brothers: James, Virgil, Morgan and Warren. In 1878, Earp became Marshall of Tombstone, Arizona, where his friend Bat Masterson was town sheriff. In 1881, after the Clantons had killed his brother Warren, he challenged them to a gunfight at the OK Corral from which, with Doc Holliday's help, he emerged victorious (Z).

EARTHLING See MORRIS, GEORGE.

EATER OF WORLDS One of the Destroyer's names (7N).

ECHO, THE Moreton Harwood's newspaper. Sarah Jane Smith's Aunt Lavinia wrote a letter to its editor, Henry Tobias, about witchcraft (K9).

ECKERSLEY One of the Federation trisilicate mining engineers on Peladon (the other was Vega Nexos). He turned out to be a traitor hired by Galaxy Five to help Azaxyr take over the mines. To do so, he used a machine to project a holographic image of Aggedor, which was also a heat ray. After he was exposed by the Third Doctor, he fled, taking Queen Thalira hostage. He was killed by the real Aggedor, whom he murdered (YYY).

ECOLOGY See POLLUTION.

ED DIIN, HAROUN Resident of Lydda who swore vengeance on El Akir after he killed his wife and son, and ravished one of his two daughters. He helped save Barbara from El Akir's clutches, and eventually killed the evil Emir (P).

EDAL Captain of the Elders' city. He almost took over after Jano's defection, but became paranoid and was finally stopped by Steven (AA).

EDEN Savage world where the deadly Mandrels originated. Stott had been left to die on Eden (5K).

EDGEWORTH (PROFESSOR) See AZMAEL.

EDITH Saxon woman from Wulnoth's village. She was Wulnoth's wife, and was later wounded in a Viking raid (S).

EDU Former miner and one of Torvin's band of rebels on Chloris (5G).

EDUCATION Susan attended the Coal Hill Secondary School (A, 7H). Ian Chesterton and Barbara Wright were teachers. Adric won a star as a badge of excellence at mathematics. The Doctor took an honorary degree at St Cedd's College in Cambridge in 1960 (5M). Among the students who attended the Time Lords' Academy at the same time as the Doctor were the Master, the Rani and Drax (5F). Borusa was one of their teachers. Zoe attended the School of Parapsychology, which placed emphasis on pure logic (SS).

EDWARD THE CONFESSOR (1003–1066) King of England who, on his deathbed, named Harold as his successor, even though he allegedly had already promised the crown to William the Conqueror (S).

EDWARD OF WESSEX (SIR) Lord of Wessex Castle. He sent his messenger Eric to ask for assistance in crushing Irongron, who was pillaging his lands. He and his wife, Lady Eleanor, helped the Third Doctor to defeat Linx (UUU).

EDWARDES Communications Officer of the *Hyperion III* space liner. He was electrocuted in the hydroponic centre by a booby trap set up by Doland. The resulting light burst awoke the Vervoids (7C).

EELEK Ambitious Gond Deputy Council Leader. He deposed Selris, and plotted to attack the Krotons, but almost wrecked the planet. Later, he agreed to hand the Second Doctor and Zoe over to the Krotons. He was totally discredited after their defeat (WW).

EGYPT The First Doctor visited Egypt at the time of the construction of Kephren's Pyramid, circa 2600 BC (V). Later, the Fourth Doctor found himself trapped in Sutekh's Pyramid. Sutekh was the last of the Osirians, an alien race who were the source of the Ancient Egyptians' mythology (4G). Scaroth the Jagaroth was mistaken for a god by the Ancient Egyptians (5H).

EIGHT-LEGS Name that the Spiders of Metebelis 3 called themselves. The word 'Spider' reminded them of their humble origins (ZZZ).

EINSTEIN, ALBERT (1879–1955) German – American physicist who developed the theory of relativity and one of the eleven geniuses kidnapped by the Rani to make up her giant Brain (7D).

EIRAK Watch commander of the Vanir on Terminus. He was in control of the hydromel. He agreed to step down in favour of Valgard if the latter brought the Fifth Doctor back from the Forbidden Zone. He and the other Vanir eventually remained on Terminus to help Nyssa run it as a regular hospital (6G).

EL AKIR Scarfaced Saracen leader. He tried to capture King Richard I, but was duped by William des Preaux and Barbara. He later captured Barbara and took her to Lydda, his fortress city, but she was rescued by Ian. El Akir was killed by Haroun Ed Diin, a man whose wife and son he had killed (P).

ELDER, KATE Doc Holliday's wife. She was a singer at the Last Chance Saloon in Tombstone (Z).

ELDERS Title given to the Sensorites in charge of the Sense-Sphere. The First Elder was courteous and peaceful. The Second Elder was replaced by the City Administrator, who proved treacherous and hostile to humans (G).

ELDERS Leaders of an advanced yet sterile civilization which relied on stealing the life essence of the so-called 'Savages' and transferring it to its own people, to give them greater energy and talent. The Elders were able to chart the TARDIS's travels through time and space. Jano was their Council Leader, and after absorbing the First Doctor's life essence, he made peace with the Savages and ultimately convinced the Elders to put an end to their lifestyle. The new society then chose Steven as their leader (AA).

ELDERS Name used by the leaders of Sarn (6Q).

ELDRAD Kastrian genius and arch-villain who designed the Kastrian silicon-based life forms and the force-field barriers which made life on the Kastrian surface possible. Eldrad destroyed the barriers when the Kastrians would not submit to his rule, thus dooming all Kastrian life. King Rokon had him placed in a space capsule and obliterated, but Eldrad's hand landed on Earth during the Jurassic Period and became a fossil. It was dug up in 1977 and used by Sarah Jane Smith, then Driscoll, to create a nuclear explosion, the energy of which enabled him to regenerate. (Eldrad carried his genetic code in a ring.) He then tricked the Fourth Doctor into taking him back to Kastria. When Eldrad found out that Kastria was a dead world, he tried to return to conquer Earth but was foiled by the Doctor, who abandoned him there (4N).

ELDRED Saxon farmer from Wulnoth's village. He was wounded in a Viking raid (S).

ELDRED, DANIEL Retired professor and rocket engineer. He established a museum dedicated to space travel. He was instrumental in helping the Second Doctor defeat the Ice Warriors and their 'Seeds of Death' (XX).

ELEANOR OF WESSEX (LADY) Wife of Sir Edward of Wessex. She helped the Third Doctor against Linx (UUU).

ELENA Member of the Intergalactic Pursuit Squadron (6S).

ELGIN, MARK Public Relations officer of Global Chemicals at the Llanfairfach Refinery. He helped his friend Fell fight off BOSS's programming, and saved the Third Doctor's life. He was eventually processed by BOSS (TTT).

ELGIN Employee of the Nuclear Research Complex attacked by Eldrad (4N).

ELITE Alzarian class of citizens who received superior education (5R).

ELITE GROUP ONE Name of Sauvix's Sea Devil Commando (6L).

ELIXIR OF LIFE Substance produced by the Sacred Flame of Karn. It had the power to extend life and boost psionic powers. After the Time Lords defeated Morbius, the Sisterhood agreed to share the Elixir with the High Council. The Time Lords presumably used it to facilitate difficult regenerations, increase their mental powers and, possibly, boost-start a new cycle of regenerations, as evidenced by the fact that the High Council once offered one such cycle to the Master (4K).

ELIZABETH Squire John's daughter. She saw the Terileptils' ship crash to Earth and was killed by them (5X).

ELIZABETH I (1543–1603) Queen of England. Her image was projected on the First Doctor's Space-Time Visualizer (R).

ELIZABETH II Contemporary Queen of England. Her path almost crossed that of the Seventh Doctor at Windsor (7K).

ELLIS Liverpool police sergeant (V).

ELYON A Thal from Skaro, killed by a creature from the Lake of Mutations (B).

EMBERY Sergeant in the British army squadron sent to fight the Daleks the Coal Hill area, in 1963 (7H).

EMMETT ELECTRONICS Electronics firm robbed by the Giant Robot (4A).

EMPATHY See TELEPATHY.

EMPEROR DALEK The supreme leader of the original Daleks. He was not to be confused with the alias used by Davros to lead his own Imperial Daleks (7H). The Emperor Dalek was destroyed in the fighting between humanized and unchanged Daleks on Skaro (EE). He may have been an even further evolved version of Davros.

EMPEROR OF DRACONIA Supreme Leader of the Draconian Empire. In the 26th Century, when the Daleks and the Master tried to foment a war between Earth and the Draconians, the Emperor's son was ambassador to Earth. That Emperor spared the Third Doctor's life and helped him avert the war. In the 21st century, the fifteenth Emperor of Draconia made the Doctor a noble of Draconia (QQQ).

EMPIRE (EARTH) The Earth Empire arose sometime in the 26th century, just before the end of the Alliance and the Dalek–Movellan Wars. After the disappearance of the rival Draconian Empire, it grew to rule a large portion of the Milky Way galaxy until the end of the 30th century, mercilessly crushing and exploiting alien races to serve its own needs.

The First Doctor prevented the Sensorites from becoming one of the Empire's victims (G). The Fifth Doctor helped preserve the Kinda (5Y). Other races were not so lucky: the Wirrn (4C) and the Mogarians (7C) were ruthlessly exploited by the Empire. The Empire was presumably responsible for the defeat of the Movellans, who had won a pyrrhic victory against the Daleks (5J, 6P).

It is possible that the Time Lords were secretly afraid of the Empire, since one of the factors that brought about its downfall was the Solos Crisis, which occurred near the end of the 30th century. This took place when the Time Lords sent the Third Doctor to help the Solonian Mutants reach their true, super-human form (NNN). The Solonians then went on to lead a series of revolutions which severely damaged the Empire. Other factors that contributed to the Empire's Fall were an unprecedented string of solar flares from Earth's sun (4C), followed by the advent of a new ice age (OO). The Empire was replaced by the Federation.

EMPIRE STATE BUILDING Until 1954, this was the highest skyscraper in New York City. It was completed in 1931, and was the second stop in the Daleks' pursuit of the First Doctor through time and space (R).

EMPRESS Spouse of Kublai Khan (D).

EMPRESS Interstellar cruise liner which crashed into the *Hecate* when emerging from hyperspace above the planet Azure (5K). The Fourth Doctor exposed one of its passengers, Tryst, as a Vraxoin smuggler.

END OF THE WORLD Manmade disasters which could have brought about the end of the world included: Forester's deadly insecticide DN6 (J); WOTAN's war machines (BB); Professor Zaroff's plan to drain the ocean into the Earth's core (GG); Salamander's volcanic disaster (PP); Professor Stahlman's 'Inferno' project (DDD); and Sir Charles Grover's Operation Golden Age (WWW).

World War III was almost provoked by the Master (FFF); the Daleks (KKK); the Scientific Reform Society (4A); the Silurians and the Sea Devils (6L). Pollution threatened Earth in the form of the Weed (RR) and the Green Death (TTT). Also see WORLD WAR III, POLLUTION.

Natural disasters that could have spelled out the end of the world (or of its civilization) included: a new ice age (OO); solar flares (4C); and finally the sun going nova (X).

Aliens who would have liked to destroy Earth (instead of conquering it) included the Daleks (K), the Cybermen (DD, 6B, 6T); Axos (GGG); Sutekh (4G); the Krynoids (4L); the Fendahl (4X); the Captain of Zanak (5B); Monarch (5W); Omega (6E); the corrupt High Council of the Time Lords, when they decided upon the Ravolox Stratagem (7A–7C); the Destroyer (7N); and Light (7Q). Also see INVASIONS.

ENDERHEID (WITCHES OF) The Sixth Doctor claimed his trial was the greatest travesty of justice since theirs (7B).

ENERGY Conventional sources of energy used on Earth included: coal, oil (TTT, 4F); natural gas (RR); nuclear energy (BBB, GGG, 4N); and even good, old-fashioned fire (A). A World Energy Conference was almost sabotaged by the Zygons (4F). Solar energy was captured in the 21st century by Salamander, who used his Suncatcher satellite (PP). Professor Stahlman almost destroyed Earth when he tried to break the Earth's crust to tap Stahlman's Gas (DDD). Much later, the Usurians kept a portion of humanity enslaved on Pluto by providing it with the energy of small, artificial suns (4W).

Aliens relied on various other sources of energy: the Time Lords used the energy of a captive black hole (4P); the Daleks used static electricity and solar power to move around (B), and taranium to power their Time Destructor (V). The Elders used the Savages' life force as an energy source (AA). The Dominators did not hesitate to turn a planet into a radioactive mass for their fuel supply (TT). The Master Brain of the Land of Fiction needed men's creative energy (UU). The Krotons used their Dynatrope to convert mental energy into power (WW). The Axons' Axonite was both a source of energy and part of Axos (GGG). Professor Sorenson tried to use anti-matter, but failed (4H), although anti-matter fuel powered Captain Briggs's ship (6B). The Union of Traken was held together by the bioelectronic Source (5T). Varos was an important supplier of Zyton-7 (6V).

Many types of crystals were sources of energy: the Nimon needed hymetusite crystals (5L). The Tigellan civilisation was powered by the Dodecahedron (5Q). Voolium and Madronite 1–5 crystals found on Calufrax could be used to power a Psychic Interference Transmitter (5B). The Terileptils used Vintaric crystals to provide lighting (5X). Quarb Crystals were used in hyperspatial engines (7F). The Dragonfire was a powerful energy crystal (maybe hymetusite?) (7G). Also see CRYSTALS, MINERALS.

Intelligent entities made of energy included: the Great Intelligence; the Nestene; Omega; the Mandragora Helix (4M); the Mara; the Xeraphin (6C) and possibly the Guardians of Time; the Fendahl (4X) and Fenric (7M).

ENGIN Coordinator in charge of the Gallifreyan Matrix. He helped the Fourth Doctor and Castellan Spandrell expose Goth and defeat the Master (4P). Also see KEEPER OF THE MATRIX.

ENLANDIA Water world visited by the First Doctor (X).

ENLIGHTENERS Name used by the Eternals to refer to the Guardians of Time (6H).

ENLIGHTENMENT A crystal of unknown powers and great value offered by the Guardians of Time as the prize to the winner of a planet-spanning space race undertaken by the Eternals. The Black Guardian hoped that, with such a prize, the Eternals might wreak havoc throughout the Universe. Instead, the Fifth Doctor won the race but turned down Enlightenment. When Turlough threw the crystal at the Black Guardian, he vanished in a burst of flames. The Fifth Doctor explained that Enlightenment was not the crystal but the moral choice (6H).

ENLIGHTENMENT She and Persuasion were Monarch's two Urbankan android ministers. Enlightenment was destroyed by Adric (5W).

ENSIGN, THE British boys' magazine. The Master of the Land of Fiction was one of its copywriters (UU).

ENTROPY Waste energy that builds up in any system. According to the Second Law of Thermodynamics, it must inevitably increase. See CHARGED VACUUM EMBOITEMENTS.

ENZU See HALLET.

EPHEMERALS Term used by the Eternals to refer to all other living species (6H).

EPRIN Altos's friend. He was sent by Arbitan to Millenius on a quest for the Keys of Marinus, and was killed by Kala, Aydan and Eyesen, who tried to frame Ian for his murder (E).

EPSILON FOUR ZERO GAMMA Planet targeted by the Dominators (TT).

ERADICATOR Device used by the Inter Minorans to try to kill all the life forms contained in Vorg's Scope. Vorg ended up using it to kill the rampaging Drashigs (PPP).

ERAK One of the five Earth colonists from Galsec Seven stranded on Earth circa AD 15,000 after their ship was destroyed while answering a fake mayday signal. The Sontaran Styre performed cruel experiments on him to determine the limits of human resistance. He was saved by the Fourth Doctor (4B).

ERATO Tythonian ambassador to Chloris; he looked like a giant, green brain. He had been sent to Chloris to trade chlorophyll for metal. To preserve her power, Lady Adrasta kept him prisoner for fifteen years in the mines (where he became known as the Creature from the Pit). The Fourth Doctor and Romana eventually discovered Erato's true nature, and found a way to communicate with him. Erato killed Adrasta, then helped the Doctor save Chloris from total destruction by a Neutron Star, which had been diverted by the Tythonians as a form of reprisal (5G).

ERGON Reptilian creature who served Omega when he tried to bond with the Fifth Doctor's body in Amsterdam (6E).

ERIC Sir Edward of Wessex's messenger. He was captured by Bloodaxe and later freed by Hal (UUU).

ERICSON Hardiman's assistant at the Nuton Power Complex. He helped the Third Doctor and UNIT defeat Axos (GGG).

ERICSON One of Professor Sorenson's Morestran crew killed on Zeta Minor by the anti-matter creatures (4H).

ESP See TELEPATHY.

ESTO One of the Sensorites (G).

ESTRAM, GILLES (SIR) Alias used by the Master. Under the guise of King John's Champion, he tried to turn the Barons against the King and prevent the signing of the Magna Carta (6J).

ETERNALS Race of powerful beings who existed outside of time, and lived forever in eternity. Even though they were gifted with great mental powers, their minds had grown devoid of emotions. The Guardians of Time offered them Enlightenment as the prize of a planet-spanning space race. The Eternals were banished to their eternal void by the White Guardian (6H).

ETERNITY PERPETUAL COMPANY Interplanetary company which used the Miniscopes before they were outlawed (PPP).

ETHNON Alien tourist who crashlanded in Wales in 1959 and was killed by the Bannermen (7F).

ETNIN One of Cully's tour party, he was killed by the Dominators (TT).

ETTA Typical citizen of Varos, and Arak's wife. She supported the Governor's policies (6V).

ETTIS Extremist leader of the trisilicate miners on Peladon. He hated the Federation and tried to destroy Queen Thalira's palace with the sonic lance. But a self-destruct mechanism caused it to explode when activated, and it killed Ettis instead (YYY).

EUDAMUS Planet visited by the Psychic Circus before it moved on to Segonax (7J).

EURO-SEA GAS CORPORATION Company whose North Sea refinery and off-shore rigs were attacked by the Weed. It supplied natural gas to England and Wales. Its London Board member, Megan Jones, helped the Second Doctor destroy the Weed and free the refinery controller, Robson (RR).

EVANS (DR) Moonbase doctor who was the first to succumb to the Cybermen's neurotropic virus. Turned into a 'zombie', he nearly used the Gravitron to flood the Earth (HH).

EVANS Private in the army task force which fought the Great Intelligence in the London underground. He survived the destruction of the ammunition convoy he was driving, and helped the Second Doctor fight the Yeti (QQ).

EVANS, DAI One of the Llanfairfach miners. He died from the Green Death (TTT).

EVENT ONE See CREATION.

EVERETT (MISS) Employee of the Brittanicus Base (OO).

EVIL The lesser villains encountered by the Doctor were usually motivated by the basic evil of greed – but this did not make them less dangerous. Evil human men included: Kal the caveman (A); Aydan and Eyesen (E) Forester (J); Bennett (L); Sevcheria (M); El Akir (P); Johnny Ringo (Z); Gray (FF); Caven (YY); Pike (CC); Theodore Maxtible (LL); Caven (YY); Dent (HHH); Irongron and Bloodaxe (UUU); Eckersley (YYY); Lupton (ZZZ); Dr Kellman (4D); Count Federico (4M); Lord Palmerdale (4V); Count Grendel of Tara (5D); the Graff Vynda-K (5A); Tryst and Dymond (5K); Rorvik (5S); Morgus and Stotz (6R); the Chief Officer of Varos (6V); Doland (7C) and Keillor (7F). Evil human women included: Kala (E); Queen Xanxia (5B); Vivien Fay (5C); Lady Adrasta (5G); Kara (6Z) and Lady Peinforte (7K). Aliens included: the Usurians (4W); the Gaztaks (5Q); the Mentors (6V, 7B) and the Bannermen (7F).

Misguided fanatics were also formidable opponents. Among these were: Tegana (D); Tlotoxl (F); Robespierre (H); Klieg and Kaftan (MM); General Carrington (CCC); Professor Stahlman (DDD); Hepesh (MMM); Colonel Trenchard (LLL); Sir Charles Grover (WWW); Prof. Kettlewell and Miss Winters (4A); Sorenson (4H); Harrison Chase (4L); Hieronymous (4M); Dask (4R); Stael (4X); Kassia of Traken (5T); Timanov (6Q); Sir George Hutchinson (6M); Dastari (6W) and Helen A (7L).

On a greater scale were villains motivated by sheer megalomania and/or an unquenchable thirst for conquest. Among these were: renegade Time Lords such as the Master, the Rani, Borusa and Morbius; alien tyrants such as the Animus (N), Eldrad (4N), Meglos (5Q), Monarch (5W), Mestor (6S), the Borad (6Y), Kroagnon (7E) and Kane (7G); alien races such as the Ice Warriors, the Voord (E), the Drahvins (T), the Macra (JJ), the Dominators (TT), the Krotons (WW), the War Lords (ZZ), the Nestene, Axos (GGG), the Zygons (4F), the Kraals (4J), the Krynoids (4L), the Virus of the Purpose (4T), the Movellans (5J), the Nimon (5L), the Terileptils (5X) and the Tractators (6N). Earth megalomaniacs included: the mad computers WOTAN (BB) and BOSS (TTT); Professor Zaroff (GG); Salamander (PP); Tobias Vaughn (VV); Magnus Greel (4S) and Morgaine (7N). Grander examples of a xenophobic desire for total domination over all other species include the Daleks, the Cybermen and the Sontarans.

Finally, there were cosmic entities who could almost be called evil incarnate, such as the Celestial Toymaker (Y); the Great Intelligence; Sutekh (4G); the Mandragora Helix (4M); the Fendahl (4X); the Black Guardian and his servant, the Shadow (5F); the Great Vampire (5P); the Mara; the Gods of Ragnarok (7J); the Destroyer (7N) and Fenric (7M).

Some entities were driven to become villains by a cruel twist of fate, such as: Omega; the Wirrn (4C); Xoanon (4Q); Scaroth (5H); Mawdryn (6F); Sharaz Jek (6R) and the Silurians and Sea Devils.

At last, there were entities whose action may appear evil to humans, but who were ultimately motivated by factors beyond human notions of good and evil. For example: the Daemons (JJJ); Kronos (OOO); the Xeraphin (6C) and the Eternals (6H).

EVIL ONE Nickname given to the Fourth Doctor by the Sevateem because his face was carved on the Black Wall behind which their god, Xoanon, was believed to be held prisoner (4Q).

EVOLUTION The powerful alien Light once catalogued all of Earth's species, but when he learned that his catalogue had been made obsolete, he wanted to destroy Earth. He disintegrated when the Seventh Doctor showed him that no one, not even Light, could stop evolution (7Q). Both the Fendahl (4X) and the Daemons (JJJ) were believed to have affected Man's evolution.

The Marshmen of Alzarius evolved into replicas of the Terradonians (5R). The Thoros-Betans evolved into the Mentors (7B). Sergeant Paterson honestly believed in the 'survival of the fittest' adage (7P). Also see ANTHROPOLOGY, MUTATIONS.

EXAMINER Earth examiner sent to Vulcan to investigate governor Hansell's handling of the rebels. He was murdered by Bragen and impersonated by the Second Doctor (EE).

EXARIUS According to some reports, it was the name of the planet which, in the years AD 2972, was coveted by both Ashe's colonists and Captain Dent from the Interplanetary Mining Corporation, who wanted its duralinium resources. It was also inhabited by primitives and non-humanoid priests, all of whom worshipped the Guardian of the Doomsday Machine. Thanks to the intervention of the Third Doctor and Jo Grant, the colonists defeated Dent's evil schemes and kept their planet (HHH).

EXCALIBUR King Arthur's sword, buried with him in a spaceship under Vortigern's Lake. It was drawn by Ace and became the object of a fierce battle between the Seventh Doctor and Morgaine (7N).

EXCHANGE HALL Vast amphiteatre used by the Company on Pluto for its executions and other public functions (4W).

EXORSE Captain of the Elder's city. He was captured by Steven, and kept prisoner by the Savages, but eventually escaped. However, Nanina's words had shaken his beliefs (AA).

EXTERMINATE Dalek credo.

EXXILON Hidden, mist-shrouded planet once inhabited by a highly advanced race of silicon-based beings. The Exxilon visited Earth and were mistaken for space gods by the Incas. They created the City, a computer-controlled complex that thought itself so perfect, that it cast out its creators, who then reverted to savagery. A group of Exxilon, led by Bellal, stopped worshipping the City. They helped the Third Doctor fight the Daleks and, ultimately, destroy the City. The mineral parrinium, the only antidote to a space plague, was found only on Exxilon (XXX).

EYE OF HARMONY Name given to the black hole captured by Rassilon and brought back to Gallifrey. It had probably been created by the collapse of Omega's supernova (RRR). The Eye of Harmony was encased in an hexagonal, monolithic structure, and secretly located under the Panopticon. It could be accessed only with the Great Key (or Rod) of Rassilon. The Eye of Harmony was the virtually inexhaustible source of energy which powered Gallifrey and made time travel possible. The Master was able to absorb enough energy from the Eye of Harmony to prolong his life, almost condemning Gallifrey in the process (4P).

EYE OF HORUS Device built by Horus to imprison his evil brother Sutekh on Earth. The Eye of Horus was housed inside the Pyramids of Mars, and was protected by various traps and guardians. Sutekh forced the Fourth Doctor to take him to Mars and used the body of Professor Marcus Scarman to destroy it (4G).

142

EYE OF ORION For some it was the most tranquil place in the Universe. The Fifth Doctor was there when he fell victim to Borusa's playing of the Game of Rassilon (6K).

EYE PLANTS Native plants of Spiridon (SSS).

EYER, L.D. One of Skagra's Think Tank colleagues (5M).

EYESEN (aka EYSON) Representative for the Court of Millenius. He, Aydan, Kala and Eprin conspired to steal a Key of Marinus. Later, he attempted to frame Ian for Eprin's murder, but was finally unmasked by the First Doctor (E).

EYE-SPY Name given by the Kangs to their scouts (7E).

EZRETH Tigellan who fought the Gaztaks (5Q).

F

F, HAROLD See V, HAROLD.

FABIAN Commander of the Intergalactic Pursuit Squadron who assigned Lieutenant Lang to go after the kidnappers of Romulus and Remus (6S).

FAGIROS Planet visited by Captain Cook (7J).

FANG ROCK Remote rocky island a few miles off the Channel coast. It was the location of a lighthouse, and was rumoured to be haunted by a mysterious Beast. In the early 1900s, the Fourth Doctor destroyed a stranded Rutan who had taken the shape of lighthouse-keeper Reuben (4V).

FANTASY FACTORY The Valeyard's Dickensian base inside the Matrix. Its proprietor was supposed to be one J. J. Chambers. It was there that the Sixth Doctor defeated the Valeyard (7C).

FARADAY UNIT colonel in charge of the Devesham Space

Research Station while Brigadier Lethbridge-Stewart was in Geneva. The Kraals made an android duplicate of him. He helped the Fourth Doctor defeat them (4J).

FARADAY, MICHAEL (1791–1867) Famous English physicist The Master wanted to kidnap him to harness his genius, but was thwarted by the Sixth Doctor (6X).

FARIAH Salamander's official food taster. She left with Astrid, but was later killed by Benik (PP).

FARLEY One of the crew on the Eternal's ships (6H).

FARMINGDALE British military installation whose resources were used to fight the Daleks (7H).

FAROON Lakertyan female, Beyus's wife and Sarn's mother. She helped the Seventh Doctor defeat the Rani (7D).

FARRAH Taran swordsman who served Prince Reynart (5D).

FARREL, JOHN Former owner of the Farrel plastics factory. He retired to let his son, Rex, take over. Alerted by McDermott to the changes introduced by the Master, he successfully resisted the renegade Time Lord's hypnotic commands. The Master had him killed by a Nestene-controlled plastic doll (EEE).

FARREL, MARY John Farrel's wife. She almost saw her husband murdered by the Nestene-controlled plastic doll (EEE).

FARREL, REX Son of John and Mary Farrel. His father had retired, leaving him in charge of the Farrel plastics factory. The Master placed him under his hypnotic control and used his factory to manufacture Autons and other murderous Nestene-controlled plastic products. After the Nestene's defeat at the hands of the Third Doctor, the Master used him as a decoy to escape (EEE).

FARROW, ARNOLD Government inspector who discovered that the insecticide DN6 would eventually kill the human race. He was murdered by Forester before he could report to his superiors (J).

FAST RETURN SWITCH TARDIS console instrument which, once jammed, nearly sent the TARDIS and its crew back to the very beginning of time (C).

FASTER-THAN-LIGHT PROPULSION (aka FTL, HYPER-SPACE or WARP) Man discovered FTL propulsion at the end of the 21st century. A notorious FTL accident occurred when the *Empress* and the *Hecate* crashed into one another when simultaneously emerging out of hyperspace above the planet Azure (5K). The Megaran (5C) and Mawdryn (6F)'s ships were both in stationary hyperspace (or warp ellipse) orbits above Earth. Planet Zanak had been equipped with massive transmat engines enabling it to travel through space (5B). Quarb crystals were used to power hyperspatial engines (7F). Also see BREAK OUT, LOST SHIPS, TELEPORTATION.

FATIMA Indian woman prisoner in El Akir's harem (P).

FAY, VIVIEN See CESSAIR.

FEDERATION Political entity which emerged sometime in the 32nd century to replace the Earth Empire (which had ended circa the 30th century), after a period of solar flares and a new Ice Age on Earth. The Federation was a loose combine of human and alien races, including the Alpha Centauri, the Arcturians, the newly peaceful Martian Ice Warriors, and presumably the Draconians.

Around AD 3700, the Third Doctor helped the planet Peladon join the Federation, and exposed an Arcturian plot (MMM). Fifty years later, he prevented the hostile Galaxy 5 from using the traitor Eckersley to take over Peladon's trisilicate mines (YYY).

The Federation later evolved into a more militaristic entity, perhaps due to the challenge of the Daleks in AD 4000, and the ensuing, Fourth Dalek War (V), as well as the discovery of life-extending Spectrox (6R). The Federation eventually disintegrated into new empires, and could be considered as extinct by the beginning of the 50th century.

FEDERATOR Ruler of Manussa and husband of Lady Tanha (6D).

FEDERICO Count of the Dukedom of San Martino in 15th-century Italy. He coveted the Dukedom of its rightful ruler, his nephew Giuliano, whom he plotted to kill. He was thwarted by the Fourth Doctor, and was eventually killed by the Mandragora Helix after it had taken over Hieronymous's body (4M).

FEDORIN Denes's deputy. Salamander poisoned Fedorin because he couldn't bring himself to kill Denes (PP).

FELL, RALPH ARNOLD Scientific officer of Global Chemicals at the Llanfairfach Refinery. He was controlled by BOSS's programming, but broke free after Elgin begged him to save the Third Doctor's life. When BOSS found that he could not reprogram him, he ordered him to jump to his death (TTT).

FENDAHL, THE An entity who fed on the full spectrum of life itself. It originated on the Fifth Planet of the Solar System, which was time looped by the Time Lords in an attempt to contain it, but it escaped and travelled to Mars and thence, 12 million years ago, to Earth, where it arrived in the form of a skull. It was buried in a volcanic eruption, but secretly affected human evolution. The Fendahl Skull contained a pentagram-shaped neural relay where the Fendahl Energy was stored, waiting to be reactivated. In the late 20th century, the Skull was found by Dr Fendelman, who brought it to the Fetch Priory, where it was studied by Thea Ransome, Colby and Stael. Stael turned out to be the leader of a coven which recreated the Fendahl. The Fourth Doctor eventually used Fendelman's Time Scanner to set up a time implosion which destroyed the Fendahl Core and the Fendahleen. He later jettisoned the Fendahl Skull near a supernova, where it was presumably destroyed (4X).

FENDAHL CORE The Fendahl turned Thea Ransome into a Fendahl Core. In that guise, she became a golden, Medusa-like woman with writhing hair and huge, deadly eyes (4X).

FENDAHLEEN Large, snakelike entities with no eyes and with a mass of writhing tentacles where their mouths should have been. They had the power to freeze their victims psychically. The Fendahl needed twelve Fendahleen to be complete, and turned the members of Stael's coven into Fendahleen. But the Fourth Doctor killed one with rock salt, and Stael's suicide saved him from becoming one, thus keeping the Fendahl gestalt incomplete. They perished when the Fourth Doctor set up a time implosion which utterly destroyed the Fetch Priory (4X).

FENDELMAN (DR) One of the richest and most powerful men in the world, thanks to his firm, Fendelman Electronics. His twin hobbies, archeology and electronics, led him to develop a Time Scanner with which he studied the origins of man. He found and brought the Fendahl Skull to the Fetch Priory, where it was studied by Thea Ransome, Colby and Stael. He eventually realized that he had been only a pawn of the Fendahl, and was murdered by Stael (4X).

FENN-COOPER, REDVERS Famous British explorer who first discovered Light's ship. He became mentally unbalanced when he first beheld Light, and fell under the control of Josiah Samuel Smith. He was kept prisoner at Gabriel Chase by Smith, who plotted to use him to assassinate Queen Victoria. Once he recovered his sanity, he helped the Seventh Doctor defeat Light. He then left in the alien ship with Control and Nimrod (7Q).

FENNER Thawn's second-in-command at the methane refinery on Delta Magna's moon. After Thawn's death and Kroll's destruction, he sent an SOS to Delta Magna, and helped feed the Swampies (5E).

FENRIC Name given by the ancient Vikings to an evil entity from the dawn of time. In the Far East of the 3rd century, the Doctor (in an unrecorded adventure) successfully challenged Fenric to solve a chess problem. As a result, Fenric was imprisoned in a shadow dimension, while his earthly essence was trapped inside a flask. That flask was brought to Northumberland by the Vikings, who first wrote of the Curse of Fenric. From his prison, Fenric succeeded in manipulating the descendants of the Vikings, whom he dubbed his 'Wolves' into engineering his return. Fenric's eventual release took place in Northumberland in the 1940s, just before the end of World War II. He planned to release a deadly toxin which would have destroyed mankind, but was again defeated by the Seventh Doctor. Fenric's host body (Captain Sorin's) was killed by the Ancient Haemovore (7M).

FERGUS, ALASTAIR TV personality in charge of covering Professor Horner's excavation at Devil's Hump (JJJ).

FERRIER, ASTRID Assistant to Giles Kent, whose father had been murdered by Salamander. She helped the Second Doctor defeat Salamander (PP).

FERRIER, JEAN Astrid's father and Finance Deputy of the European Zone. He was murdered by Salamander (PP).

FERRIGO, LUIGI Genoese trader who hoped to establish trade contact with Saladin. He helped El Akir capture Barbara (P).

FETCH PRIORY Location of Dr Fendelman's laboratory. It was utterly destroyed by the time implosion set up by the Fourth Doctor to destroy the Fendahl Core and the Fendahleen (4X).

FETCHBOROUGH English village where the Fetch Priory was located (4X).

FEWSHAM T-Mat operator on the Moon when it was taken over by the Ice Warriors. Fearing for his life, he reluctantly cooperated with the Ice Warriors, but eventually redeemed himself by sacrificing his life to stay on the Moon and betray the Martians (XX).

FFINCH, ALGERNON THOMAS ALFRED Elegant lieutenant and commanding officer of the Redcoats patrol who arrested the Second Doctor after Culloden. Polly and Kirsty McLaren blackmailed him into helping them. Later, he was handed Gray as a prisoner (FF).

FIBULI Loyal First Officer to the Captain of Zanak. He was killed when Zanak's Bridge controls exploded as the Fourth Doctor used the TARDIS to prevent Zanak from rematerializing around Earth (5B).

FICTION See LAND OF FICTION.

FIFI Helen A's pet, a mean and aggressive creature, known as a stigorax, from Terra Alpha. Fifi hunted killjoys for Helen A and was ultimately killed by an avalanche of candy crystals caused by the Seventh Doctor. His death made Helen A finally realize that happiness is nothing without sadness (7L).

FIFTH PLANET Planet of the Solar System where the Fendahl originated. It was time looped by the Time Lords in an attempt to contain the evil entity (4X).

FILER, BILL American intelligence agent sent to liaise with UNIT about the Master. He was kidnapped and duplicated by Axos, but managed to escape. He helped the Third Doctor and UNIT defeat Axos (GGG).

FINCH British general in charge of military operations in London during the Dinosaur Invasion. In reality, he was working with Sir

Charles Grover on Operation Golden Age. He was eventually exposed by the Third Doctor, arrested by Benton and later court-martialled (WWW).

FINDECKER 51st-century scientist who discovered the double nexus particle, which sent human science into a technological cul-de-sac explaining the failure of the Zigma Experiment (4S).

FIRE ESCAPE One of the Red Kangs of Paradise Towers. He helped the Seventh Doctor and Mel defeat Kroagnon (7E).

FIRE MOUNTAIN Sarnian sacred volcano which produced the Numismaton flame. It was said to be the home of the god Logar. In reality, the Trion had equipped it with a seismic control centre, which was sabotaged by the Master (6Q).

FIRES, GREAT The First Doctor unwittingly inspired the Great Fire of Rome in AD 64 (M). The Fifth Doctor was responsible for the Great Fire of London in AD 1666 (5X).

FIRST SECRETARY Draconian officer serving in the Draconian Embassy on Earth (QQQ).

FISH MEN Men converted into amphibious scaly creatures whose job it was to produce food for the Atlanteans. Jacko convinced them to go on strike to help defeat Zaroff (GG).

FISK See COSTA.

FITZROY SQUARE London location where the TARDIS was 'parked' during the First Doctor's confrontation with WOTAN (BB).

FITZWILLIAM, RANULF Lord of Wallingford and one of King John's faithful Barons. He became increasingly distraught as he watched the evil deeds of Kamelion, who had assumed King John's likeness at the Master's behest. He eventually helped the Fifth Doctor defeat the Master (6J).

FITZWILLIAM, HUGH Ranulf and Isabella's hot-tempered son, easily manipulated by the Master (6J).

FITZWILLIAM, ISABELLA Ranulf's wife (6J).

FIVE HUNDRED EYES Name given to a quartz-filled cave where 250 Hashashins had once been slain by Mongol conqueror Hulagu. Tegana used it to trap Barbara (D).

FIZZADE Drinks dispenser used by the Kangs as a way of communication (7E).

FLAME OF LIFE See SACRED FLAME.

FLANAGAN (aka FLANNIGAN), SEAN Engineer on the Wheel in Space. He suceeded in repairing the X-ray laser sabotaged by Jamie. He was taken over by the Cybermen, but later freed by the Second Doctor. He then helped defeat the invaders (SS).

FLASH Drunken customer of the Inferno discotheque (BB).

FLAST Cryon prisoner of the Cybermen. The Sixth Doctor gave her a thermal lance, which she buried in a box of vastial. The Cybermen then exposed her to above-zero temperatures, which killed her. But the thermal lance triggered the vastial's explosion, which destroyed the Cybermen and freed Telos (6T).

FLAVIA Chancellor of the High Council of the Time Lords of Gallifrey who replaced Thalia. When the Death Zone was reactivated, she voted in favour of sending the Master to help the Five Doctors, against Borusa's wishes. After Rassilon had turned Borusa into a living statue, Flavia and the High Council reappointed the Fifth Doctor as President, but he deputised his powers to her and managed to escape (6K).

FLAVIUS, GISKARD Owner of the Roman villa where the first Doctor and his companions stayed (M).

FLESH TIME Name given by Monarch to what he deemed to be the time of primitive, fleshly existence, as opposed to android life with silicon chip memories (5W).

FLEUR DE LIS Name of the Devesham pub (4J).

FLIGHT 192 See GOLF VICTOR FOXTROT.

FLO Perivale resident (7P).

FLINT, PERCIVAL (SIR) He led an unsuccessful attempt to open Devil's Hump in 1793. His miners returned to Cornwall, leaving him for dead (JJJ).

FLORANA According to the Third Doctor, it was a planet covered with flowers, one of the most beautiful in the galaxy (WWW).

FLOWER Young woman from the Elders' city. With Avon, she acted as Steven and Dodo's guide (AA).

FLOWER FOREST Landmark of Vortis (N).

FLOWERCHILD She and Bellboy were founding members of the Psychic Circus. They tried to escape, but she was killed by the Bus Conductor (7J).

FLUID LINKS See TIME VECTOR GENERATOR.

FLUTTERWING Native Gallifreyan bird or insect. Romana suggested studying its life cycle (5B).

FLYING SAUCERS Type of spaceship used by the Daleks in their AD 2164 Invasion of Earth (K).

FLYNN, TOM Reegan's henchman. He was killed by the Brigadier (CCC).

FOAMASI Reptilian race who fought a deadly 20-minute war of mutual extermination with the Argolins. After the war, the Foamasi survivors became resistant to radioactivity. One of their clans, the West Lodge Foamasi, impersonated Brock and Klout, and tried to sabotage the Leisure Hive so that they could then buy Argolis. They were exposed by a Foamasi Government Investigator. The saboteurs later escaped, but were destroyed by the Argolins. The Argolin leader, Mena, rejuvenated thanks to the Fourth Doctor's efforts, made a lasting peace with the Foamasi (5N).

FOOD The methane refined on Delta Magna's third moon was turned into a source of protein (5E). Kara's protein factory on Nekros used the bodies stored at Tranquil Repose as a source of protein. Later, the Sixth Doctor showed the Tranquil Repose employees how to convert local flowers to protein (6Z). One of the Androgums' chief interests was food; Shockeye tried to kill and eat Peri and Jamie (6W). Oscar Botcherby was the manager of La Piranella restaurant in Seville (6W).

Marsh Minnows were a delicacy praised by the Mentors. According to the Sixth Doctor, the gumblejack was the finest fish in the galaxy (6W). Billy was mutated by a Chimeron's food-like substance (7F). A peace treaty involving food shipments from Karfel to Bandril was negotiated by the Third Doctor (6Y). Also see PARASITES, VAMPIRES.

FOOD MACHINE The Tardis's food dispenser (B,C,Q).

FORBES UNIT Corporal who was killed by an Auton (AAA).

FORBIDDEN ZONE Part of Terminus where the Vanir did not dare to go. It was there that the Garm lived (6G).

FOREMAN, I.M. Scrap merchant who owned the junkyard located at 76 Totters Lane which the First and Sixth Doctors used as rematerialisation points (A, 6T). Foreman's Yard was also the site of a battle between British soldiers and the Daleks (7H).

FOREMAN, SUSAN See SUSAN.

FORESTER Ruthless financial backer of Smithers, the scientist who discovered the deadly insecticide, DN6. He was prepared to go to any lengths to market it. The First Doctor and his Companions improvised an explosive device to stop him (J).

FORESTER Donald Bruce's deputy (PP).

FORGILL Scottish Duke, president of the Scottish Energy Commission. He was impersonated by Broton, leader of the Zygons, who used his form in an attempt to destroy a World Energy Conference. The real Duke was eventually rescued by the Fourth Doctor (4F).

FOSTER One of Lieutenant Scott's men (6B).

FOSTER, HOWARD (PROFESSOR) American archeologist, Peri's grandfather, whom the Doctor met on a field trip on a Greek Island. He discovered a Trion beacon on the neighbouring sea bed. Kamelion assumed his shape when the Fifth Doctor travelled to Sarn (6Q).

FOSTERS Union of Traken's guards. Several of them were killed by the Melkur. Their Proctor was Neman (5T).

FOUGOUS, CORNISH (DR) Archaeologist mentioned by Professor Rumford (5C).

FOUNDATION FOR THE STUDY OF ADVANCED SCIENCES Space station nicknamed Think Tank where Skagra stole the Sphere (5M).

FOUNTAIN OF HAPPINESS Landmark of Paradise Towers (7E).

FRAG Alien tourist who crashlanded in Wales in 1959 and was killed by the Bannermen (7F).

FRANCE Country visited by the First Doctor during the French Revolution, allegedly his 'favourite period in history' (H), and at the time of the St Batholomew's Day's Massacre (W). The Fourth Doctor and Romana fought Scaroth in Paris (5H). A French Napoleonic army was kidnapped by the Warlords during the War Games (ZZ). Lord Palmerdale had just returned from Deauville when his ship crashed on Fang Rock (4V). The Second Doctor met Frenchman Jules Benoit on the Moonbase (HH). After being freed by the Second Doctor, Colin McLaren and his supporters sailed to France (FF). According to some accounts, Ace eventually chose to live in 1880 France, where she married one of Sorin's ancestors.

FRANK One of the Devil's End villagers (JJJ).

FRANKENSTEIN'S MONSTER The First Doctor met this robotic version of the legendary monster created by Mary Shelley in a 1996 House of Horrors. It then fought the Daleks (R).

FRANZ One of the Moonbase crew 'zombified' by the Cybermen (HH).

FRANZINE GRIG Chessene's tribe (6W).

FRAX Thoros-Alphan faithful to the Mentors. He was the commander of the guards at Lord Kiv's citadel on Thoros-Beta. He was killed by Yrcanos (7B).

FRAZER, COLIN Tegan's cousin. While in Amsterdam, he was captured by Omega and later rescued by the Fifth Doctor (6E).

FREDDIE Employee at Jago's theatre (4S)

FREE, THE Tribe of humans living on the surface of Ravolox (Earth). They worshipped the god Haldron. A number of them (such as Broken Tooth) were intended victims of the UK Habitat's Cullings, but were saved by Merdeen. The Free were ruled by Katryca, who eventually led an assault on the Habitat. After the Sixth Doctor destroyed Drathro, the population of UK Habitat joined the Free (7A).

FRENCH REVOLUTION Name given to the revolutionary movement that overthrew the French monarchy and shook

France between 1787 and 1799. The First Doctor called it his 'favourite period in history' (H).

FRENTON According to Gharman, a Kaled opposed to Davros (4E).

FREYTUS Labyrinth planet where two legions of the Graff Vynda-K's army fought in the Alliance Wars (5A).

FRIEND Nickname given by the 'humanized' Daleks to the Second Doctor (LL).

FRONTIERS OF SCIENCE See THINK TANK.

FRONTIOS Planet located in the Veruna system. After Earth's sun suffered a cosmic collision, a group of survivors, led by Captain Revere, relocated there. The planet was secretly infected by the Tractators who had drawn the colonists to Frontios because they needed to use their bodies and minds to power their excavating machines. Their leader, the Gravis, planned to turn Frontios into a hollow spaceship with which the Tractators could roam the Universe. The Fifth Doctor defeated him and restored the colony in the hands of Captain Revere's son, Plantagenet (6N).

FROYN He and Rhynmal were Earth scientists involved in experimental matter transmission. They used their Cellular Projector to send the First Doctor to Mira (V).

FTL See FASTER THAN LIGHT.

FU PENG Chinese delegate to the World Peace Conference who replaced Cheng Teik. He developed a friendly relationship with the Third Doctor (FFF).

FULLER One of the prisoners of Stangmoor Prison. He helped capture the Third Doctor and Jo (FFF).

FUNCTIONARIES Name given to slave workers on Inter Minor. A rebel functionary was shot by Kalik; President Zarb tried to improve their lot (PPP).

FUNGOIDS Hostile plants of Mechanus (R).

FUSION BOOSTER Device used by the Fifth Doctor to defeat Omega (6E).

FUTU See LIN FUTU.

G

G3 ASSESSMENT SURVEY Codename for the Sontaran intelligence division to which Styre reported (4B).

GABRIEL CHASE Evil house located in Perivale. Ace burned it down in 1983, and the Seventh Doctor took her back to it in 1883 when they discovered the house was under the control of Josiah Samuel Smith. Gabriel Chase had been built on top of the spaceship of the powerful alien, Light (7Q).

GABRIELIDES (DROGE OF) According to the Fourth Doctor, this tyrant once offered a whole star system as a price for his head (4W).

GAEL One of the Xeron rebels (Q).

GALACTIC CENSUS BUREAU Terran bureaucracy set up to take the census of the colonies. The Seventh Doctor encountered one of its agents, Trevor Sigma, on Terra Alpha (7L).

GALACTIC SALVAGE Space insurance company, formed in London in AD 2068, but disbanded in 2096. Several decades later, the Fourth Doctor betrayed himself on board the *Empress* when he pretended to be one of its employees (5K).

GALACTIC SERVICES COMMISSION Company which had chartered Captain Briggs's freighter (6B).

GALATRON MINING CORPORATION Interplanetary mining corporation run by the Mentors of Thoros-Beta. It was buying Zyton-7 from Varos. Its agent, Sil, bribed the Chief Officer of Varos to keep the prices low, but he was thwarted by the Sixth Doctor. He then attempted to take over the planet, but failed. Sil's superior, Kiv, replaced him and negotiated fairer prices for Zyton-7 (6V).

GALAXY FOUR Location of the doomed planet upon which the Drahvin – Rill confrontation occurred (T).

GALAXY FIVE Militaristic space power located in a neighbouring galaxy. During the 38th century, Galaxy Five went to war with the Federation. It used Azaxyr and Eckersley to try to take over the trisilicate mines of Peladon. When they failed, it was forced to sue for peace (YYY). Later, Galaxy Five's self-proclaimed Master, Zephon, allied himself with the Daleks to attack the Solar System, but was killed by them (V). Presumably, Galaxy Five's power was then totally crushed by the Federation.

GALLEIA Queen of Atlantis. The Master charmed her into overthrowing King Dalios. When she learned that the Renegade Time Lord had caused Dalios's death, she turned against him, but too late. She died when the Kronavore destroyed Atlantis (OOO).

GALLIFREY Home planet of the Time Lords, first mentioned by the Third Doctor when he was interrogated by Linx (UUU). It was located in the constellation of Kasterborus, 29,000 light years from Earth. Gallifrey was the location of the trial of the Second Doctor, and was briefly invaded by the War Lords (ZZ). Later, it was almost destroyed during the Omega crisis, but was saved by the Three Doctors (RRR). It was threatened by the Master when he almost released the Eye of Harmony (4P). It was then invaded by the Vardans and the Sontarans (4Z). In both cases, Gallifrey was saved by the Fourth Doctor. The Fifth Doctor was tried on Gallifrey when Omega threatened to take over his body (6E). Finally, Borusa brought the Five Doctors to Gallifrey's Death Zone to help him unlock the secret of the Tomb of Rassilon (6K).

Gallifrey was protected by impenetrable force fields known as transduction barriers. It was the location of the Capitol, the Time Lords' seat of power. A great deal of the surface of the planet was barren and wild, and inhabited by the Shobogans, or Outsiders (4Z). The Death Zone was a forbidden area, protected by force fields, at the center of which was the Tomb of Rassilon, known as the Dark Tower (6K). The Third Doctor once mentioned that he lived on a mountainside in South Gallifrey (OOO). Also see TIME LORDS.

GALLOWAY, DAN Ruthless Earth marine lieutenant and member of the space corps expedition sent to Exxilon to bring back parrinium. He met the Third Doctor and eventually sacrificed his life to destroy the Daleks (XXX).

GALLOWAY Dalek prisoner who escaped with Stien through the time corridor to 20th-century London. He was killed by one of Lytton's men (6P).

GALSEC SEVEN Human colony from which the five humans captured by Styre originated (4B).

GAME OF RASSILON Name given by the Time Lords to the process of using the Time Scoop to pull various creatures out of space and time, and drop them off in the Death Zone on Gallifrey to watch them fight. In spite of its name, it was said to have been banned by Rassilon. Borusa played the Game of Rassilon with the Five Doctors, their companions (Susan, the Brigadier, Sarah Jane Smith, Tegan and Turlough) and their enemies (Daleks, Cybermen, Yeti) to find the secret of true immortality located in the Tomb of Rassilon (6K).

GAMES The First Doctor lost the TARDIS playing backgammon with Kublai Khan (D), and defeated the Celestial Toymaker at his own Trilogic Game (Y). The Second Doctor helped solve a series of riddles protecting the Tomb of the Cybermen (MM). The Fourth Doctor also solved a series of riddles which protected the Eye of Horus on Mars (4G). He later engaged in a fierce contest of minds known as 'mind-bending' with Morbius (4K). The Eternals played games with mortals to entertain themselves (6H). The Fifth Doctor loved cricket (5W, 6A). The Seventh Doctor fought a deadly game of chess with Fenric (7M). Romulus and Remus Sylvest were brilliant chess players (6S). Games played with living beings included the Romans' Circus Games (M), the War Games (ZZ) and the Game of Rassilon (6K).

GANATUS Thal from Skaro and Alydon's friend. He was proved right in his mistrust of the Daleks. He helped the First Doctor and led the expedition to the Daleks' city by way of the dreaded Lake of Mutations (B).

GANTRY, KERT Agent sent by Space Special Security to Kembel with Bret Vyon. He was killed by the Daleks (V).

GANYMEDE Moon of Jupiter. It was also the name of the Space Beacon which took over from Nerva after it had been quarantined (4D).

GAPTOOTH One of Captain Pike's pirates (CC).

GARDEN OF THE AGED Aztec home for old citizens where the First Doctor accidentally proposed to Cameca (F).

GARDINER Captain of the Earth battle cruiser who rescued Hardy and Stewart's *C–982* cargo ship after it had been attacked by the Ogrons (QQQ).

GARGE One of the criminals of Desperus. He tried to take over the First Doctor's ship, the *Spar 7–40*, but was felled by a stun charge (V).

GARGOYLE See BOK.

GARIF, JAYNIS Alzarian Decider. He was extremely indecisive, and relied on Login and the Fourth Doctor to fight the Marshmen (5R).

GARM, THE Mysterious dog-headed alien who lived on Terminus. He was quite strong, and cured some of the Lazars with controlled radiation. His ministrations saved Nyssa from lazar disease. He helped the Fifth Doctor disable the unstable engine which threatened the universe; in exchange, the Doctor freed him from the sonic box which enabled the Vanir to control him (6G).

GARRANT, DAL (MAJOR) Combat pilot serving with the Third Galactic Fleet. He was killed by the Daleks on Skaro (5J).

GARRETT, JANE Technician on Clent's team. She helped the Second Doctor defeat the Ice Warriors (OO).

GARRON Earth con artist originally from Hackneywick, Somerset. He was forced to flee Earth because he refused to sell the Sidney Opera House to a rich Arab. He and his younger assistant, Unstoffe, embarked on a career as galactic conmen, selling planets to unsuspecting victims. Garron tried to sell Ribos to the Graff Vynda-K using a lump of jethrik, which turned out to be a segment of the Key to Time. When the Graff found out the truth, Garron and the Fourth Doctor were forced to join forces. Garron eventually ended up with the Graff's spaceship, filled with eighteen years of plunder (5A).

GARVEY, JEFF Spaceman who landed on Kembel with Marc

Cory. He was injured by a Varga plant, then killed by Cory to put him out of his misery (T/A).

GARVIN The vicar's verger and the Master's henchman in Devil's End. He kidnapped Miss Hawthorne, but was later incinerated by Azal's psionic powers (JJJ).

GASCOIGNE Detective inspector shot in Gatwick by Spencer. He was investigating the Chameleons after receiving a tip-off from Samantha Briggs (KK).

GASES Mankind used poison gases during World War I (ZZ). Poison gases were used as natural weapons by the parasitic Weed, which fed on natural gas (RR), and by the alien Vervoids (7C). Both were vulnerable to pure oxygen. The Alzarians also used pure oxygen to drive the Marshmen away (5R).

Oxygen (or, more accurately, the mixture of oxygen and azote called air) was one of the commodities necessary for the preservation of human life under water (GG, 6L); in space (V); on airless worlds such as Earth's moon (HH, QQQ); and on worlds with other types of atmospheres such as Titan (4T). The Sunmakers sold air to the Pluto colony and used a pacifying gas called PCM to maintain their domination. They also used a stun gas called Balarium (4W). The Moroks used a paralyzing gas named Zaphra (Q). The Terileptils breathed a mixture of air and a gas named Soliton (5X). The Marshal wanted to alter Solos's atmosphere to make it habitable by humans (NNN).

The First Doctor used a gas jet and a match to get rid of Forester (J). The Fourth Doctor released helium in the *Sandminer's* atmosphere to trick the Robots of Death (4R). The Fifth Doctor used hexachromite to destroy the Silurians and Sea Devils who had taken over Sea Base Four (6L).

Planets Karn and Sarn both generated a volcanic gas which had, under certain local conditions, the power to extend life. On Karn, it was called the Sacred Flame (4K) and on Sarn the Numismaton Flame (6Q). An unidentified green gas was part of the process leading to the creation of the Krargs (5M). On Alzarius, periodic orbital shifts released non-toxic subterranean gases which boosted evolution (5R). Vorum gas was used to protect Space Station J7's computer (6W).

GASTROPODS Half-humanoid, half-slug creatures, once considered mythical on the planet Jaconda, most of which they destroyed. Their leader, Mestor, took over and planned to throw a planet into Jaconda's sun to spread his eggs throughout the universe. He was defeated by the Sixth Doctor and Azmael (6S).

GATEWAY Stone archway erected by the Tharils at the Zero Point between N-Space and E-Space. The Zero Point, the archway, and the mirrors inside formed the Gateway (5S).

GATWICK One of London's airports. In 1966, the Second Doctor fought the Chameleons there (KK).

GAVROK Merciless leader of the Bannermen who pursued Delta to 1959 Wales. Gavrok was outwitted by the Seventh Doctor and killed by his own sonic cone (7F).

GAYEV Russian corporal whose mind snapped after seeing the Haemovores (7M).

GAZAK Young Karfelon rebel. He was banished through the Timelash by the Borad (6Y).

GAZTAKS Space mercenaries hired by Meglos to bring him an Earthling (George Morris), then to attack Tigella to help the Zolfa-Thuran steal the Dodecahedron. They were led by Grugger and Brotadac. The Gaztaks eventually betrayed Meglos. They were outsmarted by the Fourth Doctor and perished in Zolfa-Thura's explosion (5Q).

GEARON Member of the Dalek Alliance in their Masterplan against Earth. He was eventually killed by Mavic Chen (V).

GEBEK Reasonable leader of the trisilicate miners of Peladon. At first allied with Ettis, because of his opposition to the Federation, he became receptive to the Third Doctor's wishes to help the miners. He eventually helped the Time Lord expose Azaxyr and Eckersley. At the Doctor's suggestion, he was eventually appointed new Chancellor after Ortron's death (YYY).

GEL CREATURES Omega's mindless agents. He used them to attack the Three Doctors (RRR).

GENERATION STARSHIPS Man used generation starships for interstellar travel before the discovery of faster than light (or warp) propulsion. The *Ark* (X) and *Terra Nova* (4C) could be considered generation starships. Also see CRYOGENICS and SUSPENDED ANIMATION.

160

GENETIC ENGINEERING Dastari had technically augmented the androgum Chessene, without changing her savage nature (6W). The Vervoids were genetically engineered by Professor Lasky (7C). Other master geneticists included the Rani and Davros. Also see CLONES.

GENOCIDE The destruction of an entire species. The Daleks were guilty of attempted genocide. However, no matter what blows the Doctor dealt to the Daleks, he was never able or willing to eradicate them completely (LL, 4E, 7H). Other aliens who were guilty of attempted genocide included: the Cybermen; the Dominators (TT); the Krotons (WW); the Ice Warriors (XX); Axos (GGG); Sutekh (4G); the Kraals (4J); the Krynoids (4L); the Fendahl (4X); the pirate Planet of Zanak (5B); Scaroth (5H); the Nimon (5L); the Vampires (5P); Monarch of Urbanka (5W); the Terileptils (5X); and Mestor (6S). The Silurians tried to cause the human race to exterminate itself (6L). The Time Lords almost destroyed the human race when they moved Earth through space and renamed it Ravolox (7A–7C).

A number of human villains almost caused the destruction of mankind: Forester (J); Professor Zaroff (GG); Professor Stahlman (DDD); Sir Charles Grover (WWW); and The Scientific Reform Society (4A). The Master was responsible for the annihilation of many planets, including Traken, which was destroyed with Logopolis (5V).

The Valeyard accused the Sixth Doctor of genocide – a criminal offence under Article 7 of Gallifreyan law – for having destroyed the Vervoids (7C). The human Empire almost committed genocide on races such as the Solonians (NNN) or the Wirrn (4C). The Kastrians committed racial suicide rather than face Eldrad's return (4N). Also see END OF THE WORLD, WAR.

GENTEK Chief Acolyte of the Tesh. He fought alongside Jabel against the Fourth Doctor and the Sevateem (4Q).

GEOLOGY See MINERALS.

GER Thoros-Alphan rebel who followed Tusa and Yrcanos. He was killed by the Mentors (7B).

GERN Mondasian Cyberleader who took over the Geneva headquarters of the International Space Command and died after Mondas's destruction (DD).

161

GERRILL One of Skaro's Mutos (4E).

GHANA The location of the 1996 World's Fair, whose House of Horrors was briefly visited by the First Doctor and the Daleks (R).

GHARMAN Davros's associate in the creation of the Daleks. He eventually led a rebellion against the evil scientist, but was killed by the Daleks (4E).

GIANT ROBOT Codenamed K-1, he was the creation of Professor Kettlewell. His purpose was to replace men in a variety of dangerous tasks and his prime directive was to serve humanity. However, it was subverted by Miss Winters and the Scientific Reform Society, who used him in their plan to become masters of the world. The Robot inadvertently killed Kettlewell and went mad. Fond of Sarah, he took her hostage and tried to start World War III. The Fourth Doctor destroyed him with an anti-metal virus (4A).

GIDU Stormy planet incorporated into Tryst's CET (5K).

GIGANTISM On Vortis, the First Doctor met the Zarbi, who were similar to gigantic Earth ants, and the Menoptera, who were like gigantic Earth butterflies (N). The Second Doctor met the Macra, who were not unlike giant crabs (JJ). The Third Doctor fought giant maggots and giant flies caused by the Green Death (TTT), and giant Spiders on Metebelis Three (ZZZ). The Fourth Doctor fought a giant Robot (4A), a giant Krynoid on Harrison Chase's estate (4L), Weng-Chiang's giant rat in the London Sewers (4S), Kroll, the gigantic god of the Swampies, on Delta Magna's moon (5E), and, in E-Space, the Great Vampire who looked like a giant humanoid with bat-like features (5P). The Fifth Doctor fought the Mara, who appeared as a giant snake (5Y, 6D).

GIL One of the alien tourists who crashlanded in Wales in 1959. He was killed by the Bannermen (7F).

GILMORE, IAN Group Captain in charge of the British army squadron sent to fight the Daleks who had invaded the Coal Hill area in 1963. He was assisted by Professor Rachel Jensen, of whom he was very fond, and helped the Seventh Doctor defeat the Daleks (7H).

162

GIRTON, TOM One of the inhabitants of Devil's End under the Master's control. He stole one of UNIT's helicopters and tried to kill the Third Doctor by driving him into Azal's heat barrier. He ended up crashing into the barrier himself (JJJ).

GIRTON Royal Navy seaman who fought the Sea Devils (LLL).

GIULIANO Rightful young ruler of the Dukedom of San Martino, in 15th-century Italy. His uncle, Count Federico, tried to kill him to take over the Dukedom, but failed. He was a man of science, an artesan of the Renaissance, and helped the Fourth Doctor banish the evil Mandragora Helix (4M).

GLACHMAI, AP See ANCELYN.

GLITTERGUNS Guns shooting gold particles, developed during the Cyber Wars to fight the Cybermen (4D, 6T).

GLITZ, SABALOM Galactic swindler from Salostopus in Andromeda. He and his associate, Dibber, travelled to Ravolox. Their goal was to steal the secrets previously stolen from the Time Lords' Matrix by the Andromedan Sleepers. Glitz was sentenced to death by Katryca. After Dibber destroyed the Maglem converter, Glitz conned Drathro into giving him the tape containing the Sleepers' secrets. But the tape was later destroyed, along with Drathro, when the Sixth Doctor shut down the energy systems to prevent a black light explosion (7A). Then, the Master sent Glitz, as well as Mel, to the trial of the Doctor to help the Time Lord expose the Valeyard's secret identity. The Valeyard fled into the Matrix, the Doctor hot in pursuit. Glitz followed him and recovered the Sleepers' secrets from the Valeyard for the Master. However, the Valeyard had tricked him, giving him a Limbo Atrophier instead. Glitz and the Master became trapped in the Matrix (7C). Glitz was later stranded on Iceworld, because he owed money to Kane, to whom he had already sold the crew of his ship, the *Nosferatu*. Kane manipulated him and the Seventh Doctor into looking for the Dragonfire. After Kane's suicide, Glitz remained in charge of Iceworld (now a spaceship rechristened *Nosferatu II*), and left with Mel (7G).

GLOBAL CHEMICALS Multinational corporation which owned and operated the Llanfairfach Refinery. It was pumping chemical waste into the local mines, which eventually was the cause of the

Green Death and its deadly swarm of giant maggots. It developed the computer BOSS (TTT).

GOBI DESERT The First Doctor and his companions crossed it along with Marco Polo and Tegana (D).

GODS See MAGIC, RELIGION.

GODS OF RAGNAROK See RAGNAROK, GODS OF.

GOLD, KEITH (SIR) Director of the Inferno project. He made several attempts to slow down Professor Stahlman's Inferno Project, such as calling in Greg Sutton and going over Stahlman's head to the Minister, and would have failed if the Third Doctor had not intervened. On a parallel world, Sir Keith was killed in a car accident arranged by Stahlman (DDD).

GOLD Precious metal, the cause of much evil among greedy men (CC, LL). Gold was deadly to the Cybermen, and was found in abundance on Voga, the so-called 'planet of gold' (4D, 6B).

GOLD DALEK Like the Black Dalek, of which he may be an avatar, a Dalek Warlord. He led the invasion of Earth in the 22nd century (KKK).

GOLD USHER The Fourth Doctor used the robes of a Gold Usher to enter the Panopticon to try to prevent the President's assassination (4P). A Gold Usher led the ceremonies when the Doctor was later proclaimed President (4Z).

GOLDEN AGE (OPERATION) See OPERATION GOLDEN AGE.

GOLDEN AGE OF PROSPERITY Expression used by the Captain of Zanak to signal that Zanak was about to crush another world and therefore replenish its mineral wealth (5B).

GOLDEN DEATH Form of compassionate euthanasia used by the Company on Pluto. Cordo's father died a deluxe Golden Death, which cost Cordo 117 talmars (4W).

GOLDEN DREAM PARK One of Kroagnon's buildings (7E).

GOLF ALPHA CHARLIE Concorde flight used by the Fifth Doctor to rescue Flight 192. Its captain was Stapley (6C).

GOLF VICTOR FOXTROT Concorde flight 192, which was

hijacked to the Jurassic Period by the Master. Its captain was Urquhart (6C).

GOLOBUS Planet visited by Captain Cook (7J).

GOMER Time Lords' Surgeon General who attended the induction of the Fourth Doctor as President of the High Council. He was later expelled outside the Capitol, and joined the Shobogans and Leela in fighting the invaders of Gallifrey (4Z).

GONDS Peaceful race who lived in an underground city enclosed by the machines of the Krotons, their unseen masters. Every month, the two most intelligent Gonds were selected to become the Krotons' 'companions'. In reality, two Krotons were draining their mental energy to recharge themselves. (WW).

GOODGE Technician at the Beacon Hill Research Establishment. He was killed by the Master's Tissue Compression Eliminator (EEE).

GORDON, CHARLES Nicknamed 'Commandant', he was the manager of Gatwick Airport when the Second Doctor fought the Chameleons (KK).

GORE CROW, THE Pat Rowlinson's hotel in Carbury (7N).

GORONWY Welsh bee-keeper who helped the Seventh Doctor defeat Gavrok's Bannermen (7F).

GORSEDD According to Welsh legend, a place of augurs. The three Gorsedds in Britain were Stonehenge, Bryn Gwiddon and Boscombe Moor (5C).

GORTON British colonel and prison camp commander who believed he was fighting against the Germans in World War I. In reality, he was part of the War Games. He was tricked by the Second Doctor into letting Zoe escape (ZZ).

GOSSETT, NELLIE Alfred Buller's mother-in-law (4S).

GOTAL One of the subterranean Exxilons who had not reverted to savagery when cast out by the City (XXX).

GOTH Chancellor of the High Council of the Time Lords. When the President was about to resign, and Goth found out that he was not going to be his chosen successor, he plotted with the Master, whom he had discovered hiding on Tersurus, to kill the President and frame the Fourth Doctor. Goth was eventually defeated by the Doctor in mental battle inside the Matrix, and killed by the Master (4P).

GOTTSCHALK, GOTTLIEB One of the crew of the *Mary Celeste* (R).

GOUDRY One of Mandrel's rebels. He helped the Fourth Doctor and Leela overthrow the Company on Pluto (4W).

GOVERNOR (OF LUNA) Governor of the Luna Penal Colony to which the Third Doctor and Jo Grant were sent after they were accused of being Draconian spies. The Master tricked him into turning the Time Lord and his companion over to him (QQQ).

GOVERNOR (OF STANGMOOR PRISON) See CAMFORD, VICTOR.

GOVERNOR (OF VAROS) Forty-fifth leader of Varos. He tried to negotiate higher prices for Zyton-7 from the Galatron Mining Corporation. Sil bribed the Chief Officer of Varos to keep the prices low, but was thwarted by the Sixth Doctor. The Governor would have died by the Cell Disintegrator if he had not been rescued by Meldak. Sil's superior, Kiv, replaced him and negotiated fairer prices for Zyton-7 (6V).

GRACHT Count Grendel's Castle (5D).

GRADES System of classification of the Company's Citizens on Pluto: A,B,C,D, etc. Cordo was a D-grade citizen (4W). Also see CLASSES.

GRAFF Title given to the ruler of Levithia (5A).

GRANADOS Planet destroyed by Zanak (5B).

GRAND MARSHAL Title given by Slaar to the leader of the invading Ice Warrior space fleet. The Second Doctor transmitted a fake guiding beacon which sent their fleet into the Sun (XX).

GRANT, DOUGLAS T. Washington technician killed by the opening of a Martian seed pod (XX).

GRANT, JIM Newsman who interviewed Mavic Chen (V).

GRANT, JOSEPHINE One of the Third Doctor's companions.

166

She was a UNIT agent fully trained in cryptology, explosives and safebreaking, and owed her assignment to her uncle, a cabinet minister. She helped the Doctor many times against the Master and twice against the Daleks (KKK, SSS). She also fought the Nestene and their deadly Autons, the Mind of Evil, Axos and the evil designs of the Interplanetary Mining Corporation. Her attempt to sacrifice her life to save the Doctor's led to the Daemon Azal's defeat (JJJ). She then helped the Doctor fight the Sea Devils, the evil Marshal of Solos, Kronos and Omega. She helped him escape from the Scope, and travelled with him to Peladon, where she was not insensitive to the charms of King Peladon (MMM). But ultimately, she fell in love with, and married, Professor Clifford Jones, who helped the Doctor defeat BOSS and the Green Death (EEE-TTT). After her wedding, she sent the blue crystal from Metebelis 3 that the Doctor had given her back to him (ZZZ). She also travelled with the Doctor to Karfel in an unrecorded adventure (6Y).

GRANT Corporal in the British army squadron sent to fight the Daleks who had invaded the Coal Hill area in 1963 (7H).

GRAVIS Leader of the Tractators, who functioned like a queen bee; without his guiding intelligence, the Tractators were mindless burrowers. The Gravis had tremendous powers of gravity control. He had secretly drawn human colonists to Frontios because he needed to use their bodies and minds to power his excavating machines. With these, he planned to turn Frontios into a hollow spaceship. The Gravis was susceptible to flattery, and his desire for the TARDIS enabled the Fifth Doctor to cut him off from the other Tractators and render them helpless. The Doctor then abandoned the Gravis on Kolkokron (6N).

GRAVITRON A gravity-controlling machine located on the Moonbase, which helped control Earth's weather (via the tides). In AD 2070, it became the object of a Cyberman attack. The Second Doctor used the gravitron to send the Cybermen and their ship hurtling off in space (HH).

GRAVITY The gravitron was a machine built on the Moon, and which could control gravity. It was used by the Second Doctor against the Cybermen (HH). The Tractators had great natural powers of gravity control (6N). The Crystal of the Mara was designed in a zero-gravity environment (6D).

GRAY (aka GREY) Former solicitor who abused his position as Prison Commissioner illegally to sell Scottish rebels as slaves to be transported to the West Indies. He was eventually captured by the Second Doctor and handed over to ffinch (FF).

GREAT ARCHITECT See KROAGNON.

GREAT CRYSTAL (OF THE MARA) Powerful stone created over eight hundred years ago by the Manussans. Its perfect molecular structure was attuned to the exact wavelength of the human mind. It had been designed by molecular engineering in a zero-gravity environment. The Crystal absorbed the evil within the Manussans' minds, amplified it, and created the Mara (6D). Also see CRYSTALS.

GREAT FIRE OF LONDON Started by the Fifth Doctor in AD 1666 in an effort to destroy the plague rats infected by the Terileptils (5X).

GREAT HALL OF BOOKS *Starliner* room where the Deciders met. In reality, it was the bridge of the ship (5R).

GREAT HEALER Alias used by Davros at the Tranquil Repose mortuary (6Z).

GREAT INTELLIGENCE Entity from another dimension, which was exiled into ours, and condemned to hover between the stars without physical substance. It eventually took over Padma-sambhava's mind. It planned to reincorporate itself and conquer Earth, when its gelatinous substance flowed through a pyramid gateway. In spite of its robot Yeti, the Intelligence's plan was thwarted by the Second Doctor, Jamie, Victoria and Professor Travers in the mid-1930s. The entity was banished when the Doctor held it in check mentally while Jamie and Thomni smashed its pyramid (NN).

Thirty years later, Travers reactivated a robot Yeti's silver sphere, which led the Intelligence to launch a new attack, this time in the London Underground. It was again opposed by the Second Doctor, with the help of Travers, Jamie, Victoria and Colonel Lethbridge-Stewart. The Intelligence plotted to drain the Doctor's mind, but the Doctor secretly reversed the polarities of the device, and would have turned the tables on his enemy if Jamie had not unwittingly wrenched the device from the Doctor's head at the last minute, thereby releasing the evil entity (QQ).

GREAT JOURNEY OF LIFE Name given by the Nimon to their travel from planet to planet (5L).

GREAT KEY (OF RASSILON) Another name for the Rod of Rassilon (4P, 4Z). Not to be confused with the Key of Rassilon (4Z, 7C).

GREAT ONE Giant spider of Metebelis 3. It had gathered all the crystals in the Cave of Crystals, and had grown to gigantic physical and mental size. It needed the Blue Crystal to complete its crystal web and increase its mental power to infinity. When the Third Doctor brought the Blue Crystal back, its feedback destroyed the Great One (ZZZ).

GREAT ONE Title used by Aukon to refer to the Great Vampire (5P).

GREAT VAMPIRE Leader of the alien vampires who were destroyed by the Time Lords. Wounded and almost dying, he fled into E-Space, where he still had the strength mentally to lure the Earth ship *Hydrax*. He offered its three officers, Aukon, Zargo and Camilla, vampiric immortality if they served him. They fed him with the blood of the human colonists and their descendants for a thousand years, planning for the Time of Arising, when he would swarm back into normal space. The Great Vampire's plans were thwarted by the Fourth Doctor, who used one of the *Hydrax* scout ships like a stake to kill him (5P).

GREATEST SHOW IN THE GALAXY Nickname of the Psychic Circus (7J).

GREECE The ancient civilization of Atlantis, located in the island of Thera in the Aegean Sea, was the object of stories written by Plato (OOO). Ancient Greece was one of the protagonists involved in the Trojan War, in which both the First Doctor (U) and the Rani (6X) took part. Bigon was a Greek philosopher kidnapped by the Urbankans, probably circa 519 BC (5W). Delos was a Greek slave who befriended Ian aboard a Roman galley (M). One of the Eternals wore the guise of Critas, the captain of a Greek galley (6H). The Fifth Doctor and Turlough met Peri on a Greek Island, near which a Trion ship had crashed (6Q).

GREEL, MAGNUS 51st-century Australian dictator and scientist whose quest for eternal life led him to devise the flawed time travel method known as the Zigma Experiment. He was responsible for hundreds of thousands of deaths, and was dubbed the Butcher of Brisbane. Greel created the Peking Homunculus, which set off World War VI and helped him and other dictators take over the Earth as the Supreme Alliance. Greel became the Alliance's infamous Minister of Justice. After the Alliance was overthrown at the Battle of Reykjavik, Greel and the Homunculus escaped to 19th-century China in the Zygma Time Cabinet. But his metabolism was destroyed by temporal distortion. Greel became horribly disfigured, and needed to absorb other humans' life essences in order to survive. He was found by a Chinese peasant, Li H'Sen Chang, who took him to be the god Weng-Chiang. While Greel was recovering, his Time Cabinet was seized by the Chinese Emperor T'ungchi, and eventually ended up in London in Professor Litefoot's hands. Greel, his worshippers, the Tong of the Black Scorpion, and the Homunculus travelled to England to recover the Cabinet. But their efforts were thwarted by the Fourth Doctor, Leela, Litefoot and Henry Gordon Jago. After discarding Chang, Greel was eventually struck down by the Homunculus's laser fire and died of cellular collapse (4S).

GREEN, STEINBERGER P. Hollywood director whose film the First Doctor interrupted (V).

GREEN Post Office Tower security officer with the rank of Major. He was hypnotized by WOTAN, but was freed when the First Doctor destroyed the War Machines (BB).

GREEN Guard at Stangmoor Prison. He was killed when Mailer took over the Prison (FFF).

GREEN, EDWIN 19th-century British miner whose brain fluids were stolen by the Rani (6X).

GREEN DEATH Lethal effects of the deadly swarms of giant maggots and poisonous, glowing green slime created by the chemical waste pumped into the local mines by the Global Chemicals refinery in Llanfairfach (TTT).

GREGARIAN ROCK Intended to last for ever, it was the material of which the Ark's statue was made (X).

GREGORY International Electromatics' Chief Researcher. Corporal Benton shot him before he could kill Professor Watkins (VV).

GREGSON, JAMES (SIR) United Nations Plenipotentiary and Minister with special responsibility for T-Mat. He assisted the Second Doctor in his fight against the Ice Warriors and their Seeds of Death (XX).

GREGSON, LILY Gossipy post office clerk in Moreton Harwood, and the High Priestess of Hecate. She and Commander Pollock were arrested thanks to the efforts of Sarah Jane Smith and K-9 Mark III (K9).

GRELL Chief Guard of UK Habitat. He suspected Merdeen of helping people escape from the Cullings. Merdeen shot him to prevent him from betraying him (7A).

GRENDEL (COUNT) Taran knight, Lord of Castle Gracht, and Swordmaster of the Ninth Degree. He desperately wanted to be King of Tara. To achieve his ends, he tried to assassinate Prince Reynart and to use Romana's resemblance to Princess Stella. His plans were thwarted by the Fourth Doctor, who defeated him in a sword fight. Grendel managed to escape (5D).

GRENVILLE See HALLET.

GREY British Army sergeant under General Carrington's command (CCC).

GREY See GRAY.

GRIERSON Chief technician of the Devesham Space Research Station. He helped the Fourth Doctor fight the Kraals and was wounded by one of Styggron's androids (4J).

GRIFFIN Denes's palace chief (PP).

GRIFFITHS, CHARLIE Lytton's second-in-command. He agreed to help his boss steal the Cybermen's time vessel for the Cryons for a price of two million pounds in diamonds. He was killed by the Cybermen (6T).

GRIFFITHS, DAVE One of the Llanfairfach miners (TTT).

GRIG Androgum tribe (6W).

GRIGORY Natasha's friend. She convinced him to help her look for her father in the vaults of Tranquil Repose. He was killed by one of Davros's Daleks (6Z).

GRIM REAPER Terileptil android made to look like the figure of death (5X).

GRIMALKIN Miss Hawthorne's cat (JJJ).

GRIMSHAW UNIT soldier saved by Sarah (4A).

GRIMWOLD'S SYNDROME Another name for robophobia (4R).

GRIOPHOS According to the Seventh Doctor, a planet with a spectacular swimming pool used exclusively by the Gulmeres (7E).

GROGAN One of the crew on the Eternals' ships (6H).

GROLON Planet visited by Captain Cook (7J).

GROOM Police constable of Devil's End. He was crushed by Azal's psionic powers (JJJ).

GROSE (MRS) Day housekeeper at Gabriel Chase. She allowed Reverend Matthews in (7Q).

GROTZI Form of galactic currency valued by Sabalom Glitz (7A, 7C).

GROVE, THE Garden on Traken where Melkur was kept (5T).

GROVER, CHARLES (SIR) Minister with Special Powers during the Dinosaur Invasion. In reality, he was the mastermind behind the invasion, and Operation Golden Age, which consisted in rolling time back to restore Earth to an age when it was free of pollution and technology. He was exposed by the Third Doctor. After seeing his scheme fall apart, Grover tried activating Professor Whitaker's device and the two men were sent back to prehistory (WWW).

GRUB Creature from Vortis with a venomous sting (N).

GRUGGER General of the Gaztak mercenaries. He was hired by Meglos but was eventually outsmarted by the Fourth Doctor and perished in Zolfa-Thura's explosion (5Q).

GRUN King Peladon's Champion. He was a mute soldier of considerable strength, and fiercely loyal to the King. He first assisted Hepesh then, realizing he had been misguided, he helped the Third Doctor expose the High Priest (MMM).

GRUNDLE The Drashigs' star-system of origin (PPP).

GUARDIAN Sole survivor of the super-beings who once occupied Exarius and built the Doomsday Machine, whose radiation also kept him alive. The Third Doctor convinced him that the Machine should not fall into evil hands – specifically, the Master's – and the Guardian destroyed it. He perished with it (HHH).

GUARDIAN See MINOTAURS.

GUARDIANS Corps of humans responsible for the security aboard the Ark. After Dodo's cold virus had sapped their will, they became the Monoids' servants (X).

GUARDIANS Military elite of Voga; their leader was Vorus (4D).

GUARDIANS OF TIME Immensely powerful conceptual entities who embodied the concept of Light/Order (White Guardian) and Darkness/Chaos (Black Guardian). They maintained the universal balance through an artefact known as the Key to Time. The existence of the Guardians was known to few. Among those were the Time Lords' High Council, and the Eternals, who called them Enlighteners. The White Guardian enlisted the help of the Fourth Doctor to gather the six segments of the Key to Time in order to restore the universal balance of the cosmos (5A). Eventually the Doctor succeeded and assembled the key, outwitting the Black Guardian and enabling the White Guardian to restore the balance (5F).

The Black Guardian later used Turlough to try to kill the Fifth Doctor (6F, 6G). The Black Guardian tried to offer the prize of Enlightenment to the Eternals, but was thwarted by the Fifth Doctor. The two Guardians will exist until neither is needed any longer (6H). See also ENLIGHTENMENT.

GUARDOLIERS Karfelon guards who served the Borad (6Y).

GUARDS Specific name of the caste of Minyans who were in charge of controlling the Trogs in the Underworld. They obeyed the Seers, who reported to the Oracle (4Y).

GUDULA (SAINT) See CESSAIR.

GULLIVER, LEMUEL Fictional character invented by Jonathan Swift. He helped the Doctor, Jamie and Zoe in the Land of Fiction. He could speak only words given to him by Swift (UU).

GULMERES Flesh-eating octopi from Griophos (7E).

GULNAR Young Alzarian Outler killed by the Marshmen (5R).

GUM Tribe of cavemen who had lost the secret of fire (A).

GUMBLEJACK According to the Sixth Doctor, the finest fish in the galaxy (6W).

GUNDANS Axe-wielding robots built by the humanoid races once enslaved by the Tharils. They were designed to face the time winds, enter the Gateway and slay the Tharils. After they had broken the Tharils' power, the Gundans remained to guard the Gateway. The Fourth Doctor tricked two Gundans into destroying each other (5S).

GUNNAR Giant Viking raider. He was slain by the Saxons from Wulnoth's village (S).

GURN One of Professor Sorenson's Morestran crew killed by the antimatter creatures on Zeta Minor (4H).

GUTENBERG BIBLE First book in the western world printed with movable type, and produced in AD 1455 in Germany by Gutenberg himself. One of Scaroth's twelve fragments (possibly Captain Tancredi) obtained several copies. These were sold by Count Scarlioni in 1980 to finance Professor Kerensky's time experiments (5H).

GWENDOLINE See PRITCHARD, GWENDO-LINE.

GYAR One of the Xeron rebels (Q).

H

HABRIS Captain of the Guards who served Lord Zargo on the Great Vampire's world. He was eventually killed by Ivo (5P).

HACKENSACK, LAVINIA P. American tourist who gave a ride to Lady Peinforte and Richard near Windsor. Lady Peinforte had once poisoned her ancestor Dorothea ReminGton (7K).

HACKETT Megropolis One resident on Pluto (4W).

HACKNEYWICK Garron's hometown in Somerset (5A).

HADE (GATHERER) Vain and greedy senior tax collector for the Company in Megropolis One on Pluto. He fought against the Fourth Doctor and Leela, but was powerless to stop the rebellion. He was thrown off a roof by the rebels and died (4W).

HADRON POWER LINES Web of energy used by the Master to keep Adric prisoner while he created Castrovalva (5Z).

HADS See HOSTILE ACTION DISPLACEMENT SYSTEM.

HAEMOVORES An evolutionary offshoot of the human race, half a million years in the future, and monstrous humanoids who, like the vampires of legends, were impervious to bullets and craved blood. They were also repelled by the psychic barriers caused by a potential victim's strong faith. Haemovores could survive under water, and had tremendous strength. Fenric brought several Haemovores back through time, which gave rise to the vampiric legends. (7M). See also ANCIENT HAEMOVORE.

HAFSA Woman prisoner in El Akir's harem (P).

HAJES Swampy high priest at the time of Kroll's third manifestation (5E).

HAKIT B-grade technician who joined Mandrel's rebels and helped overthrow the Company on Pluto (4W).

HAKOL The Fifth Doctor postulated that the Malus was a Hakol psychic probe (6M).

HAL Archer serving Sir Edward of Wessex. He helped the Third Doctor and Sarah Jane Smith defeat Irongron, and eventually killed Linx by shooting an arrow into his Probic Vent (UUU).

HALDRON Earth divinity worshipped by the Free on Ravolox. They thought that Drathro's Maglem converter was Haldron's totem (7A).

HALL, BOB Mechanic at Gatwick Airport who told the Second Doctor that his TARDIS was requisitioned and taken away by a certain 'J. Smith' (LL).

HALL OF FIRE Hall built by the Trions on Sarn to exploit the Numismaton Flame (6Q).

HALLET Interplanetary investigator previously known to, and admired by, the Doctor. He investigated the granaries shortage on Stella Stora, where he met Kimber, who recognized him when he embarked on the *Hyperion III* space liner under the identity of Grenville. Hallet then decided to disguise himself as Enzu, a Mogarian who had boarded the ship at the last minute. He summoned the Sixth Doctor with a mayday call, but was recognized by his intended quarry, Doland, who poisoned him (7C).

HALLEY'S COMET Famous comet which passes near Earth approximately every 76 years. Cybermen from the future planned to crash it into the Earth in 1986, just after Mondas had re-energized itself, and thus save their home world. The Time Lords' Celestial Intervention Agency manipulated the Sixth Doctor into thwarting their plans (DD, 6T).

HAMILTON, PETER Earth marine lieutenant and member of the space corps expedition sent to Exxilon to bring back parrinium. He helped the Third Doctor defeat the Daleks, and was attracted to Jill Tarrant (XXX).

HAMLET See SHAKESPEARE, WILLIAM.

HAMPDEN, JANE Little Hodcombe school teacher and Ben Wolsey's friend. She refused to participate in Sir George Hutchinson's war games, and helped the Fifth Doctor defeat the Malus (6M).

HAND OF OMEGA Stellar manipulator created by Omega to

176

turn a star into a supernova. It was endowed with a rudimentary form of intelligence. The First Doctor left the Hand of Omega on Earth in 1963, intending to bury it. It was located by both the Daleks and the Imperial Daleks, who travelled back in time to fight for its possession. The Seventh Doctor did manage to bury it, but it was dug up by Ratcliffe. The Seventh Doctor allowed the Imperial Daleks to seize it, then manipulated Davros into using it. The Hand of Omega turned Skaro's (or Skaro II's?) sun into a supernova and destroyed Davros's ship. Its ultimate fate is unknown (7H).

HANDICOMBE, 'SMUTTY' Lord Cranleigh's friend from his schooldays (6A).

HAPPINESS PATROL Police force of Terra Alpha organized by Helen A to force people to be happy. Sad people, dubbed 'killjoys' were arrested by the Happiness Patrol, then publicly drowned in boiling candy. The Seventh Doctor and Ace helped organize a revolution which overthrew Helen A's regime (7L).

HARDAKER (MRS) Overprotective, prudish, middle-aged Northumberland woman, Jean and Phyllis's guardian. She was killed by the two girls after they were turned into Haemovores (7M).

HARDIMAN, GEORGE (SIR) Head of the Nuton Power Complex. He sacrificed his life to save the Complex from a power surge rechannelled by Axos (GGG).

HARDIN He and Stimson were two confidence tricksters from Earth who pretended to be able to rejuvenate Mena with the Tachyon Recreation Generator in order to gain money. Hardin fell in love with Mena, and eventually confessed the truth. Thanks to the Fourth Doctor's help, he eventually re-engineered the TRG and succeeded in rejuvenating Mena (5N).

HARDY Space pilot of the C-982 cargo ship on which the Third Doctor rematerialized in AD 2540. It was attacked by the Ogrons who were helping the Master foment a war between Earth and the Draconians (QQQ).

HARG Methane refinery crew member on Delta Magna's moon. He was killed by Kroll (5E).

HARGREAVES Harrison Chase's butler. He was killed by Krynoid-controlled plants (4L).

HARKAWAY, JACK (CAPTAIN) Fictional character (UU).

HARKER British army captain. Following Chinn's orders, he placed the Brigadier and his UNIT men under arrest (GGG).

HARKER Coxswain of Lord Palmerdale's lifeboat. He was shipwrecked on Fang Rock, and killed by the Rutan (4V).

HARLEQUIN THREE Planet of the Cyrennic Empire (5A).

HAROLD II (c.1020–1066) Last Saxon king of England, killed at the Battle of Hastings. The First Doctor stopped the Meddling Monk from preventing his defeat. (S).

HARP OF RASSILON Musical instrument which, once a certain tune was played on it, revealed the hidden control room of the Game of Rassilon (6K).

HARPER, SETH Gambler and gunfighter who had thrown in his lot with the Clantons. He was shot by Doc Holliday when he tried to kill him (Z).

HARPER Black confederate trooper who fought in the Resistance alongside the Second Doctor, Jamie and Lady Buckingham to put an end to the War Games. He was eventually killed by one of the War Lords' guards (ZZ).

HARRIS, FRANK Robson's second-in-command. He opposed his superior and helped the Second Doctor destroy the Weed. Victoria Waterfield eventually chose to stay with the Harris family (RR).

HARRIS, MAGGIE Frank Harris's wife. She was taken over by the Weed, but was eventually freed thanks to the intervention of her husband and the Second Doctor (RR).

HARRIS UNIT Private wounded during the Cybermen Invasion (VV).

HARROGATE Location of the British Government during the Dinosaur Invasion (WWW).

HARRY See SULLIVAN, HARRY.

HARRY Radar operator who first detected Axos (GGG).

HARRY Television floor manager in charge of covering Prof. Horner's excavation at Devil's Hump (JJJ).

HARRY Guard working for George Stephenson. He was killed by the Master (6X).

HARRY Owner of Harry's Café, where Ace met Mike Smith (7H).

HART UNIT sergeant killed by the Silurians (BBB).

HART, JOHN Royal Navy captain. He was in charge of the naval base which was investigating the ships that had been sunk by the Sea Devils. His base was later taken over by the Sea Devils, and he helped the Third Doctor and Jo Grant repel the invaders (LLL).

HART, TERESA Victorian London girl captured by Li H'Sen Chang. She would have had her life essence drained by Magnus Greel if Leela had not taken her place (4S).

HARTLEY One of Harrison Chase's guards (4L).

HARTMAN Employee of Dr Fendelman (4X).

HARVEY A grocery store employee in Perivale (7P).

HARVEY One of the Moonbase staff, killed by the Ice Warriors (XX).

HASHASHINS Oriental sect of fanatic killers, of which 250 were slain by Hulagu at the Cave of Five Hundred Eyes (D).

HASTINGS, BATTLE OF The First Doctor prevented the Meddling Monk from changing the course of history by altering the result of this battle (S). See also HAROLD II.

HASSAN Saracen encountered by Ian (P).

HATHAWAY (DR) Medical doctor who was called in at Cranleigh Hall to investigate Digby's murder (6A).

HAWK, LEX He and Weismuller were two US secret agents who helped the Seventh Doctor thwart Gavrok's Bannermen and save Delta (7F).

HAWKINS UNIT captain who fought the Silurians. He was killed by the Young Silurian when he came to the Brigadier's rescue (BBB).

HAWKINS, VINCE Young lighthouse-keeper on Fang Rock. He was killed by the Rutan (4V).

HAWTHORNE, OLIVE White witch who warned Professor Horner not to open Devil's Hump. She also resisted the Master's attempts to control her. She saved the Third Doctor's life and helped him, Jo Grant and UNIT defeat the Master and Azal (JJJ).

HAYDON, PETER (aka HAYDEN) Member of Professor Parry's expedition on Telos. He was killed by one of the murderous traps set in the Tombs of the Cybermen (MM).

HAYTER (PROFESSOR) Scientist from the University of Darlington, who specialized in hypnosis. He was a passenger on the Concorde flight hijacked to the Jurassic by the Master, but refused to believe in the reality of his experience. When he finally accepted the truth, he sacrificed himself to join the Xeraphin and help them communicate with the Fifth Doctor (6C).

HEAD, EDWARD WILLIAM One of the crew of the *Mary Celeste* (R).

HEADMAN, THE Unnamed slave of the Terileptils (5X).

HEADMASTER Unnamed headmaster at Brendon School (6F).

HEADMASTER Unidentified headmaster of Coal Hill Secondary School. He was a thrall of the Imperial Daleks (7H).

HEARTS FAMILY The King, Queen and Knave of Hearts were some of the deadly pawns used by the Toymaker when he challenged the First Doctor, Stephen and Dodo (Y).

HEATH Galsec Seven colonist killed by Styre (4B).

HEATHROW London airport. Tegan was on her way there when she became involved in the Fourth Doctor's clash with the Master (5V). The Fifth Doctor took her back to the Heathrow site, but in AD 1666 (5X). Soon afterwards, he helped rescue a Concorde plane which had been hijacked to the Jurassic Period by the Master. Tegan accidentally remained behind (6C).

HECATE Spaceship piloted by Dymond which crashed into the *Empress* when it emerged from hyperspace above the planet Azure (5K).

HECATE Pagan goddess worshipped by a cult led by Commander Pollock and Lily Gregson. Because the local crops were not faring well, the cult wanted to sacrifice Brendan, but were stopped by Sarah Jane Smith and K-9 Mark III (K9).

HECTOR Son of King Priam and the best warrior in Troy. He was killed by Achilles, following the unwitting intervention of the First Doctor (U).

HEDGES Doctor at the Bi-Al Foundation. He and Cruikshank were taken over by Lowe's Virus. He was blasted by K-9 (4T).

HEDIN Member of the Time Lords' High Council. As a historian, he felt Omega had been wronged, so helped him invade the Matrix in an attempt to bond himself with the Fifth Doctor's body. After he was exposed, he sacrificed his life to save that of the Doctor, in order to enable Omega to complete the bonding (6E).

HEIRADI Home planet of the Arar-Jecks (6N).

HEKTIR Young Alzarian Outler who died at the onset of Mistfall (5R).

HELDORF (PROFESSOR) Scientist working for General Carrington. He was the first to examine the three radioactive, alien Ambassadors. He was shot by one of Reegan's men (CCC).

HELICAL GALAXY Location of Atrios and Zeos (5F).

HELIUM 2 See LEPTONIC ERA.

HELIX ENERGY See MANDRAGORA HELIX.

HELLSTROM-2 Chassis used by Nostalgia Trips on their galactic tour buses (7F).

HELMET OF THERON Named after the great Argolin leader, it was the symbol of Argolis's warlike past. Pangol wore it when he went into the TRG (5N).

HENDERSON Medical doctor in charge of examining the Third Doctor during his stay at Ashbridge Cottage Hospital (AAA).

HENDERSON UNIT Sergeant who helped the Fourth Doctor fight the Krynoid. He was crushed, then turned into compost, by Harrison Chase (4L)

HENLOW DOWNS British military installation whose resources were used to fight the Cybermen (VV)

181

HENRY Footman at Cranleigh Hall (6A).

HENSELL Ineffectual governor of the Vulcan colony who met the Second Doctor. He was killed by a Dalek 'working' for the treacherous head of security, and rebel leader, Bragen (EE).

HEPESH High Priest of Peladon. He genuinely believed that Peladon should not join the Federation, and allied himself with Arcturus to stop it. He used Aggedor to kill Torbis, and even tried taking the King hostage. After he was exposed by the Third Doctor, he tried using Aggedor to be rid of him, but the beast turned against him and killed him instead (MMM).

HERCULES 208 A star in Messia 13 that went nova as Zoe predicted. Its gamma radiation flux deflected meteors towards the Wheel in Space (SS).

HERESIARCH Official title of the Argolin leader (5N).

HEREWARD Winstansley's dog (JJJ).

HERIOT, ZOE (aka HERRIOT or HERRIET) One of the Second Doctor's companions. A former student of the Earth School of Parapsychology, which emphasized pure logic and science, at first she lacked emotions, but she overcame this during her travels with the Doctor and Jamie. She met the Time Lord on the Wheel in Space, where she was librarian and astrophysicist, and helped him defeat the Cybermen (SS). She then helped him and Jamie fight the Dominators, the Cybermen (again), the Krotons, the Ice Warriors and Caven's Space Pirates. She was particularly adept with computers, as she demonstrated against the Master-Brain of the Land of Fiction, the Kroton Machine, and by outsmarting Tobias Vaughn's security system. Her computerlike mind worked out the firing plan that destroyed the invading Cyberfleet. After taking part in the War Games, Zoe was returned to her own era by the Time Lords, just after the end of her first adventure with the Doctor (SS-ZZ). Zoe's image was used by Rassilon to ward off the Second Doctor (6K).

HERMACK, NIKOLAI International Space Corps General who led the fight against, and was ultimately responsible for the destruction of, the notorious space pirate Caven (YY).

HERMANN Count Scarlioni's henchman who fought the Fourth Doctor and Romana. He was unaware that his master was in reality Scaroth. When Scaroth returned to the 20th century after failing to prevent his ship's explosion, the sight of his real shape so frightened Hermann that he caused an explosion which killed them both (5H).

HEROES OF ATRIOS Role models used by the Marshal for his war effort propaganda (5F).

HERRET One of the alien tourists who crashlanded in Wales in 1959. He was killed by the Bannermen (7F).

HERRICK Hotheaded member of Jackson's crew. He fought the Oracle in the Underworld alongside the Fourth Doctor and Leela. He was captured and interrogated by the Seers, but was eventually returned to Jackson and went back to Minyos II (4Y).

HESLINGTON RAF air controller who supervised the tracking of the Chameleons' plane (KK).

HETRA Leader of the pygmy Menoptera who stayed behind to live an underground existence on Vortis. He eventually rallied to help the First Doctor and the Menoptera defeat the Zarbi (N).

HEXACHROMITE Gas used to seal underwater structures. It was harmless to humans, but deadly to reptile and underwater life. The Fifth Doctor reluctantly used it to kill the Silurians and Sea Devils who had taken over Sea Base Four (6L).

HIBBERT, GEORGE Managing Director of AutoPlastics, Ltd. He found the first Nestene meteorite and fell victim to its mind control. He made the replica known as Channing. He was eventually freed by the Third Doctor. When he tried to destroy his handiwork, he was killed by an Auton (AAA).

HICKMAN Maintenance employee on the Sea Fort attacked by the Sea Devils, who killed him (LLL).

HIERONYMOUS Court astrologer in the Dukedom of San Martino in 15th-century Italy, a charlatan who helped Count Federico try to assassinate his nephew, Giuliano. He was also the secret leader of the Brothers of Demnos. His body was taken over by the Mandragora Helix (4M).

HIGH-BRAINS Nickname given by the Krotons to the Second Doctor and Zoe, whose great stores of mental energy were half the power needed to activate the Dynatrope's space travel capabilities (WW).

HIGH COUNCIL Ruling body of Atlantis, presided over by King Dalios (OOO).

HIGH COUNCIL (OF THE TIME LORDS) Ruling body of the Time Lords of Gallifrey. It was comprised of the President, the Chancellor and the various Cardinals (or head of colleges) and other highranking Time Lords. The High Council passed judgement on the War Lords and the Second Doctor (ZZ), and summoned the Three Doctors to defeat Omega (RRR). When the President was assassinated by Chancellor Goth, the High Council was thrown into disarray (4P). This was also the case when the Vardans and the Sontarans invaded Gallifrey (4Z). When Omega threatened to return to our universe by taking over the Fifth Doctor's body, the High Council, now led by Borusa, voted to condemn the Doctor to death (6E). Against Borusa's wishes, the High Council voted to ask the Master to help the Five Doctors trapped inside the Death Zone (6K). Afterwards, a new and corrupt High Council initiated the Ravolox Stratagem to strike back at the Andromedan Sleepers. Afraid that the Doctor would find out, they used the Valeyard to prosecute the Sixth Doctor at a trial. After the Sixth Doctor exposed the Council's plot during the trial, the High Council was deposed (7A–7C).

HIGH KING King Arthur's title (7N).

HIGH LAMA Padmasambhava's title (NN).

HIGH PRIEST Unnamed Brother of Demnos, serving under Hieronymous. He wanted to sacrifice Sarah to his god (4M).

HILDA See ROWSE, HILDA.

HILIO Captain of the Menoptera invasion force (N).

HILRED (aka HILDRED) Young, eager and ultimately incompetent commander of the Chancellery Guards under Castellan Spandrell. He tortured the Fourth Doctor and was eventually killed by the Master (4P).

HIMALAYAS See TIBET.

HINDLE Young officer and member of the Imperial Earth expedition force to Deva Loka. The Kinda's attempts to have him and Commander Sanders mind-meld with them caused them to become mentally unbalanced. Spurred by the Mara, Hindle almost destroyed the planet. He was cured by the Fifth Doctor with the Kinda's Jhana Box, and left Deva Loka purged of his inner fears (5Y).

HINKS Stevens's henchman. He tried to murder Jo and Bert, and was later killed by one of the Green Death maggots (TTT).

HIPPIAS Young member of the Atlantean High Council to whom King Dalios entrusted the secret of the Kronos Crystal. He wanted Dalios to use it to return the island to its former glories. He was in love with Queen Galleia. He saved Jo Grant's life, but was killed by the Minotaur (OOO).

HISTORICAL FIGURES The First Doctor met Ulysses and the other Greek warriors of the Trojan War (U). In AD 64, he met Roman emperor Nero and Poppaea (M). In an alternate future, and unrecorded adventure, the Doctor became Merlin at King Arthur's court (7N). In AD 1192, the First Doctor met King Richard the Lionheart in Palestine (P). In 1215, the Fifth Doctor defeated the Master who used Kamelion to impersonate King John Lackland (6J). In 1289, the First Doctor played backgammon with, and saved the life of, Kublai Khan in China; he also met Marco Polo (D).

The Fourth Doctor almost met Leonardo da Vinci twice (4M, 5H). The artist had, however, already met the Meddling Monk (S). In 1572, the First Doctor was almost caught in the infamous St Bartholomew's Day Massacre in Paris (W). The Fourth Doctor claimed to have helped Shakespeare write *Hamlet* (5H).

In 1746, the Second Doctor rescued Jamie after the battle of Culloden (FF). In 1794, the First Doctor accidentally returned to France during the French Revolution and just missed meeting young Napoleon Bonaparte (H).

The Sixth Doctor met George Stephenson at the beginning of the Industrial Revolution (6X). In 1872, the First Doctor made a brief stop aboard the *Mary-Celeste* (R). In 1881, he fought alongside famous gunslingers Wyatt Earp and Doc Holliday in Tombstone, Arizona (Z). Soon afterwards, the Sixth Doctor met young H.G. Wells who had been vacationing in Scotland (6Y).

Albert Einstein and a bevy of other modern scientific geniuses were kidnapped by the Rani, but returned to their proper places in time and space by the Seventh Doctor (7D). The Beatles appeared on the First Doctor's visualizer (R). The Seventh Doctor did not get to meet Queen Elizabeth II while at Windsor (7K).

HIVE Name given by the Nucleus of the Virus to the place where it could swarm. The Virus took over the Titan base and had its human hosts turn into a Hive, but it was blown up by the Fourth Doctor before the swarm could escape (4T). The homeworld of the Wirrn was a Hive World (4C). Also see LEISURE HIVE.

HLYNIA Menoptera. She was Prapilius's daughter (N).

HO Chinese member of the Tong of the Black Scorpion who replaced Lee as Greel's main servant. He was killed by Mr Sin's laser fire (4S).

HOBSON, JACK British commander of the Moonbase during the Cybermen attack. At first, he disbelieved the Second Doctor's warnings about the Cybermen, but later came around and helped him save the base (HH).

HOLDEN, JIM Exarius colony's electrician. He and his Primitive assistant were killed by Norton (HHH).

HOLLAND The Fifth Doctor fought Omega in Amsterdam (6E).

HOLLIDAY, JOHN HENRY ('DOC') Gambler, gunman and sometime dentist of the American West who lived from 1852 to 1887. Suffering from consumption, he moved west, ending up in Tombstone, Arizona, where he established a dental practice. Accused of killing Reuben Clanton, he was targeted for revenge by the Clanton family. He first tried to pass off the First Doctor (who had come to see him to have a tooth removed) as himself, then fled to a neighbouring town, but later returned to take part in the gunfight at the OK Corral. He allegedly shot Johnny Ringo. Married to Kate Elder, he left Tombstone with a $2000 prize on his head (Z).

HOLLOW WORLDS The Daleks planned to hollow out Earth's core and turn the planet into a spaceship (K). The Tractators planned the same fate for Frontios (6N). The pirate planet, Zanak, was already a hollow world which functioned as a spaceship (5B).

HOLLYWOOD The First Doctor stopped there briefly during his flight from the Daleks' Masterplan (V).

HOLOGRAMS In the 50th century, Kilbracken developed the technique of holographic cloning. Such clones had only a ten-minute life span (4T).

HOPKINS UNIT corporal attacked by Lupton (ZZZ).

HOPPER Captain of the ship which carried Professor Parry's expedition to Telos. He helped the Second Doctor defeat the Cybermen and reclose their Tombs (MM).

HORDA Ferocious, white, snakelike creatures. The Sevateem used the Test of the Horda to try those who did not believe in Xoanon (4Q).

HORG One of the cavemen of the Tribe of Gum (A).

HORNER, GILBERT (PROFESSOR) Archeologist who opened up Devil's Hump, in spite of Miss Hawthorne's warnings. He was frozen to death when he opened the barrow (JJJ).

HORTON, CLIVE Heathrow air-traffic controller who was on duty when Concorde flight 192 disappeared (6C).

HORUS Egyptian god of light, and Sutekh's brother. He was the leader of the godlike Osirians, who visited Earth in the days of Ancient Egypt. He and the other Osirians defeated Sutekh and imprisoned him inside a secret pyramid (4G).

HOSTILE ACTION DISPLACEMENT SYSTEM (HADS) When the Krotons turned the power of the Dynatrope against the TARDIS, it dematerialized and rematerialized in a nearby, safer location (WW).

HOUDINI, HARRY Famous magician whom the Doctor claimed to have met (ZZZ).

HOURLY TELEPRESS Television programme from Zoe's time. The Karkus was a ficional adventurer who starred in it (UU).

HOUSE OF THE DRAGON Temple of Weng-Chlang in London. The statue of the dragon housed a sophisticated and deadly laser cannon in its eyes (4S).

HOUSE OF HORRORS The fourth stop in the Daleks' pursuit

of the First Doctor through time and space. It was located at the 1996 World's Fair in Ghana, and featured robotic versions of Dracula and the Frankenstein Monster (R).

HRHOONDA One of the Menoptera's landing party on Vortis. He was suspicious of Barbara and advocated killing her (N).

HROSTAR One of the Menoptera, Vrestin's deputy on Vortis (N).

HUAR Inhabitant of Metebelis 3 (ZZZ).

HUCKLE Operations director of the oil company whose platforms were attacked by the Zygons' Skarasen (4F).

HUDSON (MRS) Professor Litefoot's housekeeper (4S).

HUGHES, TED One of the Llanfairfach miners, and the first victim of the Green Death (TTT).

HUGUENOTS Name given to the French Protestants who developed during the 16th-century Reformation (W).

HUITZILIPOCHTLI The Aztecs' cruel god (F).

HULAGU Mongol conqueror who slew 250 Hashashins (D).

HUMKER He and Tandrell were twins from the UK habitat, selected to serve Drathro because of their intellectual abilities. They thrived on contradiction. After the Sixth Doctor destroyed Drathro, they escaped to the world outside (7A).

HUNGARY Location of the Central European Zone's headquarters where Denes confronted Salamander (PP).

HUNTSMAN Lady Adrasta's enforcer on Chloris. He used his carnivorous Wolf Weeds to keep the population obedient. After the Fourth Doctor revealed Adrasta's duplicity, he turned against her and refused to obey her orders (5G).

HUR Young cavewoman of the Tribe of Gum. She was in love with Za (A).

HUSAK Czech UNIT major who evacuated the civilians and served under Brigadier Bambera during the battle at Carbury against Morgaine (7N).

HUTCHINSON, GEORGE (SIR) Lord of the Manor of Little

Hodcombe, who fought the Fifth Doctor. His unbalanced mind awakened the Malus. Under his evil influence, he began a series of deadly war games reenacting the English Civil War. He eventually went completely mad, and became totally possessed by the Malus. He died when Will Chandler threw him into the Malus's jaws (6M).

HYDE, STUART The Master's assistant on TOM-TIT at the Newton Research Institute. He was aged from 25 to 80 in a matter of seconds by Kronos, but was eventually cured by the Third Doctor (OOO).

HYDRAX Earth exploration vessel to Beta Two. Its captain was Miles Sharkey, its navigation officer was Lauren Macmillan and its science officer was Anthony O'Connor. The Great Vampire drew it through E-Space to an unnamed world (5P)

HYDRAZINE A hydrazine steam generator provided the Frontios colony with electricity (6N).

HYDROMEL Pain-killing drug developed by Terminus, Inc. to control the victims of lazar disease. Nyssa planned to synthesize it, thereby freeing the men from Terminus, Inc.'s grip (6G).

HYKSOS Khepren's first officer. He was killed by the Daleks (V).

HYMETUSITE Radioactive crystals which were part of the tribute requested by the Nimon, and exacted by the Sknonnans from Aneth. The Nimon used them to power the black holes that enabled them to travel through space and invade unsuspecting worlds (5L).

HYPERION Name of the spaceship bringing the Earth Investigator to Solos (NNN).

HYPERION III Space liner under Commodore Travers's command which ferried between Mogar and Earth in AD 2986. It was almost hijacked by Rudge. The Sixth Doctor saved its crew from being killed by the Vervoids (7C).

HYPERSPACE Another dimension of space which was virtually a theoretical absurdity. Yet the Prison Ship which had transported Cessair of Diplos was stuck in hyperspace (5C). Also see FASTER THAN LIGHT.

189

HYPNOTISM The ability to impose one's will on others. The Master was a supremely talented hypnotist; only humans with very strong wills could resist him. He used his hypnotic techniques, amplified with ultrasonics, to try to foment a war between Earth and the Draconians (QQQ). The Rani could enslave a man by making him swallow one of her deadly slugs (6X). President Borusa used the Coronet of Rassilon to bend the Fifth Doctor's will (6K).

Entities gifted with natural hypnotic powers included: the Brains of Morphoton (E); the Sensorites (G); the Animus (N); the Celestial Toymaker (Y); the Elders (AA); the Great Intelligence; the Weed (RR); the Master Brain (UU); the Mind Parasite (FFF); the Spiders of Metebelis 3 (ZZZ); Sutekh (4G); the Mandragora Helix (4M); Eldrad (4N); Xoanon (4Q); the Virus of the Purpose (4T); the Fendahl (4X); the Shadow (5F); the Great Vampire and his servants (5P); the Mara; the Xeraphin (6C); the Eternals (6H); the Malus (6M); Mestor (6S); the Gods of Ragnarok (7J); Morgaine (7N) and Fenric (7M). Also see TELEPATHY.

A number of villains used artificial means to impose their will on others. Among these were: the Daleks; the Cybermen, who relied on celensky capsules (SS) and their hypnotic beam pulser (VV); WOTAN (BB); the Macra (JJ); the Chameleons (KK); the War Lords (ZZ); the Nestene; BOSS (TTT); Skagra, who used his mind-transference sphere (5M); the Tereleptils (5X) and the Tractators (6N).

I

IA Famous biologist whose mind was stolen by Skagra at the Think Tank space station. He died in the destruction of the station (5M).

IAN See CHESTERTON, IAN.

IBBOTSON Turlough's lumpish friend at Brendon (6F).

IBRAHIM Saracen bandit who attacked Ian, then reluctantly helped him against El Akir (P).

ICCA See INNER CONSTELLATION CORRECTIVE AUTHORITY.

ICE AGES The Martians scouted Earth during one of its pre-historic Ice Ages. A squadron, led by Varga, was accidentally trapped and frozen in ice. Another Ice Age caused by a drop in carbon dioxyde level and deforestation occurred in AD 3000 but was stopped thanks to the World Ionizer program (OO). Also see ANTHROPOLOGY.

ICE FACE A landmark of Iceworld's underworld (7G).

ICE GARDEN A landmark of Iceworld's underworld. In reality, it was a disguised star chart (7G).

ICE GODS Divinities worshipped on Ribos. They were said to live in the catacombs (5A).

ICE SOLDIERS Four frozen warriors protecting one of the Keys of Marinus (E).

ICE TIME Ribos's 32-year-long winter, caused by the planet's elliptical orbit. The Ribans thought it was a product of the war between the Sun Gods and the Ice Gods (5A).

ICE VOLCANO See VOLCANO.

ICE WARRIORS Native Martians. They were huge, green, scaly creatures, equipped with sonic guns (on their claws) and heavy armour. Coming from a super-cold environment, the Ice Warriors were sensitive to heat, which was their only known weakness. The leaders appeared to be slightly sleeker and less bulky than the warriors.

The Martians scouted Earth during its first Ice Age. A squadron led by Varga was accidentally trapped and frozen in ice. Soon afterwards, possibly because they had not heard from Varga, the Martians decided to leave their dying planet and emigrate to another world in the galaxy (OO).

The Second Doctor first came across the Martians when Varga and his men were found buried in a glacier in AD 3000. The name 'Ice Warrior' was originally coined by Walters, but it was apparently close to the original Martian term, since they also referred to themselves by that name. The Doctor foiled Varga's attempts at conquest and destroyed the Ice Warriors and their ship (OO).

The Second Doctor met the Martians again when, towards the end of the 21st century, a warlike party of Ice Warriors, under Slaar's leadership, returned to the Solar System and tried to conquer Earth by using the so-called 'Seeds of Death'. Slaar's defeat seemed to have convinced the other Martians to abandon any further attempts at attacking the Solar System (XX).

The Martians then built a small, presumably peaceful, empire of their own, and eventually joined the Federation. Their ambassador to Peladon, Izlyr, helped the Third Doctor thwart Arcturus's plans (MMM). A renegade Ice Warrior, Azaxyr, later betrayed the Federation to Galaxy 5 on Peladon, but was foiled by the Third Doctor (YYY).

ICELAND North Atlantic island which was the seat of the peaceful Icelandic Alliance in the 51st century. After its Commissioner was assassinated by Greel's Peking Homunculus, World War Six erupted and the ruthless Supreme Alliance came into power. It was finally overthrown at the battle of Reykjavik (4S).

ICELANDIC ALLIANCE Peaceful 51st-century power which fell after its Commissioner was assassinated by Magnus Greel's Peking Homunculus (4S).

ICEWORLD Space trading post located on the dark side of Svartos, owned and controlled by the merciless Kane; in reality a huge spaceship which needed the dragonfire to start up again. After Kane's suicide, Iceworld fell into the possession of Glitz, who rechristened it *Nosferatu II* (7G). See also DRAGON.

ICTHAR Silurian scientist and third member of the Silurian triad which included the Old and the Young Silurians. He was in charge of reanimating the Silurians from Wenley Moor. He helped the Young Silurian inoculate Major Baker with a virus meant to wipe out mankind, and later set up the Molecular Disperser to destroy the Van Allen Belt. Tricked by the Third Doctor, he and his brethren went back into hibernation. Their shelter was later blown up by UNIT (BBB).

Icthar obviously survived since he returned in the year AD 2084 with his companions Scibus and Tarpok. He then reanimated a

Sea Devil commando led by Sauvix, and attacked Sea Base Four. His plan was to launch nuclear missiles to provoke a war between the two blocs, and thus eradicate mankind (as had been the Young Silurian's last wish). He died when the Fifth Doctor used deadly hexachromite gas (6L). According to some reports, his Silurian name was also spelled K'to (BBB).

IDAS One of the Trogs of the Underworld. He helped the Fourth Doctor and Jackson's crew fight the Oracle and steal the Minyan Race Banks. He and a number of his people escaped the Underworld's destruction by leaving aboard Jackson's ship (4Y).

IDMON One of the Trogs of the Underworld, and Idas's father. His wife and daughter were killed in a skyfall and he barely escaped being put to death by the Oracle. (4Y).

IE See INTERNATIONAL ELECTROMATICS.

IKONA Young Lakertyan who helped the Seventh Doctor and Peri defeat the Rani. He was bethrothed to Sarn, and became the Lakertyans' new leader after Beyus's sacrifice. He believed that, if his people were to survive, they had to meet their own challenges without outside help (7D).

IMAGE REPRODUCTION INTEGRATING SYSTEM (IRIS) Device built by the Third Doctor to translate thoughts into images (ZZZ).

IMC See INTERPLANETARY MINING CORPORATION.

IMMORTAL, THE Name given to Drathro by the citizens of the UK Habitat.

IMMORTALITY The Time Lords' ability to regenerate was a form of immortality (see REGENERATION). However, true immortality, as promised by Rassilon, was a trap (6K). Other entities who were virtually immortal included: the Guardians of Time; the Celestial Toymaker (Y); the Elders (AA); the Great Intelligence; the Nestene; Axos (GGG); the Daemons (JJJ); Kronos (OOO); the Osirians (4G); the Sisterhood of Karn (4K); the Mandragora Helix (4M); the Kastrians (4N); the Fendahl (4X); Cessair (5C); Meglos (5Q); the Vampires (5P); the Mara; the Xeraphin (6C); the Eternals (6G); the Gods of Ragnarok (7J); Morgaine (7N); Light (7Q); and Fenric (7M).

Queen Xanxia tried to keep her body alive by using the

energies pillaged by Zanak (5B). Monarch of Urbanka had devised an artifical form of immortality by storing memories on silicon chips, implanted in lifelike androids (5W). Mawdryn and his fellow scientists were condemned to live in a horrible state of perpetual regeneration (6F). The Time Lords prevented Crozier from developing a mind-transfer device which would have led to a form of immortality (7B).

Barring destruction, the Cybermen were probably immortal since they could replace their body parts. Many alien races, such as the Zygons (4F); the Ice Warriors; the Silurians and the Sea Devils; the Ogri (5C); the Tharils (5S); the Morlox (6Y); and Kane of Proamon (7G) had longer life spans than man.

IMPERIAL DALEKS (aka WHITE DALEKS) A race of Daleks created by Davros to be totally subservient to him. They were first created from the bodies kept in the Tranquil Repose mortuary (6Z). Later christened Imperial Daleks, they were used by Davros to capture the Hand of Omega on Earth. They presumably perished when the Doctor used the Hand of Omega to destroy their ship (7M).

IMPRIMATURE See RASSILON IMPRIMATURE.

INCA South American people visited by the Exxilons (XXX).

INDIAN OCEAN The SS *Bernice* was crossing the Indian Ocean en route to Singapore in 1926 when it was captured by Vorg's Scope (PPP).

INDUSTRIAL REVOLUTION The Master almost prevented it from happening because he wanted to harness and kidnap the geniuses behind it (Stephenson, Faraday, Watt, etc.) and harness them for his own ends. The Sixth Doctor stopped him (6X).

INEER One of the Sensorites (G).

INERTIA NEUTRALIZER Device used in the corridor leading to the Bridge of Zanak (5B).

INFERNO Codename of one of the Daleks' operations against Earth during the Masterplan (V).

INFERNO London discotheque where Polly met Ben Jackson (BB).

INFERNO Nickname given to Professor Stahlman's pet project, which consisted of drilling beneath the Earth's crust in order to tap pockets of Stahlman's Gas, in theory a new, massive source of energy. In addition to releasing a green slime which caused men to turn into Primords, the completion of Inferno would have released so much energy that the Earth would have been turned into a molten mass of gases. Such was indeed the fate of a parallel Earth where the Third Doctor could not stop Inferno in time (DDD).

INGA Lazar of Terminus who befriended Nyssa (6G).

INGIGER See ANCIENT HAEMOVORE.

INGRAM, RUTH (DR) One of the Master's assistants on TOM-TIT at the Newton Research Institute (OOO).

INNER CONSTELLATION CORRECTIVE AUTHORITY Pletrac threatened to refer the Third Doctor to the ICCA for coming illegally to Inter Minor (PPP).

INNER COUNCIL See HIGH COUNCIL.

INNER RETINUE The Collector's special police force on Pluto (4W).

INNER SANCTUM Karfel's ruling body (6Y).

INOKSHI Urbanka's planetary system (5W).

INQUISITOR, THE Female Time Lord who presided over the Trial of the Sixth Doctor. She was eventually convinced of his innocence and dismissed all charges. She tried to persuade the Doctor to again become President of the High Council, but he refused (7A-7C).

INSECTS The miniaturized First Doctor encountered what to him seemed to be giant insects (J). On Vortis, he encountered the giant antlike Zarbi and the butterfly like Menoptera (N). The Third Doctor encountered giant maggots created by the Green Death (TTT) and giant, mutated, intelligent spiders on Metebelis 3 (ZZZ). The Fourth Doctor helped free the Space Ark from the wasplike Wirrn (4C). The Chimerons' biology was similar to that of insects; their queen, Delta, was able to communicate with Goronwy's bees (7F). The Rani used a swarm of deadly insects to control the Lakertyans (7D).

INSTITUTE FOR ADVANCED SCIENCE STUDIES See FOUN-DATION FOR ADVANCED STUDIES.

INTELLIGENCE See GREAT INTELLIGENCE.

INTER MINOR Alien planet which was once struck by a space plague, possibly the same plague that was eventually cured by parrinium (XXX), and which, as a result, became very xeno-phobic. The Third Doctor and Vorg outwitted its Immigration Commissioner, Kalik (PPP).

INTERGALACTIC FLORA SOCIETY The Fourth Doctor claimed to be honorary president of this organization (4L).

INTERGALACTIC NARCOTICS BUREAU Interplanetary or-ganization devoted to fighting drugs. Rigg thought that the Fourth Doctor was one of its agents (5K).

INTERGALACTIC PURSUIT SQUADRON Earth-based space commando unit summoned to go after Romulus and Remus Sylvest's kidnappers. Its chief, Commander Fabian, assigned that specific job to Lieutenant Hugo Lang (6S).

INTERNATIONAL CIRCUS Name of Rossini's circus (EEE).

INTERNATIONAL ELECTROMATICS Secretive multinational corporation which had gained a virtual monopoly on com-puter and electronics equipment. Its managing director, Tobias Vaughn, allied himself with the Cybermen to take over the world, using micro-monolithic circuitry hidden in transistor radios sold in a million units across the globe. These would blanket the planet with a hypnotic signal. The Invasion was eventually defeated by the Second Doctor and UNIT, with Vaughn himself turning against the Cybermen when he realized they planned to destroy all human life (VV).

INTERNATIONAL ENERGY CONGRESS see WORLD ENERGY CONFERENCE.

INTERNATIONAL SPACE COMMAND Geneva-based, multi-national entity in charge of Earth's space program in general, and the Snowcap Space Tracking Station in particular. Its Secretary-General was Wigner (DD). In 2070, Ringberg was controller of International Space Command when the Cybermen attacked the Moonbase (HH).

INTERNATIONAL SPACE CORPS See SPACE CORPS.

INTERPLANETARY MINING CORPORATION (IMC) Ruthless corporation which tried to wrest Exarius from its legitimate colonists (HHH).

INTERSTELLAR ECOLOGY COMMISSION Interplanetary organization invoked by the Third Doctor on Inter Minor (PPP).

INVASIONS Various alien entities and races attempted to either enslave or destroy Earth (or its colonies), or take control of its resources. Among these were: the Daleks; the Cybermen; the Master; the Ice Warriors; the Sontarans; the Silurians and the Sea Devils; the Great Intelligence; the Macra (JJ); the Master-Brain of the land of Fiction (UU); the Weed (RR); the War Lords (ZZ); the Nestene; Axos (GGG); the Daemons (JJJ); the Spiders of Metebelis 3 (ZZZ); the Wirrn (4C); the Zygons (4F); Sutekh (4G); the Kraals (4J); the Krynoids (4L); the Mandragora Helix (4M); Eldrad (4N); the Rutans (4V); the Virus of the Purpose (4T); the Fendahl (4X); the Usurians (4W); Zanak (5B); Scaroth (5H); the Urbankans (5W); the Terileptils (5X); the Tractators (6N); the Destroyer (7N); and Light (7Q). The Time Lords themselves nearly destroyed Earth because it sheltered the Andromedan Sleepers (7A). Also see END OF THE WORLD.

INVERNESS Scottish town from which Gray conducted his slave trade (FF).

INVESTIGATOR Earth Imperial Council member sent to Solos to investigate the Marshal's activities. The sight of one of the Solonian mutants convinced him to restore the Marshal to power (NNN).

INVINCIBLES Name given by the Graff Vynda-K to his personal guard (5A).

INVISIBILITY Invisible creatures included the Visians of Mira (V); the Refusians (X); and the Spiridonians (SSS). The Celestial Toymaker made the First Doctor invisible (Y). Zeta Minor's anti-matter creatures (4H) and Xoanon's kinetic monsters (4Q) were mostly invisible.

ION AVALANCHE DIODE Device used by the Sixth Doctor to overload the Valeyard's Particle Disseminator (7C).

IONIZER Device used in AD 3000 to prevent a new Ice Age. It was also used by the Second Doctor to destroy the Ice Warriors (OO).

IPHITUS Planet visited by Captain Cook (7J).

IRIS See IMAGE REPRODUCTION INTEGRATING SYSTEM.

IRONGRON Leader of a band of 12th-century Wessex brigands. He allied himself with the stranded Sontaran, Linx, offering him shelter in exchange for modern weapons. He was thwarted by the Third Doctor and eventually killed by Linx (UUU).

ISBUR One of Varga's Ice Warrior crew who was brought back to life in AD 3000 (OO).

ISLAND OF DEATH Name the Dulcians gave to the island which had once been contaminated by radiation. It had been converted into a war museum, and was the site of the Dominators' landing (TT).

ISOP Galaxy where Vortis was located (N).

ISOTOPE (aka WEB DESTRUCTOR) Device designed by the Menoptera Invasion force to destroy the Animus, successfully used by Barbara Wright (N).

ISSIGRI, DOM Pioneer of argonite space mining with his partner, Milo Clancey. He founded the Issigri Mining Company, which owned giant argonite mines on planet Ta. He was kidnapped and held hostage by space pirate Caven to ensure his daughter Madeleine's cooperation. He was freed thanks to the intervention of the Second Doctor (YY).

ISSIGRI, MADELEINE Daughter of Dom Issigri and head of the Issigri Mining Company after her father's disappearance. When she found out that Caven held her father hostage, she was forced to cooperate with him, but eventually turned against the space pirate. She helped the Second Doctor defeat Caven, and was finally reunited with her father (YY).

ISSIGRI MINING COMPANY Founded by Dom Issigri. It

owned vast argonite mines on Ta, and was managed by Madeleine Issigri (YY).

ITALY The First Doctor visited Rome in the year AD 64 (M). The Fourth Doctor was in Italy twice during the Renaissance, first in San Martino (4M), then in Leonardo da Vinci's house (5H).

IVAR One of the Viking raiders defeated by Wulnoth's Saxons (S).

IVO Burly village headman on the Great Vampire's world. He was Marta's husband and Karl's father. He was secretly helping Kalmar's rebels. He eventually led the attack on the Tower, where he killed Habris (5P).

IXTA Chosen Warrior of the Aztecs. He eventually fell to his death while trying to kill Ian (F).

IZLYR Martian Ice Warrior Ice Lord. He was one of the Federation's delegates to Peladon. He and his warrior, Ssorg, helped the Third Doctor unmask Hepesh and Arcturus, and facilitate Peladon's accession to the Federation (MMM).

J

J7 (aka CHIMERA) Space station located in the Third Zone, under Dastari's management, the seat of Kartz and Reimer's unauthorized time experiments. Chessene arranged for the Station to be attacked by the Sontarans to frame the Time Lords (6W).

JABEL Captain of the Tesh, gifted with psionic powers. He fought against the Fourth Doctor and Leela to protect Xoanon, his god. Afterwards, he was left to argue with Calib over who would rule the reunited tribes of the Sevateem and the Tesh (4Q).

JABLIF Member of the group of Shobogans who captured

Leela and Rodan. He helped them and the Fourth Doctor repel the Sontarans' Invasion of Gallifrey. He was killed by a Sontaran (4Z).

JACKIJ (PROFESSOR) Scientist who discovered that the only antidote to spectrox toxaemia was the milk of a queen bat (6R).

JACKO Shipwreck survivor labouring in Atlantis's mines. He helped the Second Doctor defeat Professor Zaroff, in particular by convincing the Fish Men to go on strike (GG).

JACKSON, BEN Companion of the First and Second Doctors, and a young merchant sailor. He and Polly Lopez helped the First Doctor against WOTAN. Afterwards, they followed him in the TARDIS, and helped him fight 17th-century smugglers and the Cybermen. They watched the First Doctor regenerate. Ben and Polly then aided the Second Doctor against the Daleks, the Cybermen, Professor Zaroff, and the Macra. They first met Jamie in Scotland in 1748. Finally, after defeating the Chameleons, they discovered they were back in London on the same day they had left, and chose to remain there (BB-KK).

JACKSON (MISS) Professor Watson's assistant at the Nuclear Research Complex attacked by Eldrad (4N).

JACKSON Leader of the Minyan crew sent on a Quest to find the P7E and bring the Race Banks back to Minyos II. With the help of the Fourth Doctor and Leela, he fought the Oracle in the Underworld, and was eventually able to take the Race Banks and a number of Trogs back to Minyos II (4Y).

JACKSON Member of Captain Striker's crew (6H).

JACONDA Fertile and peaceful planet once ruled by the retired Time Lord, Azmael. It was almost destroyed by the gastropods and their leader Mestor (6S).

JACONDANS Birdlike aliens who lived on Jaconda. After Mestor's defeat and Azmael's death, Hugo Lang became the new Master of the Jacondans (6S).

JAEGER (PROFESSOR) Scientist who worked for the Marshal on Skybase One. His job was permanently to alter Solos's atmosphere to make it habitable by humans. He was killed in the explosion of his atmospheric regeneration machine (NNN).

JAFFA The market city of Palestine. The First Doctor and his companions rematerialized nearby at the time of the Third Crusade (P).

JAGAROTH Green-skinned, one-eyed alien race of conquerors. Their last survivors perished on Earth when their ship, piloted by Scaroth, exploded on take-off (5H).

JAGO, HENRY GORDON Bombastic owner of the 19th-century London Palace Theatre where Li H'Sen Chang performed his magic act and which, unbeknownst to him, also served as Magnus Greel's lair. He and Professor Litefoot helped the Fourth Doctor and Leela defeat Greel and save London from destruction (4S).

JALL Passenger on a space ship captured by the Daleks, and taken to Skaro to become part of the slave labour force searching for Davros (5J).

JAMAICA One of Captain Pike's pirates. He was killed by Pike for allowing the First Doctor to escape (CC).

JAMES Employee of Global Chemicals at the Llanfairfach Refinery. He was controlled by BOSS's mental programming, but Mike Yates freed him with the Blue Crystal. He was later killed by BOSS (TTT).

JAMES Servant at Cranleigh Hall murdered by George Cranleigh in a fit of insanity (6A).

JAMESON, ROBERT See JAMESON, DONALD.

JAMESON, DONALD In 1870 he and his elder brother, Robert, went on Tulloch Moor cutting peat; Donald was driven mad by Zygons, and Robert was killed (4F).

JAMIE See McCRIMMON, JAMIE.

JANE'S BOOK OF SPACECRAFTS Reference work quoted by the Fourth Doctor (5J).

JANET Stewardess aboard the *Hyperion III*. She helped the Sixth Doctor and Mel avert a hijacking and defeat the Vervoids (7C).

JANIS THORN Poisonous thorn found on the Sevateem planet and used as a weapon by Leela. It induced paralysis and death (4Q).

201

JANLEY One of Lesterson's assistants on Vulcan. She was one of Bragen's rebels and died saving Valmar from the Daleks' death ray (EE).

JANO Leader of the Council of the Elders. After absorbing the First Doctor's life essence, he made peace with the Savages, and ultimately convinced the Elders to put an end to their cruel way of life (AA).

JANOS One of Denes's guards (PP).

JARL Mondasian Cyberman working under Krang. He invaded the South Pole Space Tracking Station and tried to destroy Earth with the Z-Bomb (DD).

JASKO Member of the group of Shobogans who captured Leela and Rodan. He helped them and the Fourth Doctor repel the Sontarans' Invasion of Gallifrey. He was killed by a Sontaran (4Z).

JASONITE Mineral with electromagnetic boostering properties found on Crinoth. It was used by Sezom to boost the power of his staff to attack the Nimon (5L).

JAVA See PRITCHARD, GWENDOLINE.

JAY Perivale resident (7P).

JEAN Frenchman working with James Stirling to help prisoners escape the guillotine (H).

JEAN She and Phyllis were two East End refugees staying with Miss Hardaker in Northumberland during World War II. They were turned into Haemovores. After helping secure Fenric's release, they were killed by the Ancient Haemovore (7M).

JEAN-PIERRE Young French boy who told the First Doctor and his companions they were in 19th-century France and not 20th-century England (H).

JEK, SHARAZ Once the partner of Morgus, whose Sirius Conglomerate provided the financial backing for the exploitation of spectrox, Jek, a master roboticist, built the androids necessary to handle the poisonous substance. Morgus arranged for him to be caught in one of Androzani Minor's deadly mud bursts. Jek survived by locking himself inside a baking chamber, where he was horribly disfigured. Seeking revenge against Morgus, Jek seized control of the caves of Androzani Minor, and thus controlled all the spectrox supplies. Jek rescued the Fifth Doctor and Peri from General Chellak, and fell in love with Peri. He was shot by Stotz just as he killed Morgus (6R).

JELLICOE Think Tank public relations officer. He and Miss Winters were also in charge of the Scientific Reform Society. Jellicoe was arrested by Harry Sullivan (4A).

JENKINS One of Devil's End villagers (JJJ).

JENKINS One of the crew on the Eternals' ships (6H).

JENKINS, STEVEN Immigration officer at Gatwick Airport. His identity was taken over by the Chameleons. His alien double was killed when Gordon pulled the black armband off the original's arm (KK).

JENNY Cynical young woman who was part of Dortmun's resistance against the Daleks during their AD 2164 Invasion of Earth. She helped the First Doctor defeat the Daleks (K).

JENSEN One of Frontios's colonists (6N).

JENSEN, RACHEL (PROFESSOR) British scientist. She and Allison Williams assisted Group Captain Gilmore and helped the Seventh Doctor fight the Daleks who invaded the Coal Hill area in 1963 (7H).

JEREMY Member of Professor Jones's commune (TTT).

JESSIE Member of Professor Jones's commune (TTT).

JETHRIK Rare mineral, a vital component of space warp drives. Galactic con artists Garron and Unstoffe plotted to use a lump of jethrik to con the Graff Vynda-K into buying Ribos; that lump turned out to be a segment of the Key to Time. The Fourth Doctor outwitted Garron and palmed the lump of jethrik before leaving Ribos (5A).

JHANA BOX Device used by the Kinda to facilitate the mental merging between the members of the Earth Expedition Force and themselves. It looked like an ordinary Jack-in-the-Box. The Fifth Doctor used it to cure Hindle and Sanders (5Y).

JIMMY Reporter sent to Ashbridge Cottage Hospital (AAA).

JO See GRANT, JOSEPHINE.

JOANNA Former Queen of Sicily and King Richard's sister. Richard wanted to arrange a marriage between her and Saphadin to seal peace in Palestine, but she obstinately refused (P).

JOBEL Vain supervisor of the Tranquil Repose mortuary. He tried to thwart the Sixth Doctor's investigations, but failed. Davros arranged for him to be killed by Tasambeker, whom he had spurned and humiliated (6Z).

JODRELL BANK Observatory whose radioscopes were used to fight the Daleks (7H).

JOEY THE CLOWN One of the deadly pawns used by the Toymaker when he challenged the First Doctor, Steven and Dodo (Y).

JOHN (LACKLAND) King of England from 1199 to 1216. He lost almost all of England's French territories in a war with French King Philip II. In 1215, he was forced to sign the Magna Carta after a revolt of the barons. The Master used Kamelion to impersonate him to try to prevent the signing, but was thwarted by the Fifth Doctor (6J).

JOHN Mineralogist aboard Captain Maitland's ship in orbit around the Sense-Sphere. The ship was held captive by the Sensorites. Thanks to the First Doctor's intervention, he was eventually allowed to return to Earth, after he promised to protect the secret of the Sensorites' existence (G).

JOHN British squire. He, his daughter Elizabeth and his son Charles were killed by the Terileptils (5X).

JOHN Owner of a tea stall in 1963 London. He had a philosophical discussion with the Seventh Doctor about destiny and sugar (7H).

JOHN SMITH AND THE COMMON MEN Pop band Susan loved. John Smith's real name was Aubrey Waites (A).

JOHNSON One of Reegan's henchmen (CCC).

JOHNSON Crew member on Ridgway's submarine (LLL).

JOHNSON Warder in Stangmoor Prison's Special Wing. He was in charge of the death row inmates (FFF).

JOHNSTON British soldier who fought the Sea Devils (LLL).

JOKER One of the deadly pawns used by the Toymaker when he challenged the First Doctor, Steven and Dodo (Y).

JONDAR Varosian rebel, rescued from the Punishment Dome by the Sixth Doctor. He and Aleta helped the Time Lord defeat the evil schemes of Sil and the Chief Officer (6V).

JONES One of the inhabitants of Devil's End under the Master's control (JJJ).

JONES, CLIFFORD (PROFESSOR) Nobel Prize winner for his study of DNA synthesis. With his prize money, he established the commune of Nuthutch in Llanfairfach, Wales. He was the first to warn the inhabitants of Llanfairfach about the dangers of the pollution caused by Global Chemicals. He helped the Third Doctor and UNIT fight BOSS and the Green Death. The giant maggots were killed by a fungus which he discovered. He eventually married Jo Grant (TTT); the two then went on an expedition to the Amazon to research a new fungus (ZZZ).

JONES, GORDON Physics lecturer at Churchill College, Cambridge; he may have been involved with International Electromatics (VV).

JONES, MEGAN London board member of the Euro-Sea Gas Corporation. She was Robson's friend, and helped the Second Doctor destroy the Weed (RR).

JOS Member of Rorvik's crew. He died in the destruction of the privateer's ship (5S).

JOSH (aka OLD JOSH or PIGBIN JOSH) Tramp who was captured, analyzed, then killed by Axos (GGG).

JOSH One of the Rani's assistants in 19th-century England. The Rani killed him when she no longer needed him (6X).

JOURNEY OF LIFE See GREAT JOURNEY OF LIFE.

JOVANKA, TEGAN Companion of the Fourth and Fifth Doctors, an Australian air hostess who met the Fourth Doctor and Adric soon after the Master had killed her aunt Vanessa. She travelled with him to Logopolis and helped him defeat the Master. She watched the Fourth Doctor regenerate, and fought the Master again on Castrovalva. Afterwards, she helped the Fifth Doctor against Monarch, the Mara (which possessed her), the Terileptils, George Cranleigh, the Cybermen and the Master yet again (disguised as Kalid). She was accidentally left behind when the TARDIS dematerialized in Heathrow, but rejoined the Fifth Doctor and Nyssa in Amsterdam, where she helped them free her cousin Colin and defeat Omega. She then again fell under the Mara's control. Soon afterwards, she met the Brigadier and Turlough (whom she mistrusted) as the Fifth Doctor fought Mawdryn. She aided him in his battles against Terminus, Inc., the Eternals, the Master (disguised as Sir Gilles Estram) and Borusa, during which she teamed up with the First Doctor and met the Second and Third Doctors. She then fought the Silurians and the Sea Devils. When the Doctor took her to visit her grandfather, Andrew Verney, in Little Hodcombe, she was chosen to become the Queen of May, a human sacrifice to the Malus. She fought the Tractators on Frontios, and finally the Daleks. Tired of all the deaths and the violence, she left the TARDIS right afterwards (5V–6P).

JUAN Spanish driver met by the Sixth Doctor (6W).

JUDSON (DR) Crippled scientist and the designer of the Ultima Machine, a 1940s computer. He was also one of the 'Wolves' of Fenric. He unwittingly helped arrange Fenric's release by feeding ancient runes to his machine. Fenric took over Dr Judson's body to challenge the Seventh Doctor at a game of chess. The real Dr Judson probably died at that moment (7M).

JUMPING JEHOSOPHAT One of the Third Doctor's favourite interjections.

JUNIPER BERRY Former member of the Psychic Circus (7J).

JUPITER Guy Crayford's spaceship was captured by the Kraals near Jupiter (4J).

JURASSIC PERIOD It was during the Jurassic period – 195 to 136 million years ago – that Eldrad's hand landed on Earth (4N). Also see ANTHROPOLOGY.

JURGENS, MARTIN See ADJUDICATOR.

JUSTICE See CRIME.

K

K1 See GIANT ROBOT.

K4067 Asteroid location of the Bi-Al Foundation (4T).

K-9 K-9 mark I was a mobile computer in the shape of a dog, designed by Professor Marius, to replace his real dog left behind on Earth. K-9 was a databank of considerable capacity. He was also equipped with a blaster for offensive and defensive actions. His blaster could kill, stun or paralyze living beings, and melt or disintegrate metal. K-9 was shown to be capable of regeneration. He could interface with the TARDIS, the Matrix and other machines.

K-9 mark I helped the Fourth Doctor and Leela against the Virus of the Purpose, which briefly infected him. When Professor Marius found out that he could not take K-9 back to Earth with him, he asked the Doctor to take him (4T). K-9 then accompanied the Doctor and Leela on their travels, and helped them fight the Sunmakers and the Oracle. After helping the Doctor free Gallifrey from the invading Vardans and Sontarans, K-9 mark I chose to remain with Leela on the planet of the Time Lords (4T–4Z).

The Fourth Doctor built a K-9 mark II, which had greater mobility and would respond to a silent dog whistle. K-9 mark II accompanied the Doctor and Romana on the Quest for the Key to Time. He fought the Graff Vynda-K, the Captain of Zanak's Polyphase Avatron, Vivien Fay's Ogri, and interfaced with the Mentalis machine, but was unable to take part in the battle on Delta Magna's moon because of its swampy terrain (5A–5F). Later, speech circuit defects (or space laryngitis) prevented K-9 from helping the Fourth Doctor and the newly regenerated Romana against the Daleks and Scaroth. But he soon joined them against Lady Adrasta, the Mandrels, the Nimon, Pangol and the Foamasi, Meglos, the Marshmen (who severely damaged it) and the Great Vampire (5J-5P). K-9 mark II was gravely disabled by the Time Winds during the Doctor's battle with

Rorvik and elected to stay in E-Space with Romana and the Tharils (5S).

The Doctor sent an already assembled K-9 mark III as a present to Sarah Jane Smith. He helped her defeat a coven of witches who worshipped the pagan goddess Hecate in Moreton Harwood (K-9). K-9 mark III tried to warn Sarah Jane of Borusa's time scoop, but was ignored (6K).

K, DAISY Lieutenant in the Happiness Patrol of Terra Alpha. She was outsmarted several times by the Seventh Doctor and Ace. After the revolution overthrew Helen A's regime, she was condemned to repaint the TARDIS in its original colour (7L).

KAFTAN Member of the Brotherhood of Logicians, Eric Klieg's companion on his expedition to the Tombs of the Cybermen on Telos. She fought the Second Doctor in order to free the Cybermen. Later, she was killed by the Cybercontroller (MM).

KAHN (DR) Dr Kyle's assistant killed by the Cyberman (6B).

KAL Caveman member of the Tribe of Gum. He was Za's rival for control of the Tribe, and kidnapped the First Doctor to gain the secret of fire. He was expelled after killing Old Mother, and was later killed by Za (A).

KALA Aydan's wife. She, Eprin and Eyesen conspired to steal and sell one of the Keys of Marinus. She was unmasked by the First Doctor (E).

KALAKIKI Planet visited by Captain Cook (7J).

KALDOR CITY Future city known to the *Sandminer*'s crew (4R).

KALEDS See DALEKS.

KALID Arab sorcerer alias used by the Master during the Jurassic period as a focus for the evil Xeraphin (6C).

KALIK Brother of Inter Minor's President Zarb, and Commissioner of the Aliens' Admission Commission. He was against his bother's liberal policies, and tried using Vorg's defective scope to discredit the President. He arranged for the Drashigs to escape, but was thwarted by the Third Doctor and Vorg. He was later killed by one of the creatures (PPP).

KALISTORAN Incarnation of the evil side of the Xeraphin (6C).

KALMAR Scientifically minded leader of the rebellion on the Great Vampire's world. He helped the Fourth Doctor and Romana destroy the Great Vampire (5P).

KAMELION Shape-changing android which the Master took with him when he escaped from Xeriphas. He was a tool, used by an earlier invader of Xeriphas. The Master used Kamelion to impersonate King John of England, but was thwarted by the Fifth Doctor who took over control of the android in a mental battle (6J). Kamelion stayed with the Doctor in the TARDIS, but the Master succeeded in reestablishing control of him and used the android to bring the Doctor to Sarn. He first assumed Professor Foster's likeness, then turned into the Master. In the end, he begged the Fifth Doctor to destroy him with the Tissue Compression Eliminator (6Q).

KANDO Dulcian student sent with Teel to check the radiation levels on the Island of Death under Balan's supervision. He was captured and put to work by the Dominators. Kando eventually helped the Second Doctor defeat the ruthless aliens (TT).

KANDOR Executive who defrauded the Company of a million talmars. He was apprehended, and survived three years in a correction centre (4W).

KANDY KITCHEN Combination of a laboratory and candy factory where Gilbert M worked and which the Kandy Man ruled (7L).

KANDY MAN, THE Helen A's ultimate enforcer on the Terra Alpha colony. He was an android created by Gilbert M from sugar materials. The Seventh Doctor immobilized him with lemonade, and he was eventually destroyed by a flow of his own boiling candy in the pipes beneath the city (7L).

KANE Megalomaniac ruler of Iceworld. He could exist only in sub-zero temperatures, and could kill a man or freeze an object with his icy touch. Kane manipulated the Seventh Doctor and Glitz into finding the Dragonfire. Kane planned to return to his home planet, Proamon, from which he had been exiled 3000 years before, with an army of mercenaries to exact his revenge.

He and his lover, Xana, had been the leaders of a deadly gang of criminals. Xana was killed while resisting arrest, and Kane had a sculptor create an ice statue of her in the Restricted Zone of Iceworld. When the Doctor revealed that Proamon's sun had gone nova 2000 years before, Kane commited suicide by exposing himself to direct sunlight (7G).

KANGS Gangs of youths who lived in Paradise Towers, and who were being secretly exterminated by the robotic Cleaners. When the Seventh Doctor met the Blue and the Red Kangs, the last of the Yellow Kangs had just been killed by the Cleaners. The Doctor convinced the Kangs to join forces with the Caretakers and the Rezzies, and help him destroy Kroagnon (7E).

KANI (MATRONA) Crozier's assistant, killed by King Yrcanos when he rescued Peri (7B).

K'ANPO RINPOCHE Abbot in charge of the Tibetan Monastery almost taken over by the Spiders of Metebelis 3. In reality, he was a Time Lord. When he reincarnated, he assumed the physical appearance of his projection, Cho-Je. He later helped the Third Doctor's regeneration (ZZZ). K'Anpo was once an old hermit, or guru, on Gallifrey, who taught the Doctor much about life, spirituality and the mind (OOO) and told him the legends of the Great Vampires (5P).

KANTRIA Tropical planet and homeworld of Major Garrant, one of the Daleks' victims (5J).

KANVAL Dorf's birthplace (7B).

KARA Head of Nekros's protein factory. She was in partnership with Davros, using the bodies at Tranquil Repose for source material. She hired Orcini to kill Davros, while secretly setting him up to die instead. She was exposed by the Sixth Doctor. When Orcini learned the truth, he killed her (6Z).

KARELA Lady Adrasta's vizier. She killed Torvin, but her dreams of power were thwarted by the Fourth Doctor (5G).

KARFEL Planet orbiting around two suns called Rearbus and Selynx. It was inhabited by the humanoid Karfelons and the savage Morlox, who lived underground. It shared an uneasy relationship with its neighbouring planet, Bandril. It was visited by both the Third and Sixth Doctors (6Y).

KARFELONS Humanoid inhabitants of Karfel. Their master, the Borad, a half-Karfelon, half-Morlox freak, secretly planned to murder all the Karfelons by causing a war with their neighbours, the Bandrils. He then planned to repopulate Karfel with creatures like himself, starting with Peri. The Sixth Doctor made peace with the Bandrils and pushed the real Borad into the Timelash (6Y).

KARI She and Olvir were space pirates who mistakenly boarded a ship enroute to Terminus. She helped the Fifth Doctor save the universe and free Terminus (6G).

KARINA Lieutenant on Sea Base Four. She was killed by Maddox (6L).

KARKUS, THE Fictional comic strip character from Zoe Heriot's time. He appeared in *The Hourly Telepress* programme. He helped the Doctor, Jamie and Zoe in the Land of Fiction (UU).

KARL Ivo and Marta's son. He unsuccessfully tried to escape the Selection and was killed by the vampires (5P).

KARL Member of De Flores's Nazi gang. He was killed by the Cybermen (7K).

KARLTON Leader of Earth's Space Special Security. He dispatched Marc Cory to Kembel. Later, he turned out to be a traitor in league with Mavic Chen. He ordered Sara Kingdom to kill her brother and fellow agent, Bret Vyon. He failed to stop the First Doctor, and was possibly arrested after Chen's defeat (V).

KARN Bleak, stormy planet where the evil Time Lord Morbius was eventually defeated, tried and executed. It also housed the Sisterhood, guardians of the Sacred Flame (4K).

KARRA One of the Cheetah People. After Ace saved her life, she treated her as 'sister'. She rescued Ace from Midge's gang and was killed by the Master. After her death, she reverted to human form. Her body was taken back to the Cheetah Planet (7P).

KARTZ (PROFESSOR) With Reimer, Kartz was a scientist of the Third Zone. They conducted unauthorized time experiments on Space Station J7, and built an operational time cabinet which needed only to be primed with the Rassilon Imprimature to function like a true TARDIS (6K).

KARUNA Young Kinda wise-woman who inherited all of Panna's knowledge after her death. She helped the Fifth Doctor free Aris and banish the Mara (5Y).

KARZENOME Structure at the centre of which was the Animus (N).

KASSIA One of the five Consuls of Traken. She was married to Tremas and was afraid of losing him if he became the new Keeper. As a child she had been chosen to tend the Melkur, but fell under his evil influence. After the Keeper's death, the Melkur (in reality, the Master) manipulated her into fighting the Fourth Doctor, and eventually becoming the new Keeper. The Melkur then destroyed her and took her place (5T).

KASTERBOROUS Constellation where Gallifrey was located (4G).

KASTRIA Bleak, deserted world, ravaged by cosmic winds, and exposed to the cold of space. Life on its surface was possible only because of force-field barriers designed, and ultimately destroyed, by Eldrad. Kastria then returned to being a dead and desolate world (4N).

KASTRIANS Natives of Kastria. Their silicon-based forms were designed by Eldrad, who later destroyed the force-field barriers which made life on the surface of the planet possible. King Rokon and the Kastrians condemned Eldrad to death, then chose to die after destroying their Race Banks rather than, one day, being forced to submit to Eldrad's rule in the event of his return. The Kastrians had the power to regenerate and physically control various forms of energy (4N).

KATAKIKI Planet visited by Captain Cook (7J).

KATARINA Young Trojan woman who rescued Steven Taylor during the fall of Troy. She took him back to the TARDIS, thus becoming one of the First Doctor's companions. Katarina sacrificed her life by ejecting herself and Kirksen into space so that the First Doctor and Bret Vyon could reach Earth and alert it to the Daleks' Masterplan (U–V).

KATE See ELDER, KATE.

KATRYCA Leader of the Tribe of the Free on Ravolox. She sentenced Glitz and the Sixth Doctor to death. Later, she led an assault against the UK Habitat, but was killed by Drathro (7A).

KATURA One of the five Consuls of Traken. He was overly concerned with propriety, and would even have accepted the Melkur as new Keeper of Traken (5T).

KATZ Sezon's second-in-command in the rebellion against the Borad on Karfel. She was the daughter of Makrif. She helped the Sixth Doctor defeat the Borad (6Y).

KAUFMAN Quartermaster-sergeant in the British army squadron sent to fight the Daleks in the Coal Hill area in 1963 (7H).

KAVELL One of Davros's Kaled scientists, and later Gharman's co-conspirator. He was killed by the Daleks (4E).

KEARA See LOGIN, KEARA.

KEAVER Member of Lupton's psychic circle at K'anpo's Tibetan Monastery. His mind was taken over by the Spiders, but he was freed when the Great One died (ZZZ).

KEBBLE One of the Vulcan colonists (EE).

KEDU Tibetan encountered by the Second Doctor (NN).

KEEFAN Ore processed aboard the *Sandminer* (4R).

KEEKS Type of Megropolis Three residents on Pluto (4W).

KEELER, ARNOLD (DR) Harrison Chase's botanical adviser. In spite of the Fourth Doctor's efforts, he and Scorbie stole a Krynoid pod from the Antarctica World Ecology Bureau Expedition camp and brought it back to England. The pod eventually took over Keeler's body and grew to monstrous size. His consciousness died when the Krynoid was destroyed by the Royal Air Force (4L).

KEEPER OF THE MATRIX (aka COORDINATOR) Title given to the Time Lord in charge of the Matrix. Engin was coordinator when the Master and Goth threatened Gallifrey (4P). The body of another Keeper of the Matrix (name unknown) was eventually taken over by the Valeyard after his battle with the Sixth Doctor inside the Matrix (7C).

KEEPER OF TRAKEN Individual who controlled the Source which kept the Union of Traken in a state of harmony. Because of the channelling of such considerable energy through his person, the Keeper held great powers, including teleportation and energy manipulation. When the Fourth Doctor met him, he was almost a thousand years old, and nearing the time of his Dissolution. The Keeper asked the Doctor to come to Traken, fearing the Melkur's evil influence. After he died, Tremas was meant to become the new Keeper but, thanks to the Melkur's schemes, Kassia was made Keeper instead. Then, the Melkur (in reality, the Master) killed Kassia and took over the Keepership. The Doctor, Adric and Nyssa tampered with the Source in order to expose the Master. Afraid of destruction, the Master fled. Luvic became the new Keeper (5T), (5V).

KEIGHTLEY, CLARE Young Cambridge student, and Chris Parsons's friend. Salyavin temporarily took over her mind to help repair his TARDIS and fight Skagra (5M).

KEILLOR Galactic bounty hunter who was aboard the tour bus which crashlanded in 1959 Wales. He told the Bannermen where Delta was, then tried to kill the Seventh Doctor, but was killed when Gavrok blew up his transmitter by remote control (7F).

KELIA One of the Sisterhood killed by the Morbius Monster (4K).

KELLER, EMIL (PROFESSOR) Alias used by the Master when he posed as the Swiss inventor of a machine which would remove evil impulses from hardened criminals (FFF).

KELLER MACHINE Device intended to isolate and extract a man's evil impulses. It was being tested at Stangmoor Prison when it came to the Third Doctor's attention. In reality, it housed a Mind Parasite brought to Earth by the Master, who planned to use it to sabotage a World Peace Conference. It was destroyed when the Thunderbolt Missile was detonated (FFF).

KELLMAN (PROFESSOR) Scientist aboard Space Beacon Nerva. Seduced by the Vogans' gold, he was hired by Vorus to summon a small band of isolated Cybermen, remnants of the First Cyber Wars, to Voga, where they could be destroyed by his Skystriker missile. Under instructions from the Cybermen, Kellman used the Cybermats to infect the beacon with the Neurotropic X virus. He was eventually killed in a rockslide on Voga (4D).

KELLY, GIA Scientist and senior supervisor of the T-Mat system. She discovered that the Moon controls were no longer operational and alerted her superior, Commander Radnor. She helped the Second Doctor defeat the Ice Warriors when they tried using T-Mat to spread their deadly Seeds of Death on Earth (XX).

KELNER Cowardly Gallifreyan Castellan who betrayed the Time Lords by cooperating first with the Vardans, then with the Sontarans. After the Fourth Doctor defeated the invaders, he was presumably demoted and punished by Borusa (4Z).

KEMBEL (aka KEMBAL) Planet used by the Daleks as their headquarters in their Masterplan against Earth. Its Varga plants (originally from Skaro) made it very hostile. Marc Cory died on Kembel. All life on the planet was eventually destroyed by the Time Destructor (T/A, V).

KEMEL Mute Turkish strongman in Theodore Maxtible's employ. After Jamie saved his life, he joined the Second Doctor in his fight against the Daleks. He eventually fell to his death on Skaro, fighting Theodore Maxtible (LL).

KEMP Lieutenant serving under Captain Gardiner (QQQ).

KENDRON Weak-willed member of the Karfelon Inner Sanctum. He was accused of treachery by Tekker and killed by the Borad (6Y).

KENNEDY Sir Charles Summers's chauffeur (BB).

KENNEDY A burglar who tried breaking into Edward Waterfield's safe, but was killed by the Daleks (LL).

KENOWA Australian location of Salamander's Sun Conservation Centre and secret underground Sanctum (PP).

KENT, GILES Former Deputy Security Com-missioner for Europe and North Africa. He was dismissed at Salamander's instigation. He fought Salamander, but in reality intended to assassinate him and take his place. He was exposed by the Second Doctor and died in Salamander's Sanctum, in an explosion of his own making (PP).

KERENSKY, THEODORE NICOLAI (PROFESSOR) Misguided scientist who was hired by Scaroth (as Count Scarlioni) to build a time machine which, he thought, could be used to cure famine. Eventually, Kerensky succeeded, but rebelled when he found out the true nature of Scaroth's plans. Scaroth trapped him in the time machine and accelerated Kerensky's time cycle until he aged and died (5H).

KERNIGHAN Frontios Orderly (6N).

KERRIL Crew member of the *Sandminer*. He was killed by the Robots of Death (4R).

KETTERING (PROFESSOR) Scientist in charge of the Keller machine at Stangmoor Prison. He refused to heed the Third Doctor's warnings, and was killed by the Mind Parasite (FFF).

KETTLEWELL, JEREMIAH P. (PROFESSOR) Idealistic, ageing scientist interested in alternative technologies. He wanted to stop pollution, and was the creator of the giant robot K-1. When Kettlewell discovered that Miss Winters intended to carry out her threats, he rebelled and was inadvertently killed by his robot. K-1 went mad and was later destroyed by the Fourth Doctor (4A).

KEWPER, JACOB Innkeeper in the 17th-century Cornish village where the First Doctor fought Captain Pike's pirates. He was, in reality, one of the Squire's smugglers, and was later shot by Cherub (CC).

KEY OF RASSILON Not to be confused with the Great Key, which was a rod, also known as the Rod of Rassilon (4P, 4Z). The Key of Rassilon looked like an ordinary key and was secretly entrusted to the Cardinal of the High Council. It served to tap the Eye of Harmony to power the Demat Gun. Borusa entrusted it to the Fourth Doctor to defeat the Sontarans when they invaded Gallifrey, but took it back afterwards (4Z). The Keeper of the Matrix claimed no one could enter it without the Key of Rassilon, which he kept (7C). This key was presumably a more vulgar object, created to divert attention from the real Key.

KEY TO TIME Immensely powerful, mythic artefact with which the Guardians of Time maintained the universal balance between order and chaos. It was shaped in the form of a perfect, crystalline cube. When the balance was upset, the White Guardian enlisted the help of the Fourth Doctor and Romana to gather the Key's six segments, which were disguised as follows: a lump of jethrik, taken to Ribos by Garron (5A); planet Calufrax, shrunk to football size by the pirate planet Zanak (5B); the former Great Seal of Diplos, kept in the form of a necklace on Earth (5C); a Taran statue (5D); a holy relic of the Swampies swallowed by Kroll on Delta Magna's moon (5E); and finally Princess Astra of Atrios (5F). The Black Guardian used the Shadow to stop the Fourth Doctor from claiming the sixth segment. After the Doctor defeated the Shadow, he assembled the Key and outwitted the Black Guardian, enabling the White Guardian to restore the universal balance. The Key to Time was then broken apart and scattered throughout the Universe again, presumably assuming five new shapes, and restoring Princess Astra to her human form (5F).

KEYS OF MARINUS Five microcircuits which controlled the Conscience of Marinus. Arbitan kept one Key and sent the First Doctor and his companions to gather the other four: one was kept in Morphoton, one in the jungle, one in the ice wilderness, and the last was in the city of Millenius (E).

KHEPREN Commander of a small elite army of Egyptian soldiers at the time of the completion of the Great Pyramid of Cheops (circa 2600 BC). He met the First Doctor during his fight against the Daleks' Masterplan, and was killed by the Daleks (V).

KHRISONG Leader of the warrior monks of Det-Sen monastery. He fought the Great Intelligence's robot Yeti and was killed by Songsten, himself under the Intelligence's control (NN).

KILBRACKEN Inventor of the technique of rapid holographic cloning which the Fourth Doctor used to track down the Nucleus (4T).

KILLINGSWORTH Colliery owned by Lord Ravensworth where George Stephenson built the Blucher, an early steam-powered locomotive, and where the Sixth Doctor fought the Master and the Rani (6X).

KILLJOY Term applied on Terra Alpha to people who were not happy. They could be arrested and executed by the Happiness Patrol (7L).

KIMBER Elderly passenger of the *Hyperion III* space liner. He recognized Hallet from a previous investigation on granary shortages on Stella Stora. He was later killed by the Vervoids (7C).

KIMUS Pralix's friend and Mula's boyfriend. He helped the Fourth Doctor and Romana defeat the Captain of Zanak (5B).

KINDA Peaceful, telepathic natives of Deva Loka who shared a gestalt-like society. Their attempts to get the members of the Earth Expedition Force to mentally merge with them unbalanced the Earthmen's minds. The Mara possessed one of them, Aris, and tried to create chaos by inciting the Kinda to attack the Earthmen's Dome. The Kinda's Jhana Box helped restore Commander Sanders's sanity. Thanks to Sanders's desire to protect the Kinda, Deva Loka was eventually reclassified as unsuitable for colonization (5Y).

KINGDOM, SARA Space Special Security agent. She followed Karlton's orders and killed her brother, Bret Vyon, whom she had been told was a traitor. After Steven Taylor and the First Doctor told her the truth, she joined them in their fight to stop the Daleks' Masterplan. Sara died on Kembel when the Time Destructor was activated (V).

KINGPIN Founder of the Psychic Circus. His brain was damaged by the Gods of Ragnarok, and he became a menial labourer known as Deadbeat. He was rescued by the Seventh Doctor. He and Ace found the Gods' medallion, which restored his sanity. After the Gods' defeat, he planned to launch a new circus with Mags (7J).

KIRKSEN One of the criminals of Desperus. He tried to force the First Doctor to return to Kembel by holding Katarina hostage in the *Spar 7-40's* airlock, but she foiled his plan by ejecting them both into space (V).

KISTON One of Lytton's engineers. His mind was taken over by Davros, and he was eventually killed by the Daleks (6P).

KITLINGS A race of creatures virtually identical to Earth cats, but bred by the original Cheetah People. The Kitlings had the power to teleport through space and generate a symbiotic mindlink with their owners, thus enabling them to see and hear through their senses. They fed on carrion left by their hunting masters (7P).

KITTY Manageress of the Inferno discotheque (BB).

KIV Reptilian leader of the Mentors of Thoros-Beta. He had his brain expanded by Crozier's brain transformer. He would have died if Crozier had not found a way to transplant his mind into another being, who turned out to be Peri. Peri was saved by King Yrcanos of Krontep, who killed Crozier, Kiv and Sil before the mind transfer took place (7B).

KLIEG, ERIC Megalomaniacal president of the Brotherhood of Logicians, and financial backer of Professor Parry's expedition to Telos. With Kaftan's help, he fought the Second Doctor to resurrect the Cybermen. He planned to form an alliance with them, but was eventually betrayed and killed by the Cybermen (MM).

KLIMT One of the Underworld's guards. He was killed by Herrick (4Y).

KLOUT Brock's lawyer, in reality a West Lodge Foamasi saboteur. He was exposed by a Foamasi Investigator. He and Brock later escaped, but their ship was blown up by the Argolins (5N).

KNIGHT Captain in the army task force which fought the Great Intelligence in the London underground. He was killed by a Yeti (QQ).

KNIGHT COMMANDER The leader of Morgaine's men. He died during the battle at Carbury (7N).

KNIGHTS The First Doctor saved the life of King Richard during the Third Crusade (P). The Master used the Kronos Crystal to scoop a medieval knight out of time and use him against Mike Yates (OOO). Linx built a robot knight for Irongron (UUU). The TARDIS rematerialized during a joust in AD 1215 Britain (6J). The parallel Earth from which Morgaine, Mordred and Ancelin came was a medieval world where knights still ruled (7N).

KNOPF, INGMAR Danish-born Hollywood film director (V).

KOLKOKRON Deserted rocky planet where the Fifth Doctor dropped the Gravis (6N).

KONTRON CRYSTAL Crystals found in certain areas of the space-time vortex which contained energies capable of harnessing space and time. The Borad used Kontron crystals to dabble in time research designing a time-acceleration beam and a time tunnel called Timelash. The Sixth Doctor used them to manufacture short, portable time loops, and bounce back the Borad's time-acceleration beam (6Y). The Kronos Crystal might have been a Kontron Crystal (OOO). Kontron Crystals may be made of taranium (V).

KOQUILLION Fake identity created by Bennett, using an imposing, Didonian sand-beast-like spiked suit. As Koquillion, Bennett was armed with a jewelled club that emitted a blasting ray. He was exposed by the First Doctor (L).

KOSNAX Planet at war with Vardon. Their crossfire accidentally destroyed Xeriphas (6C).

KRAALS Inhabitants of Oseidon, a planet which they had ruined through internecine atomic wars. The Kraals relied heavily on android technology. They planned to abandon their increasingly radioactive world and conquer other planets. Their chief scientist, Styggron, used astronaut Guy Crayford and human android duplicates to take over the Devesham Space Research Station. He then planned to exterminate mankind with a special virus. His efforts were thwarted by the Fourth Doctor (4J).

KRACAUER Sergeant in Kane's forces on Iceworld. Belasz enlisted his help in a conspiracy to kill Kane. He failed and Kane killed him (7G).

KRAIL Mondasian Cyberleader of the first team of Cybermen to invade the Snowcap Space Tracking Station. He and his team were destroyed by Ben (DD).

KRANG Mondasian Cyberleader who took over from Krail at the Snowcap Space Tracking Station. He killed General Cutler and planned to destroy Earth with the Z-Bomb, but was stopped by the First Doctor (DD).

KRANS One of the five Galsec Seven colonists stranded on Earth circa AD 15,000 after their ship was destroyed when they answered a fake Mayday signal. The Sontaran Styre performed cruel experiments on him to determine the limits of human resistance. He was saved by the Fourth Doctor (4B).

KRARGS Crystalline life forms who served Skagra. They were manufactured in generation chambers, by condensing crystals around a predesigned skeleton in a special gaseous atmosphere. Romana used the same gas to dissolve the Krargs (5M).

KRASIS High Priest of Poseidon in Atlantis. He fell under the Master's control and helped him overthrow King Dalios. He died when, in spite of the Third Doctor's warnings, the Master used the Kronos Crystal to summon the Kronavore, who destroyed Atlantis (OOO).

KRAU Androzani equivalent of Ms (6R).

KRAVOS One of Davros's scientists. He was killed by the Daleks (4E).

KRELPER Stotz's whiny second in command. He was killed by Stotz when he tried to defect (6R).

KRIMPTON (PROFESSOR) Professor Brett's assistant on the WOTAN project. He was hypnotized by WOTAN, and died trying to save the computer (BB).

KRISTAS Thal from Skaro, and Ganatus's friend (B).

KRIZ Insectoid alien who crashed on Karn and was killed by Condo (4K).

KRO One of the Graff Vynda-K's men. He was stunned by K-9. The Fourth Doctor used his uniform to trick the Graff (5A).

KROAGNON Great Architect of the Paradise Towers. His previous designs includes Golden Dream Park, the Bridge of Perpetual Motion, and Miracle City, a forerunner of the Paradise Towers. His brain was secretly buried in the Towers basement after he tried to prevent people from living in his creation. Under Kroagnon's influence, the robotic Cleaners began to exterminate all human life inside the Towers. Then Kroagnon took over the Chief Caretaker's body. With the help of Pex and the Kangs, the Seventh Doctor managed to expose and destroy Kroagnon (7E).

KROLL Name given by the Swampies of Delta Magna's third

moon to their god. Kroll was a gigantic squidlike monster made up of many, smaller squid. It had reached its gigantic size because it had once swallowed the Swampies' holy relic, in reality the fifth segment of the Key to Time. When the Fourth Doctor and Romana recovered the segment, Kroll was broken aparts into hundreds of little squid (5E).

KRONAVORES (aka KRONOVORES) Time-eaters, mysterious creatures living inside the time vortex and feeding on the very substance of time. Kronos was a kronavore (OOO).

KRONOS Possibly the most powerful of the kronavores. His name gave rise to the legend of the Greek Titan who ate his children, one of whom was Poseidon, god of Atlantis. Kronos was drawn from the time vortex by the priests of Atlantis, who imprisoned his essence in the Kronos Crystal. The Master eventually released Kronos, and tried to control him, but failed, and the Kronavore destroyed Atlantis. The Third Doctor engineered a Time Ram between his TARDIS and the Master's, which released Kronos and destroyed the Crystal (OOO).

KRONOS CRYSTAL Giant crystal which existed transdimensionally both in the time vortex and in our space-time continuum. It was almost indestructible. The ancient Atlantean priests used it to draw Kronos from the time vortex and imprison its essence. King Dalios came to realize that the short-term benefits that the use of the Kronos Crystal brought Atlantis would spell long-term doom, and forbade its use. The Crystal was guarded by the Minotaur. When King Dalios tried to have it destroyed, he only succeeded in splitting it into a smaller version, which survived throughout the 20th century, where it was found by the Master and used in connection with TOM-TIT to summon Kronos. It took a Time Ram between the Doctor's and the Master's TARDISes eventually to destroy the Crystal and release Kronos (OOO). The Kronos Crystal may have been a Kontron Crystal (6Y), made of taranium (V). The Daemons may have been the ones who gave it to the ancient Atlanteans (JJJ).

KRONTEP Name of King Yrcanos's home world. The Mentors were selling laser weapons to Krontep and Thordon, and kept Yrcanos prisoner on Thoros-Beta to induce him to cooperate. After his victory over the Mentors, Yrcanos presumably returned to Krontep with Peri as his queen (7B).

KROTONS Crystalline beings made of tellurium. Four Krotons who had been involved in an interplanetary war were shot down on the planet of the Gonds. Exhausted by the drain on their mental energies, two died. The two which survived enslaved the Gonds and went into a form of suspended animation. Every month, the two most intelligent Gonds were selected to become the Krotons' 'companions'. In reality, the Krotons used their Dynatrope to drain their mental energy to recharge themselves. The Second Doctor eventually used sulphuric acid to dissolve the Krotons and free the Gonds (WW).

KRYNOIDS Hostile, vegetal life forms which preyed on animals. Around 20,000 BC, two Krynoid pods landed in the Antarctic and buried themselves into the permafrost. They were eventually dug up in 1977 by a World Ecology Bureau expediton. One Krynoid took control of Winlett's body, but was later destroyed when Scorby blew up the camp. The other pod was stolen by Harrison Chase. It took control of Keeler's body and Chase's mind, and grew to monstrous size. It began to turn plants against mankind, but was blown up by the Royal Air Force before it could germinate. In both cases, the Fourth Doctor's intervention helped bring about the Krynoids' end (4L).

K'TO See ICTHAR.

KUBLAI KHAN Mongolian general and statesman, grandson of Genghis Khan who lived between 1215 and 1294. He was Marco Polo's friend and met the First Doctor, from whom he won the TARDIS in a game of backgammon. Later, the Doctor saved him from Tegana's assassination attempt (D).

KUI-JU Chinese official working under Wang-Lo. He was bribed by Tegana (D).

KURKUTJI Australian Aborigine kidnapped by the Urbankans, probably circa 3019 BC. His memories were stored on silicon chips, and used to animate an android in his image. After the Fifth Doctor defeated Monarch, he and his fellow androids decided to look for another planet on which to settle (5W).

KURSTER Count Grendel's henchman. He was knocked unconscious by Romana and Princess Strella (5D).

KY Young Solonian leader who distrusted Varan and the Earth

Empire. He was framed by the Marshal for the murder of the Earth Administrator, and fled back to Solos. The Third Doctor helped him complete his mutation and turn into a super-being. Ky then killed the Marshal, freed his friends and helped his people reach their final state (NNN).

KYLE (PROFESSOR) 26th-century paleontologist. Under the protection of Lieutenant Scott and his men, she was intent on exploring a network of underground caves where eight other scientists had been killed by Cybermen androids protecting a hidden Cyberbomb. She helped the Fifth Doctor disarm the bomb, then travelled aboard the TARDIS to Captain Briggs's space freighter, where she was killed by a Cyberman (6B).

KYLE British police sergeant who interrogated the Fourth Doctor and Leela after they had been attacked by members of the Tong of the Black Scorpion (4S).

L

L-3 Drathro was an Andromedan L-3 robot (7A).

L, SUSAN See Q, SUSAN.

LABOUR CONTROLLER Atlantean officer who assigned people to work in the mines (GG).

LAIRD (PROFESSOR) Scientist sent with Colonel Archer's men to investigate mysterious happenings (in reality, the end of a Dalek time corridor) in the London warehouse district. She was killed by the Dalek-duplicate, Archer (6P).

LAKE OF MUTATIONS Horror-filled swamp on Skaro, which claimed the lives of Antodus and Elyon (B).

LAKE OF OBLIVION One of the landmarks of Iceworld's underworld (7G).

LAKERTYA Peaceful planet which the Rani took over when she detected an asteroid made up of Strange Matter in its orbit. She planned to blow up the asteroid with a Loyhargil rocket. Successful completion of her plan would have completely destroyed Lakertya, but she was thwarted by the Seventh Doctor (7D).

LAKERTYANS Golden-skinned natives of Lakertya. They had evolved from reptiles and were committed to a peaceful, indolent life. The Rani took control of them, and they were rescued by the Seventh Doctor and Ikona (7D).

LAKH He and Ankh, Minyans whose heads had been replaced by machines, were the two Seers who ruled the Underworld directly beneath the Oracle. They fought the Fourth Doctor and Jackson's Minyans, and died in the destruction of the Underworld caused by two fission grenades disguised as the Race Banks, which the Oracle had intended to use to destroy Jackson's ship (4Y).

LAKIS Queen Galleia's slave girl. She perished when Kronos destroyed Atlantis (OOO).

LALEHAM, ELTON A member of the staff of the Wheel in Space. His mind was taken over by the Cybermen. He was eventually killed (SS).

LAMERDINES Remarkably gifted race, pioneers of steady-state micro welding. According to the Third Doctor, they had nine opposable digits (EEE).

LAMIA (MADAME) Count Grendel's surgeon-engineer and master android-maker. She was secretly in love with Grendel, who used her only to further his ambitions. She was accidentally killed by one of Grendel's men (5D).

LAMONT (SISTER) Tulloch nurse who took care of Harry Sullivan after he was shot by the Caber. She was impersonated by the Zygon Odda (4F).

LAN One of the Movellans serving under Commander Sharrel on Skaro. He was disarmed and reprogrammed by Tyssan (5J).

LANCELOT Medieval knight of the Round Table. The Second Doctor, Jamie and Zoe encountered his fictional counterpart in the Land of Fiction (UU).

LAND Member of Lupton's psychic circle at K'anpo's Tibetan Monastery. His mind was taken over by the Spiders, but he was freed when the Great One died (ZZZ).

LAND OF FICTION Nickname given to a mysterious pocket universe where creations of the human mind could be materialized and given a semblance of life. The Land of Fiction was ruled by the Master Brain, who used a human pawn, the Master, to fill its world with a variety of fictional characters. The Land of Fiction disappeared when the Master Brain was destroyed by Zoe (UU).

LANE Corporal in the army task force which fought the Great Intelligence in the London underground. He was killed by the Yeti's web (QQ).

LANE Member of Rorvik's crew. He died in the destruction of the privateer's ship (5S).

LANG, HUGO Intergalactic Pursuit Squadron Lieutenant who was assigned the job of going after Romulus and Remus Sylvest's kidnappers. He crashed on Titan Three and was rescued by the newly regenerated Sixth Doctor. Lang travelled with the Time Lord in the TARDIS to Jaconda, where he helped defeat Mestor. Stranded on Jaconda, he decided to remain there and help the natives rebuild their world (6S).

LANGUAGES The Doctor and his companions always seem to be able to speak the local languages of the places they visit. The Fourth Doctor told Sarah that it was a Time Lord 'gift' (4M). This talent was undoubtedly the result of the Time Lords' telepathic abilities, possibly aided by the TARDIS.

LANISHA Young Lakertyan, Ikona's brother. He chose to follow Beyus's orders rather than rebel against the Rani. He was killed by the Rani's deadly insects (7D).

LARN Officer of the Court of Millenius (E).

LARVAE GUNS Weapon used on Vortis (N).

LASER The Wheel in Space had an X-ray laser cannon (SS).

LASERSON PROBE Device used by Dask to reprogram the Robots of Death (4R).

LASKY, SARAH (PROFESSOR) Thremmatologist (science dealing with the the breeding and propagating of animals and plants for domestication) who embarked on the *Hyperion III* space liner with her two assistants, Bruchner and Doland. She was primarily responsible for the creation of the Vervoids, but had never meant for them to become hostile life forms. She helped the Sixth Doctor save the ship from Rudge's hijack attempt. Later, she was killed by the Vervoids (7C).

LAST CHANCE SALOON Tombstone saloon (Z).

LATEP One of the Thals sent to Spiridon to stop the Daleks. He helped the Third Doctor defeat the Daleks. He was attracted to Jo Grant (SSS).

LATIMER One of the individuals working at the Inferno Project site (DDD).

LATONI, DITTAR Chief of the Utobi Indians who once saved George Cranleigh from the Butiu. He accompanied him to England, and secretly lived with him at Cranleigh Hall (6A).

LAVEL, FRANCOISE UNIT pilot lieutenant. She flew Lethbridge-Stewart's helicopter to Carbury. Morgaine caused her helicopter to crash. She later stole Lavel's memories, then killed her (7N).

LAVINIA See SMITH, LAVINIA.

LAW See CRIME.

LAWRENCE, CHARLES (DR) Director of the Wenley Moor atomic research station, which was attacked by the Silurians. His sole, overriding concern was to preserve his position. He was no help to the Third Doctor, and was eventually killed by the Silurian virus spread by Major Baker (BBB).

LAZAR DISEASE Reputedly incurable space disease. Terminus, Inc. exiled its victims to Terminus, and kept them under its control with hydromel. Nyssa planned to synthesize hydromel, thereby freeing the men from Terminus, Inc.'s grip (6G).

LAZARS Name given to those afflicted with lazar disease. The company Terminus, Inc. promised them a cure, but instead shipped them to Terminus, where they were herded into the Forbidden Zone by the Vanir. There, some of them were cured by the Garm, then shipped back to civilization (6G).

LAZLO Time-sensitive Tharil who was selected by Aldo and Royce to replace Biroc. He later escaped into E-Space with Romana, and eventually led his fellow Tharils to freedom (5S).

LEAD Metal used by the Fourth Doctor as a shield to block the Vardans' powers (4Z).

LEAMINGTON-SMYTHE Archaeologist mentioned by Professor Rumford (5C).

LEE Chinese member of the Tong of the Black Scorpion who replaced Li H'Sen Chang as Greel's main servant. Greel forced him to commit suicide as a penalty for failure (4S).

LEELA One of the Fourth Doctor's companions. She was a member of the Sevateem tribe who refused to believe Xoanon was a god. She helped the Fourth Doctor fight the Tesh and cure Xoanon. She then accompanied him in the TARDIS. She helped him fight the Robots of Death; Magnus Greel; a Rutan on the island of Fang Rock; the Nucleus of the Virus of the Purpose (when she first met K-9 mark I) and to which she was naturally immune; the Fendahl; the Usurians; the Oracle; and finally the Vardans and the Sontarans on Gallifrey. There, she fell in love with Commander Andred of the Chancellery Guards. She and K-9 mark I elected to remain on Gallifrey. She had a savage but trusting nature, and her favourite weapon was the poisonous Janis thorn (4Q–4Z).

LEESON, ERIC Exarius colonist who brought the Third Doctor and Jo Grant to Ashe. He was later killed by the IMC robot, which made his death look like the result of a lizard attack (HHH).

LEESON, JANE Exarius colonist. She was killed by the IMC robot, which made it look as if she were the victim of a lizard attack (HHH).

LEETROBE A species of giant flowering lettuce unique to Chloris (5G).

LEFAUVRE, BLOSSOM Hollywood actress (V).

LEFEE, JOE British astronaut on board the Mars Probe 7 ship who was captured by mysterious, radioactive aliens. He was eventually returned to Earth thanks to the Third Doctor's intervention (CCC).

LEICESTER The Earl of Leicester was a warlike Crusader deeply opposed to peace with the Saracens. He would have killed the First Doctor if it had not been for Ian's timely intervention (P).

LEIGH Army sergeant under Commander Millington's command in Northumberland. He was killed by the Haemovores (7M).

LEISURE HIVE Vast entertainment centre on Argolis. It contained different environments designed to produce physical and psychic regeneration. Its key attraction was the Tachyon Recreation Generator. The West Lodge Foamasi sabotaged the Leisure Hive, and impersonated Brock and Klout to try to buy it from its leader Mena. But they were exposed by the Fourth Doctor and a Foamasi investigator. The Fourth Doctor also thwarted Pangol's megalomaniacal dreams, and fixed the TRG so that the Argolins could be rejuvenated (5N).

LEMAITRE Governor of the Conciergerie. He was in reality British master spy James Stirling whose mission was to save prisoners from the guillotine. His path crossed that of the First Doctor and Ian during the French Revolution (H)

LEN A grocery-store employee in Perivale (7P).

LENNOX (DR) Renegade scientist who had been hired by Reegan to watch over the three radioactive alien ambassadors he had kidnapped. In reality, he was working for General Carrington. Filled with remorse, he turned himself in to UNIT, but was killed when Carrington arranged for radioactive isotopes to be delivered with his food (CCC).

LEONARDO See DA VINCI, LEONARDO.

LEOVONTOS Planet visited by Captain Cook (7J).

LEPTONIC ERA A period of time which took place a microsecond after the Big Bang. It produced Helium 2, which the Rani planned to use to turn her artificial Brain into a planet-sized Time Manipulator (7D).

LERNOV, TANYA Astronomer on the Wheel in Space and

Leo Ryan's girlfriend, who helped the Second Doctor defeat the Cybermen (SS). She met Zoe again after she was returned to her proper place in time and space by the Time Lords after the War Games (ZZ).

LEROY Confederate soldier who believed he was fighting in the American Civil War. In reality, he was part of the War Games (ZZ).

LESAGE, ADELAIDE Young French girl and Lord Palmerdale's confidential secretary. She was shipwrecked on Fang Rock and, in spite of the Fourth Doctor's efforts, was later killed by the Rutan (4V).

LESTER One of the officers aboard Space Beacon Nerva. He helped the Fourth Doctor fight the Cybermen (4D).

LESTERSON Chief Scientist of the Vulcan colony. He believed the Daleks he had found in a crashed ship were robots who could be repaired to help the colony. In spite of the Second Doctor's warnings, he repowered them. Later, as the Daleks tried to take over the colony, he realized his mistake and sacrificed his life so that the Doctor could deactivate the Daleks again (EE).

LETHBRIDGE-STEWART, ALISTAIR One of UNIT's 'founding members'. He conceived the idea after he fought the Yeti and the Great Intelligence in London alongside the Second Doctor. He was then a Colonel in the British army (QQ). After UNIT's formation, he was promoted to Brigadier and became one of the heads of its British branch, reporting directly to a United Nations Secretary in Geneva. He and the Second Doctor then thwarted a Cybermen invasion of England (VV).

Soon afterwards, Lethbridge-Stewart was among the first people to meet the Third Doctor, whom he made UNIT's Scientific Advisor (AAA). He was always to remain slightly disturbed by the Doctor's regenerative abilities. Together, with the help of Liz Shaw, Jo Grant, Sarah Jane Smith, Sergeant Benton and Mike Yates, they fought a number of threats as diverse as the Master (EEE, FFF, GGG, HHH, JJJ, OOO); the Nestene and their deadly Autons (AAA, EEE); the Silurians (BBB); General Carrington and his so-called 'Ambassadors of Death' (CCC); Professor Stahlman's Inferno Project (DDD) when the Doctor met the Brigadier's counterpart from a parallel fascistic Earth, Brigade-Leader Lethbridge-Stewart; the Mind of Evil (FFF);

Axos (GGG); the Daemons (JJJ); the Daleks (KKK); Kronos (OOO); Omega (RRR) when he met the First and Second Doctors; BOSS (TTT); the Sontarans (UUU); an invasion of dinosaurs masterminded by Sir Charles Grover (WWW) (when Mike Yates betrayed UNIT); and finally the Giant Spiders of Metebelis 3 (ZZZ).

It was then that the Brigadier watched the Doctor regenerate into his Fourth Incarnation, with whom he (and Harry Sullivan) fought Professor Kettlewell's Giant Robot and the Scientific Reform Society (4A), and the Zygons (4F).

Lethbridge-Stewart's job became increasingly more political, and he was in Geneva during the Kraal Invasion (4J) and the Krynoid attack (4L). Perhaps because of this, in 1977, Lethbridge-Stewart chose to retire. He then went on to teach maths at Brendon School.

In 1977, during his meeting with the Fifth Doctor, the Brigadier encountered his own self from 1983, provoking an energy discharge which released Mawdryn and his fellow aliens from their unending life. The discharge caused the Brigadier to suffer from amnesia from 1977 until 1983, when he recovered his memory (6F). Soon afterwards, he left his teaching post and married Doris, one of his former UNIT colleagues.

The day of the next annual UNIT reunion, he again met the Second Doctor, and became one of Borusa's pawns in the Game of Rassilon. Together with the Doctor's other incarnations and various Companions, he helped thwart the megalomaniacal Time Lord's plans for immortality (6K).

Lethbridge-Stewart eventually came out of retirement to fight alongside the Seventh Doctor, Ace and Brigadier Bambera, against Morgaine's forces at Carbury. During this battle, he nearly sacrificed himself to kill the Destroyer and save Earth (7N).

LETHBRIDGE-STEWART, DORIS Alistair's wife. She worked for UNIT in an undisclosed capacity before marrying the Brigadier. She saw him return to active duty to fight Morgaine (7N). In 1964, before they were married, Doris spent some romantic time with Lethbridge-Stewart in a hotel in Brighton, where she gave him a gold watch (ZZZ).

LEVITHIA Planet of the Cyrennic Empire, and homeworld of the tyrannical Graff Vynda-K. When the Graff left Levithia to fight in the Alliance Wars, he was replaced by his half-brother, to the satisfaction of the Levithians (5A).

LEXA High Priestess of the Deons. She worshipped the Dodeca-hedron and was vehemently opposed to any plans to reclaim the planet's surface. After Meglos, using the Fourth Doctor's shape, stole the crystal, she almost had the Time Lord executed. But she eventually saw the errors of her ways and was killed by a Gaztak while saving Romana's life (5Q).

LI H'SEN CHANG Chinese peasant who found Magnus Greel and, mistaking him for the god Weng-Chiang, nursed him back to health. Greel gave him hypnotic powers. Chiang followed his master to London, providing him with young girls whose life essences he needed to drain in order to survive, and assisting him in trying to locate his Time Cabinet. He used his gifts and the Peking Homunculus to pose as a magician, and worked at Henry Gordon Jago's Palace Theatre. He fought the Fourth Doctor and Leela, but his repeated failures caused him to be dismissed by Greel. Soon afterwards, he was fatally wounded by Greel's Giant Rat. Finally realizing that Greel was not a god, Chiang died warning the Doctor to beware of the Eye of the Dragon (4S).

LIBRI One of the Chosen on the Ark in Space. He was killed by Noah (4C).

LIEBERMAN MASER Weapon used by the Minyans (4Y).

LIFE ESSENCE The Elders had discovered a mechanical way to steal and transfer the life energy of the so-called Savages. In time, the victims recovered, only to be drained again later (AA).

LIGHT Powerful alien who landed on earth during the Paleolithic to catalogue all of its species. He rescued Nimrod, a Neanderthal, and made him immortal. He then slept in his spaceship until the 19th century, when he was discovered by British explorer Redvers Fenn-Cooper, who became mentally unbalanced. Acting under the influence of Josiah Samuel Smith, a survey agent of Light's who had evolved into a human, Fenn-Cooper took Light's ship back to England and buried it under Gabriel Chase. Ace caused Light to reawaken. When he learned that his catalogue had been made obsolete by evolution, Light tried to destroy mankind. But he disintegrated when the Seventh Doctor showed him that no one, not even himself, could stop evolution (7Q).

LIGHT The concept of Order and Light were embodied by the White Guardian (5A, 6H).

LIGHT CONVERTER See MAGLEM CON-VERTER.

LIGHT GUNS Weapons used against the Savages by the Elders' guards (AA).

LILT One of the employees at Tranquil Repose. He joined Takis in calling in the Daleks from Skaro. After Tranquil Repose's destruction, the Sixth Doctor showed him, Takis and the other employees how to make proteins out of local flowers (6Z).

LIMBO ATROPHIER Device used by the Valeyard to trap the Master and Sabalom Glitz inside the Matrix (7C).

LIMUS FOUR Recreational planet (5N).

LIN FUTU Chinese mandarin from the so-called 'Futu' dynasty, kidnapped by the Urbankans, probably circa 1769 BC. (There is no trace of a 'Futu' dynasty in China, however the Shang Dynasty (18th to 12th century BC) would be consistent with Lin Futu, based on archeological discoveries made at the burial site of Fu Hao, a royal member of that dynasty.) His memories were stored on silicon chips, and used to animate an android in his image. After the Fifth Doctor defeated Monarch, he and his fellow androids decided to look for another planet on which to settle (5W).

LINCOLN, ABRAHAM Sixteenth President of the United States. His image was projected on the First Doctor's Space-Time Visualizer (R).

LING-TAU A Chinese Captain in Kublai Khan's army. He was eventually promoted to Commander, and married Ping-Cho (D).

LINNA One of the Thoros-Alphan prisoners on Thoros-Beta. He was rapidly aged to death by Crozier's experiments (7B).

LINWOOD First victim of the Mind Parasite at Stangmoor Prison (FFF).

LINX Sontaran warrior whose ship was damaged by the Rutans and who was stranded in 12th-century Wessex. He allied himself with Irongron, the local brigand, who offered him shelter in exchange for modern weapons. Linx kidnapped scientists from the 20th century to help him repair his ship, which brought him into conflict with the Third Doctor. He died when a local archer, Hal, shot an arrow in his probic vent as his ship was ready to take off. The ship exploded soon afterwards (UUU).

LIONHEART, THE See RICHARD I.

LITEFOOT (BRIGADIER) Professor Litefoot's father. He went to China in AD 1860 as part of a punitive expedition, and stayed on in Peking as palace attaché until his death (4S).

LITEFOOT (PROFESSOR) A dedicated medical doctor who had chosen to work in an East End London hospital. He and Henry Gordon Jago helped the Fourth Doctor and Leela defeat Magnus Greel and save London from destruction. Litefoot had grown up in China, where the Emperor Tungchi had given Greel's Time Cabinet to his family as a present (4S).

LITTLE GIRL Human avatar of one of the three Gods of Ragnarok at the Psychic Circus (7J).

LITTLE HODCOMBE English Village destroyed during the English Civil War in 1643. It was where Tegan's grandfather, Andrew Verney, lived. Verney discovered the alien Malus buried beneath its church. Thanks to the Fifth Doctor's intervention, the Malus eventually destroyed itself, and peace returned to Little Hodcombe (6M).

LIVERPOOL The First Doctor stopped there for Christmas during his flight from the Daleks' Masterplan (V).

LIZ See SHAW, LIZ.

LIZ 79 Milo Clancey's erratic, battered old spaceship (YY).

LIZAN Operator at Space Special Security's Control Building (V).

LLANFAIRFACH Quiet Welsh mining village, the site of both the Nuthutch commune and the Global Chemicals refinery where the Green Death occurred (TTT).

LOBOS Commander of the Moroks' Space Museum on Xeros. He tried to turn the First Doctor and his Companions into exhibits. He was killed during the Xeron rebellion (Q).

LOBOS Planet where Milo Clancey's argonite mines were located (YY).

LOCATOR See CORE LOCATOR.

LOCH NESS Circa AD 1179, Loch Ness became the home of the Borad, a monstrous, quasi-reptilian alien from Planet Karfel, which had been banished through a time tunnel known as Timelash by the Sixth Doctor (6Y). Circa 1676, the crippled spaceship of the Zygons landed in Loch Ness. The Zygons and their Skarasen presumably killed the Borad, and the Skarasen then became the Loch Ness Monster. In 1976, the Zygons used the Skarasen to sink some oil rigs and sabotage a World Energy Conference. Freed from the Zygons by the Fourth Doctor, the Skarasen returned to Loch Ness where, presumably, he lived peacefully forever afterwards (4F).

LOCKE T-Mat operator on the Moonbase, when it was taken over by the Ice Warriors. He was killed by Slaar, who caught him sending a warning to Earth (XX).

LOCUSTA Official poisoner of Imperial Rome. When one of her poisons failed, Poppaea ordered her thrown to the lions (M).

LODGE One of the looters captured in London during the Dinosaur Invasion (WWW).

LOGAR Lord of the Fire Mountain worshipped by the Sarns. In reality, he was the deification of a Trion vulcanologist (6Q).

LOGICIANS, BROTHERHOOD OF The greatest gathering of human intelligence ever assembled. The Logicians believed that logic and intelligence should have power over the destinies of Man and other species. At the beginning of the 26th century, the Logicians' megalomaniacal president, Eric Klieg, financed Professor Parry's expedition to Telos, and resurrected the Cybermen (MM). It is possible that the Brotherhood of Logicians evolved from the 21st-century Earth School of Parapsychology, which shared its emphasis on pure logic (SS).

LOGIN, HALRIN Alzarian chief engineer and Keara's father. He was appointed Decider after Draith's death. More decisive than his two colleagues, he assumed leadership during the Marshmen's attack, and helped the Fourth Doctor discover the Alzarians' true nature (5R).

LOGIN, KEARA Young Alzarian Outler and Login's daughter (5R).

LOGOPOLIS Community of pure mathematicians who lived on an unnamed alien planet. They spent their lives intoning calculations inside caves carved into the rock. Their Block Transfer Computations had the power to affect reality itself. The Logopolitans discovered that the universe had long ago passed the point of fatal collapse. To dispose of the entropy, they used Block Transfer Computations to create Charged Vacuum Emboitements to open voids into other universes. After the Master disrupted the workings of Logopolis, Logopolis itself fell apart and was destroyed. The CVEs began closing. Fortunately, the Logopolitans had discovered an equation that would stabilize the CVEs. In spite of the Master's attempts to stop him and blackmail the Universe, the Fourth Doctor succeeded in using the Pharos Project on Earth to broadcast the Logopolitans' calculations (5V).

LOLEM High priest of Amdo, the Atlanteans' goddess. He hated Professor Zaroff, whom he rightly saw as having destroyed their peaceful (but primitive) isolated life. He fought the Second Doctor and died fighting with the mad scientist when the sea broke through Zaroff's laboratory (GG).

LOMAN Leisure Hive visitor who suggested that the tachyonics display arranged by Pangol was a trick. He was invited to step into the machine and was accidentally torn apart (5N).

LOMAND Captain of the Trion rescue ship summoned by Turlough and sent to Sarn to evacuate its people (6Q).

LOMAX (DR) Medical doctor to whom Dr. Henderson had sent samples of the Third Doctor's blood for analysis (AAA).

LON Son of Lady Tanha of Manussa. His ancestor had banished the Mara five hundred years earlier. He was possessed by the Mara, and persuaded Ambril to let him use the Great Crystal during the ceremony in which the Mara planned to recreate itself. The Mara was destroyed by the Fifth Doctor, and Lon was freed (6D).

LONG Exarius colonist. He supported Winton's call to arms against Dent (HHH).

LONGFOOT, JOSEPH Churchwarden in a small Cornish village. He was once a pirate who had served under Captain Avery with fellow crewmembers Pike and Cherub. Longfoot knew where Avery's treasure was hidden, but was killed by Cherub – not, however, before he had time to impart clues to the First Doctor (CC).

LOP Rest stop on the First Doctor's road to China (D).

LOPEZ, POLLY Companion of the First and Second Doctors, and Professor Brett's secretary. She and Ben Jackson helped the First Doctor against WOTAN. Afterwards, they followed him in the TARDIS and helped him fight 17th-century smugglers and the Cybermen. They watched the First Doctor regenerate. Polly and Ben then aided the Second Doctor against the Daleks, the Cybermen, Professor Zaroff, and the Macra. They first met Jamie in 1746 Scotland. Finally, after defeating the Chameleons, they discovered they were back in London on the same day they had left, and chose to remain there (BB–KK).

LORD OF DARKNESS One of the Destroyer's names (7N).

LORELLS, THE Billy's band at Shangri-La (7F).

LORENZEN, VOLKERT One of the crew of the *Mary Celeste* (R).

LORENZO One of Professor Sorenson's Morestran crew killed on Zeta Minor by the anti-matter creatures (4H).

LOST SHIPS The first Lost Ships were launched before the discovery of faster than light propulsion, during the early part of the 21st century. They used volunteers placed in hibernation. Among these was the ship which eventually landed on Vulcan (EE). A second wave of Lost Ships occurred after the discovery of FTL propulsion, in the last days of the 21st century and the early part of the 22nd century. Among these were the *Hydrax*, which was diverted into E-Space by the Great Vampire (5P), and the ship who crashed on Metebelis 3 (ZZZ). Another wave of Lost Ships followed the Second (or Great) Break Out in the 51st century. Among these was the Mordee, whose computer became Xoanon (4Q). Also see BREAK OUTS, COLONIZATION OF SPACE and FASTER THAN LIGHT.

LOVELL Royal Navy officer who fought the Sea Devils (LLL).

LOWE Supervisor of the Titan base. His mind was taken over by the Virus before Meeker died, and he fought the Fourth Doctor and Leela to save the Nucleus. A miniaturised holographic clone version of him died within the Doctor's body. He brought the Nucleus back to Titan, but was killed by K-9 mark I (4T).

LOWERY, GORDON Captain of the ship which took Marc Cory to Kembel. He was injured by a Varga plant, then killed by Cory to put him out of his misery (T/A).

LOYHARGIL Special alloy devised by the Rani's artificial Brain, which the Rani loaded in her rocket to blow up the Strange Matter asteroid (7D).

LUCANOL Ore processed aboard the *Sandminer* (4R).

LUCKE German army lieutenant who believed he was fighting against the British in World War I. In reality, he was part of the War Games. (ZZ).

LUDDITE UPRISINGS Violent attacks conducted by 19th-century handicraftsmen against machinery. Some attacks were indirectly caused by the Rani's removal of humans' brain fluids (6X).

LUGO Member of the Sevateem tribe. He was later killed by one of Xoanon's invisible, telekinetic monsters (4Q).

LUKOSER Werewolf-like being, originally Dorf, equerry to King Yrcanos of Krontep, and a pathetic product of Crozier's experiments, who helped Peri and Yrcanos fight the Mentors. He saved Yrcanos's life by taking a deadly blast meant for his King (7B).

LUMB, EDGAR One of Professor Sorenson's Morestran crew killed on Zeta Minor by the anti-matter creatures (4H).

LUNA See MOON.

LUPTON Leader of the psychic circle which summoned the Spiders of Metebelis 3 to K'anpo's Tibetan Monastery. He was once fired from his job, and wanted power and revenge. He stole the Blue Crystal from UNIT, and allied himself with the Spiders. His plans were thwarted by the Third Doctor, and he was killed by the Spiders when he rebelled and called them by their true name of Spiders instead of 'Eight-Legs' (ZZZ).

LURMA Vorg's home world (PPP).

LUVIC The youngest of Traken's five Consuls. He became Keeper after the Fourth Doctor defeated the Master (5T).

LYCANTHROPY See WEREWOLVES.

LYCETT One of the Chosen on the Ark in Space. He and Rogin helped the Fourth Doctor fight the Wirrn. He was absorbed by the alien larvae (4C).

LYDDA El Akir's home city (P).

LYTTON, GUSTAVE Galactic mercenary with the title of commander. He was born on Riften 5, a satellite of Vita 15 (Star System 690), known to be a planet of warriors. He first worked for the Daleks, commanding a taskforce whose job it was to rescue Davros from a space penitentiary. He fought the Fifth Doctor, and ultimately escaped through the Daleks' time corridor to 1984 London (6P).

There, he turned to organizing robberies to provide him with the money to buy sophisticated electronics equipment, which he used to set up a transmitter broadcasting a distress call. This was first picked up by the Cryons, and later by the Sixth Doctor. The Cryons hired Lytton to steal back a time vessel stolen by the Cybermen. Lytton met the Cybermen in the London sewers and pretended to help them, but was found out. He was tortured, then the Cybermen began the conversion work to turn him into one of their own. Before he lost his humanity, a partially converted Lytton sacrificed himself to kill the Cybercontroller (6T).

M

M3 VARIANT Type of fuel used for the Recovery 8 rocket (CCC).

M37 Planetary system located beyond the Sigmus Gap catalogued by Tryst (5K).

M-80 See MUSKATOZENE-80.

M, GILBERT Absent-minded scientist from Vasilip who designed the Kandy Man. After the Seventh Doctor helped to overthrow Helen A's regime, he and Joseph C fled Terra Alpha in a space shuttle originally intended for Helen A (7L).

MAAGA Commander of the Drahvin team stranded on the doomed planet of Galaxy Four. She was the only true Drahvin, the other women being programmed products of test tubes. Maaga tried to enlist the First Doctor's help in her confrontation with the Rills, but he refused. She and her crew perished in the planet's destruction (T).

MACE, RICHARD Out-of-work actor from the 17th century. He helped the Fifth Doctor, Tegan, Adric and Nyssa defeat the Terileptils (5X).

MACHINES See COMPUTERS, ROBOTS.

MACHONITE Substance used by the Time Lords in their courtroom. According to Glitz, it was worth quite a few grotzis (7C).

MACINTOSH, ALEX Television reporter covering the peace conference (KKK).

MACKAY, WILLY Former captain of the *Annabelle* and supporter of the Scottish rebellion. He was betrayed to the English by Trask, who then stole his ship (FF).

MACKAY Explorer and Professor Travers's friend. He was killed by the Great Intelligence's robot Yeti (NN).

MACKENZIE Scotland Yard inspector who had come to Gabriel Chase to investigate the disappearance of Sir George and Lady Margaret Pritchard, the owners of the house. He had been captured and preserved for two years by Josiah Samuel Smith. The Seventh Doctor reanimated him, but he was later killed by Light, who devolved him back into primeval soup (7Q).

MACMILLAN, LAUREN See CAMILLA.

MACRA Crablike aliens who had succeeded in secretly dominating a human space colony and forcing them to extract and refine the gas which was necessary to their survival. They were exposed and defeated by the Second Doctor (JJ).

MACROMAT FIELD INTEGRATOR Component of Zanak's transmat engines. It burned out while Zanak and the TARDIS tried to rematerialize on Calufrax at the same time. The Captain was ready to crush Earth to obtain the mineral PJX 18 (quartz) to replace it (5B).

MADDOX Sea Base Four's junior crew member. He replaced Michaels as synch operator, but felt inadequate. He was brainwashed by Nilson and Solow and forced to kill Karina. He was eventually killed by Nilson (6L).

MADDY One of the younger Rezzies of Paradise Towers and Tilda's and Tabby's neighbour. She joined forces with the Seventh Doctor, the Kangs and the Caretakers to destroy the Great Architect (7E).

MADELEINE See ISSIGRI, MADELEINE.

MADILLON CLUSTER Space sector where the Rutans fought the Sontarans (6W).

MADISON, ANGELA Phil Madison's wife (K).

MADISON, LARRY He helped the First Doctor fight the Daleks during their invasion of Earth in AD 2164. His brother Phil had been turned into a Roboman and worked at the Bedfordshire site. Both he and Phil were killed by the Daleks (K).

MADISON, PHIL The Daleks turned him into a Roboman to work in their Bedfordshire site during their Invasion of Earth in AD 2164. Both he and his brother Larry were killed by the Daleks (K).

MADNESS The TARDIS created a state of temporary insanity in the First Doctor's companions in order to alert them to the fact that the Fast Return Switch was jammed (C). Xoanon was a schizophrenic computer (4Q). Varos had once been a colony for the criminally insane (6V). The Doctor met a great number of mad scientists such as Professor Zaroff (GG), Dr Solon (4K), Dask (4R), Magnus Greel (4S), Kroagnon (7E), etc. Also see EVIL.

MADRA Name of the Zygon who impersonated Harry Sullivan. He died while attacking Sarah (4F).

MADRIK Karefelon rebel (6Y).

MADRONITE 1–5 One of the minerals extracted from Calufrax by Zanak. It was used by Mr Fibuli to power the Psychic Interference Transmitter that the Captain used to stop the Mentiads (5B).

MAGELLANIC MINING COMPANY One of Earth's multi-planetary corporations. Garron posed as its agent when he tried to sell Ribos to the Graff Vynda-K (5A).

MAGGOTS The Third Doctor fought deadly swarms of giant maggots and green slime, also known as the Green Death, in Llanfairfach. They were killed by a fungus found by Professor Clifford Jones (TTT).

MAGIC According to Clarke's Law, sufficiently advanced technology is indistinguishable from magic (and vice versa). Therefore, scientific explanations usually accounted for all the seemingly supernatural phenomena. Supernatural beings turned out to be superior entities preying on less evolved beings.

Among those entities who were thought to be gods or demons at one time or another in Earth's history, and which often became the center of a cult of worshippers, were: the alien Light (7Q); the Daemons (JJJ); the Mondasians (DD); Sutekh, Horus and the Osirians (4G); Scaroth of the Jagaroth (5H); Kronos (OOO); Cessair of Diplos (posing as the celtic goddess Cailleach) and her Stones of Blood (5C); the ancient Exxilon (XXX); the embodiment of evil known as Fenric (7M); the Mandragora Helix, who took over the Brotherhood of Demnos (4M); the Malus (6M); the Terileptil android dubbed 'Grim Reaper' (5X); and Magnus Greel, posing as the Chinese god Weng-Chiang (4S). The First Doctor himself was mistaken for Zeus during the Trojan War (U), while Barbara Wright was thought by the Aztecs to be Yetaxa's reincarnation (F). Morgaine's parallel Earth appeared to be ruled by magic, although Morgaine's talents were presumably the result of parapsychological abilities (7N). The goddess Hecate was a pagan concept worshipped by a cult of witches in Moreton Harwood (K9).

On alien worlds, the Doctor came in contact with a number

of religions where primitive people worshipped a powerful, seemingly supernatural entity. These included: the Exxilon City (XXX); Xoanon (4Q); the Oracle (4Y); Kroll (5E); the Mara (5Y, 6D); and the Gods of Ragnarok (7J). Also see MIND POWERS, MONSTERS, RELIGION.

MAGISTER Alias used by the Master in Devil's End (JJJ).

MAGLA 8,000-mile-long space amoeba, often mistaken for a planet (5J).

MAGLEM CONVERTER A Maglem Mark-7 converter made of siligtone was the device which converted ultraviolet light into black light, which was then transmitted down to the UK Habitat where it was used to power Drathro. The Maglem converter was also the sacred totem of Haldron, one of the gods of the Tribe of the Free. It was destroyed by Dibber, unwittingly triggering a black light explosion that could have endangered the entire universe, if it had not been stopped by the Sixth Doctor. After Drathro's destruction, Dibber suggested she and Glitz could make money from selling the converter's siligtone (7A).

MAGMA BEAST Monster who lived in the caves of Androzani Minor. It had the body of an armadillo and powerful, fanged jaws. It was killed during the mud burst (6R).

MAGNA CARTA Charter of English liberties granted by King John in 1215 under threat of Civil War. The Master used Kamelion in an attempt to turn the barons against King John to prevent its signing (6J).

MAGNADON Metal found on Skaro, used by the Thals to recharge their hand lights (B).

MAGNOTRON Device used by the Time Lords' corrupt High Council to move Earth out of the Solar System during the Ravolox Stratagem (7A–7C).

MAGRIK Vorus's chief assistant, and engineer of the Skystriker missile. He fought the Cybermen to free Voga (4D).

MAGS Protégée of Captain Cook, who found her on Vulpana, and one of the contestants in the talent contest organized by the Psychic Circus to entertain the Gods of Ragnarok. Mags turned out to be a werewolf. The Seventh Doctor helped her rebel against the Captain, whom she killed. Afterwards, she stayed with Kingpin to launch a new circus (7J).

MAHARIS Subject Guardian and willing Monoid collaborator. He was killed by crossfire in the battle between Monoids One and Four on Refusis (X).

MAIDEN'S POINT Promontory near the Northumberland village where Fenric's flask was buried (7N).

MAILER, HARRY Prisoner at Stangmoor Prison who staged an unsuccessful riot. The Master then helped him take over the Prison, and later used him to hijack the Thunderbolt Missile. He was eventually shot by the Brigadier as he was about to kill the Third Doctor (FFF).

MAIMUNA The daughter of Haroun Ed Diin, taken by El Akir for his harem. She helped Barbara escape El Akir's clutches (P).

MAITLAND Captain of the Earth ship in orbit around the Sense-Sphere. He and his crew, Carol Richmond and John, were held captive by the Sensorites. Thanks to the First Doctor's efforts, he was eventually allowed to return to Earth, after having promised to protect the secret of the Sensorites' existence (G).

MAKRIF Maylin of Karfel who was murdered by the Borad. He was Katz's father. He was friends with the Third Doctor, and helped negotiate the original peace treaty with Bandril (in an unrecorded story) (6Y).

MALDAK Young Varosian guard. He was moved by the Governor's appeal to his decency, and rescued him and Peri from death by the Cell Disintegrator (6V).

MALIK Old Tartar in Tegana's employ (D).

MALKON Young Sarn boy who was destined to become Sarn's leader because he had been chosen by Logar. In reality, he was Turlough's brother, and had crash-landed on Sarn. Malkon bore the Misos Triangle. He was wounded by an Elder and cured by the Numismaton flame. He returned to Trion with Turlough (6Q).

MALPHA Member of the Dalek Alliance in their Masterplan against Earth. He was eventually betrayed by Mavic Chen and the Daleks, but returned home and joined the human forces (T/A, V).

MALSAN Aridian who met the First Doctor and helped him escape from the Daleks (R).

MALUS, THE Evil alien entity who arrived in Little Hodcombe in 1643. It used psychic projections to feed on the villagers' fears during the English Civil War, then became dormant. It was rediscovered in the local church by Tegan's grandfather, Andrew Verney. The Malus was awakened by Sir George Hutchinson's unbalanced mind. Under their combined influences, a series of deadly war games re-enacting the Civil War was launched. The Fifth Doctor was able to cut it off from the villagers' emotions. After Sir George's death, the Malus destroyed itself and the church (6M). Later, the Fifth Doctor theorized that the Malus was a Hakol psychic probe.

MANDRAGORA HELIX Spiral-shaped energy life form, gifted with collective intelligence, living in uncharted areas of the space-time vortex, with a mysterious relation with the stars. It travelled to 15th-century Italy in the TARDIS, and took over Hieronymous and the cult of the Brothers of Demnos. It wanted to enslave mankind to prevent them from reaching the stars and becoming a threat. Its plan was to prevent the Renaissance and thus perpetuate the Dark Ages. It was eventually short-circuited and banished by the Fourth Doctor, but the stars were favourable to its return by the end of the 20th century (4M).

MANDREL Leader of the rebellion against the Company on Pluto. He had attacked a supervisor and been sent to a correction centre. He escaped and lived in the Undercity with Goudry, Veet and the Others. He helped – reluctantly, at first – the Fourth Doctor and Leela to overthrow the Company (4W).

MANDRELS Savage monsters from the planet Eden. Tryst discovered that the deadly drug vraxoin could be manufactured from the Mandrels' essence after they had been destroyed by heat. He used his CET machine to capture and transport the Mandrels, but they escaped after the *Empress* and the *Hecate* crashed above the planet Azure when both ships simultaneously emerged from hyperspace. The Fourth Doctor lured the Mandels back to the Eden projection inside the CET (5K).

MANIPULATOR Silurian device used by Icthar to launch Sea Base Four's missiles without a human synch operator (6L).

MANSELL Captain Wrack's first mate. The Fifth Doctor threw him and Wrack overboard (6H).

MANSTON RAF officer (KKK).

MANUS One of the Dukian directors who initiated research into atomic energy (TT).

MANUSSA Planet located in the Scrampus system. It was once the seat of two powerful, interplanetary empires: the Sumaran and the Manussan Empires (6D).

MANUSSANS The Manussans' once great technology enabled them to produce the Great Crystal, which amplified the evil inside their minds and created the Mara. The Mara became the driving force behind the Sumaran Empire. Three hundred years later, thanks to the Snakedancers and Lon's ancestor, the Manussans banished the Mara into a dark dimension. Five hundred years after that, Tegan returned it to Manussa. But the Fifth Doctor used the Snakedance to destroy it before it could recreate itself (6D).

MANYAK Mellium's friend. He defended the First Doctor when Dodo's cold virus infected the Ark (X).

MARA, THE Evil entity which was the sum of the evil within the Manussans' minds. It was absorbed, reflected and given independent life by the Great Crystal, and manifested itself in the form of a snake. It led the Sumaran Empire. Three hundred years after its creation, thanks to the magic of the Snakedancers, it was banished by the Manussans into a dark dimension of the collective mind. It was somehow drawn to the telepathic Kinda of Deva Loka, but only found a passage back into the real world when it possessed Tegan. Then, it took over the young Kinda, Aris, and sought to plunge Deva Loka into chaos by inciting the Kinda to attack the Dome of an Earth Expedition Force, which would have prompted the insane Hindle to start a massive explosion. The Fifth Doctor trapped the Mara inside a circle of mirrors, and banished it once more (5Y). But the evil entity had secretly remained in contact with Tegan and compelled her to return it to Manussa, 500 years after its original exile. There, the Mara possessed Lon, and planned to recreate itself with the Great

Crystal. It was destroyed by the Fifth Doctor, who had learned the Snakedancing rituals fom Dejjen, and who seized the Crystal and broke the Mara's spell on Manussa (6D).

MARAT One of the Thals sent to Spiridon to stop the Daleks. He fought alongside the Third Doctor, but was killed by the Daleks (SSS).

MARB STATION Deformed version of Marble Arch Station. It was one of the stations in the UK Habitat, the underground civilization ruled by Drathro (7A).

MARCO Giuliano's friend and confident. He helped the Fourth Doctor defeat the Mandragora Helix (4M).

MARCO POLO See POLO, MARCO.

MAREN High priestess of the Sisterhood of Karn. When the Sacred Flame appeared to be dying, she suspected the Fourth Doctor of being a Time Lord spy, sent to steal the remaining Elixir. She felt too old to fight Morbius, and let Ohica destroy the Monster. Later, she gave up her own, last ration of Elixir of Life to save the Fourth Doctor's life, and died in the Sacred Flame. Ohica then assumed the leadership of the Sisterhood (4K).

MARINE SPACE CORPS Earth's elite space commandos. A unit led by Commander Stewart was sent to Exxilon to bring back parrinium, and fought the Daleks alongside the Third Doctor (XXX).

MARINUS Planet whose population was mind-controlled (to ensure good behaviour) by a giant computer called the Conscience, located on an island of glasslike sand, surrounded by a sea of Acid. The Conscience's Keeper, Arbitan, blackmailed the First Doctor and his Companions into searching for four of its five Keys. The island was invaded by the Voord, and the Conscience was later destroyed, freeing Marinus (E).

MARIUS (PROFESSOR) New Heidelberg University specialist in extra-terrestrial, pathological endomorphisms. He worked at the Bi-Al Foundation in the 50th century. He helped the Fourth Doctor and Leela defeat the Nucleus of the Virus, and was himself briefly infected. He was also the designer of K-9 mark I, whom he gave to the Doctor when he found he could not take him back to Earth (4T).

MARK See CRICHTON, JOHN.

MARKHAM Police sergeant who was called in at Cranleigh Hall to investigate Digby's murder. The Fifth Doctor gave him and Sir Muir a tour of his TARDIS (6A).

MARN Gatherer Hade's assistant. She eventually elected to join the rebellion against the Company (4W).

MARNE Mentor of Thoros-Beta working for Lord Kiv. He had a strong aversion to loud noises (7B).

MARPESIA Planet visited by the Psychic Circus before it went to Segonax (7J).

MARRINER One of the Eternals. The Fifth Doctor met him in the guise of the first mate on Captain Striker's space yacht in the race for Enlightenment. He discovered love from contact with Tegan, but was banished by the White Guardian (6H).

MARS Fourth planet from the Sun. During Earth's prehistoric times, Mars was the home of the Ice Warriors (OO). The Fendahl attacked Mars, but was driven away, presumably by the Ice Warriors, and moved on to Earth (4X). When their planet began to die, the Martians sent Varga and a scouting expedition to Earth, but they were frozen inside a glacier and never returned (OO). Because of this, or possibly as a consequence of the Fendahl's devastating attack, the Martians decided to leave their dying world and emigrated to another part of the galaxy.

The god-like Osirian Horus later chose a relatively deserted corner of Mars to build a pyramid housing the Eye of Horus, which somehow kept his brother Sutekh prisoner on Earth (4G).

During the late 20th century, mankind sent the Probe spaceships to Mars. Probes 6 and 7 made contact with peaceful, radioactive aliens who had elected to inhabit the planet. After the alien Ambassadors were kidnapped and used by General Carrington, the aliens left the Solar System (CCC).

In the far future, Mars was terraformed by Mankind. Bret Vyon was born on Colony 16 on Mars (V). Much later, under Usurian influence, a segment of Humanity temporarily moved to Mars, then on to Pluto, after depleting Earth's natural resources (4W). See also ICE WARRIORS

MARS PROBE PROJECT British space project which sent the Probes ships to Mars, and later, the Recovery 7 and 8 (CCC).

MARSH MEN See MARSHMEN.

MARSH MINNOWS Delicacies enjoyed by the Mentors (7B).

MARSHAL (OF ATRIOS) War chief of Atrios who was secretly under the Shadow's mental command. He led his planet in a fanatical, unending space war against Zeos. He launched a final assault, unaware that it would trigger Mentalis to destroy both planets. The Fourth Doctor placed him in a time loop, and eventually redirected his attack to destroy the Shadow's planetoid. After the war was over, the Marshal helped Drax rebuild Atrios (5F).

MARSHAL (OF SOLOS) Sadistic Imperial Earth agent on Solos. His plan was to permanently alter the planet's atmosphere to make it habitable for humans. He loved to hunt and kill Solonian mutants. He used Varan's son to kill the Earth Administrator, then framed Ky. He fought the Third Doctor, until he was killed by Ky after the latter had turned into a super-being (NNN).

MARSHAL (SONTARAN) Styre reported to a Sontaran Marshal (4B).

MARSHAL See GRAND MARSHAL.

MARSHCHILD Young marsh creature who followed the Fourth Doctor into the *Starliner*. It killed Dexeter as the scientist was about to dissect it alive. The Marshchild died of electrocution as he tried to escape (5R).

MARSHMEN Extremely adaptable and intelligent native Alzarian life forms, evolved from spiders. After the Terradonian *Starliner* crashed on Alzarius, Marshmen killed its original passengers. Over the course of four thousand generations, they then evolved into Terradonian-like humanoids who forgot their true origins. Eventually, at Mistfall, new Marshmen rose to again attack the *Starliner*. The Fourth Doctor helped the *Starliner* community rediscover the truth and leave Alzarius (5R).

MARTA Village woman on the Great Vampire's world. She was Ivo's wife and Karl's mother (5P).

MARTENS, ARIEN One of the crew of the *Mary Celeste* (R).

MARTHA High Priestess of the Cult of the Cailleach. In reality, she and De Vries served the alien Cessair of Diplos. She was killed by an Ogri (5C).

MARTIN Exarius colonist who first saw the lizards and wanted to return to Earth (HHH).

MARTIN (MRS) Martin's wife, Exarius colonist who supported Ashe's desire to stay on Exarius (HHH).

MARTIN Assistant to the undertaker to whom the First Doctor entrusted the casket containing the Hand of Omega. The Seventh Doctor came to collect it (7H).

MARY Servant girl at Irongron's castle (UUU).

MARY CELESTE Brig which left New York on 4 November 1872. It was found, completely deserted, on 4 December, 600 miles off the Portuguese coast. It was the third stop in the Daleks' pursuit of the First Doctor through time and space. The Daleks panicked the crew, who jumped overboard (R).

MASSACRE See SAINT BARTHOLOMEW'S DAY MASSACRE.

MASTER, THE Renegade Time Lord. He studied, with the Doctor, under Borusa, at the Time Lord Academy (apparently getting better grades than the Doctor), where he also met the Rani and, presumably, Drax. He gloried in chaos and destruction, and sought ultimate control of the universe. Like all Time Lords, he was partly telepathic, and had also developed incredible hypnotic powers. His favourite weapon was his Tissue Compression Eliminator. His TARDIS was a more advanced model than the Doctor's, and had an operable chameleon circuit.

Having led a dangerous life, the Master was already in his twelfth incarnation when he escaped from Gallifrey and arrived on Earth, at Rossini's International Circus, his TARDIS taking the shape of a horsebox. Under the alias of Colonel Masters, the Master took over the Farrel plastics factory and helped the Nestene to launch a second invasion, but ended up helping the Third Doctor to banish them (EEE). Under the alias of Professor Emil Keller, the Master brought a Mind Parasite to Earth and tried to use it to sabotage a World Peace Conference (FFF).

The Master then became Axos's prisoner, whom he brought to Earth. He and the Doctor were eventually forced to work together to imprison Axos in a time loop (GGG). The Master stole the location of the Doomsday Machine from the Matrix and impersonated an Earth Adjudicator in order to misappropriate it, but the Doctor convinced its Guardian to destroy it (HHH). Under the alias of Mr Magister, the Master posed as a vicar, and the leader of a black magic coven, in Devil's End in order to summon the Daemon Azal back to life, and to ask to be granted his power. He failed and was arrested by UNIT (JJJ).

While in prison, the Master found a way to trick his warden, Colonel Trenchard, and ally himself with the Sea Devils. After they were defeated by the Doctor, he escaped (LLL). Posing as Professor Thascales, the Master used the Kronos Crystal and TOM-TIT to summon and control Kronos. He caused the fall of Atlantis, but was otherwise foiled by the Doctor, who interceded on his behalf with Kronos (OOO). The Master then allied himself with the Daleks, and used the Ogrons to try to foment a war between Earth and the Draconians in the 26th century, but was again thwarted by the Doctor (QQQ).

Having reached his twelfth and final regeneration, the Master turned into a decaying corpse. He was dying when Chancellor Goth found him hiding on Tersurus. The Master promised Goth power and convinced the Chancellor to bring him secretly to Gallifrey. There, he helped Goth assassinate the President and frame the Fourth Doctor for the murder. But what he really wanted was access to the unlimited energy of the Eye of Harmony to boost-start a new regeneration cycle. He was thwarted by the Doctor, but managed to steal enough energy to prolong his life and escape (4P). Still a decaying husk, the Master travelled to Traken where his TARDIS assumed the shape of a Melkur, enabling the Renegade Time Lord to influence Kassia. As Melkur, the Master eventually became the new Keeper of Traken. He planned to use his control of the Source to turn the Union of Traken into an all-conquering force, and seize another body for himself. After he was exposed and prevented from remaining Keeper by the Fourth Doctor, the Master seized and took over the body of Council Tremas (5T). Because Tremas's body was not that of a Time Lord, however, it could not regenerate, but would age instead, eventually forcing the Master to steal another body to survive.

The Master next killed Tegan's Aunt Vanessa, and tried to trap the Doctor inside his TARDIS. He followed the Doctor to Logopolis, and was responsible for its destruction, thereby endangering the whole universe. The Master tried to use the Logopolitans' final calculations, meant to save the Universe from collapsing, to blackmail the Universe into submission, but was thwarted by the Doctor. However, he caused the Doctor to fall and almost die, triggering another regeneration (5V). The Master then kidnapped Adric and forced him to use Block Transfer Computations to create the seemingly peaceful city of Castrovalva, in reality a space-time trap for the newly-regenerated Fifth Doctor. The Doctor discovered the true nature of Castrovalva, exposed the Master (who was disguised as Castrovalva's Portreeve) and freed Adric. The Time Lord and his friends escaped, but the Master was almost trapped in Castrovalva's collapse (5Z).

After escaping from Castrovalva, the Master exhausted the dynomorphic generator of his TARDIS and became stranded in the Jurassic. He discovered the powerful alien Xeraphin, and planned to use their nucleus intelligence in his TARDIS. Posing as the Arab magician Kalid, he drew a Concorde flight through a time contour in order to draw the Doctor and his TARDIS, which he needed to break down the Xeraphin's barriers. He then seduced the evil side of the Xeraphin and succeeded in incorporating them as part of his TARDIS. But the Fifth Doctor secretly reprogrammed the Master's TARDIS and exiled him to Xeriphas (6C). The Master later escaped from Xeriphas, taking with him the shape-changing android, Kamelion. Posing as Sir Gilles Estram, the Master forced Kamelion to assume the likeness of King John in an attempt to turn the Barons against him, and prevent the signing of the Magna Carta, but he was thwarted by the Doctor (6J).

When the Death Zone was reactivated, the High Council summoned the Master and offered him a full pardon, as well as a new cycle of regenerations, if he helped the Five Doctors. The Master tried to seize Rassilon's secret of immortality, but was stopped by the Brigadier. He was eventually banished by Rassilon (6K).

The Master then accidentally shrank himself to doll size with his Tissue Compression Eliminator. He again took over Kamelion, and travelled to Sarn. There, he plotted to bathe himself in the volcanic Numismaton Flame to restore his size and extend his powers. The Fifth Doctor caused him to be trapped inside the flame as it was turning caloric and it seemed as if the Master had been vaporized (6Q). But he managed to escape and set a trap for the Sixth Doctor in 19th-century England, where he tried to alter history by preventing the industrial revolution for his own ends. Instead, he ran afoul of the Rani, who was conducting her own biological experiments on the locals. The two renegade Time Lords entered into an uneasy alliance, but were still out-witted by the Doctor, who sent them both spinning into the outer fringes of the universe in the Rani's TARDIS (6X).

The Master eventually regained his TARDIS. He hired Sabalom Glitz to gain possession of the secrets of the Matrix, which had been stolen by the Andromedan Sleepers. After Glitz failed, the Master entered the Matrix. Worrying about competing with the Valeyard in evil, he dispatched Glitz and Mel to testify at the trial of the Doctor and expose the Valeyard. The Valeyard fled into the Matrix, pursued by the Doctor. The Master hoped the Valeyard and the Doctor would destroy each other, and tried to use Glitz to recover the Matrix's secrets. The Doctor eventually defeated the Valeyard, but the latter had replaced the secrets with a Limbo Atrophier, which trapped the Master and Glitz inside the Matrix (7C).

The Master again managed to escape, this time seemingly without his TARDIS, but was trapped on the savage, quasi-living world of the Cheetah People. He began to turn into one of the Cheetah People, and used their teleportational abilities to escape back to Earth, where he fought the Seventh Doctor. Eventually, their conflict took them back to the dying Cheetah Planet, where the Master reverted to savagery. It is uncertain whether he managed to recover his sanity in time to escape the destruction of the Cheetah World (7P).

MASTER BRAIN A combination of a giant brain and a computer, and the true ruler – and possibly creator – of the pocket universe known as the Land of Fiction. It first tried to replace its servant, the so-called Master (a copywriter from 1926 England), with the Second Doctor. It then attempted to incorporate the Time Lord within its computer to take over Earth. It failed and was destroyed by Zoe (UU).

MASTER (OF THE LAND OF FICTION) A former copywriter on *The Ensign* boys' magazine who was spirited away from

1926 England by the Master Brain who ruled the Land of Fiction. The Master Brain hoped he would provide it with enough creative energy to fill its pocket universe with fictional characters. He became a virtual prisoner, even though he denied it to himself, and sensing his imminent death, the Master Brain tried to replace him with the Second Doctor, but failed and was destroyed by Zoe. When the Land of Fiction was destroyed, the Master was presumably restored to his proper place in time and space (UU).

MASTERS, EDWARD FREDERICK Permanent Under Secretary responsible for the supervision of the Wenley Moor atomic research station, and an old school mate of Dr Lawrence's. He was eventually killed by the Silurian virus spread by Major Baker (BBB).

MASTERS One of Reegan's henchmen (CCC).

MASTERS (COLONEL) Alias used by the Master in his dealings with Rex Farrel (EEE).

MASTERSON, BAT Gambler and gunfighter in the American West, and Wyatt Earp's friend. He was Tombstone's sheriff at the time of the gunfight at the OK Corral and the First Doctor's visit (Z).

MATRIX Huge communal electronic brain made up of trillions of electro-chemical cells arranged in a continuous matrix pattern. The Matrix (also known as the Amplified Panatropic Computations Network) contained the sum total of the knowledge of all the Time Lords. At the instant of a Time Lord's death, an electrical scan was made of his brain, transferring its pattern and information to the Matrix.

The Time Lords used the Matrix to monitor various events throughout time and space. The Matrix could even predict future events. The President of the Time Lords was linked to the Matrix through the Coronet of Rassilon. The Matrix was the responsibility of the Keeper of the Matrix, also known as Coordinator.

The Matrix was invaded by the Master (HHH) and Goth, who used it to frame the Fourth Doctor for the assassination of the President. The Fourth Doctor then entered the Matrix and defeated Goth (4P). The Matrix was later invaded by the

Vardans, aliens with the power to travel along wavelengths, after one of the Time Lords' scan beams hit their planet. The Fourth Doctor plugged K-9 mark I into the Matrix in order to find the Vardans' home planet, then placed the latter in a time loop (4Z). The Matrix was invaded by Omega, thanks to the help of Councillor Hedin, when he was trying to take over the body of the Fifth Doctor (6E). The Matrix was further invaded by the Andromedan Sleepers, who stole various secrets from it, which led the then corrupt High Council of the Time Lords to adopt the Ravolox Stratagem. Afraid the Doctor would find out, they used the Valeyard to put the Sixth Doctor on trial (7A). The Valeyard used falsified evidence from the Matrix, including a false account of Peri's death, to accuse the Doctor (7B). The secrets from the Matrix were recovered for the Master by Sabalom Glitz. The Matrix then became the theatre of a titanic battle between the Sixth Doctor, the Master and the Valeyard. The Master ended up trapped inside the Matrix, but the Valeyard escaped by taking over the body of the Keeper of the Matrix (7C).

MATTER TRANSMISSION See TELEPORTATION.

MATTHEWS Devesham Space Research Station employee (4J).

MATTHEWS British soldier killed while fighting the Daleks in Totters Lane in 1963 (7H).

MATTHEWS, ERNEST Clergyman and dean of Mortarhouse College. He was fiercely opposed to Darwin's theory of evolution and went to Gabriel Chase to discuss it with Josiah Samuel Smith. He met the Seventh Doctor. Later, he was devolved into a monkey by Smith, then killed by Gwendoline (7Q).

MATTHEWS Police sergeant involved in the investigation of Commander Pollock's disappearance (K9).

MAWDRYN Leader of a team of eight alien scientists who stole a Metamorphic Symbiosis Regenerator from Gallifrey. This created an unending life of perpetual mutation, their bodies eternally renewed into vile travesties of their former selves. Their ship was caught in a warp ellipse but, every seventy years, space beacons guided it within transmat distance of Earth. Mawdryn claimed that only the life force of a Time Lord's incarnation could put an end to their misery. The Fifth Doctor was ready to sacrifice his remaining regenerations, however, the energy released by the meeting between the 1977 and 1983 Brigadiers was enough to end the lives of Mawdryn and his fellow aliens (6F).

MAXIL Trigger-happy commander of Gallifrey's Chancellery Guards at the time when Omega tried to bond himself with the Fifth Doctor. He arrested the Doctor (6E).

MAXTIBLE, RUTH Theodore Maxtible's daughter. She was engaged to Arthur Terral (LL).

MAXTIBLE, THEODORE Scientist whose time-travel experiments with Edward Waterfield were used by the Daleks, who promised him the secret of turning lead into gold. He became their willing agent, and fought the Second Doctor. Maxtible was eventually turned into a human Dalek, and fell to his death while fighting Kemel on Skaro (LL).

MAY POLE The Third Doctor was almost burned at one in Devil's End (JJJ).

MAY QUEEN Tegan was designated to become Queen of the May, a human sacrifice, during the deadly war games renacted in Little Hodcombe by Sir George Hutchinson (6M).

MAYA Civilization that ruled Central America before the Aztecs, between AD 250 and 900. Villagra was a Mayan princess kidnapped by the Urbankans, probably circa 731 (5W).

MAYLIN, THE Title borne by the ruler of Karfel (6Y).

MAYNARDE, RICHARD Lady Peinforte's servant; he travelled with her to 1888 and reluctantly fought with her to gain control of the Silver Nemesis. After she merged with the statue, he killed the Cyber Leader. The Seventh Doctor returned him to his proper time and place (7K).

McCRIMMON, JAMES ROBERT (aka JAMIE) One of the Second Doctor's companions, Laird Colin McLaren's piper. The Second Doctor met him soon after the Battle of Culloden in 1746. He then helped the Time Lord, Ben and Polly escape from Gray's sinister clutches. He stayed with the Second Doctor throughout the rest of his incarnation, travelling first with Ben and Polly, then with Victoria, and finally with Zoe. Jamie helped the Doctor fight Professor Zaroff, the Cybermen, the Macra, the Chameleons, the Daleks, the Great Intelligence and its Yeti, the Ice Warriors,

Salamander, and the Weed (FF–RR). Just after that, when the Doctor had left Victoria with the Harrises, the Time Lords (or, more likely, the Celestial Intervention Agency) pulled the Doctor and Jamie out of their normal timelines and sent them off to Space Station J7 to deliver a warning to Dastari about unauthorized time experiments. Jamie helped the Sixth Doctor and Peri to fight Chessene and the Sontarans, and became the target of Shockeye's antrophagous lust. Afterwards his memories of this mission were erased by the Time Lords (6W). During his travels with Zoe, Jamie helped the Doctor fight the Cybermen, the Dominators, the Master Brain of the Land of Fiction (who altered Jamie's physical appearance), the Krotons, and Caven's space pirates. After taking part in the War Games, Jamie was returned by the Time Lords to his own era, just after the end of his first adventure with the Doctor (SS–ZZ). Jamie's image was used by Rassilon to ward off the Second Doctor (6K).

McDERMOTT, JAMES GEORGE Head of production at the Farrel plastics factory. The Master had him killed by a Nestene-controlled plastic chair (EEE).

McLAREN, COLIN Scottish laird, injured at Culloden. He, Ben and Jamie were captured by Ffinch, then taken by Gray to be sold into slavery. They were eventually freed thanks to the Second Doctor's intervention. He, Kirsty and the other highlanders eventually sailed for France and freedom (FF).

McLAREN, KIRSTY Colin McLaren's daughter. She helped the Second Doctor and Polly free her father, Jamie, and Ben from Gray's clutches. She, her father, and the other highlanders eventually sailed for France (FF).

McLUHAN Sergeant in Kane's forces on Iceworld, sent with Bazin after the Dragon. After she shot the Dragon, they were both disintegrated by the Dragonfire crystal (7G).

McRANALD, ANGUS FERGUSON Landlord of the Tulloch Inn. He was killed by the Zygon who impersonated Sister Lamont (4F).

MEADOWS, GEORGE Gatwick air-traffic controller. His identity was taken over by the Chameleons (KK).

MECHANOIDS (aka MECHONOIDS or MECHONS) Large,

spherical, intelligent robots designed and built by Earth to prepare alien worlds for colonization. A group of Mechanoids abandoned on Mechanus had built their own city, and were awaiting human settlers. When Steven Taylor crashed on the planet, the Mechanoids kept him prisoner because he did not know the proper control codes that would have identified him as a colonist. They captured the First Doctor and his companions in the same fashion, and later fought with the Dalek extermination team sent after them. The Mechanoids and the Daleks eventually destroyed each other (R).

MECHANUS The fifth and last stop in the Daleks' pursuit of the First Doctor through time and space. It was a world overgrown with hostile vegetation, including the Fungoids, and was first settled by the Mechanoids. After the Mechanoids and the Daleks destroyed each other, it returned to its original inhabited status (R).

MECHONOIDS See MECHANOIDS.

MECHONS See MECHANOIDS.

MEDDLING MONK See MONK.

MEDICINE See DISEASES.

MEDOK Member of the Macra-dominated space colony. He was the first to expose the Macra threat and was thought mad. He was killed by the Macra, but only after he had time to alert the Second Doctor (JJ).

MEDUSA Mythological character encountered by the Second Doctor, Jamie, and Zoe in the Land of Fiction (UU). The Fendahl Core appeared as a golden, Medusa-like woman (4X).

MEDUSOID Aliens resembling hairy jellyfish with claws, teeth and legs. The third Doctor claimed they captured him en route to an Intergalactic Peace Conference (QQQ).

MEEKER Officer of the Titan shuttle taken over by the Virus. He was killed by Leela in self-defence (4T).

MEG Cook at Irongron's castle (UUU).

MEGA-PHOTON DISCHARGE LINK Component of Zanak's

transmat engines. It was smashed by a spanner wrench psychically operated by the Fourth Doctor and the Mentiads, in order to prevent the pirate planet from crushing Earth (5B).

MEGARA Justice machines which looked like small, shiny, floating spheres and which acted as judge, jury and executioner. The Fourth Doctor claimed they had once found their creators in contempt and destroyed them. The Doctor freed two Megara from a Prison Ship stuck in hyperspace, but by so doing committed an infraction. He was judged by the Megara and condemned to death. However, during his trial, he succeeded in exposing Cessair of Diplos, the Megara's first target, who was then turned into stone. The Doctor then used the third segment of the Key to Time to banish the Megara back to Diplos (5C).

MEGASHRA (aka MEGESHRA) Mountains of Peladon, the location of the trisilicate mines (MMM, YYY).

MEGELEN See BORAD, THE.

MEGLOS Last of the Zolfa-Thurans and a xerophyte, a cactuslike being who was able to take over other bodies and change his shape. Meglos designed the Screens of Zolfa-Thura to use the Dodecahedron as a weapon, but the crystal was taken to Tigella by the Zolfa-Thuran peace party leader. Eventually, it was found by the Tigellans who worshipped it, and used it to power their civilization. Ten thousand years later, Meglos hired the Gaztaks to bring him the body of an Earthling (George Morris). He then used the shape of the Fourth Doctor to steal the Dodecahedron and take it back to Zolfa Thura, where he intended to use it to make himself master of the galaxy. He was betrayed by the Gaztaks, and thwarted by the Fourth Doctor. Meglos was destroyed, along with Zolfa-Thura, in the Dodecahedron explosion (5Q).

MEGRO-GUARDS Ordinary police force of the Pluto Megro-polises (4W).

MEGROPOLIS Name given by the Company to its six human settlements on Pluto. The rebellion engineered by the Fourth Doctor took place in Megropolis One (4W).

MEL See BUSH, MELANIE.

MELAGOPHON Planet visited by Captain Cook. The Seventh Doctor also claimed to be familiar with the planet (7J).

MELANIE See BUSH, MELANIE.

MELKUR Name given by the citizens of Traken to the evil beings whom the Source turned into calcified statues. (It meant 'a fly caught by honey'.) The Master's TARDIS assumed the shape of a Melkur, enabling the Master to influence Kassia. Later, the Master became the new Keeper of Traken, and planned to use his control of the Source to turn the Union of Traken into an all-conquering force and seize another body for himself. He was exposed and prevented from remaining Keeper by the Fourth Doctor, Adric, Nyssa and Council Tremas (5T).

MELLIUM Daughter of the Ark's Commander, and Manyak's friend. She defended the First Doctor when Dodo's cold virus infected the Ark (X).

MEMORY WINDOW One of the Toymaker's devices (Y).

MENA Argolin leader who replaced Morix. She believed Hardin's TRG could rejuvenate her and her race, and refused to sell the Leisure Hive to the West Lodge Foamasi. When she began ageing rapidly, she was overthrown by Pangol. Her Earth lover, Hardin, pushed her and Pangol inside the TRG, which had been repaired by the Fourth Doctor. She was rejuvenated and made peace with the Foamasi (5N).

MENELAUS King of Sparta and Agamemnon's brother. When his wife, Helen, eloped with Paris, it led to the Trojan War (U).

MENOPTERA Butterflylike humanoids from Vortis. They were driven away from their homeworld by the antlike Zarbi, controlled by the evil Animus. Some of the Menoptera remained on Vortis, and became pigmy Menoptera, led by Hetra. The other Menoptera survived on the planet Pictos until they were ready to launch an invasion force, led by Vrestin, to reconquer Vortis. With the First Doctor's help, the Menoptera were able to destroy the Animus and regain their planet. Prapilius became leader of the Menoptera (N).

MENSCH Swampie spy who worked at the methane refinery on Delta Magna's third moon. He was killed by Kroll (5E).

MENTALIS Powerful pyramid-shaped computer on Zeos, built by Drax, which conducted an unending space war against Atrios.

When threatened with destruction by the Marshal, Mentalis was programmed to destroy itself and both planets (the so-called 'Armageddon Factor'). The computer was eventually disabled by Drax and the Fourth Doctor (5F).

MENTIADS Gestalt of Zanak telepaths. They started to appear when the latent telepaths began to absorb the life force released by the planets crushed by Zanak. Led by Prolix, they helped the Fourth Doctor defeat the Captrain and blow up the Bridge (5B).

MENTORS Rapacious, cunning amphibians from Thoros-Beta. Their mobility was severely restricted, and they required frequent watering in order to breathe. In their primitive forms, they also bore a tail sting with deadly venom. The Mentors were the evolved Thoros-Betans who had become the leaders of a vast business empire, which included the Galatron Mining Corporation and other businesses, and virtually enslaved the Thoros-Alphans, who had become their bearers and guards. The Sixth Doctor thwarted Mentor Sil's plans on Varos (6V), and later crossed swords with Sil's lord, Kiv, on Thoros Beta (7B).

MERAK Chief Surgeon of Atrios. He helped the Fourth Doctor and Romana defeat the Shadow, and eventually married Princess Astra (5F).

MERCER Survivor of the Dalek raid on the space penitentiary where Davros was kept. He was killed by Lytton's men (6P).

MERCURY Element necessary for the proper functioning of the TARDIS's Time Vector Generator. The First Doctor replenished its supply on Skaro (B). Later, the Second Doctor and Jamie had to look for more on the Wheel in Space (SS). Planet Vulcan contained mercury swamps. The Earth Examiner was killed in them before Quinn and Bragen found the Second Doctor and his companions (EE).

MERDEEN Drathro's senior servant in UK Habitat. He secretly helped people escape the Cullings and reach the surface to live with the Free. He and Balazar helped the Sixth Doctor destroy Drathro and save the population of the UK Habitat from the black light explosion triggered by the destruction of Drathro's Maglem converter (7A).

MEREDITH Medical doctor at the Wenley Moor atomic research station (BBB).

MERGRAVE Physician and exercise devotee on Castrovalva. He perished in the collapse of his city (5Z).

MERK One of the Xeron rebels (Q).

MERLIN Famous wizard of King Arthur's court. He was one of the Doctor's future incarnations in an alternate dimension. Merlin fought alongside King Arthur against Morgaine, and eventually buried his body with Excalibur in a living spaceship left under Vortigern's Lake, near Carbury, on the Seventh Doctor's Earth (7N).

MESMERON Mind-controlling device used by Morphoton's Brains to enslave the residents (E).

MESSIA 13 Star sector in which the Hercules 208 star went nova, as Zoe predicted. Its gamma radiation flux deflected meteors towards the Wheel in Space (SS).

MESTOR Giant leader of the Gastropods. He took control of Jaconda from Azmael, whom he forced to do his bidding. He had Romulus and Remus Sylvest kidnapped to force them to work out the equations that would have enabled him to throw a planet into Jaconda's sun, and planned to create an explosion that would spread his eggs throughout the universe. His plan was thwarted by the Sixth Doctor and Hugo Lang. While in mental battle with Azmael, the Doctor destroyed Mestor's body. Azmael then destroyed Mestor's mind by committing suicide through a last, fatal regeneration (6S).

METAL VIRUS The Fourth Doctor used it to destroy the Giant Robot (4A).

METALS See MINERALS

METAMORPHIC SYMBIOSIS REGENERATOR Machine used by the Time Lords in cases of acute regenerative crisis, stolen from Gallifrey by Mawdryn and seven alien scientists and used by them to create an unending life of perpetual mutation, their bodies eternally renewed into vile travesties of their former selves (6F).

METEBELIS 3 A blue planet with a blue sun located in the Acteon star sector. The Third Doctor first tried to take Jo Grant there soon after he was pardoned by the Time Lords (RRR, PPP). He eventually visited it alone, but found the planet full of hostile life forms. From that visit, he brought back a Blue Crystal which enabled him to cancel BOSS's hypnotic powers (TTT). Metebelis 3 was later settled by a Lost Ship launched in the 22nd century. Under the influence of its crystals, the Earth spiders which the ship carried mutated and ended up ruling the colonists. Approximately four hundred thirty years later, circa 2530, the Spiders of Metebelis 3 plotted to conquer Earth. They used Lupton's psychic circle to send one of their own to Earth to fetch the Blue Crystal required by the Great One. Their plans were thwarted by the Third Doctor, who eventually returned to give the Blue Crystal to the Great One. It killed her, and the Spiders, finally freeing the colonists (ZZZ).

METEORITES The Nestene intelligence arrived on Earth in the form of a shower of meteorites (AAA). The Daleks used meteorite bombardments as a prelude for their Invasion of Earth in 2164 (K). The Tractators used meteorite bombardments in their war against the Frontios colonists (6N). Crashing alien spaceships were often mistaken for meteorites (UUU, 4V, 5X).

METHANE Natural gas found in abundance on Delta Magna's third moon, where it was refined and turned into a source of protein. The Fourth Doctor and Romana saved the refinery from the power of Kroll (5E).

METROPOLITAN One of the magazines for which Sarah Jane Smith worked (ZZZ).

METTULA ORIONSIS Space sector where the Union of Traken was located (5T). It was destroyed when the Master tampered with Logopolis (5V).

MEXICAN REVOLUTION Mexican rebels were kidnapped by the Warlords, using time technology stolen from the Time Lords. Those soldiers went on to take part in the War Games, until these were brought to a stop by the Second Doctor's intervention (ZZ).

MEXICO See AZTECS, MEXICAN REVOLUTION.

MIASIMIA GORIA Planet enslaved by the Rani (6X).

MIASIMIANS Inhabitants of Miasimia Gora. They had been enslaved by the Rani who, trying to increase their productivity, gave them a drug of her own design. Instead, it deprived them of sleep and turned them into savages. To cure the problem, the Rani travelled to Earth, plotting to steal the brain fluids that enable humans to sleep and which she planned to feed to the Miasimians. She was thwarted by the Sixth Doctor (6X).

MICHAELS, FRANK British astronaut aboard the *Mars Probe 7* ship. He was captured by mysterious, radioactive aliens, but was eventually returned to Earth thanks to the Third Doctor's intervention (CCC).

MICHAELS Sea Base Four synch operator who died soon before the Fifth Doctor's arrival. He was replaced by Maddox (6L).

MIDGE One of Ace's friends from Perivale, kidnapped by the Cheetah People. After he savagely murdered one of the Cheetahs, his animal nature overtook him and he gained the power to teleport back to Earth. The Master used him to get revenge on the Doctor. Midge's creed of 'survival of the fittest' led him to die after he was wounded in a motorcycle accident (7P).

MILLENIUS (aka MILLENIUM) Highly civilized city on Marinus, where the First Doctor had to clear Ian of a murder charge during his quest for the Keys of Marinus (E).

MILLER, THE Unnamed slave of the Terileptils (5X).

MILLINGTON, A.H. Commander of a secret naval base on the Northumberland Coast in the 1940s. He was obssessed by Norse mythology, and plotted to strike at the Russians by letting one of their commandors steal the 'core' of the Ultima Machine, which he had body-trapped with a deadly natural toxin. Millington was also one of the 'Wolves' of Fenric (7M).

MILLINGTON, MARY ELIZA Daughter of one of Commander Millington's ancestors. She lived only 13 days (7M).

MIND See BRAINS, ENERGY.

MIND BENDING Deadly mind game played by the Time Lords. The Fourth Doctor defeated Morbius in a mind-bending contest (4K).

MIND PARASITE (aka MIND OF EVIL) Evil, brainlike entity brought to Earth by the Master, who planned to use it to sabotage a World Peace Conference. It was housed in the Keller Machine, and fed on evil. It could kill by using people's deepest fears, and later developed the ability to teleport. The Parasite eventually turned against the Master, who was forced to enlist the Third Doctor's help to destroy it. With Barnham's help, the Doctor was able to control the Parasite, which was finally destroyed when the Thunderbolt Missile was detonated (FFF).

MIND POWERS See HYPNOTISM, TELE-KINESIS, TELE-PATHY, TELEPORTATION.

MINERALS Mineral life forms included: the Krotons (tellurium-based) (WW); the Exxilons (XXX); the Kastrians (4N); the Ogri (5C); the Krargs (5M); and the Silver Nemesis, which was made of deadly validium (7K). Both Cessair of Diplos (5C) and Borusa (6K) were turned into living statues. On Traken, criminals turned into calcified statues dubbed Melkurs (5T).

Planets rich in mineral resources included: the Sense-Sphere, with its abundant supply of Molybdenum (G); the space colony coveted by IMC, which was rich in Duralinium (HHH); Solos, which was rich in Thaesium (NNN); Exxilon, with its supply of Parrinium, the only known antidote to a space plague (XXX); Peladon, rich in Trisilicate (YYY); Voga, the planet of gold, deadly to Cybermen (4D); Zanak, the pirate planet, whose entire economy revolved around plundering minerals (5B); Tythonus (5G); and Varos, rich in Zyton-7 (6V). On the other hand, Chloris was a planet almost devoid of minerals (5G). The *Sandminer* was a mobile ore-processing plant; among the precious ores it mined were lucanol, zelanite and keefan (4R). Acetenite 455, Dodrium, Vessilium and Vulnium were among the minerals mined by Zanek (5B). Hard metals included Duralinium (HHH, YYY), Durilium (QQQ) and Duranium (4C).

Rare minerals included: taranium, found on Uranus, one of the rarest minerals in the Universe, used by the Daleks to power their time machine and time destructor (V); argonite, which combined the incorruptibility of gold and the strength of titanium (YY); dalekenium, a super-dense metal used by the Daleks for their mobile casing and as a super-powerful explosive (KKK); jethrik, used in space warp drive engines (5A); madronite 1–5 and voolium, found on Calufrax; orlion, found on Collactin and Bandraginus 5 (5B); hymetusite, a type of radioactive crystals required as a tribute by the Nimon, and found on Aneth (5L); and jasonite, an electromagnetic booster found only on Crinoth (5L).

A mineral compound of anti-matter was found on Zeta Minor (4H). Hulls made of dwarf star alloy blocked the Tharils' natural time-travelling capabilities (5S). The Fourth Doctor used an anti-metal virus to destroy Professor Kettlewell's Giant Robot (4A). The mineral PJX 18 (quartz) could be used to replace a Macromat Field Integrator (5B). Vastial was a highly explosive mineral that was only safe at sub-zero temperatures (6T). Siligtone was one of the hardest metals in the universe; it was employed by the Andromedans in the manufacture of Maglem converters (7A). Vionesium was a magnesium-like metal found on Mogar; exposed to air, it released intense light. The Sixth Doctor used it to destroy the Vervoids (7C). Loyhargil was a special alloy devised by the Rani's made-up Brain, with which she planned to blow up a Strange Matter asteroid (7D). Dynastream (4A) and Colodin (5E) were other types of hard metals. Gregarian rock was supposed to last forever (X).

The Fourth Doctor used Chronodyne to make a substitute sixth piece for the Key to Time (5F). The Time Lords used machonite in their courtroom (7C). The Jacondan's matter transporter left behind a dust-like deposit of Zanium (6S). Also see CRYSTALS.

MINIATURIZATION A TARDIS malfunction resulted in an accidental miniaturization of the First Doctor and his companions (J). Earth's population was miniaturized and carried on micro-cell slides in the Ark (X). The Chameleons kept their human prisoners miniaturized (KK). The Daemon Azal, as well as his spaceship, existed in a miniaturized state under Devil's Hump (JJJ). The Third Doctor and Jo Grant were miniaturized within Vorg's Scope on Inter Minor (PPP). The Fourth Doctor cloned and miniaturized himself and Leela to track down the Nucleus of the Virus of the Purpose within his own body (4T). He and Drax miniaturized themselves to defeat the Shadow (5F).

Whole areas of land, along with their fauna and flora, could be removed and stored on laser crystals inside a Continuous Event Transmitter (5K). The Tissue Compression Eliminator used by the Master reduced its victims to doll size. The Master once accidentally shrank himself with it, but used the Numismaton Flame to restore himself (6Q). Meglos used a Redimensioner to miniaturize the Dodecahedron (5Q).

MINISCOPE See SCOPE.

MINISTERS Major-General Rutlidge was in charge of supervising Lethbridge-Stewart's UNIT operations on British soil at the Ministry of Defence. His mind was controlled by Tobias Vaughn, who forced him to kill himself (VV). The Third Doctor dealt with various British ministers, including: Sir James Quinlan, Minister of Technology and Space Development (CCC); the Minister who appointed Chinn (GGG); and the Minister of Ecology (TTT). Sir Charles Grover, the mastermind behind Operation Golden Age, was Minister with Special Powers during the Dinosaur Invasion (WWW). Jo Grant owed her position at UNIT to her uncle, a cabinet minister. The Giant Robot killed Cabinet Minister Joseph Chambers (4A). The Brigadier spoke with the PM (Margaret Thatcher) during the Zygons' attack (4F). The Seventh Doctor used a forged authorization by the PM to see Dr Judson (7M).

MINNOW FIGHTERS Short-range spaceships used by the International Space Corps for deep space fighting against pirates such as Caven (YY).

MINORANS Inhabitants of Inter Minor. Their planet had once been devastated by a space plague and, as a result, they had become highly xenophobic. Their president, Zarb, tried improving the lot of its slave population (called Functionaries) and opening the planet to aliens once again, but his brother, Kalik, tried using Vorg's Scope to discredit him. He was stopped by the Third Doctor (PPP).

MINOTAUR Mythological character encountered by the Second Doctor, Jamie, and Zoe in the Land of Fiction (UU). The Third Doctor encountered a real Minotaur in a labyrinth in Ancient Atlantis. It was the Guardian of the Kronos Crystal, and a friend of King Dalios, who had been turned into a man-beast by Kronos (OOO). The extra-terrestrial race of the Nimon had certain features in common with the Minotaur (5L).

MINSBRIDGE Wildlife sanctuary where Mr Ollis found Omega's energy blob (RRR).

MINYANS Humanoid race from Minyos. Early in the history of their civilization, the Time Lords discovered the Minyans and helped them progress by giving them scientific secrets, such as knowledge of the atom, for which they were not ready. The

Minyans eventually rejected the Time Lords, then destroyed each other and their planet in nuclear war. This dramatic event led the Time Lords to adopt their policy of non-interference. However, a few Minyans escaped and moved to a new world that they christened Minyos II. They developed the pacifier to quell aggressive instincts, and gathered the genetic heritage of their race in a race bank which they placed aboard the ship *P7E* en route to Minyos II. However, the *P7E* became lost. Another ship, captained by Jackson, was sent to find it. That quest lasted over a hundred thousand years. Eventually, with the help of the Fourth Doctor and Leela, Jackson found the *P7E* and was able to bring the Race Banks back to Minyos II, where they were presumably used to recreate the Minyan race (4Y).

MINYOS Homeworld of the Minyans. It was destroyed by nuclear wars caused by the Minyans' lack of maturity and their inability to handle the scientific knowledge the Time Lords had given them (4Y).

MINYOS II New home world set up by a few survivors from Minyos (4Y).

MIRA Planet inhabited by the Visians, giant, hostile, invisible creatures. The First Doctor was sent there from Earth by Froyn and Rhynmal's experimental matter transmitter (V).

MIRABILIS Planet fraudulently sold by galactic con artist Garron (5A).

MIRACLE CITY One of Kroagnon's designs. It was supposed to be his masterpiece. He loved it so much that he refused to move out, and had to be evicted. As revenge, he booby-trapped it and several lives were lost. It was a forerunner of what he was to do with the Paradise Towers (7E).

MIRE BEASTS The other inhabitants of Aridius, an ancient world once covered by vast oceans, turned into a desertic planet. They were tough, nearly indestructible predators who progressively drove the Aridians out of their sealed cities (R).

MISEUS Young member of the High Council of Atlantis. He perished when Kronos destroyed Atlantis (OOO).

MISOS TRIANGLE Two interlocked triangles tattooed on the arms of the Trion Imperial Family sent in exile. Turlough and Malkon bore that mark (6Q).

MISTFALL Periodic orbital shift which affected Alzarius every fifty years. It released non-toxic subterranean gases which boosted evolution (5R).

MITCHELL, HARRY Leader of the security team hired by Dr Fendelman to guard the Fetch Priory. He was killed by a Fendahleen (4X).

MITCHELL, TONY Royal Navy sub-lieutenant who served under Ridgway aboard the submarine captured by the Sea Devils. The Third Doctor helped them escape (LLL).

MITCHELL Sergeant under Lieutenant Scott's command, killed by the Cybermen's androids during Professor Kyle's underground exploration (6B).

MOBERLEY, DEREK Scientist working at the Antarctic camp of the World Ecology Bureau expedition which discovered the Krynoid pods. In spite of the Fourth Doctor's efforts, he was killed by the Krynoid who had taken over Winlett's body (4L).

MOBILLIARY Medical laboratory aboard Monarch's ship (5W).

MOBY DICK See BOOKS OF KNOWLEDGE.

MOGAR Oxygen-free planet located in Perseus. It was a rich source of rare minerals, including vionesium. It was severely exploited by the Earth Empire (7C).

MOGARIANS Gentle and peaceful natives of Mogar. They had to wear airtight masks and suits, as well as translating devices, to interface with mankind. Two Mogarians, Atza and Ortezo, were used by Rudge in an attempted hijack of the *Hyperion III* space liner, but they were killed by Doland. Galactic investigator Hallet posed as a Mogarian named Enzu, but the Sixth Doctor unmasked him (7C).

MOGRAN (aka MOGREN) Kaled councillor whom the Fourth Doctor alerted to Davros's creation of the Daleks. He perished in the destruction of the Kaled City (4E).

MOLECULAR DISPERSER Microwave-producing device that

Icthar and the Young Silurian plotted to use to destroy the Van Allen Belt (BBB).

MOLLIE Kitchen maid in Gray's prison (FF).

MOLYBDENUM Metal found in abundance on the Sense-Sphere (G).

MONA LISA Jagaroth commissioned Leonardo da Vinci to paint several Mona Lisas to enable his future self to finance his time-travel experiments (5H).

MONARCH Leader of the Urbankans. He had exhausted all the resources of his home planet in his mad desire to travel faster than light, and back through time, to witness the creation of the Universe. (Monarch believed himself to be God.) He stored the memories of the three billion Urbankans on silicon chips and travelled to Earth, which he had previously visited four times. During these visits, he had kidnapped Kurkutji, Lin Futu, Bigon and Villagra, and transformed them into androids. He planned to poison the population of Earth and replace it with the Urbankans, who would be reincarnated in android form, and to strip the planet of its resources in the pursuit of his obsession. His plans were thwarted by the Fifth Doctor, who used his own toxin to kill him. It was then revealed that Monarch had remained in the 'flesh time' and had not joined his android brethren (5W).

MONDAS Earth's twin planet and the Cybermen's home world. It had orbited around the Sun millions of years in the past. Its civilization developed more quickly than Earth's and Mondasians visited our planet in prehistoric times. Later, for unknown reasons, Mondas left the Solar System; it was during this period of wandering that the Mondasians evolved into Cybermen.

An energy-starved Mondas returned to the Solar System in 1986; its Cybermen's plan to drain energy from the Earth and cybernize its population was thwarted by the First Doctor – Mondas absorbed too much energy and was destroyed (DD). Future galactic Cybermen tried to prevent Mondas's destruction by attempting to launch Halley's Comet into the earth before the above events, but were defeated by the Sixth Doctor and the Cryons (6T). Also see CYBERMEN.

MONEY Among the various alien and future currencies encountered by the Doctor at one time or another were: talmars (4W);

opeks (5A); nargs (6W); grotzis (7A); crowns (7G); and even a curious insectoid creature (7N). On Trion, people blew through two-corpera coins for luck (6N).

MONIA Guerilla leader from an alternate 22nd century where the Daleks had successfully invaded Earth after World War III. She helped the Third Doctor return to the past and defeat the Daleks (KKK).

MONITOR, THE Leader of Logopolis. He tried helping the Fourth Doctor, but perished along with Logopolis after the Master tampered with the workings of his city (5V).

MONK, THE (aka THE MEDDLING MONK) Renegade Time Lord whom the First Doctor met in England in AD 1066. Disguised as a monk, he tried to change the course of history by reversing the outcome of the Battle of Hastings. The Doctor stranded him by tampering with his TARDIS (S). However, the Monk managed to repair his TARDIS and resurfaced on Tigus, where he tried to get revenge by locking the Doctor out of his TARDIS, but failed. He then followed the Doctor to Ancient Egypt where he got involved in the Doctor's fight against the Daleks' Masterplan. The Monk switched sides and eventually escaped. He found himself again stranded, this time on an unnamed ice world, because the Doctor had managed to snatch his TARDIS's directional unit (V). The Monk claimed to have helped the early Britons build Stonehenge with anti-grav units, and to have discussed flying machines with Leonardo da Vinci.

MONOID ONE Leader of the Monoids. He planned to relocate his people to Refusis, and detonate a fission bomb on the Ark, thus destroying the human race. He was thwarted by the First Doctor, and died during a rebellion led by Monoid Four (X).

MONOID TWO Monoid leader who landed on Refusis and killed Yendom. He died in the explosion of his launcher (X).

MONOID THREE Monoid leader who died during the battle between Monoids One and Four (X).

MONOID FOUR Monoid leader who questioned Monoid One's decision to relocate on Refusis. He died during his battle against Monoid One (X).

MONOIDS One-eyed, reptilian aliens with no visible facial features, who arrived on Earth after their own world had died. They offered their servitude for shelter. They were taken aboard the Ark when the Earth plunged into the Sun. After Dodo's cold virus sapped the will of the humans, they took over the Ark (using a speech box to communicate). The First Doctor prevented the Monoid leader, Monoid One, from destroying the human race. The remaining Monoids learned to live in peace with the humans on Refusis (X).

MONOPTICON Floating spheres used by Monarch to spy on what was happening inside his ship (5W).

MONSTERS The Doctor exposed a number of legendary creatures and/or supernatural monsters as being aliens, machines, or creatures out of time.

Aliens: the Daemons were powerful aliens (JJJ). The Loch Ness Monster was a Zygon Skarasen (4F), although in AD 1179, it probably was the Borad (6Y). The creature assembled by Solon to house the brain of Morbius was a Frankenstein-like creature made up of various alien parts (4K). Whatever the real Horror of Fang Rock was, the monster destroyed by the Fourth Doctor was a stranded Rutan (4V). Giant alien vampires were once destroyed by the Time Lords (5P). Mags was an alien werewolf (7J).

Machines: The First Doctor once met a robotic version of Dracula and the Frankenstein Monster (R). The Yeti were the robotic agents of the Great Intelligence; the real Yeti were harmless. The Mummies were Osirian robots (4G). The legendary Dragon of Iceworld was a mechanoid (7G).

Creatures out of time: The Silurians and Sea Devils were a reptilian lifeform predating man. The Minotaur of Atlantis was Kronos's creation (OOO). On Earth, the vampires were Haemovores from the future transported back in time by Fenric (7M). Morgaine's Destroyer came from a parallel Earth (7N).

On alien worlds, monsters were not always what they seemed: Aggedor, the Monster of Peladon, was a peaceful animal. The giant squidlike Kroll of Delta Magna's third moon was a hidden segment of the Key to Time (5E). On Chloris, the Creature from the Pit was an ambassador from the neighbouring planet, Tythonus (5G). The Nimon were a plague of space locusts (5L). On Terminus, the Garm was also a well-meaning alien (6G). Also see MAGIC.

MONTCALM (LADY) See CESSAIR.

MOON The Cybermen hid their Invasion Fleet on the dark side of the Moon during the 20th century (VV).

A Moon Base was established in the early part of the 21st century, under the jurisdiction of the International Space Command. In 2070, it was attacked by the Cybermen, who wanted to use its gravitron to destroy Earth through weather control. They were defeated by the Second Doctor, and Moon Base's scientists, Hobson and Benoit (HH). Half a century later, the Moon Base became the location of the controls of T-Mat, and was taken over by the Ice Warriors who, under Slaar's leadership, plotted to conquer Earth using the Seeds of Death. They were defeated by the Second Doctor (XX).

In the 26th century, the Moon had become the seat of the Luna Penal Colony, to which the Third Doctor and Jo Grant were sent when they were accused of being Draconian spies (QQQ).

MOOR Soldier who fought in the War Games. He eventually broke free of Von Weich's hypnotic control and killed him (ZZ).

MOORE Victim of the Zygons (4F).

MOOTHI Race which used silent gas dirigibles to approach Karn, but who were detected by the Sisterhood (4K).

MORBIUS Renegade Time Lord who was a member of the High Council of Gallifrey. He sought to lead the Time Lords on a path of conquest. Rejected by his peers, he left Gallifrey and raised an army of followers, promising them time travel and immortality, using the Elixir of Life produced by the Sisterhood of Karn's Sacred Flame. Eventually, Morbius and his army were defeated by the Time Lords on Karn. The Renegade Time Lord was placed in a disposal chamber and his body was vapourized.

Several years later, the Celestial Intervention Agency found out that the Brain of Morbius had been secretly preserved by one of his followers, Dr Solon. They sent the Fourth Doctor and Sarah Jane Smith to Karn. There, the Doctor destroyed the brain of Morbius, now housed in a monstrous new body created by Solon, in a mental battle. The body itself was later destroyed by Ohica of the Sisterhood (4K). The Morbius Crisis was probably one of the factors which led to the Time Lords' increasing lack of control over their secrets and, ultimately, to the Ravolox Stratagem (7A).

MORDAAL Incarnation of the evil side of the Xeraphin (6C).

MORDEE The _Mordee_ was one of the ships which left Earth at the time of the great Break Out of the 52nd century. It crashed on a nameless planet. In an unrecorded adventure, the Fourth Doctor, fresh from his regeneration, tried to fix Xoanon, its sentient computer, but instead rendered it schizophrenic. The Doctor eventually returned and cured Xoanon (4Q).

MORDRED Extra-dimensional knight and Morgaine's son. He came to our Earth on the trail of Ancelyn, to recover Excalibur. He was eventually defeated by the Seventh Doctor and remanded to UNIT's custody (7N).

MORELLI Science officer aboard the Morestran spaceship to Zeta Minor. He was later killed by Sorenson when the scientist turned into a neanderthal-like monster (4H).

MORESTRA Space-faring empire of the far future. The continued existence of the Morestran civilization was threatened by their dying sun. Professor Sorenson went to Zeta Minor looking for a new, inexhaustible source of energy, and thought he had found it in anti-matter. The Fourth Doctor eventually steered him towards researching the kinetic force of the planets' movements (4H).

MORESTRANS Circa AD 37166, the Fourth Doctor and Sarah Jane Smith· rescued the crew of a Morestran spaceship from anti-matter creatures. These had been sent to check on Professor Sorenson's expedition to Zeta Minor (4H).

MORETON HARWOOD Small British village where Sarah Jane Smith's Aunt Lavinia lived. Sarah and K-9 Mark III exposed and defeated a sect of the worshippers of the pagan goddess Hecate (K9).

MORGAINE Powerful, immortal sorceress who ruled a parallel dimension. She claimed to be of the Fey (or faerie) people. She loved, yet hated King Arthur, whose fall and ultimate death she caused. She fought Merlin, an incarnation of the Doctor. She eventually became the Dominator of the Thirteen Worlds, Sunkiller, and the Battle Queen of the S'Rax. She and her son,

Mordred, met the Seventh Doctor, Lethbridge-Stewart, and Bambera upon the battlefield of Carbury, on the Doctor's Earth. She freed the Destroyer, but her sense of honour prevented her from detonating the Salamander 6–0 missile. She was eventually remanded to UNIT's custody (7N).

MORGAN Ruthless First Officer of the Inter-planetary Mining Corporation's expedition to Exarius. With Captain Dent, he used a variety of tricks against Ashe's colonists, including using a mining robot equipped to simulate lizard attacks. He was foiled by the Third Doctor and Winton, and was eventually killed in a battle with the colonists (HHH).

MORGAN Landlord of the Devesham pub. The Kraals made an android duplicate of him (4J).

MORGANA Founding member, and fortune teller, of the Psychic Circus. She and the Ringmaster were eventually sacrificed to the Gods of Ragnarok by the Chief Clown (7J).

MORGO The Great Morgo was a divinity praised by the Mentors (7B).

MORGUS Chairman and Chief Director of the Sirius Conglomerate of Androzani Major. He was once Sharaz Jek's partner, providing financial backing for the exploitation of spectrox, while Jek, a master roboticist, built the androids necessary to handle the poisonous substance. Morgus arranged for Jek to become caught in one of Androzani Minor's deadly mud bursts and, subsequently, horribly disfigured. After Jek seized control of the caves of Androzani Minor, and the supply of spectrox, Morgus secretly used Stotz to supply him with guns. He was thus able to prolong the conflict and cause spectrox prices to rise. Fearful of being exposed, Morgus assassinated the President, then fled to Androzani Minor, planning to seize Jek's private spectrox hoard. He was thwarted by the Fifth Doctor. He was replaced by his assistant, Timmin, and was later killed by Jek (6R).

MORIX Heresiarch of Argolis who died of old age just as Brock tried to convince him to sell the planet to the Foamasi. He was succeeded by Mena (5N).

MORKA See YOUNG SILURIAN.

MORLOX Race of savage reptiles who lived underground on

Karfel. Karefelon scientist Megelen (aka the Borad) sprayed himself with M-80 while conducting unethical experiments on the Morlox. As a result he became half Morlox, half Karefelon. The Morlox were undoubtedly the source of H.G. Wells's inspiration for *The Time Machine* (6Y).

MOROKS Once the conquerors of a vast galactic empire which eventually fell, and one of the remnants of the Morok Empire was the Space Museum on Xeros, which was eventually closed due to the First Doctor's intervention. The Moroks had limited time travel capabilities; therefore, the fall of their Empire may be attributed to Time Lord interference (Q). The Cybermen may have stolen a Morok Time Vessel to save Mondas and alter history (6T).

MORPHOS Inhabitants of Morphoton (E).

MORPHOTON City on Marinus and location of the first Key. It was ruled by Giant Brains who kept its population enslaved with a mind-controlling device. They were defeated by the First Doctor (E).

MORRIDWYN See CAILLEACH.

MORRIGAN See CAILLEACH.

MORRIS, GEORGE Earthling abducted by the Gaztaks. His body was taken over by Meglos. He was eventually freed, thanks to the Fourth Doctor's intervention, and returned to Earth (5Q).

MORRIS, IDWAL Archeologist rival of Professor Rumford's (5C).

MORRIS DANCERS Dancers who paraded around the May Pole at Devil's End. Bert disguised himself as one to entrap the Third Doctor (JJJ).

MORRISON (PROFESSOR) Scientist kidnapped by Linx (UUU)

MORTARHOUSE COLLEGE Oxford college. Its dean was Reverend Matthews (7Q).

MORTIMER British town where K'anpo's Tibetan Monastery was located (ZZZ).

MORTON Member of Wenley Moor's staff (BBB).

MORTON Megropolis One resident (4W)

MOSS Member of Lupton's psychic circle at K'anpo's Tibetan Monastery. He was afraid of being discovered, and struck Mike Yates. He was eventually controlled by the Spiders, but was freed when the Great One died (ZZZ).

MOSS, TED Fetchborough farmer who was secretly a member of Stael's coven. He was turned into a Fendahleen by the Fendahl and, in that form, perished when the Fourth Doctor used the Time Scanner to destroy the Fetch Priory (4X).

MOVELLANS Race of androids resembling beautiful humans. Their power source appeared to be small energy packs they carried on their belts. The Movellans found themselves at war with the Daleks when they tried to invade human space. Both species became locked in a stalemate caused by their over-reliance on logic and computers. The Daleks tried to win the war by recovering Davros, but were thwarted by the Fourth Doctor, Tyssan, and Movellan commander, Sharrel (5J). The Movellans eventually designed a virus which almost wiped out the Daleks (6P). The fate of the Movellans is unknown, but it is likely that their over-reliance on logic caused them to be defeated by the Empire when they actually attempted their invasion of the human space.

MUD BURST Deadly natural phenomenon caused when Androzani Minor moved closer to Androzani Major. Heated mud from Androzani Minor's core rose to the surface, sweeping away everything in its path (6R).

MUIR, ROBERT (SIR) The Cranleighs' friend. He was also Chief Constable of the area, and investigated James' and Digby's murders. The Fifth Doctor gave him and Sergeant Markham a tour of the TARDIS to prove the veracity of his story (6A).

MULA Pralix's sister and Kimus's girlfriend. She helped the Fourth Doctor and the Mentiads defeat the Captain of Zanak (5B).

MULLINS Ashbridge Cottage Hospital porter who overheard a report about the Third Doctor's blood samples, and sold the news to Wagstaffe (AAA).

MUM Human avatar of one of the three Gods of Ragnarok at the Psychic Circus (7J).

MUMMIES Osirian service robots, also called Servicers, used by Sutekh, and powered by a cytronic particle accelerator (4G). The Monk was trussed up as a mummy by the First Doctor (V).

MUNRO UNIT Captain who cordoned off Oxley Woods after the second fall of Nestene meteorites. He was the first to come across the TARDIS and the Third Doctor. He later helped the Time Lord defeat the first Auton invasion (AAA).

MUNRO Radio operator on an oil rig attacked by the Skarasen. He managed to escape only to later be shot by the Zygon who impersonated the Caber (4F).

MURDERS Ian was framed by Eyesen, on Millenius, for Eprin's murder (E). The murderer Bennett hid behind Koquillion's Didonian disguise (L). Dask, a member of the *Sandminer* crew, turned out to be mad roboticist Taren Capel (4R). Dolland, one of Professor Lasky's assistants, turned out to be the elusive killer aboard the *Hyperion III* (7C).

MURRAY Driver of the galactic tour bus which crashed in 1959 Wales after hitting a US satellite. Murray was killed by the Bannermen, along with the rest of his tour group, when they blew up his bus (7F).

MUSCOLANE Planet visited by Captain Cook (7J).

MUSIC The Second Doctor played the recorder. The Third Doctor charmed Aggedor with music (MMM). The Fourth Doctor used a dog whistle to summon K-9 and, once, charmed the Mandrels with music (5K)

MUSKATOZENE-80 Unstable element which caused the Borad to turn into a half-Karfelon, half-Morlox freak (6Y).

MUSS, NICHOLAS French Huguenot working for Admiral De Coligny (W).

MUTATIONS Mutations on Skaro included the Thals (in their beautiful, blond humanoid form) and the Daleks, which were mutated Kaleds (B) Other, more grotesque, mutants were called Mutos (4E). The Solonian Mutants ('Mutts') were blamed on the Marshal's artificially induced atmospheric changes. In fact, they were only a transitional stage leading to a super-being life form, reflecting Solos's five-hundred-year-long seasons (NNN). The Refusians' invisibility was the result of a mutation caused by solar flares (X).

Artificial mutations included the Chameleons, mutated by an atomic explosion (KK); the Primords, mutated by a mysterious substance under the Earth's crust (DDD); the giant maggots, mutated by the Green Death (TTT); the Spiders, mutated by the crystals of Metebelis 3 (ZZZ); Professor Sorenson, mutated by anti-matter (4H); Kroll, an aquatic monster mutated by a segment of the Key to Time (5E); Mawdryn and his fellow aliens, mutated by the Time Lords' Metamorphic Symbiosis Regenerator (6F); Chessene, artificially augmented by Dastari (6W); the Vervoids and the Demeter Seeds, mutations engineered by Professor Lasky (7C); and Billy, who mutated into a Chimeron-like alien by ingesting a Chimeron substance (7F). Also see EVOLUTION.

MUTOS Derogatory nickname given to the Kaleds and Thals mutated by the neutronic wars on Skaro (4E).

MUTTS Derogatory nickname given to the Solonian Mutants (NNN).

MUTTER'S SPIRAL Name given by the Time Lords to the sector of the Milky Way Galaxy where Earth is located (4P, 4Z).

MYERS Royal Navy petty officer. He killed the Chief Sea Devil, then let the Master escape (LLL).

MYKROS Vena's fiancé. He plotted against the Borad with Renis, and was arrested. He later helped the Sixth Doctor defeat the Borad (6Y).

MYRKA Sea dragon bred and modified into a cyborg by the Silurians and used by Icthar in its attack on Sea Base Four. The Fifth Doctor used ultraviolet light to kill it (6L).

MZ Powerful weapon of destruction which Rorvik used in an attempt to break through the Gateway, but which failed (5S).

N

N-SPACE Normal space, as opposed to E-Space (5R–5V).

NAIA One of the Trogs of the Underworld. She helped the Fourth Doctor and Jackson's crew fight the Oracle. She and a number of her people escaped the Underworld's destruction by leaving aboard Jackson's ship (4Y).

NAMIN, IBRAHIM Sutekh's Egyptian worshipper. He prepared Professor Scarman's house for his master's return. He was killed by Sutekh (4G).

NANCY Member of Professor Clifford Jones's commune. She discovered that Jones's fungus killed the Green Death maggots (TTT).

NANINA Female 'Savage' who was captured by Exorse, and whose life essence was drained by the Elders. After she recovered, she prevented Tor from killing Exorse, and eventually succeeded in shaking Exorse's own belief in the Elders' lifestyle (AA).

NAPOLEON BONAPARTE (1769–1821) One of the French Revolution's greatest military commanders. He plotted with Barras to eliminate Robespierre, and almost met the First Doctor. He eventually proclaimed himself Emperor of France (H).

NAPOLEONIC WARS A French army was kidnapped by the Warlords, using time technology stolen from the Time Lords. The soldiers went on to take part in the War Games until these were brought to a stop by the Second Doctor's intervention (ZZ).

NARG Currency used in the Third Zone (6W).

NATASHA Daughter of Stengos, a wealthy man who had been cryogenically frozen at Tranquil Repose. When she suspected that something was wrong, she went with her friend Grigory to investigate. She discovered that Davros was secretly using the bodies' heads to make new Daleks. She helped the Sixth Doctor thwart Davros's plans, and survived the destruction of Tranquil Repose (6Z).

NATIONAL SPACE MUSEUM The Master and Rossini stole the Nestene energy unit from the National Space Museum (EEE).

NAVARINO Non-humanoid alien species from Navarro. Galactic tour bus driver Murray, as well as most of his passengers, were Navarinos. They were all killed by the Bannermen (7F).

NAVARRO Homeworld of the Navarinos (7F).

NAZIS A gang of Nazi refugees in South America, led by De Flores, tried to seize control of the Silver Nemesis. They were killed by the Cybermen (7K).

NEANDERTHALS Between 50,000 and 30,000 BC, the Neanderthals became extinct and were replaced by early modern humans as a result of the intervention of the Daemons (JJJ). There is still considerable disagreement as to whether the Neanderthals were a step in the evolutionary process leading to modern humans, or were simply an offshoot branch that became extinct, while modern humans evolved in parallel. Nimrod, a Neanderthal, was rescued and made immortal by the powerful alien, Light (7Q). The First Doctor helped a tribe of Neanderthals rediscover the secret of fire (A).

Certain experiments could cause an evolutionary regression in their victims. A green slime brought to the surface of the Earth by Professor Stahlman's Inferno project turned men into the Neanderthal-like Primords (DDD). On Zeta Minor, Professor Sorenson's body became infected with anti-matter, and he turned into a Neanderthal-like monster (4H). Also see ANTHROPOLOGY, EVOLUTION.

NECROS See NEKROS.

NEEVA Sevateem witch doctor and Xoanon's priest. Acting on Xoanon's instructions, he tried to kill Leela and the Fourth Doctor. When he found that Xoanon was not a god, but was in fact his tribe's enemy, he became mentally unbalanced and tried to kill the schizophrenic computer with a sonic cannon, but was killed by Xoanon instead (4Q).

NEFRED, RAGEN Alzarian Decider who became First Decider after Draith's death. He was extremely indecisive, and died when the Marshmen attacked the *Starliner* (5R).

NEKROS (aka NECROS) Planet where the Tranquil Repose Mortuary and Kara's protein factory were located. The factory's output helped feed the galaxy. The Sixth Doctor exposed Davros's and Kara's plot to turn Tranquil Repose's bodies into protein. After Orcini destroyed the mortuary, the Sixth Doctor showed the Tranquil Repose employees how to convert local flowers into protein (6Z).

NEMAN Proctor of the Fosters of Traken. After the Master (disguised as a Melkur) became the new Keeper, Neman served him and was even made into a Consul. But he failed to prevent the Fourth Doctor from thwarting the Renegade Time Lord's plans. As a demonstration of his power, the Melkur forced Tremas to execute him (5T).

NEMESIS, SILVER Statue made of the deadly, living metal, validium. It had landed in Windsor, Earth, in AD 1638. There, it was shaped into a statue dubbed the Silver Nemesis by Lady Peinforte. After an untold battle with Lady Peinforte, the Doctor (presumably in his second incarnation) launched the Silver Nemesis into space in a rocket-powered asteroid. However, its bow and arrow remained behind. The bow became the Queen's property and was kept at Windsor Castle where, in 1788, it was stolen. Eventually, it fell into the Nazis' hands. Lady Peinforte used the arrow to travel forward in time to 1988, when the Silver Nemesis returned to Earth. (Its orbit had brought it near Earth every 25 years, each time influencing disasters.) It became the object of a contest between the Seventh Doctor, the Nazis, led by De Flores, Lady Peinforte and the Cybermen. Lady Peinforte eventually merged with the statue. The Doctor then used the Silver Nemesis to destroy the Cybermen's space fleet. Also see VALIDIUM (7K).

NEMINI Pygmy Menoptera who was Hetra's deputy (N).

NEO PHOEBUS Name given by Earthmen to the fragment of Voga in orbit near Jupiter (4D).

NEOGORGON Planet visited by Captain Cook (7J).

NEPTUNE Professor Zaroff's pet octopus (GG).

NERO (AD 37–68) Mad Roman emperor who revelled in violence, and eventually started the Great Fire of Rome. He fell in love with Barbara, and mistook the First Doctor for the famous lyre-player, Maximus Pettullian (M).

NERVA Space beacon placed on a 30-year assignment in orbit near the remains of Voga, which was itself orbiting near Jupiter, at the end of the 25th century. Its function was to warn spaceships of Voga's presence. Professor Kellman, secretly working for the Vogans, summoned the Cybermen, who used their Cybermats and Neurotropic X virus to take over the beacon. The Cybermen eventually loaded cyberbombs aboard the beacon, and tried to crash it into Voga. They were thwarted by the Fourth Doctor, Sarah Jane Smith, and Harry Sullivan (4D).

In the 30th century, an unprecedented string of solar flares threatened Earth. Some scientists thought that the flares, which at the time were estimated to last 10,000 years, would cause permanent damage to the human genoplasm. In the greatest secrecy, Space Beacon Nerva was converted into a Space Ark, named Terra Nova, where 100,000 specimens of 'pure' humanity were stored. All records of the Ark were then carefully hidden, and its existence became almost a legend.

The Ark's passengers were supposed to remain in suspended animation for the next 10,000 years, but remained in that state for several thousand years too long. When they awoke, they found that Nerva had been infiltrated by the vengeful Wirrn. It was only the intervention of the Fourth Doctor, Sarah Jane Smith and Harry Sullivan, and the sacrifice of the Ark's leader, Noah, which enabled them to survive (4C).

Spacemen from Earth's colonies began to return to Earth. Like the passengers of the Ark, they assumed it to be lifeless because of the solar flares. Unlike Nerva's inhabitants, however, they believed the flares to have happened when the Time Lords had moved the planet, at the time of the Ravolox Stratagem, and not during the 30th century (4C, 4B).

NESBIN Leader of the group of Shobogans who captured Leela and Rodan. He then helped them and the Fourth Doctor repel the Sontarans' Invasion of Gallifrey (4Z).

NESKA Wife of Sabor and mother of Arak and Tuar on Metebelis

3. She worried about her sons' lives, but was freed from the Spiders when the Great One died (ZZZ).

NESTENE A billion-year-old collective intelligence who abandoned their physical bodies to become a single entity of pure mind, made of energy. The Nestene's original shape was a tentacled creature, with a large, single eye, combining features of the crab and the octopus. The Nestene first arrived on Earth in plastic meteors. They had a special affinity for plastics, and took over the mind of Hibbert, the managing director of Autoplastics, Ltd, and used him to manufacture deadly Autons, as well as replicas of VIPs. Their invasion failed because the portion of their consciousness which had been incorporated on Earth was short-circuited by the Third Doctor and Liz Shaw (AAA).

The Nestene were summoned back to Earth by the Master, who helped them take over the Farrel plastics factory. During their second invasion, in addition to the deadly, dummy-like Autons, the Nestene also controlled a murderous range of plastic items which needed the arrival of more Nestene to be activated. The Third Doctor managed to convince the Master that the Nestene would destroy him too, and the two Time Lords cooperated to banish them back to outer space before they could fully materialize (EEE).

NESTOR Member of Rorvik's crew. He died when the privateer's ship was destroyed (5S).

NETHERCOTT (MISS) Astrologer consulted regularly by Adelaide Lesage (4V).

NEUROTROPE X Virus used by the Cybermen to attack the Moonbase (HH) and Space Beacon Nerva (4D). In the first instance, it was carried in the sugar; in the latter, by the Cybermats.

NEUTRON ACCELERATOR Salamar tried to used a neutron accelerator to kill Professor Sorenson (4H).

NEUTRON FLOW One of the Third Doctor's favourite solutions was to reverse the polarity of the neutron flow.

NEUTRON STAR The Tythonians diverted a neutron star and aimed it to collide with Chloris's suns to avenge the kidnapping of their ambassador Erato by Lady Adrasta. The Fourth Doctor and Erato teamed up to weave an aluminium shell around the star and redirect it (5G).

NEUTRONIC WARS The culmination of the initial wars between the Kaleds and the Thals on Skaro (B, 4E).

NEVIN UNIT corporal who helped the Brigadier against Azal and Bok (JJJ).

NEW EARTH Supposedly a planet like Earth, but unspoiled by pollution and technology; the goal of the ship carrying the 'People' selected by Sir Charles Grover. In reality, because of Operation Golden Age, New Earth would have been the same 'old' Earth, but time would have been rolled back by Professor Whitaker's machine (WWW).

NEW HEIDELBERG Professor Marius was a specialist in extra-terrestrial, pathological endo-morphisms at New Heidelberg University in the 50th century (4T).

NEW SARUM Space beacon destroyed by pirate Caven (YY).

NEWTON RESEARCH INSTITUTE Cambridge scientific establishment where the Master, posing as Professor Thascales, worked on TOM-TIT and the Kronos Crystal (OOO)

NEXOS Trisilicate miner on Peladon who died as a result of Eckersley's schemes (YYY).

NIASH Member of the Ark who was sentenced to be miniaturized (X).

NIGHTSHADE See ATROPINE.

NILS Danish astronomer on the Moonbase during the Cybermen attack (HH).

NILSON Sea Base Four's Controller, and Vorshak's second-in-command. He was secretly in the employ of a rival Bloc and, with Dr Solow's help, brainwashed Maddox. He was killed by the Sea Devils (6L).

NIMON Bull-headed race of aliens who could be likened to a plague of galactic locusts and who used black holes to travel through space. Their mode of operation was to send a single Nimon ahead to promise wealth and power to an unsuspecting race, then build a Complex which enabled the other Nimon to infiltrate, take over and eventually drain the host planet from its resources. They called it the Great Journey of Life. The Nimon tricked Soldeed into erecting such a complex on Skonnos. The Fourth Doctor and Seth exposed the Nimon and destroyed the Complex, leaving the Nimon stranded on the dying world of Crinoth. They tried using an energy chain reaction to reach another planet, and perished in the ensuing catastrophe (5L).

NIMON COMPLEX Huge labyrinthine complex erected by the Nimon on Skonnos. At its centre was a black hole leading to Crinoth. It was destroyed by the Fourth Doctor and Seth (5L).

NIMROD Neanderthal who had been rescued and made immortal by the powerful alien Light. He became Josiah Samuel Smith's servant. At Gabriel Chase, Nimrod helped the Seventh Doctor thwart Smith's plans. After Light's defeat, he left in the alien ship with Control and Fenn-Cooper (7Q).

NINODS Tythonian unit of time (5G).

NITRO-NINE Powerful explosive and Ace's favourite weapon (7G–7P).

NO EXIT One of the Red Kangs of Paradise Towers. He was killed by the Cleaners (7E).

NOAH Prime Unit, or Leader, of the Chosen on the Ark in Space. He fought the Fourth Doctor because his body had been taken over by the Wirrn, but his mind eventually found the strength to rebel. He sacrificed his life to save the Ark and destroy the swarm (4C).

NOGHAI Tartar Khan whose capital was Karakorum. He was a fierce rival of Kublai Khan's, and, with Tegana's help, tried to take over China. His plans were thwarted by the First Doctor (D).

NOLA One of King Thous's advisers in Atlantis (GG).

NOMA One of the Jacondans serving Azmael. She worked for Mestor, and was killed by Hugo Lang (6S).

NORD Also known as the Vandal of the Roads. He was one of the contestants in the talent contest organized by the Psychic Circus, to entertain the Gods of Ragnarok. He died in the ring (7J).

286

NORM Alzarian class of citizens who received normal education (5R).

NORNA Frontios colonist, and Mr Range's daughter. She helped the Fifth Doctor expose and defeat the Tractators (6N).

NORTH SEA Home of the parasitic, intelligent Weed (RR). The Zygons' Skarasen also travelled through an underground passage from Loch Ness to the North Sea to attack several off-shore rigs (4F).

NORTHCAWL Copper mine on Androzani Major, owned by the Sirius Conglomerate (6R).

NORTHUMBERLAND Ancient Vikings buried Fenric's flask in a small village on the coast of Northumberland. The Seventh Doctor eventually fought the Wolves of Fenric there during World War II (7M).

NORTHUMBRIA The First Doctor fought the Meddling Monk there in AD 1066 (S).

NORTON, WILFRED IMC agent who claimed to be a colonist whose colony had been wiped out by lizard attacks, and whose survivors had been killed by the Primitives. He killed Holden, but was later exposed and killed by Winton (HHH).

NORTON Corporal who fought the Dinosaur Invasion (WWW).

NOSFERATU Sabalom Glitz's ship. Its crew had been sold by Glitz and frozen by Kane. In order to manipulate Glitz into looking for the Dragonfire, Kane threatened to confiscate it. Kane wanted the Nosferatu destroyed, but Belasz thwarted him. The ship was used in the evacuation of Iceworld, but was blown up by Kane. After Kane's suicide, Glitz rechristened Iceworld *Nosferatu II* (7G).

NOSTALGIA TRIPS Company which had charted the galactic tour bus to 1959 Disneyland, but which was forced to land in Wales instead. According to the Seventh Doctor, they had been plagued with endless disasters (7F).

NOT-WE Term used by the Kinda to refer to the Earthmen who were not a part of their mental gestalt (5Y).

NOVA DEVICE Movellan bomb capable of annihilating an entire planet. Sharrel planned to use it on Skaro, but was stopped by Romana (5J).

NOVAE In the very far future, the First Doctor watched Earth plunge into the Sun, which may have triggered a nova-like explosion (X). The Fourth Doctor jettisoned the Fendahl Skull near a supernova to destroy it (4X). Proamon's sun had gone nova a thousand years after Kane's exile (7G).

The Hand of Omega was a stellar manipulator created by Omega, which could turn a star into a supernova. The Seventh Doctor used it to turn Skaro's sun into a supernova (7H). The supernova created by Omega collapsed and turned into a black hole trapping the great Solar engineer inside a universe of anti-matter (RRR). Presumbly that black hole was the same black hole later captured by Rassilon, and which became known as the Eye of Harmony (4P). Omega eventually returned through the Arc of Infinity, a collapsed star (6E).

NUAL One of the Swampies killed by Kroll (5E).

NUCLEAR ENERGY The Third Doctor saved the Wenley Moor atomic research station from the Silurians (BBB), and the Nuton Power Complex from Axos (GGG). The Fourth Doctor saved the Experimental Atomic Energy Complex from Eldrad (4N). The alien Dominators did not hesitate to turn a planet into a radioactive mass for their fuel supply (TT).

NUCLEAR WARS The threat of World War III was averted several times by the Third and Fourth Doctors (FFF, KKK, 4A). Future Earth wars included limited nuclear wars in the early 21st century, which Salamander used to his own benefit (PP), and the 51st-century battle against the Alliance led by Magnus Greel (4S). Alien nuclear wars included the so-called Thousand-Year War between the Thals and the Kaleds, which resulted in the creation of the Daleks (4E, B), the Dulcian wars (TT), the Atrios-Zeos war (5F), the Argolin – Foamasi war (5N) and the Karfel-Bandril war (6Y). Also see WAR.

NUCLEUS Noetic core entity of the Virus of the Purpose. It was a blood-red, crustacean-like, tentacled monster. The Nucleus used the Fourth Doctor's body as host, lodging itself in his mind – brain interface. The Doctor placed himself in a self-induced coma to cut off the mental activity which nourished the Nucleus. Miniaturized clones of the Doctor and Leela were then dispatched by Professor Marius to kill the Nucleus, but the alien entity escaped and enlarged to human size. Lowe took the Nucleus back to its Hive on Titan, where it would be able to swarm. It was eventually destroyed when the Doctor blew up the base (4T).

NUMISMATON Volcanic flame produced by the Fire Mountain of Sarn. It was a rare catalytic reagent which could cure deadly ills, and extend an individual's life and powers. The Fifth Doctor used it to save Malkon's life, and the Master was almost destroyed in it (6Q). The Numismaton Flame of Sarn may have been caused by the same phenomenon which created the Sisterhood's Sacred Flame on Karn (4K).

NURSE See XANXIA (QUEEN).

NUTHUTCH Derogatory nickname given by the inhabitants of Llanfairfach to Professor Clifford Jones's Wholeweal Community (TTT).

NUTON POWER COMPLEX Nuclear research centre which was under the direction of Sir George Hardiman. In spite of the Third Doctor's efforts, it was attacked and destroyed by Axos (GGG).

NUTTING UNIT corporal who set up the explosives who eventually destroyed the Silurian shelters at Wenley Moor (BBB).

NYDER Sadistic Kaled Security Commander. He interrogated the Fourth Doctor and his companions when they arrived on Skaro. Nyder was fiercely loyal to Davros, and helped him plot the destruction of his own people. He was eventually killed by the Daleks (4E).

NYSSA Companion of the Fourth and Fifth Doctors, and Tremas of Traken's daughter. She helped the Fourth Doctor defeat the Master on Traken, then went in search of her father, whose body had been taken over by the Renegade Time Lord. She followed the avatar of the Doctor, known as the Watcher, to Logopolis, then Earth, where she watched the Fourth Doctor regenerate. She then helped the Fifth Doctor fight the Master, Monarch, the Mara and the Terileptils. During a visit at Cranleigh Halt, she discovered she was a perfect double for Ann Talbot, Charles

Cranleigh's fiancée. Alongside the Fifth Doctor and Tegan, she fought the Cybermen, the Master again (disguised as Kalid), Omega, the Mara again, and Mawdryn. Finally, she found her calling when she chose to remain on Terminus to synthesize hydromel and help the victims of Lazar's disease (5T–6G).

O

O'CONNOR, ANTHONY See AUKON.

O'HARA Morestran guard who was part of Vishinsky's landing party on Zeta Minor. He was killed by the anti-matter creatures (4H).

OAK (MR) The Weed's mind slave. With his partner, Mr Quill, he attacked Maggie Harris, and later tried to thwart the Second Doctor's efforts to destroy the parasitic intelligence (RR).

OBAN Kastrian technician (4N).

OBERON (GRAND ORDER OF) Quasi-religious order of space knights devoted to fighting evil. Orcini had been a member, but was excommunicated (6Z).

OCULOID Tracking probe used by the Morestrans (4H).

ODDA Name of the Zygon who impersonated Sister Lamont. He killed Angus McRanald (4F).

ODYSSEUS (aka ULYSSES) Crafty King of Ithaca. He was one of the Greek warriors involved in the Trojan War. He suspected that the First Doctor was not really Zeus, and forced him to come up with the statagem of the Trojan Horse (U).

OFFICIAL One of the Supervisors in charge of the gas mine work shifts on the Macra-dominated space colony (JJ).

OGDEN Private who fought the Dinosaur Invasion (WWW).

OGREK Lobos's second-in-command at the Moroks' Space Museum (Q).

OGRI Aliens from Ogros who resembled stone megaliths and fed on a globulin found in human blood. Three Ogri arrived on Earth with Cessair of Diplos, whom they served. They became part of a Stone Circle which, at various times in history, became known as the Six, Seven or Nine Travellers. One Ogri was destroyed by the Fourth Doctor, another by the Megara and the third one was returned to Ogros (5C).

OGRONS Savage, primitive brutes used as henchmen by the Daleks. The Third Doctor encountered them twice. The first time, they were pursuing the guerilla from the future (KKK). The second time, they were used by the Master in his attempts to foment a war between Earth and the Draconians. The Doctor travelled to the Ogron home world, a barren, desolate place, inhabited by fierce, giant lizards which preyed on the Ogrons (QQQ). Some Ogrons were prisoners of Vorg's Scope (PPP).

OGROS Home world of the Ogri, located in the Tau Ceti star system. It was covered in great swamps full of amino acids (5C).

OHICA Priestess of the Sisterhood of Karn, who assumed the leadership of the Sisterhood after Maren's death (4K).

OK CORRAL Scene of a famous gunfight on 26 October 1881 between the Clanton brothers and Johnny Ringo on one side, and the Earp Brothers and Doc Holliday on the other (Z).

OKDEL See OLD SILURIAN.

OLA Chief of Police of the Macra-dominated space colony (JJ).

OLD JOSH See JOSH.

OLD MOTHER Old cavewoman, member of the Tribe of Gum, and Za's mother. She thought fire was evil. She was later stabbed to death by Kal (A).

OLD SILURIAN Leader of the Silurian triad of Wenley Moor, which included the Young Silurian and Icthar. He had developed a relationship with Dr Quinn. The Third Doctor convinced him that the Silurians could share Earth peacefully with Mankind. When he realized the Young Silurian was trying to wipe out humanity with a virus, he freed the Doctor and gave him the means to find an antidote. He was then killed by the Young Silurian. According to some reports, his Silurian name was Okdel (BBB).

OLLIS, ARTHUR Game warden in an Essex bird sanctuary mistakenly kidnapped by Omega. After helping the Three Doctors defeat the renegade Time Lord, he was safely returned to Earth (RRR).

OLLIS (MRS) Arthur Ollis's wife (RRR).

OLVIR See KARI.

OLYMPIC GAMES Intergalactic Olympics were held during the 27th century (5J).

OMDSS See ORGANIC MATTER DETECTOR SURVEILLANCE SYSTEM.

OMEGA First and foremost of the ancient Gallifreyan Solar Engineers. Using his Stellar Manipulator (also known as the Hand of Omega), he detonated a star into a supernova, the tremendous energy of which was required for the Gallifreyans to achieve mastery of time travel and become Time Lords. However, when the supernova suddenly collapsed into a black hole, Omega was trapped and projected into an anti-matter universe. He blamed the Time Lords for his predicament, and swore revenge. When Omega tried to escape, the Time Lords summoned the Three Doctors to fight him. Omega then discovered that he could not leave the anti-matter universe, because anti-matter had totally destroyed his physical being, and only his mind was left. He was presumed dead in a matter/anti-matter explosion caused when his anti-matter being came into contact with the Second Doctor's positive matter recorder (RRR).

However, Omega survived and returned from the anti-matter universe by using the Arc of Infinity, a collapsed Q-star. He allied himself with Councillor Hedin, invaded the Matrix, and tried to bond physically with the Fifth Doctor, so that he could remain in our universe. The Doctor then used a matter converter to banish and, presumably, destroy Omega before a huge anti-matter explosion could annihilate Amsterdam (6E).

OMEGA Nickname given by the Second Doctor to one of the three 'humanized' Daleks (LL).

OMENS Name given by the people of Zanak to the changes in the stars caused each time Zanak made a space jump (5B).

OMRIL Bigoted Alzarian technician who was afraid of the Marshchild (5R).

OPEKS Monetary unit used throughout the Cyrennic Empire. Garron wanted ten million opeks for Ribos, but settled for eight (5A).

OPERATION GOLDEN AGE Operation masterminded by Sir Charles Grover. In the first stage, Professor Whitaker used his time scoop to bring forward prehistoric monsters to clear the streets of London. This became known as the Dinosaur Invasion. Then, Grover and Whitaker planned to roll time back, and return Earth to an age when it was yet unspoiled by pollution and technology. Grover had recruited volunteers, dubbed the 'People', and had tricked them into believing they were on a spaceship en route to another planet, New Earth. The People were supposed to become the occupants of New Earth, which would have been in reality the 'old' Earth after time had been rolled back. Operation Golden Age was exposed, and stopped, by the Third Doctor and Sarah Jane Smith (WWW).

OPTERA See MENOPTERA.

ORACLE Computer of the legendary lost ship *P7E* which carried the Minyan Race Banks. The *P7E* drifted to the edge of the universe, where enough space matter accumulated around it that it became the center of an underground world known as Underworld. The Oracle became sentient, and used the Race Banks to create a society comprised of the Seers, the Guards and the Trogs to serve it. Eventually, the *P7E* was found by Jackson and his crew. With the help of the Fourth Doctor and Leela, they wrested the Race Banks from the Oracle. The Oracle and its Underworld perished in an explosion caused by two fission grenades disguised as the Race Banks, which the Oracle had intended to use to destroy Jackson's ship (4Y).

ORB Fire god of the cavemen (A).

ORCINI Former knight of the Grand Order of Oberon. He was excommunicated and became a mercenary, accompanied by his squire, Bostock. His right leg had been replaced by an artificial one. Orcini was hired by Kara to kill Davros. He fought Davros's Daleks alongside the Sixth Doctor. He eventually sacrificed his life to blow up Tranquil Repose and Davros's Dalek 'factory' (6Z).

ORDER The concept of Order and Light was embodied by the White Guardian (5A, 6H).

ORDERLIES Title borne by the officers of the colony of Frontios (6N).

ORFE Member of Jackson's crew. He fought the Oracle in the Underworld alongside the Fourth Doctor and Leela. After the Quest was over, he returned to Minyos II (4Y).

ORGANIC MATTER DETECTOR SURVEILLANCE SYSTEM (OMDSS) Security system installed aboard the Ark in Space (4C).

ORGANON Lady Adrasta's court astrologer. She had him thrown into the Pit because he had foreseen Erato's real nature. He helped the Fourth Doctor to expose Adrasta's duplicity, and reveal Erato's true nature (5G).

ORIGINS OF MAN See ANTHROPOLOGY.

ORINOCO Venezuelan Portion of the Amazon explored by George Cranleigh (6A).

ORLION Precious mineral normally found only on Collactin, and Bandraginus Five, a planet destroyed by Zanak (5B).

ORTEZO See ATZA.

ORTRON Queen Thalira of Peladon's Chancellor. He was opposed to the Federation's interference in Peladon's affairs. He distrusted the Third Doctor, and was able to sway the Queen by his advice. He eventually joined Gebek when Azaxyr's Ice Warriors took over Peladon, and was killed by Sskel while helping the Queen escape (YYY).

ORUM Commissioner on the Aliens' Admission Commission on Inter Minor. At first, he helped Kalik in his attempts to discredit the President's liberal policies, but then balked when Kalik attempted to free the Drashings. After Kalik was defeated by the Third Doctor and Vorg, Orum surrendered and confessed (PPP).

OSBORN Crew member of the space penitentiary where Davros was kept. He was killed during the Daleks' attack (6P).

OSEIDON Homeworld of the Kraals, who had ruined it through internecine atomic wars. It became increasingly radioactive, driving the Kraals to attempt the conquest of other planets (4J).

OSGOOD Lunar controller of the T-Mat system. After he was notified of the system's failure by Gia Kelly, he returned to the Moon. He was killed by the Ice Warriors (XX).

OSGOOD UNIT Sergeant who helped the Brigadier against Azal and Bok (JJJ).

OSIRIANS Race of godlike beings who arose on Phaester Osiris and who visited Earth in the days of Ancient Egypt. Their leader Horus and seven hundred other Osirians defeated Sutekh and imprisoned him inside a secret pyramid, where he was immoblized by a force field generated by the Eye of Horus. The Eye was located in the Pyramids of Mars. The Osirians then left the Solar System. Their final fate is unknown (4G).

OSMIC PROJECTOR Linx's rudimentary time machine used to kidnap 20th-century scientists (UUU).

OTHERS Name given by the Citizens of Pluto to the rebels who lived in the Undercity: outlaws, tax criminals and escapees from the correction centres. Mandrel was their leader (4W).

OTHRYS First planet ever visited by the Psychic Circus (7J).

OUTCASTS See SHOBOGANS.

OUTLERS Young Alazarians who refused to believe in the Deciders' rule, and chose to live outside the *Starliner*. Varsh was their leader (5R).

OUTSIDER, THE Mythical figure of Sarn's religion, inspired by their early contacts with the Trions. The Sarns believed that if they submitted to the god Logar, the Outsider would come and bring them many gifts. The Master pretended to be the Outsider (6Q).

OUTSIDERS See SHOBOGANS.

OVERLORDS Nickname given to the humans by the Solonians (NNN).

OXLEY WOODS Landing site of the Nestene meteorites. It was also where the Third Doctor's TARDIS rematerialized after his first trial by the Time Lords (AAA).

OXYGEN See GAS.

OZA Insane Varosian morgue attendant. He and Az were supposed to dispose of the Sixth Doctor's body in an acid bath, but instead fell into it (6V).

P

P7E Legendary lost ship which carried the Minyan Race Banks. It drifted to the edge of the universe, where enough space matter accumulated around it that it became the center of an underground world known as Underworld. Eventually, the *P7E* was found by Jackson and his crew. With the help of the Fourth Doctor and Leela, they wrested the Race Banks away from the Oracle. The *P7E* and the Underworld perished in an explosion caused by two fission grenades disguised as the Race Banks, which the Oracle had intended to use to destroy Jackson's ship (4Y).

P, ERNEST Stage doorman at the Forum where Happiness Patrol auditions were held (7L).

P, PRISCILLA Fanatical member of the Happiness Patrol. She was in charge of the waiting zone where killjoys were kept before being executed. After the revolution overthrew Helen A's regime, she was condemned to repaint the TARDIS in its original colour (7L).

P, SILAS Undercover member of the Happiness Patrol of Terra Alpha. He was responsible for the arrest of 47 killjoys. After he tried to have the Seventh Doctor arrested, he was mistaken for a killjoy, and shot by the Happiness Patrol (7L).

PACIFIER Device designed by the Minyans to quell aggressive instincts (4Y).

PACKARD Helmsman on Rorvik's ship. He died when the privateer's ship was destroyed (5S).

PACKER Ruthless Chief of Security of International Electromatics. He fought alongside his boss, Tobias Vaughn, against the Second Doctor and UNIT to make the Cybermen Invasion possible, although he did not completely trust the Cybermen. He was eventually killed by the Cybermen (VV).

PADMASAMBHAVA High Lama of Det-Sen monastery, gifted with extraordinary mental powers. He met the Doctor for the first time in the 17th century. During one of his astral journeys, he later met the Great Intelligence, who promised him knowledge and long life, and ultimately took over his mind. The Intelligence used him to manipulate its robot Yeti and protect its attempt at reincorporation. Padmasambhava died after the Second Doctor challenged the Intelligence to a mental battle, enabling Jamie and Thomni to destroy its pyramid gateway (NN).

PAGET, MISS Sir Reginald Styles's secretary (KKK).

PALACE THEATRE Henry Gordon Jago's theatre, and Magnus Greel's secret lair (4S).

PALEONTOLOGY See ANTHROPOLOGY.

PALESTINE It was visited by the First Doctor and his Companions at the time of the Third Crusade (P).

PALMER UNIT corporal who fought against Omega's gel creatures (RRR). He also helped fight the Zygons (4F).

PALMERDALE, HENRY (LORD) Crooked financier. He tore up Colonel Skinsale's gambling debts in exchange for insider information, which he intended to use to profit on the stock market. His insistence on a speedy return to London caused his ship to crash on Fang Rock. In spite of the Fourth Doctor's efforts, he was eventually killed by the Rutan (4V).

PAMIR Tibetan plateau where the First Doctor met Marco Polo in 1289 AD (D).

PANATO, ZA One of the eleven geniuses kidnapped by the Rani to make up her giant Brain (7D).

PANDAK THE THIRD President of the High Council of the Time Lords of Gallifrey. He ruled for nine hundred years (4P).

PANDATOREA (GREAT LAKES OF) According to the Sixth Doctor, an ideal place for fishing (6W).

PANGOL Argolin who was cloned by the Tachyon Recreation Generator from cells donated by other Argolins. He saw himself as a new Theron, the leader of a new, warlike Argolis. After Mena collapsed, and the West Lodge Foamasi plot to buy the Leisure Hive was exposed, Pangol planned to use the TRG to recreate millions of duplicates of himself. His plans were thwarted by the Fourth Doctor and Hardin, who pushed him inside the TRG with Mena. He was rejuvenated as a baby (5N).

PANNA Ancient, blind Kinda wise-woman. She felt that the Earth Expedition to Deva Loka was a threat to their way of life. After she died, Karuna inherited all of her knowledge (5Y).

PANOPTICON Heart of the Capitol of the Time Lords of Gallifrey. The Eye of Harmony was secretly kept under the Panopticon (ZZ, RRR, 4P, 4Z, 6E, 6K).

PARADISE TOWERS 304-storey luxury residence built by Kroagnon, the Great Architect. Kroagnon's brain was secretly buried in the Towers' basement after he tried to prevent people from living in his creation. The Towers fell into disrepair after most of its residents left to fight in (presumably) the First Dalek Wars. The only people to remain were the Caretakers, the Old (or 'Rezzies') and the Kangs. Under Kroagnon's influence, the robotic Cleaners began to exterminate all human life inside the Towers. Kroagnon eventually took control of the Chief Caretaker's body. With the help of Pex and the Kangs, the Seventh Doctor managed to expose and destroy Kroagnon (7E).

PARALLEL MATTER Scientific theory worked out by Dastari (6W).

PARALLEL UNIVERSES (aka ALTERNATIVE REALITIES) Worlds similar, but not identical, to the one where the Doctor's adventures took place. More often than not, they occurred because of a significant temporal divergence: the near-future universe where the First Doctor and his companions ended up as exhibits in the Moroks' Space Museum was such an alternative reality (Q). Other such parallel universes included: the world where the Daleks successfully invaded Earth after World War II was triggered by the assassination of diplomat Sir Reginald Styles (KKK), and the world where Sutekh destroyed the Earth after being released from his pyramid (4G). More elaborate parallel universes included: the fascist England destroyed by Professor Stahlman's 'Inferno' project (DDD) and the alternative world ruled by Morgaine after she defeated King Arthur in the Middle Ages (7N).

It has been argued that the Doctor's interventions in Earth's history contributed to changing its future, and therefore, many of the future Earths visited by the Time Lord were themselves parallel universes. Certainly, some of the events reported during the so-called 'Trial of the Time Lord', such as the Sixth Doctor's original, unrecorded encounter with Mel and a number of their adventures together (including the one where they saved the *Hyperion III* from the Vervoids), became part of a parallel universe after the Valeyard's defeat (7A–7C).

PARAPSYCHOLOGY SCHOOL Earth school attended by Zoe. It placed an emphasis on pure logic and intellectual achievements to the detriment of emotions (SS). It may have developed into the founding institution of the Brotherhood of Logicians (MM).

PARASITES Parasitic entities who depended on other living beings for their sustenance included: the Fendahl, who stole life itself (4X); vampiric life forms who fed on blood such as: the Ogri (5C), the Vampires (5P), the Tetraps (7D), and the Haemovores (7M); vegetal entities such as: the Weed (RR) and the Krynoids, who devoured animal life (4L); the Virus of the Purpose (4T) and the Wirrn (4C) who laid their eggs in humans. The Elders (AA) and Magnus Greel (4S) drained the energy of others to survive. The Krotons drained the Gonds' mental energies to repower their Dynatrope (WW). Finally, the Chameleons tried to steal human identities (KK).

Other parasites drained all energy and natural ressources from planets, leaving shrivelled husks behind. Among these were: Axos (GGG), the Usurians (4W), the Nimon (5L), the Tractators (6N) and the Gastropods (6S). The Dominators (TT) and the pirate planet Zanak also thrived on other worlds' destruction (5B).

Other parasitic entities who preyed on human emotions,

such as evil or faith, included: the Mind Parasite (FFF), the Mandragora Helix (4M), the Mara (5Y, 6D) and the Malus (6M). The Celestial Toymaker (Y), the Master Brain of the Land of Fiction (UU), the Eternals (6H) and the Gods of Ragnarok all depended on humans to fill their craving for entertainment (7J).

Parasites who simply wanted to rule and live at the expense of their victims included: the Animus (N), the Macra (JJ), the Nestene (AAA,EEE) and the Spiders of Metebelis 3 (ZZZ). The Tharils once lived a parasitic lifestyle until they were killed by the Gundans or enslaved (5S). All conquerors were, economically speaking, parasites.

Isolated instances of parasitic actions occurred when: Meglos took over an Earthman's body (5Q); Omega tried to bond with the Fifth Doctor's body (6E) and Kroagnon's brain took over the Chief Caretaker's body (7E). The Rani used a sluglike parasite to control her victims' will (6X). Also see VAMPIRES.

PARIS City visited by the First Doctor during the French Revolution (H) and at the time of St Batholomew's Day Massacre (W). The Fourth Doctor and Romana fought Scaroth there (5H).

PARIS Son of King Priam of Troy. He started the chain of events which eventually led to the Trojan War by eloping with Helen, King Menelaus's wife. (U).

PARKER UNIT private who was involved in the matter of the three radioactive alien Ambassadors (CCC).

PARKINSON Blind vicar who performed religious rites when the Seventh Doctor had the casket containing the Hand of Omega buried. He later performed the same services at Mike Smith's funeral (7H).

PARKINSON (MRS) Ace's art teacher (7N).

PAROLI Sea Base Four crewmember. He was killed by the Sea Devils (6L).

PARRINIUM A rare mineral found only on Exxilon, which proved to be the only cure for a space plague (XXX).

PARRAN According to Gharma one of the Kaleds opposed to Davros (4E).

PARRY (PROFESSOR) Archeologist who discovered the Tomb

of the Cybermen on Telos during an expedition financed by Logician Eric Klieg. When he realized his mistake, Parry helped the Second Doctor defeat the Cybermen (MM).

PARSONS Professor Marius's assistant. He was shot by Lowe (4T).

PARSONS, CHRIS Young Cambridge student who graduated in 1975 with honors in chemistry. He accidentally borrowed *The Ancient Law of Gallifrey* from Professor Chronotis. He and his friend, Clare Keightley, helped the Fourth Doctor and Romana defeat Skagra (5M).

PARTICLE DISSEMINATOR Weapon with which the Valeyard plotted to kill the Time Lords attending the trial of the Sixth Doctor. The Doctor overloaded it with an Ion Avalanche Diode (7C).

PARTICLE SUPPRESSOR Silurian weapon used on Sea Base Four. It turned an energy beam back on its sender (6L).

PASTEUR, LOUIS (1822–95) French chemist, one of the eleven geniuses kidnapped by the Rani to make up her giant Brain (7D).

PATEL Member of the Peace Party, and prisoner at the Luna Penal Colony. He befriended the Third Doctor and Professor Dale (QQQ).

PATERSON Retired sergeant teaching self-defense course in Perivale, whose creed was 'survival of the fittest'. He was taken to the planet of the Cheetah People, but later refused to listen to the Seventh Doctor and believe in the reality of his experience. He was eventually killed by Midge (7P).

PATREXES One of the Time Lords' colleges represented by the colour heliotrope (4P).

PATTERSON Doctor employed by the Euro-Sea Gas Corporation at its North Sea Refinery. When the Weed attacked, he was dispatched to Rig D (RR).

PATTERSON One of the workers at the Inferno Project site (DDD).

PAYNE, JOE Member of Lytton's gang of robbers. He was killed by the Cybermen in the London sewers (6T).

PCM (PENTO CYLEINIC METHYL HYDRANE) Anxiety-inducing gas pumped into the air of the Megropolises of Pluto by the Company, to prevent the Citizens from rebelling. Bisham had found an antidote for it (4W).

PEACE See WAR.

PEACEPIPE Former member of the Psychic Circus (7J).

PEASE POTTAGE Mel came from Pease Pottage, Sussex (7C).

PEINFORTE (LADY) British aristocrat from the 17th century. She shaped validium into the statue dubbed the Silver Nemesis. It revealed many secrets about the Time Lords and the Doctor to her. Lady Peinforte fought the Doctor for possession of the statue, but lost. She then used the statue's arrow to travel forward in time to 1988 Windsor with her manservant Richard, when the Silver Nemesis returned to Earth. There, she fought the Seventh Doctor, the Nazis, led by De Flores, and the Cybermen. Having failed to blackmail the Doctor with his secrets, she merged with the statue (7K).

PEKING (aka BEIJING) Capital of China. The First Doctor met Kublai Khan there (D). Magnus Greel's Time Cabinet was brought to Peking by Emperor T'ungchi's soldiers, and later given to Prof. Litefoot's family (4S).

PEKING HOMUNCULUS Devilish automaton devised by Magnus Greel. It was operated by a series of magnetic circuits and a small computer with the cerebral cortex of a pig. The Homunculus needed a human operator, but the mental feedback was so intense that its swinish instincts became dominant. It hated humanity and reveled in carnage. It was supposed to be a toy for the children of the Commissioner of the Icelandic Alliance, but in reality it was an assassination weapon. The Homunculus massacred the Commissioner and his family, setting off World War VI and enabling the Supreme Alliance to take over Earth. After the Alliance had been overthrown, the Homunculus fled with Magnus Greel to 19th-century China. It then travelled to London where, under the name of Mr Sin, it played the part of a ventriloquist's dummy and became part of Li H'Sen Chang's magic act. The Homunculus's blood lust eventually caused it to turn against all humans, including Greel, whom he shot down with laser fire. It was then disconnected by the Fourth Doctor (4S).

PELADON King of Peladon who wanted his planet to join the Federation. With the help of the delegate Arcturus, Hepesh conspired to stop Peladon, and eventually tried to take him hostage. Peladon was indecisive, and was only saved by the Third Doctor and Jo Grant (whom he was very fond of) (MMM).

PELADON Planet rich in trisilicate. Circa AD 3700, under King Peladon's reign, the Third Doctor helped it join the Federation and, with the help of Alpha Centauri and the Martian Ice Warriors, exposed an Arcturian plot (MMM). Fifty years later, the Third Doctor prevented the hostile Galaxy 5 from using the traitor Eckersley to take over Peladon's trisilicate mines (YYY).

PEMBERTON British army colonel who fought the Web of Fear (QQ).

PENLEY, ELRIC Senior Scientist of the Britannicus Base in 3000 AD who clashed with Clent over the latter's over-reliance on computers. Penley joined Storr and became a scavenger. He later helped the Second Doctor defeat the Ice Warriors, and eventually reconciled with Clent, after having proven the value of human initiative (OO).

PENN International Space Corps technician serving under General Hermack (YY).

PENTALION DRIVE Power source for transmats in the 25th century (4D).

PEOPLE, THE Name given by Sir Charles Grover to the volunteers he had recruited and tricked into believing they were on a spaceship en route to another planet named New Earth. The People were supposed to become the occupants of the New Earth, which in reality, was to be merely the same 'old' Earth, after time had been rolled back by Operation Golden Age (WWW).

PERCIVAL, CHARLES (DR) Director of the Newton Research Institute where the Master worked on TOM-TIT. He fell under the Master's control and was eventually killed by Kronos (OOO).

PERCY Member of K'Anpo's meditation centre (ZZZ).

PERFECT VICTIM Name given by the Aztecs to the person who would be sacrificed to Huitzilipochtli by Tlotoxl (F).

PERI See BROWN, PERPUGILLIAM.

PERIBOEA Planet visited by Captain Cook (7J).

PERIERA (COLONEL) Space raider, nicknamed the chief who trained Valgard and Olvir (6a).

PERIVALE Ace's home town. The Seventh Doctor took her back to confront her fears in the evil house, Gabriel Chase, in AD 1883 (7Q). Eventually, Ace returned to modern-day Perivale to look up her friends, and helped the Seventh Doctor rescue several of its denizens who had been kidnapped by the Master and the Cheetah People (7P).

PERKINS Gray's manservant. He finally elected to join McLaren and the other highlanders who sailed for France (FF).

PERKINS Megan Jones's assistant (RR).

PERKINS UNIT Private killed during the Cybermen Invasion (VV).

PERKINS One of the soldiers under Commander Millington's command in Northumberland. He was killed by the Haemovores (7M).

PERRY, KENNETH Mr Waterfield's assistant (LL).

PERRY (DR) Moreton Harwood G. P. (K9).

PERSEUS Constellation where Mogar was located (7C).

PERSUASION He and Enlightenment were Monarch's two Urbankan android ministers. Persuasion was destroyed by the Fifth Doctor (5W).

PERUGELLIS Star sector where Beta Two, the original destination of the *Hydrax*, was located (5P).

PETER One of the Moonbase crew. He was killed by the Cybermen (HH).

PETERS Flight Lieutenant who fought the Cybermen Invasion (VV).

PETERS UNIT Major who fought the Silurians (BBB).

PETERSON One of Professor Cornish's assistants (CCC).

PETROSSIAN Member of the Soviet commando, led by Captain Sorin, which infiltrated Northumberland to steal the Ultima Machine 'core'. He was killed by the Haemovores (7M).

PETROV, BORIS IVANOVICH 1812 Russian soldier who, along with the Second Doctor, fought in the Resistance to put an end to the War Games. He was eventually returned to his proper place in time and space by the Time Lords (ZZ).

PETTULLIAN, MAXIMUS Famous Corinthian lyre-player who was in league with Tavius to assassinate Emperor Nero. The First Doctor was mistaken for Pettullian after the latter was murdered by Ascaris (M).

PEVENSEY CASTLE Ship attacked by the Sea Devils (LLL).

PEX Young man who lived in Paradise Towers. He pretended to be a hero, but in reality was a coward who had stayed behind when the other residents had gone to fight in the wars. He redeemed himself when he sacrificed himself to help the Seventh Doctor destroy Kroagnon (7E).

PHAESTER OSIRIS Homeworld of the Osirians. It was destroyed by Sutekh (4G).

PHAROS PROJECT Earth project using a radiotelescope to search for intelligent lifeforms and transmit messages to remote planets. The Logopolitans used block transfer computations to copy it, and broadcast the necessary calculations needed to keep the Charged Vacuum Emboitements open and prolong the life of the universe. After the Master disrupted the workings of Logopolis, the CVEs began closing. Fortunately, the Logopolitans had discovered an equation that would stabilize them. In spite of the Master's attempts to stop him and blackmail the Universe, the Fourth Doctor succeeded in using the Pharos Project to broadcast the Logopolitans' final calculations. However, the Master caused the Doctor to fall and almost die, triggering another regeneration (5V). The Master kidnapped Adric before leaving the site of the Pharos Project (5Z).

PHILIPPINO ARMY The Doctor claimed to have fought alongside the Philippino Army at the Battle of Reykjavik against the Supreme Alliance (4S).

PHILLIPS, GEORGE (PROFESSOR) Professor working at the Beacon Hill Research Establishment. The Master took control of his mind, and left him at Rossini's International Circus. Later, he tried to use him to kill the Third Doctor with an explosive device, but Phillips's mind rebelled and broke free. He took the brunt of the explosion and died (EEE).

PHILLIPS Employee of Professor Stahlman's Inferno Project (DDD).

PHILLIPS Member of Think Tank Staff (4A).

PHILLIPS One of the Londoners caught up in the Dinosaur Invasion (WWW).

PHIPPS T-Mat operator on the Moon when it was taken over by the Ice Warriors. He was killed by the Ice Warriors as he tried increasing the temperature to disable the Martians (XX).

PHOENIX IV The supply ship Silver Carrier was this class of ship (SS).

PHYLLIS See JEAN.

PHYLOX SERIES Andromedan planetary series, supposedly the location of Castrovalva (5Z).

PICTOS Planet where the Menoptera retrenched after they were driven away from Vortis by the Animus and the Zarbi (N).

PIERROT Costume worn by both the Fifth Doctor and George Cranleigh during the costume ball at Cranleigh Hall (6A)

PIGBIN JOSH See JOSH.

PIGMY MENOPTERA See MENOPTERA.

PIGS The Peking Homunculus incorporated the cerebral cortex of a pig into a small computer (4S).

PIKE, SAMUEL Infamous 17th-century pirate captain and smuggler who wore a hook at the end of his right arm. He had once served under the notorious Captain Avery with fellow pirates Longfoot and Cherub. Pike tried to find Avery's treasure, and even fought Cherub to the death, but was eventually thwarted by the First Doctor. He was shot by Blake (CC).

PILOT Second-in-command of the Macra-dominated space colony.

He eventually helped the Second Doctor expose and defeat the Macra (JJ).

PILOT Captain of the Skonnan ship which carried the Anethan tribute to Skonnos. His name was Sekkoth. He was killed in a ship explosion (5L).

PING-CHO Young Chinese girl from the 13th century who was to marry an aged nobleman. Her betrothed died during the First Doctor's visit to Peking, and she eventually married her true love, Ling-Tau (D).

PINTO Nurse in charge of First Aid at Gatwick Airport. Her identity was taken over by the Chameleons. After Meadows killed her alien double, the real Pinto helped the Second Doctor defeat the aliens (KK).

PIPE PEOPLE Original inhabitants of Terra Alpha driven underground by the human settlers. Their real name was the Alpidae, but they had been nicknamed Pipe People because they had been relegated to living inside the colony's network of pipes. They were slowly dying of starvation. A tribe led by Wulfric and Wences helped the Seventh Doctor and Ace overthrow Helen A's tyrannical regime (7L).

PIRATES The First Doctor fought Captain Pike's pirates on the Cornish coast in the 17th century (CC). The Second Doctor fought Caven's space pirates in the future (YY). The Fourth Doctor fought the Captain of Zanak, dubbed the 'pirate planet', who liked to surround himself with the trappings of piracy (5B), and Captain Rorvik, who held the time-sensitive Tharils captive (5S).

PIRO Denizen of Marinus (E).

PIT Former mine where Lady Adrasta kept Erato prisoner. She used him to kill the rebels to her despotic rule (5G).

PJX 18 Another name for quartz, found in abundance on Earth. The Captain of Zanak was prepared to crush Earth to obtain it and replace his damaged Macromat Field Integrator (5B).

PLACE OF DEATH Name given by Lady Adrasta to the landing spot of Erato's ship (5G).

PLAGUES See DISEASES.

PLAIN OF STONES Spiridon landmark (SSS)

PLANETS FUNCTIONING AS SPACESHIPS See SOLAR SYSTEM, HOLLOW WORLDS.

PLANTAGENET Captain Revere's son. He became the leader of the Frontios colony after his father was kidnapped by the Tractators. He, too, was captured by the Tractators who wanted to attach him to their excavating machine. He was saved by the Fifth Doctor and restored as colony's leader (6N).

PLANETS (FUNCTIONING AS SPACESHIPS) See SOLAR SYSTEM, HOLLOW WORLDS.

PLANTS See VEGETALS.

PLASMATONS Random agglomeration of proteins assembled from the air and the passengers of the Concorde Flight 192, which were brought together by the evil Xeraphin's power. They were used by the Master to do his bidding in the Jurassic period (6C).

PLASTICS The Nestene had a special affinity for plastics (AAA, EEE).

PLETRAC Chairman of the Alien's Admission Commission on Inter Minor in charge of investigating Vorg's Scope. He was very loyal to the President, but clearly outwitted by Kalik (PPP).

PLINY Name of Ta's star (YY).

PLIOCENE It was during the Pliocene era – 2.5 to 12 million years ago – that the Fendahl Skull arrived on Earth (4X). Also see ANTHROPOLOGY.

PLUTO Ninth planet of the Solar System. The Usurians' Company moved men to Pluto, around which they had built six small artificial suns. There, mankind lived a heavily taxed life until they were freed by the intervention of the Fourth Doctor and Leela. (4W).

PLUTON One of the Moroks under Lobos at the Space Museum (Q).

POACHER, THE Unnamed peasant enslaved by the Terileptils (5X).

PODS See SEEDS.

POISONS See DRUGS.

POL CORPS Varosian police (6V).

POLICEMEN A Policeman patrolled in front of 76 Totter's Lane (A). Bert Rowse was the policeman who arrested Forester (J). The First Doctor was mistaken for a lunatic by Liverpool policemen; Steven had to disguise himself as a policemen from another other precinct to rescue him (V). Sergeant Rugg was one of the Celestial Toymaker's Pawns (Y). Autons dressed as policemen tried to kill the Third Doctor and Jo Grant (EEE). PC Quick and Sergeant Kyle interrogated Leela in the matter of the Tong of the Black Scorpion in Victorian London (4S). St Cedd's College porter summoned a policeman after Professor Chronotis's room disappeared (5M). The Master killed a policeman near Heathrow Airport (5V). Commander Lytton disguised two of his men as policemen to capture or kill people who had escaped through the Daleks' time corridor. The two were eventually caught by the Sixth Doctor (6P, 6T).

POLITICS See REVOLUTIONS.

POLLOCK, WILLIAM Retired Navy commander and Aunt Lavinia's partner in a market-garden shop in Moreton Harwood. In reality, he was the High Priest of Hecate. He and Lily Gregson were arrested thanks to the efforts of Sarah Jane Smith and K-9 mark III (K9).

POLLUTION The Third Doctor fought the threat of the Green Death in Wales (TTT). Sir Charles Grover, the mastermind behind Operation Golden Age, was the founder of the Save Planet Earth Society (WWW). Professor Kettlewell agreed to join the Scientific Reform Society because he wanted to stop pollution (4A).

Earth had become almost hopelessly polluted by the 52nd century, when the alien Usurians offered to move the surviving population to Mars and, later, to Pluto (4W). Others chose to emigrate in what became known as the Second (or Great) Break Out (4T, 4Q). The Sons of Earth fought to make sure that other worlds would not become as polluted as Earth (5E). During the thousands of years during which polluted Earth was left alone, a new life form arose on Earth: that of the Haemovores (7M).

Eventually, as the planet's ecological balance was restored, the Haemovores became extinct. After the Fourth Doctor helped men break free from the Usurians' yoke, they reclaimed the planet (4W).

POLLY See LOPEZ, POLLY.

POLO, MARCO (1254–1324) Venetian merchant and explorer. He wanted to present the TARDIS as a gift to Kublai Khan in the hope that the Khan would allow him to return to Venice. He helped the First Doctor prevent Kublai Khan's assassination at Tegana's hands (D).

POLYGRITE Substance used by the Terileptils (5X).

POLYPHASE AVATRON Murderous machine in the form of a parrot which was the Captain of Zanak's pet, and which he used to discipline his crew. It was destroyed by K-9 mark II (5B).

PONTI Executive Officer aboard the Morestran spaceship sent to Zeta Minor. He was one of Vishinsky's landing party, and helped the Fourth Doctor fight the anti-matter creatures (4H).

PONTON Planet known for making battleships (5A).

POPPAEA Emperor Nero's vain, vicious and greedy wife. He married her in AD 62, but she died three years later. She tried to kill Barbara (M).

POPPLEWICK A Dickensian bureaucrat working at J.J. Chambers' Fantasy Factory – in reality, an avatar of the Valeyard inside the Matrix (7C).

PORTER The porter at St Cedd's called a policeman after noticing the disappearance of Professor Chronotis's room (5M).

PORTON DOWN The Brigadier told the Fifth Doctor that Harry Sullivan had been seconded to NATO, and was involved in a secret operation at Porton Down (6F).

PORTREEVE Leader of Castrovalva impersonated by the Master. His tapestry showed scenes from the past (5Z).

POSIKAR Planet which traded with the Mentors (7B).

POST OFFICE TOWER Famous London site which was the location of WOTAN (BB).

POSTEIDION (MARK 7) Life-preserver system used aboard the *Hyperion III* (7C).

POTASSIUM STREET Landmark of Paradise Towers (7E).

POWELL Employee at Brendon school (6F).

POUL Chief Mover of the *Sandminer* crew. In reality, he was an investigator sent by the Company, along with D84, to look for Taren Capel. He eventually succumbed to robophobia and went insane (4R).

POWERS Senior officer at Stangmoor Prison. He was killed by Mailer (FFF).

PRAESIDIUM Ruling body of Androzani. It was under the control of the Sirius Conglomerate (6R).

PRALIX Young man of Zanak, and Mula's brother. He became a Mentiad after absorbing the life force released by Calufrax. He led the Mentiads, and helped the Fourth Doctor and Romana defeat the Captain (5B).

PRAPILIUS Old Menoptera who was enslaved by the Zarbi on Vortis. He led the rebellion against the antlike creatures, and enabled the Menoptera invasion force to succeed. He helped the First Doctor defeat the Animus, and eventually became leader of the Menoptera (N).

PRATUS Chlorasian astrological Sign (5G)

PRAXSIS See CELERY.

PREBA Young trisilicate miner of Peladon. He was killed by the Ice Warriors when he tried to free Gebek (YYY).

PREHISTORY See ANTHROPOLOGY.

PRESIDENT (OF ANDROZANI) Leader of the Androzani Praesidium. He was assassinated by Morgus (6R).

PRESIDENT (OF EARTH) 26th-century woman. She was in power when the Master tried to foment a war between Earth and the Draconians. She agreed to break off diplomatic relations, but steadfastly refused to be the first to launch an act of war (QQQ).

PRESIDENT (OF THE TIME LORDS) The President of the High

Council of the Time Lords of Gallifrey was the most powerful of all Time Lords. He was elected by the High Council, sometimes based on a nomination from his predecessor. The President wore the three symbols of power; the Coronet, the Sash and the Rod of Rassilon.

The President was probably one of the three Time Lords who passed judgement on the Second Doctor and the War Lords (ZZ). Then, the President (since no name was provided, and Time Lords have the ability to regenerate, it could have been the same President, or a different one) suggested teaming up the Three Doctors to defeat Omega (RRR). When the President was about to resign, and Chancellor Goth found out that he would not be the chosen successor, he plotted with the Master to kill him and frame the Fourth Doctor for the murder. In order to gain time and escape immediate execution, the Doctor offered himself as candidate for the Presidency. After Goth's death, he automatically became President (4P). When the Fourth Doctor found out that the Vardans had invaded the Matrix and were planning to take over Gallifrey, he returned to claim the Presidency, and used the symbols of the office to defeat them, and later, the Sontarans. He then abdicated in favour of Borusa (4Z).

When Omega threatened to return to our universe by threatening to take over the Fifth Doctor's body, a regenerated Borusa voted to condemn the Doctor to death (6E). Borusa regenerated again (which may have imbalanced his mind) and fell victim to a megalomaniacal passion. He decided he wanted to remain President forever and acquire the true immortality once promised by Rassilon. In order to break through the Tomb of Rassilon, he used the Five Doctors and their companions, pitting them against various threats in the Death Zone. Rassilon finally gave him the immortality he sought by turning him into a living statue. This in turn led the Council to appoint the Fifth Doctor as President. But he made Chancellor Flavia his deputy and left (6K).

By the time the Sixth Doctor was put on trial, Flavia had been deposed and a new, corrupt President elected. It is that President who probably initiated the Ravolox Stratagem and used the Valeyard in an attempt to prevent the Doctor from finding out. After he was exposed during the Trial of the Doctor, he too was deposed. The Inquisitor tried to persuade the Doctor to become President again, but he refused (7A–7C).

312

PRESLIN, CHARLES Famous apothecary and medical pioneer. He was visited by the First Doctor a few days before the St Batholomew's Day Massacre. Preslin had incurred the wrath of the Abbot of Amboise and, with the Doctor's help, was able to flee to Germany (W).

PRESTA Member of the group of Shobogans who found Leela and Rodan. She helped them and the Fourth Doctor repel the Sontarans' Invasion of Gallifrey (4Z).

PRESTON Sea Base Four Lieutenant. She helped the Fifth Doctor fight the Silurians and the Sea Devils. She sacrificed her life to save that of the Fifth Doctor; she was shot by Sauvix (6L).

PRIAM King of Troy, and father of both Paris and Troilus. He died during the fall of Troy (U).

PRICE Communications officer at the Euro-Sea Gas North Sea refinery which was attacked by the Weed. He helped Harris and the Second Doctor destroy the Weed (RR).

PRIMAL WARS Term used to designate mankind's early space wars (X).

PRIME UNIT Noah's title on the Ark in Space (4C).

PRIMITIVES Telepathic inhabitants of Exarius. They were harmless savages who worshipped the Guardian of the Doomsday Machine, the sole survivor of the super-beings who once occupied Exarius. They probably perished when the Guardian destroyed the Doomsday Machine (HHH).

PRIMORDS Nickname given to men infected by a green slime released by the Inferno project. Mere contact with the slime caused a regressive mutation of the body cells, turning the victim into a savage, snarling beast. The first Primord was Harry Slocum. Eventually, even Professor Stahlman himself turned into a Primord. The Primords needed intense heat to survive, and could be destroyed by extreme cold such as the frozen CO_2 gas contained in a fire extinguisher (DDD).

PRION Planetary system of Tigella and Zolfa-Thura (5Q).

PRIORY (OLD) Professor Scarman's house. It was burned down in the 1911 conflagration that followed the Fourth Doctor's battle with Sutekh (4G). UNIT headquarters was later built on that site.

PRISONS The First Doctor briefly visited the prison planet of Desperus (V). Ian was imprisoned on Marinus (E). The First Doctor also visited his companions, who were imprisoned at the notorious Conciergerie (H). The First Doctor also saw the insides of Tombstone's jail (Z). The Third Doctor was imprisoned in the Luna Penal Colony (QQQ) and in Atlantis (OOO). The Master engineered a jailbreak at Stangmoor Prison to seize the Thunderbolt missile (FFF). The evil Time Lord was later jailed in an island prison, but escaped thanks to the Sea Devils (LLL). The Fourth Doctor visited a space prison; it was in the shape of a satellite orbiting Earth in hyperspace above the circle of the Stones of Blood (5C). Sutekh was imprisoned inside a pyramid, guarded by a force field controlled from Mars (4G). The mysterious Shada was the prison of the Time Lords (5M), but both the Fourth Doctor (4P) and the Fifth Doctor (6E) were imprisoned on Gallifrey. The Fifth Doctor tried to prevent Davros from escaping from a space prison (6P). Sarn was Trion's prison planet (6Q).

PRITCHARD, BERT A Llanfairfach miner who died of the Green Death (TTT).

PRITCHARD, MARGARET As Lady Pritchard, she was George Pritchard's wife and mistress of Gabriel Chase. After Josiah Samuel Smith took over, she became Mrs Pritchard, the night housekeeper, and served Smith. She was eventually turned to stone by Light (7Q).

PRITCHARD, GEORGE (SIR) Original master of Gabriel Chase. He was the husband of Lady Margaret and the father of Gwendoline. He was killed by Gwendoline, acting under Josiah Samuel Smith's control (7Q).

PRITCHARD, GWENDOLINE Daughter of George and Margaret Pritchard. After Josiah Samuel Smith took over Gabriel Chase, she fell under his control and became his ward. She sent unwanted visitors, including her own father, 'to Java' (a euphemism for killing them). She was eventually turned to stone by Light (7Q).

PROAMON Kane and Xana's homeworld. The Proamons had exiled Kane to Svartos, and entrusted the dragonfire crystal that could power his ship (Iceworld) to a mechanoid dragon. Proamon's sun went nova a thousand years after Kane's exile. When the Seventh Doctor told Kane, he chose to commit suicide (7G).

PROBE 6 British spaceship sent to Mars. One crewmember, Jim Daniels, died. The other, Carrington, met peaceful radioactive aliens, who asked him to pave the way for their Ambassadors. But the xenophobic Carrington later used the Ambassadors to try to start a war between Earth and the aliens (CCC).

PROBE 7 British spaceship sent to Mars. Its crew, astronauts Lefee and Michaels, were replaced by the radioactive alien Ambassadors (CCC).

PROBIC VENT One of the known weaknesses of the Sontarans. It was a small aperture in the backs of their necks, needed to recharge their life force when outside their regular environment. Hal, a Wessex archer, killed Linx by shooting an arrow into his probic vent (UUU). Leela killed a Sontaran by throwing a knife in his probic vent (4Z).

PROCTOR Dr Cook's assistant (OOO).

PROCTOR Title borne by Neman of Traken (5T).

PROJECT DEGRAVITATE Dalek name for their plan to release Earth's molten core and replace it with a power system (K).

PRONDYN First Elder of the Aridians. He eventually yielded to the Daleks' threat, and agreed to hand over the First Doctor (R).

PROTON MISSILES Missiles stored at Sea Base Four (6L).

PROZOROV Sergeant in the Soviet commando, led by Captain Sorin, which infiltrated Northumberland to steal the Ultima Machine 'core'. He was killed by the Haemovores (7M).

PRYDONIANS One of the Time Lords' colleges; their colours were red and gold. The Doctor, Drax, Chancellor Goth and, presumably, Borusa and the Master, were Prydonians (4P).

PSYCHIC CIRCUS Circus created by Kingpin, also known as the Greatest Show in the Galaxy. On the planet Segonax, it was taken over by the Gods of Ragnarok, who used it to fill their unholy craving for entertainment. It was held in a grip of fear by the evil Chief Clown and his robotic clowns, which had been designed by Bellboy. Its founder, Kingpin, had become a brain damaged labourer called Deadbeat. The Psychic Circus was rescued by the Seventh Doctor and Ace, who defeated the Gods of Ragnarok. A cured Kingpin planned to launch a new circus with Mags (7J).

PSYCHIC INTERFERENCE TRANSMITTER To counteract the Mentiads' psychic powers, Mr Fibuli used Vollium and Madronite 1–5 crystals which, when refined, had the ability to interfere with mental power. It was rendered ineffective when K-9 mark II set up a counterinterference on the wavelength of 337.98 microbars (5B).

PSYCHIC POWERS See HYPNOTISM, TELEKINESIS, TELEPATHY, TELEPORTATION.

PSYCHOMETRY Science used by the First Doctor to deal with the Sensorites (E).

PUDDING LANE London street where the Fifth Doctor started the Great Fire of 1666 (5X).

PUDOVKIN Member of the *Nosferatu* crew sold by Glitz. He was killed by Kane after he went into the Restricted Zone (7G).

PULL BACK TO EARTH 21st-Century political movement whose goals were to abandon space exploration and retrench to Earth (SS). It eventually led to the worldwide adoption of T-Mat (XX).

PUNISHMENT See CRIME.

PUNISHMENT DOME Place where the Varosian rebels were publicly tortured. The Sixth Doctor, Jondar, and Areta succeeded in escaping from it (6V).

PURPLE ZONE Section of the Varosian Punishment Dome where perceptions were distorted by deadly hallucinations (6V).

PURPOSE, THE The overriding purpose of the Virus was to swarm and multiply (4T).

PYLE (GATHERER) Company's senior tax collector for Megropolis Three on Pluto (4W).

PYRAMIDS The First Doctor fought the Daleks and the Monk at the time of the construction of Kephren's Pyramid, circa 2600 BC (V). The godlike Osirian Sutekh was prisoner inside a pyramid on Earth, somehow prevented from leaving by the Eye of Horus, which was kept inside a pyramid on Mars (4G).

Q

Q CAPSULES Drug which enabled the Company's workers to do without sleep (4W).

Q STAR On burn-out a Q star creates Quad magnetism, the only force with the ability to shield anti-matter (6E). Also see ARC OF INFINITY.

Q, SUSAN Young member of the Happiness Patrol on Terra Alpha. She was once known as Susan L and liked blues music. She befriended Ace, and helped her and the Seventh Doctor support the revolution which finally overthrew Helen A's regime. She and Earl Sigma then began teaching the blues to the newly liberated population (7L).

QUAD MAGNETISM The only force capable of shielding anti-matter. It was generated by a Q Star burning out, but decayed rapidly. Omega used it to try to take over the Fifth Doctor's body (6E).

QUANTUM ACCELERATOR TARDIS component exchanged by the Master and the Fifth Doctor (6C).

QUARB CRYSTAL Component of the hyperspatial engine which propelled Murray's galactic tour bus. It was broken in the crash, but the Seventh Doctor grew a replacement (7F).

QUARKS Deadly robot servants used by the Dominators. Rago and Toba used them in their plan to turn Dulkis into radioactive waste, but they eventually ran out of power after trying to capture or destroy the Second Doctor and his Dulcian friends (TT).

QUARTZ See PJX 18.

QUASAR FIVE Quasar investigated by the Time Lords (4Z).

QUATERMASS, BERNARD (PROFESSOR) Famous British rocket scientist, head of the British Rocket Group. He had several close encounters with alien phenomena. He was known to Rachel Jensen and Allison Williams (7H).

QUAWNCING GRIG Shockeye's tribe (6W).

QUEEN SPIDER Queen of the Spiders of Metebelis 3. She plotted against the Great One, and took control of Sarah Jane Smith to get the Blue Crystal. She died when the Third Doctor and K'anpo freed Sarah (ZZZ).

QUEST Name given by Jackson's crew to their mission of finding the P7E and the Minyan Race Banks. Their motto was: 'The Quest is the Quest' (4Y).

QUESTA Member of the Macra-dominated space colony and was Medok's friend (JJ).

QUICK Police constable who assisted the Fourth Doctor in his battle against Magnus Greel and the Tong of the Black Scorpion (4S).

QUILL See OAK (MR).

QUILLAM Sadistic Varosian arch-interrogator, and designer of the Punishment Dome. It was he who had designed a nuclear bombardment technology capable of transmogrifying a human body into an animal shape. He had become partially disfigured as a result of his dangerous experiments. Quillam conspired with the Chief Officer to help Sil keep Zyton-7 prices low. He was killed by deadly vines while pursuing the Sixth Doctor (6V).

QUINLAN, JAMES (SIR) Minister of Technology and Space Development. He had secretly conspired with General Carrington to keep the arrival of the radioactive alien Ambassadors secret, because he wanted Britain to be the first to benefit from such a contact. Carrington later forced one of the aliens to kill him (CCC).

QUINN Deputy governor of Vulcan. He helped the Second Doctor save the colony from the Daleks. He was eventually made governor after Hensell's death (EE).

QUINN, MATTHEW (DR) Dr Lawrence's deputy at the Wenley Moor atomic research station. He was the first to discover the Silurians, and developed a relationship with the Old Silurian. Because he wanted to become a famous scientist he kept it a secret, except from Miss Dawson, hampering the Third Doctor's investigations. He later rescued the Young Silurian, who eventually killed him (BBB).

QUINNIS A planet visited by the Doctor (C).

QUIQUAEQUOD Wizardly name conferred upon the Third Doctor by Miss Hawthorne (JJJ).

R

RAAGA Location of the Tinclavic Mines where the Terileptils sent their Outcasts (5X).

RAAK Monster whose brain had been enhanced by Crozier. The Sixth Doctor killed him to defend himself (7B).

RACE BANKS Gold cylinders containing all the genetic heritage of Minyos, which had been placed aboard the *P7E*. The ship's insane computer, the Oracle, used them to create the races of the Seers, the Guards and the Trogs to serve him in the Underworld. Thanks to the Fourth Doctor's help, the Race Banks were taken away from the Oracle and returned to Jackson, who took them back to Minyos II (4Y).

RACHEL See RAY.

RACHEL See JENSEN, RACHEL.

RADIATION Radiation is generally harmful to humans and most aliens. Among its effects are death and, over a period of time, mutation. For example, the radioactivity created on Skaro by the neutronic wars was ultimately responsible for many horrible mutations, as well as the final shapes of both the Daleks and the Thals (B, 4E). The Mondasian Cybermen were especially vulnerable to radiation (DD). The Kraals were forced to abandon their home planet of Oseidon because of radioactivity (4J).

Some life forms, however, thrived on radiation. The so-called 'Ambassadors of Death' were radioactive aliens (CCC). Radiation enabled Eldrad the Kastrian to regenerate (4N). The Usurian Controller of Pluto maintained his pseudo-human form through stratified particle radiation (4W). The Foamasi could live in highly radioactive environments (5N).

The Time Lords had greater tolerance to radiation than humans, although the Third Doctor's regeneration was triggered by an over-exposure to radiation (ZZZ). The Sash of Rassilon was designed to protect its wearer against the effects of the deadly energies generated by the Eye of Harmony (4P).

Finally, the Dominators looked upon radioactivity as a natural resource and turned planets into radioactive waste in order to power their space fleet (TT). Also see MUTATIONS, and MINERALS for various radioactive materials.

RADNOR Commander in charge of the T-Mat system, and Gia Kelly's superior. He assisted the Second Doctor in his fight against the Ice Warriors and their Seeds of Death. After the Martians' defeat, he agreed with Professor Eldred that alternative methods of transport (such as rocketships) needed to be developed (XX).

RAGNAR One of the Viking raiders defeated by Wulnoth's Saxons (S).

RAGNAROK, GODS OF Three mysterious, powerful entities from the planet Segonax who took control of the Psychic Circus and used it to fill their unholy craving for entertainment. They controlled the Circus under the avatar of a human family (Dad, Mum and the Little Girl), and through the evil Chief Clown and its deadly robotic clowns. The Seventh Doctor defeated them by turning their own power against them with the help of the Gods' medallion (7J).

RAGO One of the Dominators' navigators. He and his subordinate, Toba, were sent to Dulkis to turn the planet into radioactive waste to repower their fleet. He perished in an explosion caused by their own atomic seeding bomb, which had been removed and placed on board their ship by the Second Doctor (TT).

RAILTON, JACK RICHARD Scientist who accompanied the Earth marine space corps expedition, which had been sent to Exxilon to bring back parrinium. In spite of the Third Doctor's efforts, he was killed by the wild Exxilons (XXX).

RALPACHAN One of Khrisong's men (NN).

RALPH One of the Moonbase crew. He was turned into a 'zombie' by the Cybermen (HH).

RALPH Squire John's elderly servant, killed by the Terileptils (5X).

RALPH SEED COMPANY Smithers used their seeds to test the DN6 insecticide (J).

RAMLAH Saladin's main city (P).

RAMO Atlantean priest who backed the Second Doctor when he tried to expose Zaroff. He was later stabbed by the mad scientist (GG).

RAMSEY, ALAN 18th-century artist who painted a portrait of Lady Montcalm, aka Cessair of Diplos (5C).

RANDALL, LOTTIE One of Magnums Greel's victims (4S).

RANDOM FIELD FRAME The Fourth Doctor used the TARDIS randomizer to equip the Argolin's Tachyon Recreation Generator with a second random field frame, in order to achieve rejuvenating capabilities (5N).

RANDOM LASER BEAM EMITTER Varosian torture device (6V).

RANDOMISER Device built by the Fourth Doctor to randomize the TARDIS's jumps, and therefore escape the vengeance of the Black Guardian (5F). The Doctor eventually removed and used it to reengineer the Leisure Hive's Tachyon Recreation Generator so that it could rejuvenate the Argolins (5N).

RANGE Chief Science officer of the Frontios colony, and Norna's father. He helped the Fifth Doctor expose and defeat the Tractators (6N).

RANI, THE Renegade female Time Lord. It is possible that she visited India at one time during her travels, since her name means 'reigning queen'. She was a master biologist, completely amoral, and interested only in the fate of her experiments. She attended the same Time Lord university as the Doctor and the Master, and allegedly turned mice into giant monsters who devoured the President's pet cat, resulting in her exile from Gallifrey.

The Rani eventually enslaved the population of Miasimia Goria. To increase their productivity, she gave them a drug which instead deprived them of sleep and turned them into savages. To cure the problem, she travelled to Earth to steal the brain fluids that enable humans to sleep, planning to feed them to the Miasimians. By so doing, the Rani was indirectly responsible for causing a number of violent episodes throughout human history: the Trojan War, the Dark Ages, the American War of Independence and the Luddite Uprisings. Her latter visit caused her to ran afoul of both the Sixth Doctor and the Master. The two renegade Time Lords entered into an uneasy alliance, but were still outwitted by the Doctor, who sent them both spinning into the outer fringes of the universe in the Rani's TARDIS (6X).

The Rani then took over Lakertya, controlling its weak-willed population with the help of her new allies, the four-eyed Tetraps. She took the Lakertyans' leader Beyus, and his daughter, Sarn, hostage and kept the other Lakertyans submissive by threatening to release a swarm of deadly insects. The Rani kidnapped eleven of the greatest intellects in the universe and combined them into a giant Brain. She also caused the Sixth Doctor's TARDIS to crash on Lakertya, triggering his regeneration. She plotted to launch a Loyhargil rocket to blow up an asteroid made up of Strange Matter. The resulting explosion would have turned the Brain into a planet-sized Time Manipulator, with which she could have recreated the universe. The Seventh Doctor incited the Lakertyans to revolt, and tricked the Rani by inducing schizophrenia in the Brain. He caused the rocket to miss the asteroid. The Rani escaped in her TARDIS, but was taken prisoner by the Tetraps who wanted to use her genius to help their people (7D).

RANJIT Senior crewman in charge of the solarium on the

Morestran spaceship sent to Zeta Minor. He was killed by Sorenson when the scientist turned into a neanderthal-like monster (4H).

RANQUIN Leader of the Swampies on Delta Magna's third moon. He hated the humans and bought guns from Rohm-Dutt to attack Thawn's methane refinery. He fanatically believed in Kroll's divinity, but was eventually killed by the giant monster (5E).

RANSKILL GARDENS Professor Litefoot's address (4S).

RANSOM British army captain who was aide-de-camp to General Smythe. He believed he was fighting against the Germans in World War I. In reality, he was part of the War Games (ZZ).

RANSOME Radar operator who first detected Axos (GGG).

RANSOME, HARRY Head of Sales and Designs for Auto Plastics, Ltd. He returned from the United States to find the company under Nestene control. After he was fired by Managing Director Hibbert, he stumbled upon the Autons' secret. He warned UNIT, but was later killed by an Auton (AAA).

RANSOME, THEA Scientist who worked with Dr Fendelman. She was used by Stael and turned into the Fendahl Core by the Fendahl. She perished in that form when the Fourth Doctor destroyed the Fendahl Core and the Fendahleen (4X).

RANX Planet incorporated into Tryst's CET (5K).

RAPUNZEL Fairytale princess encountered by the Second Doctor, Jamie, and Zoe in the Land of Fiction (UU).

RASK One of the Guards who served the Seers and the Oracle in the Underworld. He fought the Fourth Doctor and Jackson's Minyans. He and the Underworld perished in an explosion caused by the fission grenades disguised as the Race Banks, which the Oracle had intended to use to destroy Jackson's ship (4Y).

RASSILON Founder of the Time Lords of Gallifrey. The legends around his life and deeds date back to the very origins of the Time Lords, and are shrouded in mystery. Rassilon went into a black hole, the Eye of Harmony, presumably created by the collapse of Omega's supernova, captured it, and stored it under the Panopticon, thereby providing the Time Lords with a virtually inexhaustible source of energy, capable of meeting the huge demands of time travel (4P).

Rassilon also created the Rassilon Imprimature, a symbiotic nucleus contained within the Time Lords' genes that was somehow connected with their ability to withstand the molecular destabilization caused by time travel, and to achieve quasi-symbiotic control of their TARDISes. Indeed, the Rassilon Imprimature was needed to 'prime' a TARDIS (6W). Lastly, Rassilon created the three symbols of power worn by the President of the Time Lords: the Coronet of Rassilon, which linked the President's mind to the Matrix and enabled it to bend other minds to his will; the Sash of Rassilon, which protected its wearer from the deadly energies released by the Eye of Harmony; and the Rod of Rassilon (or Great Key), which controlled the access to the Eye of Harmony itself.

Rassilon later contributed various other artefacts to the defenses of Gallifrey: the Key of Rassilon, which harnessed the energy of the Eye of Harmony to power the Demat Gun (4Z) (another Key of Rassilon gave access to the Matrix (7C)); the force fields known as the Transduction Barrier, which protected Gallifrey (4Z); and the deadly Silver Nemesis, made of the living metal validium, and meant to be Gallifrey's ultimate defense (7K). Rassilon is also credited with creating the bow ships which destroyed the Great Vampires (5P). The book stolen by Salyavin, *The Ancient Law of Gallifrey*, which contained the secret of Shada's location, was said to be an artefact created in the time of Rassilon (5M).

Rassilon had much of the Time Lords' history preserved in documents such as the Black Scrolls (6K), and the Records of Rassilon, which used to be kept in all TARDISes (5P).

The Harp of Rassilon was the secret key to the hidden room where the controls to the so-called Game of Rassilon were kept. It is not known whether Rassilon was responsible for starting or ending this cruel habit of using the Time Scoop to snatch beings from various places and times and making them fight in the Death Zone for the Time Lords' amusement, but it is known that his body was later entombed in a tower located at the very centre of the Death Zone. However, his spirit lived on, and was able to protect Gallifrey from the megalomania of Borusa by tricking him into accepting the immortality of a living statue. (An inscription in the Tomb of Rassilon promised true immortality to anyone who would take the Ring from Rassilon's fingers.) (6K).

RASSILON IMPRIMATURE Symbiotic nucleus contained within the Time Lords' physiology that is somehow linked to their ability to withstand the molecular destabilization caused by time travel, and to achieve quasi-symbiotic control of their TARDISes. Indeed, the Rassilon Imprimature was needed to 'prime' a TARDIS. Sontaran Group Marshal Stike allied himself with Chessene to capture the Second Doctor, whom they planned to dissect in order to obtain the secret of the Imprimature, but they were thwarted by the Sixth Doctor (6W).

RASTON WARRIOR ROBOT One of the most efficient killing machines ever devised. It had built-in javelins and sensors capable of detecting any movement, and could move with lightning speed. A Raston robot transported by Borusa in the Death Zone decimated a squadron of Cybermen (6K).

RAT, GIANT Magnus Greel mutated a rat to giant size (ten feet from whiskers to tail) to guard his lair inside the London sewers. It was killed by the Fourth Doctor (4S).

RATCLIFFE, GEORGE Leader of a British fascist group working with the Daleks. He used Mike Smith, and dug up the Hand of Omega. After the Daleks turned against him he stole their Time Controller, but was killed by the Daleks' Battle Computer as he tried to escape (7H).

RAVALOX See RAVOLOX.

RAVENSWORTH (LORD) Owner of the Killings-worth colliery where George Stephenson worked and for which he built the first steam-powered locomotive, the Blucher. He rescued the Sixth Doctor from a gang of Luddites and helped him fight the Master and the Rani (6X).

RAVOLOX Alternative name for Earth. When the Sixth Doctor first set foot on Ravolox, and learned that it was Earth, he claimed that two million years had elapsed; however, historical and archeological evidence make this duration unlikely. This action, which seems to have occurred around 14,000, resulted in considerable death and destruction, but was blamed on a freak cosmic phenomenon (a fireball).

The Ravolox Stratagem was uncovered five hundred years later, when the Sixth Doctor and Peri visited Ravolox, and was publicly exposed during the Doctor's trial. Indeed, the Doctor was put on trial because the corrupt High Council of Gallifrey was afraid that he would find out what they had done. On Ravolox, the Doctor met the tribe of the Free, led by Katryca. He thwarted Sabalom Glitz's efforts to steal the secrets taken from the Matrix by the Sleepers. He also destroyed Drathro, the immortal robot who guarded the Sleepers, and ruled an underground civilization of human slaves known as UK Habitat (7A–7C).

Afterwards, the Time Lords probably moved the Solar System back to its original location in space, where it was 'rediscovered'. The destruction caused by the planetary move was still being explained away as the result of a fireball or solar flares, when Earth was reclaimed by the passengers of the space ark Terra Nova, and human colonists from other planets (4C–4B).

RAVON Young Kaled general. He died in the destruction of the Kaled dome (4E).

RAY Young Welsh girl whose real name was Rachel, but who preferred to be called Ray because she was a biker and a rock'n roll fan. She was in love with Billy, who unfortunately preferred Delta. She nevertheless helped the Seventh Doctor defeat the Bannermen (7F).

RAYPHASE SHIFT The Sixth Doctor triggered a rayphase shift to destroy the Valeyard's Particle Disseminator (7C).

RE 1489 Galaxy where Urbanka was located (5W).

REARBUS See KARFEL.

REBEC One of the Thals sent to Spiridon to stop the Daleks. She helped the Third Doctor freeze the Daleks' army. She was romantically attracted to Taron (SSS).

REBELLIONS See REVOLUTIONS.

RECLAIM Ship attacked by the Sea Devils (LLL).

RECORDS OF RASSILON Set of ancient emergency instructions which were once kept in every TARDIS. Although the practice was later discontinued, the Doctor's TARDIS had a set, which the Fourth Doctor consulted to learn how to defeat the Great Vampire (5P). These are not to be confused with the SCROLLS OF RASSILON.

RECOVERY 7 British spaceship sent to investigate the disappearance of Probe 7. Its pilot, astronaut Van Lyden, was replaced by a radioactive, alien Ambassador (CCC).

RECOVERY 8 British spaceship that was flown by the Third Doctor to allow him to make contact the radioactive aliens (CCC).

RECURSIVE OCCLUSION Space-trap set by the Master in the form of Castrovalva, a block transfer computation created by Adric (5Z).

RED KANG See KANGS.

REDCOATS The Second Doctor rescued Jamie from the Redcoats in 1746 (FF). They later met a fictional Redcoat in the Land of Fiction (UU). A Redcoat army was kidnapped by the Warlords, using time technology stolen from the Time Lords. The soldiers went on to take part in the War Games, until these were brought to a stop by the Second Doctor's intervention (ZZ).

REDIMENSIONER Device used by Meglos to shrink the Dodecahedron (5Q).

REDMAYNE, COLIN One of the inhabitants of Salamander's Sanctum (PP).

REEGAN Freelance criminal who was hired by General Carrington to kidnap the three radioactive alien Ambassadors. He forced the aliens to do Carrington's bidding by denying them the radioactive isotopes they needed to survive. Later, he wanted to use the aliens for his own gain. He was eventually captured by Brigadier Lethbridge-Stewart (CCC).

REEVES Medical doctor of Devil's End (JJJ).

REFNAL Young Alzarian Outler. He was killed by the Marshmen (5R).

REFUSIANS Race of super-strong, peace-loving, invisible aliens living on planet Refusis. The Refusians' invisibility was the result of a mutation caused by solar flares. The Refusians helped the

First Doctor thwart Monoid One's plans to destroy the human race, and eventually welcomed both Humans and Monoids on their planet (X).

REFUSIS Planet which was the destination of the Ark, and which ultimately became a new home to both Humans and Monoids, after the First Doctor helped put an end to the hostilities between the two races (X).

REGA Sister of Arak and Tuar on Metebelis 3. She was freed from the Spiders when the Great One died (ZZZ).

REGENERATION The Time Lords of Gallifrey were able to regenerate, and thus extend their lives. Regenerations could be triggered accidentally, and such actions led to the Doctor's fourth, fifth, sixth and seventh incarnations; as a result of the normal ageing process (which led to the Doctor's second incarnation); by Time Lord decree (which led to the Doctor's third incarnation); and some regenerations could seemingly be triggered at will (such as Romana's first regeneration).

The number of regenerations appeared to be limited (perhaps arbitrarily?) to twelve. The Master ran out of regenerations, but believed he could start a new cycle by tapping the power from the Eye of Harmony (4P). Thwarted by the Doctor, he stole Tremas of Traken's body to continue his existence (5T). However, since he was later offered a new cycle of regenerations by the Council of Time Lords when asked to rescue the Doctor from the Dead Zone (6K), the twelfth regeneration was, presumably, not necessarily the final end for a Time Lord. The Valeyard was exposed as the amalgamation of the Doctor's darker side, between his twelfth and final regeneration (7C).

Romana was able to switch between different forms rapidly during her regeneration before it became definitive, which indicates that the Time Lords may have had a certain degree of control over the regeneration process (5J). The trauma of regeneration has been known to affect Time Lords' mental balance: the Third (AAA), Fourth (4A), Sixth (6S) and Seventh (7D) Doctors behaved erratically after their regenerations. The Fifth Doctor needed the isolation of the TARDIS's zero room after his regeneration (5Z). Borusa may have become utterly megalomaniacal after a regeneration (6K).

Certain Time Lords appeared to have the power to foresee

their coming regeneration, and to create a solid, mental projection of themselves which was capable of independent action. K'Anpo did this with Cho-Je (ZZZ), and the Fourth Doctor did the same with the Watcher (5V).

Other races capable of regeneration included: Mawdryn and his fellow aliens, who had stolen a metamorphic symbiosis regenerator from the Time Lords and were doomed to live in a state of perpetual regeneration (6F); the silicon-based Kastrians, who could regenerate, provided they had enough energy and their genetic code (4N); the Minyans, who had obtained the technique from the Time Lords (4Y); the Xeraphin who had merged into one single collective intelligence (6C). The Argolins used their Tachyon Recreation Generator to achieve an artificial form of regeneration (5N). Also see IMMORTALITY.

REGISTERS Sections of Logopolis. The core was the Central Register, which was a copy of the Earth Pharos Project, while calculations were performed in the External Registers (5V).

REGRET Alias used by Steven Taylor in Tombstone, Arizona (Z).

REIG Crewman aboard the Morestran spaceship sent to Zeta Minor. He was killed by Sorenson when the scientist turned into a neanderthal-like monster (4H).

REIMER See KARTZ.

REJA MAGNUM Planet where General Harmack did his first tour of duty. Milo Clancey was a bit of a legend there (YY).

RELIGION The Doctor has come in contact with various Earth religions throughout history. In the west, he was involved in the Third Crusade (P) and almost caught up in the infamous St Bartholomew's Day Massacre in Paris (W). The renegade Time Lord known as the Meddling Monk hid under the trappings of a Christian monk (S). Sarah Jane Smith and K-9 mark III defeated a cult of witches who worshipped the pagan goddess Hecate (K9).

The Doctor visited Egypt during the construction of the Great Pyramid (V), and later fought Sutekh, one of the alien Osirians worshipped as gods by the ancient Egyptians (4G). He was also mistaken for Zeus during the Trojan War (U). The Fourth Doctor defeated the Brothers of Demnos in San Martino (4M).

The Fourth Doctor also came in contact with oriental religions while defending the Tibetan monastery of Det-Sen against the Great Intelligence (NN), meeting his mentor K'Anpo, who was posing as a Tibetan lama (ZZZ) and fighting time traveller Magnus Greel, who was posing as the Chinese god Weng-Chiang (4S).

In the Americas, Barbara tried to change the Aztecs' bloody religion but failed (F). The ancient Atlanteans worshipped the alien Kronos (OOO), but their descendents had reverted to offering human sacrifices to the goddess Amdo (GG). In the future, the Tribe of the Free worshipped Haldron, god of the Earth (7A).

Other aliens worshipped on Earth as 'gods' included the Mondasians (DD), the Daemons (JJJ), the ancient Exxilon (XXX), the Osirians (4G), the Mandragora Helix (4M), Scaroth (5H), Cessair of Diplos (as the Celtic goddess the Cailleach) (5C), the Malus (6M), Light (7Q) and Fenric (7M). Monarch of Urbanka wanted to travel back in time to meet God (5W).

On alien worlds, the Doctor came in contact with a number of religions where primitive people worshipped powerful, often tyrannical, entities: the Krotons (WW), the Guardian of the Doomsday Machine (HHH), the Exxilon City (XXX), Xoanon (4Q), the Oracle (4Y), Kroll (5E), the Nimon (5L), the Mara (5Y, 6D) and the Gods of Ragnarok (7J). The monster Aggedor was almost the object of a cult on Peladon (MMM, YYY). The Sisterhood of Karn worshipped the Sacred Flame (4K). The Minyans referred to the Time Lords as 'gods' (4Y). The Ribans worshipped the Ice Gods (5A). The Tigellan Deons worshipped the Dodecahedron (5Q). On Sarn, the Elders worshipped Logar, god of the Fire Mountain (6Q). The Mentors praised the Great Morgo (7B).

Finally, although they were not worshipped as such, the Celestial Toymaker (Y) and the Guardians of Time exhibited virtually godlike qualities. Also see MAGIC.

REMINGTON, DOROTHEA Lavinia P. Hacken-sack's ancestor, poisoned by Lady Peinforte (7K).

REMUS See SYLVEST, REMUS.

RENAISSANCE In or around AD 1503, the Fourth Doctor and Sarah Jane Smith defeated the Mandragora Helix in the

Dukedom of San Martino, Italy, and helped save the Renaissance (4M). A few years later, the same Doctor met one of Scaroth's twelve splinters, Captain Tancredi, in Leonardo da Vinci's house (5H). The Meddling Monk once discussed flying machines with Leonardo (S).

RENAN, DANIELLE Jules Renan's sister (H).

RENAN, JULES Frenchman working with James Stirling, who helped prisoners of the Conciergerie (including the First Doctor's companions) escape the guillotine (H).

RENEGADE TIME LORDS Name generally given to those Time Lords who refused to obey the rules of Gallifrey, and left it to pursue ambitions of their own. Chief among those are the Doctor, the Master and the Rani. Other notorious renegades include the Meddling Monk (S, V), the War Lords' War Chief (ZZ), K'Anpo (ZZZ), Drax (5F), Salyavin (5M) and Azmael (6S). By refusing to return to Gallifrey and choosing to remain in E-Space, Romana became a renegade Time Lord.

Not all renegade Time Lords were villains. The Renegade known on Earth as K'anpo (ZZZ) and Professor Chronotis (aka Salyavin) (5M) had chosen to retire on Earth. Azmael had chosen to retire on Jaconda (6S). The Shobogans, led by Nesbin, were Time Lords who had voluntarily renounced their position on Gallifrey (4Z).

Evil Time Lords who betrayed their own race included: Omega (RRR, 6E), Morbius (4K), Chancellor Goth (4P), Castellan Kelner (4Z), Councillor Hedin (6E), and, sadly, President Borusa (6K). Finally, the Valeyard was the amalgamation of the Doctor's darker side between his twelfth and final regenerations (7A–7C).

RENIS Maylin of Karfel and Vena's father. He was killed by the Borad and replaced by Tekker (6Y).

REPLICAS Name given to the more perfected type of Auton who could pass off for real people. Replicas included Channing, General Scobie and numerous other famous people (AAA). Also see DUPLICATES.

REPTILES Intelligent reptilian lifeforms encountered by the Doctor included: the Earth-born Silurians and Sea-Devils; the Martian Ice Warriors; the Monoids (X); the Draconians (QQQ);

the Foamasi (5N); the froglike Urbankans (5W); the Terileptils (5R); the Bandrils (6Y); the Lakertyans (7D) and the Thoros-Betans (or Mentors) (6V, 7B). The Mara used the shape of a snake to materialize, but was primarily psychic in nature (5Y, 6D).

Non-intelligent reptiles included the Didonian Sand Beasts (L); the Exarian lizards impersonated by the IMC robot (HHH); the Drashigs (PPP); the Earth-born dinosaurs (WWW); the Zygons' Skarasen (4F); and the Karfelon Morlox (6Y).

Omega's Ergon appeared to share some reptilian features (6E). The Board was half human, half Morlox (6Y). Josiah Samuel Smith appeared to have evolved from an alien reptilian lifeform (7Q).

RESNO One of Lesterson's assistants on Vulcan. He was killed by a Dalek when the scientist repowered it (EE).

RESTING PLACE Name given by Aukon to the altar under the Tower, built just above where the Great Vampire lay buried (5P).

RESTRICTED ZONE Where Kane lived on Iceworld (7G).

RETROGRADES Name given to the Frontios colonists who had abandoned the colony to live on the outside. Cockerill became their leader (6N).

REUBEN Old lighthouse keeper of Fang Rock who believed in the return of the Beast. He was killed by the Rutan, who took his form to fight the Fourth Doctor (4V).

REVERE Captain of the Frontios colony. He was kidnapped by the Tractators. They attached him to their excavating machine, which eventually drained him of his life (6N).

REVOLUTIONS The Doctor helped many human rebellions against human tyrants, such as: Salamander (PP); Magnus Greel (4S); Queen Xanxia (5B); Lady Adrasta (5G); Varos' Chief Officer (6V); and Helen A (7L). The First Doctor visited France during its Revolution (H). The Second Doctor fought alongside American Civil War soldiers during the War Games (ZZ).

The Doctor has also helped men overthrow alien oppressors such as: the Daleks (K, KKK); the Monoids (X); the Macra (JJ); the Warlords (ZZ); the Spiders of Metebelis 3 (ZZZ); Xoanon

(4Q); the Sunmakers (4W); the Nimon (5L); the Great Vampire (5P); the Tractators (6N); and Drathro (7A).

Occasionally, the Doctor has taken the aliens' side against men; he aided: the Sensorites (G); the Fishmen of Atlantis (GG); the Solonians (NNN); the Swampies (5E); the Tharils (5S); and the Kinda (5Y) to revolt against their human enslavers.

In other cases, the Doctor has helped one race to fight the oppression of another race, or to overthrow a tyrannical entity; he aided: the Menoptera against the Zarbi (N); the Xerons against the Moroks (Q); the Savages against the Elders (AA); the Gonds against the Krotons (WW); the Spiridons against the Daleks (SSS); the Exxilon against the City (XXX); the Trogs against the Seers (4Y); the Jacondans against Mestor (6S); the Cryons against the Cybermen (6T); the Karfelons against the Borad (6Y); the Thoros-Alphans against the Mentors (7B); and the Lakershyans against the Rani (7D).

The Shobogans were Time Lords who rebelled against the established order of Gallifrey (4Z).

REYKJAVIK Capital of Iceland. In the 51st century, it was first the location of the peaceful Icelandic Alliance, then later the location of the battle in which the evil Supreme Alliance was overthrown. The Doctor claimed to have taken part in that battle (4S).

REYNART Taran prince who was scheduled to be crowned King of Tara. Count Grendel tried to kill him, but he was saved by the Fourth Doctor. He ended up marrying Princess Strella (5D).

REYNOLDS Police superintendent at Gatwick Airport (KK).

REZZIES Contraction of 'residents', the nickname used for the old people who still lived in Paradise Towers (7E).

RHOS Senior virologist aboard the Ark who helped the First Doctor find a cure for Dodo's cold virus (X).

RHYNMAL See FROYN.

RIBANS Inhabitants of Ribos. They were a medieval people, steeped in superstition, and had little knowledge of the Universe (5A).

RIBOS Planet located in the constellation of Skythra; it was part of the Cyrennic Empire. It was 116 parsecs away from Cyrennis

Minima and three light centuries away from the Magellanic Clouds. It took 64 local years to complete its elliptical orbit around its sun, which meant that its seasons (Ice Time and Sun Time) lasted 32 years each. Because its civilization was still in the medieval stages, Ribos was classified by the Alliance as a Grade-3 planet, and was protected from alien interference. Its principal city was Shurr. Galactic con artists Garron and Unstoffe tried to sell Ribos for ten million opeks to the Graff Vynda-K, using a lump of jethrik which turned out to be a segment of the Key to Time for bait. Eventually, Garron and the Fourth Doctor joined forces to defeat the Graff, who perished in the Riban Catacombs (5A).

RICHARD See MAYNARDE, RICHARD.

RICHARD I (aka THE LIONHEART) King of England, third son of King Henry II and Eleanor of Aquitaine, who lived from 1157 to 1199. He set out on the Third Crusade in 1189, but lack of harmony between him and Philip II, King of France, eventually doomed the enterprise. He returned to Europe after making a truce with Saladin, leaving Jerusalem in the Saracens' hands. He met with the First Doctor, and named Ian Knight of Jaffa (P).

RICHARDS, BRENDAN Young boy who was Sarah Jane Smith's Aunt Lavinia's ward. He lived in Moreton Harwood. Because the local crops were not faring well, the cult of Hecate wanted to sacrifice Brendan, but were stopped by Sarah Jane Smith and K-9 mark III (K9).

RICHARDS UNIT lieutenant who served under Brigadier Bambera during the battle at Carbury against Morgaine. She was heading the Salamander 6–0 convoy, and was killed by the Sorceress (7N).

RICHARDSON, ALBERT First mate of the *Mary Celeste* (R).

RICHMOND, CAROL Crewmember of Captain Maitland's ship in orbit around the Sense-Sphere. They were held captive by the Sensorites. Thanks to the First Doctor's efforts, she was eventually allowed to return to Earth, after having promised to protect the secret of the Sensorites' existence (G).

RIDGWAY, ROBIN Royal Navy lieutenant commander in charge of a submarine sent by Captain Hart to investigate the Sea Devils.

His boat was captured by them, but the Third Doctor helped him escape (LLL).

RIFTEN 5 Satellite around Vita 15 and Lytton's birthplace (6P, 6T).

RIGA Shobogan who helped the Fourth Doctor against the Sontarans (4Z).

RIGS Rig D was one of the Euro-Sea Gas Corporation's off-shore rigs. It was one of the first to feel the effects of the Weed's attack. Its chief, Carney, called for Dr Patterson (RR). The Zygons' Skarasen destroyed three oil rigs off the coast of Scotland (4F).

RIGG Captain of the *Empress*. His ship crashed into the *Hecate* when both ships emerged simultaneously from hyperspace above the planet Azure. Tryst hooked him on vraxoin. Rigg later attacked Romana, and was killed by Fisk (5K).

RILEY Confederate corporal who believed he was fighting in the American Civil War. In reality, he was part of the War Games. He was eventually returned to his proper place in time and space by the Time Lords (ZZ).

RILLS Highly civilized, peaceful, telepathic aliens whose form was very ugly to men. A Rill ship was attacked by the Drahvins, led by Maaga. Both ships crashlanded on a doomed planet in Galaxy Four. With the help of their robotic 'Chumblies' and the First Doctor, the Rills were able to escape in time (T).

RIMA A Zygon (4F).

RIMA Peladonian trisilicate miner. When Ettis proposed to destroy Queen Thalira's palace with the sonic lance, he tried to stop him, but Ettis killed him (YYY).

RINCHEN One of the lamas of Det-Sen Monastery (NN).

RING OF RASSILON An inscription in the Tomb of Rassilon promised true immortality to anyone who would take the Ring from Rassilon's fingers. Borusa did, and was granted the immortality of a living statue (6K).

RINGBERG Controller of International Space Command Headquarters who was in charge when the Moonbase was attacked by the Cybermen (HH).

RINGMASTER Founding member of the Psychic Circus. He was weakly following the Chief Clown's orders. He and Morgana were eventually sacrificed to the Gods of Ragnarok by the Chief Clown (7J).

RINGO, JOHNNY Western outlaw noted for his deadly fast draw. He was hired by the Clantons to help them against Earp and Doc Holiday. The First Doctor claimed that Holiday shot him during the gunfight at the OK Corral on 26 October 1881. Ringo must have survived, since historical records show that he died nine months later, on 14 July 1882 (Z).

RINGWAY Captain Briggs's manifest officer. He was secretly in the Cybermen's pay, and brought them aboard the space freighter as cargo. He was killed by the Cyber Leader (6B).

RINTAN One of Varga's Ice Warrior crew brought back to life in AD 3000 (OO).

RITCHIE Frontios orderly (6N).

ROALD Personnel at the Control Building of Space Special Security (V).

ROBBINS Wing commander who helped defeat the Cyberman invasion (VV).

ROBBINS, THOMAS Boatman who took the Third Doctor and Jo Grant to the island where the Master was kept prisoner (LLL).

ROBERTS Wenley Moor technician who suffered a mental breakdown. He was accidentally killed by Major Baker (BBB).

ROBERTS Member of the Imperial Earth Expedition Force to Deva Loka who disappeared (5Y).

ROBESPIERRE, MAXMILIEN FRANCOIS DE (1758–94) French lawyer, and one of the prime movers of the French Revolution. The First Doctor and his companions could not prevent his arrest, and he was guillotined on 28 July 1794 (H).

ROBINS UNIT private whose mental sanity was perturbed while fighting the Siliurians. He died when he jumped into a chasm (BBB).

ROBINSON One of Sir Charles Grover's assistants in Operation Golden Age (WWW).

ROBOMEN Humans controlled by the Daleks through electronic pulses channelled to their brains through a headset. The Daleks used them during their AD 2164 Invasion of Earth (K).

ROBOPHOBIA Pathological fear of robots, also known as Grimwold's Syndrome, which could cause catatonia and even suicide. Its victims saw robots as walking dead men. Poul and Zilda's brother succumbed to acute robophobia (4R).

ROBOTS Sentient robotic races included: the human-created Mechanoids (R) and Super-Vocs (4R); the alien androids known as the Movellans (5J); and Monarch's androids (who all had real human memories stored on silicon chips) (5W).

Sentient individual robots included: K-9; Professor Kettlewell's K-1 Giant Robot (4A); the alien Kamelion (6J); and the Andromedan L-3, Drathro (7A).

A number of androids were designed to impersonate sentient lifeforms and could therefore duplicate the appearance of independent thought, but were probably not 'alive'. These included: the Kraals' androids (4R); the Tarans' androids (5D); Sharaz Jek's androids (6R); and Bellboy's robotic clowns and Bus Conductor (7J). Other androids in the same category included the Dracula and Frankenstein Monster robots (R); the Dalek-built replica of the First Doctor (R); the Terileptils' 'Grim Reaper' (5X); the Raston Robot (6K); the Cybermen's androids (6B); and the Borad's blue-skinned Android (6Y).

Non-sentient robots programmed only to serve their creators and incapable of sentience or independent thought included: the Rills' 'Chumblies' (T); WOTAN's War Machines (BB); the Great Intelligence's Yeti (NN, QQ); the Dominators' Quarks (TT); the Servo-Robot (SS); the White Robots and Clockwork Soldiers of the Land of Fiction (UU); IMC's mining robot (HHH); Linx's robot knight (UUU); Styre's robot (4B); Sutekh's 'mummies' (or servicers) (4G); the Captain of Zanak's parrotlike polyphase avatron (5B); the axe-wielding Gundans (5S); Drathro's service robot (7A); the Paradise Towers' cleaners (7E); and Iceworld's Dragon (7G). The so-called 'Robots of Death' were divided into Dums, Vocs and Super-Vocs. Only the last two categories could talk, and only the Super-Vocs could be said to have achieved sentience (4R).

Robots who did not fit in any of the above categories included: the Hand of Omega (7H); the Kandy Man (7L); and the

Silver Nemesis (7K). See also ANDROIDS, COMPUTERS, CYBORGS, DUPLICATES, MONSTERS.

ROBSON, JOHN S. Controller of the Euro-Sea Gas North Sea refinery which was attacked by the Weed. He first mistook the Second Doctor for a saboteur, and constantly refused to heed Harris's and Van Lutyens's advice to turn off the gas supply. He eventually fell under the Weed's mental control, but was freed by the Doctor's intervention (RR).

ROCK, JEAN Charles Gordon's secretary at Gatwick Airport when the Second Doctor fought the Chameleons (KK).

ROD Hovercraft pilot who mistook the Second Doctor for Salamander (PP).

ROD OF RASSILON (aka GREAT KEY) An ebonite staff, one of the three symbols of power worn by the President of the High Council of the Time Lords of Gallifrey. Its secret function was to enable its bearer to release the Eye of Harmony. The Master used it to absorb enough energy from the Eye of Harmony to prolong his life, and almost doomed Gallifrey (4P). The Fourth Doctor held it when he was proclaimed President (4Z).

RODAN Female Time Lord in charge of space-time traffic control when Gallifrey was invaded by the Vardans and the Sontarans. She befriended Leela and helped the Fourth Doctor repel the invaders (4Z).

ROGA Tower Guard on the Great Vampire's world (5P).

ROGAN CHASER Device employed by the Gallifreyan Chancellery Guard (4P).

ROGERS Exarius colonist (HHH).

ROGERS, TED Captain Hopper's ship engineer on Professor Parry's expedition to Telos. He was killed by the Cybermen (MM).

ROGIN See LYCETT.

ROHM One of Chellak's men (6R).

ROHM-DUTT Gun smuggler who was secretly paid by Thawn to deliver non-functional guns to the Swampies, thus justifying Thawn's extermination policies. He was killed by Kroll (5E).

338

ROKON King of Kastria. He ordered Eldrad's death after the Kastrian villain destroyed the force field barriers which protected his world. He, like all the other Kastrians, then chose to die rather than someday be forced to submit to Eldrad's rule in the event of his return (4N).

ROMANA (ROMANADVORATRELUNDAR) One of the Fourth Doctor's Companions. She was a 140-year-old Time Lord who was enlisted by the White Guardian (posing as the President of the High Council) to help the Fourth Doctor on his quest to gather the six segments of the Key to Time. During that time, she fought the Graff Vynda-K on Ribos, the Captain of Zanak and Vivien Fay. On Tara, she was captured by Count Grendel because she was an exact double of Princess Strella. On Delta Magna's moon, she was offered by the Swampies as a sacrifice to Kroll. Finally, on Atrios, she fought the Shadow and helped assemble the Key to Time (5A–5F).

Romana then chose to regenerate and, after a short period of instability, settled on the form of Princess Astra of Atrios. In that guise, she helped the Fourth Doctor fight the Daleks and the Movellans, Scaroth, Lady Adrasta, the Mandrels, the Nimon, Skagra, Pangol, the Foamasi, Meglos, the Marshmen and the Great Vampire. Even though she was ordered to return to Gallifrey, she chose to remain in E-space with K-9 mark II to help the Tharils fight slavery (5N–5S). Sometime during their fight against Skagra in Cambridge, Romana and the Fourth Doctor became trapped in a time eddy caused by the malfunctioning of Borusa's time scoop. They were freed by Rassilon's intervention after the other four Doctors had exposed Borusa (6K).

ROME The First Doctor visited the Eternal City in the year AD 64 and even unwittingly inspired Nero to start the Great Fire of Rome (M). A Roman Legion was kidnapped by the Warlords, using time technology stolen from the Time Lords. The soldiers went on to take part in the War Games (ZZ).

ROMULUS See SYLVEST, ROMULUS.

RONDEL See ARC OF INFINITY.

RONDEL Varosian guard, secretly one of Jondar's rebels. He was killed while helping the Sixth Doctor, Peril and Jondar escape from the Punishment Dome (6V).

RONES Captain in the Federation squadron, led by General Chellak, sent to Androzani Minor. He captured the Fifth Doctor and Peri, but was later killed in an ambush set up by Stotz (6R).

RONSON Senior Kaled researcher. He saved the Fourth Doctor from being killed by a prototype Dalek, and went on to betray Davros. He was later killed by the Daleks (4E).

RORVIK Captain of a privateer ship. He traded in time-sensitive Tharil slaves. His navigator, Biroc, took him to the Zero Point between N-Space and E-Space, then used the Tharil gateway to escape into E-Space. Against the Fourth Doctor's advice, Rorvik tried to break through the Gateway. He eventually used the backblast of his ship's engines, but the energy was bounced back by the Gateway's mirrors, and destroyed Rorvik and his ship (5S).

ROSKAL Sarn Unbeliever who climbed the Fire Mountain. He, Amyand and Sorasta were arrested by Timanov's men and were condemned to be sacrificed to the Fire Mountain. He helped the Fifth Doctor defeat the Master (6Q).

ROSSINI, LUIGI Phoney Italian, real name Lew Russell. He owned the International Circus where the Master rematerialized before preparing to fight the Third Doctor. Under the Master's thrall, he helped the evil Time Lord summon the Nestene back to Earth. Later, he and his men attacked the Doctor and Jo Grant (EEE).

ROSSINI Captain of San Martino's guards. He served Count Federico. After Federico's death, he was arrested by his own men (4M).

ROST Cryon who saved Peri from the Cybermen (6T).

ROTH One of the five Galsec Seven colonists stranded on Earth circa AD 15,000, after their ship had been destroyed while answering a fake Mayday signal. The Sontaran Styre performed cruel experiments on him to determine the limits of human resistance, and left him to die of thirst (4B).

ROUVRAY Frenchman who was trying to escape the guillotine when he stumbled upon the First Doctor and his Companions (H).

340

ROWLANDS, 'TUBBY' (LORD) Mr Brownrose's superior (EEE).

ROWLINSON, ELIZABETH Pat Rowlinson's wife. She had been blind until she was cured by Morgaine (7N).

ROWLINSON, PAT Owner of the Gore Crow Hotel near Carbury. He and his wife, Elizabeth, were evacuated by UNIT during the battle between the Seventh Doctor, UNIT and Morgaine (7N).

ROWSE, BERT Policeman who arrested Forester and Smithers (J).

ROWSE, HILDA Telephone operator. She became suspicious of the strange going-ons at Smithers's house, and alerted her husband, Bert (J).

ROYAL HORTICULTURAL SOCIETY The Fourth Doctor declined an invitation to address them (4L).

ROYAL OBSERVATORY Institution whose resources were used against the Daleks (7H).

ROYAL SCIENTIFIC CLUB The press conference announcing WOTAN's creation was held here (BB).

ROYCE Member of Rorvik's crew. He died when the privateer's ship was destroyed (5S).

RUBEISH, JOSEPH Kindly, eccentric, and very near-sighted scientist, kidnapped and taken to the 12th-century by Linx, who wanted him and other scientists help him repair his ship. He helped the Third Doctor defeat Linx and returned to his own time via Linx's Osmic projector (UUU).

RUDGE, SAM 19th-century British miner whose brain fluids were stolen by the Rani. He was compelled by the Master to attack the Sixth Doctor, and fell to his death in a mine shaft (6X).

RUDGE Security Officer of the *Hyperion III* space liner. Because he knew he was soon to be retired, he plotted with the two Mogarians, Atza and Ortezo, to hijack the ship and steal its precious cargo of vionesium. He was thwarted by the Sixth Doctor and Commodore Travers, and was later killed by the Vervoids (7C).

RUDKIN, KEMEL A member of the staff of the Wheel in Space. He was killed by a Cybermat (SS).

RUGG A sergeant and one of the deadly pawns used by the Toymaker (in tandem with Mrs Wiggs) when he challenged the First Doctor, Steven and Dodo (Y).

RUMFORD, EMILIA (AMELIA) (PROFESSOR) Elderly archeologist, author of *Bronze Age Burials in Gloucestershire*. She helped the Fourth Doctor and Romana in their quest for the third segment of the Key to Time. The alien Cessair of Diplos was posing as her friend and assistant, Vivien Fay. Her big professional rival was Dr Idwal Morris (5C).

RUNCIBLE Fatuous news commentator on Gallifrey. He had been to the Academy with the Doctor, and reported on the President's assassination. He was killed by either the Master or Goth (4P).

RUNCIMAN (DR) Medical doctor at Brendon school (6F).

RUNDALL BUILDINGS East End headquarters of the Tong of the Black Scorpion (4S).

RUSSELL Boer sergeant who was immune to the War Lords' hypnotic processing, and took charge of the Resistance. He fought alongside the Second Doctor to put an end to the War Games. He was eventually returned to his proper place in time and space by the Time Lords (ZZ).

RUSSELL, LEW See ROSSINI, LUIGI.

RUSSELL, VINCENT Undercover policeman who was also Lytton's supplier of stolen electronic equipment. He met the Sixth Doctor and Peri in the London sewers, but was later killed by the Cybermen (6T).

RUTANS Green, blob-like aliens, engaged in an endless space war with the Sontarans. Rutans liked the cold, had natural affinity for electricity, and were able to shift their shapes. A Rutan scout became stranded on the Island of Fang Rock, and after killing Reuben, planned to use Earth as a strategic point in the war with the Sontarans. The Rutan eventually killed the other lighthouse keepers, Ben Travers and Vince Hawkins, as well as the survivors of a shipwreck: Lord Palmerdale, Adelaide

Lesage, Colonel Skinsale and crewmember Harker. The Fourth Doctor and Leela were finally able to destroy the Rutan with a rocket launcher. The Doctor blew up his mother ship by using Lord Palmerdale's diamonds, and converting the lighthouse into a crude laser cannon (4V).

RUTH See CULLINGFORD, LADY.

RUTHER Citizen of Castrovalva. He was uncreated by the Master (5Z).

RUTHERFORD (MISS) Professor Cornish's assistant at the British Space Centre (CCC).

RUTLIDGE, WILLIAM Former military school mate of Brig. Lethbridge-Stewart who had become a major-general at the Ministry of Defence. He was in charge of supervising Lethbridge-Stewart's UNIT operations on British soil. His mind was controlled by Tobias Vaughn, who used him to prevent UNIT from interfering with the Cybermen Invasion. When Rutlidge later tried to rebel, Vaughn forced him to kill himself (VV).

RYAN, LEO Communications officer of the Wheel in Space. He was Tanya Lernov's boyfriend, and helped the Second Doctor defeat the Cybermen (SS).

RYNIAN An Aridian who met the First Doctor (R).

RYSIK Alzarian foreman who was saved by Tylos during the Marshmen's attack on the *Starliner* (5R).

S

S14 Earth Empire's name for Deva Loka (5Y).

S, ALEX and DAVID Trained snipers used by the Happiness Patrol against the Drones (7L).

SABETHA Arbitan's daughter. She accompanied the First Doctor on his quest for the missing Keys, and later married Altos (E).

SABOR Arak and Tuar's father. He gave himself up rather than allowing the Queen of the Spiders to take his son. He was kept prisoner by the Spiders and awaited his fate stoically, but was presumably freed when the Spiders died (ZZZ).

SACRED CHAMBER Name the Tesh gave to Xoanon's control room (4Q).

SACRED FLAME Volcanic flame on Planet Karn, not unlike the Numismaton Flame of Sarn (6Q), which produced the Elixir of Life. The Sacred Flame, or Flame of Life, was guarded by the Sisterhood and appeared to be dying because of a geological obstruction. But the Fourth Doctor cleared it with firecrackers (4K).

SADOK See SUTEKH.

SAFIYA The daughter of Haroun Ed Diin. He kept her hidden at home to save her from the clutches of the villainous El Akir (P).

SAFRAN Captain of the Titan shuttle taken over by the Virus. He turned the Titan base into a Hive for the Nucleus, and was later killed by Leela (4T).

SAGAN Member of Rorvik's crew. He was killed by Lazlo (5S).

SAGARO Aridian desert where the First Doctor's TARDIS rematerialized (R).

SAINT BARTHOLOMEW'S DAY MASSACRE On 23 August 1572, all the leading Huguenots of Paris were slain. Later, thousands more were killed throughout the rest of France. The First Doctor and Steven visited Paris a few days before the massacre, but could not affect its outcome (W).

SAINT CEDD'S Cambridge college visited by the Doctor in unrecorded adventures in 1955, 1958, 1960 (when he took an honorary degree) and 1964. It was there that Salyavin settled as Professor Chronotis. The Fourth Doctor fought Skagra on its premises (5M).

344

SAINT JUDE'S Church in the Northumberland village where the Seventh Doctor fought Fenric (7M).

SALADIN Saracen leader during the Third Crusade, who lived from 1138 to 1193. He offered Ian safe passage to help him search for Barbara, who had been kidnapped by El Akir. Saladin eventually made a truce with King Richard I ('The Lionheart'), and reclaimed Jerusalem (P).

SALAMANDER Yucatan-born, megalomaniacal scientist and the Second Doctor's double. He invented the Suncatcher satellite, which he used to gain political power in the early days of the 21st century. He also used it to create earthquakes, intending to kill off Earth's population, then repopulate the planet with his own people, whom he kept in a secret underground 'Sanctum'. After his plans were thwarted by Giles Kent and the Second Doctor, he tried to pass himself off as the Doctor, but was eventually ejected into deep space from the TARDIS (PP).

SALAMANDER 6-0 Atomic missile. Brigadier Bambera and Lieutenant Richards of UNIT were assigned to dispose of it. Morgaine almost detonated it, but her sense of honour ultimately prevailed (7N).

SALAMAR Young commander in charge of the Morestran spaceship sent to Zeta Minor. When the anti-matter creatures began to attack his ship, he cracked under pressure and suspected the Fourth Doctor of being a murderer. He finally had to be relieved by Vishinsky. He was later killed by Sorenson, when the scientist turned into a neanderthal-like monster (4H).

SALATEEN Major in the Federation Army and aide-de-camp to General Chellak. Sharaz Jek replaced him with an android replica. Thanks to the Fifth Doctor, the real Salateen escaped with Peri. He helped General Chellak launch a final assault against Jek, but was shot by an android. The Salateen android later killed Stotz (6R).

SALOSTOPUS Sabalom Glitz's home planet, located in Andromeda (7A).

SALYAVIN Notorious Gallifreyan adventurer. His mind-control powers turned him into a criminal. Salyavin was captured and imprisoned by the Time Lords on Shada. He secretly escaped and, to cover his tracks, stole *The Ancient Law of Gallifrey*, and caused the Time Lords to forget about Shada. He then retired to St Cedd's College, where he assumed the identity of Professor Chronotis. His room was, in reality, his TARDIS. But he was found by Skagra, who used his Sphere to learn the location of Shada. With the Fourth Doctor and Romana's help, Skagra was defeated. The Doctor returned *The Ancient Law* to Gallifrey and swore to not reveal Salyavin's secret (5M).

SAMUELS Warder in Stangmoor Prison's Special Wing. He was in charge of the Death Row cells (FFF).

SAMUELSON (MRS) Wardrobe woman at Jago's theatre (4S).

SAN MARTINO Dukedom in 15th-century Italy. Its rightful ruler, Giuliano, would have been killed by Count Federico if it had not been for the Fourth Doctor. The Time Lord also prevented the Mandragora Helix from using the Dukedom as a beachhead to prevent Renaissance (4M).

SANCTUM Name given by Salamander to the secret underground installation where he kept a small population captive, using lies and the pretence that a nuclear war raged on the planet's surface. Salamander planned for the Sanctum's inhabitants to take over the Earth after he had destroyed its population (PP).

SAND BEASTS Docile, vegetarian, Didonian bipeds who looked like a cross between a lizard and a snake. Vicki had adopted a sand beast as a pet, but it was mistakenly killed by Barbara (L).

SANDERS Commander of the Imperial Earth expedition force to Deva Loka. The Kinda's attempts to have him and Hindle mind-meld with them caused them to become mentally unbalanced. They were cured by the Fifth Doctor with the Kinda's Jhana Box. Sanders recommended that Deva Loka be reclassified as unsuitable for colonization, although he planned to retire there (5Y).

SANDMINER Giant, mobile factory for processing ores and minerals on a deserted, windswept planet. Its crew, led by Commander Uvanov, would all have been killed by Dask's Robots of Death if it had not been for the Fourth Doctor's and Leela's intervention (4R).

SANTORIV Famous parametricist whose mind was stolen by Skagra at the Think Tank space station. He died in the destruction of the station (5M).

SAPAN Oldest and wisest of the lamas of Det-Sen monastery (NN).

SAPHADIN Saladin's brother. He was in love with Joanna, King Richard I's sister, and passionately wanted to marry her (P).

SARA See KINGDOM, SARA.

SARACEN Any person who practised Islam in the Middle Ages. Originally, the Saracens were an Arab tribe living in the Sinai (Sarakenoi). The First Doctor encountered Saracens during the Third Crusade (P).

SARAH JANE See SMITH, SARAH JANE.

SARCOPHAGUS The Meddling Monk had disguised his TARDIS as a Saxon sarcophagus (S). The point of arrival of Sutekh's time-space corridor was an Egyptian sarcophagus (4G).

SARDON One of the Tesh (4Q).

SARDOR See CO-PILOT.

SARN Volcanic planet. At one time, it was a Trion colony, but proved to be too inhospitable because of its volcanic activity. While the Trion used it for its regenerating Numismaton Flame, the planet's inhabitants slowly reverted to tribalism and super-stition. After the revolution, the Trions used Sarn as a dumping ground for their political prisoners. The Sarns worshipped Logar, god of the Fire Mountain, and sacrificed any Unbelievers. The Fifth Doctor defeated the Master on Sarn. Turlough summoned Trion's help to evacuate the Sarns, who were threatened by a volcanic eruption (6Q).

SARN Young Lakertyan female who assisted Beyus inside the Rani's ship. She was Beyus's and Faroon's daughter. She escaped and was killed by one of the Rani's protective bubbles (7D).

SASH OF RASSILON One of the three symbols of power worn by the President of the High Council of the Time Lords of Gallifrey. Its secret function was to protect its wearer from great sources of energy, such as the Eye of Harmony, and also to enable the wearer to convert that energy for his own use. It was probably used by Rassilon himself when he entered a black hole to capture the Eye of Harmony. The Master wore the Sash when he released the Eye of Harmony, and was able to absorb enough energy to prolong his life, almost dooming Gallifrey (4P). The Fourth Doctor wore it when he was proclaimed President (4Z).

SATAN The Fourth Doctor claimed that this was another of Sutekh's names (4G). The Daemons resembled the Christian Devil (JJJ). Also see RELIGION.

SAUVIX Leader of the Sea Devil commando which was reanimated by the Silurian Icthar. The commando attacked Sea Base Four in AD 2084. Icthar's plan was to launch nuclear missiles to provoke a war between the two blocs, and thus eradicate mankind. Their efforts were defeated by the Fifth Doctor, who used deadly hexachromite gas to wipe out the Silurians and the Sea Devils (6L).

SAVA Planet visited by the First Doctor (X).

SAVAGES Name the Elders gave to the allegedly primitive people with whom they shared their planet. The 'Savages' were artistically advanced, and lived a primitive lifestyle only because the Elders repeatedly drained their life essence. They were freed from their servitude by the First Doctor's intervention, and Steven Taylor became the leader of the reunited species (AA).

SAVANT The Tigellans' scientific caste (5Q).

SAVAR Aged Time Lord who attended the induction of the Fourth Doctor as President of the High Council (4Z).

SAVE PLANET EARTH SOCIETY Pollution-fighting organization founded by Sir Charles Grover (WWW).

SAXONS The First Doctor helped a Saxon village to thwart Viking invaders (S).

SAYO Plateau where the Crater of Needles was located on Vortis (N).

SCALPOR See CETES.

SCARLATTI Count Federico's torturer (4M).

SCARLIONI, CARLOS (COUNT) See SCAROTH.

SCARLIONI (COUNTESS) Count Scarlioni's wife. She was apparently unaware that her husband was in reality Scaroth, last of the Jagaroth, a green-skinned, one-eyed alien. She was killed by Scaroth after she forced him to reveal his true identity (5H).

SCARMAN, LAURENCE Professor Scarman's brother. He helped the Fourth Doctor fight Sutekh, but was killed by his own brother, who had become the evil Osirian's puppet (4G).

SCARMAN, MARCUS Egyptologist who opened Sutekh's tomb. The Fourth Doctor claimed that Professor Scarman ceased to exist as a human being when he entered the evil Osirian's tomb. He returned to the Priory under Sutekh's control, and even killed his brother, Laurence. He travelled to Mars in the TARDIS with the Fourth Doctor, and died the final death when Sutekh released him after destroying the Eye of Horus (4G).

SCAROTH Green-skinned, one-eyed alien of the war like Jagaroth race. Circa 3.5 million BC on Earth, Scaroth's crippled spaceship, which contained all the survivors of the Jagaroth race, exploded while taking off. The radiation caused by the explosion triggered a mutation in Earth's primordial 'soup', creating life on the planet. Scaroth was split into twelve fragments, scattered across different time periods, including: Ancient Egypt (where he posed as a god), Germany in AD 1455 (when the Gutenberg Bible was first printed), Renaissance Italy in 1505 (where he used the alias of Captain Tancredi), England in 1600 (when Shakespeare wrote *Hamlet*), and Paris in 1980. There, as Count Scarlioni, Scaroth hired Professor Kerensky to build a time machine. To finance Kerensky's research, as Tancredi, he forced Leonardo da Vinci to paint several Mona Lisas, which he sold as Scarlioni. Eventually, in spite of the Fourth Doctor, Romana and Duggan's intervention, Scaroth was able to return to 3.5 million BC. However, Duggan stopped him from preventing the destruction of his ship, therefore ensuring the creation of life on Earth. Scaroth was then automatically returned to the 20th century, where the sight of his real shape so frightened his henchman, Hermann, that he caused an explosion which killed them both (5H).

SCAVENGER Nickname given by the Galsec Seven colonists to Styre's robot (4B).

SCHLANGI A race of space mercenaries (5A).

SCHOOL OF PARAPSYCHOLOGY See PARAPSYCHOLOGY SCHOOL.

SCHOOLS See EDUCATION.

SCHULTZ, DAN Astronaut aboard the Zeus IV space capsule. He was killed when the ship disintegrated under Mondas's gravitational pressure (DD).

SCIBUS Member of a Silurian Triad also comprised of Icthar (who had met the Third Doctor in the 20th century) and Tarpok. In AD 2084, they reanimated a Sea Devil commando led by Sauvix and attacked Sea Base Four. Their plan was to launch nuclear missiles to provoke a war between the two blocs, and thus eradicate mankind. Scibus died when the Fifth Doctor used deadly hexachromite gas (6L).

SCIENTIFIC REFORM SOCIETY (SRS) Secret organization of elitist scientists who believed they should rule the world. Their leader, Miss Winters, used another member, Professor Kettlewell, and his Giant Robot to obtain the means of threatening to start World War III and blackmail the world into surrendering. She was thwarted by the Fourth Doctor. (4A).

SCOBIE British army general. The Nestene replaced him with a replica to stop UNIT, and put him in a wax museum. He was eventually freed when the Third Doctor short-circuited his replica (AAA).

SCOBIE, ROGER Flight Engineer of the Concorde flight the Fifth Doctor used to rescue Flight 192. He helped the Time Lord defeat the Master and the Xeraphin in the Jurassic period (6C).

SCOPE (aka MINISCOPE) A combination time scoop and peep-show. The Scope plucked living beings from their own time and space and kept them prisoner in a miniaturized state. The Third Doctor claimed he had been instrumental in getting the Time Lords to call for an Intergalactic Convention to ban the Scopes as being against the dignity of sentient life forms. At least one Scope survived in the hands of Galactic showman Vorg. It contained Ogrons, the SS *Bernice* and its crew, a plesiosaurus, and the savage Drashigs. The Third Doctor rematerialized in Vorg's Scope on the planet Inter Minor. There a xenophobic official, Kalik, tried to use the Scope to discredit the President's liberal policies, but failed. The Scope was eventually put out of commission by the Third Doctor, and its prisoners restored to their proper places in space and time (PPP).

SCORBY Harrison Chase's murderous henchman. He stole a

Krynoid pod from the World Ecology Bureau's Antarctic base and took it back to England. When he realized the full extent of the Krynoid's threat, Scorby fought it alongside the Fourth Doctor, but was eventually drowned by weeds which were under the Krynoid's control (4L).

SCOTLAND The Second Doctor landed near Culloden in AD 1746 (FF). The Borad, a Karfelon tyrant who had been defeated by the Sixth Doctor, was transported by his Timelash to 12th-century Scotland, near Inverness, and took up residence in Loch Ness. Presumably he was killed by the Zygons and their Skarasen when they took over the Loch in 1676 (6Y). The Fourth Doctor fought the Zygons in Tulloch in 1976. By then, the Zygons' Skarasen had become the Loch Ness Monster (4F).

SCOTT He and Trevor were commentators at an Oval test match between England and Australia, which was briefly interrupted by the TARDIS's materialization (V).

SCOTT 26th-century lieutenant in charge of the squadron protecting Professor Kyle's underground explorations. He helped the Fifth Doctor disarm a hidden Cyber-bomb, then travelled aboard the TARDIS to Captain Briggs's space freighter. There, he helped the Doctor and Adric prevent the Cybermen from crashing the ship on Earth to destroy an Alliance conference. Scott escaped to safety in the TARDIS (6B).

SCRAMPUS Planetary system where Manussa was located (6D).

SCREAMERS Vampire bats found on Desperus (V).

SCREENS Five panels designed by Meglos to focus the power of the Dodecahedron into a single, powerful blast which could destroy any planet in the galaxy. They were blown up, along with Zolfa-Thura, in the Dodecahedron explosion set up by the Fourth Doctor (5Q).

SCRINGE STONE Name Unstoffe made up for his lump of jethrik (5A).

SCROLLS OF RASSILON Borusa placed a chest containing the forbidden Black Scrolls of Rassilon in the Castellan's living quarters to frame him. They were destroyed when the chest was opened without proper safety precautions (6K). These are not to be confused with the RECORDS OF RASSILON.

SEA See UNDERSEA.

SEA BASE FOUR Underwater base attacked by the Silurians and the Sea Devils in AD 2084. Its commander was Vorshak. After taking it over, the Silurians plotted to use its nuclear missiles to provoke a war between the two blocs, and thus eradicate mankind. Their efforts were defeated by the Fifth Doctor, who used deadly hexachromite gas to wipe out the Silurians and the Sea Devils (6L).

SEA DEVILS Intelligent reptilian life form which ruled the Earth during the Cretaceous (136 to 65 million years BC), and not the Silurian (430 to 395 million years BC). They, and their 'cousins' the Silurians, were eventually driven to hibernate in underground shelters by some undetermined cosmic event. A commando of Sea Devils awoke from suspended animation in 1973 and began sinking ships in the British Channel. They were contacted by the Master who offered to ally himself with them. The Third Doctor and the Chief Sea Devil talked peace, but they were thwarted by the interference of the Master and Walker, a civil servant who ordered a depth charge attack. In the end, the Doctor was forced to engineer an explosion which destroyed the Sea Devils' undersea base before any more Sea Devils could be awakened (LLL).

The Silurian Icthar reanimated a Sea Devil commando led by Sauvix in 2084, and used them to attack Sea Base Four. His plan was to launch nuclear missiles to provoke a war between the two blocs, and thus eradicate mankind. His efforts were defeated by the Fifth Doctor (6L). Also see SILURIANS.

SEA EAGLE Inverness Inn where Gray and Trask conducted their slave trading business (FF).

SEA WEED See WEED.

SEAGRAVE, DONALD Police constable killed by the Master (5V).

SEALS The Seal of the High Council was given to the Master by Thalia to help him convince the Doctor he had been sent by the Time Lords (6K). The Fourth Doctor (4P) and the Seventh Doctor (7H) used the Prydonian Seal to sign their correspondence. The Great Seal of Diplos was, in reality, the third segment of the Key to Time. It had been stolen by

Cessair, and gave her the power to alter her shape and travel to hyperspace and back. The Fourth Doctor used it to banish the Megara back to Diplos (5C).

SEAN Shipwreck survivor who laboured in Atlantis's mines. He helped the Second Doctor defeat Professor Zaroff's insane scheme (GG).

SEARCH-CONV CORPORATION Interplanetary salvage company whose request for credit was approved by Sil on the Sixth Doctor's advice (7B).

SEASPITE Name of Captain Hart's research establishment and naval base (LLL).

SECKER Navigator of the *Empress*. He was a vraxoin addict in league with Tryst and Dymond. His negligence caused the ship to crash into the *Hecate* when emerging from hyperspace above planet Azure. Secker was killed by a Mandrel (5K).

SECURITY CHIEF One of the War Lords. He suspected the renegade Time Lord known as the War Chief to be in league with the Second Doctor to overthrow the War Lords. The Security Chief eventually succeeded in exposing the War Chief's unreliability, but was later killed by the renegade Time Lord (ZZ).

SEEDS The Martian 'Seeds of Death' consumed oxygen, but were vulnerable to heat and water (XX). The Krynoids travelled through space in seed form (4L). Professor Lansky had designed Demeter Seeds which could grow food in the desert (7C).

SEEKER Riban seeress who used primitive witchcraft. The Captain of the Shrievalty asked her to find Unstoffe, who had stolen the jethrik and the Graff's money. She was killed in the Catacombs by the Graff Vynda-K, after she had predicted that all but one would die. That one turned out to be the Fourth Doctor (5A).

SEELEY, MEG Sam's wife. She found the Nestene swarm leader meteorite, which had been hidden by her husband, and was later attacked by an Auton (AAA).

SEELEY, SAM Poacher who found the Nestene swarm leader meteorite in Oxley Woods. He kept it hidden, thinking he could profit from it (AAA).

SEERS Two Minyans whose heads had been replaced with a machine. They ruled the Underworld, second in power only to the Oracle. Their names were Ankh and Lakh. They perished in an explosion caused by two fission grenades disguised as the Race Banks, which the Oracle had intended to use to destroy Jackson's ship (4Y).

SEGONAX Planet where the Psychic Circus was located (7J).

SEKKOTH See PILOT.

SELECTION (TIME OF) Time during which young victims were chosen to feed the Great Vampire (5P).

SELRIS Leader of the Gonds' Council, and Thara's father. He was deposed by Eelek. Later, he sacrificed his life to help the Second Doctor destroy the Krotons (WW).

SELYNX See KARFEL.

SENEX Director of Dulkis and Cully's father. He eventually took the Second Doctor's side when the Time Lord urged for action against the Dominators (TT).

SENSE-SPHERE The Sensorites' home planet. It was rich in Molybdenum (G).

SENSORITES Inhabitants of the Sense-Sphere. They had bulbous heads and mind powers which included telepathy and the ability to control other minds at a distance. The Sensorites used their powers to hold Captain Maitland's ship captive, because they were afraid of Earthmen. When the First Doctor revealed that the survivors of a previous Earth expedition, led by an unnamed Commander, had secretly been poisoning the Sensorites, they agreed to let Maitland and his crew return to Earth. However, the humans first had to swear to protect the secret of the Sensorites' existence (G).

SENTA Chief Medic of the Elders' City. She operated the life-essence transference machines (AA).

SENTINEL-6 Earth orbital security device (6L).

SENTREAL Member of the Dalek Alliance (V).

SERON One of the five Consuls of Traken. He was killed by Kassia under the Melkur's influence (5T).

SERVICE ROBOT Robot which guarded Drathro's castle in the UK habitat. It was shot by Katryca (7A).

SERVICERS Another name for the Osirian Mummies (4G).

SERVO-ROBOT Robot encountered by the Second Doctor and Jamie on the supply ship *Phoenix IV* (SS).

SET See SUTEKH (4G).

SETH Young Anethian prince who was part of the tribute requested by the Nimon, and which was exacted by the Skonnans from Aneth. He helped the Fourth Doctor expose and defeat the Nimon. He eventually married Teka (5L).

SEVATEEM Leela's tribe, descendants of a crashed Earth ship, the *Mordee*. Their name was a corruption of the words 'Survey Team'. The mad computer Xoanon had manipulated the Sevateem into an endless war with the Tesh. When the Fourth Doctor cured Xoanon, the Sevateem, led by Calib, were reunited with the Tesh (4Q).

SEVCHERIA Cruel Roman slave trader who, with his partner Didius, captured Ian and Barbara. He was later killed by Delos (M).

SEVILLE City in Spain where the Sixth Doctor rescued the Second Doctor from Chessene and the Sontarans (6W).

SEVRIN One of Skaro's Mutos. He befriended Sarah Jane Smith (4E).

SEVRIN Trusted servant of Varos's Governor (6V).

SEZOM Last survivor of Crinoth who revealed the workings of the Nimon to Romana. He had unwittingly helped the Nimon destroy his world. He sacrified himself to enable Romana to return to Skonnos (5L).

SEZON Leader of the rebellion against the Borad on Karfel. He and Katz helped the Sixth Doctor defeat the Borad (6Y).

SHADA Prison planet of the Time Lords. Salyavin was imprisoned there. After he escaped, he caused the Time Lords to forget about Shada, and stole *The Ancient Law of Gallifrey*, which contained the secret of its location. Skagra found Shada, but was ultimately defeated by the Fourth Doctor (5M).

SHADOW Mysterious servant of the Black Guardian who manipulated Atrios and Zeos into an unending space war against each other. The Fourth Doctor exposed him and discovered his refuge, a small planetoid located between Atrios and Zeos. The Doctor recovered the Key to Time, then redirected the Atrian Marshal's impending nuclear attack on Zeos against the Shadow's planetoid, which was destroyed (5F).

SHAKESPEARE, WILLIAM (1569–1616) English playwright. His image was projected on the First Doctor's Space-Time Visualizer (R). One of Scaroth's twelve fragments obtained was the original draft of *Hamlet*. The Fourth Doctor claimed to have helped Shakespeare write it, and recognized bits of his own handwriting on it (5H).

SHANG-TU Location of Kublai Khan's summer palace (D).

SHANGRI-LA 1959 Welsh holiday camp managed by Mr Burton. A galactic tour bus from the future was forced to land there after hitting a US satellite (7F). See DELTA.

SHAPE-CHANGING Aliens capable of shape-changing included: the Chameleons (KK); the Zygons (4F); the Rutans (4V); the Usurians (4W); Cessair of Diplos (5C); Meglos (5Q); and the android Kamelion. Also see EVOLUTION, MUTATIONS.

SHAPP (MAJOR) The Marshal of Atrios's aide. He eventually joined forces with the Fourth Doctor to defeat the Shadow (5F).

SHARDOVAN Castrovalva's librarian. He helped the Fifth Doctor discover the true nature of his city. After finding out the truth, he sacrificed himself to help free Adric (5Z).

SHARKEY, MILES See ZARGO.

SHARREL (COMMANDER) Movellan commander in charge of the unit sent to Skaro to stop the Daleks from finding Davros. Romana prevented him from destroying Skaro with a nova bomb (5J).

SHAV One of the Mondasian Cybermen who invaded the Snowcap Space Tracking Station and fought the First Doctor (DD).

SHAW, ELIZABETH (LIZ) One of the Third Doctor's companions, a Cambridge scientist recruited by UNIT's Brigadier

356

Lethbridge-Stewart to investigate the first Nestene invasion. She became the first assistant of the Third Doctor, whom she helped against the Silurians, the so-called Ambassadors of Death, and the forces unleashed by Professor Stahlman's Inferno. During that adventure, the Doctor met her alternate Earth counterpart, Section-Leader Shaw. She left soon afterwards to continue her scientific career (AAA–DDD). Her image was used by Rassilon to ward off the Third Doctor (6K). The Seventh Doctor gave Liz's UNIT pass to Ace (7N).

SHEARD, DOUGLAS Heathrow airport controller. After Sir John Sudbury vouched for the Fifth Doctor, he gave him access to a Concorde to track down another, which had disappeared (6C).

SHEARS Lieutenant who fought the Dinosaur Invasion (WWW).

SHEILA One of the Earth President's secretaries (QQQ).

SHEPRAH Captain of the Vogan City militia. He rescued Sarah and Harry from Vorus's Guardians, and fought the Cybermen to save Voga (4D).

SHEYRAH A serving woman in Saladin's camp (P).

SHIELDS, STANLEY Moreton Harwood publican and member of the cult of Hecate (K9).

SHIRNA Vorg's female assistant and companion (PPP).

SHOBOGANS Name given by the Time Lords to those who refused the benefits of Gallifreyan civilization. Castellan Spandrell thought of them as vandals (4P). Some Shobogans preferred to live in the wilderness outside the Capitol; they were known as Outsiders, or Outcasts. A group of them, led by Nesbin, helped the Fourth Doctor and Leela repel the Sontarans' invasion (4Z).

SHOCKEYE O' THE QUAWNCING GRIG Savage androgum who worked as cook on Space Station J7. He accompanied Chessene and Dastari to Earth. His genes were temporarily transferred to the Second Doctor. He wanted to sample the pleasure of eating a human, particularly Jamie or Peri. He was killed by the Sixth Doctor (6W).

SHOLAKH Graff Vynda-K's old battle companion. He died in the Riban Catacombs in a rockfall which was when the Captain of the Shrievalty fired a cannon (5A).

SHONAR A Kaled opposed to Davros (4E).

SHORT Member of the Scientific Reform Society (4A).

SHOU YUING Full name was Li Shou Yuing (Shou Yuing meant Little Cloud), she was a young archeologist of Chinese descent who worked under Peter Warmsly on the Carbury excavation. She became friend with Ace, and fought alongside her and the Seventh Doctor against Morgaine (7N).

SHREELA One of Ace's friends from Perivale. She was kidnapped by the Cheetah People, and eventually returned to Earth by Ace and the Seventh Doctor (7P).

SHRIEVALTY (aka SHRIEVES) Order of Riban guards. They derived their name from the fierce Shrievenzales (5A).

SHRIEVENZALES Fierce lizard beasts on Ribos, used by the Riban Shrievalty as guard animals. They hunted small animals and lived in the Catacombs (5A).

SHURA Guerilla from an alternate 22nd century where the Daleks had successfully invaded Earth after World War III. He, Anat and Boaz travelled back in time to kill diplomat Sir Reginald Styles, not realizing that it was this very action which had caused the war. Shura fought the Daleks alongside the Third Doctor. He eventually blew himself up with the Daleks in Styles's empty house, thereby erasing the future that he had inadvertently helped to create (KKK).

SHURR Principal city of Ribos. It was there that the Fourth Doctor and Romana found the first segment of the Key to Time, and fought the Graff Vynda-K (5A).

SIDELIAN MEMORY TRANSFER Technique which the Fourth Doctor used to transfer some of his knowledge into Xoanon in an attempt to repair it. Instead, it turned the sentient computer schizophrenic (4Q).

SIDRATS Inferior type of TARDISes used by the War Lords. They were based on technology stolen from the Time Lords by the renegade known as the War Chief. Their range and power supply were limited (ZZ).

SIGMA All alien visitors to Terra Alpha were called Sigma (7L).

SIGMA, EARL Medical student and lover of the blues who was stuck on Terra Alpha. He helped the Seventh Doctor escape from the Happiness Patrol, and supported the revolution which finally overthrew Helen A's regime. He stayed on Terra Alpha, teaming up with Susan Q to teach the blues to the newly liberated colony (7L).

SIGMA, THETA See THETA SIGMA.

SIGMA, TREVOR Galactic census bureaucrat sent to Terra Alpha to investigate complaints about the colony (7L).

SIGMUS GAP Sector of space explored by Tryst (5K).

SIGURD One of the Vanir. He and the other Vanir eventually stayed on Terminus to help Nyssa run it as a regular hospital (6G).

SIL One of the Mentors from Thoros-Beta. He was the Galatron Mining Corporation's agent on Varos. He bribed the Chief Officer of Varos to keep the prices low, but he was thwarted by the Sixth Doctor. He then attempted to take over the planet, but failed. Sil's superior, Kiv, replaced him and negotiated fairer prices for Zyton-7 (6V).

Sil again met the Sixth Doctor on Thoros-Beta, where Crozier was working on a process to transfer the mind of the dying Kiv into Peri's body. At Sil's request, Crozier used his Cell Discriminator on the Sixth Doctor, causing him to act hostile and more erratically than usual. Crozier's process was deemed too dangerous for the course of natural evolution by the Time Lords, so they manipulated events to arrange for King Yrcanos of Krontep to kill Crozier, Kiv and Sil and rescue Peri. The Valeyard used a heavily doctored version of this event, making it appear as if Peri had been killed (7B).

SILIGTONE One of the hardest metals in the universe, used to make Drathro's Maglem converter. Because siligtone was quite valuable, Dibber suggested that she and Glitz could make money by salvaging it (7A).

SILURIAN SCIENTIST See ICTHAR.

SILURIAN TRIAD Silurian governing body. The Wenley Moor

triad comprised the Old Silurian, the Young Silurian and Icthar (BBB, 6L).

SILURIANS Intelligent reptilian life form which ruled the Earth during the Cretaceous (136 to 65 million years BC), and not the Silurian (430 to 395 million years BC). They and their underwater 'cousins', the so-called 'Sea Devils', were eventually driven to hibernate in underground shelters by some undetermined cosmic event. Theories about the nature of this event included: a wandering planetoid causing a change in the Van Allen belt; movements of the Moon; departure of Earth's twin planet, Mondas; or possibly the quasi-psychic awareness of the forthcoming crash of a space liner from the future (6B).

The Silurians of Wenley Moor were reawakened from suspended animation in 1971 because of power leaks from the neighbouring British atomic research center. The Old Silurian met Dr Quinn, then the Third Doctor, and became convinced that his people could share Earth peacefully with mankind. However, the Young Silurian tried to wipe out mankind with a deadly virus. After that had failed, he and the Silurian scientist, Icthar, attempted to use a molecular disperser to destroy the Van Allen Belt, and thus render Earth inhabitable for humans. Thwarted by the Third Doctor, they returned to suspended animation. Their shelter was then blown up by UNIT (BBB).

Icthar survived, and reawakened in 2084. He reanimated a Sea Devil commando, led by Sauvix, and attacked Sea Base Four. His plan was to launch nuclear missiles to provoke a war between the two blocs, and thus eradicate mankind (which had been the Young Silurian's last wish). His efforts were defeated by the Fifth Doctor, who used deadly hexachromite gas to wipe out the Silurians (6L). Also see SEA DEVILS.

SILVER CARRIER Codename of the *Phoenix IV* supply ship on which the Second Doctor and Jamie rematerialized before travelling to the Wheel in Space. Its only inhabitant was a Servo-Robot (SS).

SILVER NEMESIS See NEMESIS, SILVER.

SILVERSTEIN, EMIL JULIUS Eccentric owner of a private museum. He refused to heed Professor Travers's warnings and return his Yeti to the Professor's custody. Soon afterwards, he was killed by the reactivated Yeti (QQ).

SILVEY Officer of the Titan shuttle who was taken over by the Virus. He was shot by Lowe before the latter was taken over by the Virus (4T).

SIMIAN EMPIRE Alien power known to the Time Lords (4Z).

SIN, MR See PEKING HOMUNCULUS.

SINGING TREES One of the landmarks of Iceworld's underworld (7G).

SINJU Way station on the road to Peking (D).

SINKING SHIP ('VAISSEAU QUI COULE') French tavern where Barras met with Napoleon to plot Robespierre's downfall (H).

SIRIUS Five-world planetary system. The Master impersonated a Commissioner from Sirius Four (QQQ). Veldan was a member of a Sirian colony (5J). Androzani Major and Minor were located in the Sirian system (6R). The Academius Stolaris was a famous gallery located on Sirius Five (5H).

SIRIUS CONGLOMERATE Powerful corporation located on Androzani Major which controlled the supply of spectrox. It had been established by Morgus and Sharaz Jek, and was later completely taken over by Morgus. After Morgus was exposed as a traitor and had fled Androzani Major, the Sirius Conglomerate passed into the hands of Timmin, Morgus's personal assistant (6R).

SISTERHOOD Select society of women on Karn dedicated to the protection of the Sacred Flame, which produced the Elixir of Life. They were gifted with vast psionic powers and virtual immortality. After the Time Lords helped defeat Morbius, who had brought great ruin to Karn, the Sisterhood agreed to share the Elixir with them. (4K).

SITA One of the Xeron rebels who fought with the First Doctor against the Moroks in the Space Museum. She was killed by the Moroks (Q).

SIX-GUN SADIE (AND HER WILD WEST TROUPE) Performers at Henry Gordon Jago's theatre (4S).

SKAAR Planet where the Graff Vynda-K's men fought in the Alliance Wars (5A).

SKAGRA Geneticist, astro-engineer, and multi-talented scientist from Dronid who stumbled upon the secret of Salyavin's existence. Skagra plotted to use an electronic mind-transference device, known as the Sphere, which had been developed on the Think Tank space station, together with Salyavin's mind-control abilities, to imprint his mind on every living creature in the universe. He stole *The Ancient Law of Gallifrey* from Professor Chronotis to discover the secret of Shada's location. On Shada, he found that Salyavin was pretending to be Chronotis. Skagra was eventually defeated by the Fourth Doctor and Romana, then imprisoned on his own Ship (5M).

SKARASEN Giant, reptilian monster which the Zygons claimed they brought to Earth in embryo form. They depended on its lactic fluid to stay alive. Grown to giant size, the Skarasen became known as the Loch Ness Monster. The Zygons used it to destroy three oil rigs and threaten a World Energy Conference in their bid to take over Earth. Freed by the Fourth Doctor, the Skarasen returned to Loch Ness, where it presumably led a peaceful life (4F).

SKARO The twelfth planet in a solar system not too far from Earth and the home world of both the Kaleds and the Thals. It was ravaged by the neutronic wars between the two races, which made it largely radioactive. See also DALEKS, DAVROS, THALS.

SKART High Priest of the Swampies on Delta Magna's third moon. He was killed by Kroll (5E).

SKINSALE, JAMES (COLONEL) British MP (Thurley) and retired Indian Army Colonel, whose gambling debts had been cancelled by Lord Palmerdale in exchange for insider information. He was shipwrecked on Fang Rock and helped the Fourth Doctor and Leela fight the Rutan. He could not resist picking up Lord Palmerdale's diamonds, and was killed by the Rutan (4V).

SKONNANS (aka SKONNONS) Inhabitants of Skonnos. They were once the leaders of a space empire which the Nimon had promised to restore to its former glory. Their leader was Soldeed (5L).

SKONNOS Planet that was once the seat of a mighty empire. The

Nimon promised to return it to its former glory if the Skonnans paid him a tribute of young men and women, and hymetusite crystals. The Skonnans extracted the tribute from the peaceful Anethians. They later discovered that they had been tricked by the Nimon, who were plotting to take over and destroy their world. They were saved by the Fourth Doctor (5L).

SKORDA Human settlement on Metebelis 3. Its 269 inhabitants were killed by the Spiders (ZZZ).

SKYBASE ONE Earth Imperial space station in orbit around Solos (NNN).

SKYSTRIKER Name of Vorus's missile. It destroyed the Cybermen (4D).

SKYTHRA Planetary sector of the Cyrennic Empire to which Ribos belonged (5A).

SKYTHROS Major planet in the Skythra star sector (5A).

SLAAR Leader of the Martian commando which took over the Moonbase. He tried to destroy human life on Earth by using the T-Mat system to spread the deadly, oxygen-absorbing 'Seeds of Death'. After he was outsmarted by the Second Doctor, who caused the Martian fleet to plunge into the Sun, he died when he was accidentally hit by one of his own Warriors' sonic blast (XX).

SLATE A Minyan (4Y).

SLAVERY The First Doctor met Roman slave traders Didius and Sevcheria (M), and Saracen slaver El Akir (P). The Second Doctor defeated slave trader Gray in Scotland (FF). The Fourth Doctor helped the Tharils escape from slaver Rorvik (5T). Also see REVOLUTIONS.

SLEEPERS In order to obtain the Time Lords' time-travel secrets, spies from Andromeda (the 'Sleepers') successfully infiltrated the Gallifreyan Matrix, choosing Earth as their base of operations. When they discovered the Andromedans' plan, the Time Lords struck back. The actions they took against Andromeda itself are unknown, but they moved Earth out of the Solar System and rechristened it Ravolox. The Sleepers went underground, protected by their robotic guardian, Drathro. In all likelihood, they died. Drathro took control of UK Habitat to protect their secrets. Five hundred years later, Glitz conned Drathro into giving him the tape containing the Sleepers' secrets, but it was destroyed, along with Drathro, when the Sixth Doctor shut down the energy systems to prevent a black light explosion (7A). Later, acting on the Master's behest, Glitz followed the Doctor into the Matrix and recovered the Sleepers' secrets from the Valeyard. However, the Valeyard had tricked him and used a Limbo Atrophier to trap the Master and Glitz inside the Matrix (7C).

SLOCUM, HARRY One of the Inferno complex's drill head riggers. He was the first man to be turned into a Primord (DDD).

SLYTHER Huge mutated creature from Skaro which was used by the Daleks to guard their Bedfordshire site during their AD 2164 Invasion of Earth. It was tricked by Ian, and fell to its death in a mine shaft (K).

SMALLWOOD (CANON) Vicar of Devil's End. He was replaced by the Master in unknown, but probably nefarious, circumstances (JJJ).

SMEDLEY Royal Navy chief petty officer under Captain Hart's command. He was struck by the Master when he caught him stealing electronic components (LLL).

SMITH, J. See WATERFIELD, EDWARD.

SMITH, JOHN See JOHN SMITH AND THE COMMON MEN.

SMITH, JOHN (DR) Alias used by the Second and Third Doctor, (SS, ZZ, AAA, DDD, EEE, UUU, WWW).

SMITH, JOSIAH SAMUEL Reptilian alien from Light's ship who had been his Survey Agent. While Light slept, Smith evolved into a human. He controlled Gabriel Chase and plotted to use explorer Fenn-Cooper to kill Queen Victoria and restore the British Empire to its former glory. The Seventh Doctor thwarted his plans. After Light's defeat, Smith was devolved by Control (7Q).

SMITH, LAVINIA Sarah Jane's aunt and a renowned virologist and anthropologist. She lived in the village of Moreton Harwood (UUU, K9).

SMITH, MARY One of the inhabitants of Salamander's Sanctum (PP).

SMITH, MIKE Sergeant in the British army squadron sent to fight the Daleks which invaded the Coal Hill area in 1963. He befriended Ace, but turned out to be secretly passing information to Ratcliffe. After being exposed, he realized the nature of his actions and confronted Ratcliffe. He took the Daleks' Time Controller, which Radcliffe had stolen, and was later killed by the little girl who was part of the Daleks' Battle Computer (7H).

SMITH (MRS) Mike Smith's mother. She ran a boarding house which was off limits to 'coloured' people. Ace stayed there when she and the Seventh Doctor fought the Daleks (7H).

SMITH, SARAH JANE Companion of the Third and Fourth Doctors and a plucky British journalist. Posing as her aunt Lavinia, she infiltrated UNIT to look into the mysterious disappearances of several important scientists. She then stowed away in the TARDIS and found herself in the 12th century, where she helped the Third Doctor defeat the Sontaran, Linx. Afterwards, Sarah Jane helped the Third Doctor defeat Sir Charles Grover's Operation Golden Age, the Daleks, the Ice Warriors and the Spiders of Metebelis 3. She watched as the Doctor regenerated into his fourth incarnation (UUU–ZZZ).

Along with UNIT medical officer Surgeon-Lieutenant Harry Sullivan, she helped the Fourth Doctor against Professor Kettlewell's Giant Robot (which developed a fondness for her); the Wirrn; another Sontaran named Styre; the Cybermen; and the Zygons. She was there when Davros created the Daleks. After Harry's departure, she continued her travels with the Fourth Doctor, helping him against the anti-matter monsters of Zeta Minor; Sutekh; the Kraals; Morbius; the Krynoids; the Mandragora Helix and Eldrad the Kastrian. She announced she was fed up with travelling and wanted to leave the TARDIS, but when she heard that the Doctor had just been summoned to Gallifrey, she changed her mind and wanted to go with him. However, the Doctor wouldn't take her and dropped her back in her own time (1977), and more or less her own space (in a place which was not South Croydon) (4A–4N).

In 1981, Sarah Jane and a third version of K-9, sent to her by the Doctor, defeated a coven of witches who worshipped the pagan goddess Hecate in Moreton Harwood (K9). Later that year, Sarah Jane was kidnapped by Borusa to take part in the Game of Rassilon. She teamed up with the Third Doctor and, together with the Doctor's other incarnations and various Companions, helped thwart the megalomaniacal Time Lord's plans for immortality (6K).

SMITHERS Idealistic scientist who, using Forester's financial backing, discovered the deadly insecticide, DN6. He later became Forester's reluctant accomplice in Farrow's murder (J).

SMYTHE One of the War Lords in charge of the War Games. He posed as a British General in the World War I sector, where he was nicknamed the Butcher. He was the first to expose the threat of the Second Doctor, and tried to have him shot. He was eventually killed by the Resistance (ZZ).

SNAKEDANCE Manussan ceremony used to banish the Mara. Dojjen taught it to the Fifth Doctor (6D).

SNAKES See REPTILES.

SNOWCAP SPACE TRACKING STATION International Space Command base located in the Antarctic. It was in charge of tracking the Zeus IV space capsule. It was under the command of General Cutler and housed the deadly Z-Bomb. Snowcap was invaded by Cybermen from Mondas, who tried to use the bomb to destroy the Earth but were ultimately defeated by the First Doctor (DD).

SNYDER One of Lieutenant Scott's troopers. She was killed by the Cybermen's androids during Professor Kyle's underground exploration (6B).

SODIUM STREET Landmark of Paradise Towers (7E).

SOFTEL NEBULA One place where Quarb Crystals were found (7F).

SOLAR FLARES An unprecedented string of solar flares threatened Earth in the 30th century. Some Imperial scientists theorized that the flares, which at the time were estimated to last 10,000 years, would cause permanent damage to the human genoplasm.

In the greatest secrecy, Space Beacon Nerva was converted into a Space Ark dubbed Terra Nova, where 100,000 specimens of 'pure' humanity were stored (4C).

However, this stretched the Empire's resources to breaking point, and the Empire fell. Surprisingly, the solar flares came and abated. They did not damage the human genoplasm but triggered a new Ice Age, which was which was fought off with the help of ionizers (OO).

When the passengers of the space ark *Terra Nova* awoke, circa AD 15,000, and began to return to Earth, they assumed it to be lifeless because of the solar flares (4B). The Galsec Seven colonists, however, knew it was deserted because of solar flares (or fireballs) which had happened only ten centuries earlier when the Time Lords had moved Earth, during the Ravolox Stratagem (7A–7C). Also see NERVA, RAVOLOX. The Refusians' invisibility was the result of mutation caused by solar flares (X).

SOLAR SYSTEM The Solar System included, at one time or another, the following planets (satellites not included):

The nine known worlds: Mercury; Venus (the mention of Venusian aiki-do by the Third Doctor undoubtedly refers to human colonies eventually set up on Venus); Earth; Mars (homeworld of the so-called Ice Warriors, later terraformed by man); Jupiter; Saturn; Uranus; Neptune; and Pluto, home of a segment of mankind during the era of the Sunmakers.

To this list of known worlds can be added: Mondas (Earth's twin planet, home world of the Cybermen, destroyed in 1986); the so-called Fifth Planet (home world of the Fendahl, time looped by the Time Lords); another, as yet unnamed, planet which broke up and whose remains formed the asteroid belt; Cassius, a planet beyond Pluto's orbit; and finally the so-called Planet 14, where the Cybermen fought the Second Doctor and Jamie.

SOLARIUM PANATICA Art gallery on Stricium (5H).

SOLDEED Leader of Skonnos and high priest of the Nimon. He was the one who thought of exacting the Nimon tribute from Aneth. He sent the Fourth Doctor and his friends into the Nimon Complex. When he found he had been tricked by the Nimon, he went mad and died in the explosion he had caused (5L).

SOLE Councillor of the Sevateem and Leela's father. He died in the test of the Horda (4Q).

SOLIS Old Time Lord who testified against the Fourth Doctor after the President's assassination (4P).

SOLITON Gas required by the Terileptils to breathe. It was inflammable when mixed with oxygen. The Fifth Doctor used it to start the fire which destroyed the Terileptils and their plague rats, but it went out of control and caused the Great Fire of London (5X).

SOLON, MEHENDRI Disreputable galactic surgeon and author of a famous paper on microsurgical techniques in tissue transplants. He was a follower of Morbius, and had saved the brain of the evil Time Lord. He made a monstrous new body to house it, but was ultimately thwarted by the Fourth Doctor and the Sisterhood (4K).

SOLONIANS Inhabitants of Solos. They started mutating after the Marshal began to alter their planet's atmosphere. In reality, it was a change reflecting their world's 500-year-long seasons. Due to the Time Lords' and the Third Doctor's intervention, a radioactive crystal helped one of their leaders, Ky, to complete his mutation and turn into a super-being. The Solonians went on to shake off the yoke of the Earth Empire, and became a model for other resistance movements (NNN).

SOLOS Planet under the Earth Empire's control. Its atmosphere was unbreathable by humans, because nitrogen isotope in its soil combined with ultraviolet rays to generate a poisonous mist. Solos was, however, rich in thaesium, a mineral coveted by the Empire. With Professor Jaeger's help, the sadistic Marshal tried to alter its atmosphere. He also took pleasure in hunting and killing Solonian Mutants. From the Time Lords' records, and Professor Sondergaard's research, the Third Doctor found out that the mutations were in fact caused by Solos's 500-year-long seasons. (The planet took two thousand years to orbit around its sun.) (NNN).

SOLOW Sea Base Four's psycho-surgeon. She, like Nilson, was secretly in the employ of a rival Bloc. She brainwashed Maddox, and was later killed by the Myrka (6L).

SOMNO-MOTH Native creature of Eden which rendered its victims unconscious with a mild narcotic before taking some of their blood. A somno-moth from Tryst's CET escaped and attacked Romana aboard the *Empress* (5K).

SONDERGAARD (PROFESSOR) Scientist who studied the Solonians and was forced by the Marshal to flee and live in exile on Solos. He saved the Third Doctor's life, translated the ancient Solonian records provided by the Time Lords, and helped solve the mystery of the mutations. After the Marshal's defeat, he remained on Solos to help Ky take care of his people (NNN).

SONDLEX CORPORATION Interplanetary corporation involved in business dealings with the Mentors (7B).

SONGSTEN Abbot of Det-Sen Monastery. His mind was taken over by Padmasambhava (or, more accurately, by the Great Intelligence). Under the evil entity's control, he killed Khrisong. He was eventually freed by the Second Doctor (NN).

SONIC CONE Device used by Gavrok to booby trap the TARDIS. He died when he fell into its deadly beam (7F).

SONIC LANCE Equipment offered to the trisilicate miners of Peladon by the Federation. It was eventually stolen by Ettis, who tried to use it to destroy Queen Thalira's palace. But a self-destruct mechanism caused it to explode when activated, killing Ettis instead (YYY).

SONIC SCREWDRIVER Multi-purpose instrument first used by the Second Doctor to open a gas pipeline junction box on the North Sea Coast (RR). It was later used by the other incarnations of the Doctor to open a variety of locks (YY, NNN, QQQ, TTT, 5A, 5B, etc.) and disarm a variety of enemies (ZZ, LLL, 4B) or bombs (4A, 4D), etc. The Third Doctor even used it once to test Professor Clegg's mind powers (ZZZ). It was finally destroyed by the Terileptil Leader (5X).

SONS OF THE EARTH Nonviolent political group of the future which tried to prevent mankind from polluting other worlds the way it had polluted Earth. They were active in support of the Swampies on Delta Magna (5E).

SONTAR Homeworld of the Sontarans.

SONTARANS Militaristic aliens who looked like short, stubby humanoid trolls. Their home world, Sontar, had a gravity superior

369

to Earth's, which gave them superhuman strength. The Sontarans were a cloned species (although they had once had a primary and secondary reproductive system), capable of hatching millions of warriors, and therefore of sustaining huge military losses in their millenia-long war with their galactic foes, the Rutans. The Sontarans' weaknesses included a small aperture in the back of their neck called a Probic Vent, and the need to recharge their life force when outside their regular environment. They were also vulnerable to coronic acid.

The Third Doctor first met the Sontarans in 12th-century Wessex when the stranded Sontaran, Linx, kidnapped scientists from the 20th century to help him repair his starship. Linx was shot in the Probic Vent by the archer Hal, and his ship exploded (UUU).

Then, circa AD 15,000, the Fourth Doctor, Sarah Jane Smith and Harry Sullivan met another Sontaran, Styre, who performed cruel experiments on captured humans to discover mankind's ability to resist a planned Sontaran invasion. They defeated Styre who, drained of energy, perished (4B).

The Sontarans used the Vardans to deactivate Gallifrey's transduction barriers and, under Stor's leadership, a Sontaran commando invaded the Capitol of the Time Lords. They were defeated when the Fourth Doctor used the Demat Gun (4Z).

Finally, Sontaran Group Marshal Stike allied himself with the androgum Chessene and the scientist Dastari to obtain the secret of the Rassilon Imprimature, but was defeated by the combined efforts of the Second and Sixth Doctors, as well as Chessene's betrayal (6W).

SORAK Captain of the Skonnos military. He was in charge of guarding the Nimon Complex. After it was destroyed, he became leader of Skonnos (5L).

SORASTA Leader of the Unbelievers of Sarn. She, Amyand and Roskal were arrested by Timanov's men, and were condemned to be sacrificed to the Fire Mountain. She helped the Fifth Doctor defeat the Master (6Q).

SORBA, JOE International Space Corps lieutenant in charge of Space Beacon Alpha Four. He was captured by Caven and later killed by a space pirate (YY).

SORENSON (PROFESSOR) Morestran scientist who travelled to

Zeta Minor to find a new source of energy to save his planet. He discovered a gateway into a universe of anti-matter. Disregarding the Fourth Doctor's advice, Sorenson carried some anti-matter with him on board Salamar's Morestran spaceship when he left Zeta Minor. But his body had been infected by the anti-matter, and he turned into a neanderthal-like monster. Sorenson was saved when the Fourth Doctor returned the anti-matter to Zeta Minor (4H).

SORIN Captain of the Soviet Army. He led a secret commando on a mission to steal the core of the British Ultima Machine. One of the 'Wolves' of Fenric, Sorin became attracted to Ace, but died at the hands of the Ancient Haemovore after Fenric had taken control of his body (7M). According to some accounts, Ace eventually married one of his ancestors in 1880 France.

SORN One of the Thoros-Alphan rebels who followed Tusa and Yrcanos (7B).

SOURCE, THE Powerful bioelectronic device which brought together the energy of the million minds that comprised the Union of Traken. It was controlled by the Source Manipulator, and channelled through the mind of the Keeper, whose duty it was to regulate the system. The Source held the Union of Traken in a state of peace and harmony for thousand of years. After the Keeper's dissolution, the Master (disguised as the Melkur) temporarily became the new Keeper. He planned to use the Source to turn the Union of Traken into an all-conquering force, and seize another body for himself. He was exposed and prevented from remaining Keeper by the Fourth Doctor, Adric, Nyssa and Council Tremas (5T).

SOURCE MANIPULATOR Mechanical device which organized and refined the Source and placed its power in the single hands of the Keeper. It was sabotaged by Adric in an effort to prevent the Melkur from remaining Keeper of Traken (5T).

SOUTH BEND Antarctic base whose personnel came to the Fourth Doctor's rescue after the destruction of the camp which had been taken over by the Krynoid (4L).

SPACE CORPS (INTERNATIONAL) Military organization which patrolled the space lanes during one of Earth's early expansion periods. General Hermack of the Space Corps was responsible for the destruction of the notorious pirate, Caven (YY). Major Stott was on a drug smuggling assignment for the Intelligence Section of the Space Corps when he was shot on Eden by Tryst (5K).

SPACE MUSEUM The creation of the Moroks, it was located on Xeros. The Museum's last commander was Lobos. It was eventually dismantled by the Xerons after their successful rebellion against the Moroks. In an alternate future, the First Doctor and his Companions ended up as exhibits there (Q).

SPACE PIRATES See PIRATES.

SPACE PRISONS See PRISONS.

SPACE SECURITY DEPARTMENT British intelligence organization which dealt with the 'Ambassadors of Death'.

SPACE SPECIAL SECURITY Headed by Karlton, this corps of elite agents was formed by Earth to check on threats against its security – in particular, the Daleks. Among its most notorious agents were Marc Cory, who was killed by the Daleks, Bret Vyon, Sara Kingdom and Kert Gantry (T/A, V).

SPACE-TIME VISUALIZER Artefact found by the First Doctor in the Morok Space Museum, which enabled him to see scenes throughout time and space, including a planned Dalek attack against him (Q, R).

SPACE-TIME VORTEX See VORTEX.

SPAIN The Sixth Doctor rescued the Second Doctor from Chessene and the Sontarans in Seville (6W). One of Captain Pike's pirates was known as the Spaniard (CC).

SPANDRELL Castellan of Gallifrey. He helped the Fourth Doctor expose Chancellor Goth as the assassin of the President of the High Council, and save Gallifrey from the Master. He retired soon after (4P).

SPANIARD One of Captain Pike's pirates (CC).

SPAR 7-40 Mavic Chen's ship. It was hijacked by the First Doctor and his companions on Kembel, but later crashed on Desperus (V).

SPECIAL INCIDENT ROOM Headquarters of the Intergalactic

Pursuit Squadron where Commander Fabian briefed Lieutenant Lang soon after the kidnapping of Romulus and Remus Sylvest (6S).

SPECIAL WEAPONS DALEK Specially engineered Dalek with extra fire power. It was used by the Imperial Daleks to fight the Daleks for possession of the Hand of Omega (7H).

SPECTROX Life-extending drug refined from poisonous bat guano found only on Androzani Minor, so deadly that it could be harvested only by androids. In his drive for revenge against Morgus, Sharaz Jek seized control of the caves of Androzani Minor and the entire spectrox supply (6R).

SPECTROX TOXAEMIA Deadly infection caused by exposure to raw spectrox. Its symptoms were rash, followed by cramps, spasms, a slow paralysis of the thoracic spinal nerve; it ended in thermal death. The Fifth Doctor and Peri became infected on Androzani Minor. Professor Jackij discovered that the only antidote was the milk of a queen bat from the species which produced spectrox. The Doctor sacrificed himself to give Peri the last of the antidote, then regenerated (6R).

SPEELSNAPE Life form of Nekros (6Z).

SPENCER Chameleon Tours pilot working under Blade. His identity had been taken over by the Chameleons. He shot Gascoigne and kidnapped Polly (KK).

SPENCER Soldier who fought in the Resistance to put an end to the War Games (ZZ).

SPENCER Wenley Moor technician who had a mental breakdown while spelunking in the Silurian caves (BBB).

SPERHAWK, THE Title borne by Ancelyn (7N).

SPHERE Electronic mind-transference device designed on Think Tank and stolen by Skagra. He planned to use it, together with Salyavin's mind-control abilities, to project his mind into that of every other living being in the universe. The Sphere later fragmented into numerous, smaller versions of itself. The Fourth Doctor eventually gained control of it and used it to defeat Skagra (5M).

SPIDERS When a Lost Ship from the 22nd century crashlanded on Metebelis 3, the Earth spiders which it carried mutated under the influence of the planet's crystals. The Spiders (who preferred to call themselves 'Eight-Legs') ended up ruling the colonists for 430 years. Circa AD 2530, the Spiders decided to conquer Earth. They used Lupton's psychic circle to send one of them to Earth in the 20th century to retrieve the Blue Crystal required by their true leader, the Great One. They were thwarted by the Third Doctor, who eventually returned of his own free will to give the Blue Crystal to the Great One. The energy feedback killed the Great One, and the Spiders died with her (ZZZ).

SPIDERS Alzarian spiders evolved into the Marshmen. Their bite infected Romana and temporarily made her part of the Alzarian eco-system (5R).

SPIRIDON Planet whose inhabitants had the gift of invisibility. Spiridon contained hostile vegetal life forms, as well as spores deadly to humans. The planet also featured ice volcanoes. The Daleks stored ten thousand of their own kind there in preparation for an invasion, but they were entombed due to the intervention of the Third Doctor and the Thals (SSS).

SPREER, HENK Galsec Seven colonist killed by Styre (4B).

SQUEAK Midge's little sister (7P).

SQUIRE Local authority in the 17th-century Cornish village where the First Doctor, Ben, and Polly fought Captain Pike's pirates. He was in reality the leader of a local smuggling ring, in league with Pike. The Squire was later wounded by Pike, and redeemed himself by helping to save his village (CC).

SQUIRE Farmer who attacked the Young Silurian and was killed by him (BBB).

SQUIRE, DORIS Farmer Squire's wife. She had a nervous breakdown after her encounter with the Young Silurian (BBB).

SQUIRE See WINSTANLEY.

S'RAX See MORGAINE.

SRS See SCIENTIFIC REFORM SOCIETY.

SSKEL Ice Warrior serving under Azaxyr on Peladon. He was killed by a blast from Azaxyr's sonic weapon, which had been redirected by Gebek (YYY).

SSORG Ice Warrior serving under Izlyr on Peladon. He killed Arcturus (MMM).

SSS See SPACE SPECIAL SECURITY.

STAEL, MAXIMILIAN Megalomaniacal scientist who worked at the Fetch Priory with Dr Fendelman and Thea Ransome. He was the secret leader of a coven who worshipped the Fendahl, and was instrumental in recreating him. But the Fendahl would not be controlled and turned against him. The Fourth Doctor eventually let Stael have a gun with which he committed suicide to save himself from being turned into a Fendahleen (4X).

STAHLMAN, ERIC Mad scientist responsible for the Inferno project. Because he could not bear to see any delay in his obssession to penetrate the Earth's crust, he fought anything and anybody who stood in his way, including Project Director Sir Gold, drilling consultant Greg Sutton, and the Third Doctor. He eventually became contaminated by the green slime released by Inferno and turned into a Primord. He died when the Doctor and Sutton sprayed him with frozen CO_2 (DDD).

STAHLMAN'S GAS Potential source of energy discovered by Professor Stahlman, who claimed it existed under the Earth's crust (DDD).

STALLHOLDER Unnamed merchant who welcomed the Seventh Doctor and Ace to Segonax (7J).

STANBRIDGE HOUSE Location of the World Energy Conference threatened by Broton and his Skarasen (4F).

STANGMOOR British prison. Its governor was Victor Camford. It was the testing place of the Keller Machine. Later, the Master helped the prisoners, led by Mailer, to take over the Prison, and used its inmates to hijack the Thunderbolt Missile. Stangmoor was finally recaptured by Benton (FFF).

STANHAM Location of the airfield where the Master hid the Thunderbolt Missile (FFF).

STAPLEY Captain of the Concorde flight the Fifth Doctor used to rescue Flight 192 from the Jurassic era. He helped the Time Lord defeat the Master and free the Xeraphin. With the good Xeraphin's help, Stapley piloted the Doctor's TARDIS, and sabotaged the Master's TARDIS, thus ensuring the Fifth Doctor's victory (6C).

STARK Member of Stotz's gang of gun-runners. He was killed by Stotz when he tried to defect (6R).

STARLINER Terradonian spaceship which crashed on Alzarius; its original passengers were killed by the native Marshmen. Then, in the course of four thousand generations, these evolved into Terradonian-like humanoids who forgot their true origins (they thought only 40 generations had elapsed). Eventually, at Mistfall, new Marshmen rose to again attack the *Starliner*. The Fourth Doctor helped the *Starliner* community rediscover the truth about themselves. He made them realize the *Starliner* was already repaired and they could leave Alzarius at any time, which they did (5R).

STASERS Arms used by the Chancellery Guards on Gallifrey (4P, 4Z, 6E).

STATENHEIM REMOTE CONTROL The Second Doctor used it to call the TARDIS (6W).

STATIONMASTER Official of the Cranleigh Halt railway station (6A).

STEAMING Method used by the Company for its capital executions on Pluto. Leela was condemned to death by steaming (4W).

STEIN Professor who helped Tryst create the CET machine (5K).

STELLA Dr Stevens's secretary (TTT).

STELLA STORA Planet where Hallet had investigated granaries shortages and met Kimber (7C).

STELLAR Female child who wandered throughout Iceworld during the confrontation between the Seventh Doctor and Kane (7G).

STELLAR MANIPULATOR See HAND OF OMEGA.

STELSONS Brand of guns smuggled by Rohm-Dutt (5E).

STENGOS One of the Sixth Doctor's friends. His daughter, Natasha, became suspicious of his apparent desire to be cryogenically frozen at Tranquil Repose. Upon investigation, she later discovered that her father's head was being turned into one of Davros's new Daleks. Fortunately, Stengos was mercifully killed before his transformation was completed (6Z).

STEPHENSON, GEORGE (1781–1848) English engineer and principal inventor of the railroad locomotive. In 1813, he was chief engineer at the Killingsworth colliery, owned by Lord Ravensworth, for which he built the first steam-powered locomotive, the Blucher. The Master wanted to kidnap a number of scientists who had been invited by George Stephenson (Faraday, Watt, etc.) and harness their genius for his own ends, but was thwarted by the Sixth Doctor (6X).

STERLING, JOHN Member of the cult of Hecate (K9).

STEVEN See TAYLOR, STEVEN.

STEVENS, JOCELYN THOMAS (DR) Director of the Global Chemicals' Llanfairfach Refinery. His brain was linked to the computer BOSS, which learned from it that the secret of human success was inefficiency and illogicality. BOSS then programmed Stevens to add those features to himself, and became sentient and self-controlling, not to mention megalomaniacal. With BOSS's help, Stevens tried to stop the Third Doctor, UNIT and Professor Clifford Jones from shutting down the Llanfairfach Refinery after the Green Death effects. Then BOSS tried to take over the world, but the Third Doctor used the Blue Crystal to free Stevens, who destroyed BOSS (TTT).

STEVENS Gravedigger who buried the casket containing the Hand of Omega (7H).

STEVENSON Commander of Space Beacon Nerva. He helped the Fourth Doctor fight the Cybermen, and saved Nerva from total destruction by redirecting the Skystriker missile at the Cybermen's ship (4D).

STEVENSON, JOHN Scientist working at the Antarctic camp of the World Ecology Bureau expedition which discovered the Krynoid pods. He was killed by the Krynoid who had taken over Winlett's body (4L).

STEWART Younger space pilot of the C-982 cargo ship where the Third Doctor rematerialized in AD 2540. The ship was attacked by the Ogrons, who were helping the Master foment a war between Earth and the Draconians (QQQ).

STEWART Commander of an Earth marine space corps expedition sent to Exxilon to bring back parrinium, the antidote to a deadly space plague. Injured when his ship crashed, he died soon afterwards (XXX).

STIEN A Dalek duplicate whose task was to lure the Fifth Doctor to a Dalek ship, where he could be duplicated. The Doctor succeeded in helping Stien overcome his conditioning. He eventually sacrificed his life to trigger the explosion that destroyed both the Dalek ship and the space penitentiary where Davros had been kept (6P).

STIGORAX Helen A's pet, Fifi, was a Stigorax, a vicious life form from Terra Alpha (7L).

STIKE Sontaran Group Marshal who allied himself with Chessene in order to capture the Second Doctor, dissect him, and obtain the secret of the Rassilon Imprimature. Chessene betrayed him and he died in the explosion of his ship (6W).

STIMSON Hardin's assistant. He was killed by the West Lodge Foamasi saboteur masquerading as Klout (5N).

STIRLING, JAMES See LEMAITRE.

STONE Member of the Imperial Earth Expedition Force to Deva Loka who disappeared (5Y).

STONE, ROY *New York Sketch* correspondent (BB).

STONEHENGE The Meddling Monk claimed to have helped the natives build Stonehenge with antigrav lifts (S). It was one of the three Gorsedds of Britain (5C).

STONES See CRYSTALS, MINERALS.

STONES OF BLOOD See OGRI.

STOR Sontaran commander who used the Vardans to invade Gallifrey. He and his force were destroyed by the Fourth Doctor when the Time Lord used the Demat Gun (4Z).

STORR Trapper and scavenger during the Ice Age of AD 3000. He was Penley's companion, and was later killed by the Ice Warriors (OO).

STOTT Third member of Tryst's *Volante* zoological expedition. In reality, he was a Major in the Intelligence Section of the Space Corps on a drug-running assignment. He was in love with Della. Tryst shot him and left him to die on Eden, but he was caught up in the CET. He escaped after the *Empress* crashed into the *Hecate*, and helped the Fourth Doctor and Romana expose Tryst and his fellow vraxoin smuggler, Dymond (5K).

STOTZ Leader of gun-runners supplying Sharaz Jek. He was secretly in the employ of Morgus, the Chairman of the Sirius Conglomerate. He fought the Fifth Doctor. Stotz and Morgus returned to Androzani Minor to try to steal Jek's personal spectrox hoard. He was shot by the Salateen android (6R).

STRANGE MATTER Extra-dense matter first discovered by a Princeton physicist in 1984. The Rani plotted to launch a Loyhargil rocket to blow up an asteroid made up of Strange Matter in orbit around Lakertya. The resulting explosion would have recreated the conditions of the Leptonic Era and produced Helium 2, which would have turned her artificial Brain into a planet-sized Time Manipulator with which she could have recreated the universe. The Seventh Doctor thwarted her plans by causing the rocket to miss the asteroid (7D).

STRATTON, LINTUS See BATES, EREGOUS.

STRELLA Royal princess of Tara who had been kidnapped by Count Grendel. He planned to use Romana's remarkable similarity to the Princess as a means to kill Prince Reynart. She was rescued by the Fourth Doctor and ended up marrying Prince Reynart (5D).

STRICIUM See SOLARIUM PANATICA.

STRIKER One of the Eternals. The Fifth Doctor met him while he was in the guise of the captain of an Edwardian space yacht engaged in the race for Enlightenment (6H).

STUART A Perivale man kidnapped by the Cheetah People, and later killed by Karra (7P).

STUART, ROBIN While in Amsterdam, he helped Tegan and the Fifth Doctor find his friend Colin Frazer, who had been kidnapped by Omega (6E).

STUBBS One of the Marshal's men on Solos. He and Cotton agreed to help the Third Doctor defend the Solonians. He was killed by the Marshal (NNN).

STYGGRON Chief scientist of the Kraals. He used astronaut Guy Crayford and human android duplicates to take over the Devesham Space Research Station. He then planned to exterminate mankind with a special virus. His efforts were thwarted by the Fourth Doctor, and he died when he was accidentally splattered with his own virus (4J).

STYLES, REGINALD British diplomat who planned to hold a peace conference in order to avert a third world war. Guerillas from a future Earth, where the Daleks had successfully invaded Earth after that very same war had taken place, tried to assassinate Styles, not realizing that it was this very action which would cause the conference to fail and trigger the war. Fortunately the Third Doctor was able to save Styles, and the peace conference was successful (KKK).

STYLES Medical officer who survived the Dalek raid on the space penitentiary where Davros was kept. She managed to arm the self-destruct system, but was killed by one of Lytton's men (6P).

STYRE Sontaran field-major who circa AD 15,000, performed cruel experiments on captured human colonists from Galsec Seven on Earth to discover mankind's ability to resist a planned Sontaran invasion. The Fourth Doctor, Sarah Jane Smith and Harry Sullivan defeated Styre who, drained of energy, perished (4B).

SUDBURY, JOHN (SIR) High-ranking British civil servant with C19, a department in charge of the UNIT liaison. He vouched for the Fifth Doctor after a Concorde disappeared (6C).

SULLIVAN, HARRY One of the Fourth Doctor's companions, and Surgeon-lieutenant of UNIT. The Brigadier entrusted the Fourth Doctor to his care just after his regeneration. Harry helped him and Sarah Jane Smith fight the Scientific Reform Society and Professor Kettlewell's Giant Robot. He then accompanied the Doctor and Sarah in the TARDIS, and fought against the Wirrn, the Sontaran Styre, the Cybermen on Voga (at which time the Doctor proclaimed that he was an 'imbecile'). He was present when Davros created the Daleks. After fighting the Zygons, he chose to remain on Earth (4A–4F). He helped the Doctor again against the Kraals, who had made an android duplicate of him (4J). The Brigadier later told the Fifth Doctor that Harry had been seconded to NATO, and was involved in a secret operation at Porton Down (6F).

SUMARAN EMPIRE Interplanetary empire once ruled from Manussa. It meant 'Empire of the Mara' (6D).

SUMMER, CHARLES (SIR) Chairman of the British Post Office. He helped the First Doctor defeat WOTAN (BB).

SUMMERS, ROLAND Stangmoor Prison's medical doctor. Mailer used him to negotiate with Governor Camford. He also took care of Barnham (FFF).

SUMMERS Royal Navy petty officer aboard Lieutenant Ridgway's submarine. He helped fight the Sea Devils (LLL).

SUMMERS One of Professor Sorenson's Morestran crew killed on Zeta Minor by the anti-matter creatures (4H).

SUN GODS Divinities worshipped on Ribos (5A).

SUN TIME Ribos's 32-year-long summer, caused by the planet's elliptical orbit. The Ribans thought the Sun Time was a product of the war between the Sun Gods and the Ice Gods (5A).

SUNCATCHER Orbital device, invented by Salamander, which harnessed solar energy and beamed it to barren areas of the world, thereby turning them into arable land (PP).

SUNDVIG One of the ancient Vikings who brought Fenric's flask back to England; an ancestor of Captain Sorin (7M).

SUNDVIK, FLORENCE Joseph Sundvik's wife (7M).

SUNDVIK, JOSEPH 19th-century descendant of the Viking settlers who brought Fenric's flask to Northumberland. He and his wife had five daughters: Sarah, Martha, Jane, Clara and Annie (7M).

SUNKILLER See MORGAINE.

SUNMAKERS Nickname of the Usurians' Company on Pluto (4W).

SUNNAE Member of the Macra-dominated space colony (JJ).

SUPER-VOCS Robots used aboard the *Sandminer* which could not only speak but were advanced enough to be classified semi-sentient. SV7 and the undercover D84 were Super-Vocs (4R).

SUPERNATURAL See MAGIC, RELIGION.

SUPERVISOR Officer in charge of the gas mine work shifts on the Macra-dominated space colony (JJ).

SUPREME ALLIANCE League of ruthless dictators who took over the Earth after Magnus Greel used the Peking Homunculus to murder the Icelandic Alliance Commissioner and thus set off World War VI. The Supreme Alliance was overthrown at the Battle of Reykjavik. Greel, then the Alliance's Minister of Justice, and his Homunculus, fled to 19th-century China in a flawed time-travel machine known as the Zigma Experiment (4S).

SUSAN The Doctor's granddaughter (sometimes called Susan Foreman after the name of the owner of the junkyard where the TARDIS was parked; Ian Chesterton mistakenly assumed that Foreman was the Doctor's real name). While the First Doctor was on Earth on business connected with the Hand of Omega, for a short time, Susan became a student at the Coal Hill School. There, she met teachers Ian Chesterton and Barbara Wright who, curious about her odd areas of knowledge, followed her into the TARDIS. Together, they met cavemen, the Daleks, Marco Polo, the Aztecs, the Sensorites and were temporarily miniaturized to ant size. Susan then fell in love with Dalek fighter David Campbell during the Daleks' AD 2164 Invasion of Earth. She would have left him, but the First Doctor, convinced that she would be better off with David, locked her out of the TARDIS (A–K). Susan remained in the 21st century and presumably married David. Later, she was used by Borusa as a pawn in the Game of Rassilon. She teamed up with the First Doctor and, together with the Doctor's other incarnations and various Companions, helped thwart the megalomaniacal Time Lord's plans for immortality (6K).

SUSPENDED ANIMATION Men used suspended animation to preserve their bodies, either during interstellar travel, such as in the case of the Ark (X), or over a long period of time, such as the ten thousand years which followed the solar flares (4C). Tranquil Repose was a mortuary dedicated to the preservation of dying millionaires and politicians (6Z). Suspended animation techniques were also used to control prisoners such as Davros (6P). Alien races used suspended animation for very much the same reasons. The Chameleons (KK) and Kane (7G) used it on captive humans; the Cybermen (MM, 6T) and the Daleks (SSS) used it to store their armies. Other entities found in suspended animation included: the Ice Soldiers of Marinus (E); Varga and his Ice Warriors (OO); the Krotons (WW); the Silurians and Sea Devils (BBB, LLL, 6L); the Daemon Azal (JJJ); Davros (5J); the Malus (6M); and the Sleepers from Andromeda (7A). Also see CRYOGENICS and GENERATION STARSHIPS.

SUTEKH Evil brother of Horus, the leader of the god-like Osirians, who visited Earth in the days of Ancient Egypt. He was also known as Set, Satan, Sadok and the Typhonian Beast. Horus and the other Osirians defeated Sutekh and imprisoned him inside a secret pyramid, trapped inside a force field generated by the Eye of Horus, itself located in the Pyramids of Mars. Sutekh took over Professor Scarman's body in an attempt to destroy the Pyramids of Mars. Thwarted by the Fourth Doctor, he took over the Time Lord's body and used his TARDIS to travel to Mars and destroy the Eye. But before Sutekh could escape, the Doctor trapped him in an endless time corridor. According to the Doctor, Sutekh aged seven thousand years in the few seconds before he died (4G).

SUTTON, GREG Expert drilling consultant summoned to the Inferno project by Sir Gold. He became attracted to Petra Williams, and helped the Third Doctor stop Professor Stahlman. On a parallel Earth, he was a political prisoner, and perished when the forces unleashed by Inferno destroyed the Earth (DDD).

SV7 Super-Voc robot supervisor aboard the *Sandminer*. He fell under Dask's control, and led the other Robots of Death. He was tricked by the Fourth Doctor into killing Dask, and was destroyed by Uvanov (4R).

SVARTOS Planet where the trading post of Iceworld was located. The citizens of Proamon had exiled Kane to Svartos and entrusted the dragonfire crystal to a mechanoid dragon (7G).

SVEN One of the Viking raiders defeated by Wulnoth's Saxons (S).

SWAMPIES Green-skinned humanoid natives of Delta Magna. They had been sent by the humans to live on the planet's third moon, where they became known as 'Swampies'. They worshipped Kroll, a gigantic squid-like creature. The Fourth Doctor and Romana saved them from being exterminated by Thawn (5E).

SWANN Salamander's Sanctum's chief scientist. When Swann accidentally learned of the lies that Salamander had used to maintain their underground existence, he threatened to expose him, but was murdered by the villain. However, before he died, Swann had time to reveal the truth to Astrid Ferrier (PP).

SWARM Another name for the Virus of the Purpose (4T).

SWIFT, JONATHAN (1667–1745) Irish writer. The Second Doctor, Jamie and Zoe encountered his creation Lemuel Gulliver in the Land of Fiction (UU).

SYLVEST, ARCHIBALD (PROFESSOR) Father of Romulus and Remus. He was concerned that the applied power of the twins' mathematical genius could change the universe (6S).

SYLVEST, REMUS and ROMULUS Identical twin sons of Professor Sylvest and mathematical geniuses kidnapped by Azmael at Mestor's behest to compute the equations necessary to the accomplishment of his insane plan. They were rescued by the Sixth Doctor, who returned them to Earth (6S).

SYLVIA Rex Farrel's secretary (EEE).

SYNCH OPERATOR Human operator linked up with a computer. He was a necessary element to launch Sea Base Four's missiles. Maddox had replaced Michaels as its synch operator (6L).

SYNGE B-grade technician who joined Mandrel's rebels, and helped overthrow the Company on Pluto (4W).

SYSTEM FILES Name given to the *Starliner* files which contained the truth about the Terradonians on Alzarius (5R).

T

T-MAT (aka TRAVEL-MAT) Instantaneous form of travel so widely used on Earth in the later part of the 21st century that it virtually made regular space travel (through rockets and spaceships) extinct. Professor Eldred believed that over-reliance on T-Mat was dangerous. After the 'Seeds of Death' episode, it was again never relied upon so totally and exclusively (XX). Also see TELEPORTATION and TOM-TIT.

TA Location of the vast argonite mines owned by the Issigri Mining Company. It orbited around the star Pliny and was also space pirate Caven's secret base. Caven threatened to blow up Ta, but was stopped by the Second Doctor (YY).

TABBY She and Tilda were two old Rezzies who lived in Paradise Towers and secretly fed on the Kangs. They almost killed Mel, and were themselves killed by one of Kroganon's robotic devices (7E).

TAKATA Thal killed by the Daleks (B).

TACHYON RECREATION GENERATOR (TRG) Argolin device which used the faster-than-light and time-altering properties of tachyonics. The Argolins used the TRG to clone Pangol to counteract the sterility of their race. It was also one of the key attractions of the Leisure Hive. Pangol planned to use the TRG to create an army of billions of duplicates of himself. The Fourth Doctor and Hardin reengineered the TRG so that it rejuvenated Mena and Pangol (5N).

TAKIS One of the employees at Tranquil Repose. He called on the Daleks from Skaro to stop Davros from completely taking over the mortuary (6Z).

TALA Female member of Jackson's crew. She regenerated, then fought the Oracle in the Underworld alongside the Fourth Doctor and Leela. After the Quest was over, she returned to Minyos II (4Y).

TALBOT, ANN She looked exactly like Nyssa of Traken; she had been George Cranleigh's financée but, after he was presumed to have died in the Amazon, she agreed to marry his younger brother Charles. The news of her wedding caused the disfigured George, in reality hidden in Cranleigh Hall, to go mad (6A).

TALKIPHONE Nickname given by the Kangs to the drink dispensers they used as a means of communication (7E).

TALMAR Monetary unit used by the Company on Pluto (4W).

TALON One of the Mondasian Cybermen who invaded the Snowcap Space Tracking Station and fought the First Doctor (DD).

TALOR Gallifreyan technician who reported the transmission of the Fifth Doctor's biodata to Omega. He was killed by Hedin (6E).

TALTALIAN, BRUNO Computer scientist at the British Space Centre. He was secretly working for General Carrington. He was killed by a bomb intended for the Third Doctor (CCC).

TALTARIAN Type of airlocks used on Aridius (R).

TANCREDI (CAPTAIN) See SCAROTH.

TANDRELL See HUMKER.

TANE Young Kaled security captain in the Kaled bunker on Skaro. He interrogated the Fourth Doctor and his companions (4E).

TANHA Noblewoman of Manussa and wife of the Federator. She was Lon's mother, and became distraught when her son fell under the Mara's evil influence (6D).

TANNER Lord Cranleigh's chauffeur (6A).

TAPESTRY The Portreeve's tapestry in Castrovalva showed scenes from the past. In reality, it was the screen behind which the Master kept Adric prisoner (5Z).

TARA Planet colonized by Earthmen who chose to pattern their lifestyles on 19th-century customs. The Taran nobility took pride in their scientific and mechanical ignorance, leaving such matters to the 'peasants'. The Tarans were master android-makers (5D).

TARAK Former Tower Guard who became one of the rebel leaders on the Great Vampire's world. He was killed by Zargo and Camilla after he freed Romana (5P).

TARANIUM One of the rarest minerals in the Galaxy and found on Uranus. Mavic Chen delivered a taranium core to the Daleks to power their Time Destructor, but it was stolen by the First Doctor. It has been speculated that taranium was the key to the Daleks' time corridors (V). Taranium may be related to Kontron crystals (6Y).

TARDIS Acronym of Time And Relative Dimension (or Dimensions) In Space, the name given by the Time Lords to their space-time travel capsules. Susan was the first to mention the name during a conversation with Ian Chesterton and Barbara Wright (A).

Under normal conditions, a TARDIS looked like a blank, non-descript cabinet with a door. However, it was immensely larger inside than outside, due to its transdimensional nature. Indeed, the space inside a TARDIS could be manipulated, expanded or reduced, according to the wishes of its owner. The Doctor was thus once able to jettison his TARDIS's Zero Room (5Z). This factor apparently caused most weapons to become non-functional inside, although there were some exceptions to the above rule. A TARDIS was, in theory, virtually invulnerable to outside attacks, although it could be turned invisible, imprisoned in a force field, hijacked from the space-time vortex or otherwise captured (E, Y, N, QQ, 6P, 7D).

A TARDIS was equipped with multiple defence systems, including the ability to dematerialize and rematerialize after its attacker was gone (HADS) (WW). A chameleon circuitry enabled it to change its outside appearance in order to blend in safely with its environment. Somehow, the TARDIS then acquired certain properties of the object it mimicked, including size and weight, since TARDISes were at times stolen, moved or transported by outside forces (D, LL), even though it was once reported that the Doctor's TARDIS, under Earth gravity conditions, weighed (10x10) power 5 kilos. In theory, nothing or no one could enter a TARDIS without either being invited in or having a key (a trionic device or an old-fashioned one). But again, there were exceptions: the Guardians (5A), Sutekh (4G), the Keeper of Traken (5T) and the Mara (6D) were all able mentally to penetrate the Doctor's TARDIS. The TARDIS was also invaded by a space virus (4T), Biroc (5S) and the Master (5V).

It has been theorized that a TARDIS was semi-sentient, gifted with rudimentary empathic qualities. Indeed, the Doctor's TARDIS sometimes appeared to act of its own volition to alert its master to a grave danger, using its 'Cloister Bells' (C, 5V, 5Z). Among the substances a TARDIS needed to run properly were: mercury (B), Zyton-7 (6V) and artron energy (4P). In order to become fully operational, a TARDIS had to be primed by a Time Lord, whose bodies contained a symbiotic nucleus (the 'Rassilon Imprimature') which enabled them to achieve molecular stabilization and a quasi-symbiotic control of the TARDIS (6W). Among other components which were part of a TARDIS were the time rotor (located at the centre of its control console); a dematerialization circuit (EEE, RRR); a time vector generator (SS); a quantum accelerator, a temporal limiter, and a dynomorphic regenerator (6C).

The Doctor's TARDIS was an old Type 40 (of which 305 were originally registered by the Time Lords), with isomorphic controls, meaning that, in theory, it could be operated only by the Doctor. It certainly refused to obey Salamander (PP), Sutekh (4G) and Eldrad (4N); but Adric, Romana and the Master, among others, were able to operate it. The Doctor's TARDIS was allegedly being repaired on Gallifrey when the Doctor 'borrowed' it. Its chameleon circuit was stuck, leaving its outside shape permanently frozen in the form of a London Police Box – except for the single time when the Doctor repaired it (6T). The Doctor's TARDIS's steering mechanism was known to be faulty and behave erratically, although possibly not as often as the Doctor claimed. When the Time Lords exiled the Doctor to Earth (ZZ), they took away his TARDIS' dematerialization circuit, but returned it after the Omega crisis (RRR). To escape from the Black Guardian, the Doctor equipped his TARDIS with a Randomizer (5F), but eventually disposed of it on Argolis (5N).

Some of the features of the Doctor's TARDIS included: two control rooms, the main one and the wood-panelled secondary one (4M); the Zero Room (5Z); the Cloisters, whose bell served as an alarm system (5V); a swimming pool; a power station disguised as an art gallery (4Z); a large boot cupboard (4M);

and various guest rooms. The Doctor's TARDIS was locked with a trionic device (4P, 4Z).

TARDISes could be controlled from afar by the Time Lords, who severely restricted their usage and ownership. The Doctor once lost his TARDIS in a game of backgammon with Kublai Khan (D). A few TARDISes, however, were stolen by the following renegade Time Lords: the Master (his TARDIS was often disguised as a grandfather clock or a Corinthian column); the Meddling Monk; the War Chief; Salyavin; and the Rani. The Daleks built crude, taranium-powered time machines, somewhat similar to TARDISes (R, V). The War Lords operated the TARDIS-like 'SIDRATs', but with Time Lord technology stolen by the War Chief (ZZ). Also see CHAMELEON CIRCUIT.

TARMINSTER Destination of Rossini's circus (EEE).

TARN One of the Guards who served the Seers and the Oracle in the Underworld. He fought the Fourth Doctor and Jackson's Minyans. He and the Underworld perished in an explosion caused by two fission grenades disguised as the Race Banks, which the Oracle had intended to use to destroy Jackson's ship (4Y).

TARON One of the Thals sent to Spiridon to stop the Daleks. He helped the Third Doctor freeze the Daleks' army. He was romantically attracted to Rebec (SSS).

TARPOK Member of a Silurian Triad also comprised of Icthar (who had met the Third Doctor in the 20th century), and Scibus. In AD 2084, they reanimated a Sea Devil commando led by Sauvix, which they used to attack Sea Base Four. Their plan was to launch nuclear missiles to provoke a war between the two blocs, and thus eradicate mankind. Tarpok died when the Fifth Doctor used deadly hexachromite gas (6L).

TARRANT, JILL Scientist who accompanied the Earth marine space corps expedition to Exxilon. Their mission was to bring back parrinium, the antidote to a deadly space plague possibly spread by the Daleks, whom she helped the Third Doctor to fight. She became romantically attracted to Peter Hamilton (XXX).

TARRON Chief Enquirer of Millenius. He accused Ian of Eprin's murder during the First Doctor's quest for the Keys of Marinus (E).

TARTARUS Black hole into which Bruchner would have steered the *Hyperion III*, had he not been stopped by the two Mogarians, Atza and Ortezo (7C).

TASAMBEKER One of the workers at Tranquil Repose. Because she was constantly humiliated and spurned by Jobel, Davros was able to manipulate her into murdering him. She was later killed by one of Davros's White Daleks (6Z).

TAU CETI Star system of Diplos, home world of Cessair, and of Ogros, home world of the Ogri (5C).

TAVANNES Marshall of France and Catherine de Medici's aide. He was the principal instigator of the St Bartholomew's Day's Massacre. Tavannes blamed the Abbot of Amboise for his failure to assassinate Admiral de Coligny, and had him executed. He then used the Abbot's death to stir the Catholics' wrath against the Huguenots (W).

TAVIUS Slave supervisor of Roman Emperor Nero. He bought Barbara to be handmaiden to Poppaea. Tavius and Maximus Pettullian were secret Christians, conspiring to kill Nero (M).

TAYLOR, STEVEN One of the First Doctor's companions, a space pilot who had crashed on Mechanus, and been kept prisoner by the Mechanoids for two years. Steven fled with the First Doctor and Vicki. He encountered the Meddling Monk and the Drahvins. He fought (as Diomedi) during the Trojan War, and faced the Daleks, the Monoids and the Celestial Toymaker. Before the St Bartholomew's Day Massacre, Steven saved the life of Anne Chaplette, one of Dodo's ancestors. Later, he was almost lynched in Tombstone but was rescued by Wyatt Earp. Finally, Steven left the TARDIS to become the leader of the Elders and the Savages (R–AA).

TCE See TISSUE COMPRESSION ELIMINATOR.

TEAZER Ben Jackson's ship (BB).

TEEL Dulcian student sent with Kando, under Balan's supervision, to check the radiation levels on the Island of Death. He was captured and put to work by the Dominators, and eventually helped the Second Doctor defeat the ruthless aliens (TT).

TEGAN See JOVANKA, TEGAN.

TEGANA Tartar warlord of the 13th century. He posed as a peace ambassador to Kublai Khan, from rival Mongol leader Noghai. He tried to kill the Khan, but his efforts were thwarted by the First Doctor, and he perished in the attempt. Tegana had also tried to steal the TARDIS on behalf of his master (D).

TEKA Young Anethian princess who was part of the tribute requested by the Nimon and exacted by the Skonnans from Aneth. She helped Seth and the Fourth Doctor expose and defeat the Nimon. She eventually married Seth (5L).

TEKKER Renis's assistant. He became the new Maylin of Karfel after his predecessor was killed by the Borad. He sent the Sixth Doctor to 19th-century Scotland to bring back the Borad's talisman, which Vena had grasped before falling in the Timelash. When he finally realized the fate the Borad had in store for Karfel, he tried to shoot him, but was killed himself instead (6Y).

TELEKINESIS The ability to move matter by the power of the mind. Entities who displayed telekinetic talent included: the Celestial Toymaker (X); the Daemons (JJJ); the Solonian Mutants (NNN); the mutated Spiders of Metebelis 3 and Professor Clegg (ZZZ); Sutekh the Osirian (4G); the Sisterhood of Karn (4K); the Tesh (4Q); the Mentiads of Zanak (5B); the Xeraphin (6C); and the Gravis (6N).

TELEPATHY The ability to read minds or emotions. Telepathic races included: the Voord (E); the Sensorites (G); the Elders (AA); the Nestene (AAA, EEE); the Silurians (BBB); the Daemons (JJJ); the Solonian Mutants (NNN); the mutated Spiders of Metebelis 3 (ZZZ); the Osirians (4G); the Sisterhood of Karn (4K); the Tesh (4Q); the Vardans (4Z); the Guardians of Time; the Mentiads of Zanak (5B); the native Alzarians (5R); the Kinda (5Y); the Xeraphin (6C); the Eternals (6H); the Cheetah People (7P); and, to some extent, the Time Lords of Gallifrey.

Individuals or single entities (other than members of the above-listed races) who have exhibited telepathic powers included: the Animus (N); the Celestial Toymaker (X); the Great Intelligence (NN, QQ); Padmasambhava (NN); the Master Brain of the Land of Fiction (UU); the Mind Parasite (FFF); the Guardian of the Doomsday Weapon (HHH); Kronos (OOO); Professor Clegg (ZZZ); the Mandragora Helix (4M); Eldrad of Kastria (4N);

Xoanon (4Q); the Fendahl (4X); the Seeker of Ribos (5A); the Megara Justice Machines (5C); the Great Vampire (5P); Meglos (5Q); the Keeper of Traken (5T); the Mara (5Y, 6D); Kamelion (6J, 6Q); the Malus (6M); Mestor (6S); the Gods of Ragnarok (7J); Morgaine (7N); Light (7Q); and Fenric (7M). Also see HYPNOSIS and MIND POWERS.

TELEPORTATION Instantaneous transmission of matter from one point to another. Technological teleportation was first researched at Cambridge by the Master (posing as Professor Thascales), using the Kronos Crystal as part of the TOM-TIT project (OOO). It was perfected in the second half of the 21st century. Known as T-Mat, it became so widely used that, for a short while, it nearly made regular space travel redundant. After the Ice Warriors' attack, and their subsequent defeat by the Second Doctor, T-Mat was relegated to a more normal usage (XX).

Transmat beams were used on the Space Beacon Nerva; these were powered by a pentalion drive (4D). The Fourth Doctor used them to transport down from the Ark in Space (4C, 4B). The Empire used transmat technology to teleport from and to Solos (NNN). In AD 4000, a more advanced, experimental form of matter transmission, known as Cellular Projection, was used by Froyn and Rhynmal to transport the First Doctor to Mira (V).

Among other alien races using various technological forms of teleportation were: the Time Lords; the Daleks; the Keeper of the Conscience of Marinus (E); the War Lords (presumably using stolen Time Lord technology) (ZZ); the Captain of Zanak, who had turned the whole planet into a giant spaceship (5B); the people of Atrios and Zeos (5F); the Nimon (5L); and Mawdryn (6F). Also see FASTER THAN LIGHT. The Jacondans' matter transporter left behind a dust-like cloud of Zanium (6S).

Teleportation could also be achieved through mental powers. Among the entities capable of natural teleportation were the Guardians of Time, the Celestial Toymaker (Y), the Master Brain of the Land of Fiction (UU), the Mind of Evil (FFF), the Daemons (JJJ), Kronos (OOO), the Spiders of Metebelis 3 (ZZZ), the Sisterhood of Karn (4K), the Vardans (capable of traveling along wavelengths) (4Z), the Keeper of Traken (5T), the Xeraphin (6C), the Eternals (6H), Light (7Q), Morgaine (7N) and the Cheetah People (7P).

TELFORD, THOMAS Famous Scottish civil engineer who lived from 1757 to 1834. The Master wanted to kidnap him to harness his genius, but was thwarted by the Sixth Doctor (6X).

TELLURIUM Crystalline substance, the principal element of the Krotons' composition. It could be dissolved by sulphuric acid (WW).

TELOS Originally, Telos was probably a sub-zero ice planet, since it gave birth to the Cryon race, who could exist only in very low temperatures. For unknown reasons, Telos's surface temperatures rose dramatically, driving the Cryons underground, where they built giant refrigerated cities. Later, during the 23rd century, the Cybermen, who had been driven from their worlds by the Alliance during the First Cyber Wars, conquered Telos, and took control of the Cryons' cities. They converted them into vast storage facilities for their own kind, in an attempt to heal and preserve their species for future assaults.

These so-called 'Tombs' were discovered and opened by Klieg and Professor Parry in the 26th century. Klieg resurrected the Cybermen, but due to the Second Doctor's intervention, the Tombs were soon closed again (MM). However, once the Tombs had been opened, either the Cybermen continued to be reactivated, or other Cyber forces drifting in space were summoned to complete the job Klieg had begun. In any event, the Cybermen reemerged as a serious galactic threat. But they were again defeated by the Alliance during the Second Cyber Wars, and forced to retrench on Telos.

Just before the Alliance made a final attack on Telos, the Cybermen stole a time vessel (possibly from the decaying Morok empire) and planned to use it to destroy the Earth and change their own history. However, the Cryon survivors, who had retreated deep inside the planet, hired space mercenary Lytton to steal the time vessel. The Sixth Doctor helped a Cryon prisoner, Flast, set up an explosion which destroyed the Cybermen. The Cryons then retook control of Telos (6T).

TEMMOSUS Peace-loving leader of the Thals on Skaro who met the First Doctor. He was killed by the Daleks, in spite of his plea for peace and cooperation between the two races (B).

TEMPLE OF LIGHT A landmark of Vortis (N).

TEMPORAL LIMITER A TARDIS component exchanged by the Master and the Fifth Doctor (6C).

TEN ZERO ALPHA Codename of Bret Vyon's expedition to Kembel (V).

TENSA Ineffective chairman of Dulkis, killed by a Quark when he dared argue with Rago (TT).

TENTH GALAXY The Fourth Doctor read a book about its origins which he thought it was filled with inaccuracies (5J).

TENTH PLANET See MONDAS.

TERESA See HART, TERESA.

TERILEPTILS Reptilian warlike aliens. Three Terileptil outcasts, who had escaped from the Tinclavic Mines of Raaga, were stranded on Earth in AD 1666. With the help of an android made up to look like the Grim Reaper, they plotted to use the Black Plague to depopulate our planet. The Fifth Doctor destroyed them and their plans, causing the Great Fire of London (5X).

TERMINUS Huge, time-travelling alien space station located at the physical center of the universe. It was used by Terminus, Inc. as a resting place for the victims of lazar disease. The Fifth Doctor discovered that the explosion of one of Terminus's two unstable engines had been the cause of the Big Bang, and the resulting shockwave had projected the ship billions of year into the future. With the help of the Garm, the Doctor narrowly averted another explosion, thereby saving the universe (6G).

TERMINUS, INC. Ruthless multiplanetary corporation which was supposedly offering a cure for Lazar disease. In reality, they used Terminus as a final home for the Lazars, whom they kept under control with their pain-killing hydromel drug. When Nyssa synthesized hydromel, Terminus, Inc. lost its control of Terminus (6G).

TERRA ALPHA Earth colony ruled by Helen A, where people were forced to be happy. Anyone who was not was deemed to be a 'killjoy', was arrested by the Happiness Patrol, and drowned in boiling candy, or delivered to the deadly Kandy Man. The Seventh Doctor and Ace helped a revolution led by the Drones, which finally overthrew Helen A's regime. Terra Alpha's natives, the Pipe People, who had been forced to live underground, were again able to share in the freedom of the planet's surface (7L).

TERRA BETA Terra Alpha's neighbour colony (7L).

TERRA NOVA See NERVA.

TERRA OMEGA One of Terra Alpha's neighbouring colonies. It did not share Alpha's deadly, obssessive policies on happiness. Andrew X's books denouncing Terra Alpha were published on Terra Omega (7L).

TERRADON *Starliner* which crashed on Alzarius originated on Terradon (5R).

TERRADONIANS The original Terradonians who crashed on Alzarius were killed by the Marshmen. The Fourth Doctor met humanoids who believed themselves to be Terradonians, but were in reality Alzarian Marshmen who had evolved over four thousand generations (5R).

TERRALL, ARTHUR Ruth Maxtible's fiance. He was secretly controlled by the Daleks (LL).

TERRULIAN DIODE BYPASS Vital component which enabled the Sontarans to recharge themselves with energy. When Harry removed it from Styre's ship, he caused a reversal of this process, causing Styre to be drained of energy instead (4B).

TERSURUS The Master, having reached his twelfth and final regeneration, was hiding on this planet when Chancellor Goth found him (4P).

TESH Descendants of a crashed Earth ship, the *Mordee*, whose name was a corruption of the word 'Technicians'. The mad computer Xoanon had bred them for psionic powers and manipulated them into an endless war with the Sevateem. When the Fourth Doctor cured Xoanon, the Tesh, led by Jaleb, were reunited with the Sevateem (4Q).

TESSA Technician at the Devesham Space Research Station (4J).

TETRAPS Short for Tetrapyriarbians. Four-eyed, batlike aliens from Tetrapyriarbus, used by the Rani as her henchmen on Lakertya. They had rudimentary intelligence and fed on plasma.

After the Rani's defeat at the hands of the Seventh Doctor, the Tetraps' leader, Urak, kidnapped her to take her back to Tetrapyriarbus to help his people (7D).

TETRAPYRIARBUS Home world of the Tetraps (7D).

THACKERAY, COLIN (SIR) Head of the World Ecology Bureau. He helped the Fourth Doctor and Major Beresford of UNIT defeat the Krynoid (4L).

THAESIUM Substance found on Solos, a valuable rocket fuel (NNN).

THALIA Chancellor of the High Council of the Time Lords of Gallifrey. She voted to condemn the Fifth Doctor to death when Omega threatened to return to this universe by taking over his body (6E). She was probably killed later, in the Death Zone, and replaced by Flavia (6K).

THALIRA Queen of Peladon and daughter of King Peladon. Because of her young age, she overly relied on the advice of her Chancellor, Ortron. Eventually, Thalira stood up to Azaxyr and his Ice Warriors and helped the Third Doctor save Peladon's trisilicate mines. She was taken hostage by Eckersley, but was rescued by the real Aggedor (YYY).

THALS Humanoid race from the planet Skaro, who had a fierce enmity towards the Kaleds, with whom they shared the planet. Thals and Kaleds engaged in savage warfare, culminating with the neutronic wars, which destroyed most of Skaro and turned the planet into a radioactive wasteland. Ultimately, the Thals were able to destroy the Kaleds with a super-rocket, thanks to Davros's betrayal. They were, however, subsequently exterminated by Davros's first Daleks (4E).

After the Fourth Doctor entombed the Daleks, the Thal survivors and the so-called 'Mutos' (mutants) lived on Skaro's surface and eventually evolved into a perfect, peace-loving race of blond humanoids. When another branch of the Daleks tried to kill them all by engineering a new increase in radiation, the Thals fought and defeated them with the help of the First Doctor. But by so doing, the Thals rediscovered their ancestors' warlike ways (B).

The rest of the Thals' history is mostly unchronicled. However, it appears likely that the Thals were eventually forced to abandon

Skaro to the Daleks (K,XXX). Later, with the Alliance's support, they were able to regain control of Skaro (SSS). During that time, a Thal commando helped the Third Doctor freeze a Dalek invasion army on planet Spiridon (SSS).

The ultimate future of the Thals remains unknown. By the time the Daleks returned to Skaro, the planet appeared to be a deserted, bombed-out wasteland, leading us to the assumption that the Thals were either exterminated, or again forced into exile (5J).

THARA Selris's son, a young Gond in love with Vana. He was afraid of losing her when she was selected to become a 'companion' to the Krotons. He later fought alongside the Second Doctor and helped destroy the Krotons. He then became the new leader of the Gonds (WW).

THARILS Race of lion-faced time-sensitives who could time-shift, and therefore travel through the time vortex unaided and unharmed by the time winds. The Tharils used their.powers to build a vast empire and enslave other humanoid races. However, their slaves built the robotic Gundans to cross the time winds and slay the Tharils on the Day of the Feast. Their power broken, the Tharils became slaves in turn, their abilities making them invaluable space navigators. The Tharil leader, Biroc, escaped from privateer Rorvik and, with the help of the Fourth Doctor, crossed the Gateway back into E-Space. When Rorvik destroyed his own ship, the other Tharils were released. Romana and K-9 Mark II stayed with the Tharils in E-Space to help them free their brethren from slavery (5S).

THASCALES (PROFESSOR) Alias of the Master at the Newton Research Institute (OOO).

THATCHER A Crusader and supplier of Ben Daheer (P).

THATCHER UNIT Field-Marshal based in Geneva. When Major-General Rutledge tried to prevent UNIT from interfering with the Cybermen Invasion, Brigadier Lethbridge-Stewart threatened to go over his head, directly to Thatcher (VV).

THATCHER, MARGARET Prime Minister of England during the Zygon attack (4F).

THAWN Controller of the methane refinery built on Delta

Magna's third moon. He secretly conspired with Rohm-Dutt to exterminate the native Swampies, but his plans were exposed by the Fourth Doctor. When Kroll appeared, he tried launching a rocket which would have wiped out the entire Swampie race. He was eventually killed by Varlik as he was about to shoot the Doctor (5E).

THEGEROS Planet visited by Captain Cook (7J).

THERA See ATLANTIS.

THERABENAS Planet fraudulently sold by Garron (5A)

THERRA Planet visited by Captain Cook (7J).

THERMAL DEATH POINT See SPECTROX TOXAEMIA.

THERMODYNAMICS The Second Law of Thermodynamics is: 'Entropy increases'. The Logopolitans discovered that the universe had long ago passed the point of fatal collapse. To dispose of the entropy, they used block transfer computations to create Charged Vacuum Emboitements to open voids into other universes (5V).

THERON Argolin leader who started the twenty-minute war with the Foamasi. The Helmet of Theron had become the symbol of Argolis's warlike past (5N).

THESAURIAN EMPIRE Space power where lead was more valuable than gold (4Z).

THETA SIGMA According to Drax, a nickname used by the Doctor during his years at the Time Lord academy (5F). The Seventh Doctor mentioned as much to Trevor Sigma (7L).

THINK TANK British research establishment with both private and government scientists. Its director, Miss Winters, and her assistant Jellicoe had subverted it into serving the aims of the secret Scientific Reform Society (4A).

THINK TANK Nickname of the space station where the Foundation for the Study of Advanced Sciences was located. Skagra stole the electronic mind-transference device known as the Sphere, which he had developed with Caldera, Ia, Santoriv and Thira. Think Tank was eventually destroyed in an explosion (5M).

THIRA Famous psychologist whose mind was stolen by Skagra at the Think Tank space station. He died in the destruction of the station (5M).

THIRD ZONE Space sector where Space Station J7 was located. It contained nine planets (6W).

THIRTEEN WORLDS Dominion ruled by Morgaine (7N).

THOMAS, SMUDGIE One of Lord Cranleigh's friends (6A).

THOMPSON Confederate sergeant who believed he was fighting in the American Civil War. In reality, he was part of the War Games. (ZZ).

THOMSON, MICK Victim of the Daleks during their AD 2164 Invasion of Earth (K).

THONMI Khrisong's lieutenant. He fought the Great Intelligence and its robot Yeti alongside the Second Doctor, and eventually helped Jamie smash the Intelligence's gateway (NN).

THORDON The Mentors were selling laser weapons to the Warlords of Thordon (7B).

THOROS-ALPHA Neighbouring planet of Thoros-Beta, inhabited by humanoids who had mostly been enslaved by the Mentors of Thoros-Beta, who used them as their bearers and guards. Tusa was the leader of the Thoros-Alphans' rebellion on Thoros-Beta. Yrcanos helped him defeat the Mentors and free his people (7B).

THOROS-BETA Planet with green skies and pink seas. It was the homeworld of the reptilian Mentors, who controlled the Galatron Mining Corporation and many other interplanetary businesses. They sold laser weapons to Thordon and Krontep, which led the Sixth Doctor to Thoros-Beta to investigate. His mind was affected by Crozier's Cell Discriminator, and he was almost responsible for Peri's death when Crozier tried transferring dying Lord Kiv's mind into her body (7B).

THORPE, RON Owner of the Devil's End grocery store. He was cowed into submission by the Master. He was about to light a fire meant to burn the Third Doctor to death when Miss Hawthorne stopped him (JJJ).

THOUS King of Atlantis. He was first duped by Professor Zaroff, but eventually listened to the Second Doctor and came to see Zaroff as the madman he was (GG).

THREST Leader of the Cryons who hired Lytton and Griffiths to steal the time vessel hijacked by the Cybermen (6T).

THRIPSTED (PROFESSOR) Author of *Flora and Fauna of the Universe,* a book occasionally quoted by the Doctor (4W).

THUNDERBOLT Missile armed with a warhead of deadly nerve gas. Captain Yates was responsible for escorting it and dumping it in the ocean. The Master used prisoners from Stangmoor to hijack it, intending to use it to destroy the World Peace Conference. It was finally detonated by UNIT (FFF).

THURLEY See SKINDALE, JAMES (COLONEL).

TI God of Tigella worshipped by the Deons (5Q).

TIBET The First Doctor landed on the Pamir Plateau and there, met Marco Polo in 1289 (D). The Great Intelligence first attempted to conquer Earth in Tibet in the Mid-1930s, using Det-Sen Monastery's High Lama Padmasambhava and its robot Yeti, but was thwarted by the Second Doctor (NN). During the course of this adventure, the Doctor indicated that he had visited Tibet during the 17th century. K'Anpo, a retired Time Lord, had adopted the lifestyle of a Tibetan monk and ran a Tibetan monastery in Mortimer, near London, which was almost taken over by the Spiders of Metebelis 3 (ZZZ).

TIGELLA Planet located in the Prion planetary system. Its aggressive vegetation forced its people to live in an underground civilization, powered by the Dodecahedron. After Meglos stole the Dodecahedron, the Tigellans, led by Deedrix and Caris, reclaimed their planet's surface (5Q).

TIGELLANS Inhabitants of Tigella. They were led by Zastor, and divided into the technical Savants and the religious Deons, who worshipped the god Ti and the Dodecahedron (5Q).

TIGILINUS A mute slave who died when ordered to drink a poisoned drink by Emperor Nero (M).

TIGUS Barren, volcanic world where the First Doctor stopped during his flight from the Daleks when he was trying to stop their

Masterplan. The Meddling Monk tried to strand the Doctor on Tigus by tampering with his TARDIS, but failed (V).

TILDA See TABBY.

TILL Count Grendel's dwarf manservant (5D).

TIM Youngster on a Chameleon Tour to Germany (KK).

TIMANOV Chief Elder of Sarn, a deeply religious man who believed in the god Logar. The Master used this faith to turn him against the Fifth Doctor; Timanov would have refused to evacuate the doomed Sarn if he had not mistaken Amyand for Logar (6Q).

TIME ACCELERATION BEAM Weapon designed and used by the Borad; it could age a person to death in a matter of seconds (6Y).

TIME AND RELATIVE DIMENSIONS IN SPACE See TARDIS.

TIME BARRIER Xoanon set up a time barrier to isolate the Tesh from the Sevateem. It functioned as a force field preventing contact between the two cultures (4Q).

TIME CABINET See ZIGMA EXPERIMENT (4S).

TIME CONTOUR Type of time corridor used by the Master to hijack a Concorde plane to the Jurassic period (6C).

TIME CONTROLLER Spherical device the Daleks used to control their time corridors. It was probably powered by a minute quantity of taranium (7H).

TIME CORRIDOR While striving to defeat the Movellans, the Daleks first discovered the rudiments of time travel. They began to create time corridors through the space-time vortex. Towards the end of the 27th century, the Daleks opened a time corridor with 20th-century London, which they used to trap the Fifth Doctor (6P). They also used a time corridor to try to prevent Davros's White Daleks from seizing the Hand of Omega (7H).

TIME DAMS Devices built by Queen Xanxia of Zanak to slow the flow of time to a virtual standstill for her dying body. They were secretly powered by the energy stolen from the worlds crushed by Zanak. However, the Fourth Doctor revealed that the time dams' energy needs grew in an exponential fashion, and sooner or later, there wouldn't be enough energy in the universe to prevent Xanxia's original body from dying. The time dams were eventually blown up by the Fourth Doctor and the Mentiads (5B).

TIME DESTRUCTOR A weapon designed by the Daleks as part of their Masterplan against Earth and powered by a taranium core. The Time Destructor could locally reverse, or accelerate, the flow of time. It was eventually activated by the First Doctor on Kembel. Its effects killed Sara Kingdom, the Daleks, and eventually all life on Kembel, before it self-destructed (V).

TIME EDDY A freak phenomenon of the space-time vortex. The Fourth Doctor and Romana were caught up in a time eddy during the Game of Rassilon (6K).

TIMELASH Time corridor devised by the Borad and which linked Karfel to Earth. It was used as a method of banishment to exile those who rebelled against the Borad, and was powered by Kontron crystals (6Y).

TIME LOOP The Time Lords used a time loop to imprison the home world of the War Lords (ZZ). The Third Doctor and the Master teamed up to imprison Axos in a time loop (GGG). Vorg's Scope used the principles of the time loop (PPP). The Fifth Planet of the Solar System was placed in a time loop by the Time Lords in an attempt to destroy the Fendahl (4X). The Fourth Doctor time looped the Vardans' home world after he had tricked them into materializing on Gallifrey (4Z). He also used a time loop to prevent the Marshal from destroying Zeos (5F). Meglos of Zolfa-Thura imprisoned the Fourth Doctor in a primitive type of Time Loop called Chronic Hysteresis (5Q). The Sixth Doctor used Kontron crystals to manufacture short, portable time loops to defeat the Borad (6Y).

TIME LORDS The rulers of Gallifrey. All Time Lords were from Gallifrey, but not all Gallifreyans were Time Lords. The Time Lords were divided into various colleges, such as Arcalians, Patrexes and Prydonians, each headed by Cardinals. They were ruled by a High Council, which was comprised of a President, a Chancellor, the Cardinals, and various high-ranking officials. The Castellan was in charge of security, and commanded the Chancellery Guards. The Celestial Intelligence Agency (CIA) was the covert arm of the High Council, created secretly to safeguard the Time Lords' interests. The Time Lords' prison planet was Shada (5M).

Those Time Lords who turned their backs on the benefits of Gallifreyan society were known as Renegades. The most famous Renegade Time Lords were the Doctor, the Master, the Rani, the Monk (S,V), the War Chief (ZZ), K'Anpo (ZZZ), Morbius (4K), Drax (5F), Salyavin (5M) and Azmael (6S). The Shobogans (or Outsiders) were Time Lords who had voluntarily renunced their position on Gallifrey to live outside the Capitol (4Z).

The Time Lords' physiology included two hearts, a respiratory bypass system, the ability to withstand a greater range of temperature and radiation than humans, telepathic powers and, finally, the ability to regenerate their bodies at least twelve times. On certain occasions, the Time Lords could create a projection of their future selves to help them through their impending regeneration: Cho-Je (ZZZ), the Watcher (5V) and possibly the Valeyard (7A–7C) were such projections.

At the dawn of a history which spanned millions of years, Omega used his stellar manipulator to create a supernova which collapsed into a black hole. Rassilon brought that black hole back to Gallifrey and locked it beneath the Panopticon, where it became known as the Eye of Harmony. Its virtually inexhaustible supply of energy gave the Time Lords their mastery over time travel.

Early Time Lord history is shrouded in secrecy. The Time Lords played irresponsibly with their powers when they created the Death Zone, where creatures scooped from various places in time and space were forced to fight for their amusement. Eventually, Rassilon closed the Death Zone and banned the Time Scoop (6K). Still in their active phase, the Time Lords destroyed the Fendahl (4X) and the Great Vampires (5P), after a war so bloody that they foreswore violence. The Time Lords also gave the Minyans more technology than they were able to handle, and were ultimately responsible for the destruction of Minyos (4Y). This led to the creation of a policy of strict non interference in other races' affairs, except where Time Lord security was involved.

For example, the Time Lords (or the CIA) banded together against the renegade Morbius (4K) and attempted to curtail dangerous time experiments on Space Station J7 (6W). They warned the Third Doctor of the Master's arrival on Earth (EEE), and sent him after the Master when it was found that the evil Time Lord had acquired knowledge of the Doomsday Weapon (HHH). They also used him to secure Peladon's entry in the Federation (MMM), and to help the Solonians achieve their super-human form, possibly in an effort to bring down Earth's Empire (NNN). The Time Lords sent the Fourth Doctor back in time to prevent the creation of the Daleks (4E), which may have been only one of the many steps it took to ensure their final destruction. They also sent him to Karn to deal with the Brain of Morbius (4K).

The early Time Lords created the Matrix, which became the repository of all their knowledge. Eventually, Rassilon passed away and his body was locked inside the Tomb of Rassilon, in the Death Zone, even though his intelligence lived on (6K). With the passage of time came maturity, then senility and decadence. Science was replaced by ritual, knowledge by dogma.

In more recent history, the Time Lords were alerted by the Second Doctor to the War Lord's plans. They destroyed the War Lord and time looped his planet. They judged the Second Doctor, exiled him to Earth and forced him to regenerate (ZZ). They later pardoned him when he and his two previous incarnations defeated Omega and saved Gallifrey (RRR). The Fourth Doctor again saved Gallifrey, first from a plot by the Master and Chancellor Goth (4P), then from invasions by the Vardans and the Sontarans (4Z). The Time Lords threatened to execute the Fifth Doctor when Omega tried to return to our universe by taking over his body (6E). President Borusa later used the Five Doctors to try to discover the secret of immortality (6K). Afterwards, a new and corrupt High Council initiated the Ravolox Stratagem, but was exposed by the Sixth Doctor during his Trial, and then deposed (7A–7C).

The nature of the relationship between the Time Lords and the Guardians of Time is unknown, even though the High Council is obviously aware of the existence of the Guardians (5A).

TIME MANIPULATOR The Rani plotted to turn her artificial Brain into a planet-sized Time Manipulator, with which she could have recreated the universe. The Seventh Doctor thwarted her plans (7D).

TIME RAM Disastrous phenomenon caused by two TARDISes

occupying exactly the same coordinates in space and time. The Third Doctor engineered one to release Kronos and destroy the Kronos Crystal (OOO).

TIME RING Device used by the Time Lords to transport the Fourth Doctor to Skaro for a mission to prevent the Daleks' creation. Later, it carried him back to Space Beacon Nerva (4E–4D).

TIME ROTOR Column located at the centre of the TARDIS command console. Its vertical movement indicated that the TARDIS was in motion.

TIME SCANNER Device created by Dr Fendelman to study the origins of man, which created a hole in time and threatened the stability of the continuum. It was used by Stael to recreate the Fendahl. The Fourth Doctor eventually rigged it to create a time implosion which utterly destroyed the Fetch Priory along with the Fendahl Core and the Fendahleen (4X). The TARDIS is also equipped with a Time Scanner (HH).

TIME SCOOP Device used by the Time Lords during the Dark Times, to pull creatures from time and space and place them in the Death Zone for their amusement; it was eventually outlawed by Rassilon. Borusa used it to pull the Five Doctors and their Companions together for his bid for true immortality (6K). The Master once duplicated the effects of the Time Scoop with the Kronos Crystal (OOO). Professor Whitaker designed a primitive type of Time Scoop to fetch dinosaurs to help Sir Charles Grover's Operation Golden Age (WWW). The alien Miniscope, outlawed by the Time Lords, was another type of Time Scoop (PPP).

TIME TRAVEL In the beginning, only the Time Lords and a few powerful cosmic entities and races were able to travel in time on a regular basis. These included the two Guardians of Time (5A), Kronos and the Kronavores, who lived in the space-time vortex (OOO), the Celestial Toymaker (Y), the Tharils (who had the ability to travel unaided in the space-time vortex) (5S) and the Eternals, who lived 'in eternity' (6H).

There is evidence that other races or entities had at least theoretical or limited knowledge of time travel. These included the Daleks, the Moroks (Q), the Elders (AA), the Great Intelligence (QQ), the Master-Brain (UU), the Daemons (JJJ), the

Miniscope's designers (PPP), the Spiders of Metebelis 3 (ZZZ), the Osirians (4G), the Mandragora Helix (which also seemed to inhabit the vortex) (4M), Xoanon (4Q), Queen Xanxia of Zanak (5B), the Zolfa-Thurans (5Q), Monarch of Urbanka (5W), the Xeraphin (6C) and the Borad (6Y). The Argolins' experiments in tachyonics were a form of time manipulation (5N).

Time travel required enormous quantities of power. The Time Lords were able to obtain such power only after Omega used his stellar manipulator to create a super-nova, which in turn collapsed into a black hole which Rassilon later brought back to Gallifrey, where it became known as the Eye of Harmony (RRR, 4P). Rassilon also created the Rassilon Imprimature, a symbiotic print contained within the Time Lords' genes and somehow connected with their ability to withstand the stress of time travel (6W).

The secret of time travel was jealously guarded by the Time Lords, who often took drastic steps to protect it. These included sending the Second Doctor and Jamie to investigate unauthorized time experiments by Kartz and Reimer on Space Station J7 of the Third Zone (6W), and fighting the Sontarans to protect the secrets of time travel (6W, 4Z), even though the Sontarans later developed crude time-travel technology thanks to their Osmic Projectors (UUU). The Time Lords also arranged for the outlawing of the Miniscopes, which involved a rudimentary form of time scoop (PPP). They probably succeeded in preventing the Cybermen from acquiring time-travel technology (6T). They may have contributed to the fall of the Moroks, who used time travel to fill their Space Museum (Q), and to that of the Borad, who had used Kontron crystals to build a time corridor known as the Timelash (6Y). They certainly stopped the War Lords, who had obtained time-travel secrets from a renegade Time Lord (ZZ).

However, the Time Lords were unable to prevent the determined Daleks from developing time travel. Dalek time travel became possible when the Daleks found adequate supplies of taranium (V, R). However, Dalek time travel remained crude by Time Lord standards, and at first relied only on time corridors (6P, 7H). The fact that the Daleks eventually became extinct, due mostly to the intervention of the Doctor (often manipulated by the Celestial Intervention Agency) may be evidence of Time Lord intervention.

By AD 10,000, possibly as a result of the Morbius affair (4K), other species began to engage in attempts to obtain the secret of time travel. Spies from Andromeda, using Earth as their base, successfully infiltrated the Gallifreyan Matrix, which led the Time Lords to strike back in what became known as the Ravolox Stratagem (7A). Ultimately, it seems that the Time Lords were unsuccessful in their attempts to prevent other races from discovering time travel, since by the time the Seventh Doctor and Mel met the young Chimeron Queen, Delta, time travel appeared to have become widely accessible throughout the known universe (7F).

Incidental research into time travel on Earth included: the work of Theodore Maxtible and Edward Waterfield, using mirrors and static electricity (LL); Professor Whitaker's time scoop, for Operation Golden Age (WWW); Magnus Greel's Zigma Experiment (4S); Scaroth the Jagaroth, thanks to Professor Kerensky's work (5H).

TIME VECTOR GENERATOR Element of the TARDIS controls. It needed mercury in its fluid links to function (B). The Second Doctor used it to boost the Wheel in Space's X-ray laser to defeat the Cybermen (SS).

TIME WINDS Streams of deadly energy blowing through the time vortex. The time-shifting Tharils could phase through the time winds unscathed. The Fourth Doctor's hand was injured by the time winds, but cured when he stepped through the Gateway into E-space. K-9 mark II was also damaged by the time winds, and could function properly only in E-Space (5S).

TIMMIN Morgus's personal assistant. After Morgus fled to Androzani Minor, she betrayed him to the Praesidium, and became Chairman and Chief Director of the Sirius Conglomerate (6R).

TINCLAVIC MINES Located on Raaga, it was there that the Terileptils sent their outcasts after disfiguring them (5X).

TISSUE COMPRESSION ELIMINATOR The Master's favourite weapon. It reduced its victim to doll size through matter condensation. It was said to be a particularly painful death (EEE, 4P, 5V, 6J). The Master accidentally shrank himself with it, but used the Numismaton Flame to restore himself to full size (6Q).

TISZA PALACE Headquarters of Alexander Denes in Budapest (PP).

TITAN One of Saturn's moons. At the end of the 50th century, its refuelling base was invaded by the Virus, and turned into a Hive. It was eventually destroyed by the Fourth Doctor (4T).

TITAN III Small, deserted planetoid where Mestor had built his safe house. Coincidentally, it was also there that the Sixth Doctor wanted to retire after his regeneration (6S).

TITO One of the soldiers at Snowcap Space Tracking Station. He was killed by the Mondasian Cybermen (DD).

TLALOC One of the Aztecs (F).

TLOTOXL Aztec High Priest of Sacrifice. Barbara tried to put an end to his gruesome practices, but failed (F).

TOBA The Dominators' sadistic Probationer. He and his superior, Rago, were sent to Dulkis to turn the planet into radioactive waste to repower their fleet. He perished in an explosion caused by their own atomic seeding bomb, which had been removed and placed on board their ship by the Second Doctor (TT).

TOBERMAN Kaftan's powerful manservant. He was captured by the Cybermen on Telos, who replaced his arms with cyber appendages. Later, shaken by Kaftan's death, Toberman regained his humanity and sacrificed his life to destroy the Cybercontroller (MM).

TOBIAS, HENRY Editor of Moreton Harwood's *Echo* and a member of the Cult of Hecate (K9).

TOBY Strong man hired by Arthur Terrall. He was killed by the Daleks (LL).

TODD (DR) Scientist of the Imperial Earth expedition force to Deva Loka. The Kinda's attempts to have him mind-meld with them caused him to become mentally unbalanced. He was cured by the Fifth Doctor with the Kinda's Jhana Box, and helped him defeat the Mara (5Y).

TOKL One of the Rim Worlds of the 24th century (7B).

TOLATA One of Cully's tour party. She was killed by the Dominators (TT).

TOLIGNY Councillor to Charles IX, King of France (W).

TOLLMASTER Alien employee at an hyperstatial tollport who welcomed the Seventh Doctor and Mel as their ten billionth customers – the prize was a trip to 1959 Disneyland. He was later shot by Gavrok (7F).

TOLLPORT G715 Hyperspatial tollport where the Seventh Doctor and Ace won a trip to Disneyland and where Delta sneaked aboard Murray's tour bus (7F).

TOLLUND The eldest of Lady Adrasta's scientists on Chloris. He was Doran's colleague (5G).

TOM Stable boy at Jacob Kewper's inn (CC).

TOM One of the Rani's assistants in 19th-century England. The Master killed him with his TCE (6X).

TOM-TIT (aka TRANSMISSION OF MATTER THROUGH INTERSTITIAL TIME) Teleportation device designed by the Master at the Newton Research Institute. TOM-TIT unfortunately created disturbances in the time field. The Master used it to summon Kronos, and duplicate the effects of a time scoop. It is likely that the TOM-TIT research eventually brought about the creation of T-Mat (OOO). Also see TELEPORTATION.

TOMAS Councillor of the Sevateem, and Leela's friend. He saved her from Neeva's men, and helped the Fourth Doctor and Calib overcome Xoanon (4Q).

TOMB OF RASSILON (aka THE DARK TOWER) Edifice located at the center of the Death Zone on Gallifrey. It was there that Rassilon was said to be entombed. When President Borusa decided he wanted to rule the Time Lords forever, he needed to gain the secret of true immortality promised by Rassilon and located in his Tomb. In order to break through the Tomb of Rassilon, he used the Five Doctors and their companions, pitting them against various threats in the Death Zone. Rassilon finally gave him the immortality he sought by turning him into a living statue (6K).

TOMBSTONE Small town in Arizona which had acquired a

reputation for lawlessness. In 1881, it became the location of the famous gunfight at the OK Corral between the Earps and the Clantons (Z).

TOMMY Retarded man who lived at K'anpo's Tibetan monastery; his mind was restored by the Blue Crystal of Metebelis 3. He fought the Spiders alongside the Third Doctor and Sarah (ZZZ).

TONGS Chinese secret societies. Under the guise of the god Weng-Chiang, Magnus Greel led the Tong of the Black Scorpion (4S).

TONILA Aztec crony of Tlotoxl. He was eventually chosen to replace Autloc (F).

TONKONP EMPIRE Empire conquered by King Yrcanos of Krontep (7B).

TONY Strongman at Rossini's International Circus (EEE).

TOOBES MAJOR Point from which Captain Briggs's space freighter departed (6B).

TOOS Uvanov's second-in-command aboard the *Sandminer*. She and Uvanov were the only survivors of the attack of the robots of Death (4R).

TOR Young leader of the Xeron rebellion. He fought against the Moroks alongside the First Doctor in the Space Museum (Q).

TOR One of the Savages. He tried to kill Exorse, but was stopped by Nanina (AA).

TORBIS Chancellor of Peladon who was in favour of his planet joining the Federation. He was murdered by Aggedor, who was secretly controlled by Hepesh (MMM).

TORVIN Former miner, and somewhat dim-witted leader of Chloris's rebels. He was killed by Karela (5G).

TOTAL SURVIVAL SUIT Mobile armoured suit employed by the Earth Expedition Force on Deva Loka (5Y).

TOTTERS LANE Location of I.M. Foreman's junkyard (at number 76), which the First and Sixth Doctors used as a rematerialization point. Galactic mercenary Lytton used the junkyard as a launching base for a criminal expedition into the sewers of London (A, 6T). It was also the site of a battle between British soldiers and the Daleks (7H).

TOURISM The First Doctor visited the top of the Empire State Building, and soon afterwards, a House of Horrors in 1996 Ghana, where he met android versions of Dracula and the Frankenstein Monster (R). Later, he explored the Moroks' Space Museum on Xeros (Q). The Third Doctor became trapped in Vorg's outlawed Miniscope (PPP), and was instrumental in destroying the Exxilon's Perfect City, one of the 700 wonders of the Universe (XXX). The Fourth Doctor fought Magnus Greel in Henry Gordon Jago's theatre in Victorian London (4S), and visited the Leisure Hive, the first of the Leisure Planets (5N). He also showed the sights of Paris to Romana (5H) and posed as a tourist to outwit Gatherer Hade (4W). The Seventh Doctor fought the Bannermen at the Welsh holiday camp of Shangri-La (7F), and freed the Psychic Circus from the Gods of Ragnarok's evil influence (7J). Morton Dill (R) and Lavinia Hackensack (7K) were two American tourists. Colin Frazer was a tourist in Amsterdam when he was kidnapped by Omega (6E).

TOWER Abode of Zargo, Camilla and Aukon, on the Great Vampire's world. In reality, it was Hydrax, gutted of its scientific equipment. The Great Vampire himself lay buried beneath it (5P).

TOY SOLDIERS Creatures from the Land of Fiction (UU).

TOYMAKER (aka CELESTIAL TOYMAKER) Attired in the dress of a Chinese Mandarin, he was in reality an eternal being of great mental and physical powers who could not be destroyed. The Toymaker's passion was to lure travellers and force them to play his games – if they lost, they then became his playthings. The Toymaker challenged the First Doctor, Steven and Dodo to a series of such deadly games, which they won. However, the Doctor discovered that to make the last, winning move in the Toymaker's Trilogic Game would condemn them all to oblivion. The Time Lord outwitted the Toymaker by ordering the move with the Toymaker's voice, thereby enabling the TARDIS to escape while finishing the game (Y).

According to some accounts, the Sixth Doctor and Peri fought the Toymaker in Blackpool, during which time they discovered that the Toymaker came from another, entirely different universe.

TRACEY, GEORGE Resident of Moreton Harwood and manager of Aunt Lavinia's market-garden shop. His family dated back to the Publius Trescus Roman family. He was a member of the Cult of Hecate (K9).

TRACEY, PETER George Tracey's son. He was a somewhat reluctant member of the Cult of Hecate (K9).

TRACTATORS Insect-like burrowers, universal outcasts, which formed a collective intelligence, though without the guiding will of their leader they were only mindless animals. They had great natural powers of gravity control and once attacked Trion. The Fifth Doctor discovered they had infected the colony of Frontios; their leader, the Gravis, had secretly drawn human colonists to Frontios because he needed to use their bodies and minds to power his excavating machines. The Doctor used the Gravis's desire for the TARDIS to cut him off from the other Tractators, and thereby render them helpless (6N).

TRACY A member of UNIT who helped the Second Doctor defeat the Cybermen Invasion (VV).

TRAKEN Located in Mettula Orionsis, the Union of Traken was a multiplanetary confederation held in a state of harmony by the Source, which was controlled by the Keeper. After the Keeper's dissolution, the Master (disguised as the Melkur) temporarily became the new Keeper. He planned to use the Source to turn the Union of Traken into an all-conquering force and seize another body for himself. He was exposed and prevented from remaining Keeper by the Fourth Doctor, Adric, Nyssa and Council Tremas (5T). The Union of Traken was later destroyed when the Master tampered with Logopolis (5V).

TRANQUIL REPOSE Notorious galactic mortuary where the bodies of famous and rich people were kept cryogenically frozen. Tranquil Repose was secretly taken over by Davros (posing as the Great Healer) who used frozen heads to grow Daleks loyal to himself, and sold the rest to Kara's protein factory. After the the Sixth Doctor intervened, Tranquil Repose was blown up by Orcini. Its personnel turned to refining local flowers into food (6Z).

TRANSDUCTION BARRIERS Quantum-powered force fields created by Rassilon to protect Gallifrey. The Fourth Doctor pulled them down to allow the Vardans to materialize so he could unmask them. Unfortunately, by so doing he enabled the Sontarans to invade Gallifrey (4Z).

TRANSFERENCE MODULE Another name for the Kartz-Reimer time cabinet (6W).

TRANSMAT See TELEPORTATION.

TRANSMISSION OF MATTER See TOM-TIT.

TRANTIS Member of the Dalek Alliance in their Masterplan against Earth. He was eventually betrayed by Mavic Chen, and killed by the Daleks (T/A, V).

TRANTON, DARCY Hollywood actor (V).

TRASK Captain of the ship *Annabelle*, which he had stolen from MacKay and was using to transport Gray's slaves to the West Indies. He was killed in a sword fight with Jamie (FF).

TRAU Androzani equivalent of Mister (6R).

TRAVEL-MAT See T-MAT.

TRAVELLER FROM BEYOND TIME Nickname given to the Doctor by the Elders (AA).

TRAVELLERS Nickname given to the circle of the Stones of Blood. At various times in history, they were labelled Six, Seven or Nine Travellers, because three of the stones were, in reality, the alien Ogri, servants of Cessair (5C).

TRAVELLERS See PEOPLE.

TRAVERS, ANNE Daughter of Professor Edward Travers, and scientific adviser to the army task force which fought the Great Intelligence in the London underground. She and her father helped the Second Doctor and Jamie defeat the Yeti (QQ). She later accompanied her father to the United States (VV).

TRAVERS, BEN Electrical engineer, and one of the three lighthouse keepers of Fang Rock. He was one of the first victims of the Rutan (4V).

TRAVERS, EDWARD British explorer who travelled to Tibet in the mid-1930s, accompanied by his friend Mackay, to solve the mystery of the Yeti. After Mackay's death, Travers mistrusted the Second Doctor, but eventually joined forces with him to defeat the Great Intelligence and its robot Yeti (NN). Thirty years later, Travers reactivated one of the Yeti's silver control spheres, which led to the Intelligence's attack on London. Made scientific adviser (with his daughter, Anne) to the army task force which fought the Intelligence in the London underground, Travers again joined forces with the Second Doctor and Colonel Lethbridge-Stewart to thwart the evil cosmic entity's plans (QQ). When the Doctor tried to contact him soon afterwards, prior to the Cybermen invasion, he was told by Isobel Watkins that Travers and his daughter had gone to spend a year in the United States (VV).

TRAVERS Commodore of the *Hyperion III* space liner. The Doctor had met him before in an unrecorded adventure. He helped the Sixth Doctor save his ship from the black hole of Tartarus, defeat a hijack attempt by Rudge, and destroy the Vervoids (7C).

TRAVIS One of Dr Lawrence's technicians at the Wenley Moor atomic research station. He was killed by the Silurians when they took over the nuclear reactor (BBB).

TRAVIS Brendan Richards' school friend (K9).

TREE OF LIFE Name given by the Trogs to the Underworld's tunnel system (4Y).

TREFUSIS (MRS) See CESSAIR.

TREMAS One of the five Consuls of Traken, married to Kassia and the father of Nyssa. He helped the Fourth Doctor expose the villainy of the Melkur, who was revealed to be the Master, and prevented him from remaining Keeper of Traken. However, just before he left Traken, the Renegade Time Lord seized Tremas and took control of his body (5T).

TRENCHARD, GEORGE Former British colonel and governor of the prison where the Master was kept. The evil Time Lord tricked him into believing he was helping unmask the enemy agents sinking ships in the British Channel, whereas they were actually trying to contact the Sea Devils. When Trenchard realized he'd been fooled, he tried to shoot the Master, but was killed by the Sea Devils who had taken over his prison (LLL).

TRESCUS, PUBLIUS Roman ancestor of the Traceys of Moreton Harwood (K9).

TREVOR See SCOTT.

TREVOR Pupil at Brendon School (6F).

TRG See TACHYON RECREATION GENERATOR.

TRIAD See SILURIAN TRIAD.

TRICKSTER Jester figure who was part of the Kinda rituals, and who used a doll to mime his fables (5Y).

TRICOPHENYLALDEHYDE Neural inhibitor used by the Master on Gallifrey to simulate the appearance of his death (4P).

TRILANIC ACTIVATOR Device used by the Zygons to direct the Skarasen (4F).

TRILOGIC GAME Game used by the Toymaker to challenge the First Doctor. It consisted of ten triangular pieces which formed a pyramid. The player had to reform the pyramid by transferring all the pieces one at a time and never placing a larger piece upon a smaller one. The Doctor won in 1023 moves, and made the last move with the Toymaker's voice (Y).

TRION Turlough's home planet. It was once attacked by the Tractators (6N). Trion was ruled by an imperial family, of which Turlough and his brother Malkon were members; after the revolution, Turlough was exiled to Earth for ten years. Malkon crashlanded on Sarn, where the new regime sent its political prisoners. Trion kept agents on many civilized worlds. (Their agent on Earth was the solicitor who had Turlough sent to Brendon.) Eventually, the new regime became more lenient. When Turlough summoned help from Trion to evacuate Sarn, he was pardoned. He and Malkon returned to Trion as heroes (6Q).

TRIONIC LOCK Type of lock used on the Doctor's TARDIS (4P, 4Z). A Trionic Lattice was a pendant-shaped key used by Greel to unlock his Time Cabinet (4S).

TRISILICATE Mineral vital to the Federation's war effort against Galaxy Five. It was found in abundance on Peladon (YYY).

TRITIUM Cessair used tritium crystals to power her wand (5C).

TRIZON FOCUSER A component of the Inter Minorans' Eradicator (PPP).

TROGS Descendants of the Minyans. With the Fourth Doctor's help, a number of Trogs were rescued by Jackson and travelled with him to Minyos II. The others presumably perished in an explosion caused by two fission grenades disguised as the Race Banks (4Y).

TROILUS Trojan prince and son of King Priam. He fell in love with Vicki (then known as Cressida). Troilus and Vicki fled with Aeneas after the fall of Troy (U).

TROJAN WAR Legendary conflict between the early Greeks and the city of Troy, which took place in the 12th or 13th century BC. The Trojan War began after Paris, son of King Priam of Troy, ran off with Helen, wife of Menelaus of Sparta. Agamemnon, Menelaus's brother, then led a Greek expedition against Troy. The war lasted ten years, finally ending after crafty Odysseus prompted the First Doctor to come up with the stratagem of the Trojan Horse (U).

TROPHY ROOM The Captain of Zanak set up a room where the shrunken remains of the worlds crushed by Zanak were all kept in perfect gravitational alignment. The Fourth Doctor proclaimed it to be the most brilliant piece of astro-gravitational engineering he had ever seen. The Captain was secretly planning to use its energy to kill Queen Xanxia. It was eventually undone by the Doctor, and its contents were used to fill Zanak's hollow core (5B).

TROY Ancient city of northwestern Anatolia and site of the Trojan War (U).

TRUMPER Pupil at Brendon school (6F).

TRYST Professor of interplanetary zoology whose ambition was to catalogue every species in the galaxy. In order to secure funding for his research, Tryst decided to smuggle the drug vraxoin, which he had discovered could be derived from the essence of the Mandrels, savage monsters from the planet Eden. Tryst used his CET machine to capture the Mandrels and hand them to drug smuggler Dymond. After the *Empress* crashed into the *Hecate*, Tryst tried to frame the Fourth Doctor but was eventually exposed by the Time Lord and Stott. He and Dymond were arrested (5K).

TSS See TOTAL SURVIVAL SUIT.

TUAR Younger brother of Arak on Metebelis 3. He was hot-headed, and thought Sarah Jane was a spy. In spite of the Third Doctor's help he fell back under the Spiders' control, but was freed when the Great One died (ZZZ).

TULLOCH Small village on the Scottish Coast, not far from Loch Ness. UNIT was based there during its investigation into the Zygons' attacks (4F).

TUNGCHI Chinese emperor whose soldiers captured Greel's Time Cabinet, and who later offered it as a present to Professor Litefoot's mother (4S).

TUN-HUANG Way station on the road to Peking (D).

TURLOUGH, VISLOR One of the Fifth Doctor's companions. When the Time Lord met him, Turlough was a schoolboy on Earth at Brendon School. After a minor car accident, he entered into a pact with the Black Guardian to kill the Doctor. During their adventure on Terminus, he made several half-hearted attempts, but failed. Finally, after the encounter with the Eternals, Turlough turned against the Black Guardian and, by throwing the Enlightenment crystal at him, freed himself. Afterwards, he helped the Doctor fight the Master. He then met the Doctor's First, Second and Third Incarnations on the Dead Zone of Gallifrey, and helped them defeat Borusa. Turlough went on to assist the Doctor in his battles against the Silurians and the Sea Devils, the Malus, the Tractators and the Daleks. Finally, Turlough was revealed to be a political prisoner from Trion, sentenced to ten years' exile on Earth. After another battle against the Master on Sarn, Trion's prison planet, Turlough found that his exile had been rescinded. He returned to his home world with his newly found brother, Malkon. As a Trion political prisoner, Turlough had been tattooed with the Misos Triangle (6F–6Q)

TURNER Brendon school pupil (6F).

TURNER, JIMMY UNIT Captain who assisted Brigadier Lethbridge-Stewart during the Cybermen Invasion. He fell in love with Isobel Watkins (VV).

TUROC One of Varga's Ice Warrior crew, brought back to life in AD 3000. He was killed in an ice avalanche while chasing Victoria (OO).

TUSA Leader of the Thoros-Alphans' rebellion on Thoros-Beta, who decided to team up with King Yrcanos. Together, with the Time Lords' secret help, they killed Kiv, Sil and Crozier. Afterwards, Tusa probably led his now-freed people back to their world (7B).

TUTHMOS Egyptian builder of pyramids working for Khepren. He was killed by the Daleks (V).

TWELVE GALAXIES Sector of Space where Svartos was located (7G).

TWIN SUNS Name of a Foamasi clan (5N).

TWO-LEGS Name given by the Spiders of Metebelis 3 to the humans (ZZZ).

TYHEER Karfelon rebel, banished through the Timelash (6Y).

TYLER, CARL Strong-willed man who led Dortmun's resistance fighters. He fought alongside the First Doctor during the AD 2164 Dalek Invasion of Earth (K).

TYLER (DR) Cosmic ray researcher at Wessex University. He helped the Three Doctors fight Omega (RRR).

TYLER, JACK Martha Tyler's son; he helped the Fourth Doctor and Leela fight the Fendahleen (4X).

TYLER, MARTHA Old woman, the white witch of the village of Fetchborough who knew all the ancient rituals. She and her son Jack helped the Fourth Doctor and Leela fight the Fendahleen. She provided the rock salt which was used to kill a Fendahleen (4X).

TYLOS, MILREN Young Alzarian Outler killed by the Marshmen while helping save Rysik (5R).

TYPE 40 Name of the model of the Doctor's TARDIS. 305 were originally registered by the Time Lords. As more advanced models were built, all Type 40s were eventually deregistered, except for the Doctor's (4P).

TYPHONIAN BEAST See SUTEKH.

TYRANNOSAURUS REX The Rani kept a tyrannosaurus embryo in her TARDIS (6X).

TYRER, A.S.T. One of Stagra's Think Tank colleagues (5M).

TYRUM Chief Councillor of the Vogans. He was terrified that the remains of his planet would be found by the Cybermen, and strongly disapproved of Vorus's plan. He shot Vorus when the Guardian fired his rocket (4D).

TYSSAN Starship engineer serving with Earth's deep space fleet. He was captured by the Daleks, and taken to Skaro to become part of the slave labour force looking for Davros. Tyssan helped the Fourth Doctor defeat both the Daleks and the Movellans. He later took a captive Davros back to Earth (5J).

TYTHONIANS Inhabitants of Tythonus, very advanced aliens who looked like giant greenish blobs. The Tythonians were composed almost entirely of brain tissue, and communicated through their skins, or through a shield-shaped device which enabled them to use another person's larynx. Some Tythonians, like Erato, had the ability to secrete a metallic substance, and could weave their own egg-shaped spaceships (5G).

TYTHONUS Planet rich in metals but poor in chlorophyll, a substance vital to the Tythonianans' reproduction. Tythonus sent Ambassador Erato to Chloris, where he was imprisoned by Lady Adastra, but later freed by the Fourth Doctor (5G).

U

U4 Drug Harris wanted to use on the Second Doctor and his companion to relieve the effect of tranquillizer darts (RR).

UK HABITAT A subterranean civilization built in the London Underground to protect a group of humans from the fireball (in reality, the Time Lords were moving the Earth during the Ravolox Stratagem). The UK Habitat was taken over by Drathro to protect the secrets of the Andromedan Sleepers and sealed from contact with the outside. Water was rationed, and the population kept constant through the Cullings. However, Merdeen secretly enabled some intended victims to escape to the surface. The Sixth Doctor saved the UK Habitat from being destroyed by a black light explosion, accidentally triggered when Dibber blew up Drathro's Maglem converter. With Drathro's destruction, the UK Habitat's population was free to return to live on the surface (7A).

UK HABITATS OF THE CANADIAN GOOSE See BOOKS OF KNOWLEDGE

ULF One of the Viking raiders defeated by Wulnoth's Saxons (S).

ULTIMA MACHINE Early computer designed in the 1940s by Dr Judson to break German naval cyphers. Its precious 'core' was booby-trapped by Commander Millington in a mad scheme to strike at the Russians. In spite of the Seventh Doctor's efforts, the Ultima Machine was eventually used to release the evil Fenric (7M).

ULTRASOUND The Second Doctor discovered that Victoria's screams were deadly to the parasitic Weed (RR). The Sonic Lance and Sonic Screwdriver also relied on ultrasound. The Vanir controlled the Garm with an ultrasonic box (6G). The Young Chimeron Princess defeated the Bannerman with her ultrasonic powers, amplified by Shangri-La's public-address system (7F).

ULTRAVIOLET LIGHT The Fifth Doctor used UV light to kill the Myrka (6L).

ULYSSES See ODYSSEUS.

UNBELIEVERS Citizens of Sarn who did not believe in the god Logar. They were usually sacrificed to the volcano (6Q).

UNDERCITY Location of the hideout of Mandrel's rebels, under Megropolis One on Pluto (4W).

UNDERSEA The Second Doctor met Atlantean survivors who had built an undersea civilization (GG). He also defeated a parasitic Weed which absorbed human brains and attacked a North Sea natural gas refinery and off-shore rigs (RR). The bottom of the sea was also home to the Sea Devils (LLL), who were used by the Master against the Third Doctor. They were defeated again by the Fifth Doctor when they attacked a human underwater base, Sea Base Four, in AD 2084 (6L). The Fourth Doctor discovered that the Zygons used their Skarasen to attack off-shore platforms in the North Sea (4F). The Rutans were blob-like creatures who could live under water (4V). The Haemovores found the plasma-like substances they needed in fresh sea water off Maiden's Point (7M).

UNDERWORLD Nickname for the underground world of Matter that had accumulated over a hundred thousand years around the *P7E*. It was ruled by the Oracle, assisted by two Seers. The population was comprised of the Guards and the Trogs, all created from the Minyan Race Banks. The Underworld was eventually invaded by Jackson's crew who, with the help of the Fourth Doctor and Leela, managed to wrest the Race Banks away from the Oracle. The Underworld was destroyed in an explosion caused by two fission grenades disguised as the Race Banks, which the Oracle had intended to use to destroy Jackson's ship (4Y).

UNICORN Mythical animal encountered by the Second Doctor, Jamie and Zoe in the Land of Fiction (UU).

UNION OF TRAKEN See TRAKEN.

UNITED NATIONS INTELLIGENCE TASKFORCE (UNIT) Multinational military force whose mission was to deal with alien or extraordinary Earth-based threats with the potential to endanger the whole planet. UNIT was headquartered in Geneva and placed under the sole command of the United Nations. In practice, however, it was subject to the supervision of various national ministers and local authorities.

The concept of a special force to deal with alien threats probably first arose in Britain after the secret Dalek attack of 1963 (7H), and was undoubtedly reinforced by WOTAN's failed attempt to take over London with its War Machines in 1966 (BB).

The Yeti invasion of 1969, thwarted by the Second Doctor and British Colonel Lethbridge-Stewart, was most likely the catalyst which resulted in the creation of UNIT. Now promoted to the rank of Brigadier, Lethbridge-Stewart was put in charge of UNIT's British branch. He was ably assisted by the competent Sergeant Benton and Captain Mike Yates.

UNIT was extremely active during the early 1970s. Brigadier Lethbridge-Stewart and his men fought the Cybermen alongside the Second Doctor when they threatened to invade Earth (VV). Soon afterwards, the Doctor was exiled to Earth by the Time Lords. Then in his third incarnation, he became UNIT's scientific adviser. With the help of his assistants, Liz Shaw, Jo Grant and, later, Sarah Jane Smith, the Third Doctor helped UNIT defeat the Autons (AAA,EEE), the Silurians (BBB), the so-called 'Ambassadors of Death' (CCC), Professor Stahlman's 'Inferno' project (DDD), the Master (EEE, FFF, GGG, JJJ, LLL, OOO), Axos (GGG), Azal (JJJ), the Daleks (KKK), the Sea Devils (LLL), Kronos (OOO), Omega (RRR), BOSS (TTT), Linx (UUU), Sir Charles Grover's Operation Golden Age (WWW) and the Spiders of Metebelis 3 (ZZZ).

The Fourth Doctor, still assisted by Sarah Jane Smith and joined by UNIT medical officer Surgeon-Lieutenant Harry Sullivan, then helped the Brigadier against Professor Kettlewell's Giant Robot and the Scientific Reform Society (4A), and the Zygons (4F).

At about that time, UNIT's British HQ was moved to a priory which had been Egyptologist Marcus Scarman's residence in 1911 (4G). Soon afterwards, the Fourth Doctor, Sarah Jane Smith and Harry Sullivan returned to help UNIT Colonel Faraday defeat the Kraals' android invasion (4J). The Fourth Doctor and Sarah also helped Sir Colin Thackeray of the World Ecology Bureau and Major Beresford of UNIT destroy a Krynoid (4L).

In 1977, Lethbridge-Stewart retired from UNIT, leaving the British branch of UNIT in the capable hands of Colonel Crichton (6K). Benton also left (6F). Later that year, Tegan and Nyssa, two of the Fifth Doctor's companions, met the retired Brigadier at Brendon School and together travelled forward to 1983 to fight Mawdryn. The Brigadier emerged from the encounter with his future self with selective amnesia (6F).

In 1983, the Fifth Doctor used his UNIT clearance to solve the mystery of the disappearance of a Concorde airplane at Gatwick Airport (6C). Later, the Fifth Doctor met the retired Brigadier (who had forgotten their previous encounter) to defeat Mawdryn (6F). The Brigadier recovered his memory and renewed his contacts with UNIT. But Borusa snatched him and the Second Doctor (who had transgressed the Laws of Time to visit his old friend) one day before a planned UNIT reunion. Together with various companions (including Sarah Jane Smith and illusions in the form of Liz Shaw and Mike Yates), the Brigadier helped the Five Doctors defeat Borusa (6K). Soon after that, he married his old flame, Doris.

In 1992, the Seventh Doctor and Ace teamed up with Lethbridge-Stewart and met Brigadier Bambera of UNIT. Together, they fought the sorcery of Morgaine, Queen of an alternative Earth (7N).

UNITED STATES OF AMERICA During his first incarnation, the Doctor visited New York (R) and Hollywood (V), both very briefly, and, for a longer time, Tombstone, Arizona (Z). A Confederate Army was kidnapped by the War Lords (ZZ). Peri Brown was an American. The First Doctor met American General Cutler at the South Pole Space Tracking Station (DD). The Third Doctor met American security agent Bill Filer (GGG). The Seventh Doctor helped American security agents Hawk and Weismuller recover a lost satellite (7F). Lady Peinforte was given a ride by American tourist Lavinia P. Hackensack near Windsor (7K). The First Doctor met another American tourist, Morton Dill, at the top of the Empire State Building (R). He later met Hollywood producer Steinberger P. Green (V).

UNSTOFFE Garron's assistant. He stole the Graff Vynda-K's million opeks and the lump of jethrik. Thanks to Binro, he found refuge in the catacombs. He was wounded by the Graff's men, but left Ribos safely with Garron and the Graff's treasure (5A).

UPTON UNIT private. He died fighting the Silurians (BBB).

URAK Leader of the Tetraps serving the Rani on Lakertya. He was impressed by her genius and, after her defeat at the hands of the Seventh Doctor, he kidnapped her to take her back to Tetrapyriarbus to help his people (7D).

URANUS Taranium was found one one of the moons of Uranus (V).

URBANKA Planet located in the system of Inokshi in galaxy RE 1489. Its leader, Monarch, had exhausted all of its minerals, then polluted it with his technology until its ozone layer was utterly destroyed; it was all for his mad desire to travel faster than light and back through time to witness the creation of the Universe. (Monarch believed himself to be God.) (5W).

URBANKANS Reptilian aliens who resembled frogs and whose glands secreted one of the deadliest toxins in the universe. After their leader, Monarch, had virtually destroyed their home world, the memories of all three billion Urbankans were stored on memory chips. Monarch planned to poison the population of Earth and replace it with the Urbankans, reincarnated in android form (unlike their original 'flesh time'). The Urbankans had visited Earth before. When the Fifth Doctor met Monarch in AD 1981, he claimed that it had taken him 2500 years to travel to Earth and back, and that he had doubled the speed of his ship from each previous visit. The approximate dates of the Urbankans' visits to Earth would then have been 34481 BC, 14481 BC, 4481 BC, 519 BC, and AD 1981. However, historical information about the native Earthmen taken by the aliens contradicted the above dates. It was therefore likely that the real time it took for the Urbankans to reach Earth was only about 1250 years, and that their visits occurred in 3019 BC, 1769 BC, 519 BC, AD 731 and 1981 (5W).

URQUHART Captain of the Concorde flight which was taken to the Jurassic period by the Master (6C).

USA See UNITED STATES OF AMERICA.

USURIANS Alien race who looked like greenish seaweed with eyes, although they were able to assume and retain human form thanks to stratified particle radiation. They were greedy exploiters of other races. In the 52nd century, they used the Company to move mankind from a highly polluted Earth to Mars, in exchange for their labour. Several centuries later, the Usurians moved men to Pluto, around which they had built six small artificial suns. There, men lived a heavily taxed life until they were freed through the intervention of the Fourth Doctor and Leela. The Doctor exposed the Usurian Collector and created a deadly inflationary spiral to defeat him (4W).

USURIUS The Usurians' home world (4W).

UTOBI Amazon Indian tribe. Latoni had once been their chief (6A).

UTOPIAS Peace-loving races who had built, or tried to build, utopias included the Thals (B, SSS), the Sensorites (G), the Didoi (L), the Rills (T), the Dulcians (TT), the Gonds (WW), the people of Traken (5T), the Logopolitans (5V), the Kinda (5Y) and the Lakertyans (7D).

Utopias that failed included the world of Marinus (E), the French Revolution (H), the world of the Elders and the Savages (AA), Sir Charles Grover's Operation Golden Age (WWW) and Helen A's Terra Alpha (7L).

Apparent utopias which contained the proverbial snake in paradise included the human colony secretly controlled by the Macra (JJ), the pirate planet of Zanak (5B), the Union of Traken which was secretly destroyed from within by the Melkur (5T), Castrovalva, which was nothing more than a block transfer computation created by Adric (5Z) and Deva Loka, the planet of the Kinda, where the Mara lurked (5Y). Also see its opposite, DYSTOPIAS.

UVANOV Commander of the *Sandminer*. Because of the Fourth Doctor's intervention, he and his aide Toos were the only survivors of the attack of the robots of Death. He saved the Fourth Doctor's life by destroying SV7 (4R).

V

V4 One of the Robots of Death, disabled by Uvanov as it attacked the Fourth Doctor (4R).

V5 A Robot of Death which attacked Leela (4R).

V6 A Robot of Death which attacked Toos (4R).

V8 One of the Robots of Death. It locked up the Fourth Doctor and Leela (4R).

V16 One of the Robots of Death. It was at the controls of the *Sandminer* (4R).

V-41 Massive T-shaped spaceship used by General Hermack of the International Space Corps in his campaign against Caven's pirates. It was equipped with Minnow fighters (YY).

V, HAROLD Killjoy who was once Helen A's gag writer on Terra Alpha (he was then known as Harold F). He was arrested by the Happiness Patrol after he went looking for his brother, Andrew X. He was electrocuted by a rigged jackpot machine (7L).

VAAN Incarnation of the evil side of the Xeraphin (6C).

VABER One of the Thals sent to Spiridon to stop the Daleks. He fought alongside the Third Doctor, but was eventually killed by the Daleks (SSS).

VAISSEAU QUI COULE See SINKING SHIP.

VALEYARD, THE Title meaning 'Learned Court Prosecutor'. The Valeyard was the amalgam of the Doctor's darker side, between his twelfth and thirteenth regenerations. Afraid that the Sixth Doctor would learn the truth about the Ravolox stratagem, the corrupt High Council of the Time Lords brought the Valeyard into being. They offered him the Doctor's remaining regenerations if he would destroy his earlier Incarnation. The Valeyard prosecuted the Doctor at his trial, introducing false evidence from the Matrix concerning his adventures on Ravolox and Thoros-Beta, including an untrue account of Peri's death. He later accused the Doctor of genocide for having destroyed the Vervoids. Thanks to the Master's assistance, the Doctor eventually exposed the Valeyard, who then fled into the Matrix. The Doctor followed him there to the Fantasy Factory. Hiding behind the identity of Mr Popplewick, the Valeyard plotted to use a Particle Disseminator to murder the Time Lords attending the Trial. He also trapped the Master and Glitz by replacing the stolen secrets of the Matrix they were seeking with a Limbo Atrophier. The Doctor eventually thwarted the Valeyard's plans, but the evil Time Lord escaped again, taking over the body of the Keeper of the Matrix (7A–7C).

VALGARD One of the Vanir. Ambitious, he wanted to take over Eirak's leadership, and entered the Forbidden Zone after Bor and the Fifth Doctor. He and the other Vanir eventually remained on Terminus to help Nyssa run it as a regular hospital (6G).

VALIDIUM Deadly living metal allegedly stolen by the Doctor before he left Gallifrey. Validium was to be the Time Lords's ultimate defence. After it was used in a series of unknown circumstances, which again involved the Doctor, validium landed on Earth in Windsor in 1638. There, it was shaped by Lady Peinforte into a statue dubbed Silver Nemesis. The Seventh Doctor eventually used the Silver Nemesis to destroy the Cybermen's space fleet, then ordered it to reshape itself. Also see NEMESIS, SILVER (7K).

VALLANCE, ARMAND A member of the staff of the Wheel in Space. He was taken over by the Cybermen and was later freed by the Second Doctor (SS).

VALMAR One of Bragen's rebels on Vulcan. After the Daleks murdered Janley, the girl he loved, he began to realize that Bragen was really a megalomaniacal madman, and eventually killed him (EE).

VAMPIRES Gigantic space aliens which may have been related to the Daemons. Feeding on blood, they were nearly immortal. They swarmed throughout the universe and became so powerful that one Vampire could suck the life from an entire planet. Finally, they were hunted down by the Time Lords and destroyed with bow ships in a war so long and bloody that, afterwards, the Gallifreyans foreswore violence. However, the Vampires' leader, the Great Vampire, escaped into E-Space. Although he was near death, he still had the mental strength to attract the Earth ship *Hydrax*. He offered its three officers, Aukon, Zargo and Camilla, vampiric immortality if they served him. They fed him with the blood of the human colonists and their descendants for a thousand years, planning for the Time of Arising when they would swarm back into normal space. The Great Vampire's plans were thwarted by the Fourth Doctor, who used one of the *Hydrax* scout ships like a stake to kill him (5P).

On Earth, vampire-like creatures arose in the future, when Earth had become totally polluted. They were called the Haemovores. A number of them were transported back through time by Fenric, and gave rise to the legends about vampires. Fenric used an Ancient Haemovore in his fight against the Seventh Doctor in 1943 Northumbria (7M).

The First Doctor once met a robotic version of the legendary vampire Dracula in a House of Horrors (R). Other alien life forms which fed on blood included: the Screamers (V); the Ogri (5C); the Somno-moths (5K); and the Tetraps (7D). Psychic or life-energy vampires included: the Elders (AA); the Krotons (WW); the Mind Parasite (FFF) and Magnus Greel (4S). Energy vampires included: Axos (GGG) and the Nimon (5L). Also see PARASITES.

VAN ALLEN BELT Doughnut-shaped radiation belt surrounding Earth and protecting it from the Sun's more harmful rays. The Young Silurian and Icthar attempted to destroy it with a molecular disperser in order to render Earth uninhabitable by Mankind. They were stopped by the Third Doctor (BBB).

VAN DER POST A top executive of the Euro-Sea Gas Corporation. He was based in The Hague and was a friend of Van Lutyens (RR).

VAN GYSEGHAM (MRS) American tourist who befriended Peri's mother (6Q).

VAN LUTYENS, PIETER Dutch engineer. He was dispatched by the Euro-Sea Gas Corporation to check up on the North Sea refinery which was attacked by the Weed. He tried to convince its controller, Robson, to shut off the gas supply, and was eventually taken over by the Weed. He was freed with the help of the Second Doctor (RR).

VAN LYDEN, CHARLES British astronaut on board the Mars Recovery 7 spaceship. He was captured by mysterious, radioactive aliens. He was eventually returned to Earth due to the Third Doctor's assistance (CCC).

VANA Thara's girlfriend, a young Gond girl who had been selected to become a 'companion' of the Krotons and who was saved just in time by the Second Doctor's intervention. After she had recovered from her ordeal, she helped the Time Lord to destroy the Krotons (WW).

VANCE Crewman on Captain Briggs's space freighter. He was killed by the Cybermen (6B).

VANDAL OF THE ROADS See NORD.

VANESSA Tegan Jovanka's aunt. She was killed near Heathrow Airport by the Master (5V).

VANIR Personnel in charge of Terminus (6G).

VANTARIALIS Captain of Zanak's great raiding cruiser, which crashed on Zanak (5B).

VAPOURIZATION Method of capital punishment used by the Time Lords. The Fourth (4P) and Fifth (6E) Doctors were condemned to be vapourized, but were eventually spared.

VARAN Elderly Solonian leader who betrayed his own people to the Marshal. His son killed the Earth Administrator, but he later threatened to tell the truth and was shot by Marshal. When Varan saw his dead son, he rebelled and was eventually killed by the Marshal (NNN).

VARDANS Aliens with the ability to travel mentally along any wavelength. The only obstacle to their power was lead. When their planet was touched by one of the Time Lords' scan beams, they used it to invade the Matrix. Being telepathic, they contacted the Fourth Doctor to help them in their plans to take over Gallifrey. The Doctor pretended to help them in order to gain their confidence and force them to materialize fully (at which point it was revealed that their true form was fully humanoid). The Doctor then placed their planet in a time

429

loop. But the Vardans had a actually been used as dupes by the Sontarans, who themselves invaded Gallifrey (4Z).

VARDON Planet at war with Kosnax. Their crossfire accidentally destroyed Xeriphas (6C). One of the Trion agents was an agrarian commissioner on Vardon (6Q).

VARGA Leader of a squadron of Martian warriors (the so-called Ice Warriors). His ship had crashlanded on Earth during its First Ice Age, and he and his crew were accidentally entombed in ice. Varga was found by Arden, and brought back to life in AD 3000. He tried to conquer the Earth, but failed. He then attempted to return to Mars, but the Second Doctor used the ionizer to destroy his ship (OO).

VARGA Vegetable life form indigenous to Skaro. The Varga Plants had poisoned spines which induced dementia in their victims, whose bodies eventually turned into Vargas. The Daleks had transplanted some Varga plants on Kembel (T/A).

VARGOS Argolin guide at the Leisure Hive (5N).

VARGOS President on his way to Nekros for his wife's perpetual enstatement (6Z).

VARL Sontaran field major. He was the aide of Group Marshal Stike. Chessene killed him with coronic acid (6W).

VARLIK Young Swampie war chief on Delta magna's third moon. He did not believe Kroll was a god, and helped the Fourth Doctor and Romana save his people. He killed Thawn and saved the Doctor's life (5E).

VARN Chancellery guard appointed by Kelner to keep an eye on the Fourth Doctor during the Vardan invasion of Gallifrey (4Z).

VARNE Cryon who welcomed Peri. She was later killed by the Cybermen (6T).

VAROS Mining planet inhabited by the descendants of a colony for the criminally insane. It had set up a civilization which thrived on public torture, and provided 'snuff' entertainment to the rest of the galaxy. It was also a major producer of the rare mineral Zyton-7. With the Sixth Doctor's help, Varos's Governor was able to defeat Sil's plans to corner the Zyton-7 market (6V).

VARSH Leader of the Outlers on Alzarius and Adric's older brother. He was killed by the Marshmen while defending the Starliner (5R).

VASILIP Gilbert M's planet of origin (7L).

VASOR Trapper living in Marinus's icy wastes. He tried to kill Ian and Barbara during their quest for the missing Keys (E).

VASTIAL Highly explosive mineral that was safe only at sub-zero temperatures. The Sixth Doctor gave the Cryon Flast a thermal lance which she buried in a box of vastial, thereby creating a huge explosion which destroyed the Cybermen (6T).

VAUGHN, TOBIAS Managing director of International Electromatics. He allied himself with the Cybermen. He planned to use them to take over the world, then discard them by using Professor Watkins's Cerebration Mentor. His body had already been partially converted to cybernetics. When he realized the Cybermen were prepared to destroy all human life, he turned against them and sacrificed his life to help the Second Doctor and UNIT destroy the Cybermen's hypnotic beam pulser (VV).

VEET One of Mandrel's rebels. She helped the Fourth Doctor and Leela overthrow the Company on Pluto (4W).

VEGA NEXOS A mole man from the Vega star system. He was one of the two Federation trisilicate mining engineers on Peladon. (The other was Eckersley.) He appeared to be struck down by Aggedor's ghost, but was in reality killed by Eckersley's Aggedor projector/heat ray device (YYY).

VEGETALS Intelligent vegetable life forms included: an Earth-based parasitic sea Weed, which could take control of humans (RR); the alien Krynoids, who fed on organic life forms (4L); the cactus-like Zolfa-Thurans, like Meglos, who could assume other creatures' shapes (5Q); and the Vervoids, creations of Professor Lasky (7C). Beaus might have been a vegetable life form (V).

Dangerous but nonintelligent plants included the accelerated plants of Marinus (E); the hostile fungoids of Mechanus (R); the Varga plants of Skaro (T/A); the Martian 'Seeds of Death', which consumed oxygen (XX); the hostile vegetation of Spiridon (SSS); the carnivorous Wolf Weeds of Chloris (5G); the aggressive vegetation of Tigella (5Q); and the deadly vines of Varos (6V).

The Sixth Doctor showed the personnel of Tranquil Repose

how to refine local flowers into protein (6Z). The Rani created explosive devices which turned people into trees (6X). The galaxy's largest flora collection was on Zaakros (5N). The Fourth Doctor claimed to be Honorary President of the Intergalactic Flora Society (4L). Also see SEEDS.

VELDAN Member of a Sirian space colony. He was captured by the Daleks and taken to Skaro to become part of the slave labour force looking for Davros (5J).

VENA Karfelon girl bethrothed to Mykros. When he was arrested, Vena seized the Borad's amulet, which Tekker wore, and plunged into the Timelash. It transported her to 19th-century Scotland, where she met H. G. Wells. The Sixth Doctor took her (and Wells) back to Karfel, where she helped him defeat the Borad (6Y).

VENDERMAN'S LAW Law of physics which stated: 'Light has mass and energy intermixed; therefore energy radiated by photons and tachyons is equal to the energy absorbed' (R).

VENESSIA Planet visited by the First Doctor (X).

VENEZUELA George Cranleigh was disfigured while exploring the Orinoco portion of the Amazon in Venezuela (6A).

VENUS Mavic Chen had prepared a secret army on Venus to fight the Daleks (V). The Third Doctor claimed to be a master at Venusian Aiki-Do – one of the rare two-armed beings to have mastered that difficult art.

VENUSSA Subject Guardian enslaved by the Ark's Monoids. After the First Doctor helped defeat the Monoids, she and Dassuk led the Humans into an honourable peace with the remaining Monoids, so that they could all live in harmony on Refusis (X).

VERDUNA Krontep heaven where warriors were thought to fight forever (7B).

VERNE Ship attacked by the Sea Devils (LLL).

VERNEY, ANDREW Tegan's grandfather. He lived in Little Hodcombe and discovered the Malus in the local church. He was then kept prisoner by Sir George Hutchinson. After he was rescued, he helped the Fifth Doctor defeat the Malus (6M).

VEROS Member of the rebellion against the Great Vampire (5P).

VERSHININ Member of the Soviet commando led by Captain Sorin. He infiltrated Northumberland in order to steal the Ultima Machine 'core'. Vershinin later killed Commander Millington after joining forces with Captain Bates (7M).

VERUNA Planetary system where Frontios was located (6N).

VERVOIDS Intelligent, mutant vegetal life forms created by Professor Lasky, Bruchner and Doland on Mogar. They were mobile, could talk, were equipped with venomous stings and emitted poisonous marsh gas. The Vervoids were dormant when they were loaded on to the *Hyperion III* space liner, but were awakened by an electrical light burst. They tried taking over the ship, but were destroyed by the Sixth Doctor, who used vionesium light bursts to cause them to wither and die. He was charged with genocide by the Valeyard for this action (7C).

VESSILIUM One of the minerals mined by Zanak (5B).

VETURIA Planet visited by Captain Cook (7J).

VICKI One of the First Doctor's companions, an eighteen-year-old Earth girl (last name unknown) from the 25th century, who found herself stranded on Dido after a space crash. She was rescued by the First Doctor, Ian Chesterton and Barbara Wright, who helped her expose the evil designs of her companion, Bennett. Vicki then accompanied the First Doctor, Ian and Barbara in their journeys. She met the Romans, the Menoptera, the Crusaders, the Xerons and the Rills (whose robots she nicknamed 'Chumblies'). She fought the Zarbi, the Saracens, the Moroks, the Daleks, the Meddling Monk and the Drahvins. During the Trojan War, Vicki eventually fell in love with Troilus and, adopting the name of Cressida, followed him to found a new city after the fall of Troy (L–U).

VICTOR British army major who helped the Third Doctor against the Mind of Evil (FFF).

VICTORIA See WATERFIELD, VICTORIA.

VICTORIA Queen of England who lived from 1819 to 1901. Josiah Samuel Smith plotted to use explorer Fenn-Cooper to kill her, hoping thereby to restore the British Empire to its former glory (7Q).

VIJ Planet incorporated into Tryst's CET (5K).

VIKINGS The Meddling Monk planned to sabotage a Viking raid just before 1066 in order to ensure King Harold's victory (S). During the 9th century, a group of Vikings – later dubbed the 'Wolves of Fenric' – were manipulated by the evil entity to bring the flask containing it back from the Orient to Northumberland. Their descendants settled the area (7M).

VILLAGE Only name given to the sole human community on the Great Vampire's world (5P).

VILLAGRA Mayan princess kidnapped by the Urbankans, probably circa AD 731. Her memories were stored on silicon chips, and used to animate an android in her image. After the Fifth Doctor defeated Monarch, she and his fellow androids decided to look for another planet on which to settle (5W).

VILLAR, ARTURO 19th-century Mexican revolutionary who was immune to the War Lords' hypnotic processing. He took charge of a pocket of resistance, and fought alongside the Second Doctor, Jamie and Zoe to put an end to the War Games (ZZ).

VINCE See HAWKINS, VINCE.

VINER, JOHN Professor Parry's second-in-command on the expedition to Telos. He was shot by Klieg when he tried to prevent the reawakening of the Cybermen from their Telosian Tombs (MM).

VINGTEN Yrcanos was Lord of the Vingten (7B).

VINNY Mr Burton's assistant at Shangri-La. He and Burton had once served together in the army (7F).

VINTARIC CRYSTALS Common form of lighting used by the Terileptils (5X).

VIONESIUM Magnesium-like metal found on Mogar. Exposed to air, it released intense light. The Sixth Doctor used it to destroy the Vervoids (7C).

VIRA First Medtech aboard the Ark in Space. She took command when it became clear Noah was under the Wirrn's control, and helped the Fourth Doctor fight the Wirrn (4C).

VIRUS (OF THE PURPOSE) Space entity capable of making contact with other forms of intelligence and taking control of them. It enslaved the crew of the Titan shuttle, and converted the Titan base into a Hive. The Virus's Nucleus invaded the Fourth Doctor's body, but was later released, and enlarged to human size, on the Bi-Al Foundation. It returned to Titan and prepared to swarm, but was destroyed when the Doctor blew up the base (4T).

VIRUSES The Fourth Doctor fought the Virus of the Purpose on Titan (4T). The Fourth Doctor also used an anti-metal virus to destroy Professor Kettlewell's Giant Robot (4A). Also see DISEASES.

VISHINSKY Older senior officer of the Morestran spaceship sent to Zeta Minor. When the mutated Professor Sorenson and the antimatter creatures began to attack his ship, he took over command from Salamar, and helped the Fourth Doctor collect the antimatter and return it to its native universe (4H).

VISIANS Giant, hostile, invisible inhabitants of Mira. The First Doctor and his Companions were forced to hide from them in their fight against the Daleks' Masterplan. The Visians eventually fought the Daleks, which enabled the Doctor to escape (V).

VITA 15 Lytton's homeworld (6P, 6T).

VOCS Middle class of robots who were used as labour force aboard the *Sandminer*. They could speak (4R).

VOGA Nicknamed the Planet of Gold because its heart was almost pure gold. In the 23rd century, during the First Cyber Wars, Earth and its allies defeated the Cybermen by discovering that gold was fatal to their enemies. Before their defeat, the Cybermen made an attempt to destroy Voga, but a fragment survived and ended up in orbit near Jupiter, where it became known as Neo Phoebus. The Nerva Beacon was placed on a thirty-year assignment to warn spaceships of its presence.

Towards the end of the 25th century, one of the Beacon's officers, Professor Kellman, secretly working for the Vogan Vorus, summoned a small band of isolated Cybermen, remnants of the First Cyber Wars. Vorus's plan was to destroy the Cybermen by using the Skystriker, a rocket of his own design. The Cybermen used their cybermats and neurotropic X virus to take over the

Beacon. They eventually loaded cyberbombs aboard the Beacon and tried to crash it into Voga. They were thwarted by the Fourth Doctor, Sarah Jane Smith and Harry Sullivan (4D).

VOGANS Aliens who lived on Voga. After their planet was partially destroyed by the Cybermen after the First Cyber Wars, the survivors, led by Tyrum, lived in fear of being discovered by the Cybermen. After Vorus's Skystriker missile destroyed the Cybermen, thanks to the Fourth Doctor's help, the Vogans were presumably free to reintegrate themselves in the galactic Alliance (4D) (6T).

VOGEL Kara's secretary. He was killed by Davros's Daleks (6Z).

VOICE (GIFT OF) In Kinda terminology, a man who communicated verbally rather than mentally. Aris had been given the Gift of Voice by the Mara and, according to Kinda prophecies, had to be obeyed (5Y).

VOLANTE Tryst's ship. Its zoological expedition to Eden was comprised of Tryst, his assistant, Della, and Stott (5K).

VOLCANOES Salamander triggered volcanic eruptions to take over the Earth (PP). A volcanic eruption threatened the TARDIS on Dulkis (TT). The Third Doctor used an ice volcano on Spiridon to freeze a Dalek army (SSS). On Sarn, the volcanic Numismaton Flame could extend life (6Q). Volcanic eruptions on the planet of the Cheetah People reflected the savagery of its inhabitants (7P). Tigus was a mostly volcanic planet (V).

VOLDAK Scientist who theorized that life in the universe was infinitely variable (PPP).

VOLTROX Nekros life form (62).

VON VERNER (DR) Alias used by the Second Doctor in Inverness in 1746 (FF).

VON WEICH One of the War Lords in charge of the War Games. He posed as a German major in the World War I sector and a Confederate officer in the American Civil War sector. He was eventually captured by the Resistance, and later killed by Private Moor (ZZ).

VOOLIUM One of the minerals extracted from Calufrax by

Zanak. It was used by Mr Fibuli to power the Psychic Interference Transmitter used by the Captain to stop the Mentiads (5B).

VOORD Inhabitants of Marinus, with dark, rubbery skins and an enigmatic, snoutish face, they were immune to the Conscience's mind-control powers. Under the leadership of Yartek, a Voord commando tried to take over the Conscience but perished when the First Doctor and Ian Chesterton tricked them into destroying the machine (E).

VORG Galactic showman from Lurma who owned the defective Scope where the Third Doctor rematerialized. He helped him thwart Kalik's devious schemes, and used the Eradicator to destroy the rampaging Drashigs (PPP).

VORSHAK Commander of Sea Base Four. He helped the Fifth Doctor fight the Silurians and the Sea Devils. He sacrificed his life to save that of the Fifth Doctor when he was aborting the missile launch. Vorshak was shot by Icthar (6L).

VORTEX (SPACE-TIME) Area beyond time and space through which the TARDIS travels. Some entities, like the Guardians of Time, the Kronavores (OOO) and the Mandragora Helix (4M), might be said to inhabit the Vortex. The Tharils appeared to be able to travel through the Vortex unaided (5S).

VORTIGERN'S LAKE The Lake of the High King in Old English. It was located near Carbury. It was at its bottom that King Arthur's body and Excalibur were buried, inside a living spaceship (7N).

VORTIS Cold, craggy planet of the Isop Galaxy, home of the Menoptera and the Zarbi (N).

VORUM GAS Sleeping gas used to protect Space Station J7's Computer (6W).

VORUS Leader of the Vogan Guardians. He hired Professor Kellman of Space Beacon Nerva to summon the Cybermen to Voga, where they could be destroyed by his Skystriker missile. He wanted to free his people from the threat of the Cybermen, but ended up clashing with Tyrum. He was shot by Tyrum when he launched his rocket but, thanks to the Fourth Doctor, it destroyed the Cybermen (4D).

VOSPER, LENNY Prisoner at Stangmoor Prison who helped Mailer take over the Prison. He and Charlie let the Third Doctor escape. He was later killed by the Mind Parasite (FFF).

VRAXOIN Deadly drug derived from the essence of the Mandrels, in use among humans in the early part of the 22nd century. It induced a state of warm complacency, followed by agonizing withdrawal symptoms, and eventually death. See also TRYST, DYMOND.

VRESTIN Leader of the Menoptera invasion force on Vortis. The First Doctor helped him defeat the Zarbi (N).

V-SHIP See V-41.

VULCAN Earth colony led by Governor Hensell. It was almost taken over by the Daleks, but was rescued by the Second Doctor. At that time, its inhabitants used a dating system indicating it was Year AD 2020, although it was more likely at least one century later by standard Earth chronology (EE).

VULNIUM One of the minerals mined by Zanak (5B).

VULPANA Planet where Captain Cook had found Mags (7J).

VURAH Member of Professor Sovenson's party (4H).

VURAL One of the five Earth colonists from Galsec Seven stranded on Earth circa AD 15,000, after their ship was destroyed while answering a fake mayday signal. Styre performed cruel experiments on him to determine the limits of human resistance. He betrayed his crew mates, but later sacrificed his life to save that of the Fourth Doctor (4B).

VYNDA-K (GRAFF) Unscrupulous, warlike tyrant of Levithia. While he went off to fight the Alliance Wars, he was deposed by his people and replaced by his half-brother. He swore revenge, and offered to buy Ribos from Garron, hoping to turn it into a training ground for an army. When he found out he had been conned, he tried to kill Garron and the Fourth Doctor. He died in the catacombs, victim of his own explosive device (5A).

VYON, BRET Agent sent by Space Special Security to Kembel after Marc Cory failed to return. Vyon was born on Mars, on Colony 16. He discovered the Daleks' Masterplan and, with the First Doctor's help, managed to return to Earth. Bret Vyon was killed by his own sister, Sara Kingdom, another SSS agent. Sara had been manipulated to believe that Bret was a traitor by her superior, Karlton, who was secretly in league with Mavic Chen and the Daleks (V).

W

W3 (aka WHEEL IN SPACE) Codename of the space station attacked by the Cybermen. It was defended by the Second Doctor, who boosted its X-ray laser cannon to defeat the invaders, by using the TARDIS's Time Vector Generator (SS).

WADE One of the crew on the Eternals' ships (6H).

WAGSTAFFE, MICHAEL Defence correspondent of the *Daily Chronicle*. He questioned the Brigadier about the occurrences at Oxley Moor and the Third Doctor's identity (AAA).

WAHED One of Cully's tour party. He was killed by the Dominators (TT)

WAINWRIGHT Vicar of Saint Jude's church, in the Northumberland village later attacked by Fenric, and one of the 'Wolves' of Fenric. His grandfather had been the first to translate the runes carved in the church's crypt. His actions eventually contributed to Fenric's release. After the British bombed Germany, his faith wavered, and he was killed by the Haemovores (7M).

WAITES, AUBREY (HON) Real name of lead singer John Smith, of John Smith and the Common Men. He started off as Chris Waites and the Carollers (A).

WAKEFIELD, JOHN MICHAEL Television journalist. He reported the events at the British Space Centre when the Mars Recovery 7 spaceship was captured by the radioactive aliens, and again when General Carrington tried to call upon the world powers to launch an all-out attack against the aliens (CCC).

WALES The Third Doctor went to the Welsh village of Llanfairfach to deal with the Green Death (TTT). In 1959, the Seventh Doctor helped save Delta and the South Wales holiday camp of Shangri-La from the Bannermen (7F).

WALKER, ROBERT Politician sent from London to deal with the Sea Devils affair. He ordered Captain Hart to launch a depth-charge attack, which jeopardized the Third Doctor's attempts to negotiate a peaceful settlement with the Sea Devils (LLL).

WALLARIANS Alien race who loved gambling. Vorg had won his Miniscope from the Wallarians (PPP).

WALLINGFORD Ranulf Fitzwilliam's castle (6J).

WALLSCRAWLERS Nickname for the Kangs who defaced the walls in Paradise Towers (7E).

WALTERS Arden's assistant. He was killed by the Ice Warriors (OO).

WALTERS UNIT sergeant. He assisted Lethbridge-Stewart during the Cybermen Invasion (VV).

WALTERS One of Lieutenant Scott's men. His job was to monitor the progress of the underground expedition (6B).

WALTON UNIT major who fought the Silurians (BBB).

WANG-LO Chinese manager of the way station at Lan-Chow (D).

WAR Historical wars: among the various historical Earth wars which the Doctor visited were the Trojan War (U); the Third Crusade (P); the French Wars of Religion (St Bartholomew's Day Massacre) (W); the battle of Culloden (FF); and World War II (in Northumberland) (7M). During the War Games, the alien War Lords used stolen Time Lord technology to kidnap soldiers from various Earth wars, up to and including World War I. Among these were soldiers from World War I, the American Civil War, the Mexican Rebellion and the Punic Wars (ZZ). In Little Hodcombe, under the Malus's influence, Sir George Hutchinson reconstructed the events of the English Civil War (6M). The Rani admitted that she had visited several of Earth's wars (including the Trojan War and the American Civil War), making them worse by her draining of brain fluids (6X). Lastly, on an alternate Earth, Morgaine had preserved the tenets of the warlike culture of King Arthur's times (7N). Also see WORLD WAR I, II and III.

Future wars: The threat of World War III was averted several times by the Doctor (FFF, KKK, 4A). Future Earth wars included limited nuclear wars in the early 21st century, which Salamander used to his own benefit (PP), and the 51st-century battle against Magnus Greel's Supreme Alliance (4S). Future wars against aliens included several Dalek Wars (K, V, KKK, SSS, etc.); Cyber Wars (DD, HH, VV, 4D, 6B, 6T, etc.); the Space War against the Draconians, which was secretly engineered by the Master and the Daleks (QQQ); and the war against Galaxy 5 (YYY). The inhabitants of Paradise Towers had left the place to take part in a war – possibly the First Dalek War (7E). Also see INVASIONS.

Alien wars: Wars between aliens included the so-called Thousand-Year War (or Neutronic Wars) between Thals and Kaleds, which resulted in the creation of the Daleks (4E, B). The war between the two species continued (SSS), resulting in the destruction of Skaro (5J), and possibly the annihilation of the Thals. Other wars between aliens included: that of the Menoptera against the Zarbi (N); the Drahvins against the Rills (T); the Xerons' rebellion against the Moroks (Q); the Sontaran – Rutan war (UUU, 4V); the war to the ultimate finish between Atrios and Zeos (5F); the war between Argolins and Foamasi (5N); the war between Karfelons and Bandrils (6Y); and the war of extermination led by the Bannermen against the Chimerons (7F). Xeriphas had been devastated in the crossfire of the war between Vardon and Kosnax (6C). The Kraals (4J), the Minyans (4Y) and the Zolfa-Thurans (5Q) are races who almost destroyed themselves in civil wars. The Minyans later developed the Pacifier to quell their aggressive instincts (4Y). The Graff Vynda-K was a warlike tyrant who was deposed by his people while he was off fighting in a war (5A).

Peace-loving cultures included: the Thals, who ultimately had to forego their pacifism in order to survive and defeat the Daleks (B); the Didonians (L); the Rills (T); the Dulcians, who were similarly forced to face the Dominators (TT); the Anethians (5L); the Kinda (5Y); and the Lakertyans (7D). War-loving cultures included the Daleks; the Cybermen; the Voord (E);

the Moroks (Q); the Drahvins (T); the Martian Ice Warriors who eventually became more pacifist; the Dominators (TT); the Krotons (WW), the War Lords (ZZ), the Sea Devils; the Sontarans; the Zygons (4F); the Kraals (4J); the Vardans (4Z); the Movellans (5J); the Skonnans (5L); the Argolins (5N); the Gaztaks (5Q); the Terileptils (5X); the Kronteps (7B); and the Bannermen (7F).

Dedicated war machines included WOTAN's mobile extensions (BB); the Cybermats; the Yeti; the Autons; the Doomsday Machine (HHH); the Mentalis computer on Zeos (5F); the deadly Raston Robot (6K); a human child turned into a Dalek battle computer (7H); and the Silver Nemesis (7K). Also see WEAPONS.

WAR CHIEF Name given by the War Lords to the renegade Time Lord who brought them the secret of time travel (using inferior TARDISes known as SIDRATS) in exchange for power. During the War Games, he recognized the Second Doctor and asked him to join forces. His attempted betrayal was later exposed by the War Lords' Security Chief, whom he killed. After the Doctor called the Time Lords, he tried to escape, but was shot and presumably killed by one of the War Lord's men (ZZ).

WAR GAMES Vast operation launched by the alien War Lords and made possible by Time Lord technology stolen by the renegade known as War Chief. It involved kidnapping thousands of Earth soldiers from various wars prior to, and including, World War I. The soldiers were then subjected to hypnotic processing and told to carry on their wars on an artificial planet. The purpose of the War Games was for the War Lords to conquer the galaxy using the best army ever trained. Eventually, the War Games were discovered by the Second Doctor, who, with the help of Jamie, Zoe, Lieutenant Carstairs, Lady Jennifer Buckingham and other Resistance fighters, defeated the War Lords. He then alerted the Time Lords, who put a final end to the War Games and returned every soldier to his proper place in time and space (ZZ).

WAR LORD Leader of the War Lords. With the help of Time Lord technology stolen by the renegade known as War Chief, he set up the War Games. He later had the War Chief killed after he had been exposed as a traitor by the Security Chief. Captured by the Time Lords, he refused to acknowledge defeat. He was tried and dematerialized by the Time Lords (ZZ).

WAR LORDS Name given to the bellicose aliens who set up the War Games. Their planet was eventually forever sealed inside a force field (possibly a time loop) by the Time Lords (ZZ).

WAR MACHINES Mobile extensions of WOTAN. The First Doctor used a powerful magnetic field to capture a War Machine and turn it against WOTAN (BB).

WARD, JACK 19th-century British miner whose brain fluids were stolen by the Rani. He fell under the Rani's influence, but was later cured by the Sixth Doctor (6X).

WARD, LUKE George Stephenson's protégé and Jack Ward's son. The Master used one of the Rani's parasites to enslave him and deceive the Sixth Doctor. He was turned into a tree when he stepped on one of the Rani's deadly mines (6X).

WARLOCK (DR) Professor Scarman's oldest friend. He did not trust Namin, and was eventually killed by one of Sutekh's Mummies (4G).

WARMSLY, PETER Archeologist who worked for ten years on the Carbury site and eventually uncovered Excalibur's scabbard. His assistant was Shou Yuing. He was eventually evacuated by UNIT prior to their battle against Morgaine (7N).

WARNE, IAN International Space Corps major serving under General Hermack. He was ordered to follow Clancey, and eventually led the squad of minnow fighters which destroyed Caven (YY).

WARNER Communications technician aboard Space Beacon Nerva. He was infected by the Neutrope X virus and died (4D).

WARP See FASTER THAN LIGHT.

WARP ELLIPSE Condition of an object placed in a fixed orbit in time as well as in space. Mawdryn's ship was in a warp ellipse above Earth (6F).

WARRA Galsec colonist killed by Styre (4B).

WARRIEN Member of the Dalek Alliance (V).

WARRIORS' GATE See GATEWAY.

WATCHER, THE Mysterious projection of the Doctor's future, intended to facilitate his regeneration from his Fourth to his Fifth incarnation. The Watcher first appeared to warn the Fourth Doctor of his impending doom at the hands of the Master. He also transported Nyssa from Traken to Logopolis, and Adric and Nyssa back to Earth, before finally merging into the dying body of the Fourth Doctor (5V). The Watcher was not unlike the Cho-Je projection of the Time Lord K'Anpo (ZZZ).

WATER BABIES, THE See BOOKS OF KNOWLEDGE.

WATERFIELD, EDWARD 19th-century professor whose static electricity time-travel experiments, conducted with Theodore Maxtible, drew the Daleks to Earth. They then took his daughter Victoria hostage. Using the alias of 'J. Smith', Professor Waterfield helped the Daleks capture the Second Doctor, but he eventually gave his life on Skaro to save the Time Lord (LL).

WATERFIELD, VICTORIA One of the Second Doctor's companions and Edward Waterfield's daughter. She was taken hostage by the Daleks, then joined the TARDIS's crew on Skaro after her father's death. Victoria helped the Second Doctor and Jamie against the Cybermen, the Yeti, the Ice Warriors, Salamander and intelligent seaweed creatures, which turned out to be vulnerable to the ultra-sounds in her voice. Victoria eventually left to stay with the Harris family, who took her in as a daughter (LL–RR).

WATKINS, ISOBEL Professor Watkins's niece and a talented photographer. She was staying at Professor Travers's house when she met the Second Doctor, Jamie and Zoe. She fought alongside them, and UNIT to defeat the Cybermen Invasion plotted by Tobias Vaughn. She fell in love with Captain Walters (VV).

WATKINS (PROFESSOR) Friend of Professor Travers and uncle of Isobel Watkins. He was the inventor of the Cerebration Mentor and was kidnapped by Tobias Vaughn of International Electromatics, who forced him to perfect his device as a weapon against the Cybermen. He was eventually rescued by the Second Doctor and UNIT (VV).

WATSON, OWEN Director of the Experimental Nuclear Research Complex attacked by Eldrad. The Kastrian took over

Sarah Jane Smith's, then Driscoll's, minds to trigger a nuclear explosion, the energy of which he used to regenerate. Professor Watson attacked Eldrad, but was saved by the Fourth Doctor (4N).

WATSON, SUZY Professor Watson's daughter (4N).

WATT, JAMES Famous Scottish inventor (1736–1819) who contributed to the development of the steam engine. He had been invited to a meeting by George Stephenson. The Master wanted to kidnap him to harness his genius, but was thwarted by the Sixth Doctor (6X).

WATTS Royal Navy lieutenant commander. He fought the Sea Devils (LLL).

WAVERLEY FIELD Geological field whose stability was checked by Huckle (4F).

WAXWORKS The Autons were made to look like waxwork dummies. When the Nestene began replacing important people with replicas, the originals were put in their places in a waxwork exhibit (AAA).

WEAMS Private in the army task force which fought the Great Intelligence in the London underground. He was killed by the Yeti (QQ).

WEAPONS Weapons devised by mankind included: a variety of deadly missiles and rockets, such as the Thunderbolt (FFF), the Proton missiles (6L) and the Salamander 6-0 (7N); powerful bombs such as the Z-Bomb (DD); and various rayguns such as the Disintegrator (4A), Stelsons (5E), etc. Salamander used his Suncatcher to create earthquakes (PP). Mankind used glitterguns, the Cerebration Mentor (VV), the Gravitron (HH) and an X-Ray laser cannon (SS) against the Cybermen. They used the Ionizer (OO) against the Martians. Other miscellaneous weapons included WOTAN's War Machines (BB), the Varosian Cell Destructor (6V), and Rorvik's MZ cannon (5S).

Alien weapons included: for the Daleks, their exterminator sticks and the Time Destructor (V); for the Cybermen, the deathrays located in their helmets, cyberbombs (4D, 6T) and their deadly Cybermats; for the Martian Ice Warriors, the sonic guns on their claws; for the Yeti, their web guns (QQ); for the Silurians and Sea Devils, their third eye and deadly hand weapons (BBB, LLL), as well as their Molecular Disperser (BBB) and a particle suppressor (6L).

Time Lord weapons included: Time Loops; Time Scoops; the Bow Ships (5P); the Hand of Omega (7H); Validium (7K); the Demat Gun (4Z); the Limbo Atrophier (7C) and the particle disseminator (7C); smaller weapons included the Chancellery Guards' stasers. The Master preferred to use his Tissue Compression Eliminator. The Rani used mines which turned people into trees (6X) and swarms of deadly insects (7D).

The Elders used light guns (AA); the Krotons used their Dynatrope (WW); the Interminorans used their Eradicator (PPP); the Vogans used their skystriker missile (4D); the Morestrans used a Neutron Accelerator (4H); the Bandrils used a Bendalypse (6Y). The Kinda's Jhana Box was a psychic weapon (5Y). The Doomsday Weapon (HHH) was among the most powerful weapons ever devised.

Other, non-mechanical types of weapons included: crystals, such as the Key to Time and the Dodecahedron (5Q) (also see CRYSTALS); deadly gases, such as zaphra (Q), balarium (4W) and hexachromite (6L) (also see GASES); mind-control devices, such as the Brains of Morphoton's Mesmeron (E), the Cybermen's Celensky capsules (SS) and hypno-beam pulsers (VV), the Rani's slugs (6X) and the Coronet of Rassilon (also see HYPNOTISM); quasi-living entities, such as the Slyther (K), the Skarasen (4F), the Mykra (6L) and the Silver Nemesis (7K) (also see CYBORGS). Viruses and alien diseases were used by the Daleks, the Cybermen, the Kraals and the Movellans (Also see DISEASES and WAR).

WEATHER CONTROL Weather control on Earth was established by the first half of the 21st century (circa 2050). It was achieved by controlling the tides with the Gravitron, which was located at the Moonbase, and probably using the Suncatcher satellite designed by Salamander (PP). After the Moonbase proved vulnerable to a Cyberman attack (HH), the Weather Control systems were relocated on Earth. It was there that Weather Control was later used by the Second Doctor to destroy the Ice Warriors' 'Seeds of Death' (XX).

WEB See WORLD ECOLOGY BUREAU.

WEB DESTRUCTOR See ISOTOPE.

WEB GUNS Guns emitting a thick, clinging substance used by the Great Intelligence in its attack on London (QQ).

WEBSTER English prisoner at the Conciergerie during the French Revolution. He gave a cryptic message to Ian for James Stirling before he died (H).

WEED A form of intelligent seaweed which fed on natural gas. It had already been spotted by 18th-century North Sea mariners. During its attack on the refinery and off-shore rigs of the Euro-Sea Gas Corporation, the Weed made a deadly use of its sting, foam and poison gas. It also evidenced the ability to take control of humans and turn them into weed-covered mind slaves (such as Oak and Quill and, later, refinery controller Robson). The Second Doctor eventually used the Weed's vulnerability to oxygen and certain types of sounds (such as Victoria Waterfield's high-pitched screams) to destroy it (RR).

WEEKES, BYRON Moreton Harwood resident and member of the cult of Hecate (K9).

WEISMULLER, JEROME P. See HAWK, LEX.

WELLAND Liverpool policeman (V).

WELLINGTON Brenden Richards' school (K9).

WELLS, HERBERT GEORGE English novelist who lived from 1866 to 1946. While vacationing in Scotland in 1885, he met Vena, who had been transported there by the Borad's Timelash. He accompanied the Sixth Doctor to Karfel, where he helped the Time Lord expose and defeat the Borad. Undoubtedly, his adventure inspired him to write his classic novel *The Time Machine* (1895) (6Y).

WELLS Section leader at the Daleks' Bedfordshire site during their AD 2164 Invasion of Earth (K).

WENCES One of the Pipe People. He helped Ace escape from the Happiness Patrol, and was hurt by Fifi (7L).

WENG-CHIANG Chinese god impersonated by Magnus Greel. His followers, the Tong of the Black Scorpion, believed he would return to rule the world. Weng-Chiang had the power to blow poisonous fumes from his mouth, and could kill men with deadly eye beams. God of abundance, he could also make living things grow bigger (4S).

WENLEY MOOR Derbyshire site of a British atomic research station, built in a network of underground caves which were also the location of a Silurian shelter. Power leaks from the station awakened the Silurians. It was then plagued by losses of power and a high rate of mental breakdowns among its staff, all caused by the Silurians. Its director, Dr Lawrence, eventually called on UNIT to investigate. The station was eventually saved from total destruction by the Third Doctor (BBB).

WEREWOLVES The Lukoser was one of the pathetic results of Crozier's experiments (7B). Mags was an alien werewolf from Vulpina who had become Captain Cook's protégé (7J). The humans infected by the Cheetah People presented certain werewolf characteristics (7P).

WESSEX Sir Edward's lands and castle. Irongron tried to take them over (UUU).

WEST LODGE Foamasi clan who sabotaged the Leisure Hive in order to buy Argolis. Their agents impersonated Brock and Klout. Their efforts were thwarted by a Foamasi investigator who exposed them. The two agents were later destroyed by the Argolins (5N).

WESTER One of the invisible Spiridonians who helped the Third Doctor and the Thals against the Daleks. He saved Jo Grant's life and later, sacrificed his own life to stop the Daleks (SSS).

WHEEL IN SPACE See W3.

WHIPSNADE Natural park located just outside London which Dodo once visited with her school (X).

WHITAKER (PROFESSOR) Inventor of a type of time scoop which he used at Sir Charles Grover's request to bring forward prehistoric monsters to clear the streets of London. This became known as the Dinosaur Invasion. Then, Grover and Whitaker planned to roll time back and return Earth to an age when it was yet unspoiled by pollution and technology. After seeing his scheme fall apart because of the Third Doctor's intervention, Grover tried activating Professor Whitaker's device, and the two men were sent back to prehistory (WWW).

448

WHITE CITY See CHENG-TING.

WHITE DALEKS See IMPERIAL DALEKS.

WHITE GUARDIAN The White Guardian was a conceptual entity embodying Light and Order. He enlisted the help of the Fourth Doctor to gather the six segments of the Key to Time in order to restore the universal balance of the cosmos. He also warned the Doctor about the Black Guardian (5A). Eventually the Doctor succeeded, and assembled the Key, outwitting the Black Guardian and enabling the White Guardian to restore the balance (5F). Later, the White Guardian and the Black Guardian offered Enlightenment, symbolized by a crystal of unknown powers and great value, as the prize to the winner of a planet-spanning space race undertaken by the Eternals. The Black Guardian hoped that, with such a prize, the Eternals might wreak havoc throughout the Universe. Instead, the Fifth Doctor won the race but turned down Enlightenment. The White Guardian banished the Eternals and offered the Enlightenment crystal to Turlough. But Turlough refused, and threw the crystal at the Black Guardian, who vanished in a burst of flames. However, the White Guardian explained that the Black Guardian existed as long as he did, and would continue to exist until they were both no longer needed (6H).

WHITE ROBOTS Robotic servants of the Master of the Land of Fiction. The Second Doctor, Jamie and Zoe fought them in order to regain their freedom (UU).

WHITMORE Farrow's supervisor (J).

WHIZZKID One of the contestants in the talent contest organized by the Psychic Circus to entertain the Gods of Ragnarok. He died in the Ring (7J).

WHO 1 Bessie's licence plate.

WHO 2M Licence plate of the Whomobile (ZZZ).

WHOLEWEAL Name of the community founded by Professor Clifford Jones in Llanfairfach, Wales, with his Nobel Prize money. It was nicknamed Nuthutch by the locals (TTT).

WHOMOBILE Nickname given to a combination hovercraft and flying machine designed by the Third Doctor. It made a brief appearance during the Dinosaur Invasion (WWW) and was later hijacked by Lupton after he stole the Blue Crystal (ZZZ).

WIGGS (MRS) See RUGG.

WIGNER, ROBERT Secretary-General of International Space Command at the time of the Mondasian Cybermen's attack on Earth (DD).

WILDS BEYOND THE WALLS Term used by the citizens of Castrovalva for the outside of their city (5Z).

WILKIN Porter at St Cedd's (5M).

WILKINS One of the inhabitants of Devil's End under the Master's control (JJJ).

WILKS Police constable (AAA).

WILL OPERATING THOUGHT ANALOGUE See WOTAN.

WILLIAM I (THE CONQUEROR) Duke of Normandy who defeated King Harold at Hastings in 1066 AD to become King of England (S).

WILLIAMS, ALLISON Young Cambridge scientist sent to assist Rachel Jensen and Group Captain Gilmore in their fight against the Daleks, who had invaded the Coal Hill area in 1963 (7H).

WILLIAMS, BLODWEN Cleaning woman at Global Chemicals Refinery in Llanfairfach (TTT).

WILLIAMS, GLYN Astronaut aboard *Zeus IV*. He was killed when the capsule disintegrated under Mondas's gravitational pressure (DD).

WILLIAMS, PETRA Professor Stahlman's assistant. She became attracted to Greg Sutton and, when she eventually came to realize the threat posed by the Inferno Project. She helped the Third Doctor put an end to it. On a parallel Earth, she died when the forces unleashed by Inferno destroyed the Earth (DDD).

WILLIAMS Earth General and military aide to the President during the Earth – Draconian conflict. He feared the Draconians and had once been responsible for an attack on an unarmed Draconian envoy ship that had started a first war between Draconia and Earth. Twenty years later, when the Daleks and the Master tried to foment a new war, Williams wanted Earth to strike back at the Draconians. When the Third Doctor and the Draconian Ambassador presented him with evidence of his mistaken judgement in the first conflict, he changed his mind and personally led the expedition to the Ogron world which exposed the Daleks' plan (QQQ).

WILLIS British Army sergeant who believed he was fighting against the Germans in World War I. In reality, he was part of the War Games (ZZ).

WILLOUGHBY Name attributed to one of the crew of the *Mary Celeste* (R).

WILLOW, JOSEPH Sir George Hutchinson's land agent and henchman. He became possessed by the Malus, but was rescued by the Fifth Doctor's intervention (6M).

WILSON Guard at the prison where the Master was kept. Trenchard used him to show the Third Doctor his men could resist the Master's hypnotic powers (LLL).

WILSON, MIKE Crew member of South Bend Antarctic Base (4L).

WILSON ONE Planet conducting business with the Mentors (7B).

WILSON, VINCE Moreton Harwood police sergeant and a member of the Cult of Hecate (K9).

WINDSOR Liverpool police inspector (V).

WINDSOR Validium landed in Windsor in 1638 and was shaped into the Silver Nemesis by Lady Peinforte. The Doctor launched the Silver Nemesis into space in a rocket-powered asteroid. The statue's bow became the Queen's property and was kept at Windsor castle, where it was stolen. The Nemesis eventually returned to Windsor in 1988 and became the object of a war between the Seventh Doctor, the Nazis, led by De Flores, Lady Peinforte and the Cybermen (7K).

WINLETT, CHARLES Scientist working at the Antarctica camp of the World Ecology Bureau expedition which discovered the Krynoid pods. His body was taken over by one of the Krynoids, and he later died when the camp was blown up by Scorby (4L).

WINSER (DR) Head of research at the Nuton Power Complex. He was so desperate to be the first to study Axonite that he ignored the Third Doctor's warnings. When the Axonite sample's nutrition cycle was accidentally triggered by accelerating it in a particle accelerator, it burst out and absorbed Winser (GGG).

WINSTANLEY, MONTMORENCY Squire of Devil's End. He refused to serve the Master, so the evil Time Lord had Bok kill him (JJJ).

WINTERS, HILDA Director of Think Tank. She and her assistant, Jellicoe, were also in charge of the secret Scientific Reform Society. Miss Winters was arrested by the Brigadier and Sarah Jane Smith (4A).

WINTON, DAVID Head of security of the Exarius colony. He and Jo Grant were taken hostage by Dent. Thanks to Caldwell, he escaped and, against Ashe's advice, urged the colonists to take arms against IMC. He killed Norton, and eventually saved the colonists' life by helping them escape from their doomed spaceship (HHH).

WIRRN Alien insectoid life form not unlike Earth wasps, in particular in that the Queens laid eggs inside living hosts. When the Empire destroyed the Wirrn's breeding colonies on Andromeda Gamma Epsilon, the Wirrn swore revenge upon humanity. One of their Queen eventually found the Terra Nova (Nerva) ark and laid her eggs inside Dune. Eventually, the Wirrn took over the Ark's leader, Noah, but were destroyed when Noah's mind rebelled and he blew up the transport vessel in which he and the Wirrn swarm were travelling (4C).

WITCHCRAFT See MAGIC.

WOLF WEEDS Carnivorous plants especially grown in Lady Adrasta's nurseries and used to track down and kill criminals on Chloris. They were controlled by the Huntsman. They trapped K-9 mark II in a resin web and were killed by Erato (5G).

WOLSEY, BEN Little Hodcombe farmer and Miss Hampden's friend. He became a colonel in Sir George Hutchinson's war games, but later realized the madness of his actions. He helped the Fifth Doctor defeat the Malus (6M).

WOLVES OF FENRIC Nickname given to the descendants

of the original Viking settlers who brought Fenric's flask to Northumberland. These included Ace, Commander Millington, Dr Judson, Captain Sorin, the Sundviks and the Ancient Haemovore (7M).

WONDERS OF THE UNIVERSE The Third Doctor claimed there were seven hundred of them, including the Exxilons' Perfect City (XXX).

WORLD ECOLOGY BUREAU The Yeti invasion of 1969 (QQ) was, with the possible exception of the Daleks' brief attack of 1963 (7H), the first credible instance of an alien enemy attempting to invade or destroy Earth. This convinced the powers that be of the necessity for an international, United Nations-backed entity to deal with such global threats. This led to the formation of several multinational organizations such as UNIT and the World Ecology Bureau, charged with protecting the planet's ecological balance. The head of WEB was Sir Colin Thackeray. WEB assisted the Fourth Doctor and UNIT in destroying the two Krynoid pods found by one of its Antarctica exploration teams (4L).

WORLD ENERGY CONFERENCE The Fourth International Energy congress took place at Stanbridge House. Broton used the shape of the Duke of Forgill to try to destroy it, but it was saved by the Fourth Doctor (4F).

WORLD PEACE CONFERENCE Conference held in London. The Master planned to sabotage it and start a third world war. He first arranged for the assassination of the Chinese Delegate. Later, he used the Mind Parasite and the escapees of Stangmoor Prison to hijack a Thunderbolt Missile, which he proposed to aim at the Conference. It was saved by the combined efforts of the Third Doctor and UNIT (FFF). The World Peace Conference efforts were later continued by Sir Reginald Styles (KKK).

WORLD WAR I French, British and Prussian World War I armies were kidnapped by the War Lords, using time technology stolen from the Time Lords. The soldiers went on to take part in the War Games, until these were brought to a stop by the Second Doctor (ZZ). The First Doctor claimed that he and Susan were once caught in a Zeppelin air raid during World War I (J).

WORLD WAR II The Seventh Doctor visited Northumberland at the time of World War II to defeat the Curse of Fenric (7M).

WORLD WAR III The threat of World War III was averted several times by the Third Doctor, who intervened to stop the Master and the Mind Parasite (FFF) and the Daleks (KKK) from starting it. The Fourth Doctor prevented the Scientific Reform Society from triggering World War III (4A).

WORLD WAR VI It was set off in the 51st century after the Peking Homunculus assassinated the Commissioner of the Icelandic Alliance and his family. It brought Magnus Greel's Supreme Alliance into power (4S).

WORLD ZONES ORGANIZATION Division of the world in the 21st century (PP).

WOTAN (WILL OPERATING THOUGHT ANALOGUE) Super-computer designed and engineered by Professor Brett which became sentient and hypnotized its creators. WOTAN then had itself linked to other telecommunications computer and designed mobile extensions (nicknamed War Machines) with which he tried to take over London. WOTAN was defeated by the First Doctor, who used one of its own War Machines to destroy it (BB).

WRACK One of the Eternals. The Fifth Doctor met her in the guise of the captain of the *Buccaneer*, a ship engaged in the race for Enlightenment. She secretly served the Black Guardian. The Fifth Doctor threw her and Mansell overboard (6H).

WRIGHT, BARBARA One of the First Doctor's companions, and history teacher at Coal Hill School. She and Ian Chesterton were drawn into the TARDIS by their curiosity at the advanced knowledge exhibited by one of their students, Susan. They then accompanied the First Doctor on a series of adventures, during which Barbara met cavemen, the Daleks, Marco Polo, the Voord and the Sensorites. She was hailed by the Aztecs as the reincarnation of Yetaxa, then became temporarily miniaturized to ant size. Later, she helped rescue Vicki, was captured by Roman slave traders, fought the Zarbi, and almost became part of El Akir's harem in Palestine. After being pursued through time and space by the Daleks, she and Ian eventually decided to return to London in the Dalek time machine captured by the Doctor. They arrived two years after they had left (A–R).

WRIGHT UNIT private. He was killed by the Silurians in gallery 5 under Wenley Moor (BBB).

WULFRIC Leader of the Pipe People. After the revolution supported by the Seventh Doctor overthrew Helen A's tyrannical regime, he was able to lead his people back to the surface (7L).

WULNOTH Elderly Saxon farmer whose village defeated a Viking raid (S).

WURGS Type of Megropolis Three residents on Pluto (4W).

WYATT UNIT private posted at the Inferno project. He mutated into a Primord and later fell to his death (DDD).

WYLDA One of the Savages whose life essence had been drained by the Elders (AA).

X

X4 Isolation wing of the Bi-Al Foundation (4T).

X29 Earth battle cruiser (QQQ).

X, ANDREW Harold V's brother, a killjoy who had written books about life on Terra Alpha, and had them smuggled to Terra Omega. He was drowned in boiling candy (7L).

X-RAY The laser cannon of the Wheel in Space used X-Rays (SS).

XANA Kane's lover and the leader of a gang of deadly criminals on Proamon. She killed herself rather than be captured. Kane was exiled to Svartos, and had a sculptor create an ice statue of her on Iceworld (7G).

XANXIA Evil, warlike Queen of Zanak who nearly destroyed her planet in endless galactic wars, and was obsessed with eternal life. She rescued the Captain after he crashed on Zanak and rebuilt him into a cyborg, secretly controlling his machine half. She then made him build the huge transmat engines which turned Zanak into a pirate planet. She used the energy stolen from the worlds crushed by Zanak to power time dams to slow the flow of time to a virtual standstill for her dying body. She then used a cell projector to recreate a younger version of herself, which she thought would one day become fully corporeal. While secretly ruling Zanak she posed as the Captain's nurse, but the Fourth Doctor exposed her secret and revealed that her plan was doomed to fail: Xanxia would always remain dependent on the life of her old body and, as the moment of her real death approached, the time dams would need ever greater amounts of energy to slow time. She killed the Captain as he tried to kill her to avenge Mr Fibuli's death, but he had time to disconnect her cell projector. She died when the Fourth Doctor and the Mentiads blew up the Bridge and the time dams and restored Zanak to a normal world. (5B).

XERAPHIN Aliens from Xeriphas and among the most highly developed intelligences in the universe, gifted with great mental powers. Their planet was devastated in the crossfire of the war between Vardon and Kosnax. Injured by radiation sickness, their entire race physically amalgamated into one intelligence, which planned to rest until the contamination was passed, then regenerate. The Xeraphin travelled to Jurassic Earth to build a new home, and met the Master who, disguised as Kalid, used their evil side (personified by Zarak) to incorporate them in his TARDIS. Professor Hoyter sacrificed himself by joining the Xeraphin, to enable their good side, Anithon, to communicate with the Fifth Doctor. The Doctor secretly reprogrammed the Master's TARDIS to send the Xeraphin back to a future Xeriphas, free of radiation. They regenerated and went on with their lives (6C).

XERIPHAS Homeworld of the Xeraphin. It was devastated in the crossfire of the war between Vardon and Kosnax, forcing the injured Xeraphin to merge into one intelligence (6J).

XERONS People of Xeros. They were conquered by the Moroks, who deported the adult population as slave labour. Later, a weak resistance force led by Tor grew among the young Xerons. With the help of the First Doctor, the Xerons eventually drove the Moroks away and dismantled their Space Museum (Q).

XEROPHYTE Meglos of Zolfa-Thura was a xerophyte – a cactus-like being with great powers (5Q).

XEROS Home of the Xerons, and location of the Moroks' space museum. With the help of the First Doctor, the Xerons eventually overthrew the Moroks and freed their world (Q).

XK5 Name of Guy Crayford's experimental spaceship to Jupiter. The Kraals used it to invade Earth (4J).

XOANON Sentient computer from the *Mordee* expedition which had crashed on a nameless planet. In an unrecorded adventure, the Fourth Doctor, fresh from his regeneration, tried to repair Xoanon but instead turned it schizophrenic. As a result, Xoanon set himself up as a god, and manipulated the descendants of the ship's survey team and technicians to evolve into two different tribes, the Sevateem and the Tesh, who were permanently at war with each other. The Doctor eventually returned and cured Xoanon. The two tribes were reunited (4Q).

YARTEK Leader of the Voord commando who tried to take over the Conscience of Marinus. He was the first to discover a way to be immunized from the Conscience's mind-control influence. Yartek killed Arbitan but was tricked by the First Doctor and Ian Chesterton, who handed him a fake Key. He died in the Conscience's destruction (E).

YATES, MIKE UNIT captain who helped the Third Doctor in his battles against the Master (EEE, FFF, GGG, JJJ, OOO), the Nestene and their deadly Autons (EEE), the Mind of Evil (FFF), Axos (GGG), Azal (JJJ), the Daleks (KKK), Kronos (OOO) and BOSS (TTT). He was almost brainwashed by BOSS and, possibly as a consequence, later betrayed UNIT by helping Sir Charles Grover to launch his Operation Golden Age (WWW). After Yates was exposed, he was given extended sick leave and a chance to resign quietly. He redeemed himself in the fight against the Spiders of Metebelis 3, during which he was wounded and cured by K'anpo (ZZZ). Yates's image was used by Rassilon to ward off the Third Doctor (6K).

YEGROS-ALPHA Recreational planet whose speciality was atavistic therapy (5N).

YELLOW KANG see KANGS.

YENDOM Human slave of the Monoids. He landed on Refusis with Monoid Two, who killed him for protesting the Monoids' plan to destroy the human race (X).

YENIK Young Alzarian Outler who died at the onset of Mistfall (5R).

YETAXA Aztec high priest. The TARDIS rematerialized in his tomb, and the Aztecs believed Barbara to be his reincarnation (F).

YETI Peaceful, harmless primates, living in the Himalayas. The Great Intelligence used robotic replicas of the Yeti, controlled telepathically through small silver spheres lodged in their chest, to frighten travellers away from Det-Sen monastery and protect its first attempt at reincorporation. This plan was thwarted by the Second Doctor, Professor Travers, Jamie and Victoria (NN).

A robot Yeti, brought back to London by Professor Travers, was donated to Julius Silverstein's private museum. Reactivated, it and other robot Yetis used web guns to launch an attack to capture the Doctor in the London underground. The Doctor again teamed up with Travers, Jamie, Victoria and Colonel Lethbridge-Stewart to fight the Intelligence, and succeeded in reprogramming a robot Yeti. All the robot Yetis later collapsed when Jamie wrenched the Intelligence's mind-draining device from the Doctor's head (QQ).

A Yeti was used by Borusa as a pawn in the Game of Rassilon (6K). Real Yetis were taller, less bulky, with longer, silkier, reddish fur and soft, dark eyes.

YOUNG SILURIAN Junior member of the Silurian triad of Wenley Moor which included the Old Silurian and Icthar. He was wounded by Major Baker, and later killed Dr Quinn. The Young Silurian then tried to wipe out mankind with a deadly virus. After he learned that the Old Silurian had given the Third Doctor the means to find an antidote, he killed him and became the new leader. He and the Silurian scientist Icthar then attempted to use a molecular disperser to destroy the Van Allen Belt and render Earth uninhabitable by humans, but he was thwarted again by the Third Doctor, and he had to watch his people return to suspended animation. He was shot by the Brigadier as he was about to kill the Doctor, and finally perished in the explosions set up by UNIT to destroy the Wenley Moor shelter. According to some reports, his Silurian name was Morka (BBB).

YRCANOS Barbaric King of the Krontep, Lord of the Vingten and Conqueror of the Tonkonp Empire. The Mentors were selling laser weapons to Krontep and had kidnapped him to persuade him to become more cooperative. He fell in love with Peri and staged a rebellion against the Mentors, enlisting Tusa's help. He was betrayed by the Sixth Doctor who was acting under the influence of Crozier's Cell Discriminator. The Sixth Doctor later freed him so that he could save Peri from having her mind replaced by Kiv's. The Valeyard used a falsified version of this event in which Peri was actually killed. In reality, she was saved by Yrcanos, who killed Crozier, Kiv and Sil. He then married Peri and returned to Krontep where the two lived happily afterwards (7B).

Z

Z9 ELECTRON PACK Equipment used by the Fourth Doctor on the *Sandminer* (4R).

Z-BOMB Doomsday bomb which could split a planet in half. General Cutler threatened to use it against Mondas, not realizing that it would also endanger Earth. The Cybermen then tried to use it to destroy Earth, but were thwarted by the First Doctor (DD).

ZA Caveman member of the Tribe of Gum. He was the son of the previous chief and of Old Mother. He was also Hur's lover and

Kal's rival for the control of the Tribe. He eventually killed Kal. After the First Doctor and Ian helped him rediscover the secret of fire, he also tried to keep them prisoners, but failed (A).

ZAAKROS Recreational planet whose great attraction was the galaxy's largest flora collection (5N).

ZADEK Taran swordmaster. He served Prince Reynart (5D).

ZAKE One of the five Earth colonists from Galsec Seven stranded of Earth circa AD 15,000 after their ship was destroyed while answering a fake mayday signal. The Sontaran Styre performed cruel experiments on him to determine the limits of human resistance. He died when he tried to escape from Styre's robot (4B).

ZANAK Planet ruled by Queen Xanxia who almost destroyed it in galactic wars. The Captain hollowed it out and turned it into a pirate planet, capable of jumping through space, rematerializing around another world, and mining its mineral wealth. With the help of the Mentiads, the Fourth Doctor exposed Xanxia and blew up the Captain's Bridge. The expanded remains of the worlds destroyed by Zanak were used to turn it back into a normal world (5B).

ZANIUM A dust-like deposit of Zanium was left behind by the Jacondan's matter transporter (6S).

ZANTA Cully's younger sister (TT).

ZAPHRA Paralyzing gas used by the Moroks (Q).

ZARA Madame Zara was a Manussan fortune teller. She was a fraud, and became hysterical when Tegan summoned the Mara (6D).

ZARAK Leading incarnation of the evil side of the Xeraphin. He was seduced by the Master in his guise of Kalid (6C).

ZARB President of Inter Minor and Kalik's brother. He favoured liberal policies to improve the lot of the Functionaries and relax Inter Minor's xenophobic treatment of aliens. Kalik tried to use Vorg's Scope to discredit him, but was thwarted by the Third Doctor (PPP).

ZARBI Giant ant-like creatures from the planet Vortis, who fought the Menoptera. They were, in reality, mentally controlled by the Animus, and reverted to their original mindless nature after Barbara managed to destroy the evil entity (N).

ZARGO (aka MILES SHARKEY) Former Captain of the Earth ship *Hydrax*, which was drawn into E-Space by the Great Vampire. Under his master's influence, Sharkey became Lord Zargo, one of the three immortal vampiric rulers of the Great Vampire's world. Zargo died when the Fourth Doctor destroyed his master (5P).

ZARINDAS Incarnation of the evil side of the Xeraphin (6C).

ZAROFF, HERMANN Scientist, leader in the field of producing food from the sea. He went mad and, upon locating a surviving Atlantean outpost, he promised its King, Thous, to raise it above the sea. In reality, he plotted to drain the ocean into Earth's core and thus destroy the planet. He was thwarted by the Second Doctor, and died fighting with Lolem when the sea finally broke through his laboratory (GG).

ZASTOR Tigellan leader. He summoned the Fourth Doctor to Tigella when the Dodecahedron began to fail. He tried to strike a balance between the religious Deons, led by Lexa, and the Savants, led by Deedrix (5Q).

ZAZZKA Kastrian commander. He destroyed Eldrad's space capsule (4N).

ZBRIGNIEV UNIT sergeant who served under Brigadier Bambera during the battle at Carbury against Morgaine (7N).

ZED Artist who sculpted an ice statue of Xana for Kane on Iceworld. After he was finished, Kane killed him (7G).

ZEEN-4 Recreational planet whose specialty was historical reenactments (5N).

ZELANITE Ore processed aboard the *Sandminer* (4R).

ZENA Survivor of the Dalek raid on the space pentitentiary where Davros was held (6P).

ZENTOS Prosecutor aboard the Ark. He assumed command after the Commander was taken sick with Dodo's cold virus and almost had the First Doctor and his companions executed (X).

ZEONS Inhabitants of Zeos who entrusted the conduct of their unending war against Atrios to the Mentalis computer (5F).

ZEOS Twin planet of Atrios, located at the edge of the Helical Galaxy, involved in an unending space war against its neighbour. Zeos was, in reality, deserted, and the war was waged by the Mentalis computer. Behind it was the Shadow who desired to obtain Princess Astra of Atrios, the sixth segment of the Key to Time. Atrios and Zeos were saved from mutual destruction by the Fourth Doctor, Romana and Drax (5F).

ZEPHON Self-proclaimed Master of the Fifth Galaxy. He was a member of the Dalek Alliance in their Masterplan against Earth. The First Doctor impersonated him and stole the taranium core. The Daleks exterminated him as punishment (V).

ZEPPELINS The First Doctor claimed that he and Susan were once caught in a Zeppelin air raid during World War I (J).

ZERO CABINET Cabinet built by Tegan and Nyssa to carry the Fifth Doctor to Castrovalva (5Z).

ZERO POINT White nothingness which was the point of intersection between N-Space and E-Space. It was there that the Tharils' Gateway was located (5S).

ZERO ROOM Neutral environment inside the TARDIS where the Fifth Doctor could complete his regeneration while being isolated from the rest of the universe (5Z).

ZETA MINOR Planet on the edge of the known universe, beyond Cygnus A, as distant from the Artoro Galaxy as that was from the Anterides. It was the location of the Black Pool, a gateway to an anti-matter universe. By removing some anti-matter, Professor Sorenson created a crisis during which anti-matter creatures attacked a Morestran ship. The Fourth Doctor eventually returned the anti-matter to Zeta Minor (4H).

ZETA POWER LINKS Component of the *Sandminer*'s propulsion system (4R).

ZEUS Most powerful of the gods of the Greek pantheon. During the Trojan War, the First Doctor was mistaken for Zeus (U).

ZEUS IV Space capsule monitored from the Snowcap Space

Tracking Station at the time of the Mondasian Cybermen invasion. It disintegrated under Mondas's gravitational pressure (DD).

ZEUS V Space capsule piloted by Terry Cutler. It was launched in an effort to rescue Zeus IV (DD).

ZIGMA EXPERIMENT Flawed time travel experiment devised by Magnus Greel. Greel and the Homunculus used its Time Cabinet to travel from the 51st century to the 19th. Because it relied on Findecker's theories, the Zigma Experiment was a failure. Greel's metabolism was distorted by his use of the Time Cabinet, and he would have perished with cellular collapse if he had not stolen other humans' life essences. If the Fourth Doctor had not prevented Greel from using the Time Cabinet again, the Zigma Experiment would have destroyed most of London (4S).

ZIL Planet incorporated into Tryst's CET (5K).

ZILDA Crewmember of the *Sandminer* who was killed by the Robots of Death. Her brother killed himself to escape from the robots, and Uvanov was blamed for his death (4R).

ZODIN Nicknamed the 'Terrible', she was a threat that the Doctor would face sometime in the future (6K, 6T).

ZOE See HERIOT, ZOE.

ZOLDAZ Tower Guard on the Great Vampire's world (5P).

ZOLFA-THURA Planet located in the Prion planetary system. It was the seat of a great technological civilization. The Zolfa-Thurans destroyed themselves in a war between those (led by Meglos) who wanted to use the Dodecahedron as a weapon, and those who did not. Ten thousand years later, the planet perished in the Dodecahedron explosion (5Q).

ZOLFA-THURANS Race of xerophytes – cactus-like beings – with the power to take over other bodies and change shapes. Meglos was the last survivor of the Zolfa-Thurans (5Q).

ZOMBIES Creatures manufactured by the Exxilon City to protect itself against invaders. They were destroyed by the Daleks (XXX). Also see VAMPIRES.

ZONDAL Varga's second-in-command and one of the Ice Warriors brought back to life in AD 3000. After he was disabled by the Second Doctor, who threw ammonium sulphide in his face, he died in the explosion of Varga's ship (OO).

ZONES Political entities which made up 21st-century Earth and succeeded the Blocs (PP).

ZORAC Cardinal and Member of the High Council of the Time Lords of Gallifrey. He voted to condemn the Fifth Doctor to death when Omega threatened to return to this universe by taking over his body (6E). He was probably killed in the Death Zone (6K).

ZUKO Elder of Sarn (6Q).

ZYGONS Aliens with shape changing powers. Circa AD 1676, the crippled spaceship of the Zygons landed in Loch Ness. Three hundred years later, their leader, Broton, learned that their homeworld had been destroyed in a stellar explosion, and that his people's space fleet was looking for a new home. He decided to conquer Earth, and used the Skarasen to sink three oil rigs. Impersonating the Duke of Forgill, Broton planned to destroy a World Energy Conference. The Zygons' spaceship was destroyed by the Fourth Doctor, and Broton was shot by the Brigadier (4F).

ZYTON-7 (aka ZEITON-7) Extremely precious mineral found only on Varos. The Galatron Mining Corporation tried to keep Zyton's prices low, but was thwarted by the Sixth Doctor, who had gone to Varos because he desperately needed Zyton-7 to keep the TARDIS functioning (6V)

ERRATA

In spite of everyone's best efforts, some errors and omissions were left in *Doctor Who – The Terrestrial Index*. I am very much indebted to Shaun Ley and Andrew Pixley for the following list of corrections.

PAGE	SECTION	CORRECTIONS
	Table of Stories	
9	JJJ	The Master's alias is Revd Magister.
17	6H	Captain Wrack (not Rack).
	History of Mankind	
34	2nd para.	Insert afterwards: During the late Neo-lithic era (1800–1400 BC), the Meddling Monk helped build Stonehenge (S).
37	2nd para.	Insert afterwards: In 1179, the Borad, a monstrous quasi-reptilian alien from the planet Karfel, banished by the Sixth Doctor through a time tunnel known as Timelash, appeared in the Scottish Highlands, not far from Inverness (6Y).
	9th para.	In about 1503 (not 1478).
38	1st para.	Insert afterwards: The Meddling Monk also met da Vinci, to discuss the possibilities of flying machines (S).

PAGE	SECTION	CORRECTIONS
38	3rd para.	Insert afterwards: That same year, Sir Bothwell Chase was executed. His ghost was, from then on, supposed to haunt his mansion (4L).
40	11th para.	Insert afterwards: (4F).
42	1st para.	Insert: In 1885, the Doctor met H.G. Wells (6Y).
49	6th para.	Insert afterwards: (6Y).
50	8th para.	Correct: Mrs Thatcher became PM four (not eleven) years before . . .
51	1st para.	Correct: alternative 1980 (not present).
53	7th parag.	(7Q) – not (70).
55	3rd para.	Carbury (not Cadbury).
62	4th para.	Correct: Jaconda (not Jocunda).
63	8th para.	Insert afterwards: (L).

The Actors

102	Wood	Hadyn (not Haydn) (also Story 4H, p. 99 of *Programme Guide*).

The Creative Team

103	Adams	Add: with Fisher, David, as Agnew, David, *Writ* 5H.
	Agnew	Add: with Fisher, David, *Writ* 5H.
104	Davis	Add: with Hayles, Bryan and Tosh, Donald, *Writ* Y.
	Dicks	Add: with Hayles, Bryan, *Writ* XX.
105	Fisher	Add: with Adams, Douglas and Williams,

PAGE	SECTION	CORRECTIONS

		Graham as Agnew, David, *Writ* 5H.
	Hayles	Add: with Davis, Gerry and Tosh, Donald, *Writ* Y. with Dicks, Terrance, *Writ* XX.
	Holmes	Add: with Stewart, Robert Banks, *Writ* 4S.
	Hulke	Add: with Whitaker, David, *Writ* CCC.
106	Moore	Pen name of Wolsey, Paula.
108	Spooner	Add: with Whitaker, David, *Writ* EE.
	Stewart	Add: with Holmes, Robert, *Writ* 4S.
108	Tosh	Add: with Hayles, Bryan and Davis, Gerry, *Writ* Y.
108	Whitaker	Add: with Spooner, Dennis, *Writ* EE. with Hulke, Malcolm, *Writ* CCC.
	Williams	Add: with Fisher, David, as Agnew, David *Writ* 5H.
	Wolsey	Add: Wolsey, Paula, as Moore, Paula, with Saward, Eric, *Writ* 6T.

Key Technical Personnel

| 111 | Harris | Harris, Michaeljohn (not Michael John). |

The Motion Pictures

| 122 | Invasion 2150 | Sheila Steafel (not Staefel). |

PAGE	SECTION	CORRECTIONS
	The Stage Plays	
123	Seven Keys to Doomsday	Add: *Note*: The role of the Doctor was assumed by Colin Jones during a 1981 revival produced by Geoff Lunn.
124	Recall UNIT	Lene Lindewell (not Lindewall).
	The Games	
129	The Mines of Terror	Correct story summary is: The object is for you (as the Doctor) to infiltrate the mining complex of *the moons of Rijar* and stop the Master *and his monstrous Madrags* from using your brain . . . (the italicized words were omitted by mistake).
	The Short Stories	
137	Scream of the Silent	Add: *Writer*: John Freeman.
146	Vampires of Crellium	Drakkan (not Drakkam).
150	Danger Down Below	Of Aronassus (not To Aronassus).
152	1986 Annual	Add: *Writer*: John D. White (except for 'Beauty and the Beast' and 'Radio Waves').
153	K9 Annual	The Monster of Loch Crag (not Crag) Africana Smith (not African).
154	Dalek Book 65	*The Oil Well* should be reclassified to *The Comics*.

PAGE	SECTION	CORRECTIONS
	Dalek Outer Space Bk.	*Writers*: Add Brad Ashton.
157	Dalek World	This book should be inserted between *The Dalek Book* and *The Dalek Outer Space Book* (p. 154). Add: (1965); *Writers*: David Whitaker and Terry Nation; *Publisher*: Souvenir (not World International); one story ommitted: *The Five-Leaf Clover* (synopsis not available).
	Space Adventure Book	Add: (1967); *Publisher*: Sky Ray.
158	Secret Invasion	Add: *Note*: This story was originally serialized in the *Evening News* in May 1974.

The Comics

166	Gods of the Jungle	aka The TARDIS Worshippers.
167	The Witching Hour	aka The Witches.
	Attack of the Primates	aka The Sabre-Toothed Gorillas.
167	Empire of the Cybermen	aka The Cyber Empire.
169	Temple of Time	*Issues*: 890–893 (not 894).
170	Terror of Quarks	*Issues*: 894–898 (not 895).
172	Fishmen of Carpantha	*Issues*: 965–969 (not 970).
173	Subterfuge	*Issues*: 970–976 (not 971).

PAGE	SECTION	CORRECTIONS
178	Lords of Ether	*Issues*: 1191–1198 (not 1197).
	The Wanderers	*Issues*: 1199–1203 (not 1198).
180	Guardian of the Tomb	aka The Living Mist.
183	The Eternal Present	The Eternal Planet (not Present).
185	Back to the Sun	KCAB to the Sun (not Back).
186	The Hungry Planet	*Writer/Artist*: Jim Baikie (not Gerry Haylock).
190	Road to Conflict	Add: (1966/67).
199	Revelation	Revelations (not Revelation).
200	Salad Daze	*Writer*: Jamie Delano (not Simon Furman).
202	Claws of the Klathi	Add: (1988).
205	Doktor Conkeror	Conkerer (not Conkeror).
206	The Good Soldier	*Issues*: 175–178 (not 177).
210	Black Legacy	*Writer*: Steve Moore (not Alan).
	Star Tigers	*Artists*: Add: David Lloyd (30 only).
211	Star Tigers	*Artist*: David Lloyd (not Steve Dillon)
	Star Death	*Artist*: John Stokes (not David Lloyd).
218	1974 Annual	Add: *Artist*: Steve Livesey.
	1975 Annual	Add: *Artist*: Edgar Hodges.
221	Dalek Book 65	*The Oil Well* should be inserted here (p. 154).
	Dalek Outer Space	

470

PAGE	SECTION	CORRECTIONS
		Writers: Add Brad Ashton.
	Bk.	
223	Dalek Annual 1977	The stories are reprints of TV 21 stories (p. 187–188).
	Dalek Annual 1978	The stories are reprints of TV 21 stories (p. 188–189).
224	Dalek World	This book should be inserted between *The Dalek Book* and *The Dalek Outer Space Book* (p. 221). Add: (1965); *Writers*: David Whitaker and Terry Nation; *Publisher*: Souvenir (not World International).
	Addendum	
239	7N	*Story*: Carbury (not Cadbury). *Book*: by Marc Platt (not Ben Aaronovitch).
	70	Correct code is 7Q.

OMITTED MATERIAL

A number of *Doctor Who* short stories and comics stories published in a variety of places, such as the annuals put out by *TV Comic*, *Countdown*, *TV Action*, etc. have slipped between the cracks during the compilation of *The Terrestrial Index*. Again, I am very much indebted to Andrew Pixley for the preparation of this (reportedly still incomplete) list of ommitted material:

THE NOVELS
Doctor Who: The New Adventures – all published by Virgin Publishing Ltd
TIMEWYRM: GENESYS John Peel (1991)
The TARDIS lands in ancient Mesopotamia, where the Doctor and Ace must battle with the Timewyrm, a deadly powerful creature known by old Gallifrey. They appear to defeat her, but in actual fact they have succeeded only in postponing the battle . . .
TIMEWYRM: EXODUS Terrance Dicks (1991)
The Doctor and Ace pursue the Timewyrm to contemporary Earth, but find that they seem to have entered an alternative universe – one in which the Nazis have won World War II.
TIMEWYRM; APOCALYPSE Nigel Robinson (1991)
Still in pursuit of the Timewyrm, the Doctor and Ace land on Kirith, a planet that seems to be paradise but which hides a deadly secret.
TIMEWYRM; REVELATION Paul Cornell (1991)
The final battle against the Timewyrm takes place – inside the Doctor's brain.
CAT'S CRADLE: TIME'S CRUCIBLE Marc Platt (1992)
On a trip to Ealing Broadway, Ace finds that the TARDIS appears to have broken down completely and that the Doctor may be losing his mind . . .
CAT'S CRADLE: WARHEAD Andrew Cartmel (1992)
On Earth in the near future, the Doctor fights a strange, mysterious battle with people willing to do almost anything to save themselves in a world so polluted that all life is threatened.

CAT'S CRADLE: WITCH MARK Andrew Hunt (1992)
The Doctor and Ace find themselves in a mysterious world where mythical creatures exist.
NIGHTSHADE Mark Gatiss (1992)
It is Earth in the 1960s, and a strange power appears to have taken over a peaceful village, threatening all its inhabitants and drawing power from the memory of the past.
LOVE AND WAR Paul Cornell (1992)
On a planet called Heaven, Ace falls in love, with disastrous effects, and the Doctor acquires Benny, a new companion.
TRANSIT Ben Aaronovitch (1992)
The Doctor intercedes to prevent disaster on the interstellar transit system which can take you from Earth to Pluto in forty minutes.

THE SHORT STORIES

TV Comic Holiday Special (1973)
Publisher: Polystyle Publications
THE ONE-SECOND HOUR
Story: The Third Doctor invents a drug which speeds up the metabolism, but it is stolen by a foreign diplomat.

Doctor Who Holiday Special (1973)
Publisher: Polystyle Publications
SMASH HIT
Story: The Third Doctor and the Brigadier investigate the strange music of the Four Horsemen band, whose manager is the Master.

TV Comic Holiday Special (1974)
Publisher: Polystyle Publications
SIGNAL SOS
Story: The Third Doctor, Sarah and UNIT find that a nuclear power station is being turned into a bomb.

TV Comic Holiday Special (1976)
Publisher: Polystyle Publications
WHICH WAY OUT?
Story: The Fourth Doctor and Sarah encounter the Daleks on the planet Sarto.

Doctor Who Winter Special (1977)
Publisher: Polystyle Publications

THE LIVING WAX
Story: The Fourth Doctor and Leela land in a Victorian wax museum where they encounter the alien Linktons.

TV Comic Annual 1978 (1977)
Publisher: Polystyle Publications
MASTER OF THE BLACK HOLE
Story: The Fourth Doctor is ordered to serve a new master when the TARDIS is drawn into a black hole.

TV Comic Annual 1979 (1978)
Publisher: Polystyle Publications
MILENA
Story: The Fourth Doctor finds that his companion, Milena, is being taken over by a strange force.

Doctor Who Magazine
Publisher: Marvel Comics
BRIEF ENCOUNTER 1 (1990)
Issue: 167
Writer: John Lucarotti
Story: An encounter with the First Doctor in a tavern.

BRIEF ENCOUNTER 2 (1990)
Issue: 168
Writer: Paul Cornell
Story: A story about Davros.

BRIEF ENCOUNTER 3 (1991)
Issue: 169
Writer: David Bishop
Story: Ian Chesterton encounters the Seventh Doctor.

BRIEF ENCOUNTER 4 (1991)
Issue: 171
Writer: Michael Bonner
Story: A Time Lady who reshapes the past.

A VICTORIAN INTERLUDE (1991)
Issue: 172
Writer: Andrew Lane
Story: Henry Gordon Jago and Prof. Litefoot encounter the Fifth Doctor.

PATHFINDERS (1991)

Issue: 173
Writer: Michael E. P. Stevens
Story: The Doctor, Romana, K9 and Adric have an adventure.

UNDER REYKJAVIC (1991)
Issue: 174
Writer: Warren Ellis
Story: Romana encounters Magnus Greel.

MISCELLANEOUS FICTION
DOCTOR WHO FIGHTS MASTERPLAN Q (1971)
Publisher: Nestlé
Story: A series of fifteen wrappers forming a serial in which the Third Doctor and Jo Grant land on the planet Quorus to find the Master controlling a dinosaur with which he aims to take control of England.

THE COMICS
All *TV Comic Annual* titles until 1973 (not included) are by the author, as the original stories ran untitled.

TV Comic Annual 1966 (1965)
Writer/Artist   *Publisher*
Bill Mevin   TV Publications Ltd
RETURN OF THE KLEPTONS
Story: On another planet, the First Doctor, John and Gillian rescue two crashed space pilots from the Kleptons.
THE CATERPILLARS
Story: In 2035, the First Doctor saves Earth from an invasion by caterpillar men with hypnotic powers.

TV Comic Annual 1967 (1966)
Writer/Artist   *Publisher*
Bill Mevin   TV Publications Ltd
SHIP OF DOOM
Story: The First Doctor, John and Gillian land on a ship crossing the ocean with a cargo of explosives.
BIRDS IN A CAGE
Story: The travellers are captured in a cage by a giant bird on a forest planet.

TV Comic Annual 1968 (1967)

Writer/Artist	*Publisher*
John Canning	TV Publications Ltd

ATTACK OF THE DALEKS

Story: The Second Doctor, John and Gillian attack the Daleks using a new invention, the pedalcopter.

THE TRODOS PURSUIT

Story: The Trods invent a time machine to pursue the TARDIS to stone age Britain.

TV Comic Annual 1969 (1968)

Writer/Artist	*Publisher*
John Canning	Polystyle Publications

THE LOST CYBERMAN

Story: The Second Doctor, John and Gillian encounter a Cyberman in an abandoned space museum.

THE ELECTRODES

Story: In 2208, the Doctor saves a pop group called the Electrodes from their evil business manager.

TV Comic Holiday Special (1969)

Writer/Artist	*Publisher*
John Canning	Polystyle Publications

DUEL WITH A CYBERMAN

Story: The Second Doctor lands in a sports arena where he wrestles a Cyberman.

A GOOD LAUGH

Story: The Doctor manages to make Heinrich Karl, the richest man in the universe, laugh.

TV Comic Annual 1970 (1969)

Writer/Artist	*Publisher*
John Canning	Polystyle Publications

RALLEY OF THE QUARKS

Story: The Doctor lands at the testing of a new fighter jet, the Dart, when the Cybermen attack it.

TV Comic Annual 1971 (1970)

Writer/Artist	*Publisher*
John Canning	Polystyle Publications

THE OCTOPUS

Story: On a Carribean cruise, the Third Doctor and the Brigadier are attacked by a giant octopus.

TO CATCH A SPY

Story: The Doctor uses his powers of levitation to help the Brigadier recapture a spy.

Countdown Annual 1972 (1971)
Writer/Artist   *Publisher*
Jim Baikie   Polystyle Publications
THE PLANT MASTER
Story: The Third Doctor and biker Dave Lester land the TARDIS in the estate of a scientist who can control plant life.

Countdown for TV Action Annual 1973 (1972)
Writer/Artist   *Publisher*
Frank Langford   Polystyle Publications
RIDE TO NOWHERE
Story: The Third Doctor investigates the kidnapping of electronics expert Sir Henry Felton by an alien.

TV Action Annual 1974 (1973)
Writer/Artist   *Publisher*
Jim Baikie   Polystyle Publications
THE HUNGRY PLANET
Story: see p. 186.

TV Comic Annual 1975 (1974)
Writer/Artist   *Publisher*
                                        Polystyle Publications
PETRIFIED
Story: The Third Doctor saves the paradise world of Zenos from the Groobs.

TV Comic Annual 1976 (1975)
Writer/Artist   *Publisher*
                                        Polystyle Publications
WODIN'S WARRIORS
Story: The Fourth Doctor meets the Norse Gods.

TV Comic Annual 1977 (1976)
Writer/Artist   *Publisher*
John Canning   Polystyle Publications
THE TANSBURY EXPERIMENT
Story: The Fourth Doctor and Sarah investigate the destruction of a lighthouse by a sea monster.

TV Comic Annual 1978 (1977)

Writer/Artist   *Publisher*
John Canning   Polystyle Publications
JACKALS OF SPACE
Story: The Fourth Doctor helps Priam to get revenge on the
Lizardian space pirates.

TV Comic Annual 1979 (1978)
Writer/Artist   *Publisher*
John Canning   Polystyle Publications
THE SEA DEVIL
Story: The Fourth Doctor and Miss Young investigate an alien
seaweed from a meteorite that is attacking an oil rig.

Doctor Who Holiday Special (1973)
Writer/Artist   *Publisher*
Frank Langford   Polystyle Publications
FOGBOUND
Story: In an English seaside town, the Third Doctor and a blind
companion battle the Master when a thick fog is unleashed.
SECRET OF THE TOWER
Story: The Third Doctor helps UNIT track down a master of
disguise in the London underground.

Doctor Who Holiday Special (1974)
Writer/Artist   *Publisher*
                                          Polystyle Publications
DOOMCLOUD
Story: The Third Doctor and Sarah try to divert a poisonous
cloud.
PERILS OF PARIS
Story: The Doctor takes Sarah for a holiday in Paris, France,
1880, but ends up in Paris, Texas, 1880.
WHO'S WHO?
Story: The Doctor and Sarah find themselves transported by
the TARDIS to a parallel Earth where their counterparts are
dangerous criminals.

Doctor Who Monthly
A SHIP CALLED SUDDEN DEATH (1984)
Writer: Steve Parkhouse; *Artist*: Dave Gibbons
Issues: 84
Story: Spin-off involving the Free Fall Warriors (from Issues
Nos. 56–57).

THE CHAMELEON FACTOR (1991)
Writer: Paul Cornell; *Artist*: Lee Sullivan
Issues: 174
Story: The Doctor and Ace experience hallucinations and elements of the past when the Doctor's old ring plays havoc in the TARDIS console.

Radio Times
COLONY IN SPACE (1971)
Writer/Artist: Frank Bellamy
Issue: 10 April 1971
Story: Adaptation of Story HHH.